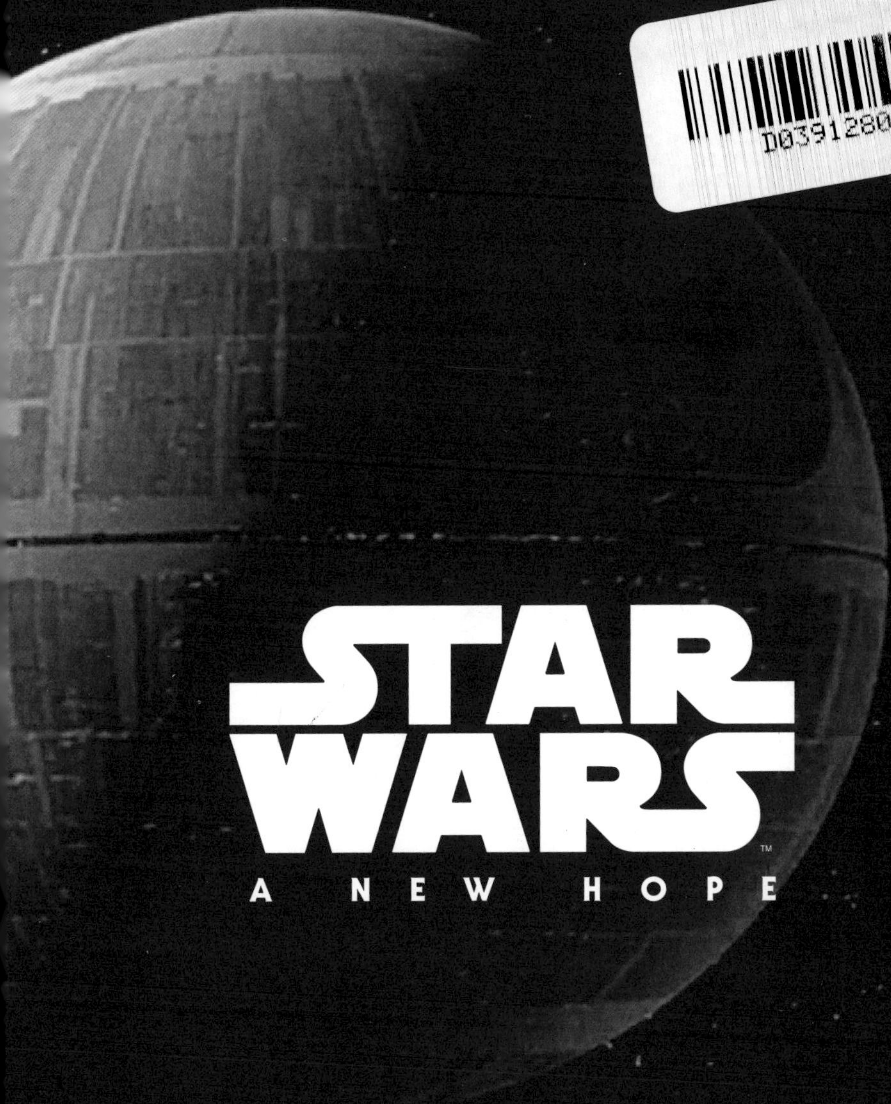

STAR WARS

A NEW HOPE

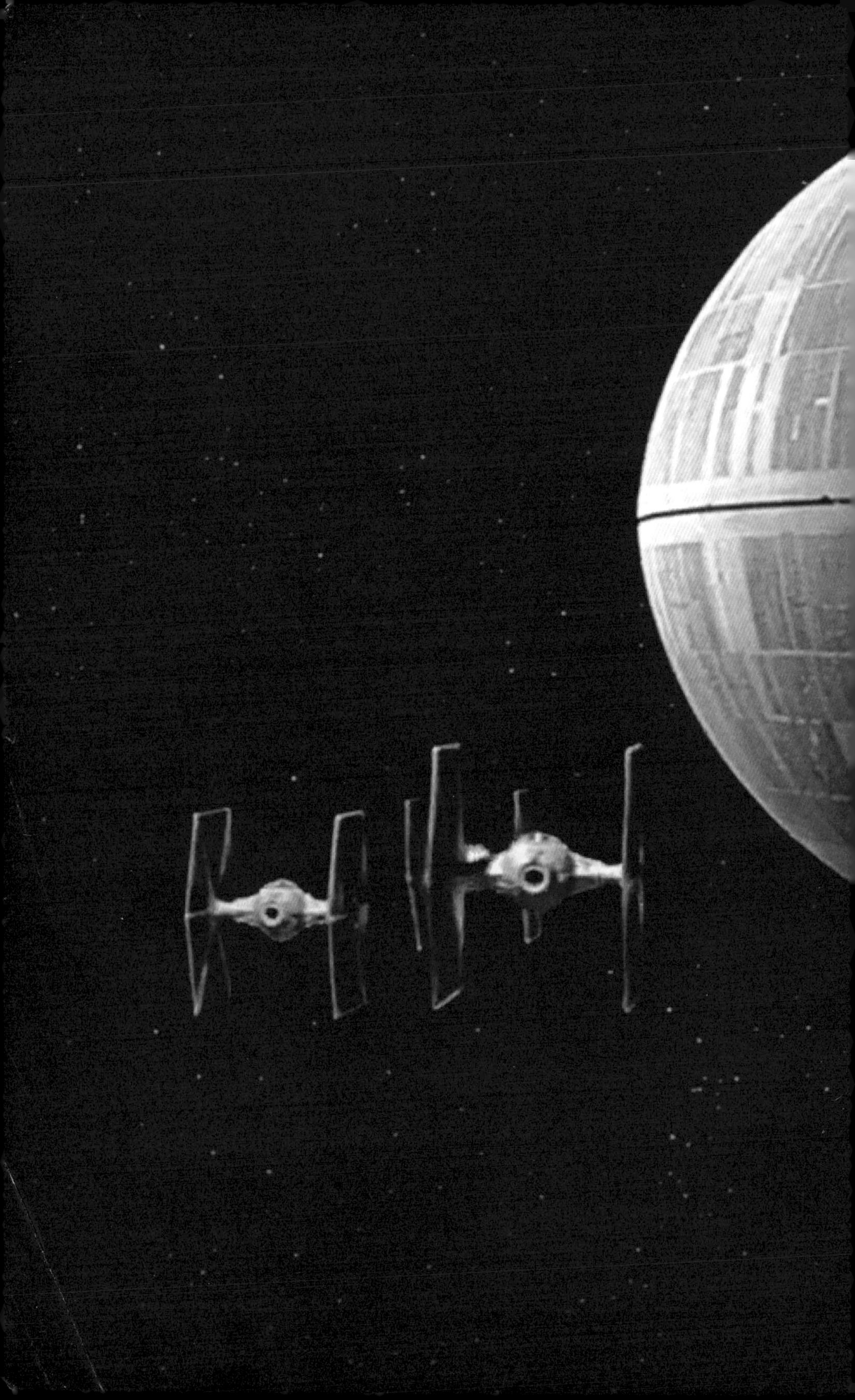

Disney · Lucasfilm Press

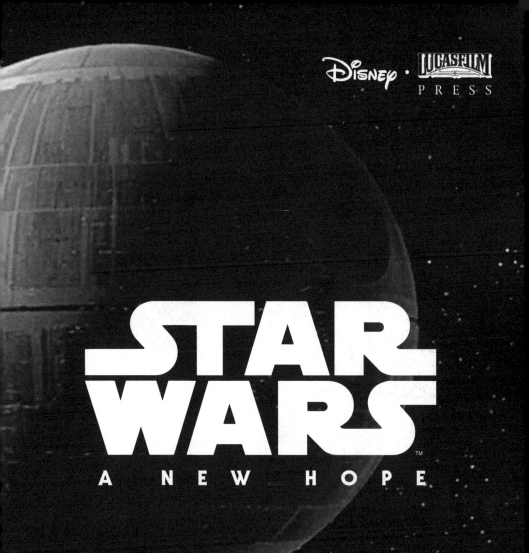

STAR WARS™
A NEW HOPE

CINESTORY COMIC

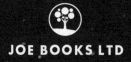

JOE BOOKS LTD

Published simultaneously in the United States and Canada by Joe Books Ltd,
489 College Street, Suite 203, Toronto, ON M6G 1A5

www.joebooks.com

First Joe Books edition: October 2017

Print IsBN: 978-1-77275-521-3
ebook IsBN: 978-1-77275-794-1

Star Wars: A New Hope
Written and directed by George Lucas
Produced by Gary Kurtz

Library and Archives Canada Cataloguing in Publication
information is available upon request

Printed and bound in Canada

1 3 5 7 9 10 8 6 4 2

A long time ago in a galaxy far, far away....

STAR WARS™

A NEW HOPE

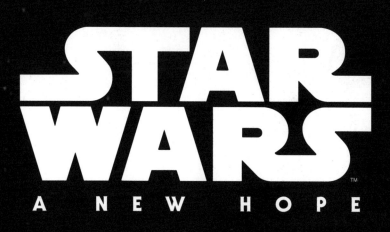

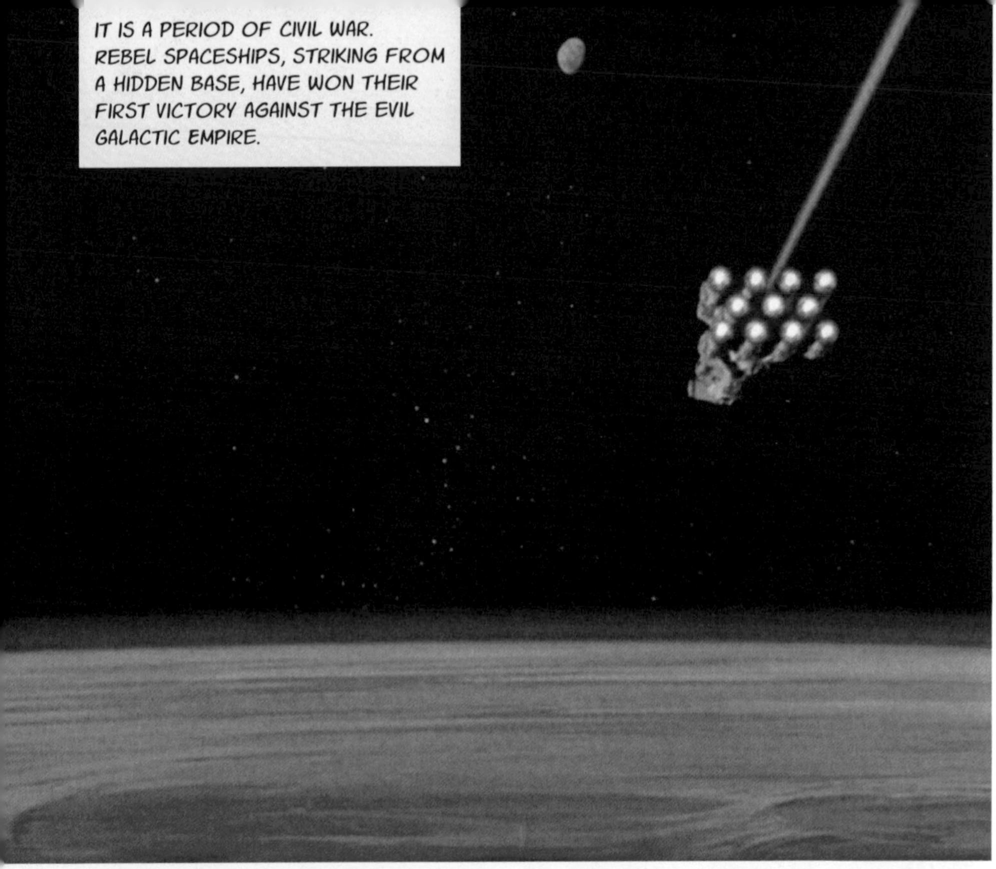
IT IS A PERIOD OF CIVIL WAR. REBEL SPACESHIPS, STRIKING FROM A HIDDEN BASE, HAVE WON THEIR FIRST VICTORY AGAINST THE EVIL GALACTIC EMPIRE.

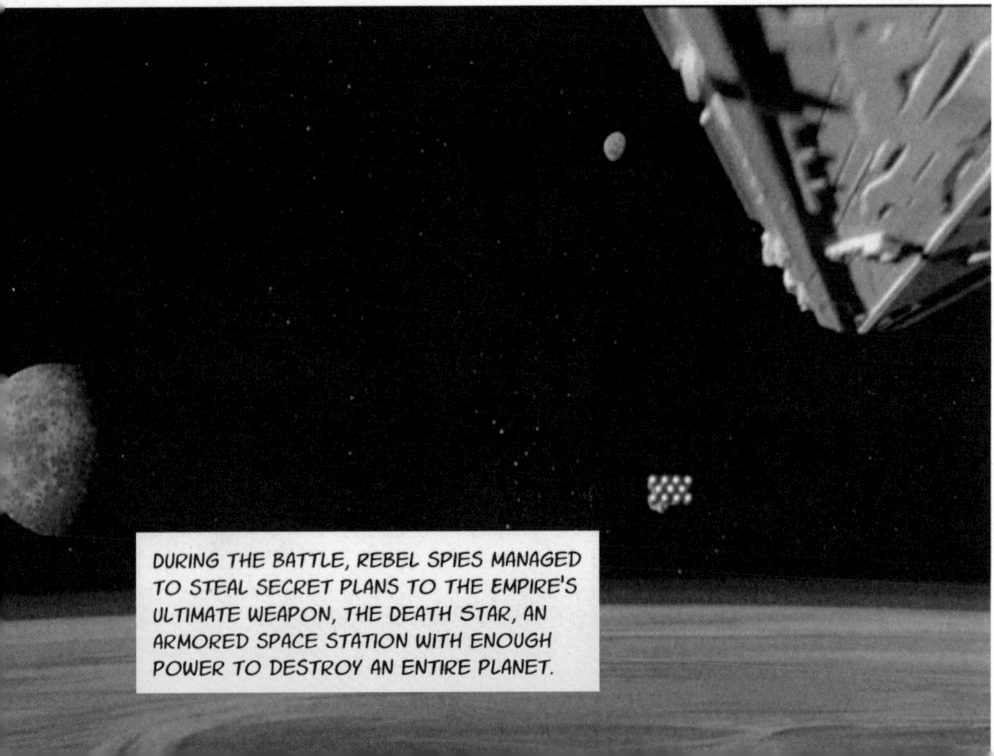
DURING THE BATTLE, REBEL SPIES MANAGED TO STEAL SECRET PLANS TO THE EMPIRE'S ULTIMATE WEAPON, THE DEATH STAR, AN ARMORED SPACE STATION WITH ENOUGH POWER TO DESTROY AN ENTIRE PLANET.

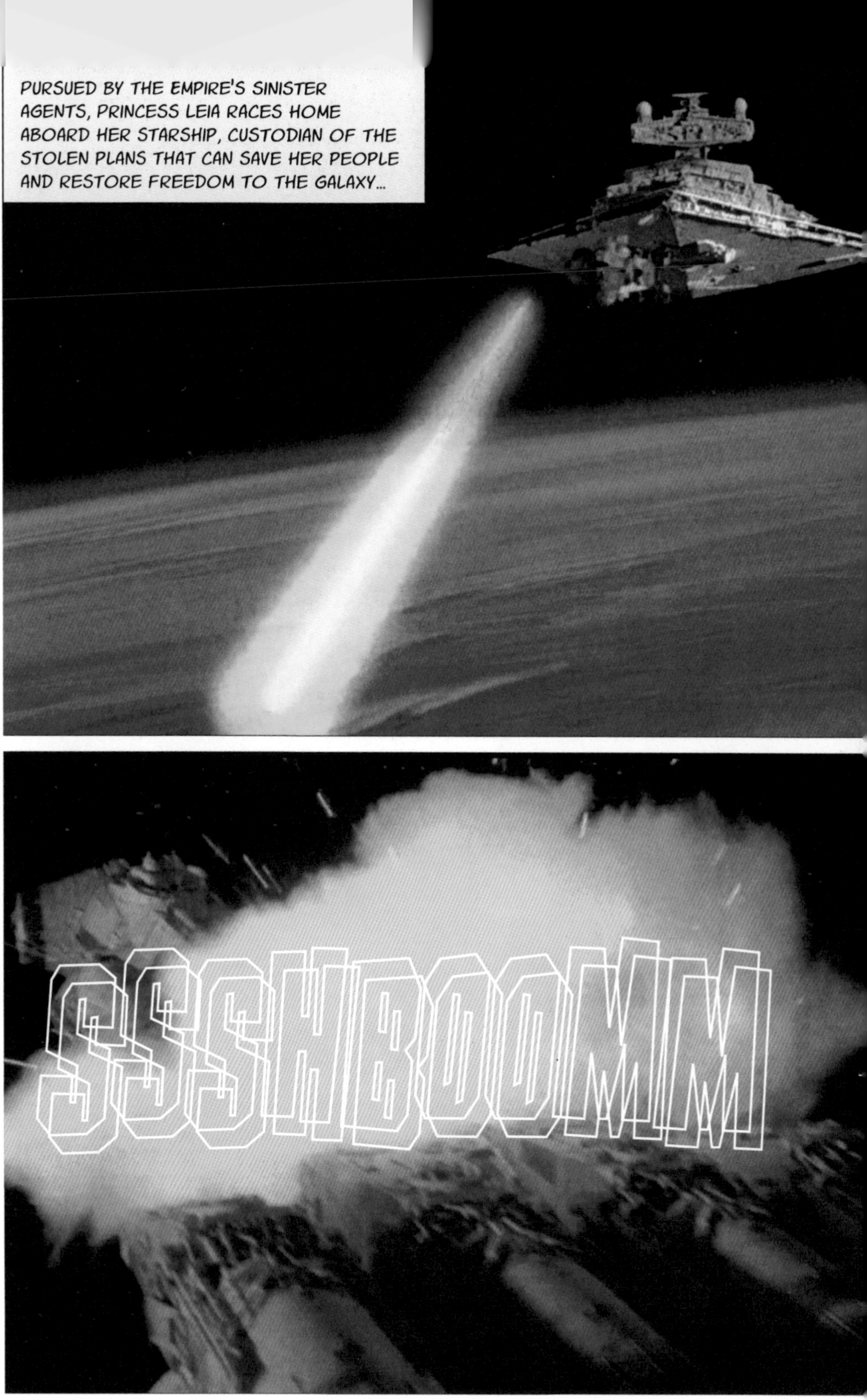
PURSUED BY THE EMPIRE'S SINISTER AGENTS, PRINCESS LEIA RACES HOME ABOARD HER STARSHIP, CUSTODIAN OF THE STOLEN PLANS THAT CAN SAVE HER PEOPLE AND RESTORE FREEDOM TO THE GALAXY...
SSSHBOOMM

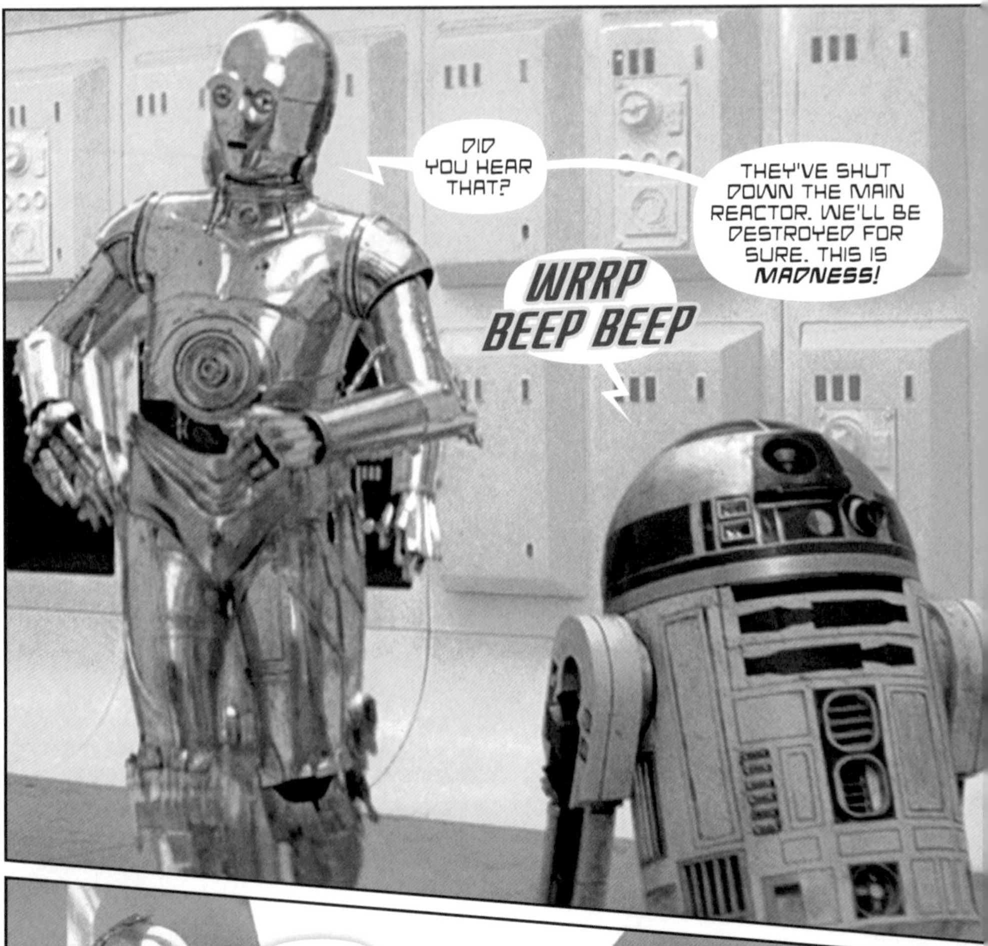
DID YOU HEAR THAT?
THEY'VE SHUT DOWN THE MAIN REACTOR. WE'LL BE DESTROYED FOR SURE. THIS IS MADNESS!
WRRP BEEP BEEP

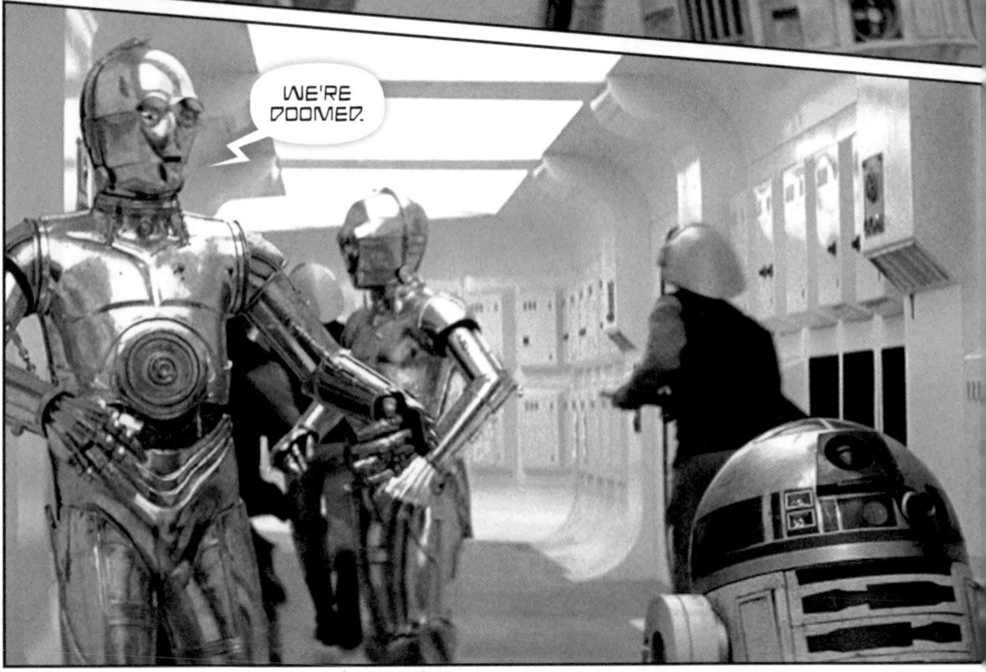
WE'RE DOOMED.

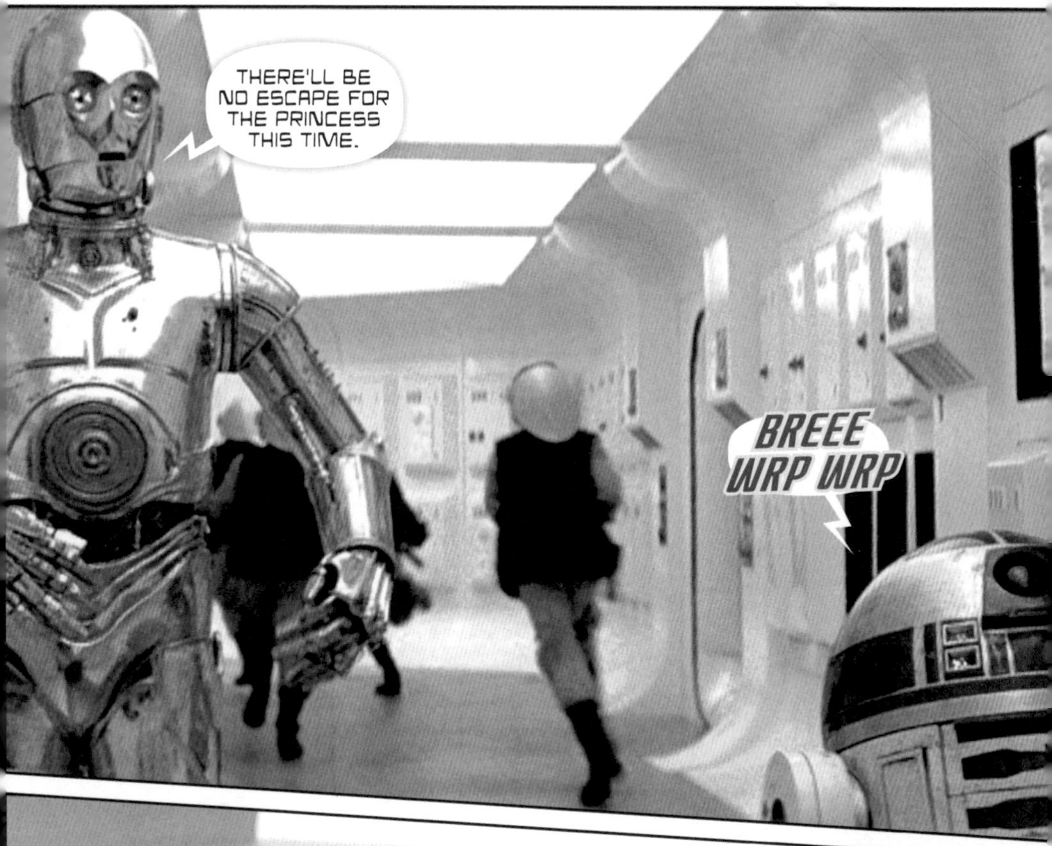
THERE'LL BE NO ESCAPE FOR THE PRINCESS THIS TIME.
BREEE WRP WRP

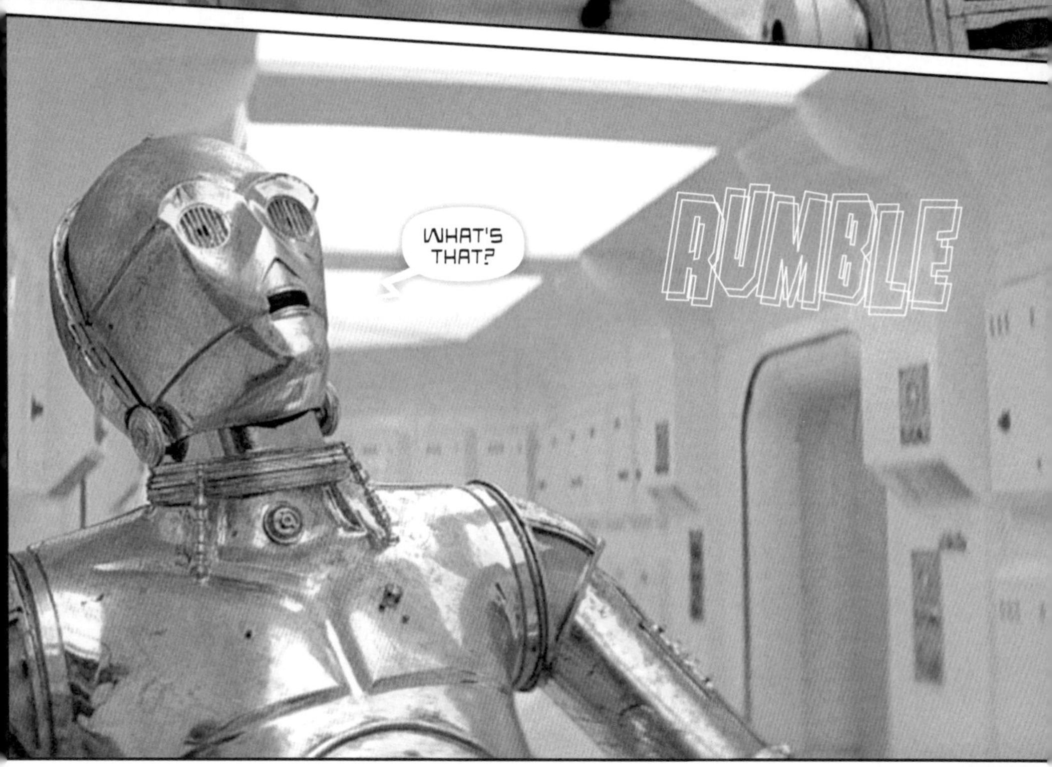
WHAT'S THAT?
RUMBLE

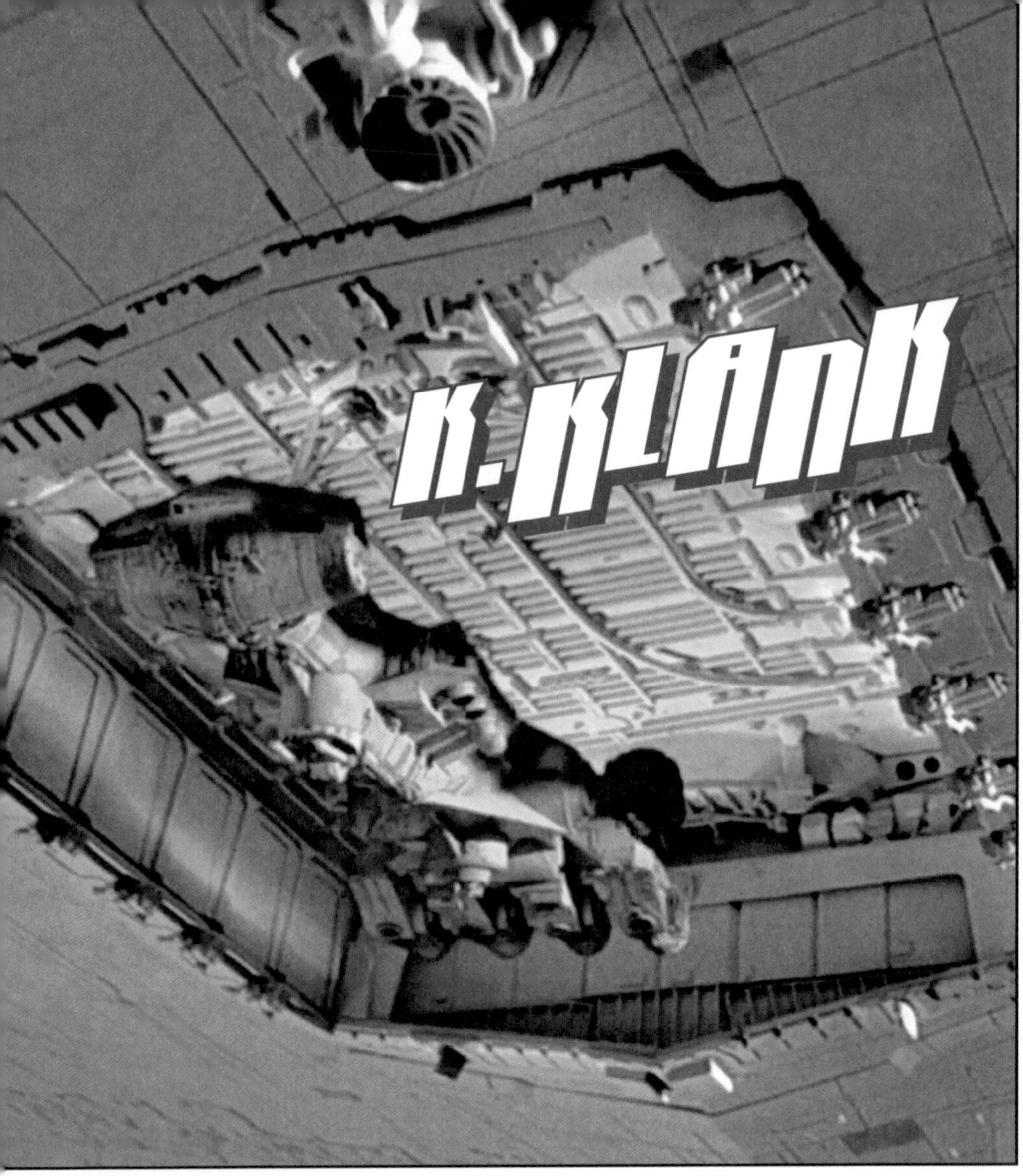
K-KLANK

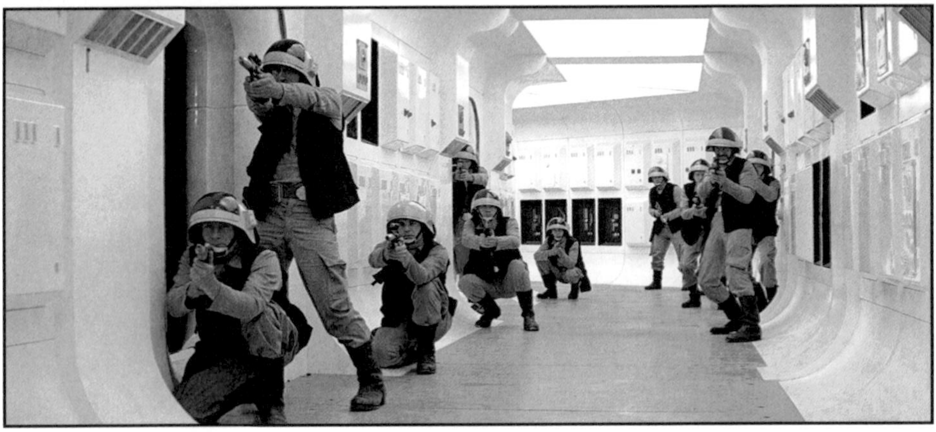

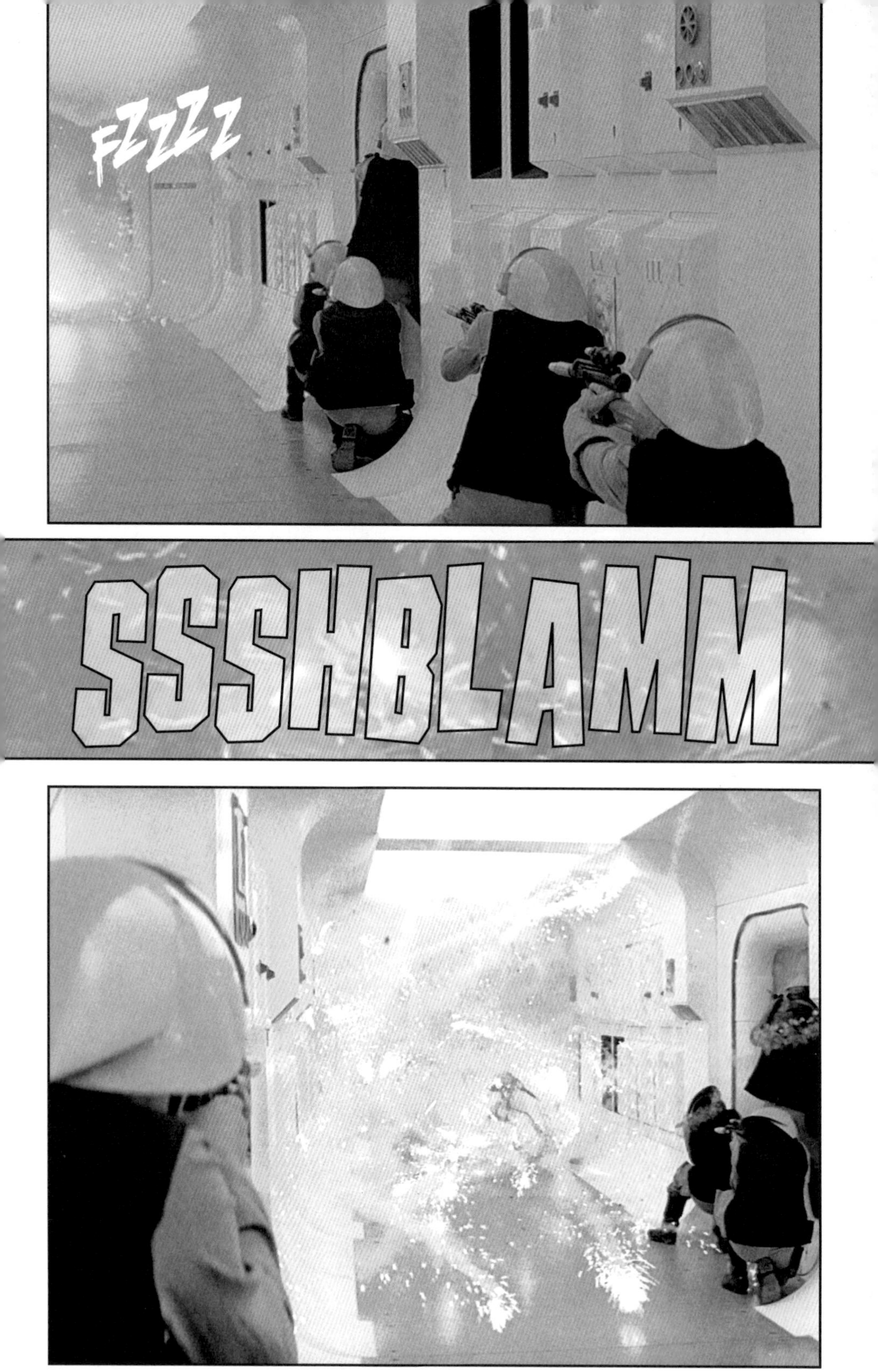
FZZZZ
SSSHBLAMM

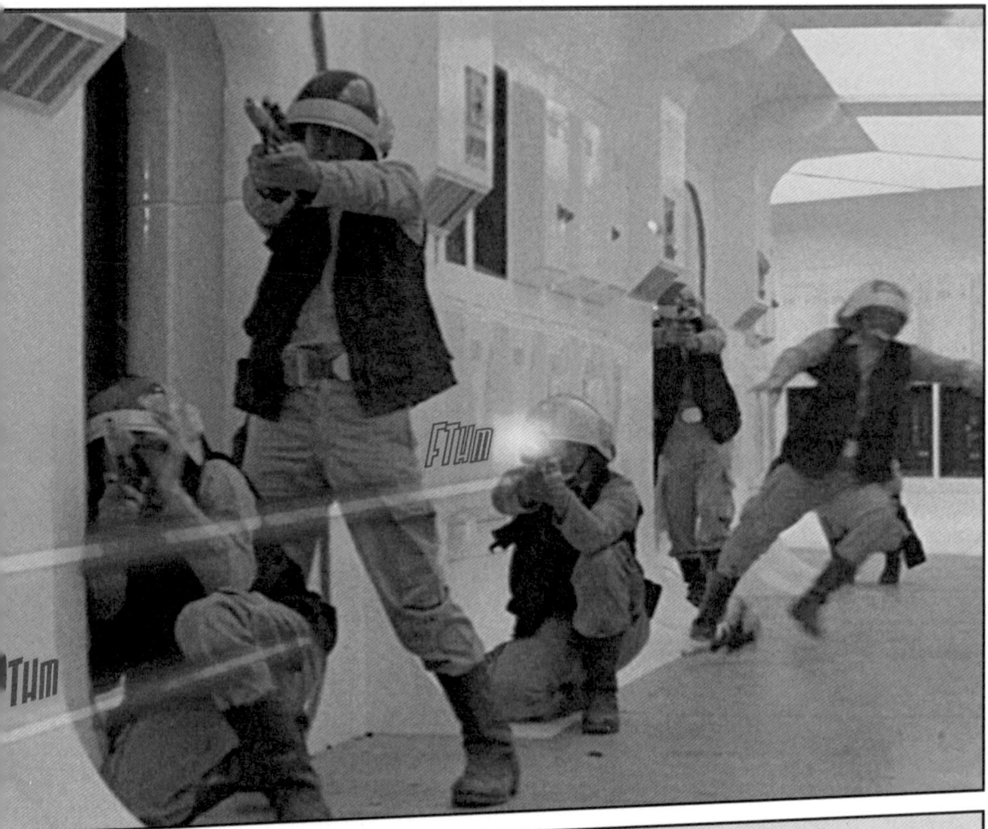
FTHM
THM

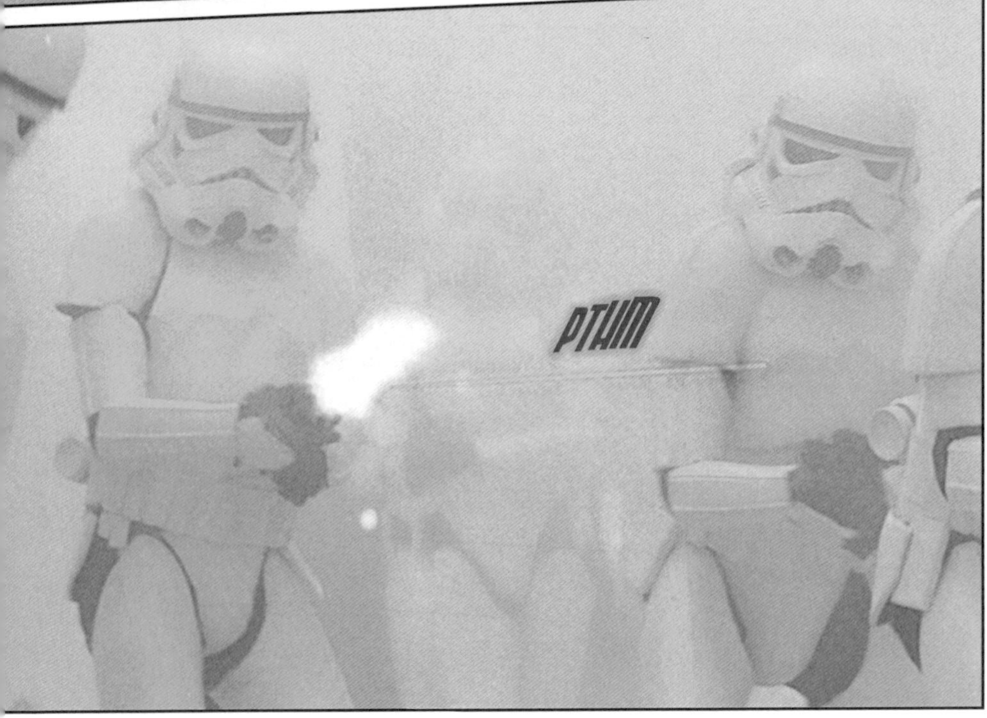
PTHM

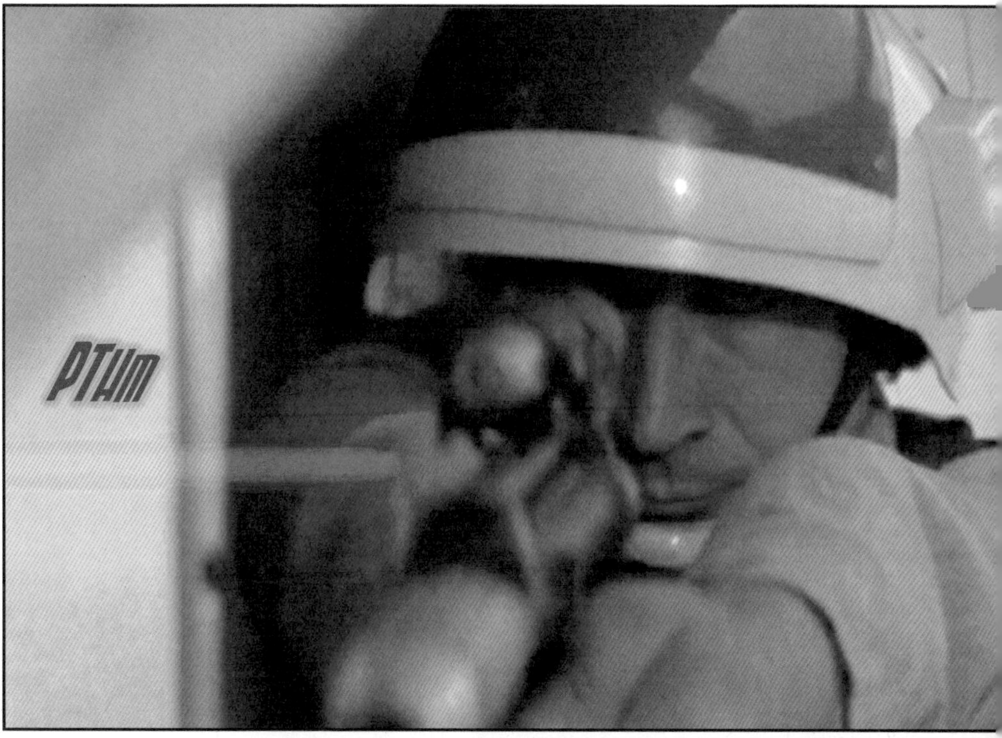

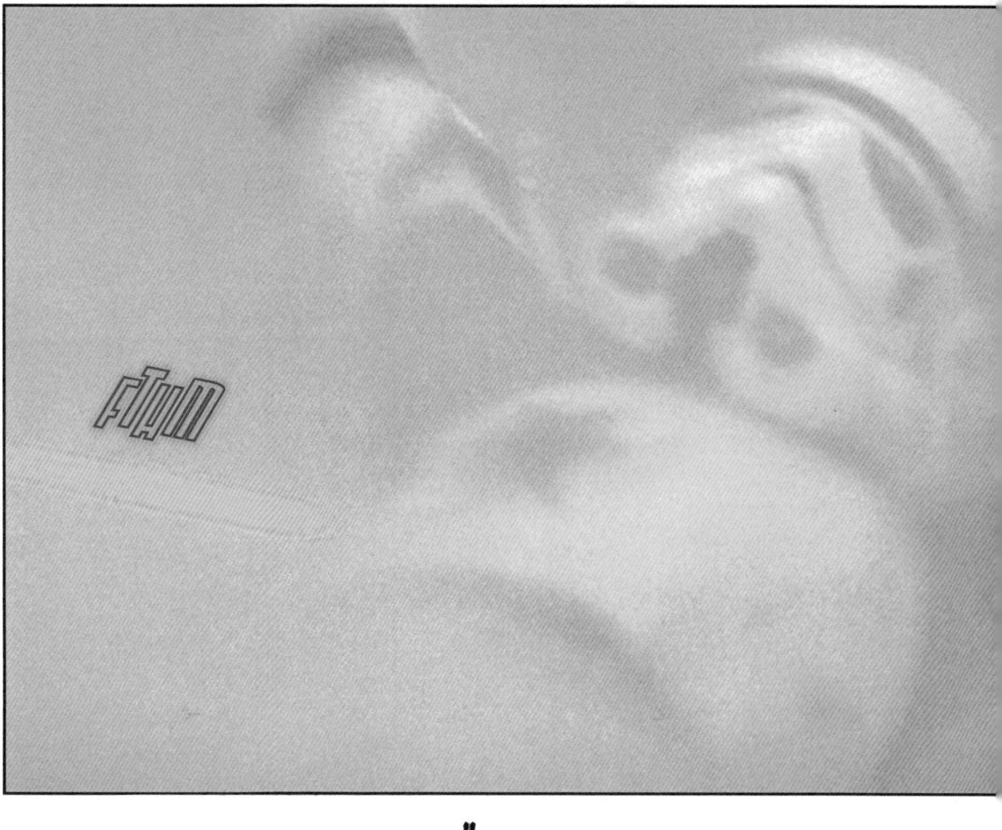

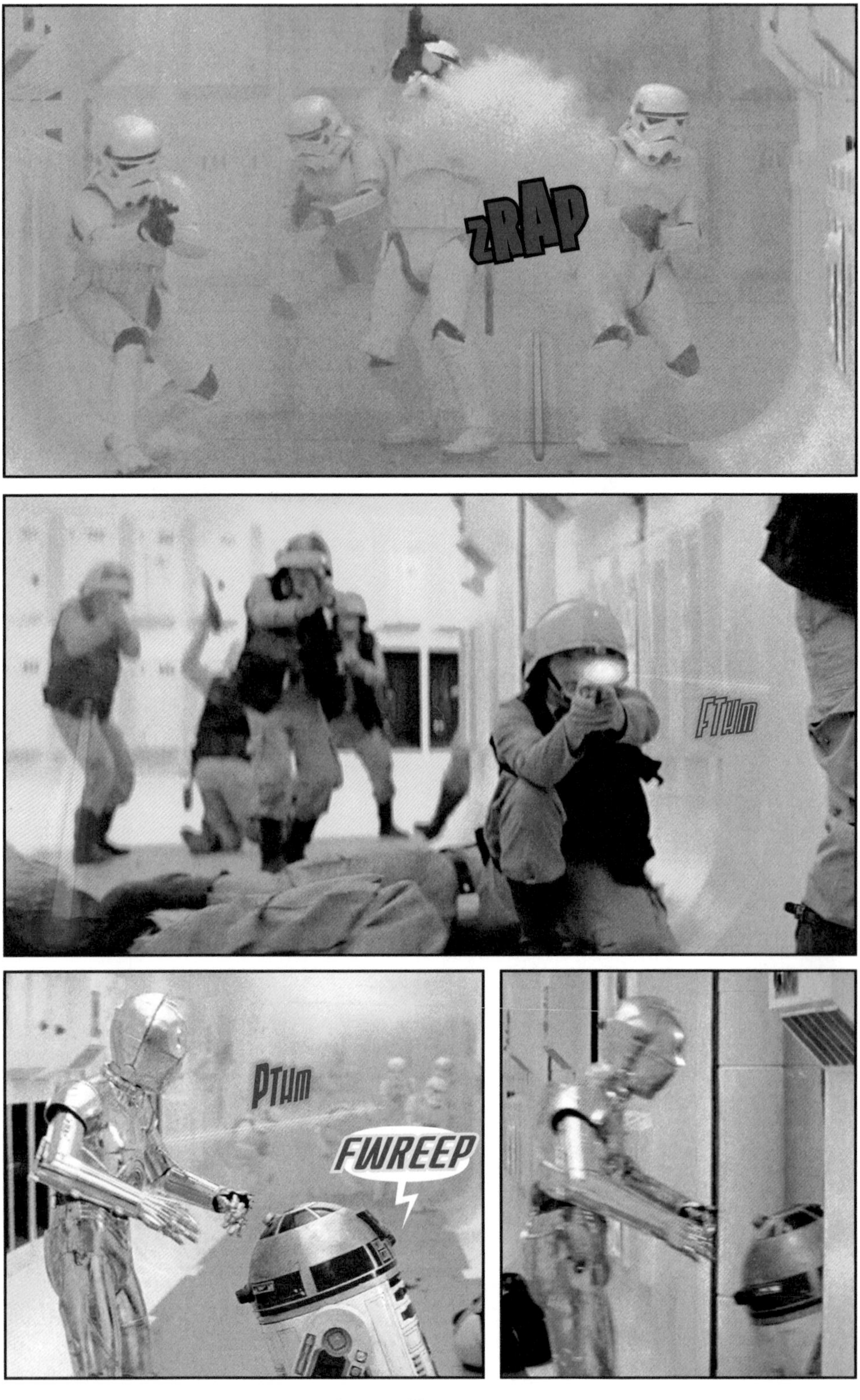
zRAP
FTHM
PTHM
FWREEP

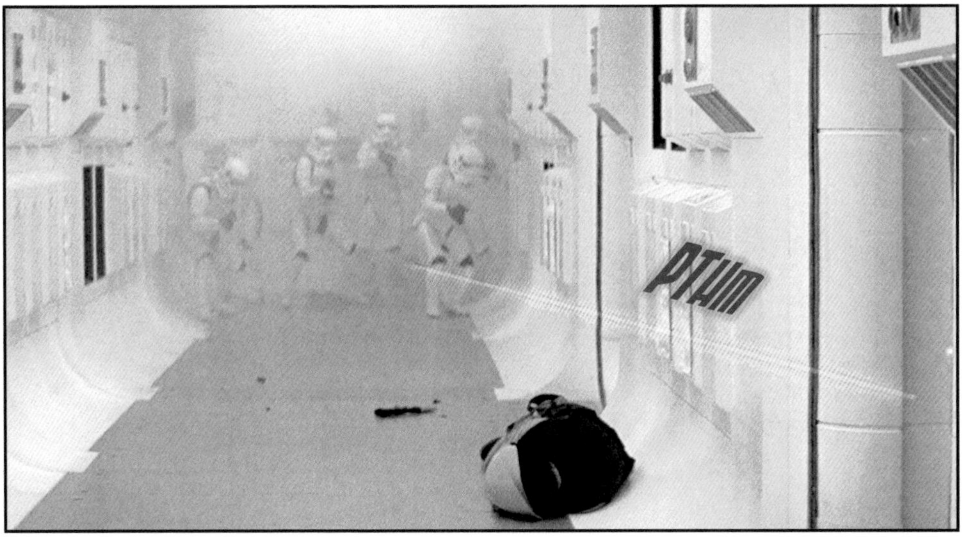
PTUM

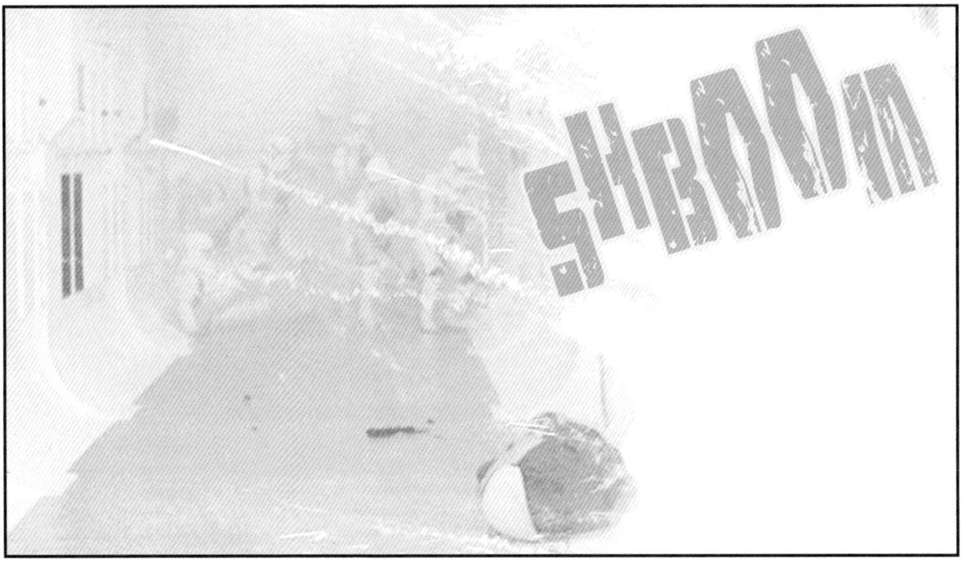
SHBOOM

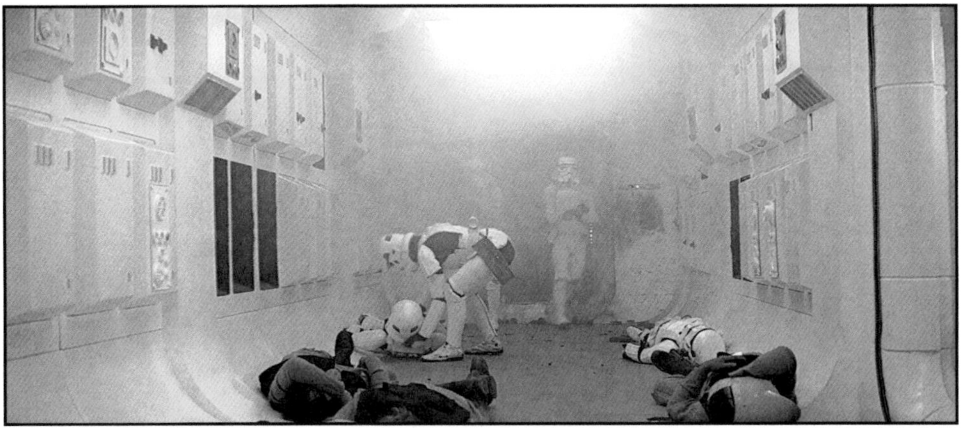

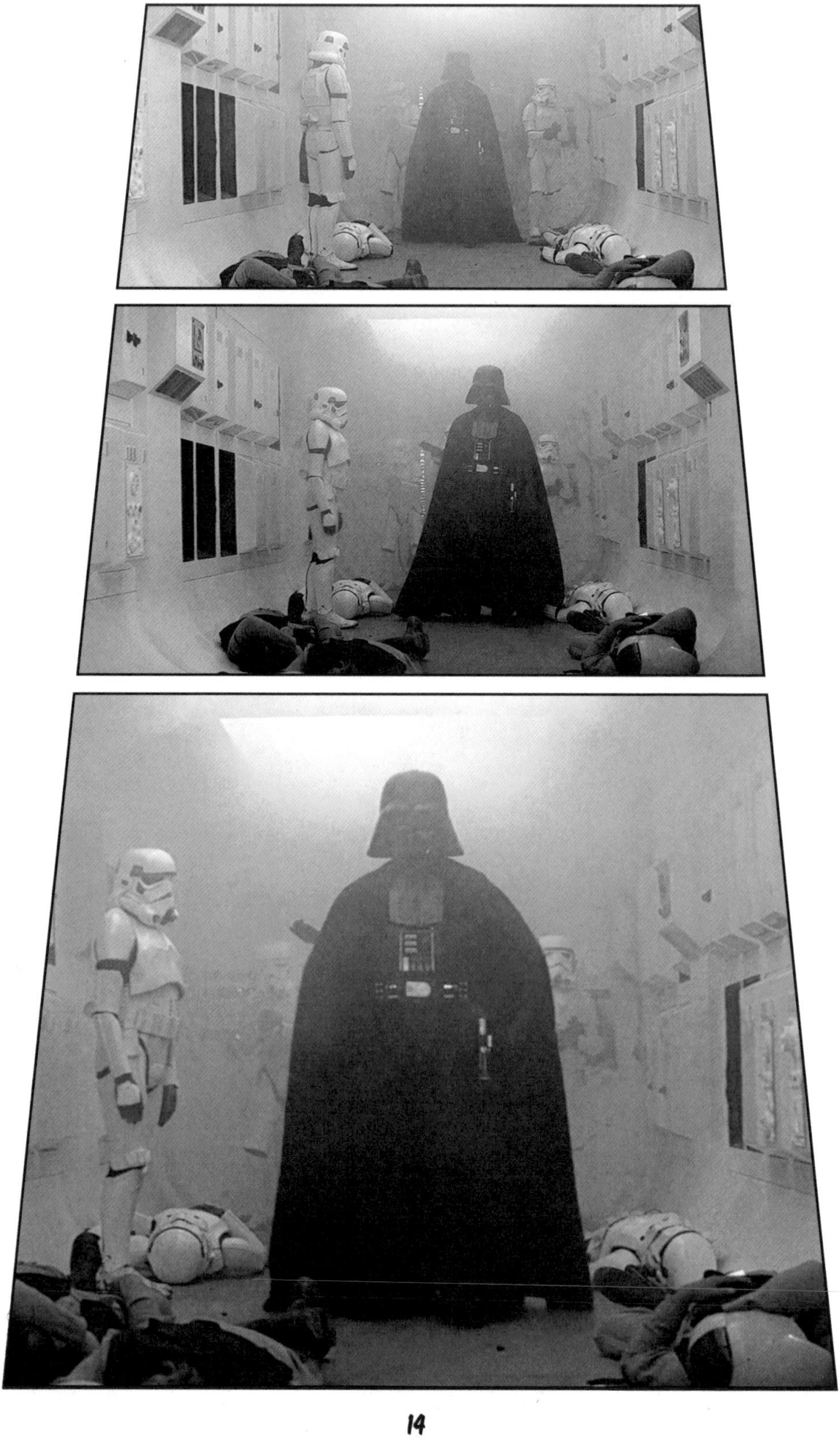

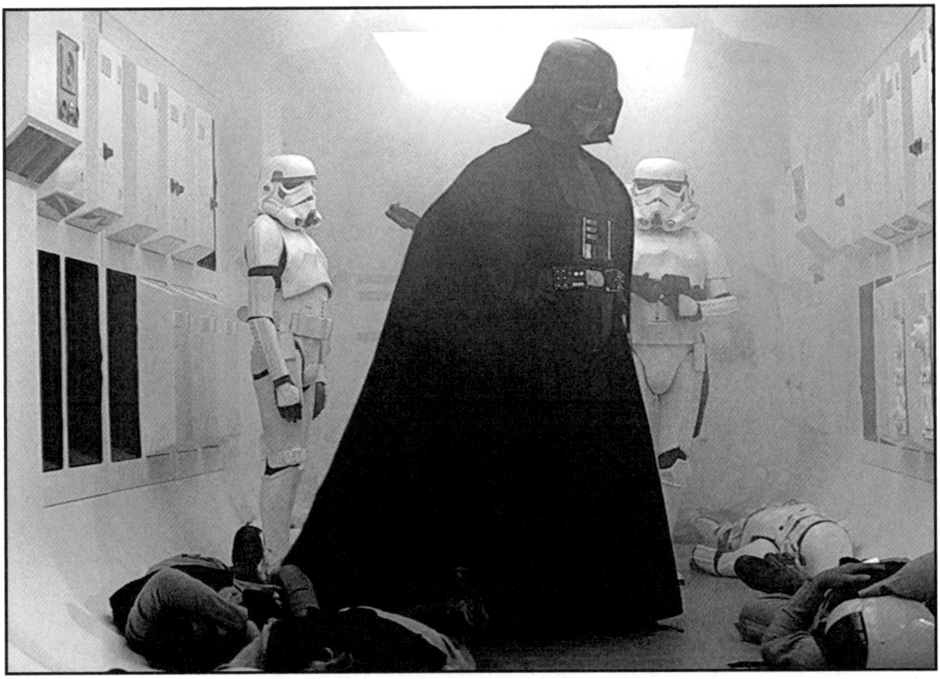

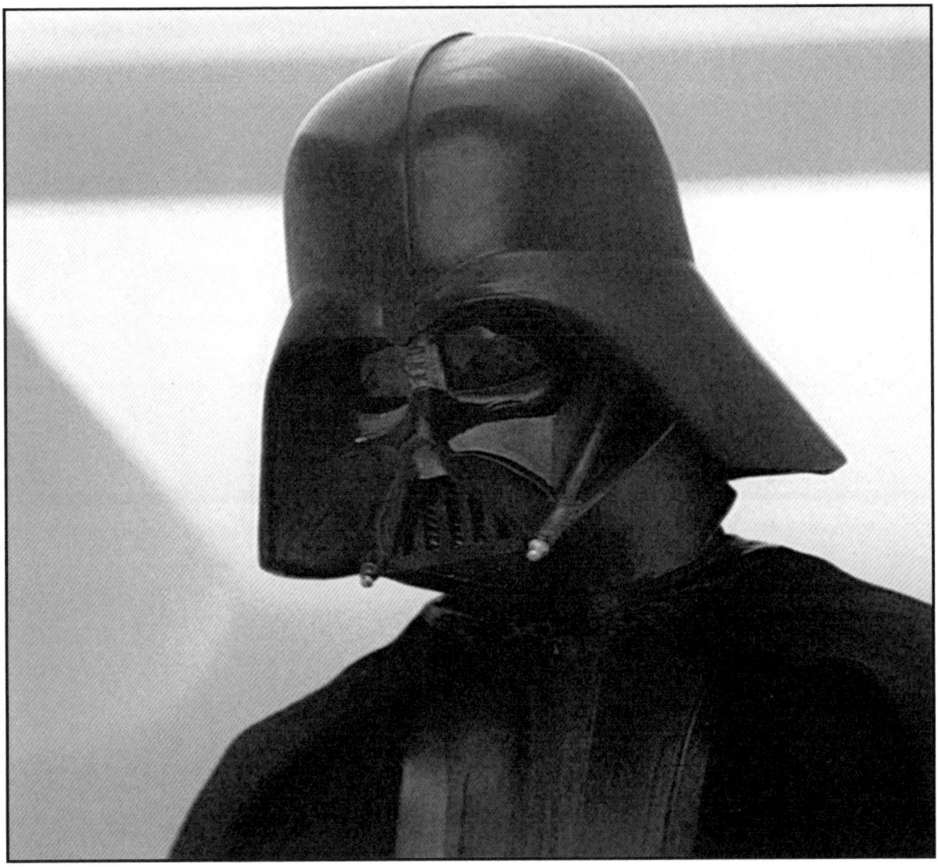

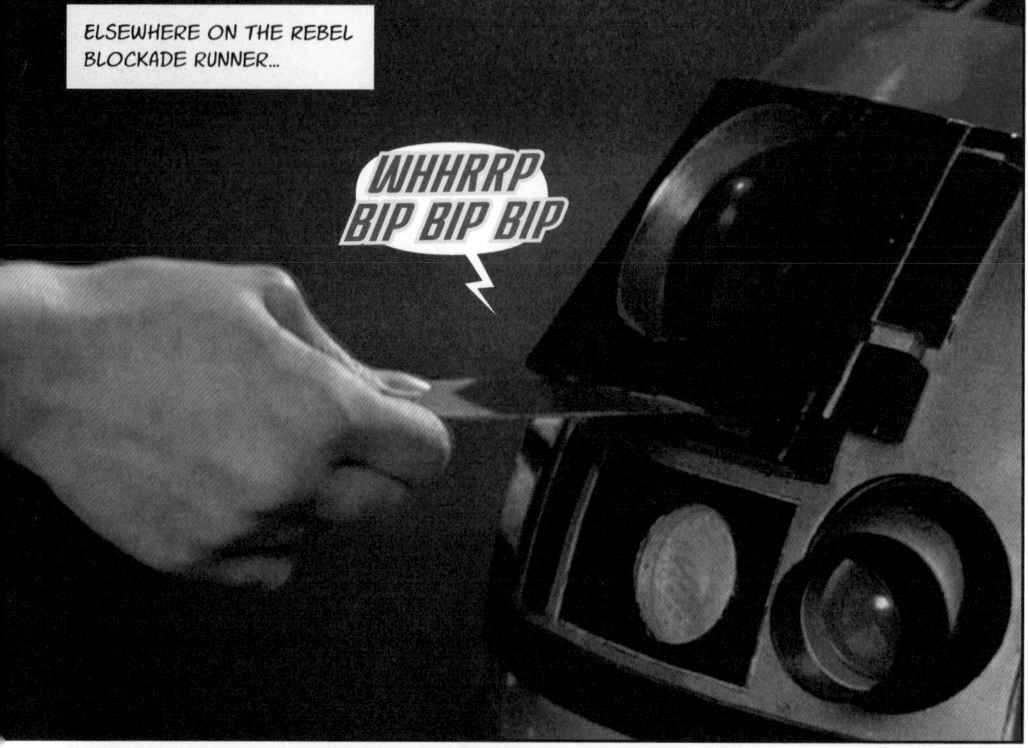
ELSEWHERE ON THE REBEL BLOCKADE RUNNER...
WHHRRP BIP BIP BIP

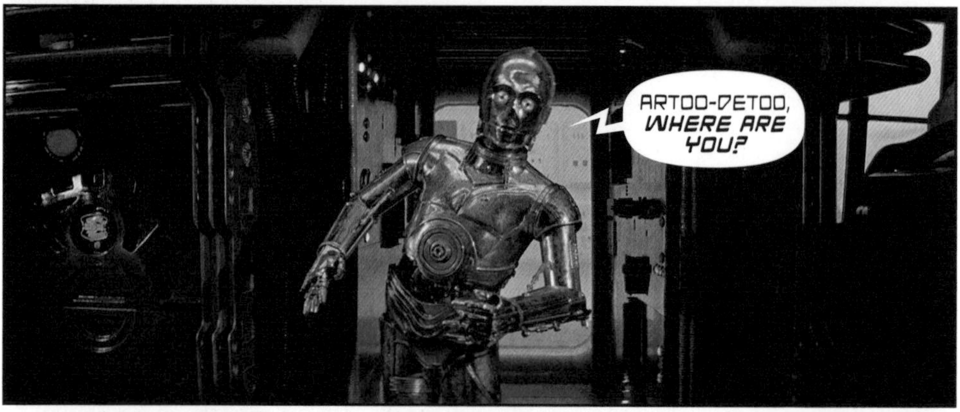
ARTOO-DETOO, WHERE ARE YOU?

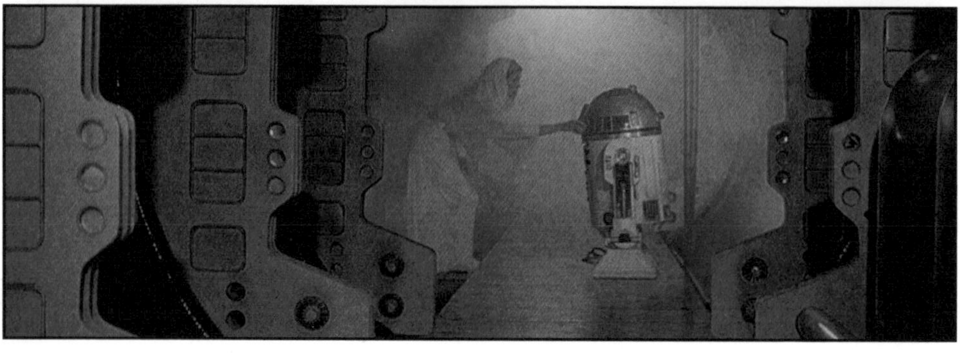

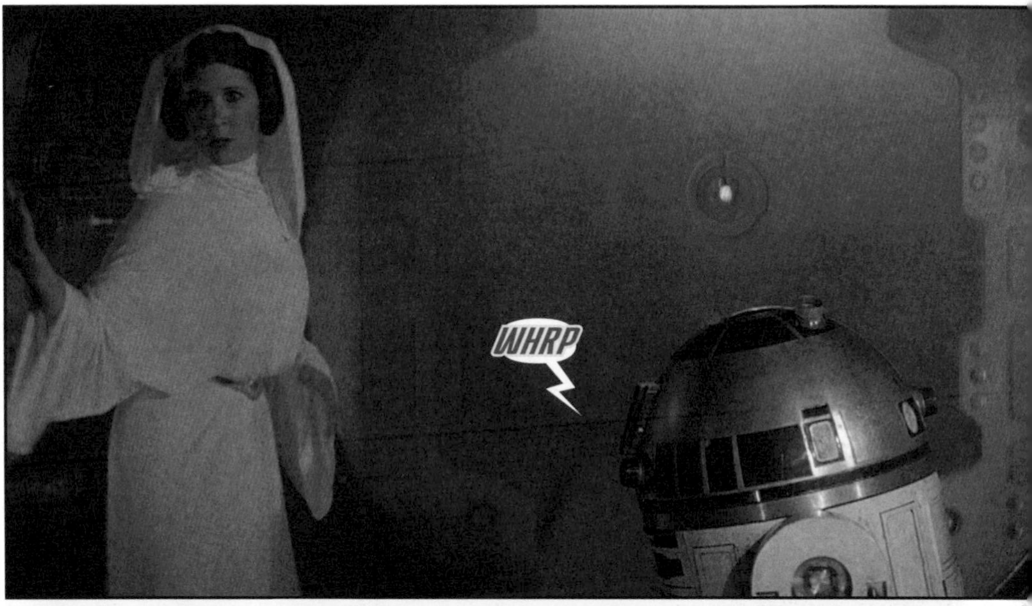
WHRP

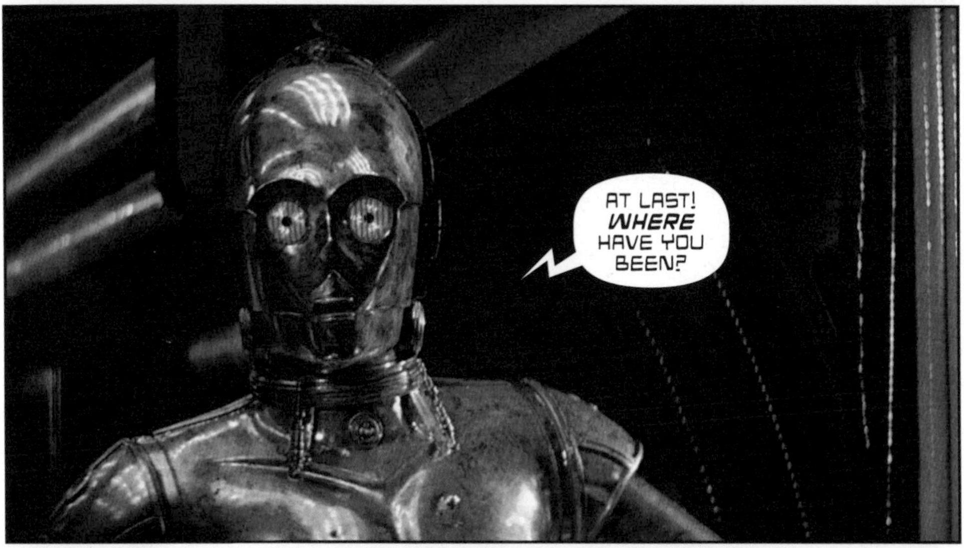
AT LAST! WHERE HAVE YOU BEEN?

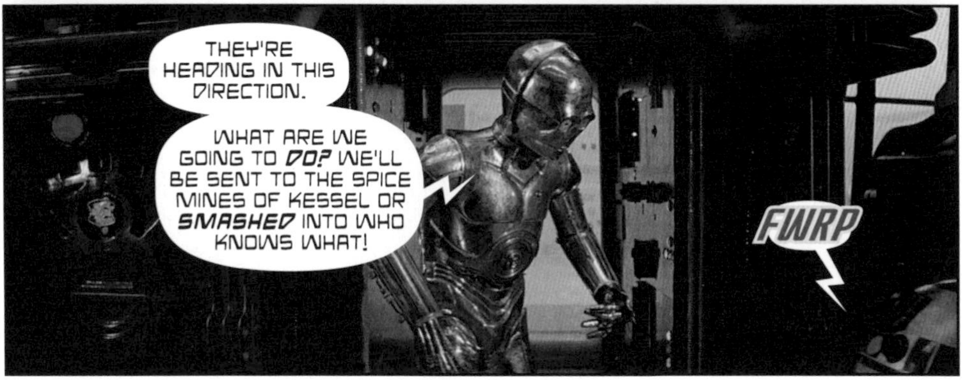
THEY'RE HEADING IN THIS DIRECTION.
WHAT ARE WE GOING TO DO? WE'LL BE SENT TO THE SPICE MINES OF KESSEL OR SMASHED INTO WHO KNOWS WHAT!
FWRP

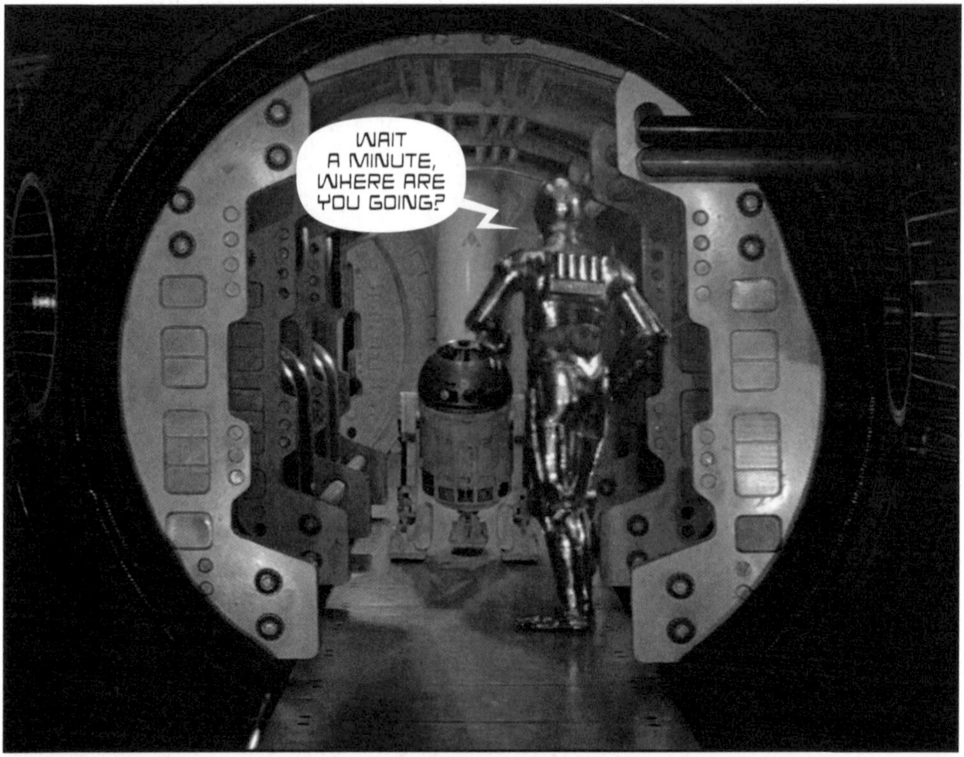
WAIT A MINUTE, WHERE ARE YOU GOING?

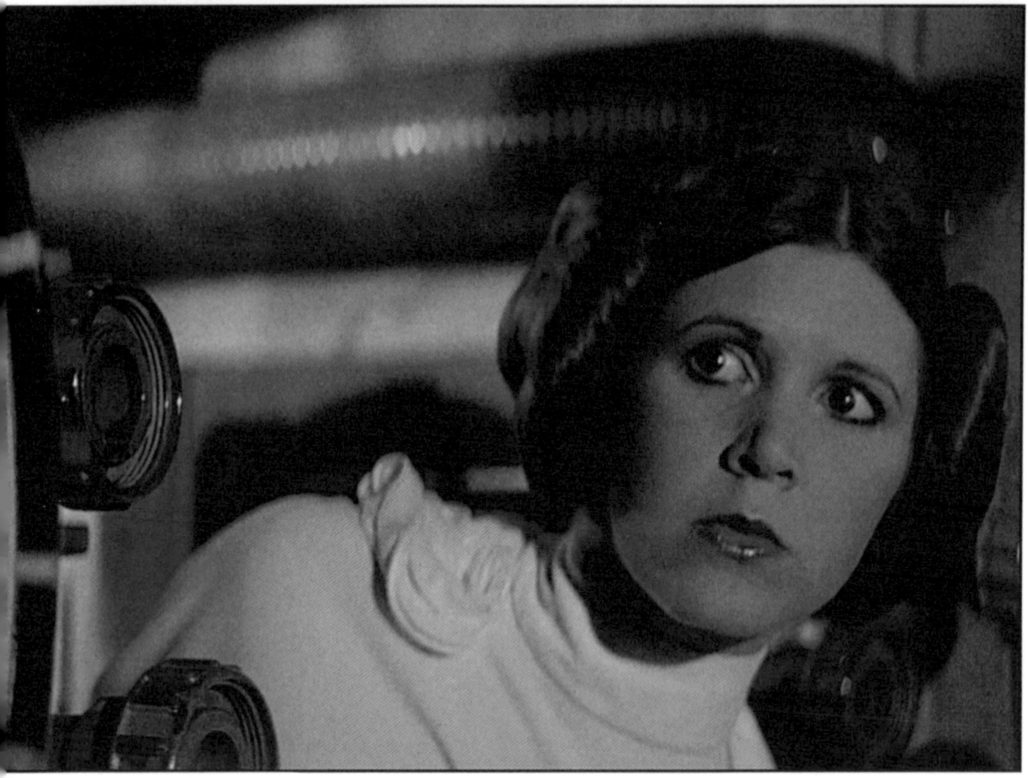

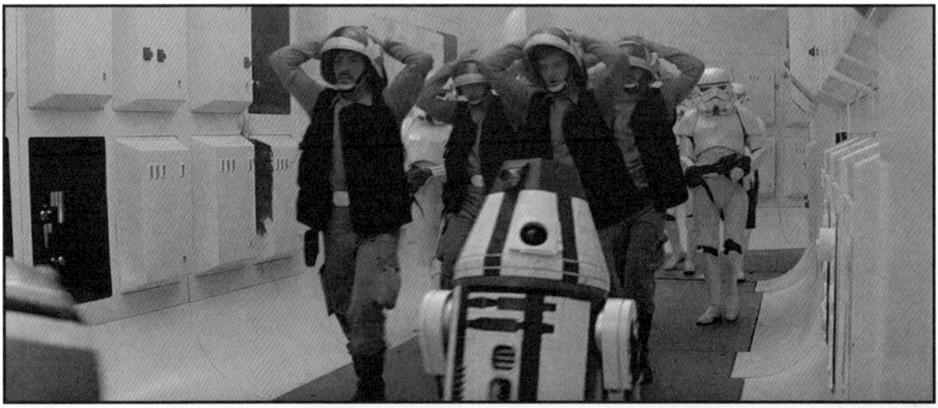

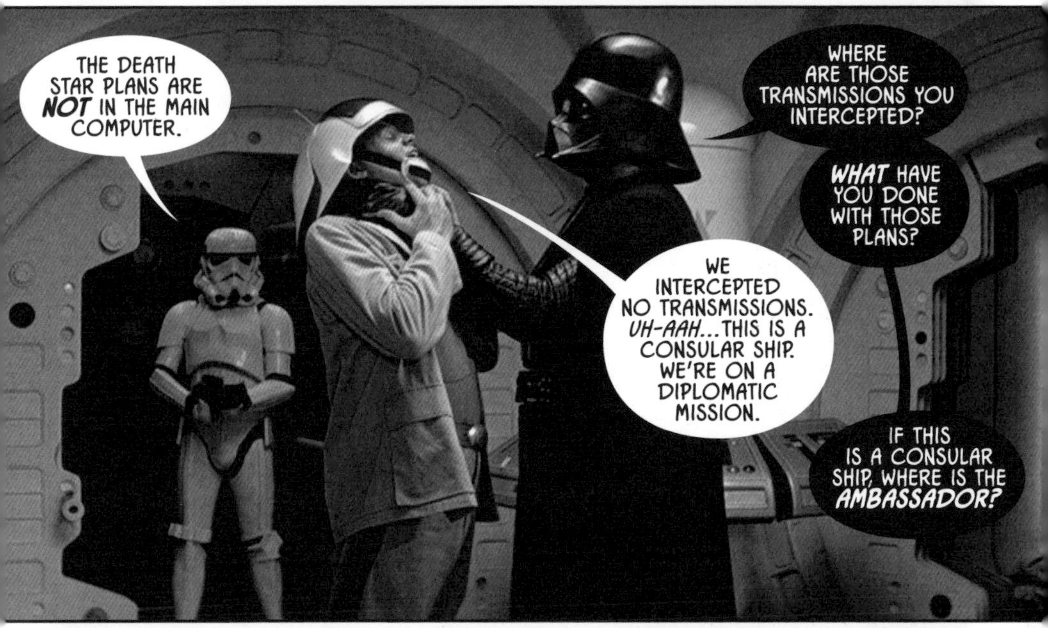
THE DEATH STAR PLANS ARE **NOT** IN THE MAIN COMPUTER.
WHERE ARE THOSE TRANSMISSIONS YOU INTERCEPTED?
WHAT HAVE YOU DONE WITH THOSE PLANS?
WE INTERCEPTED NO TRANSMISSIONS. *UH-AAH*...THIS IS A CONSULAR SHIP. WE'RE ON A DIPLOMATIC MISSION.
IF THIS IS A CONSULAR SHIP, WHERE IS THE **AMBASSADOR?**

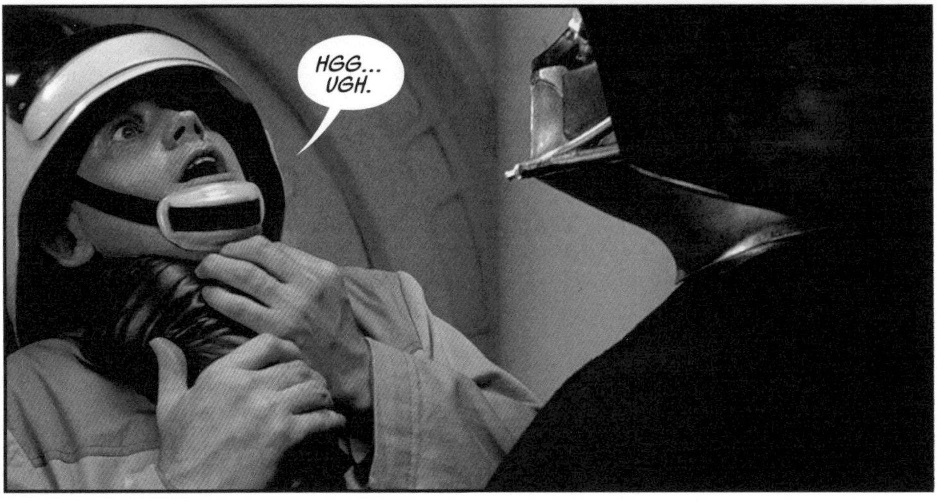
HGG... UGH.

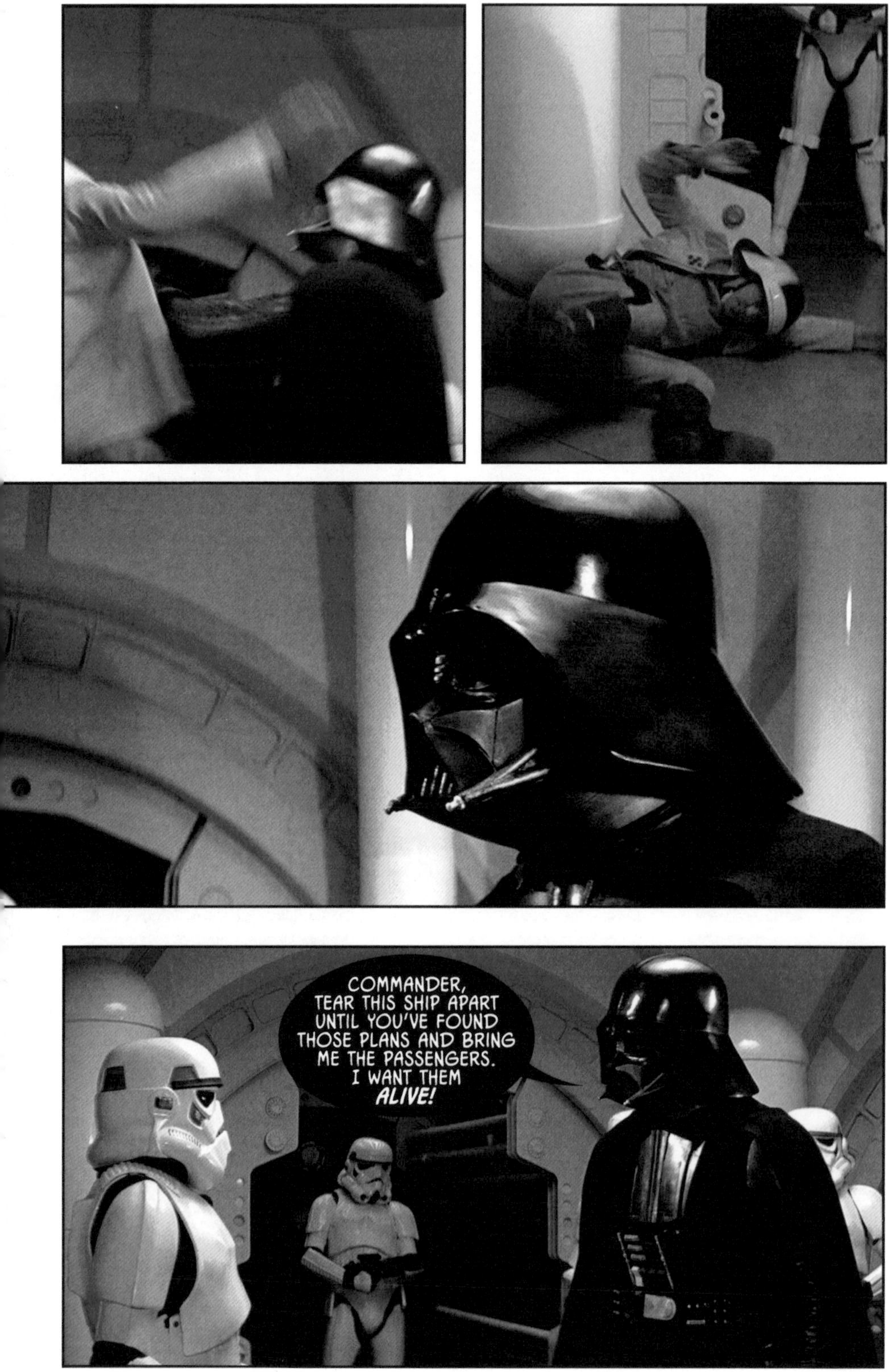
COMMANDER, TEAR THIS SHIP APART UNTIL YOU'VE FOUND THOSE PLANS AND BRING ME THE PASSENGERS. I WANT THEM *ALIVE!*

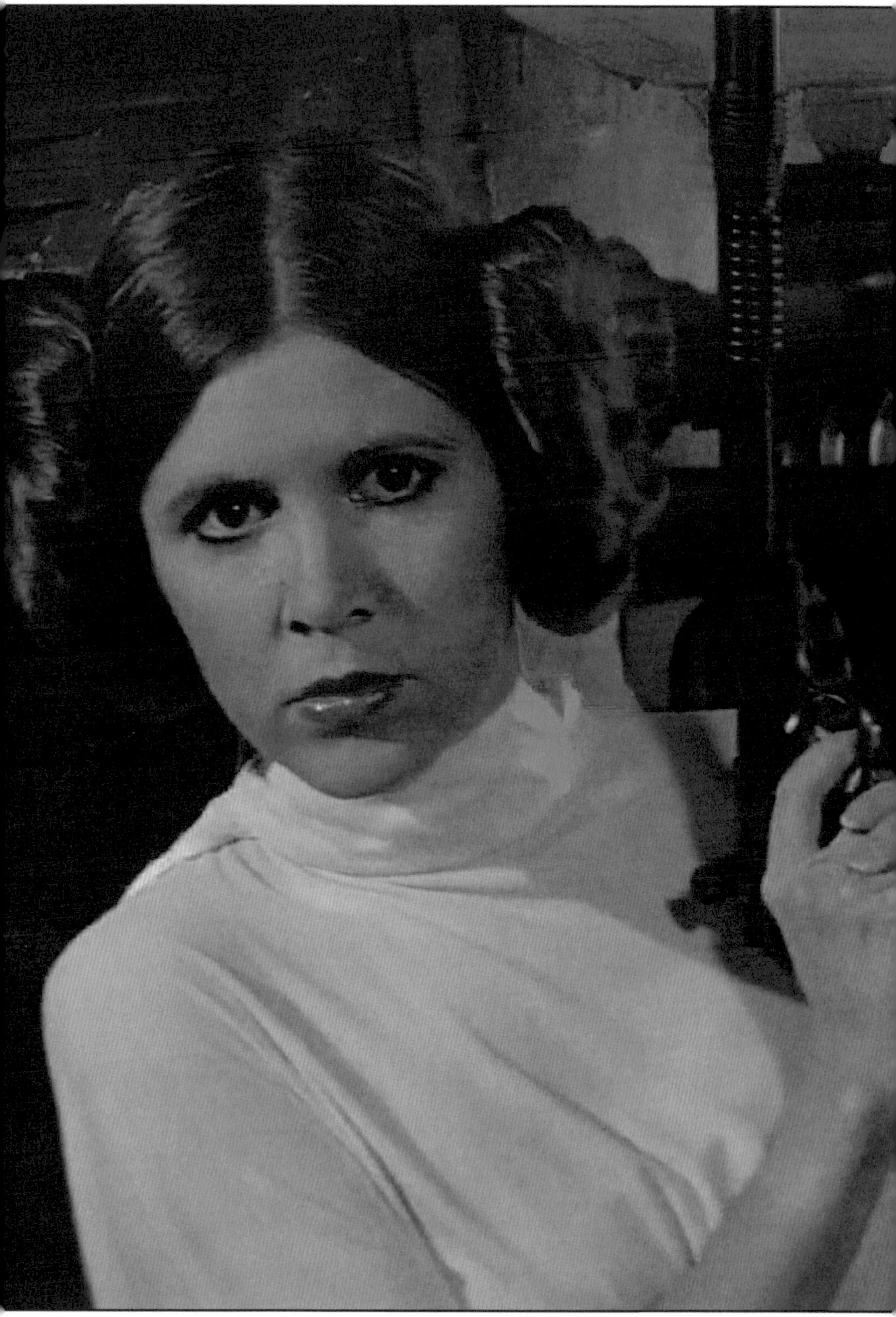

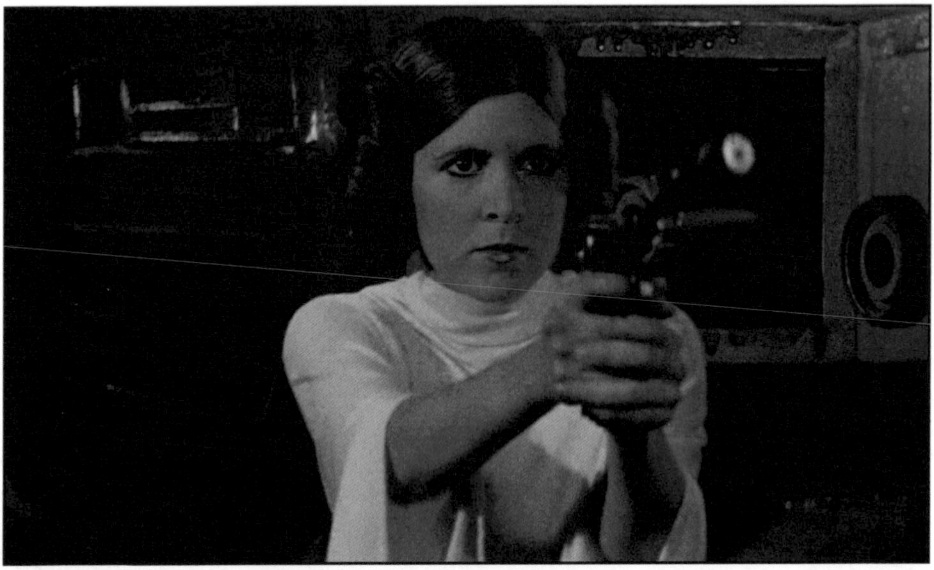

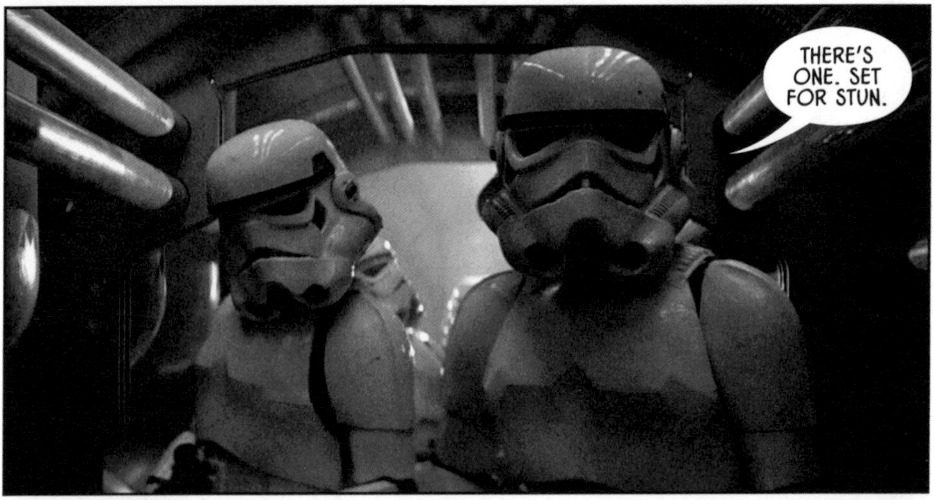
THERE'S ONE. SET FOR STUN.

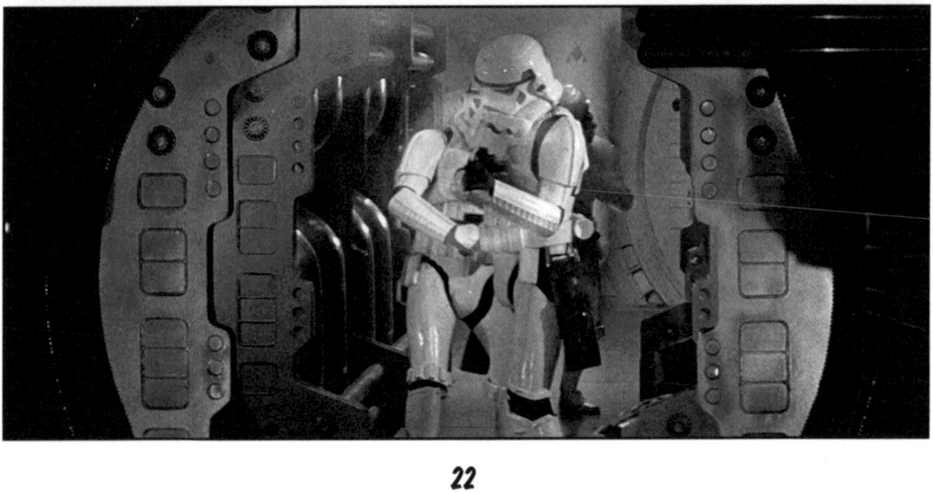

ZRAP

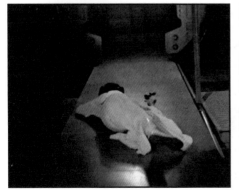

SHE'LL BE ALL RIGHT. INFORM LORD VADER WE HAVE A PRISONER.

23

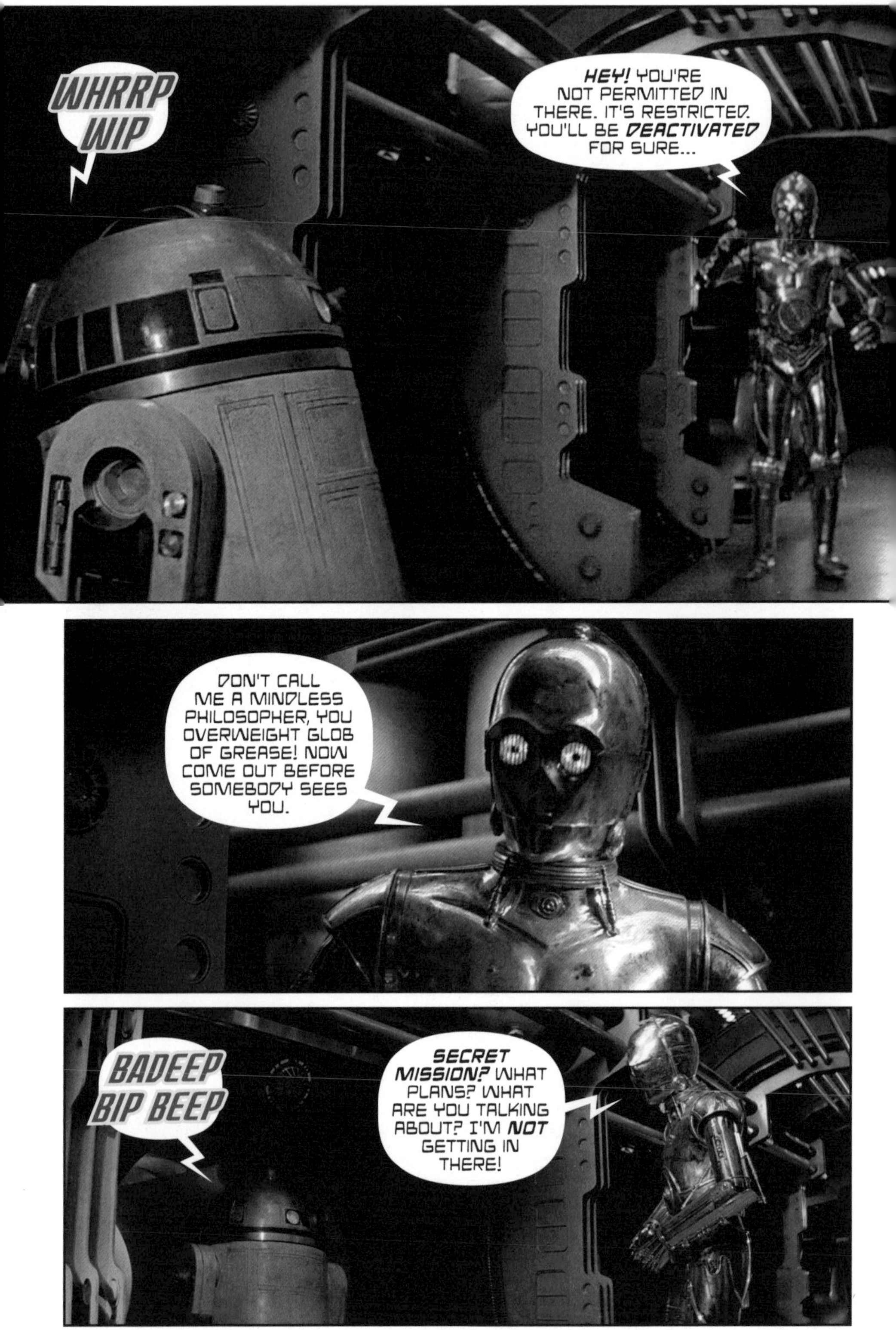
WHRRP WIP
HEY! YOU'RE NOT PERMITTED IN THERE. IT'S RESTRICTED. YOU'LL BE DEACTIVATED FOR SURE...
DON'T CALL ME A MINDLESS PHILOSOPHER, YOU OVERWEIGHT GLOB OF GREASE! NOW COME OUT BEFORE SOMEBODY SEES YOU.
BADEEP BIP BEEP
SECRET MISSION? WHAT PLANS? WHAT ARE YOU TALKING ABOUT? I'M NOT GETTING IN THERE!

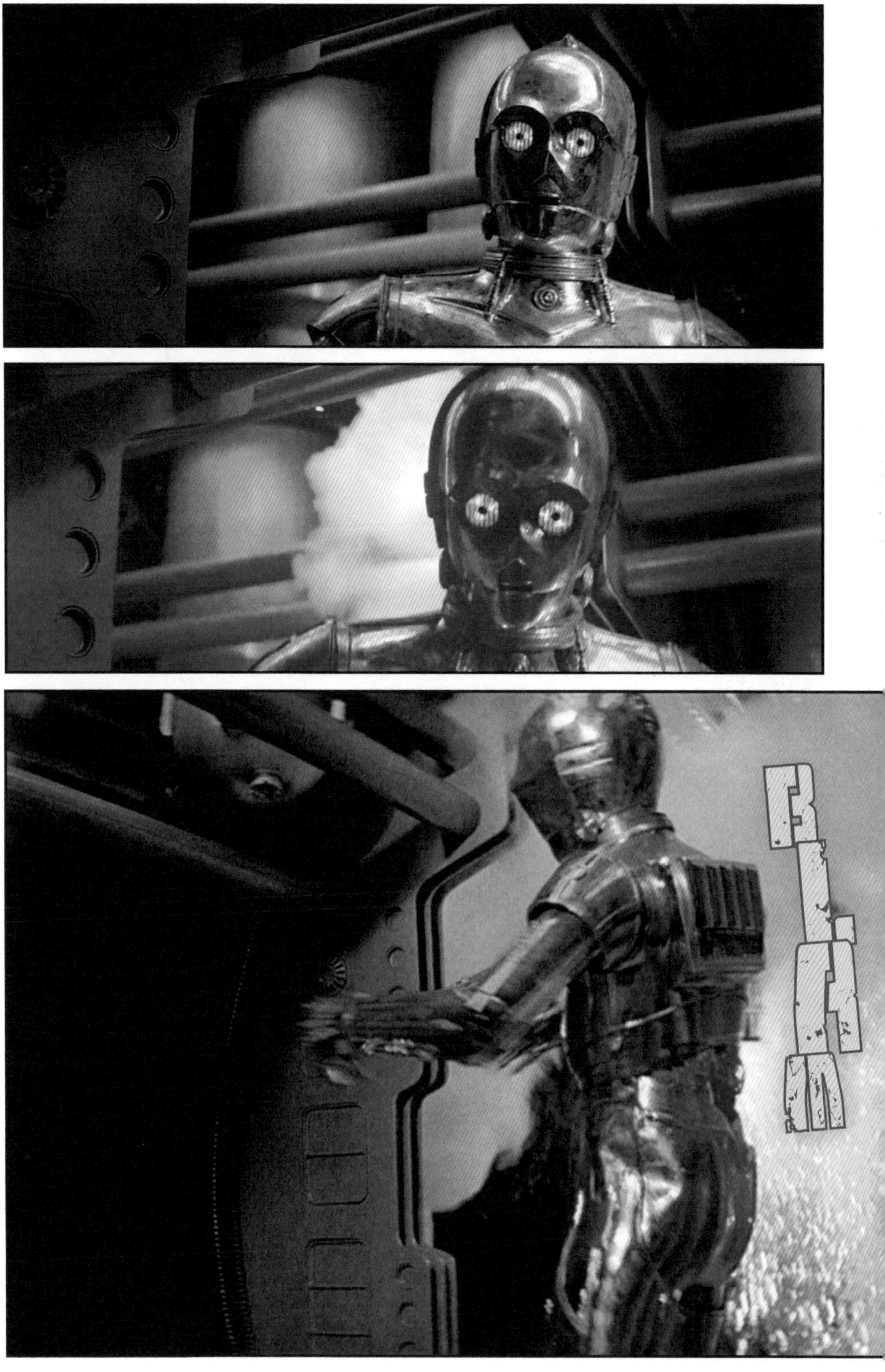
BLAM

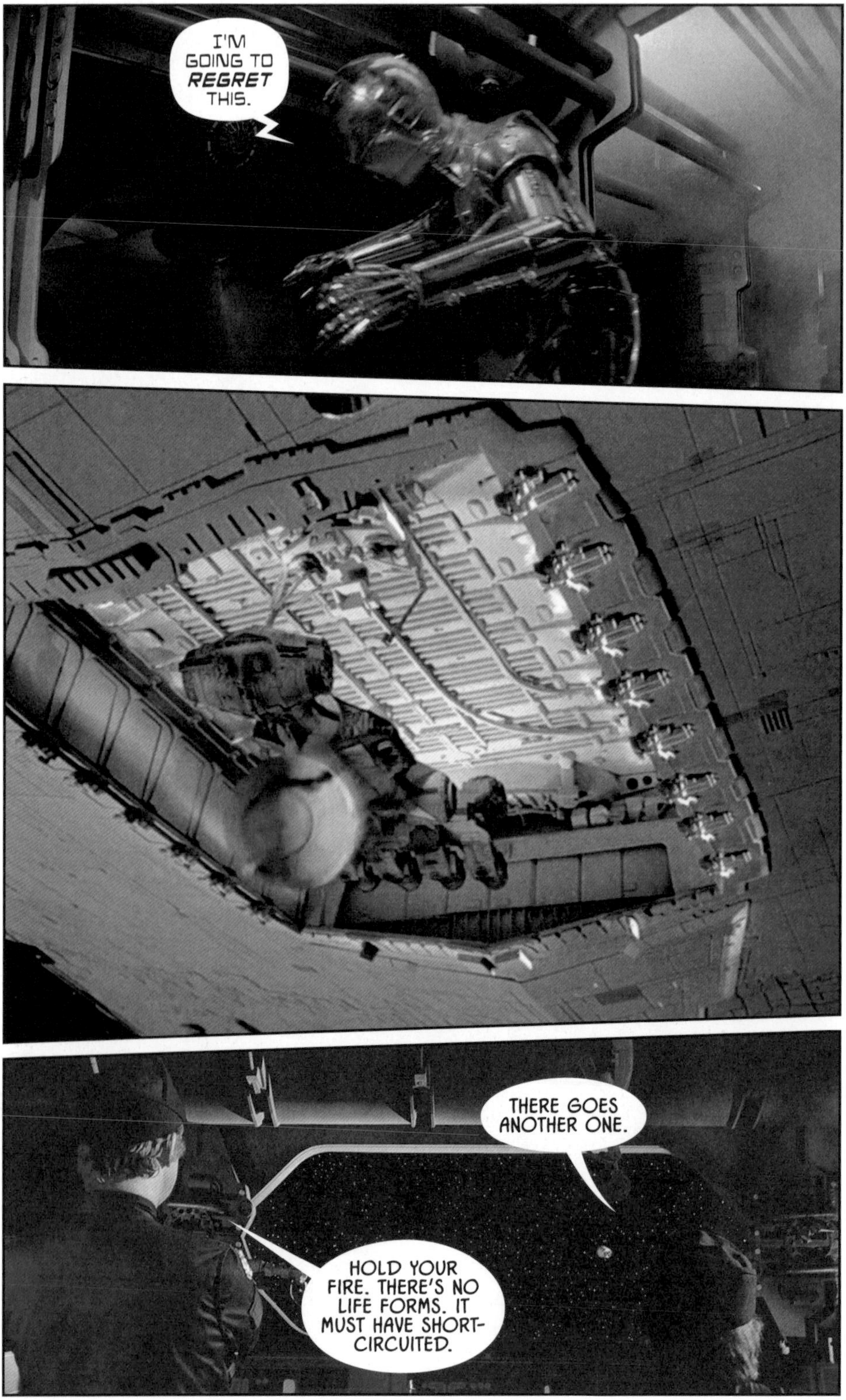
I'M GOING TO REGRET THIS.
THERE GOES ANOTHER ONE.
HOLD YOUR FIRE. THERE'S NO LIFE FORMS. IT MUST HAVE SHORT-CIRCUITED.

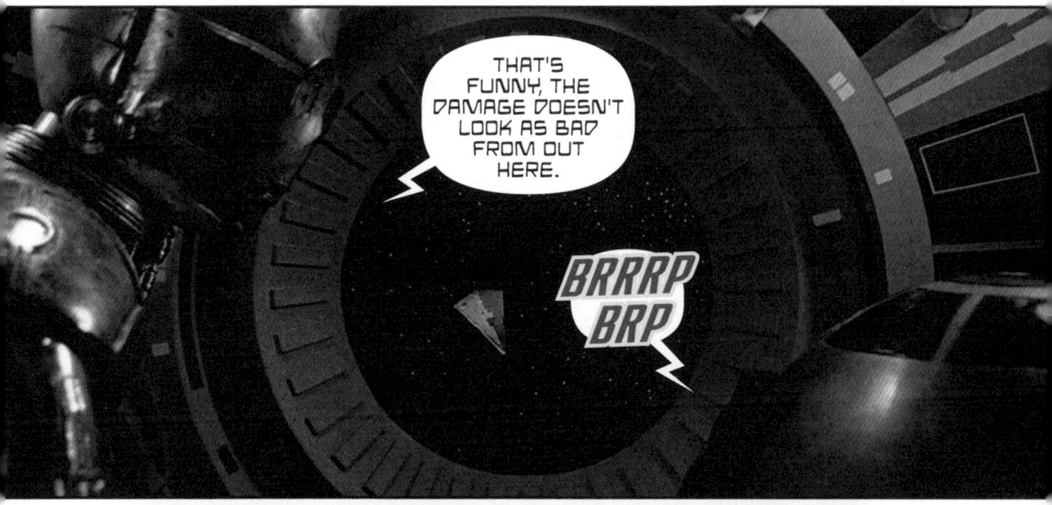
THAT'S FUNNY, THE DAMAGE DOESN'T LOOK AS BAD FROM OUT HERE.
BRRRP BRP

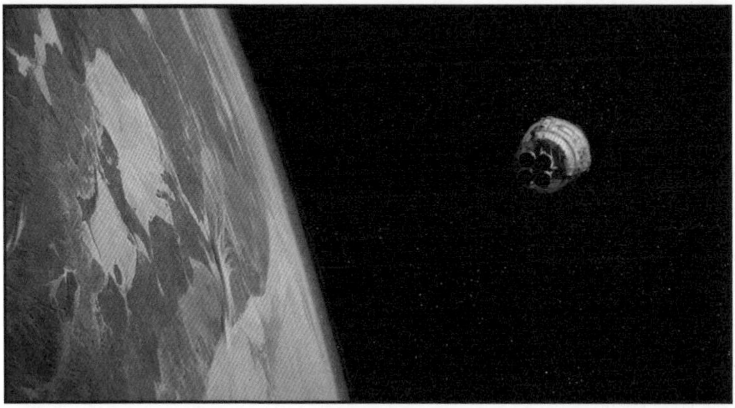

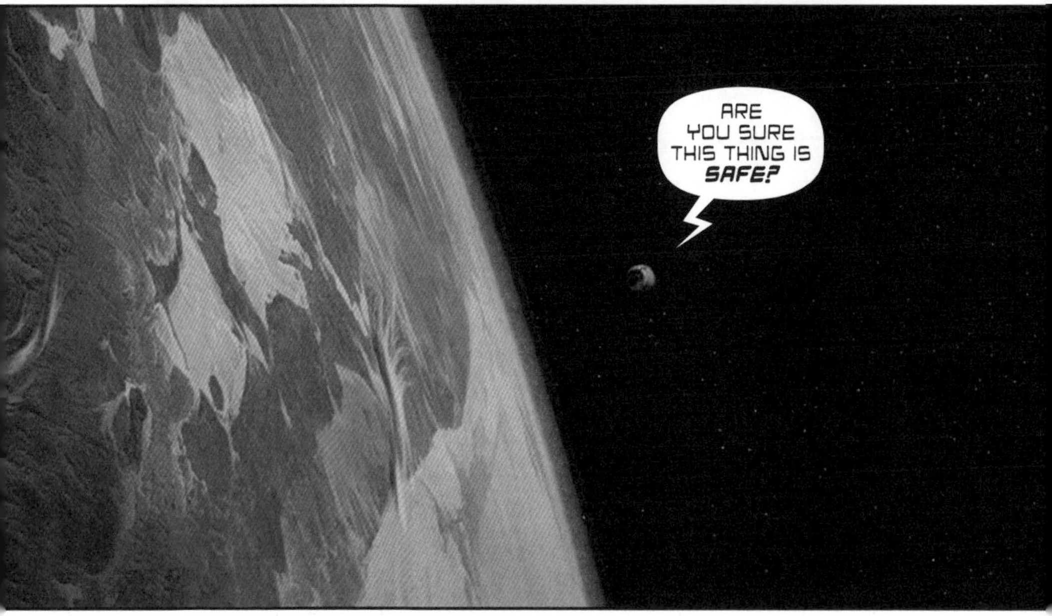
ARE YOU SURE THIS THING IS SAFE?

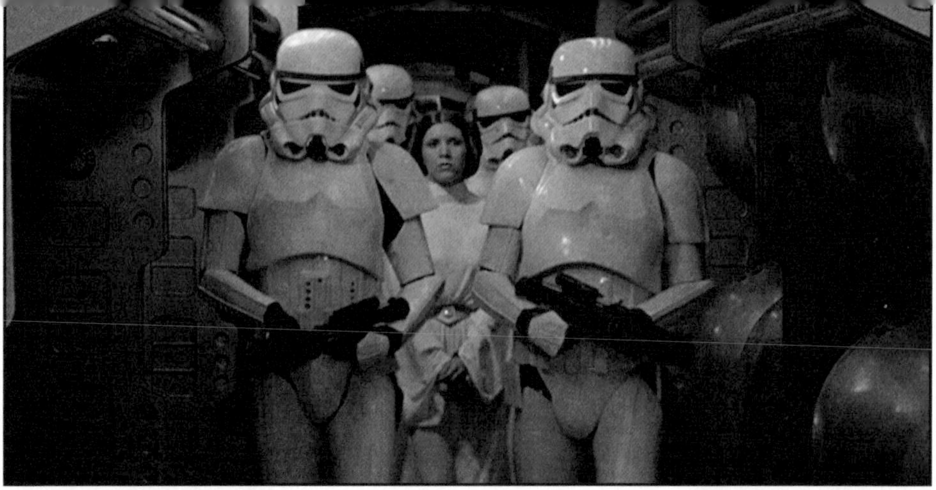

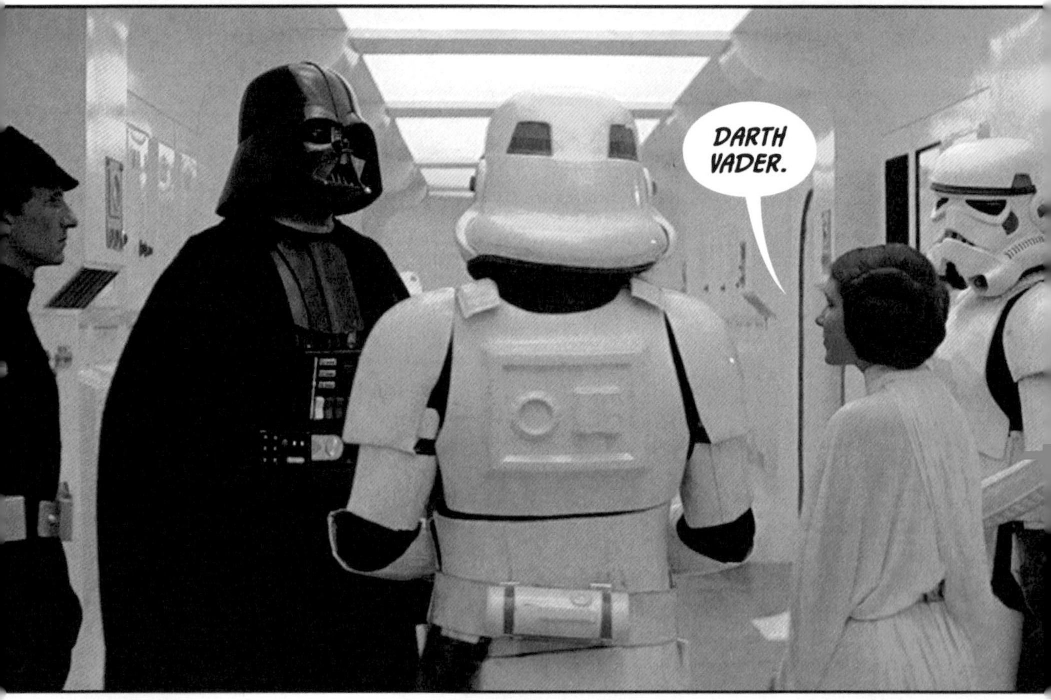
DARTH VADER.

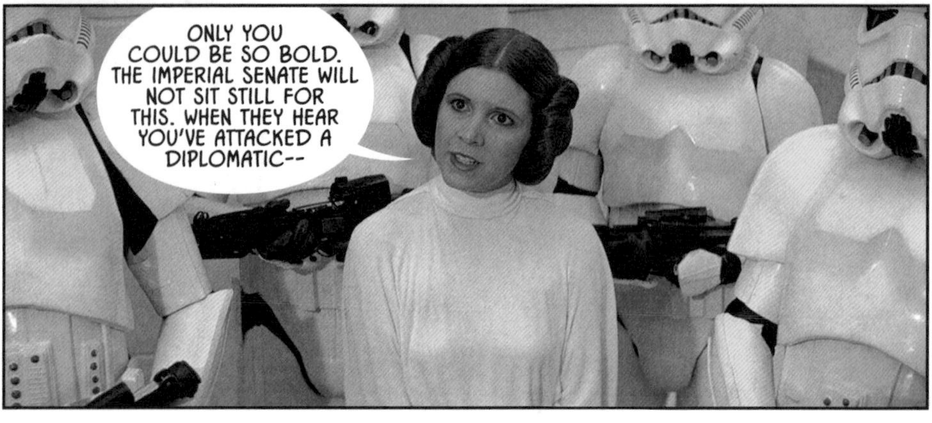
ONLY YOU COULD BE SO BOLD. THE IMPERIAL SENATE WILL NOT SIT STILL FOR THIS. WHEN THEY HEAR YOU'VE ATTACKED A DIPLOMATIC--

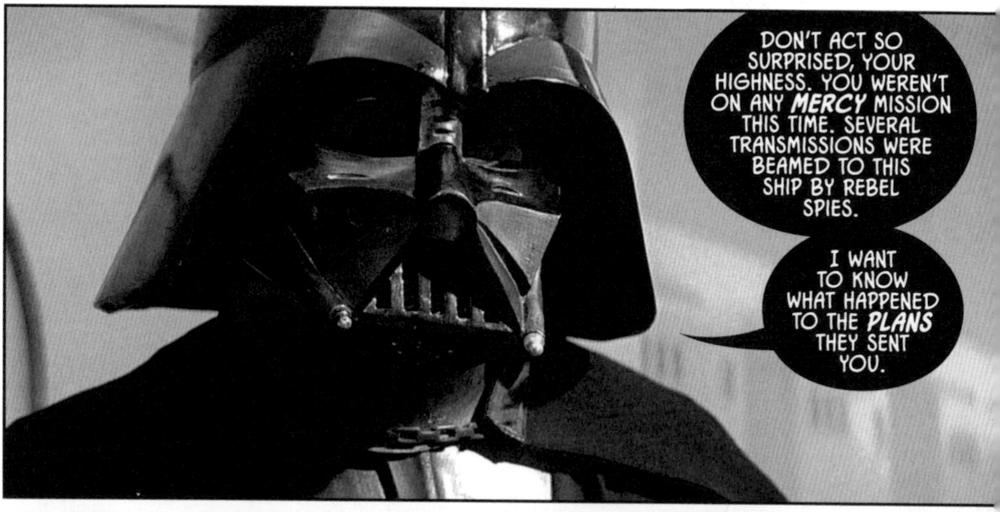
DON'T ACT SO SURPRISED, YOUR HIGHNESS. YOU WEREN'T ON ANY MERCY MISSION THIS TIME. SEVERAL TRANSMISSIONS WERE BEAMED TO THIS SHIP BY REBEL SPIES.
I WANT TO KNOW WHAT HAPPENED TO THE PLANS THEY SENT YOU.

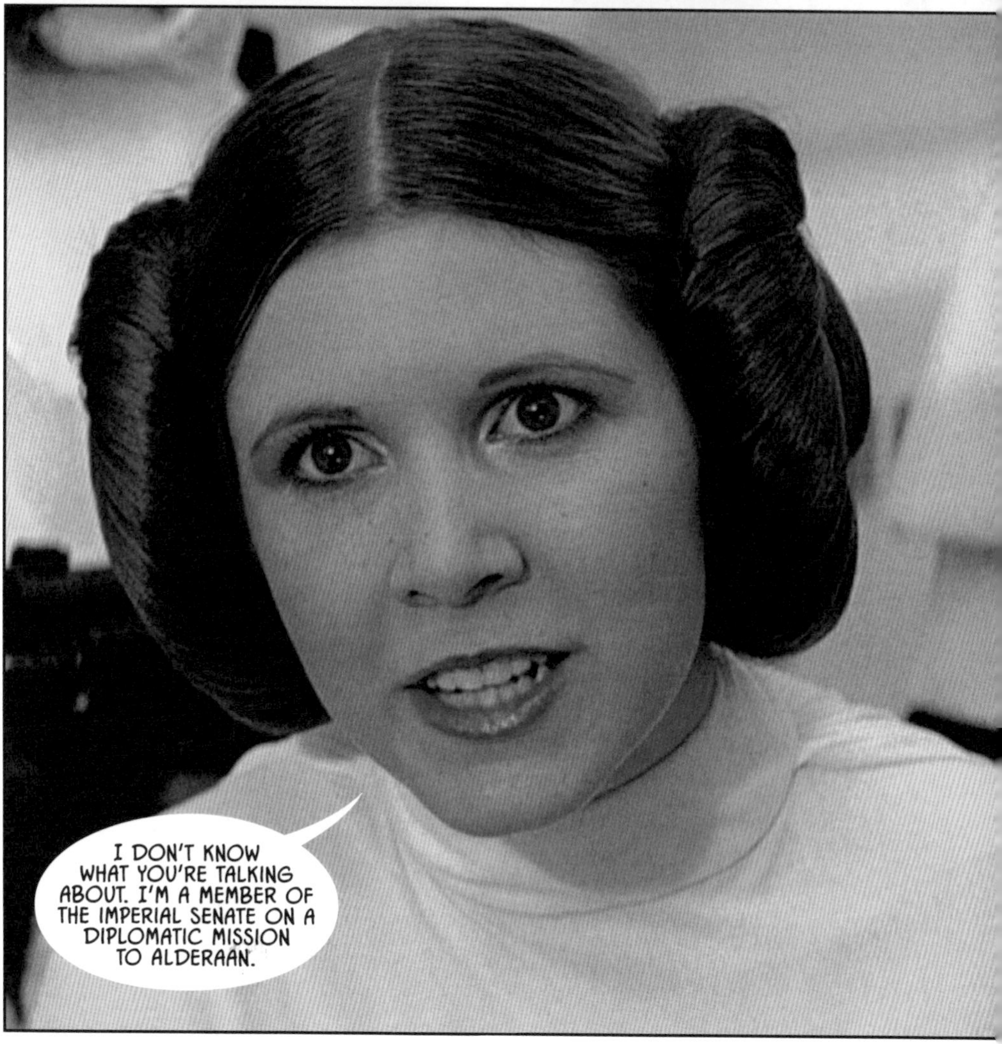
I DON'T KNOW WHAT YOU'RE TALKING ABOUT. I'M A MEMBER OF THE IMPERIAL SENATE ON A DIPLOMATIC MISSION TO ALDERAAN.

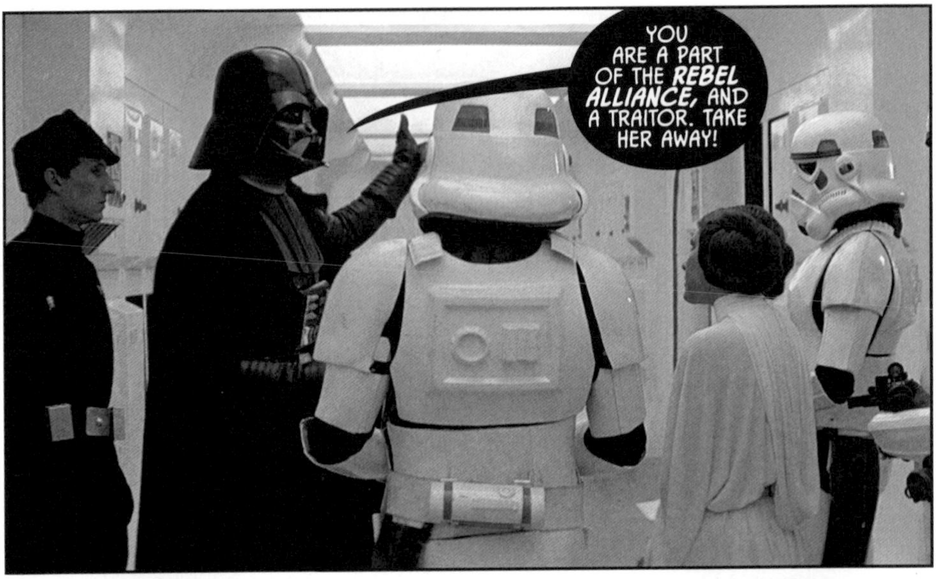
YOU ARE A PART OF THE REBEL ALLIANCE, AND A TRAITOR. TAKE HER AWAY!

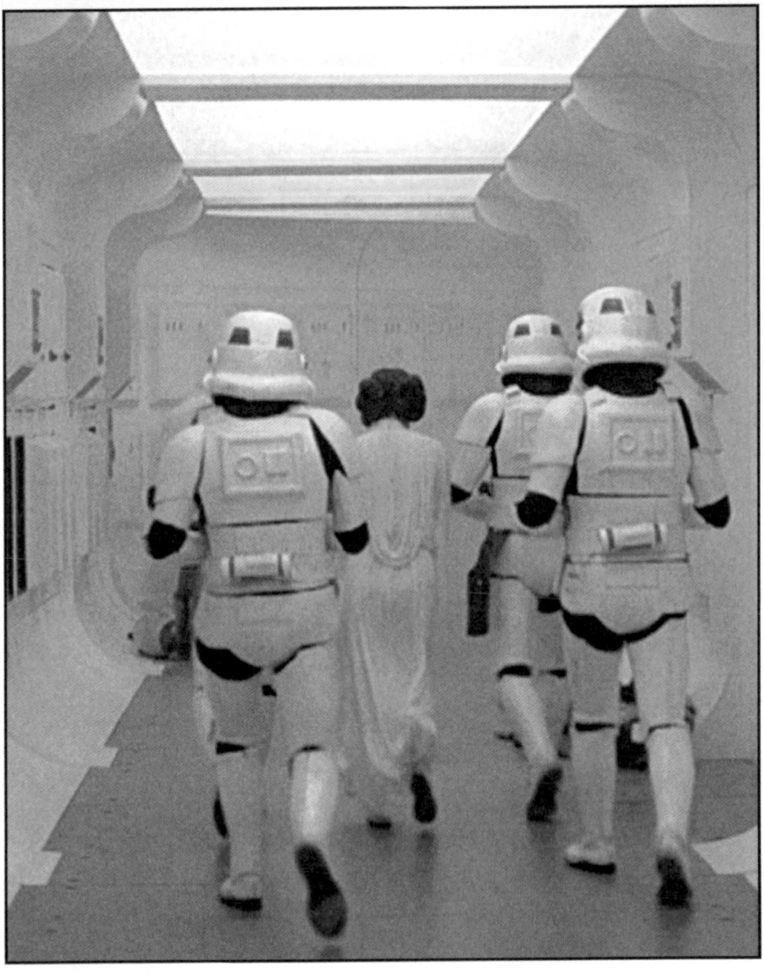

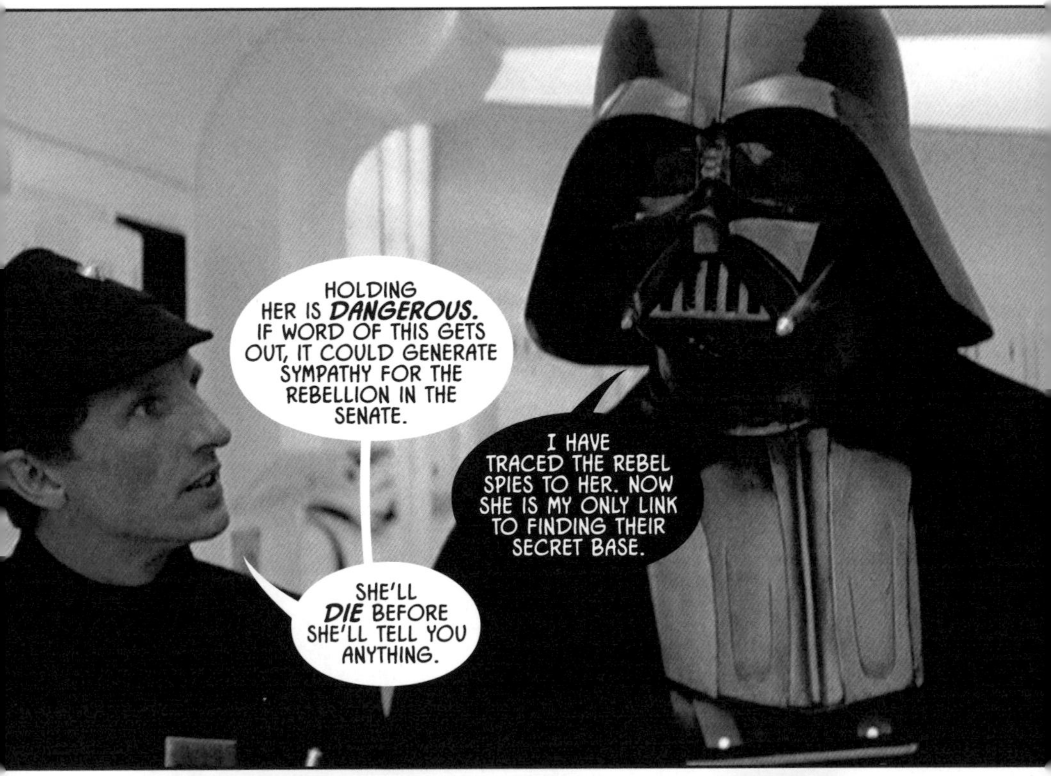
HOLDING HER IS DANGEROUS. IF WORD OF THIS GETS OUT, IT COULD GENERATE SYMPATHY FOR THE REBELLION IN THE SENATE.
I HAVE TRACED THE REBEL SPIES TO HER. NOW SHE IS MY ONLY LINK TO FINDING THEIR SECRET BASE.
SHE'LL DIE BEFORE SHE'LL TELL YOU ANYTHING.

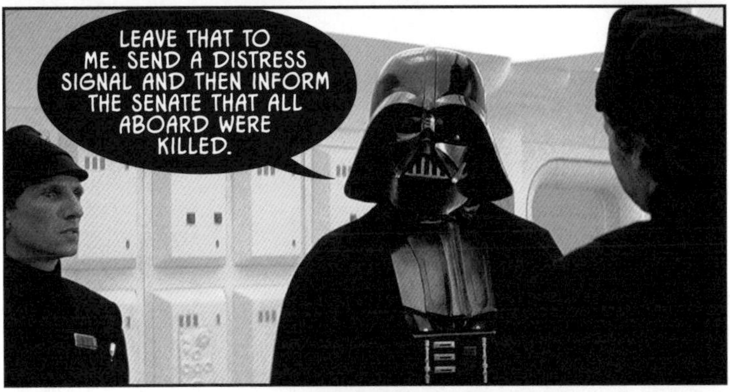
LEAVE THAT TO ME. SEND A DISTRESS SIGNAL AND THEN INFORM THE SENATE THAT ALL ABOARD WERE KILLED.

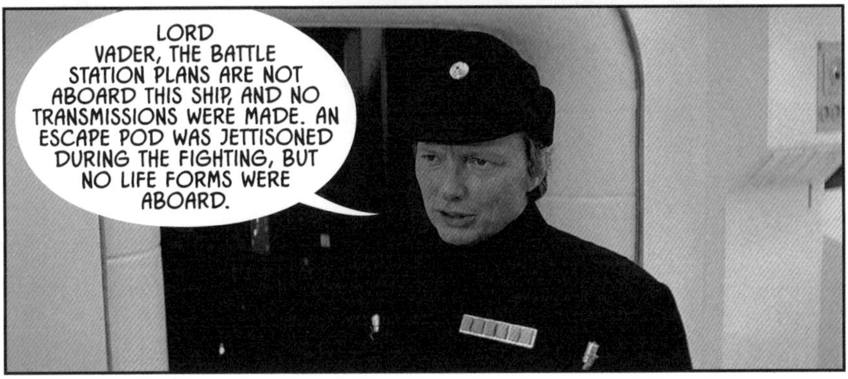
LORD VADER, THE BATTLE STATION PLANS ARE NOT ABOARD THIS SHIP, AND NO TRANSMISSIONS WERE MADE. AN ESCAPE POD WAS JETTISONED DURING THE FIGHTING, BUT NO LIFE FORMS WERE ABOARD.

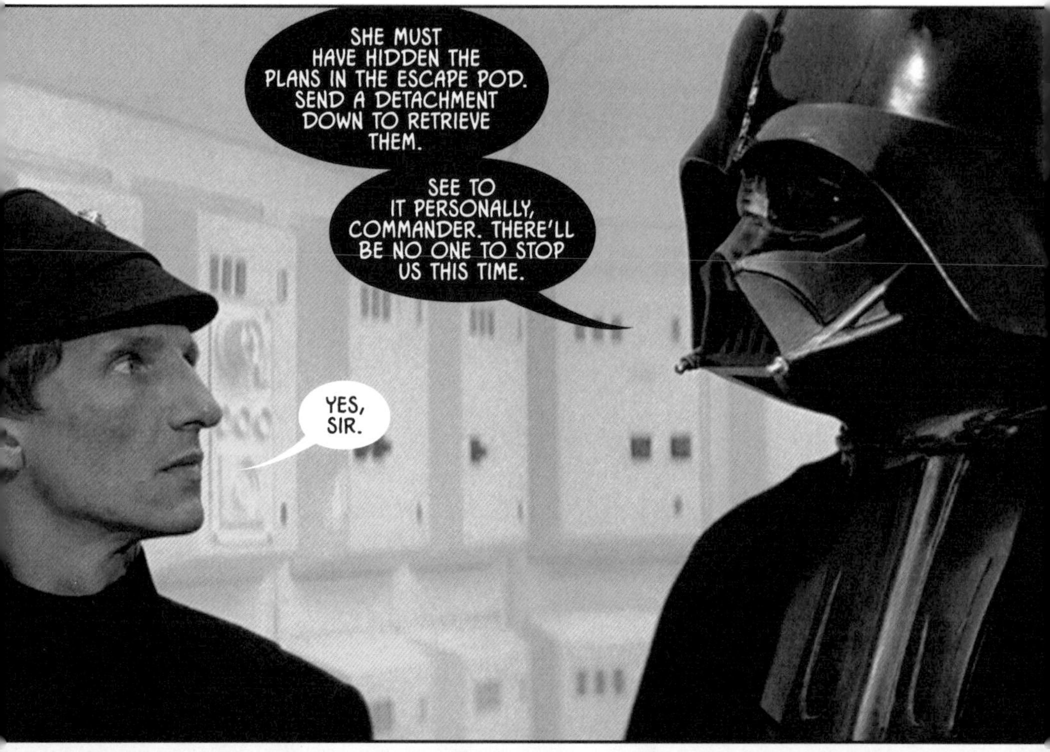
SHE MUST HAVE HIDDEN THE PLANS IN THE ESCAPE POD. SEND A DETACHMENT DOWN TO RETRIEVE THEM.
SEE TO IT PERSONALLY, COMMANDER. THERE'LL BE NO ONE TO STOP US THIS TIME.
YES, SIR.

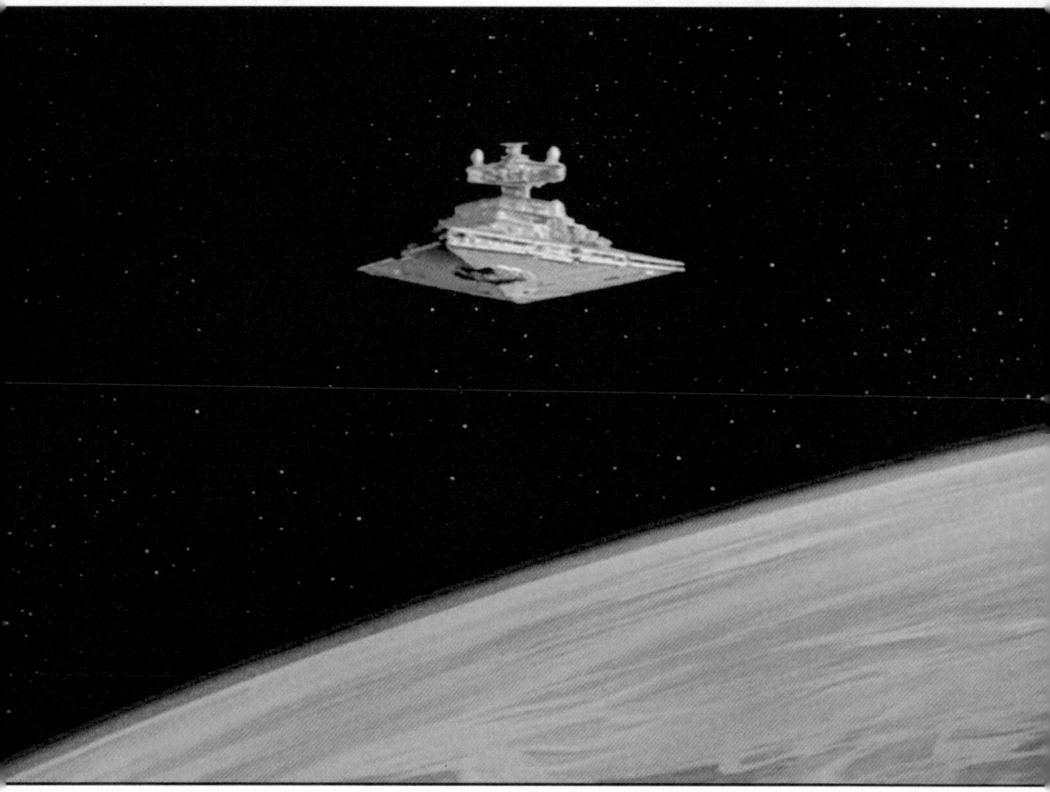

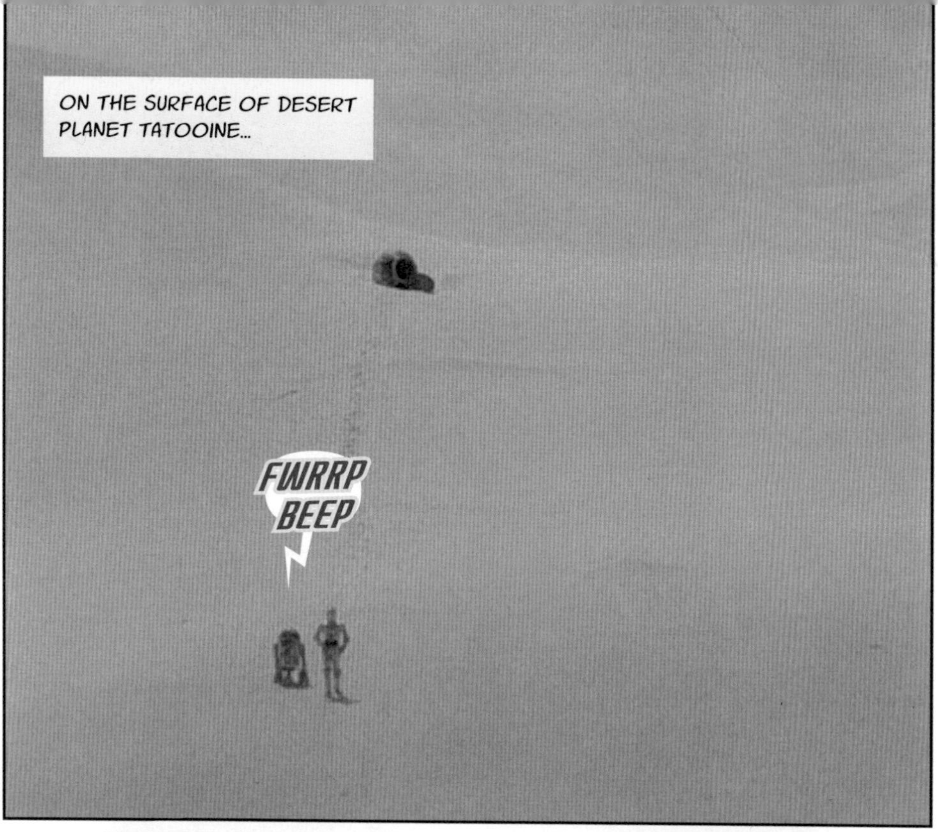
ON THE SURFACE OF DESERT PLANET TATOOINE...
FWRRP BEEP

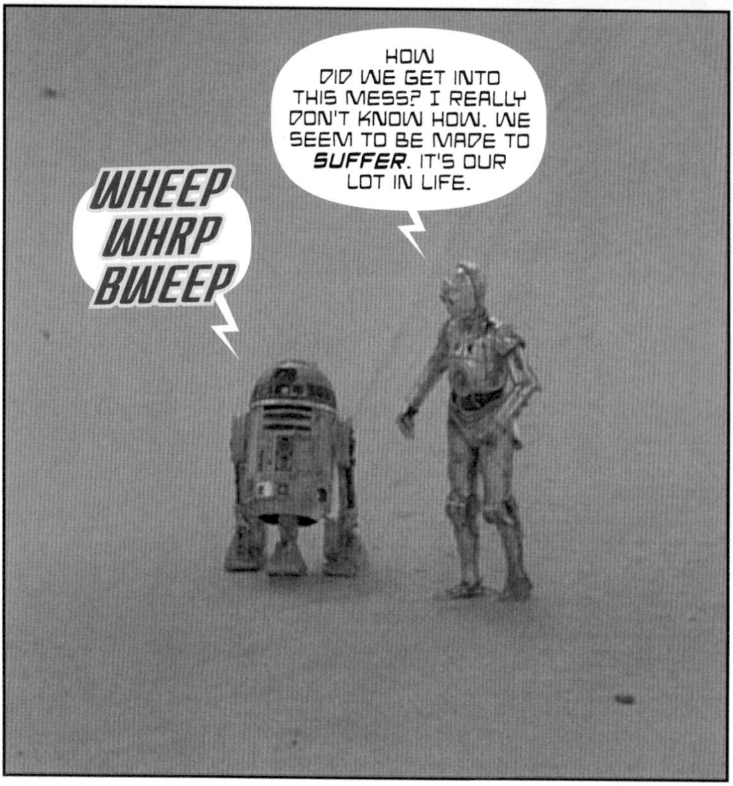
WHEEP WHRP BWEEP
HOW DID WE GET INTO THIS MESS? I REALLY DON'T KNOW HOW. WE SEEM TO BE MADE TO **SUFFER**. IT'S OUR LOT IN LIFE.

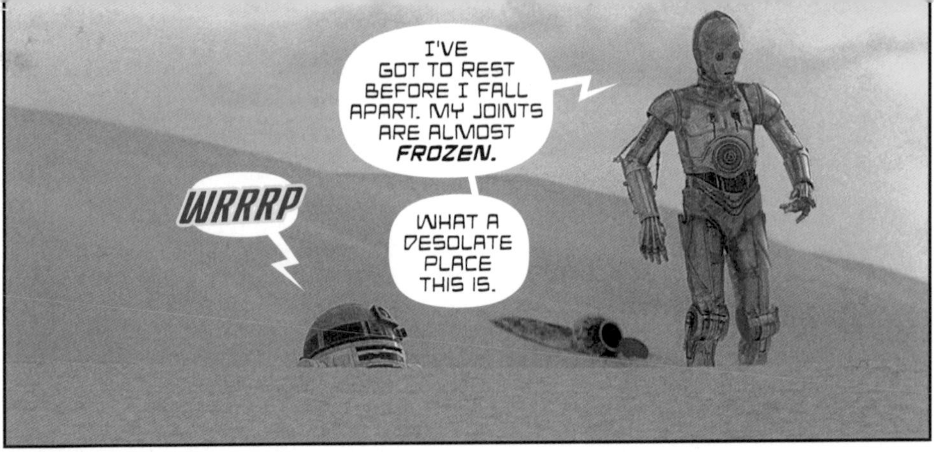
I'VE GOT TO REST BEFORE I FALL APART. MY JOINTS ARE ALMOST **FROZEN.**
WHAT A DESOLATE PLACE THIS IS.
WRRRP

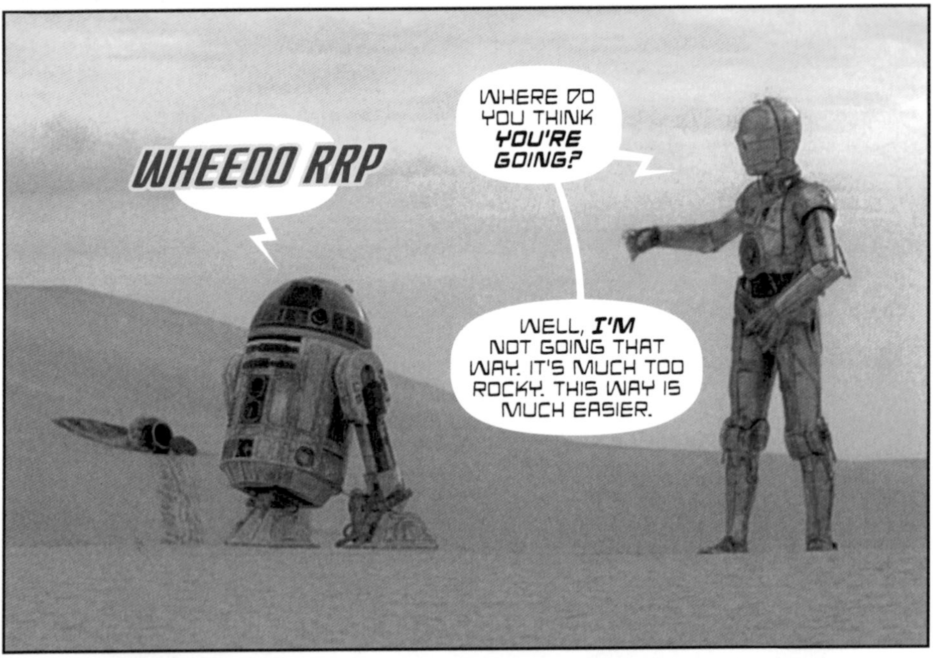
WHEEOO RRP
WHERE DO YOU THINK **YOU'RE** GOING?
WELL, **I'M** NOT GOING THAT WAY. IT'S MUCH TOO ROCKY. THIS WAY IS MUCH EASIER.

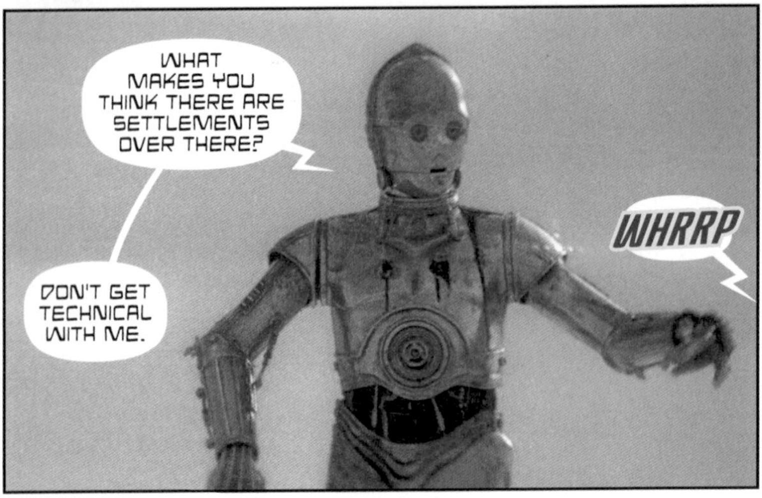
WHAT MAKES YOU THINK THERE ARE SETTLEMENTS OVER THERE?
WHRRP
DON'T GET TECHNICAL WITH ME.

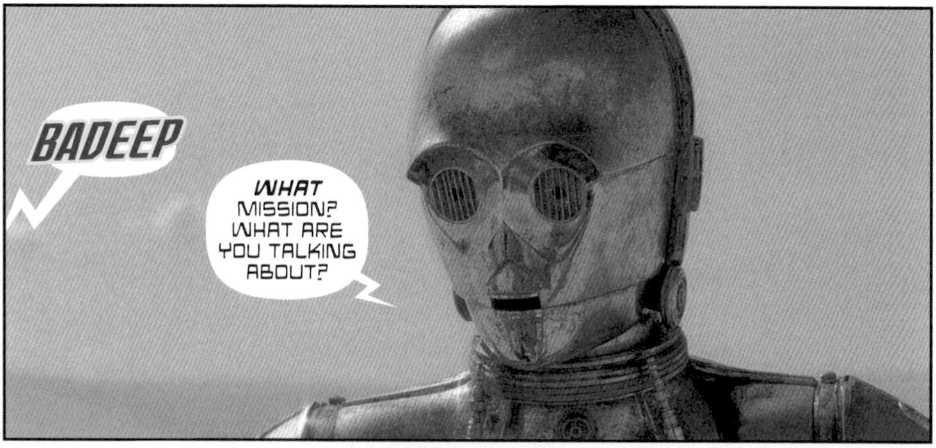
BADEEP
WHAT MISSION? WHAT ARE YOU TALKING ABOUT?

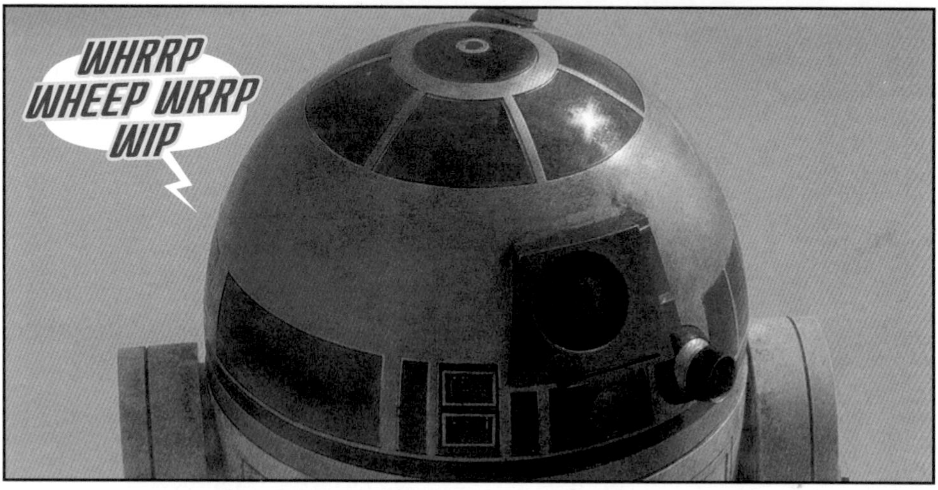
WHRRP WHEEP WRRP WIP

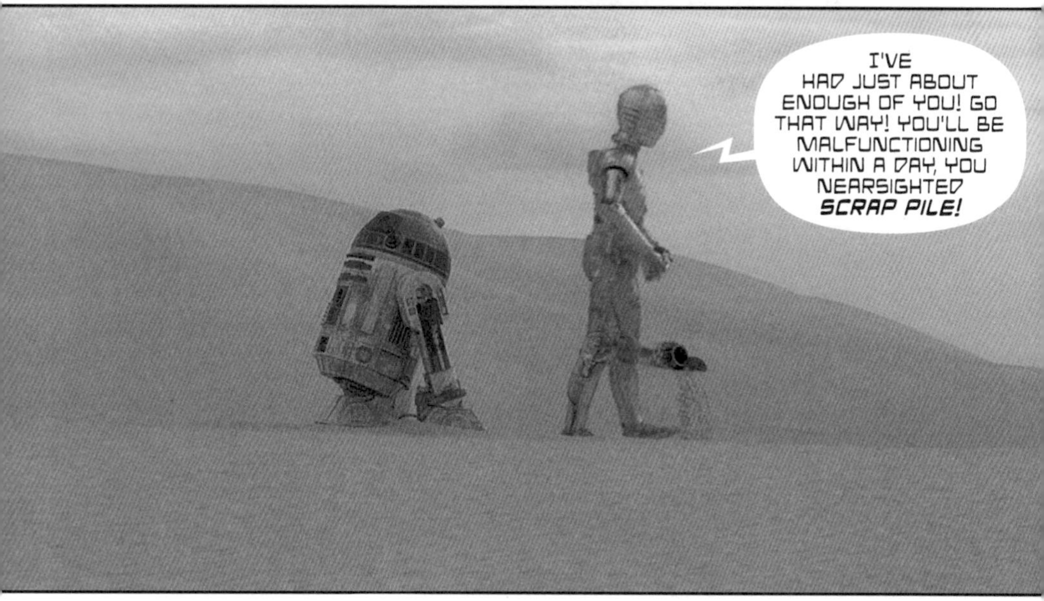
I'VE HAD JUST ABOUT ENOUGH OF YOU! GO THAT WAY! YOU'LL BE MALFUNCTIONING WITHIN A DAY, YOU NEARSIGHTED SCRAP PILE!

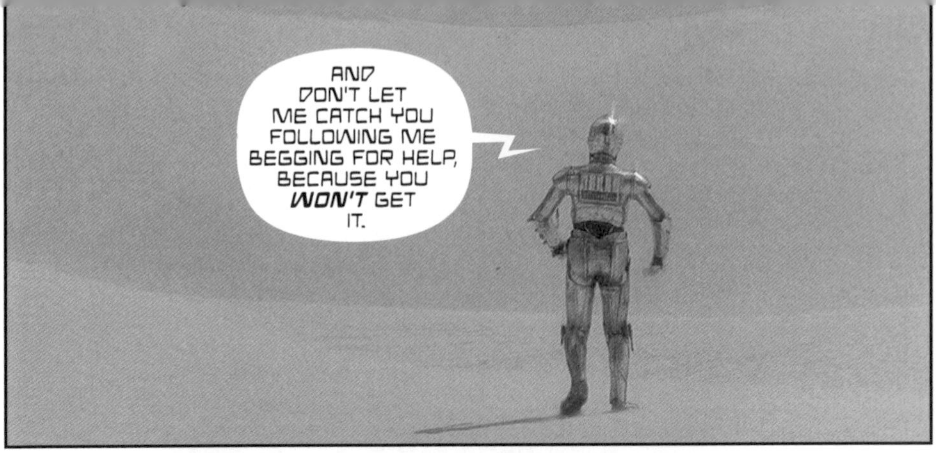
AND DON'T LET ME CATCH YOU FOLLOWING ME BEGGING FOR HELP, BECAUSE YOU *WON'T* GET IT.

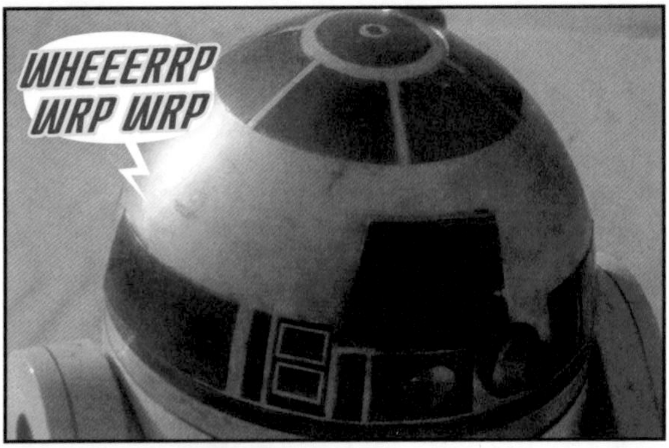
WHEEERRP WRP WRP

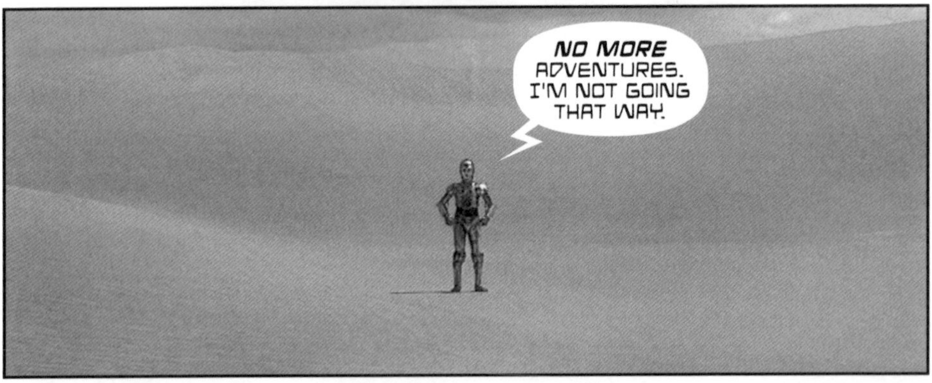
NO MORE ADVENTURES. I'M NOT GOING THAT WAY.

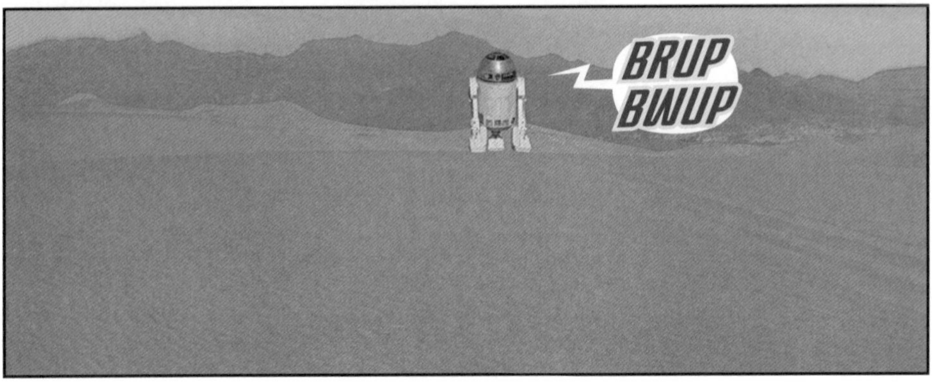
BRUP BWUP

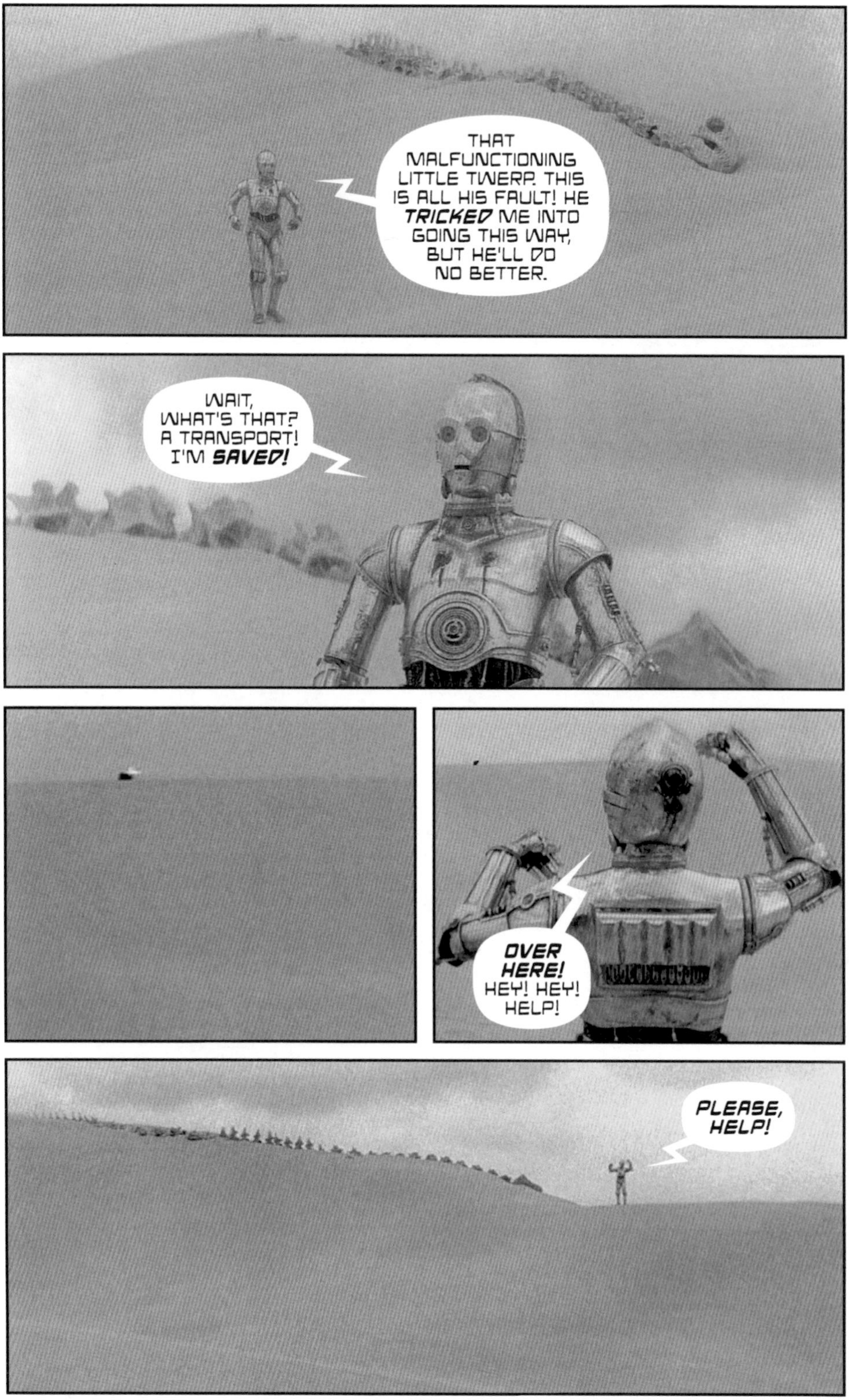
THAT MALFUNCTIONING LITTLE TWERP. THIS IS ALL HIS FAULT! HE *TRICKED* ME INTO GOING THIS WAY, BUT HE'LL DO NO BETTER.
WAIT, WHAT'S THAT? A TRANSPORT! I'M *SAVED!*
OVER HERE! HEY! HEY! HELP!
PLEASE, HELP!

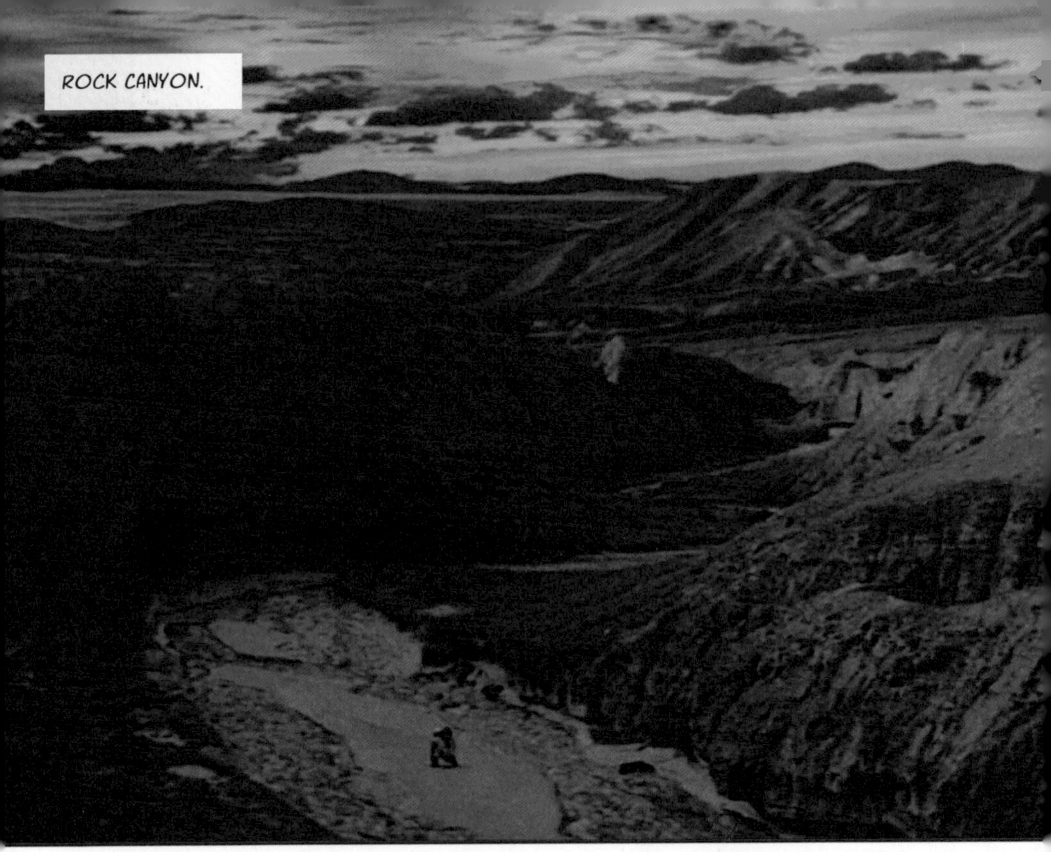
ROCK CANYON.

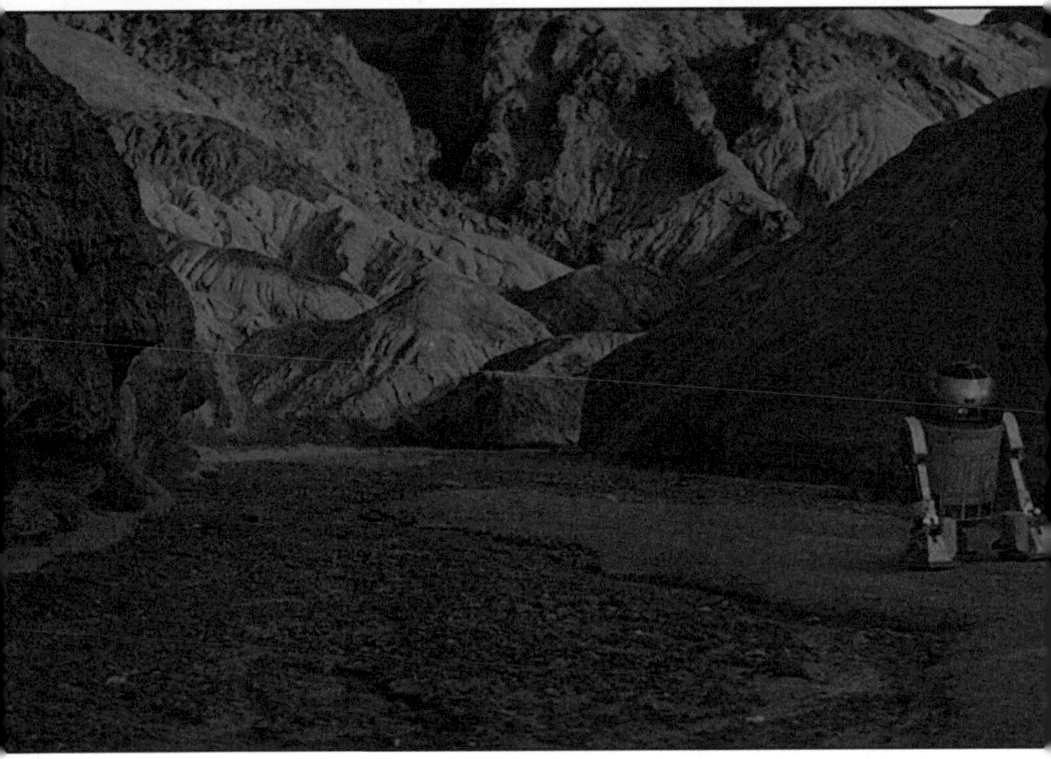

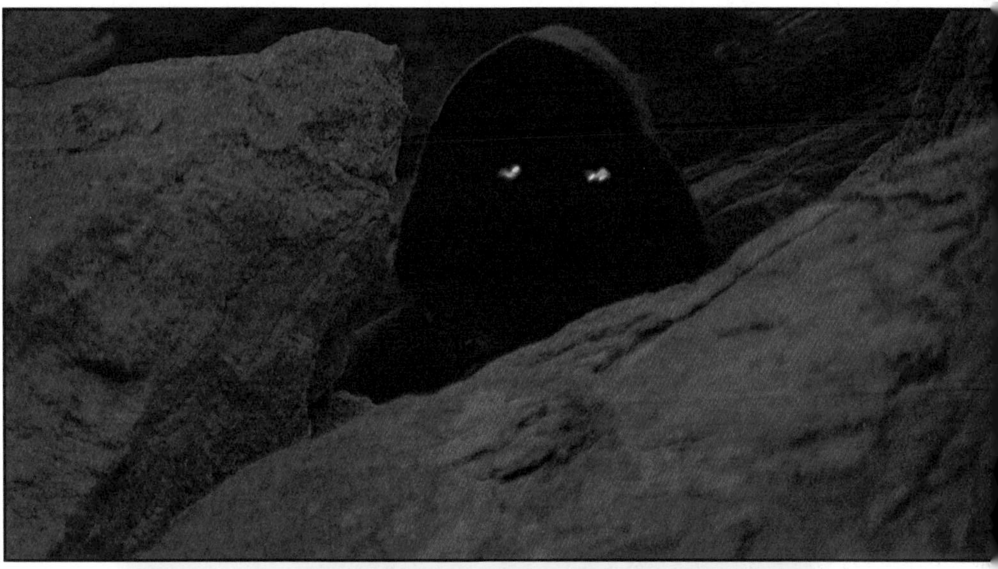

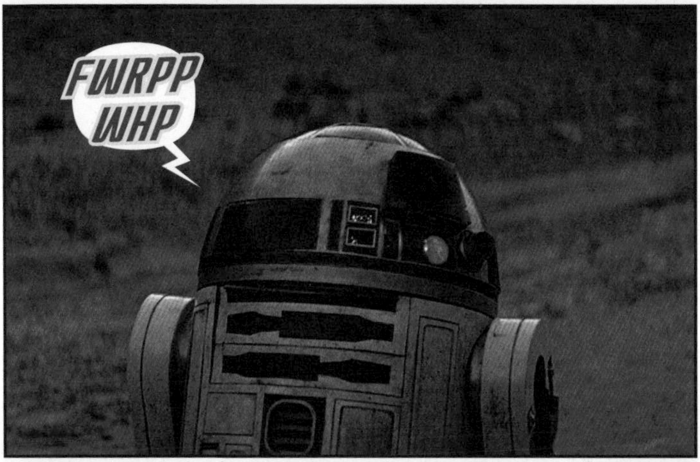
FWRPP
WHP

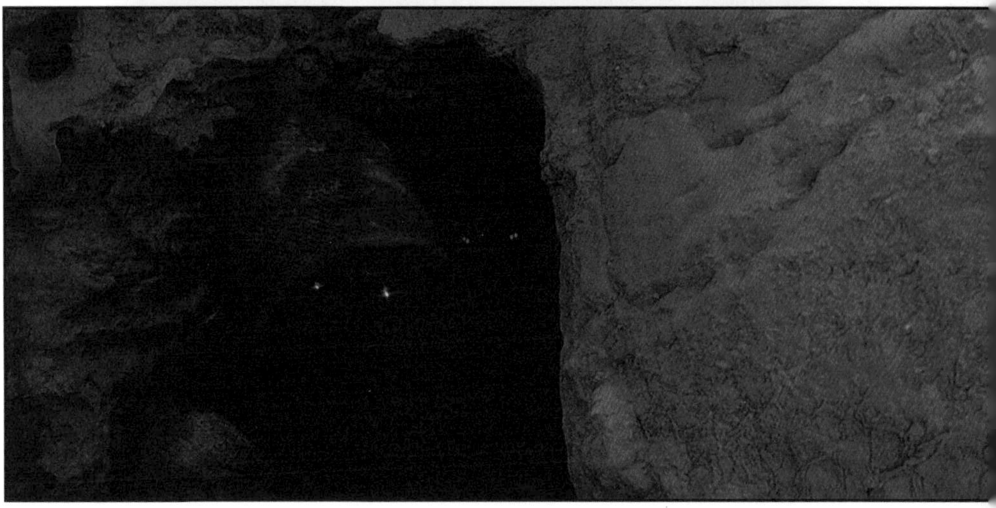

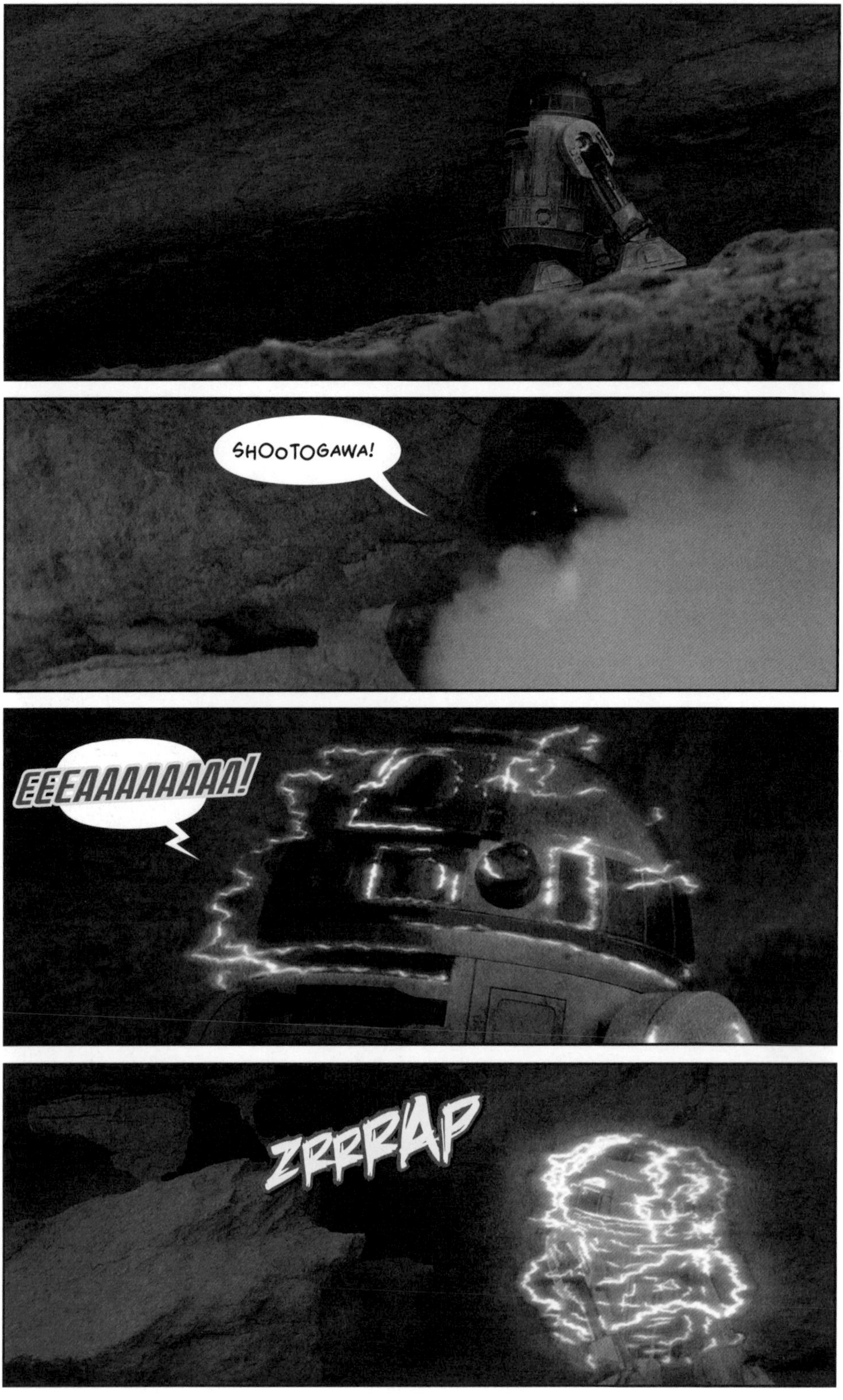
SHOOTOGAWA!
EEEAAAAAAAA!
ZRRRAP

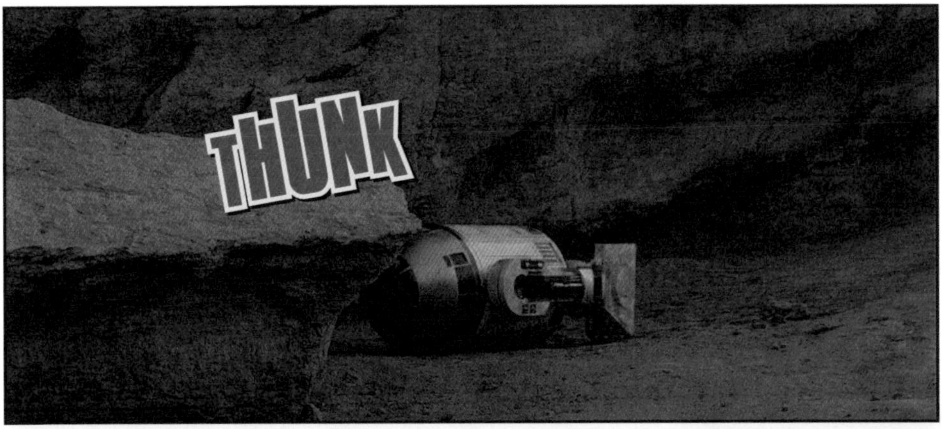
THUNK

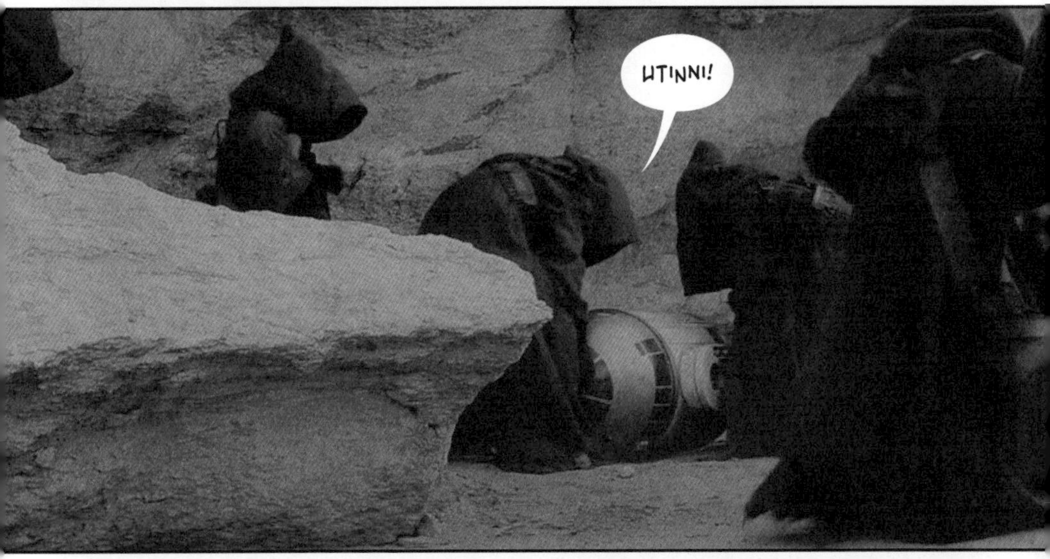
UTINNI!

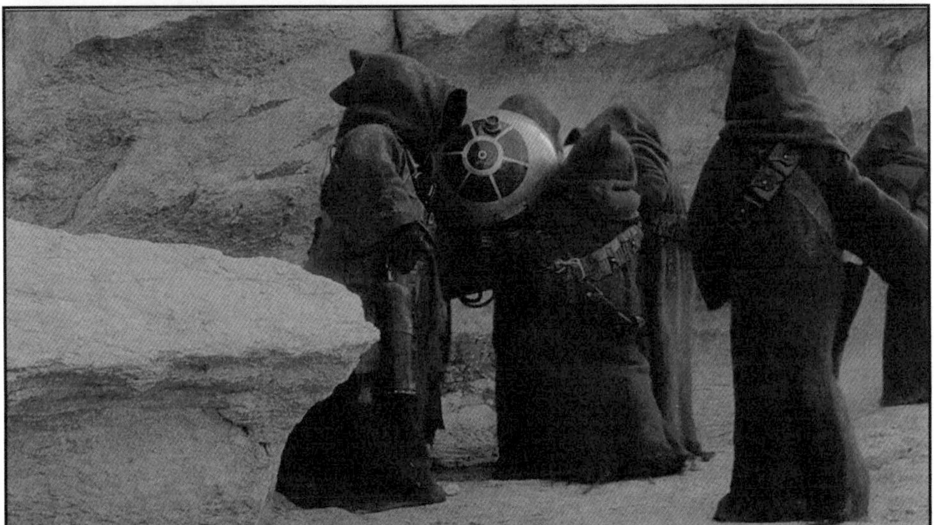

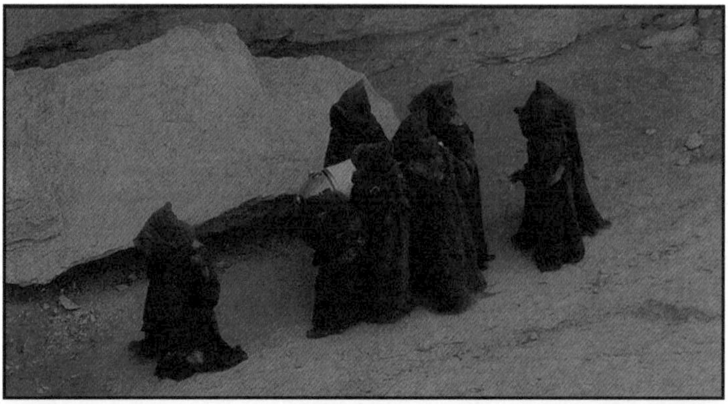

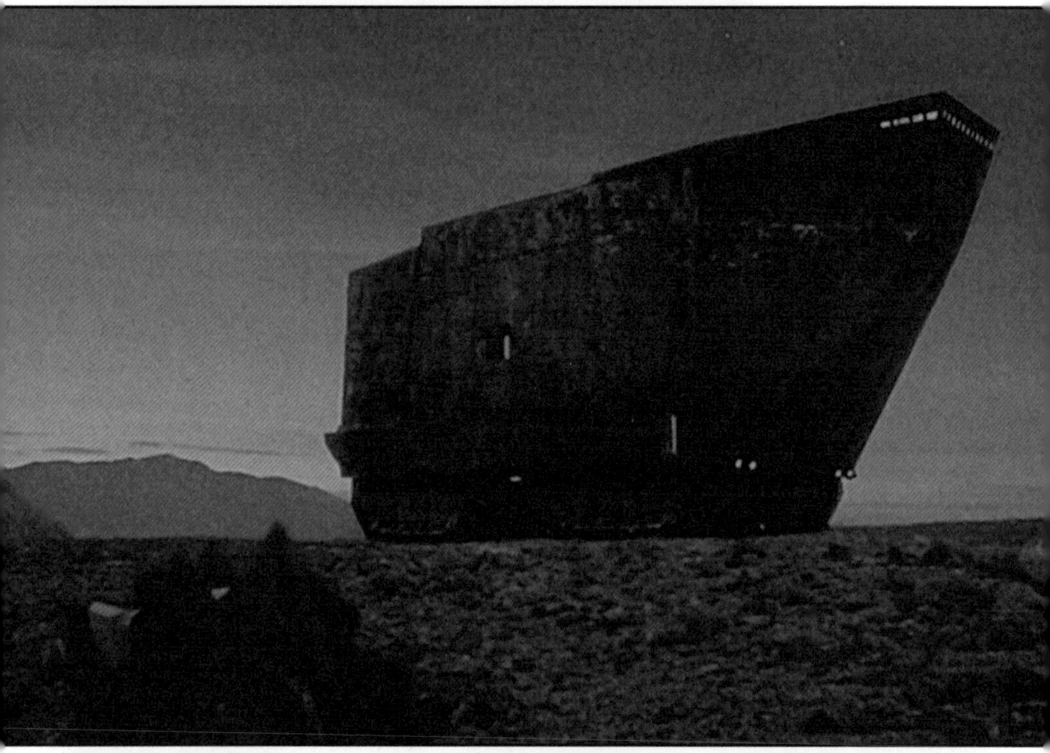

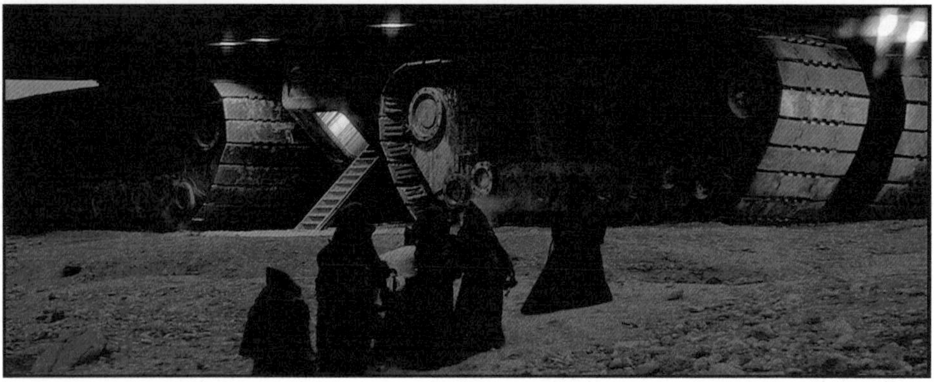

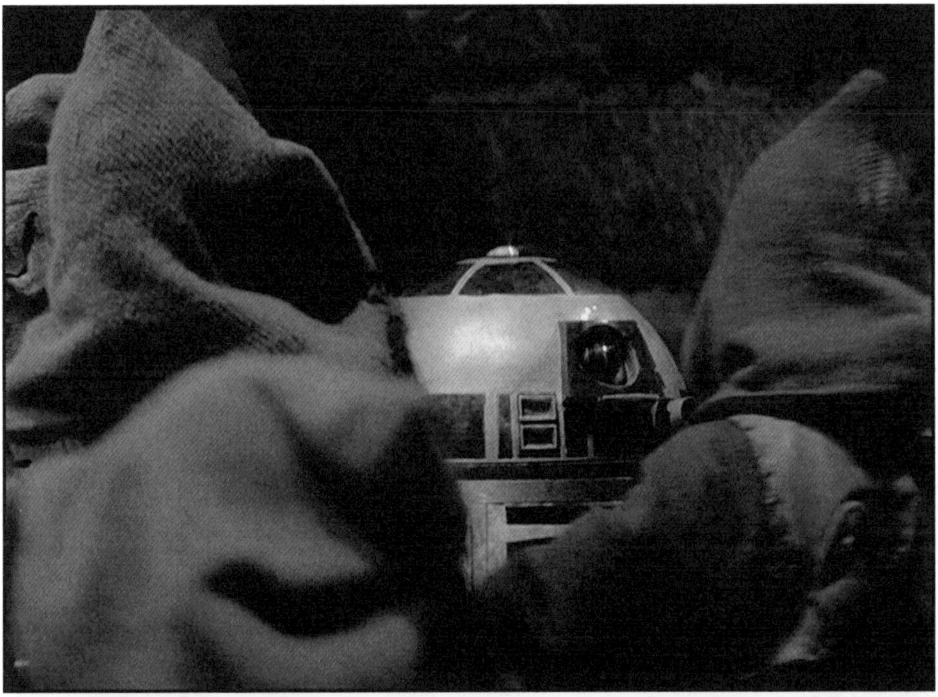

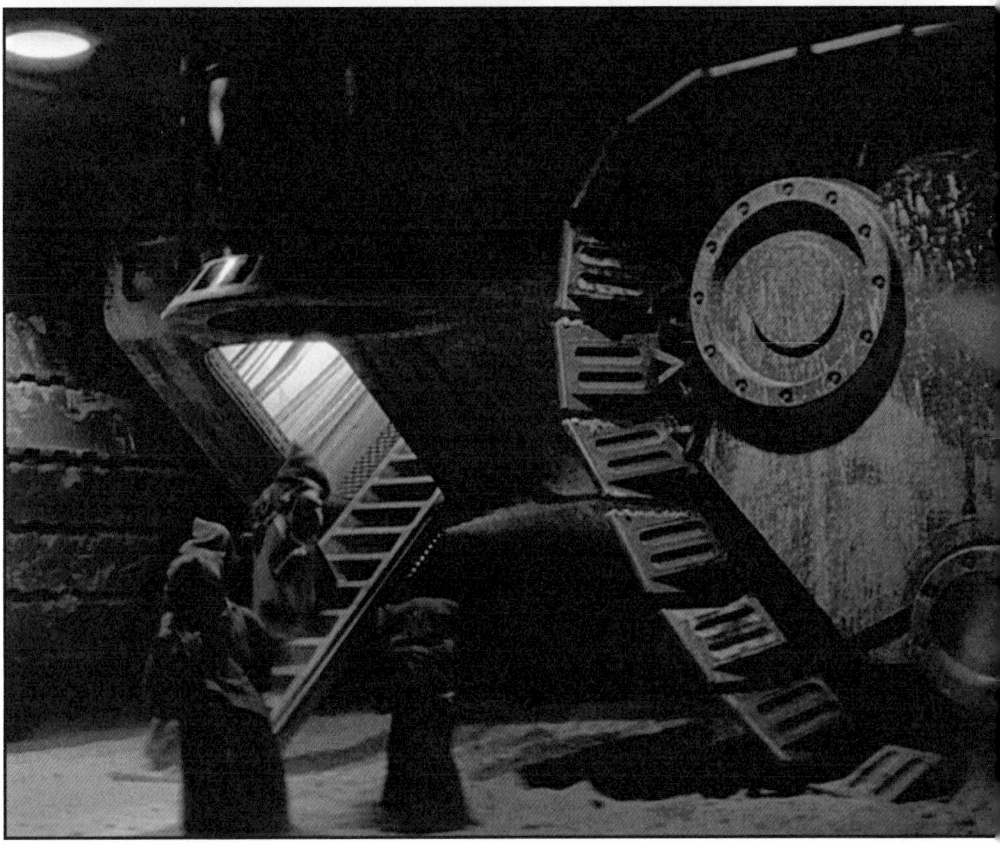

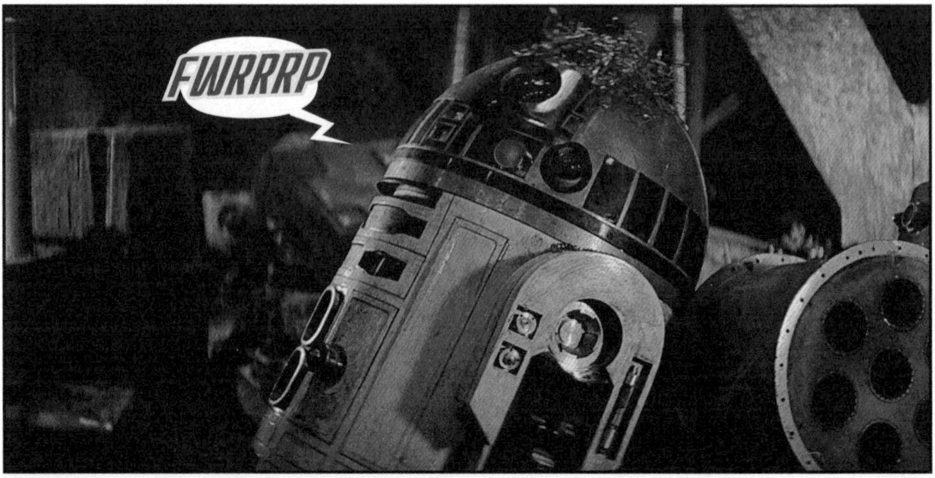
FWRRRP

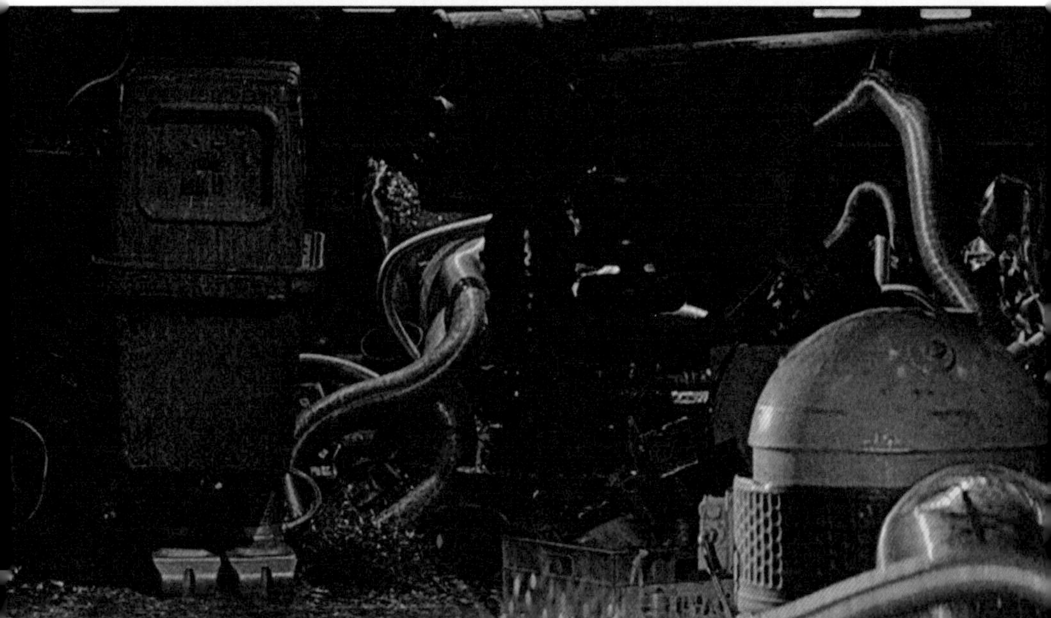

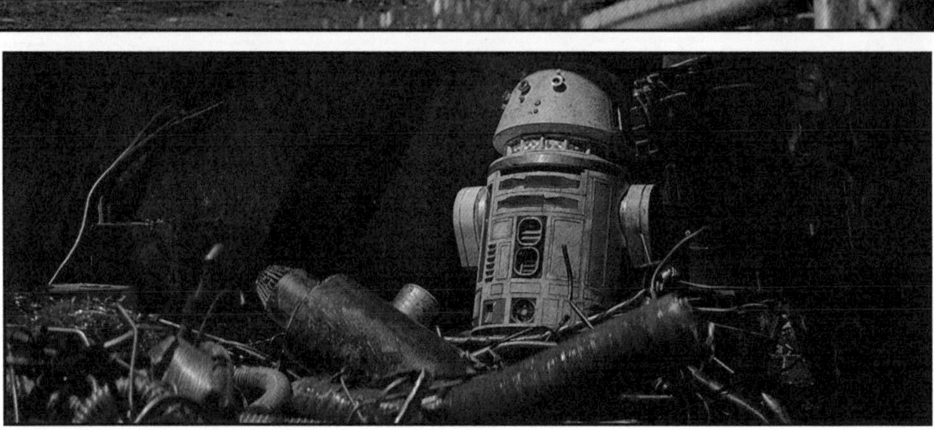

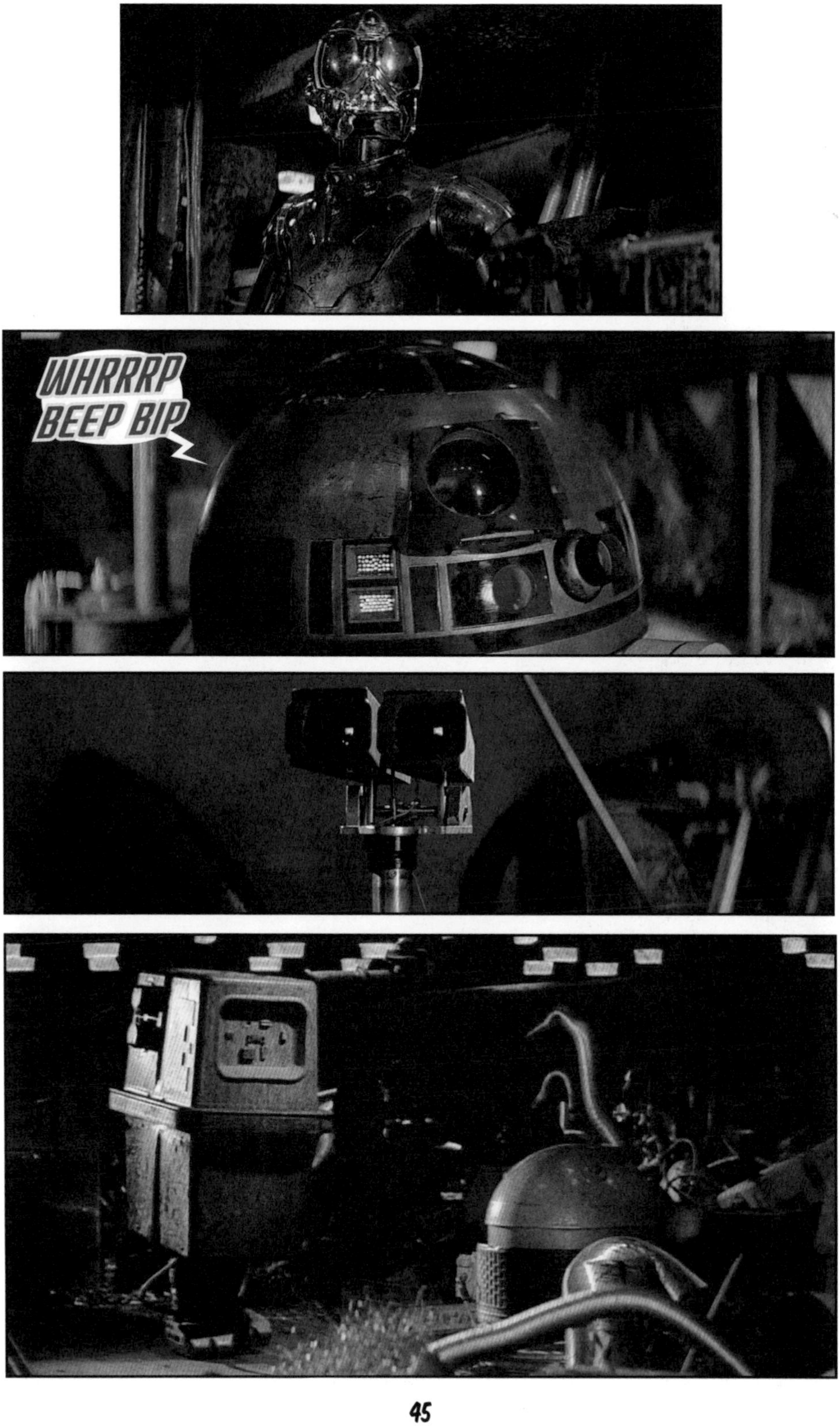
WHRRRP BEEP BIP

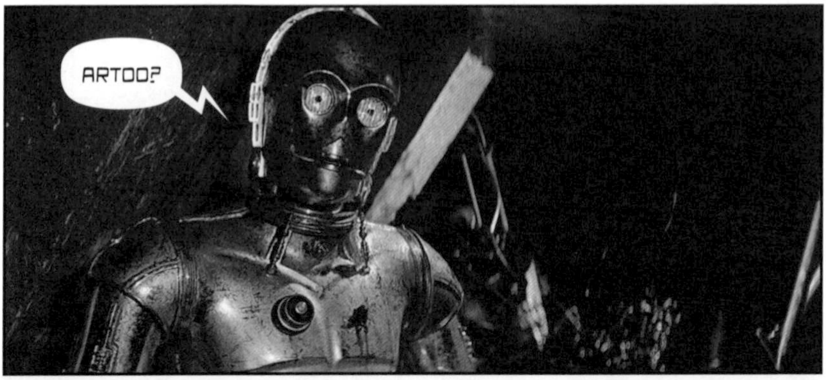
ARTOO?

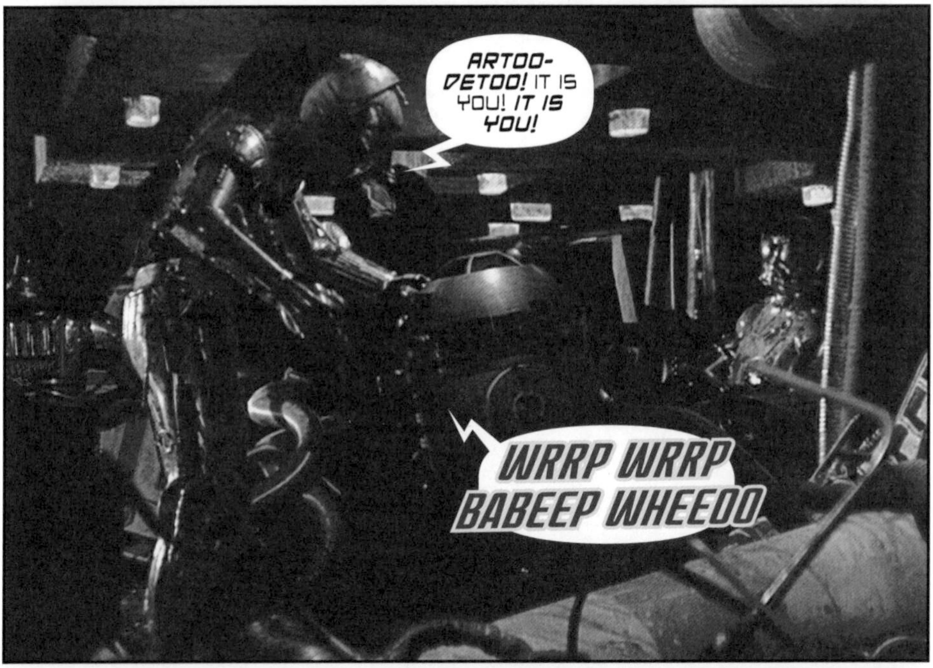
ARTOO-DETOO! IT IS YOU! IT IS YOU!
WRRP WRRP BABEEP WHEEDO

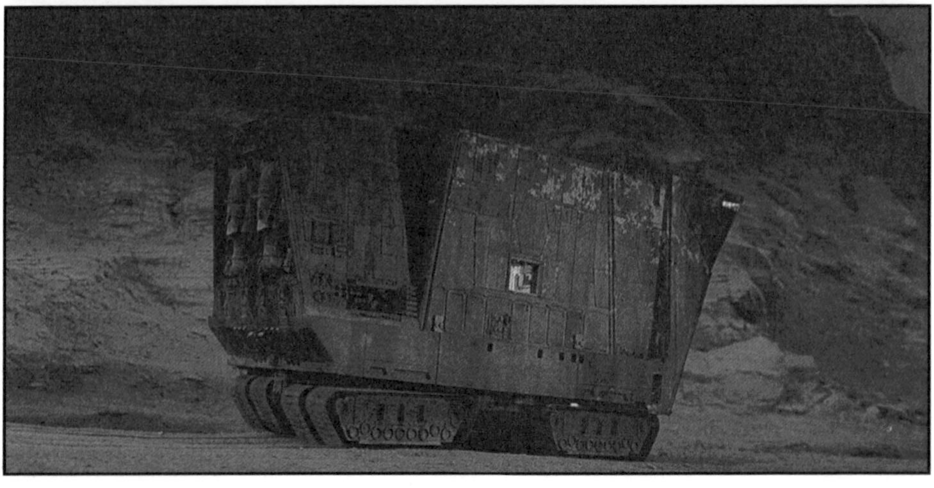

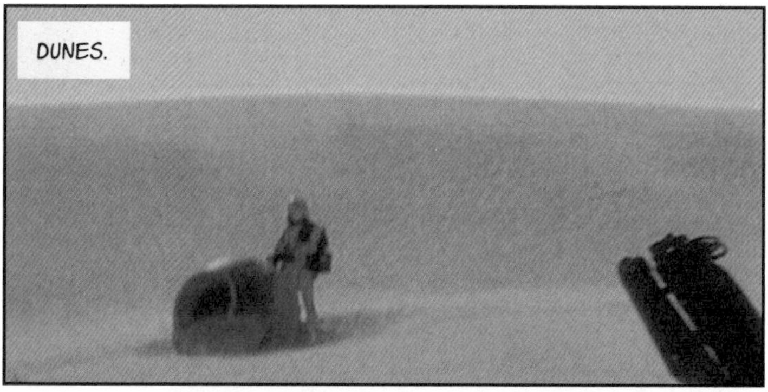
DUNES.

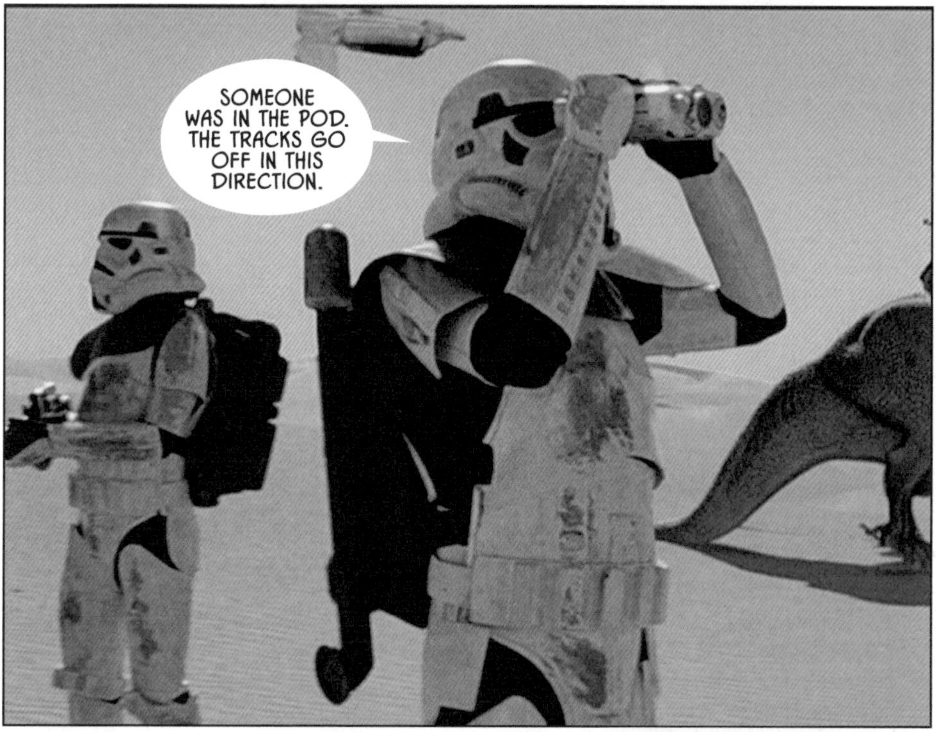
SOMEONE WAS IN THE POD. THE TRACKS GO OFF IN THIS DIRECTION.

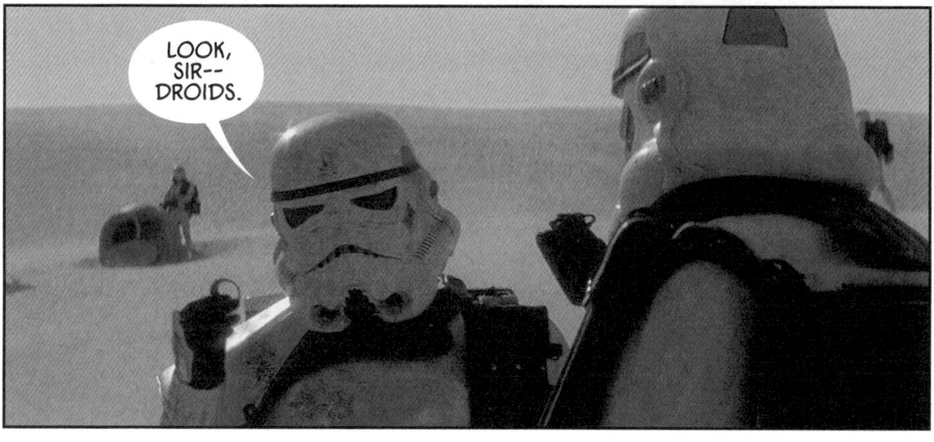
LOOK, SIR-- DROIDS.

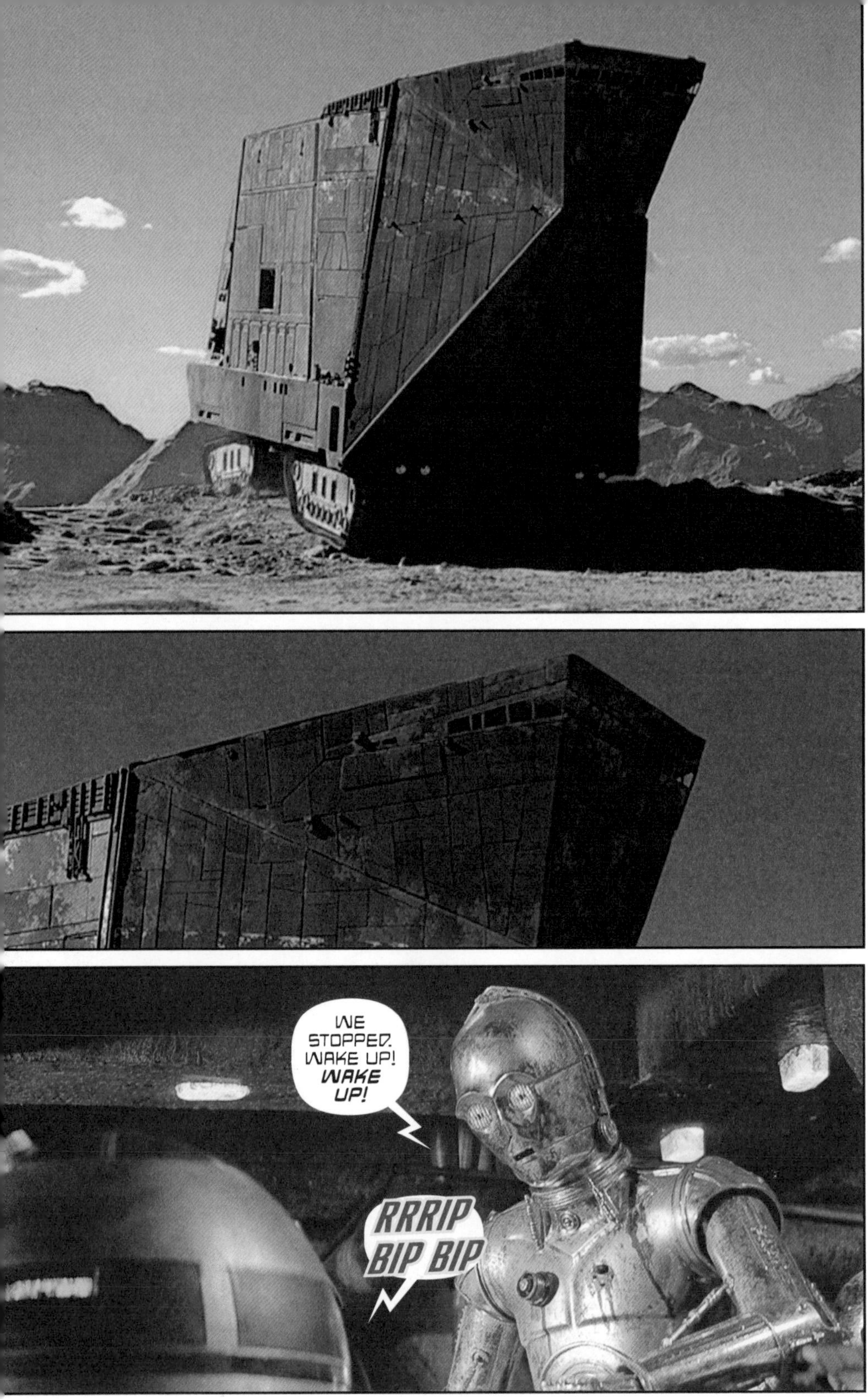
WE STOPPED. WAKE UP! WAKE UP!
RRRIP BIP BIP

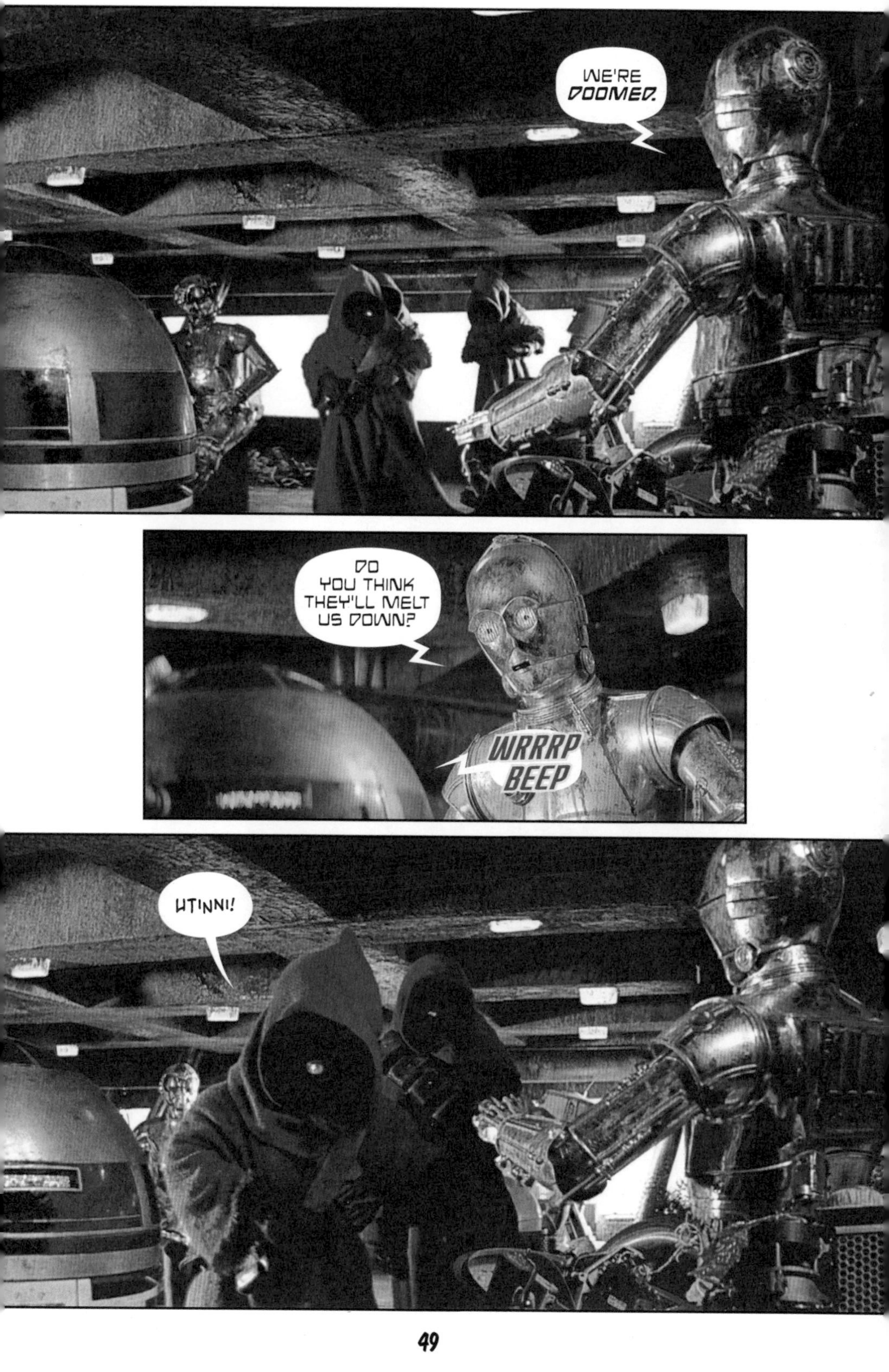
WE'RE DOOMED.
DO YOU THINK THEY'LL MELT US DOWN?
WRRRP BEEP
UTINNI!

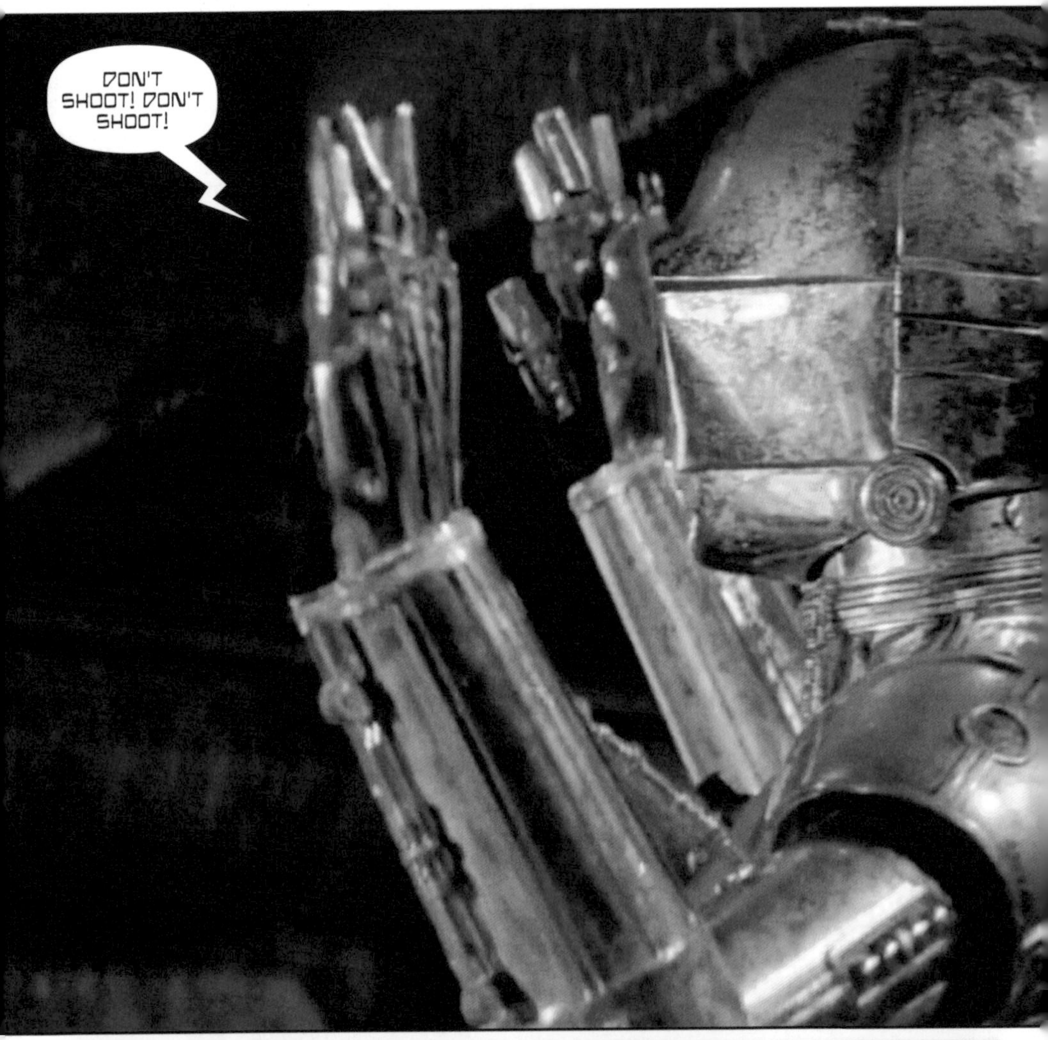
DON'T SHOOT! DON'T SHOOT!

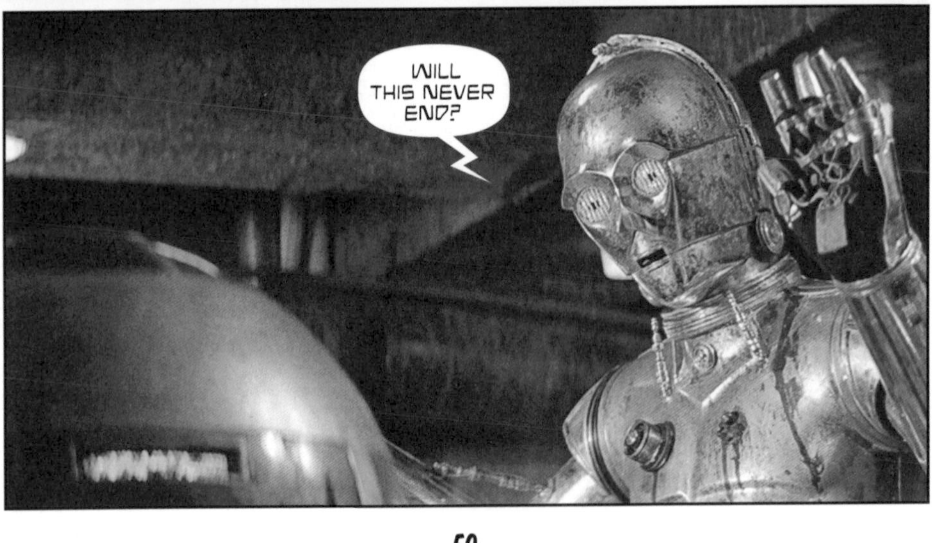
WILL THIS NEVER END?

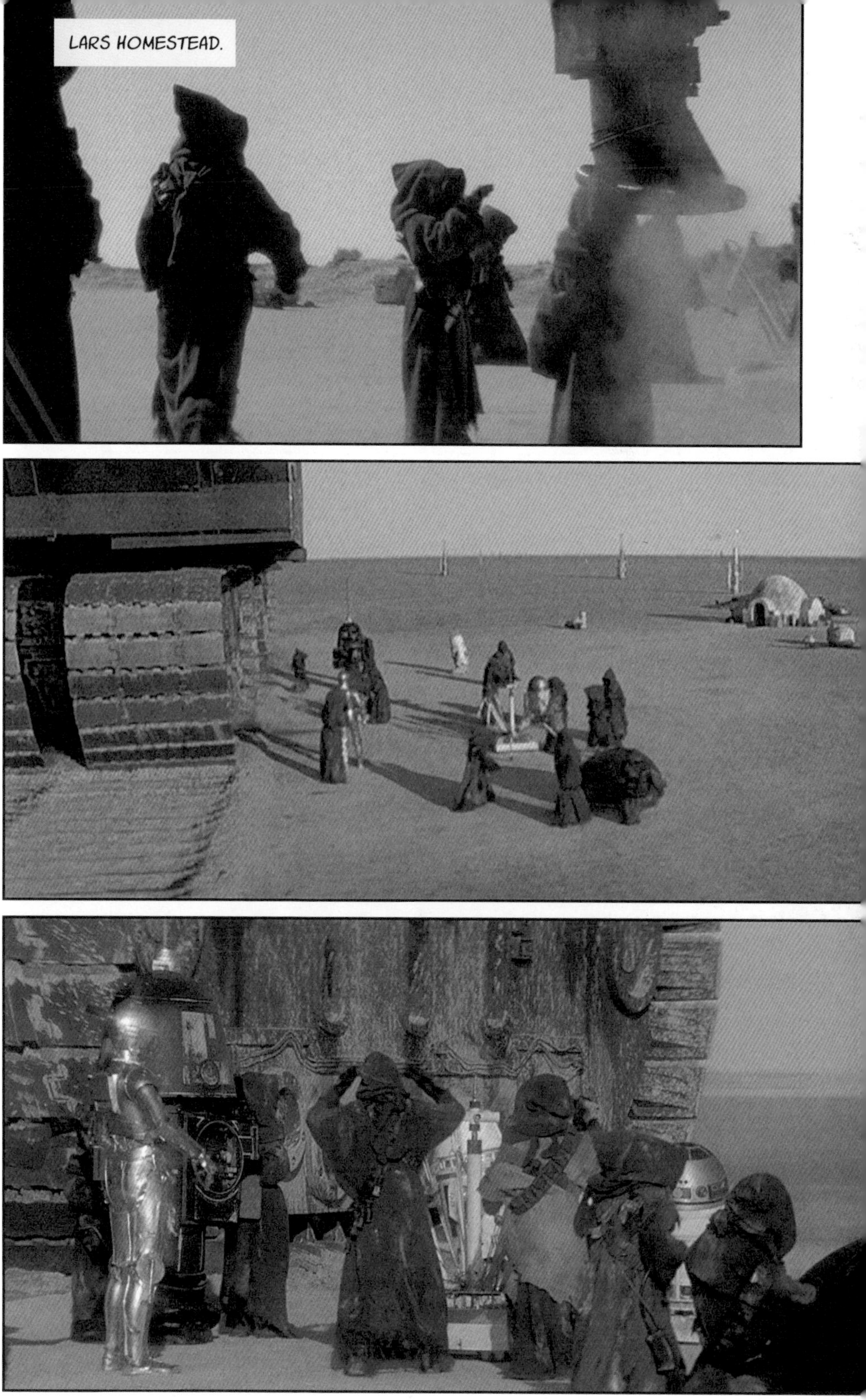
LARS HOMESTEAD.

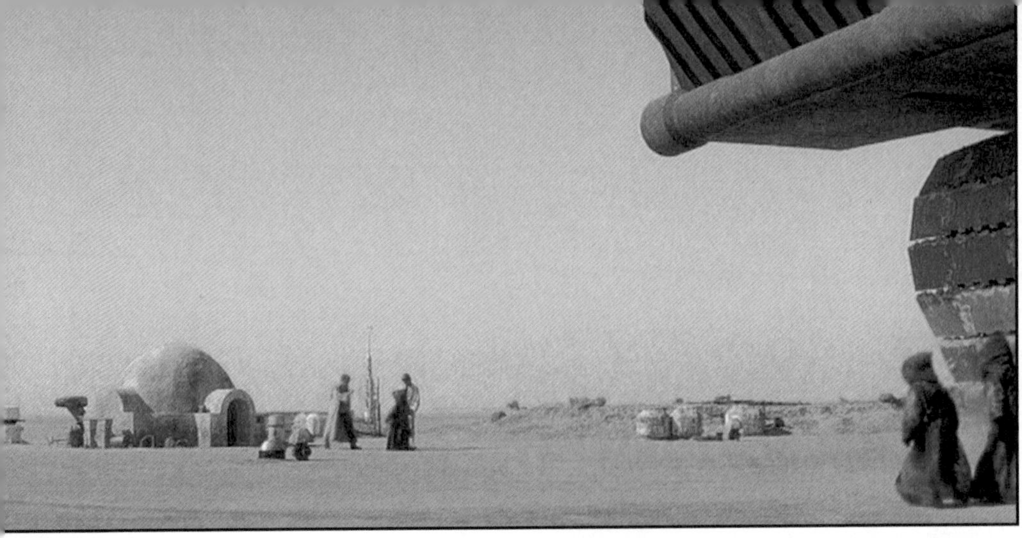

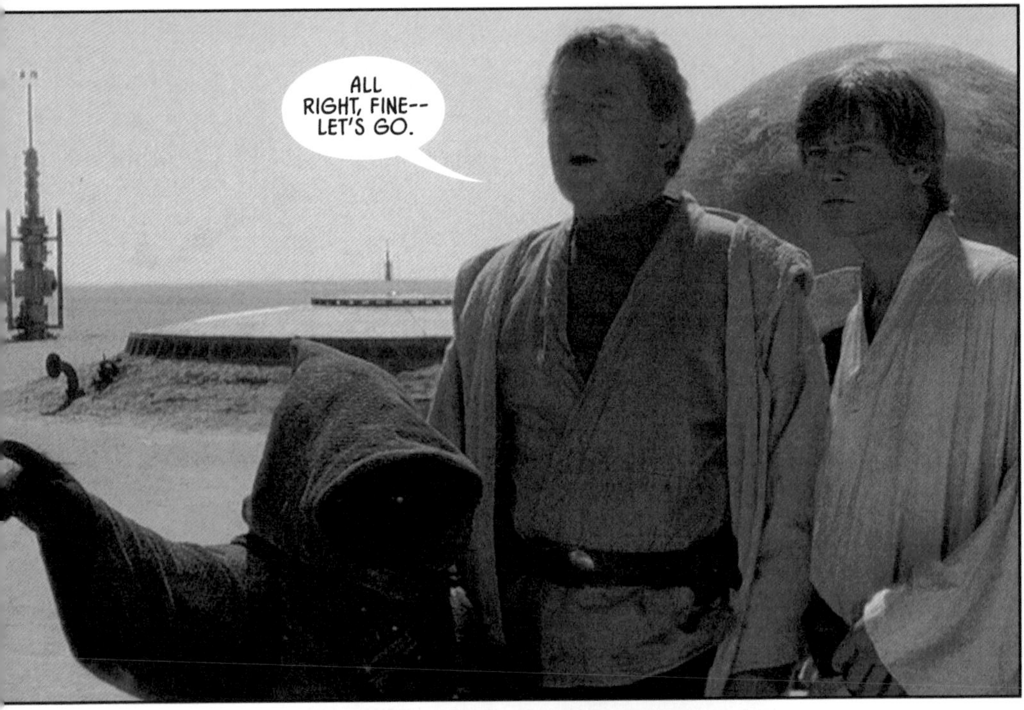
ALL RIGHT, FINE-- LET'S GO.

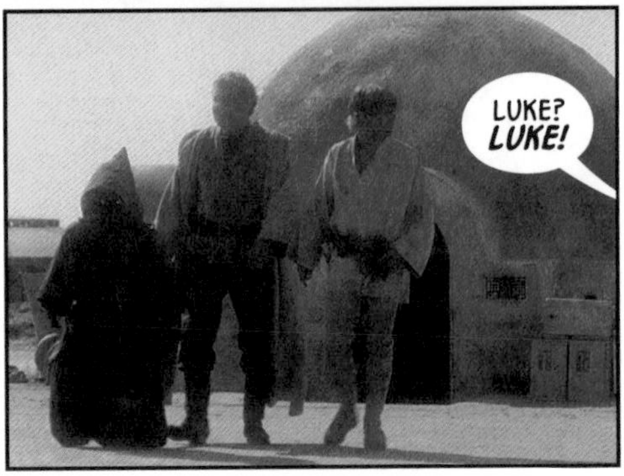
LUKE? **LUKE!**

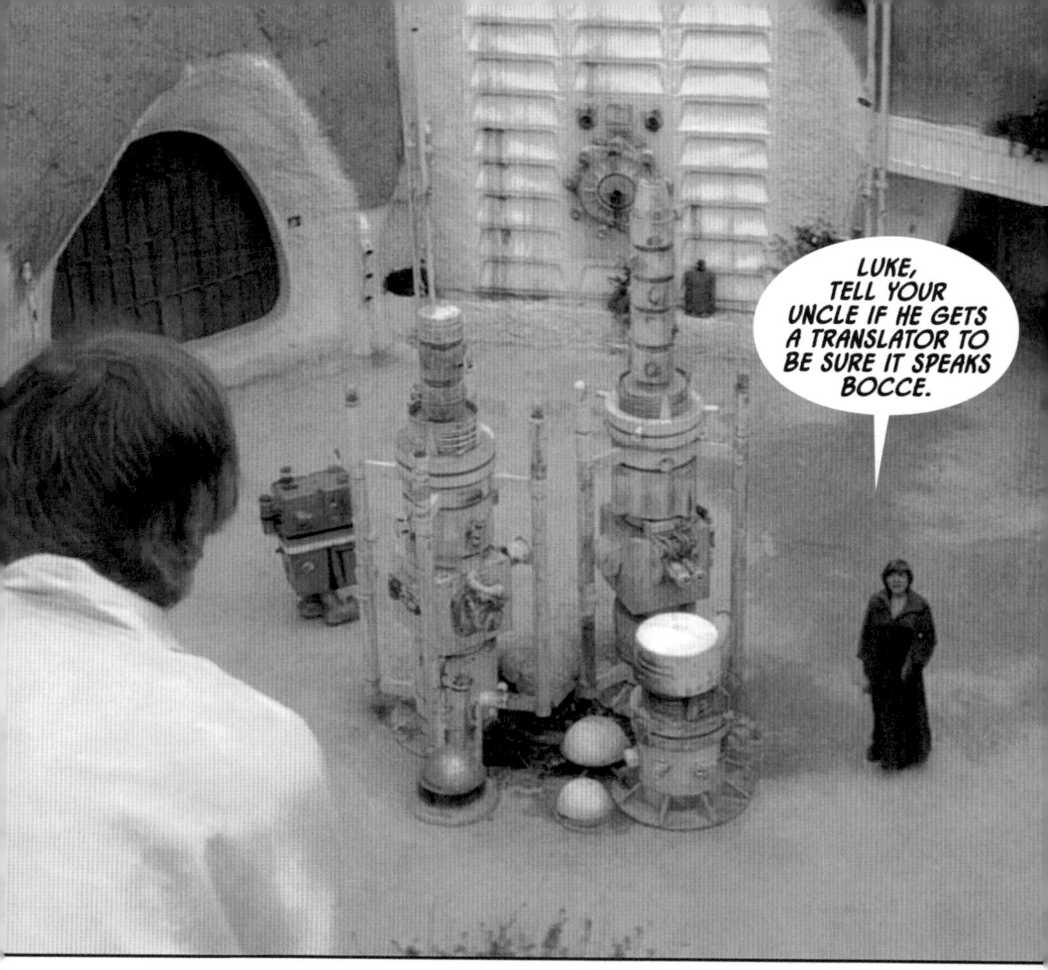
LUKE, TELL YOUR UNCLE IF HE GETS A TRANSLATOR TO BE SURE IT SPEAKS BOCCE.

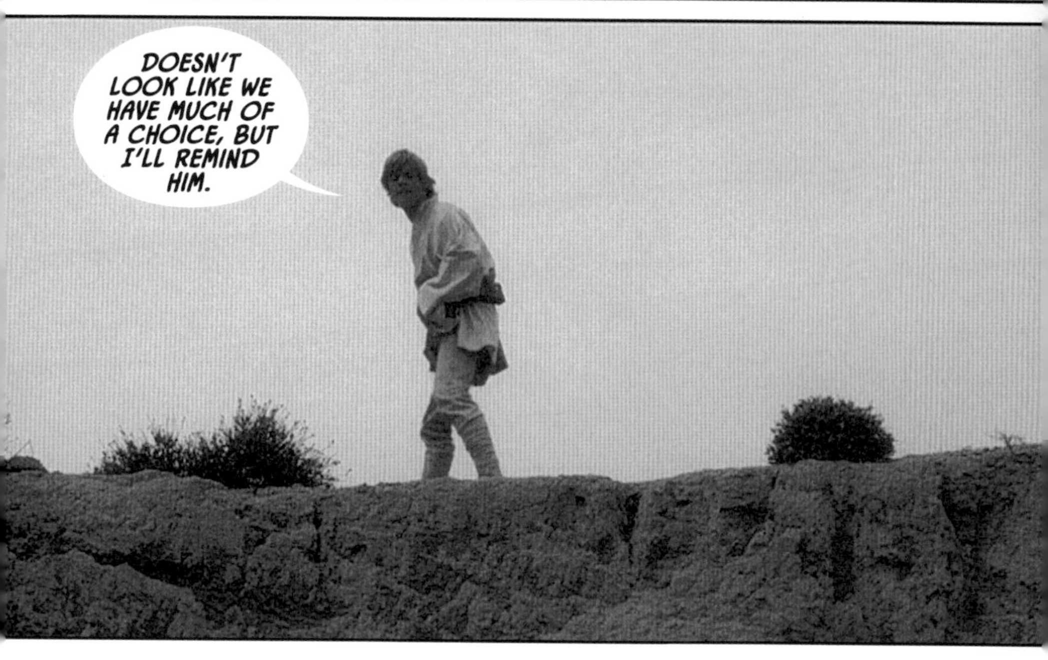
DOESN'T LOOK LIKE WE HAVE MUCH OF A CHOICE, BUT I'LL REMIND HIM.

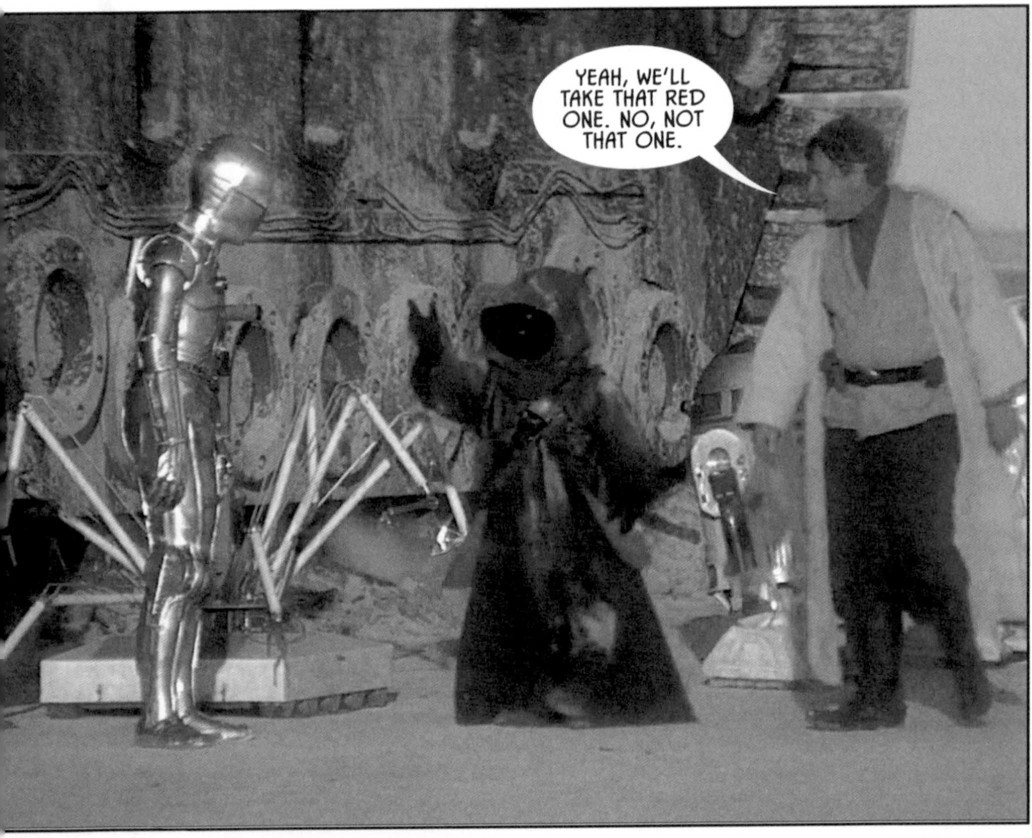
YEAH, WE'LL TAKE THAT RED ONE. NO, NOT THAT ONE.

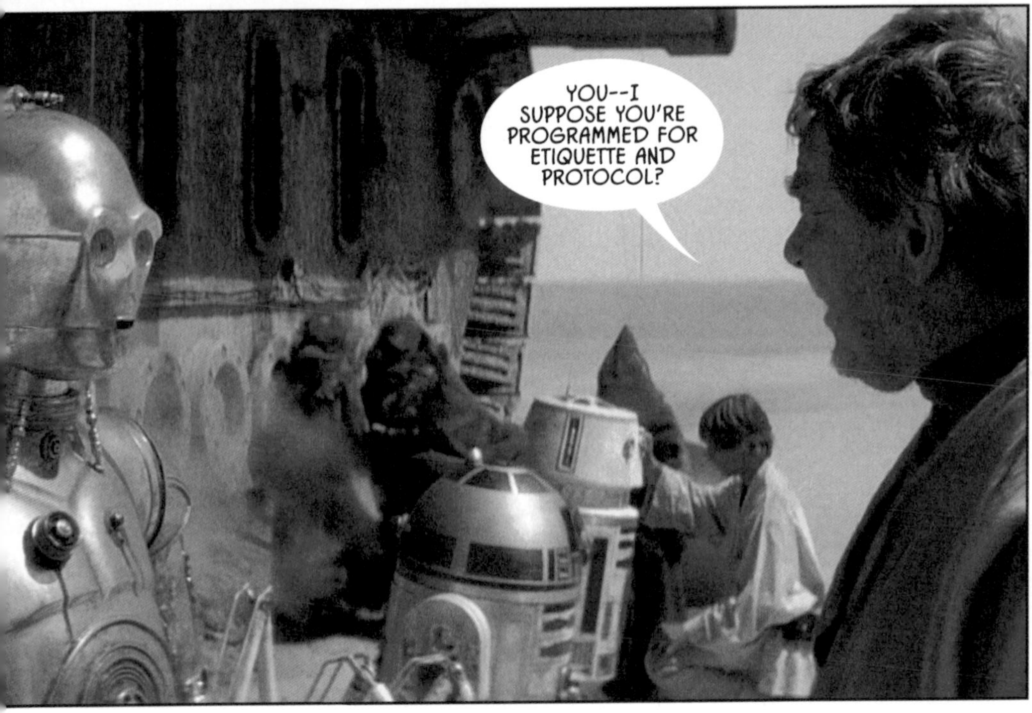
YOU--I SUPPOSE YOU'RE PROGRAMMED FOR ETIQUETTE AND PROTOCOL?

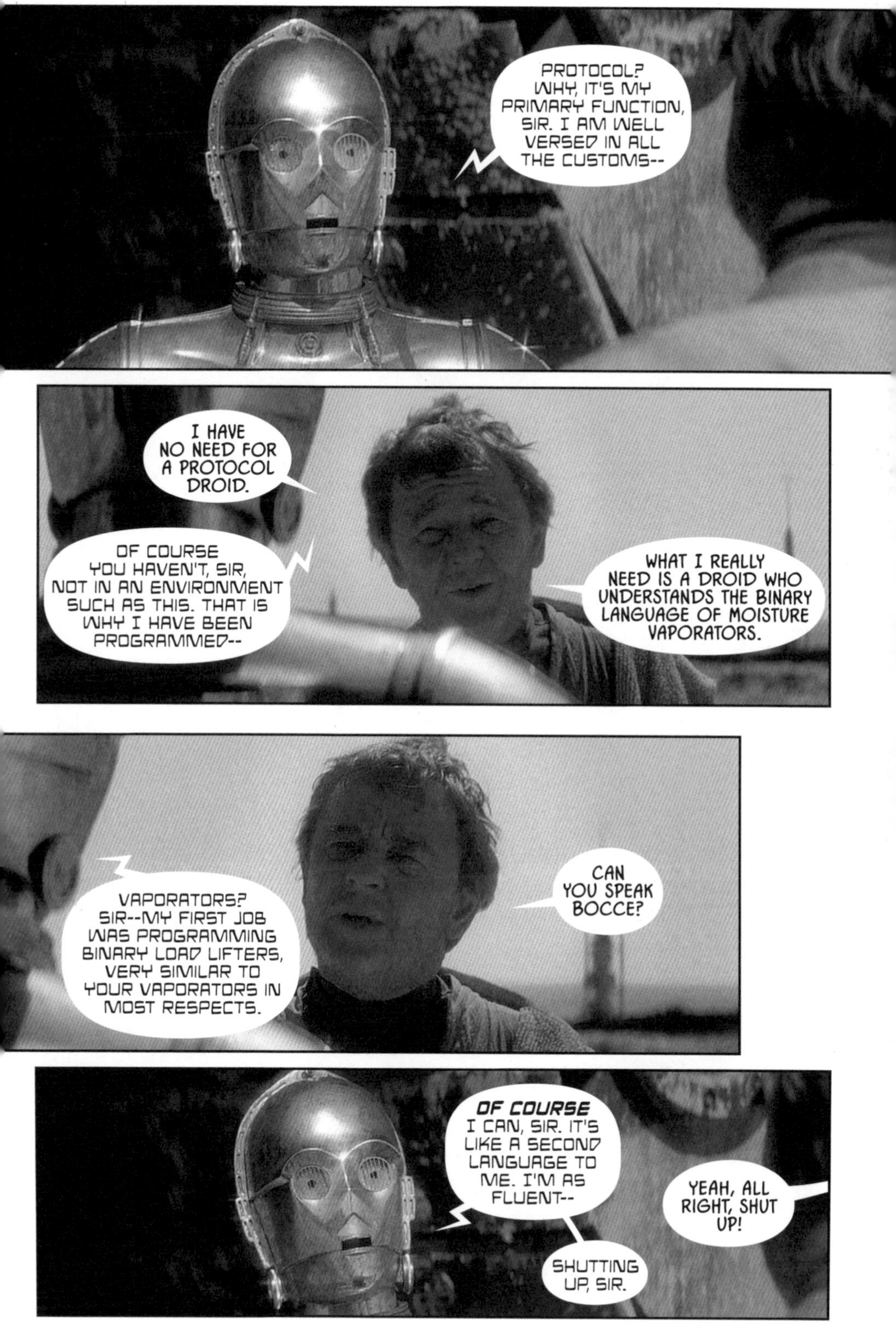
PROTOCOL? WHY, IT'S MY PRIMARY FUNCTION, SIR. I AM WELL VERSED IN ALL THE CUSTOMS--
I HAVE NO NEED FOR A PROTOCOL DROID.
OF COURSE YOU HAVEN'T, SIR, NOT IN AN ENVIRONMENT SUCH AS THIS. THAT IS WHY I HAVE BEEN PROGRAMMED--
WHAT I REALLY NEED IS A DROID WHO UNDERSTANDS THE BINARY LANGUAGE OF MOISTURE VAPORATORS.
VAPORATORS? SIR--MY FIRST JOB WAS PROGRAMMING BINARY LOAD LIFTERS, VERY SIMILAR TO YOUR VAPORATORS IN MOST RESPECTS.
CAN YOU SPEAK BOCCE?
OF COURSE I CAN, SIR. IT'S LIKE A SECOND LANGUAGE TO ME. I'M AS FLUENT--
YEAH, ALL RIGHT, SHUT UP!
SHUTTING UP, SIR.

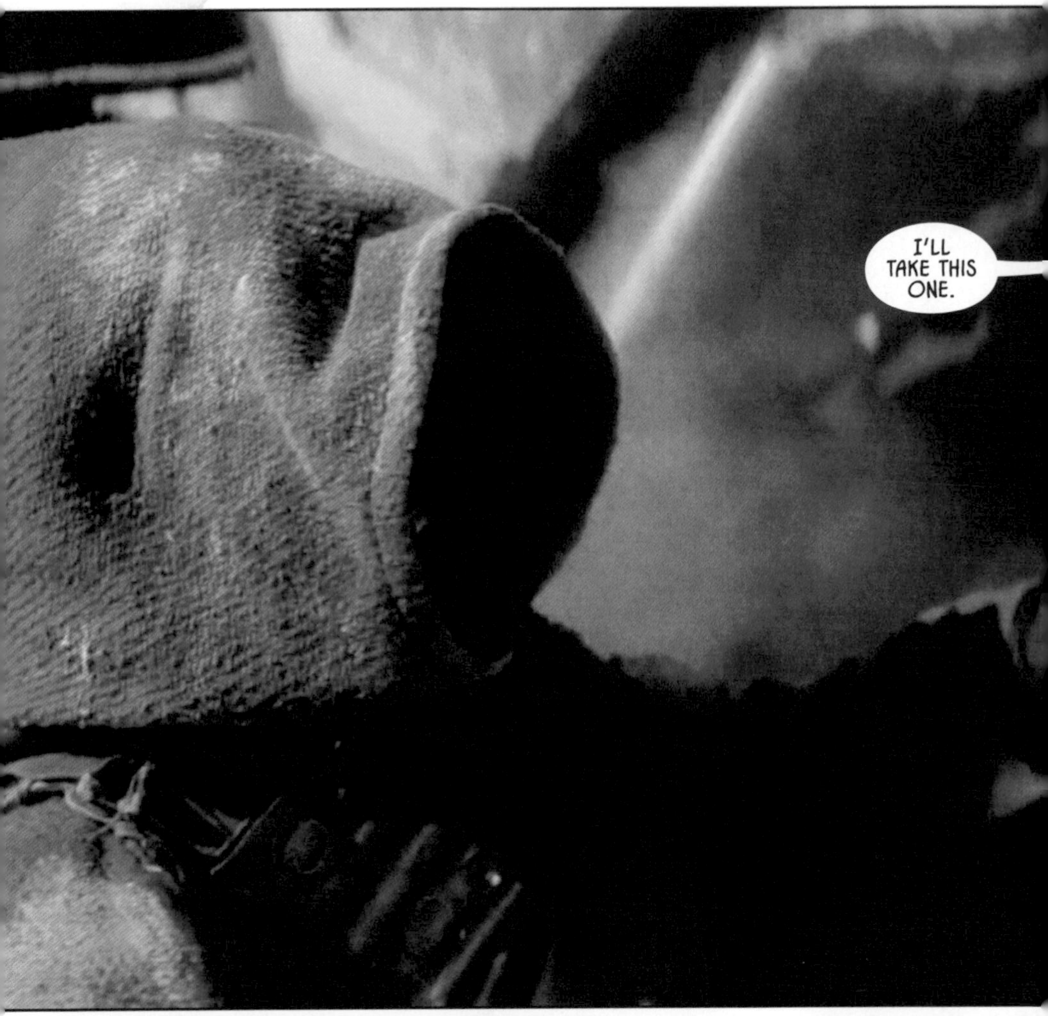
I'LL TAKE THIS ONE.

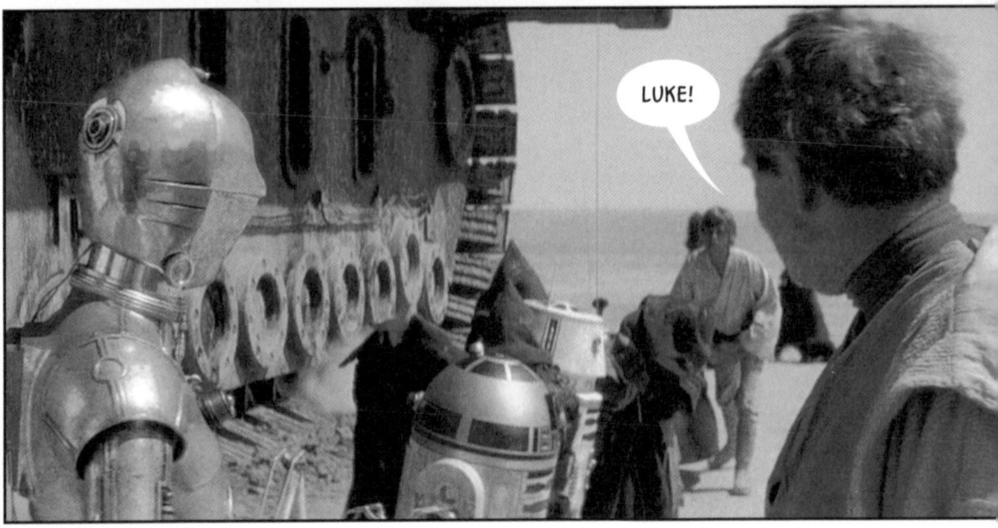
LUKE!

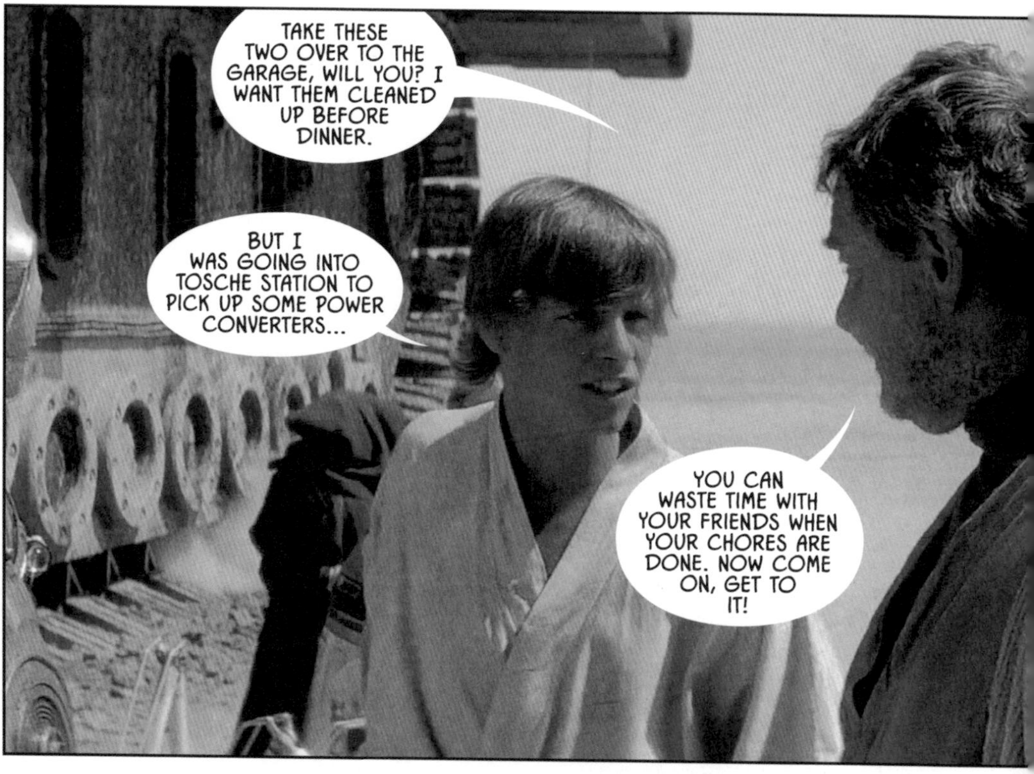
TAKE THESE TWO OVER TO THE GARAGE, WILL YOU? I WANT THEM CLEANED UP BEFORE DINNER.
BUT I WAS GOING INTO TOSCHE STATION TO PICK UP SOME POWER CONVERTERS...
YOU CAN WASTE TIME WITH YOUR FRIENDS WHEN YOUR CHORES ARE DONE. NOW COME ON, GET TO IT!

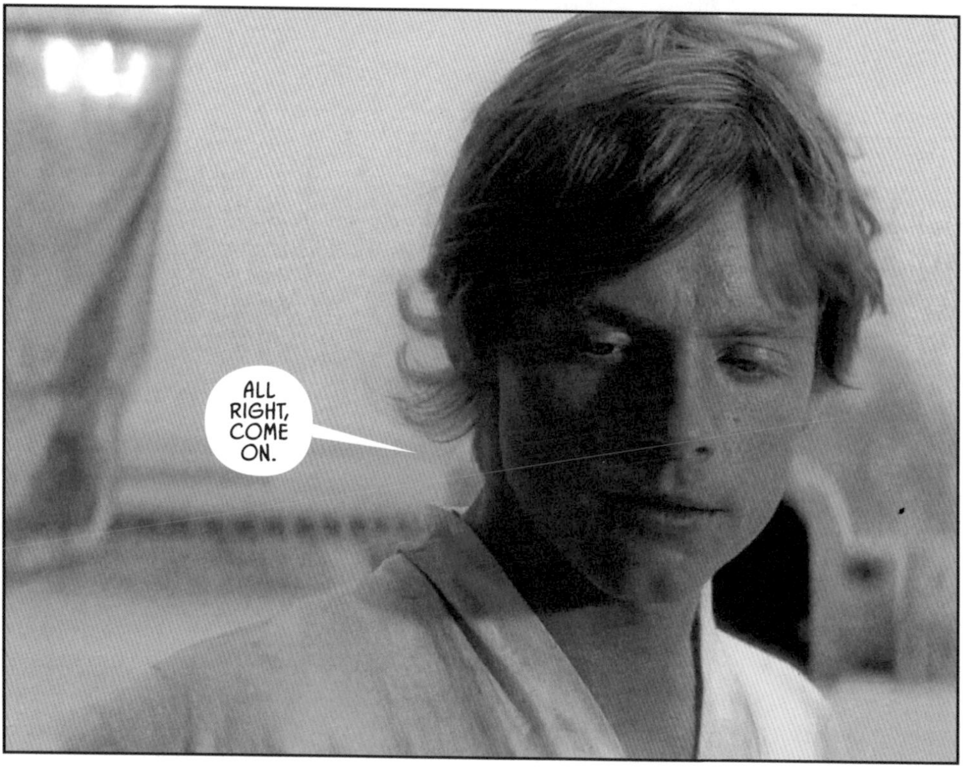
ALL RIGHT, COME ON.

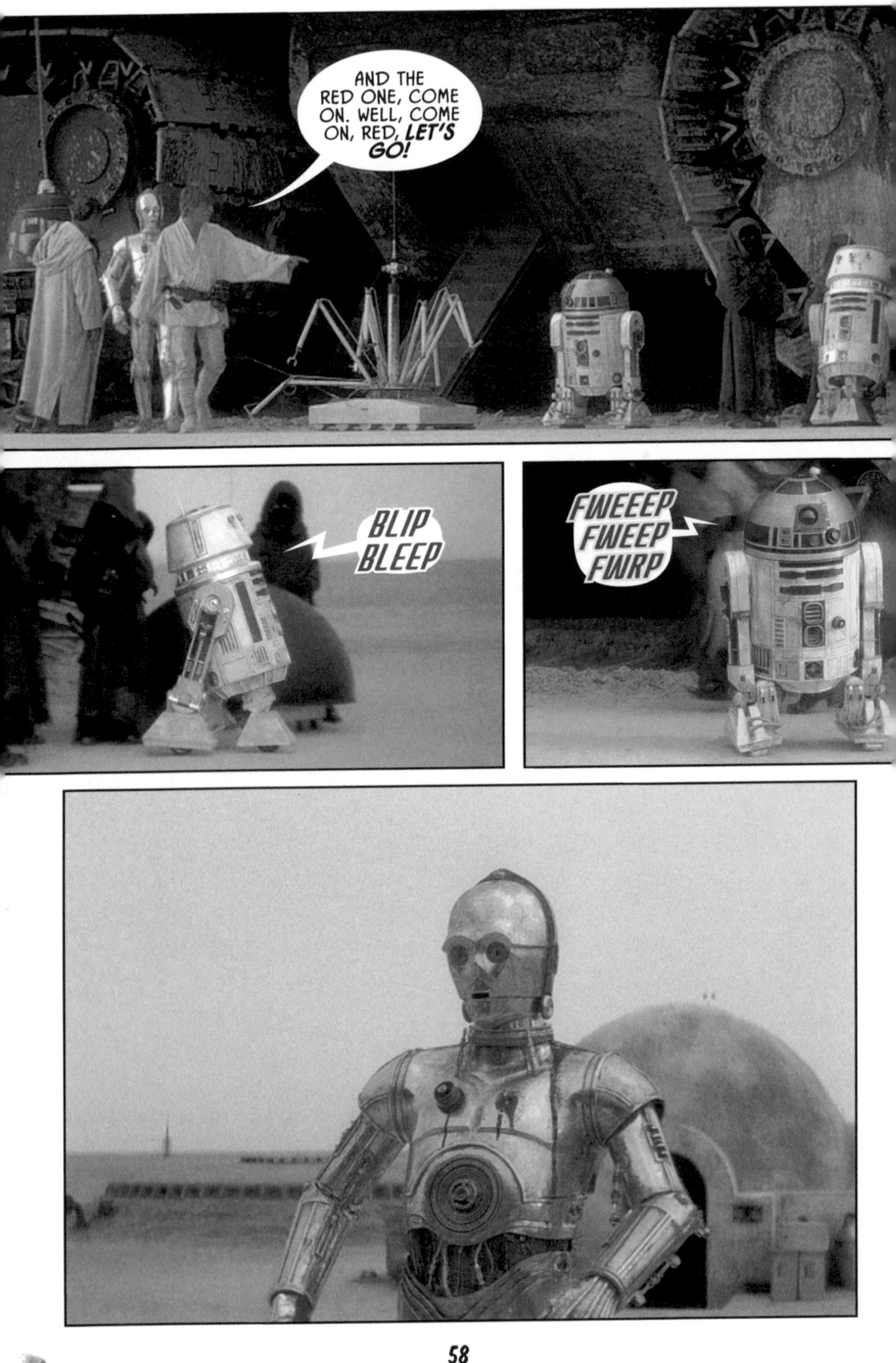
AND THE RED ONE, COME ON. WELL, COME ON, RED, LET'S GO!
BLIP BLEEP
FWEEEP FWEEP FWRP

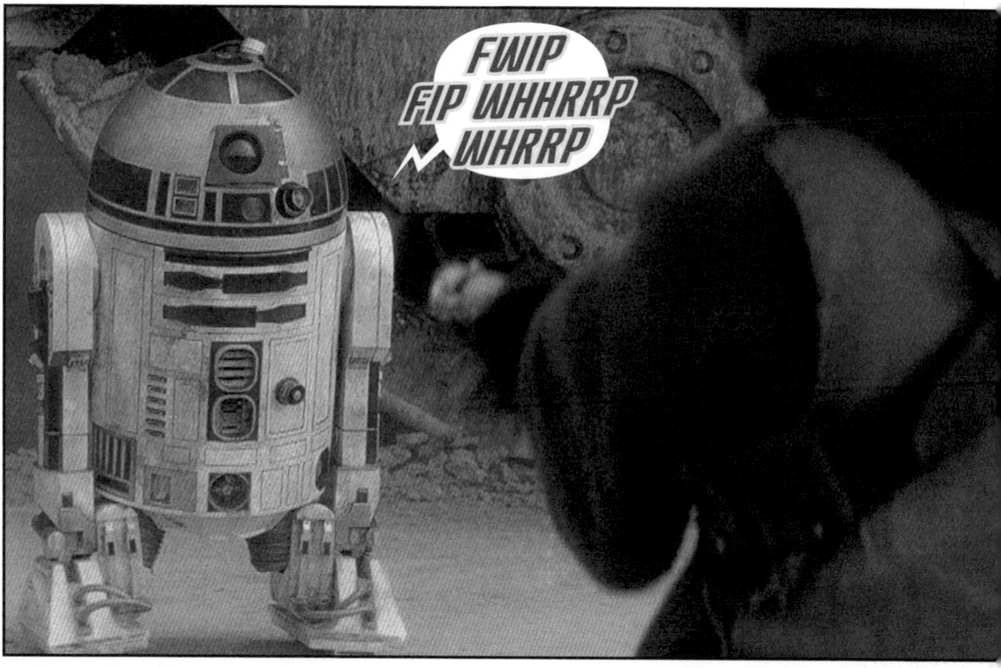
FWIP
FIP WHHRRP
WHRRP

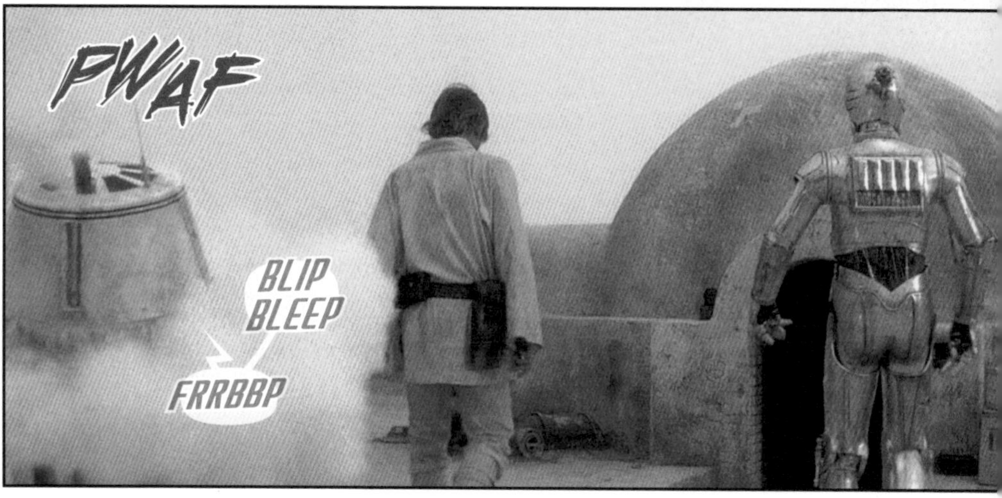
PWAF
BLIP
BLEEP
FRRBBP

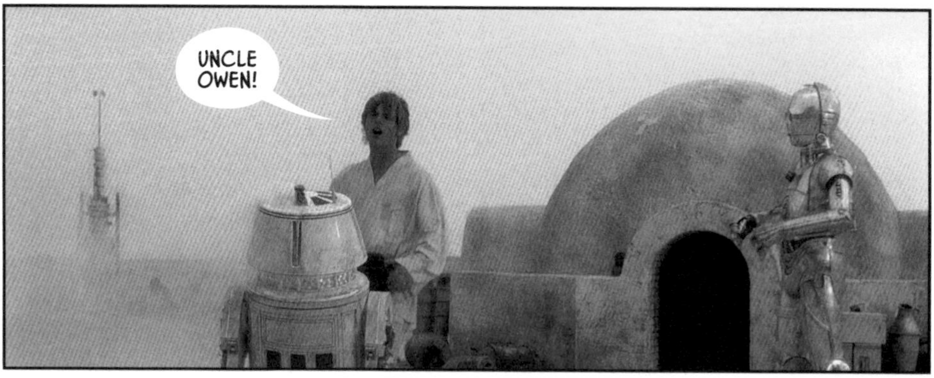
UNCLE
OWEN!

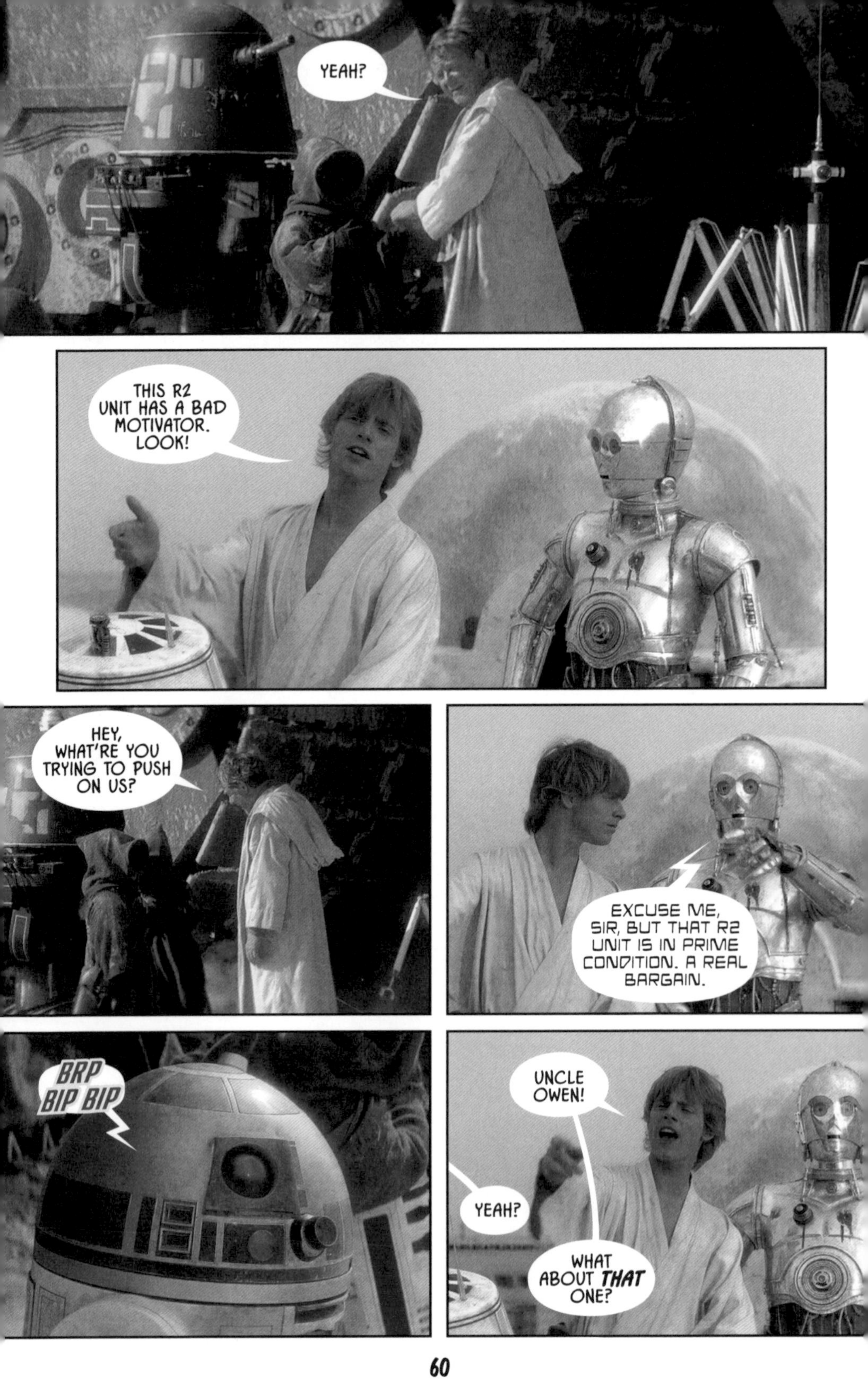
YEAH?
THIS R2 UNIT HAS A BAD MOTIVATOR. LOOK!
HEY, WHAT'RE YOU TRYING TO PUSH ON US?
EXCUSE ME, SIR, BUT THAT R2 UNIT IS IN PRIME CONDITION. A REAL BARGAIN.
BRP BIP BIP
UNCLE OWEN!
YEAH?
WHAT ABOUT **THAT** ONE?

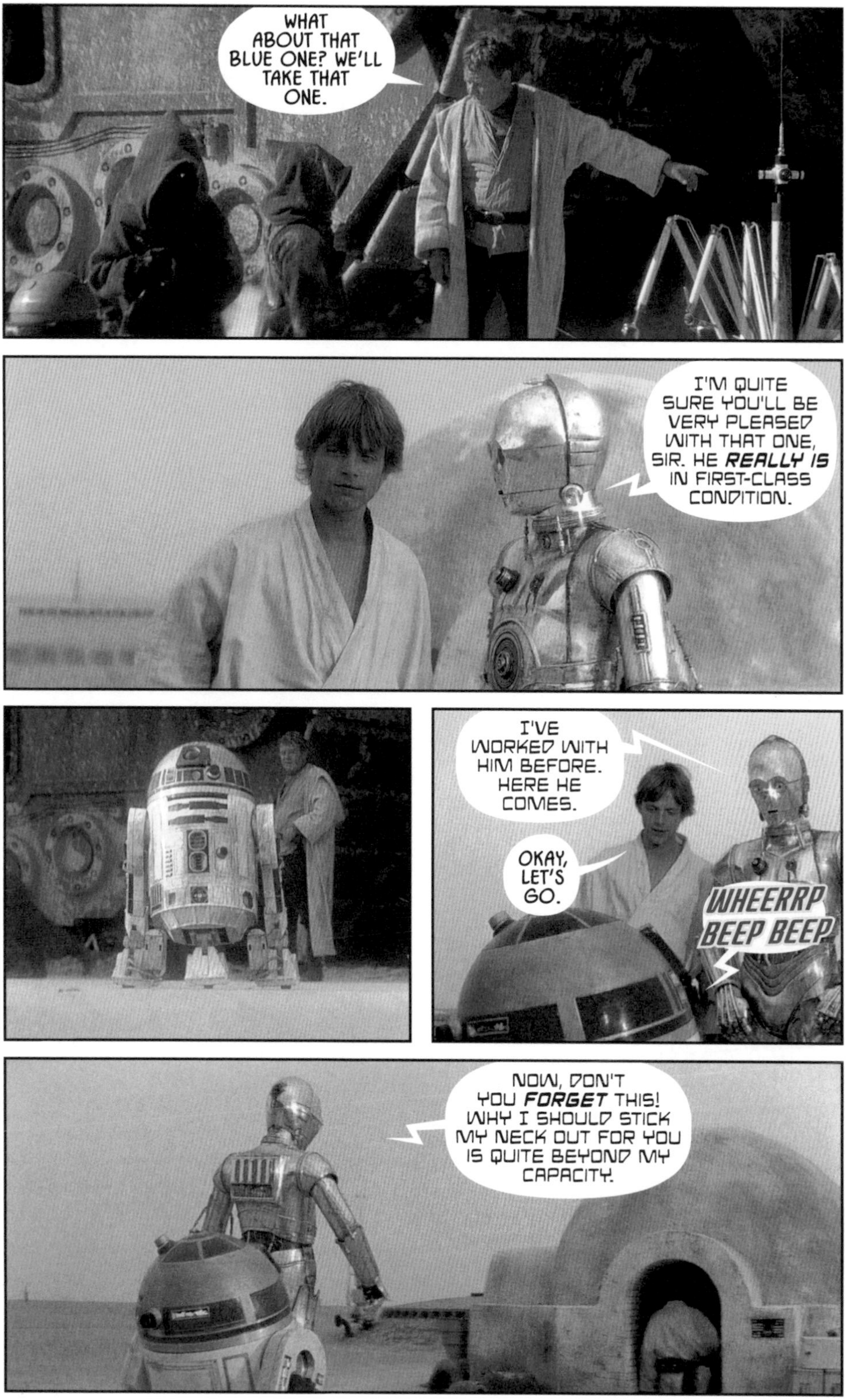
WHAT ABOUT THAT BLUE ONE? WE'LL TAKE THAT ONE.
I'M QUITE SURE YOU'LL BE VERY PLEASED WITH THAT ONE, SIR. HE *REALLY IS* IN FIRST-CLASS CONDITION.
I'VE WORKED WITH HIM BEFORE. HERE HE COMES.
OKAY, LET'S GO.
WHEERRP BEEP BEEP
NOW, DON'T YOU *FORGET* THIS! WHY I SHOULD STICK MY NECK OUT FOR YOU IS QUITE BEYOND MY CAPACITY.

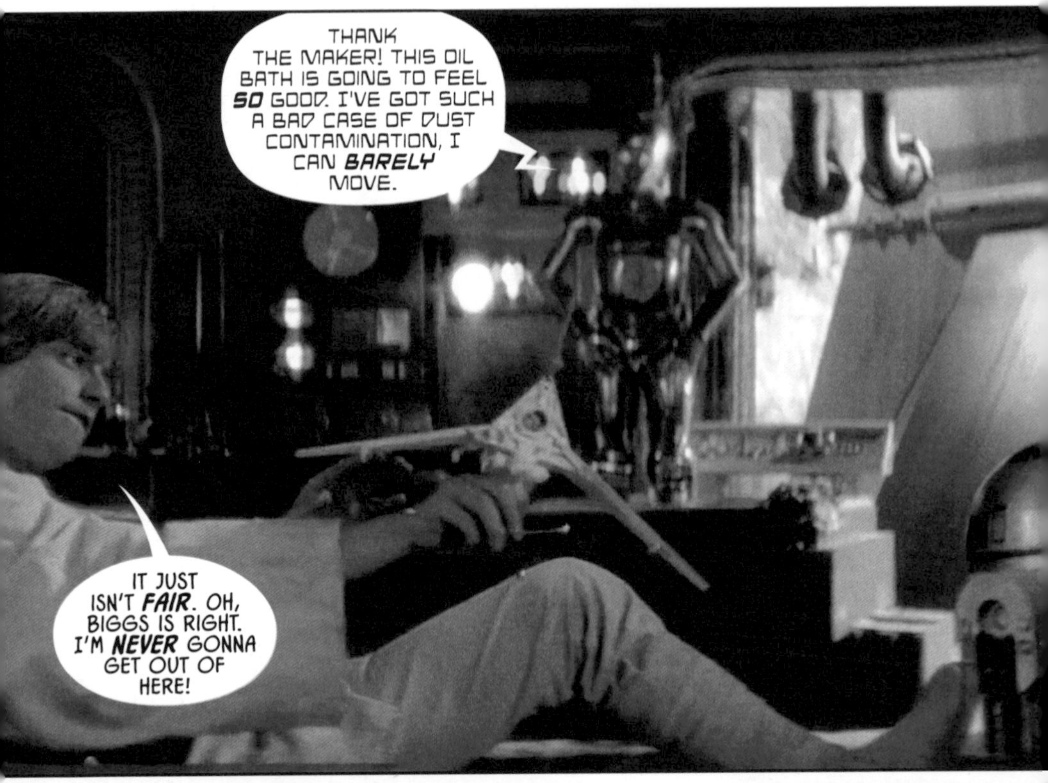
THANK THE MAKER! THIS OIL BATH IS GOING TO FEEL **SO** GOOD. I'VE GOT SUCH A BAD CASE OF DUST CONTAMINATION, I CAN **BARELY** MOVE.
IT JUST ISN'T **FAIR**. OH, BIGGS IS RIGHT. I'M **NEVER** GONNA GET OUT OF HERE!

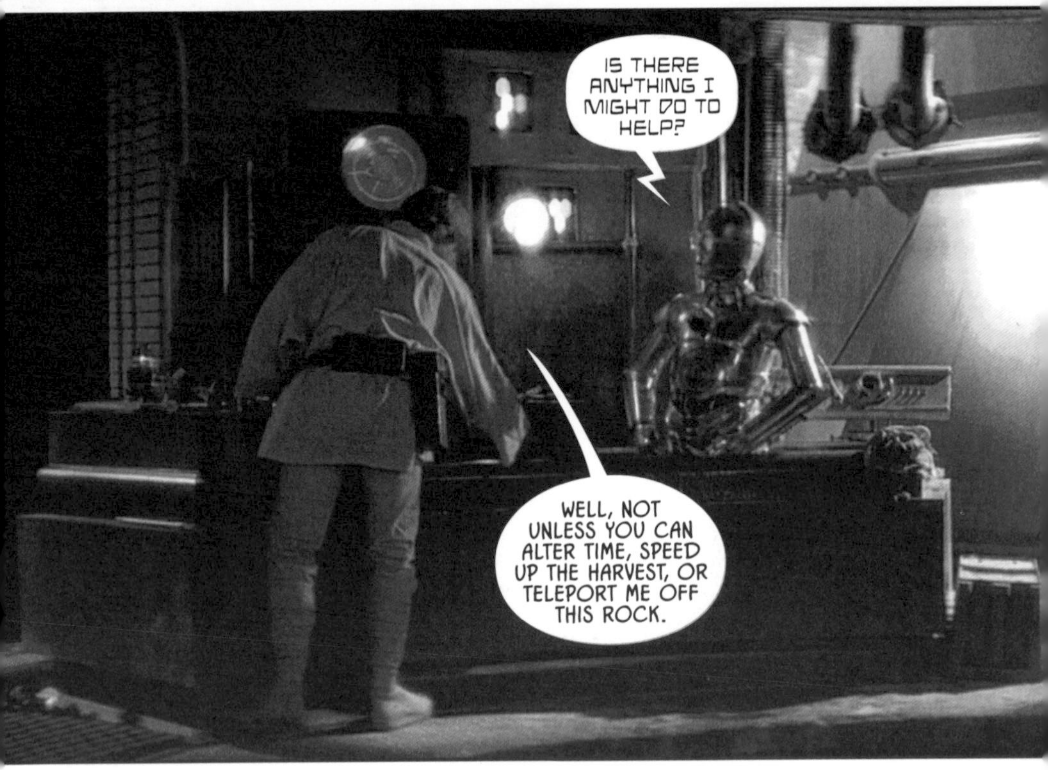
IS THERE ANYTHING I MIGHT DO TO HELP?
WELL, NOT UNLESS YOU CAN ALTER TIME, SPEED UP THE HARVEST, OR TELEPORT ME OFF THIS ROCK.

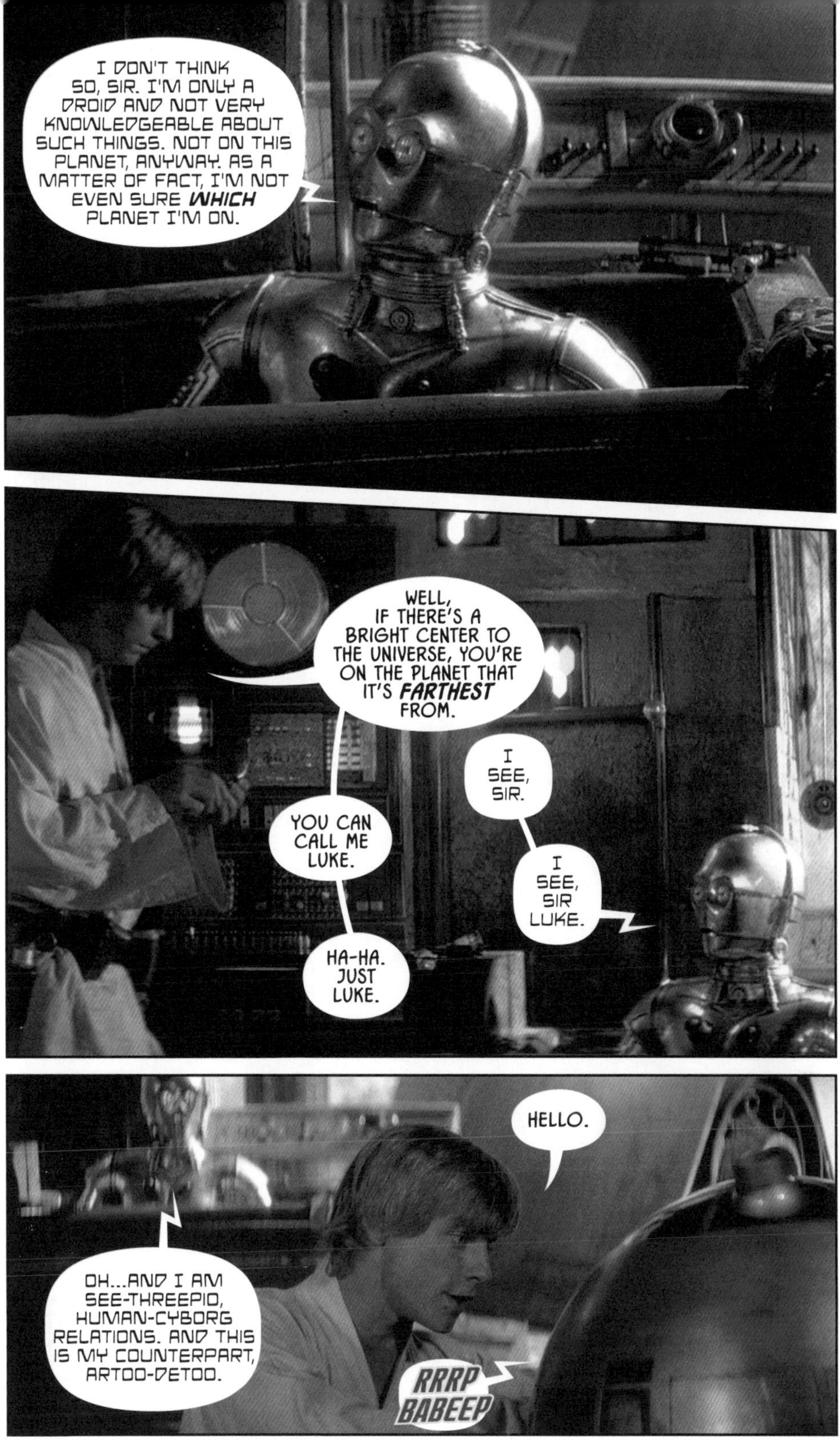
I DON'T THINK SO, SIR. I'M ONLY A DROID AND NOT VERY KNOWLEDGEABLE ABOUT SUCH THINGS. NOT ON THIS PLANET, ANYWAY. AS A MATTER OF FACT, I'M NOT EVEN SURE ***WHICH*** PLANET I'M ON.
WELL, IF THERE'S A BRIGHT CENTER TO THE UNIVERSE, YOU'RE ON THE PLANET THAT IT'S ***FARTHEST*** FROM.
I SEE, SIR.
YOU CAN CALL ME LUKE.
I SEE, SIR LUKE.
HA-HA. JUST LUKE.
HELLO.
OH...AND I AM SEE-THREEPIO, HUMAN-CYBORG RELATIONS. AND THIS IS MY COUNTERPART, ARTOO-DETOO.
RRRP BABEEP

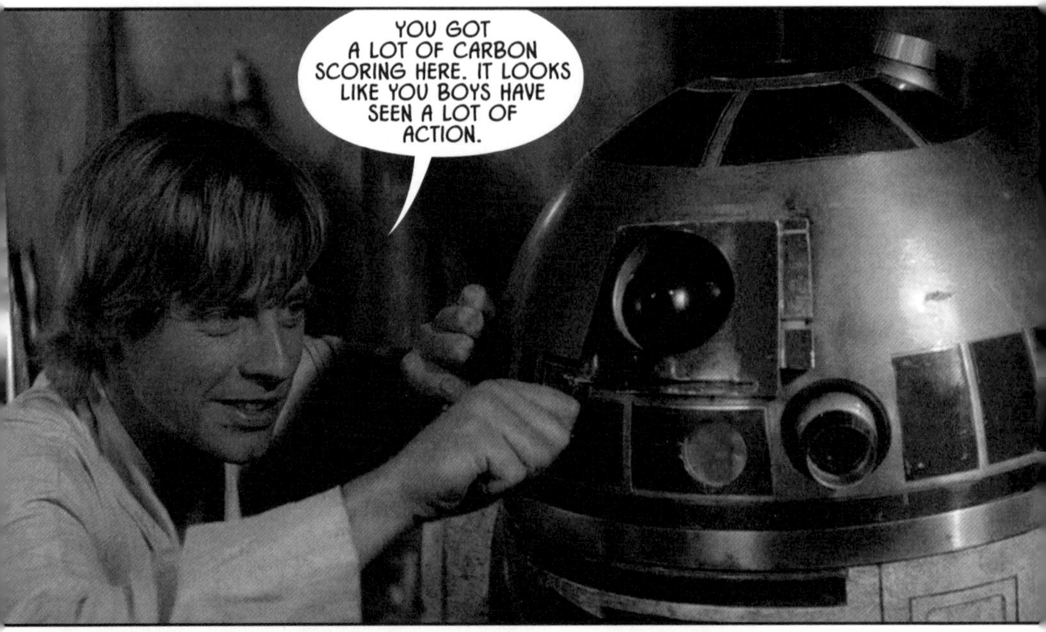
YOU GOT A LOT OF CARBON SCORING HERE. IT LOOKS LIKE YOU BOYS HAVE SEEN A LOT OF ACTION.

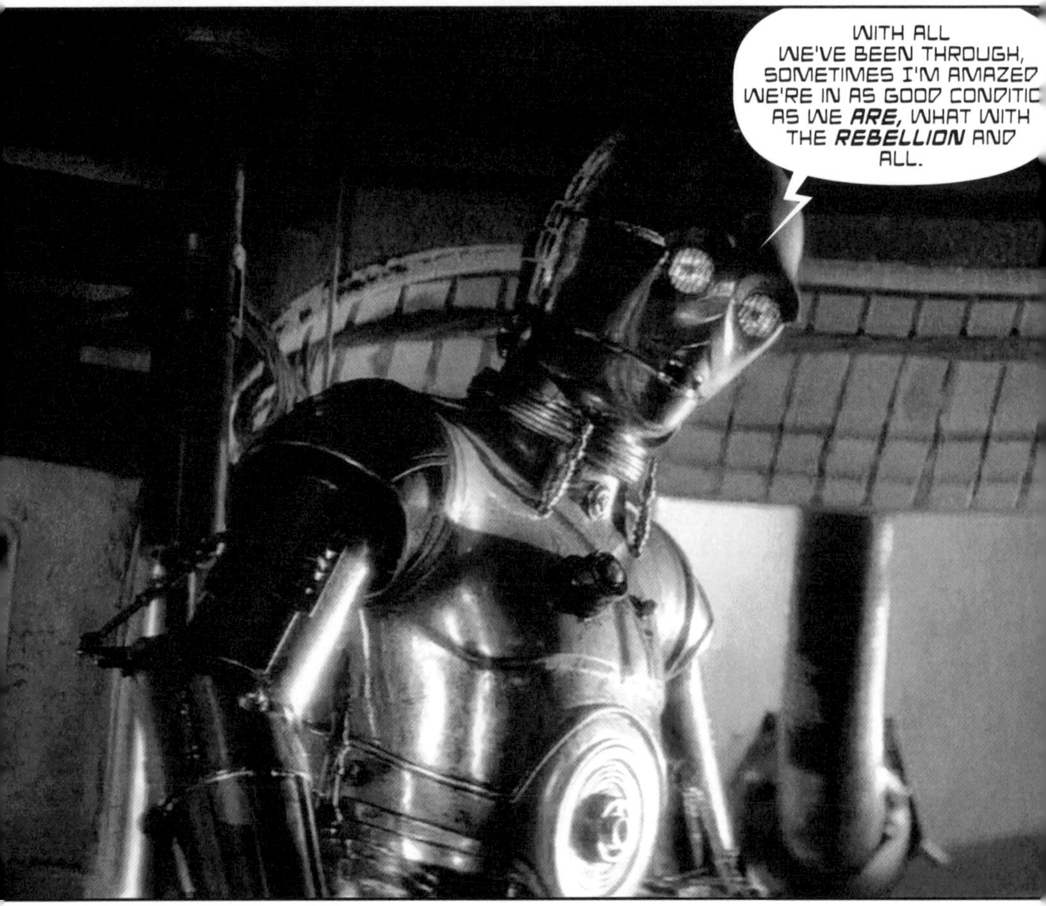
WITH ALL WE'VE BEEN THROUGH, SOMETIMES I'M AMAZED WE'RE IN AS GOOD CONDITIC AS WE *ARE*, WHAT WITH THE *REBELLION* AND ALL.

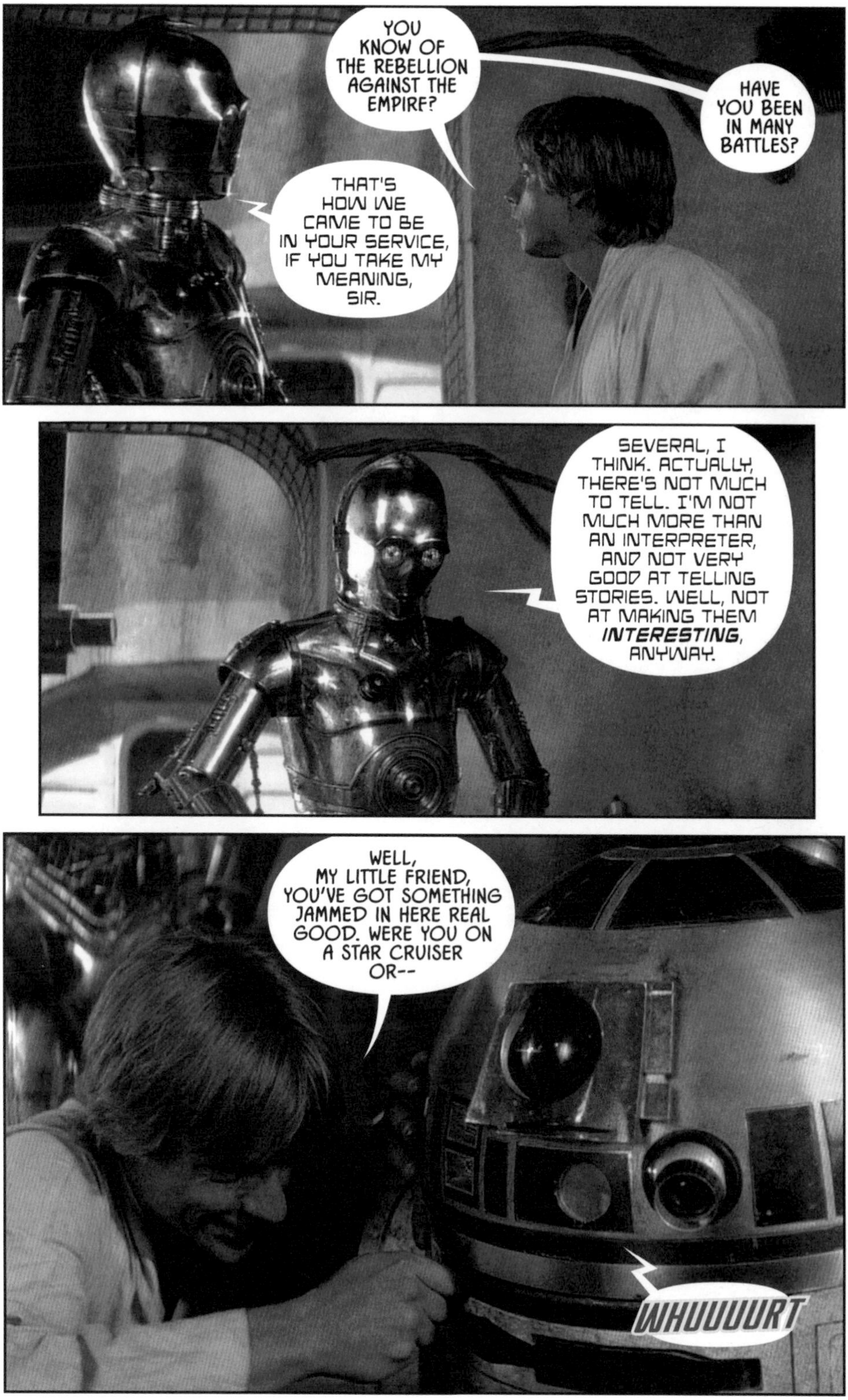
YOU KNOW OF THE REBELLION AGAINST THE EMPIRE?
THAT'S HOW WE CAME TO BE IN YOUR SERVICE, IF YOU TAKE MY MEANING, SIR.
HAVE YOU BEEN IN MANY BATTLES?
SEVERAL, I THINK. ACTUALLY, THERE'S NOT MUCH TO TELL. I'M NOT MUCH MORE THAN AN INTERPRETER, AND NOT VERY GOOD AT TELLING STORIES. WELL, NOT AT MAKING THEM *INTERESTING*, ANYWAY.
WELL, MY LITTLE FRIEND, YOU'VE GOT SOMETHING JAMMED IN HERE REAL GOOD. WERE YOU ON A STAR CRUISER OR--
WHUUUURT

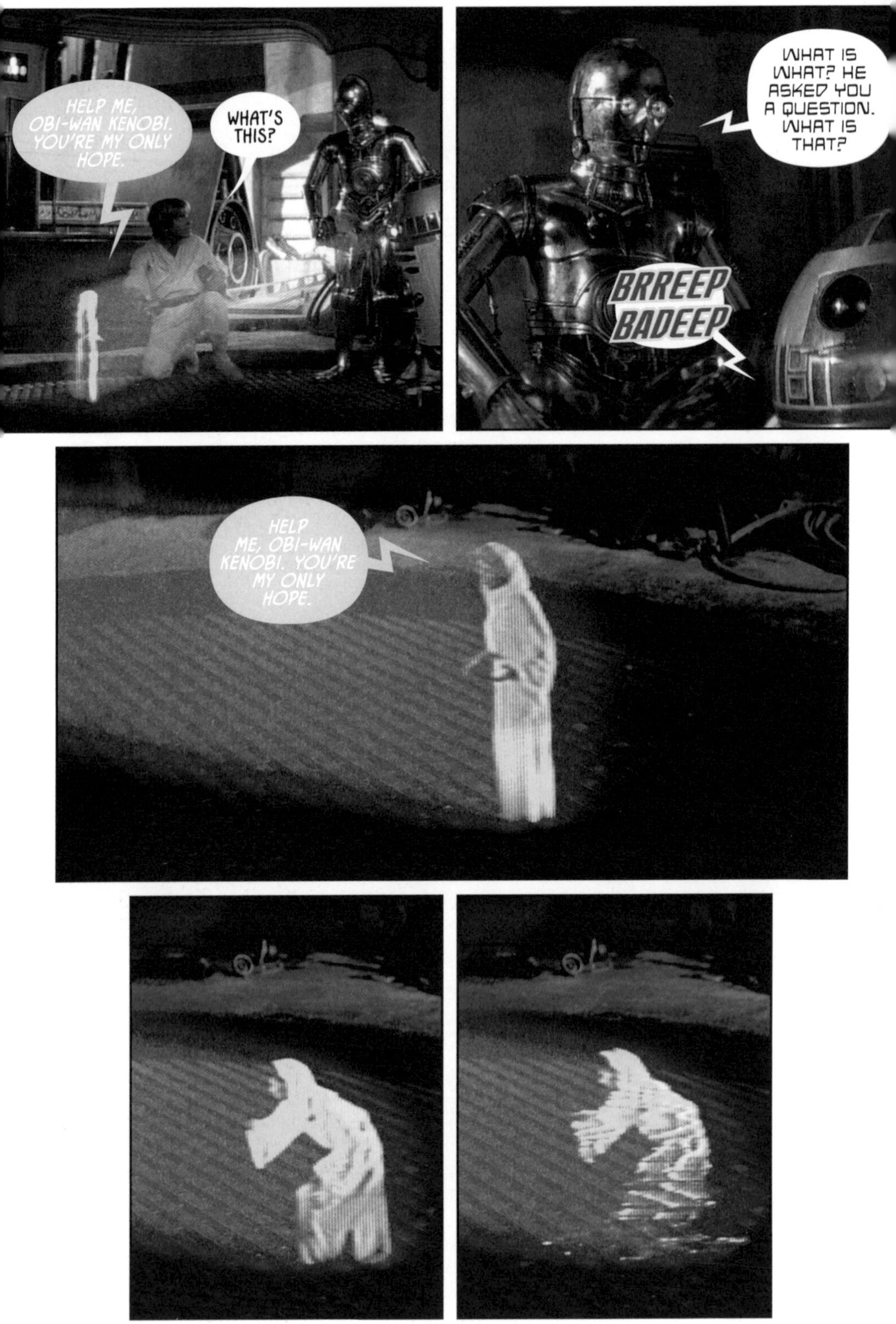
HELP ME, OBI-WAN KENOBI. YOU'RE MY ONLY HOPE.
WHAT'S THIS?
WHAT IS WHAT? HE ASKED YOU A QUESTION. WHAT IS THAT?
BRREEP BADEEP
HELP ME, OBI-WAN KENOBI. YOU'RE MY ONLY HOPE.

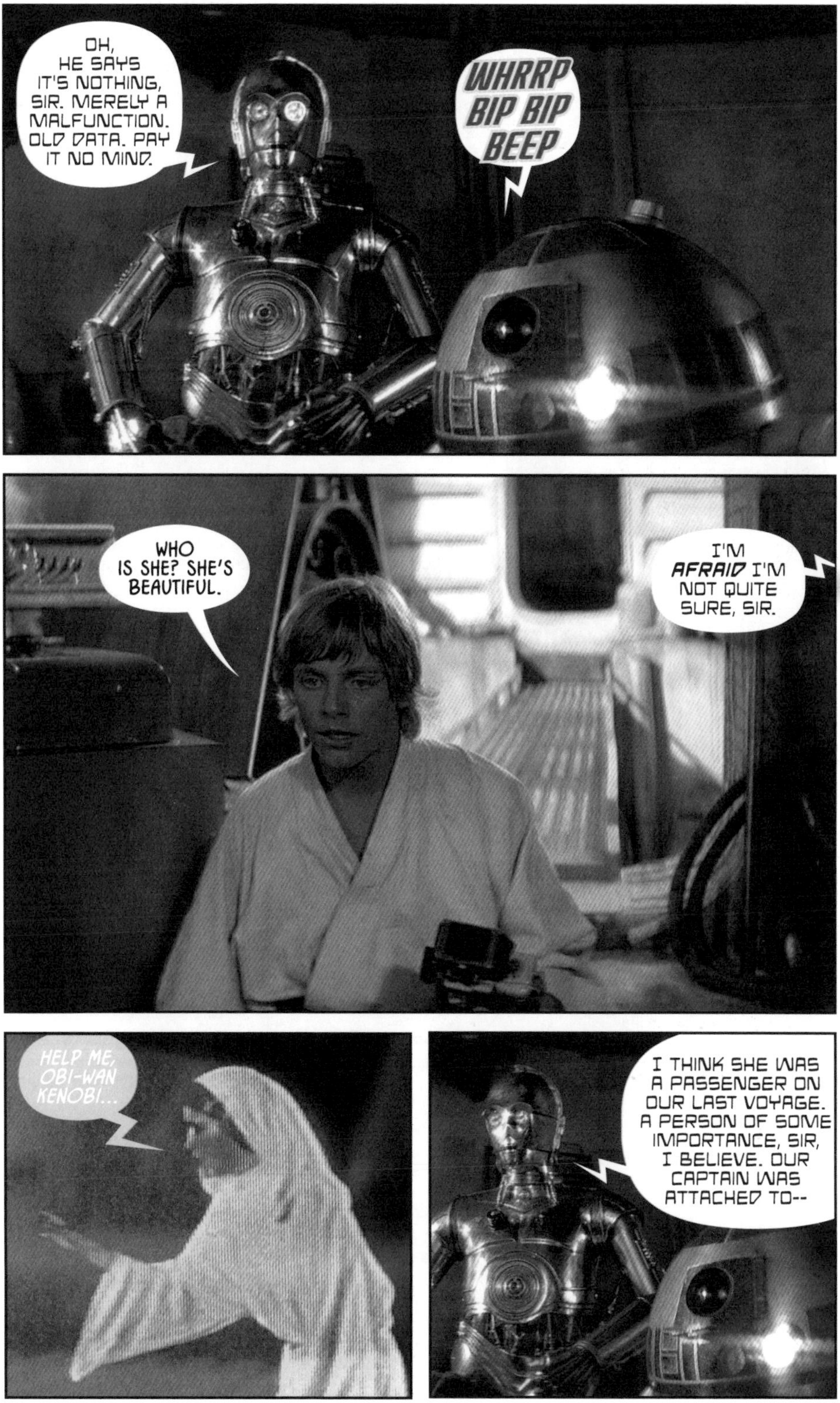
OH, HE SAYS IT'S NOTHING, SIR. MERELY A MALFUNCTION. OLD DATA. PAY IT NO MIND.
WHRRP BIP BIP BEEP
WHO IS SHE? SHE'S BEAUTIFUL.
I'M *AFRAID* I'M NOT QUITE SURE, SIR.
HELP ME, OBI-WAN KENOBI...
I THINK SHE WAS A PASSENGER ON OUR LAST VOYAGE. A PERSON OF SOME IMPORTANCE, SIR, I BELIEVE. OUR CAPTAIN WAS ATTACHED TO--

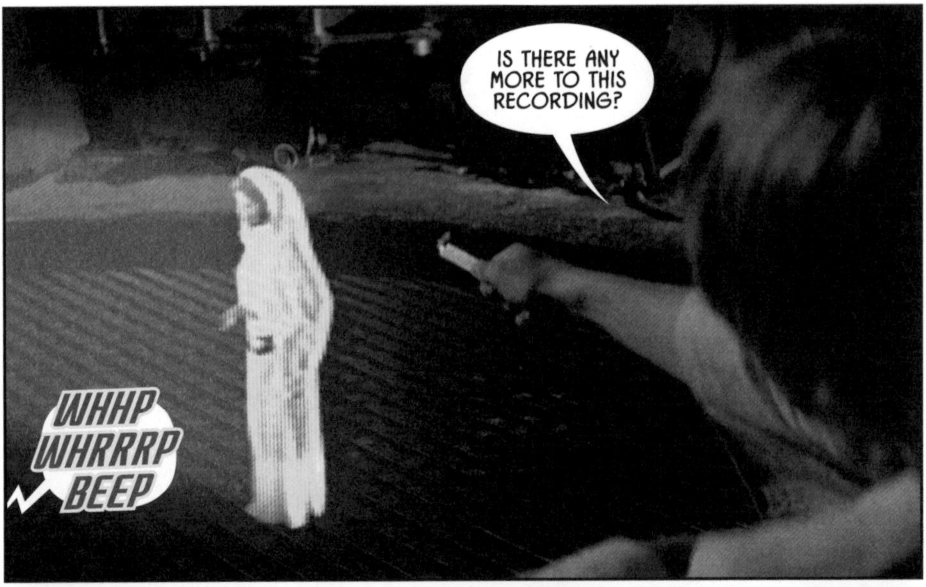
IS THERE ANY MORE TO THIS RECORDING?
WHHP WHRRRP BEEP

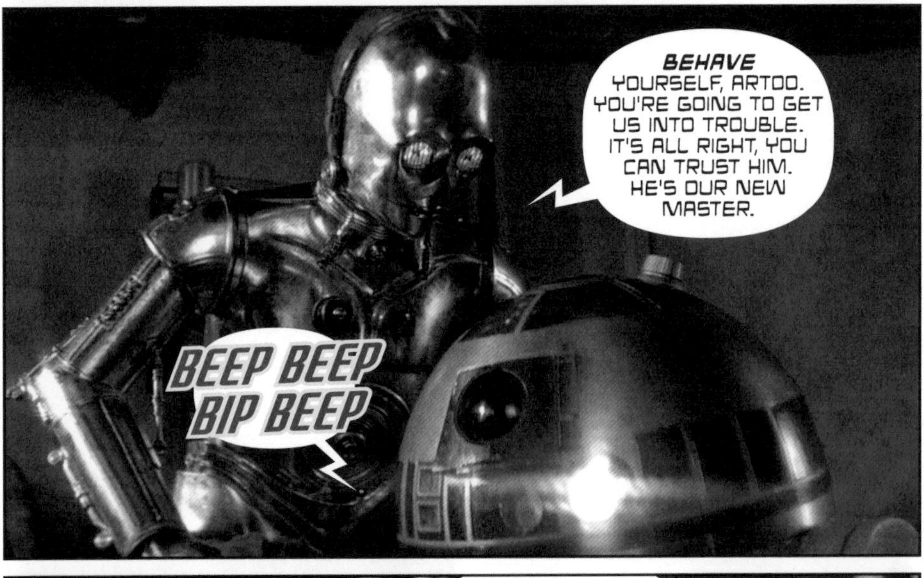
BEHAVE YOURSELF, ARTOO. YOU'RE GOING TO GET US INTO TROUBLE. IT'S ALL RIGHT, YOU CAN TRUST HIM. HE'S OUR NEW MASTER.
BEEP BEEP BIP BEEP

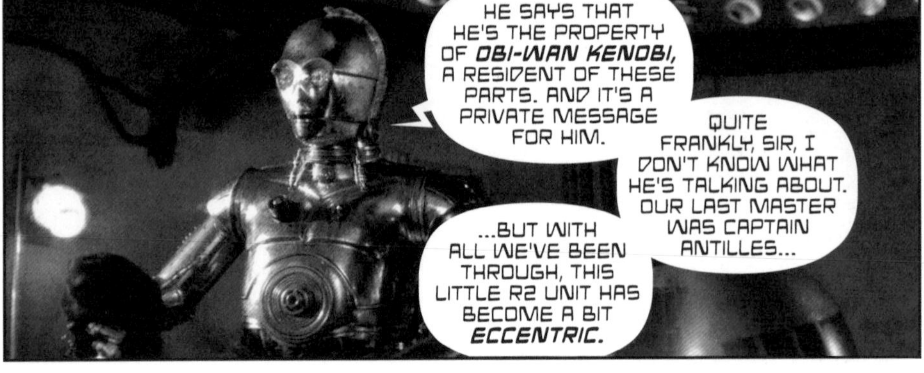
HE SAYS THAT HE'S THE PROPERTY OF OBI-WAN KENOBI, A RESIDENT OF THESE PARTS. AND IT'S A PRIVATE MESSAGE FOR HIM.
QUITE FRANKLY, SIR, I DON'T KNOW WHAT HE'S TALKING ABOUT. OUR LAST MASTER WAS CAPTAIN ANTILLES...
...BUT WITH ALL WE'VE BEEN THROUGH, THIS LITTLE R2 UNIT HAS BECOME A BIT ECCENTRIC.

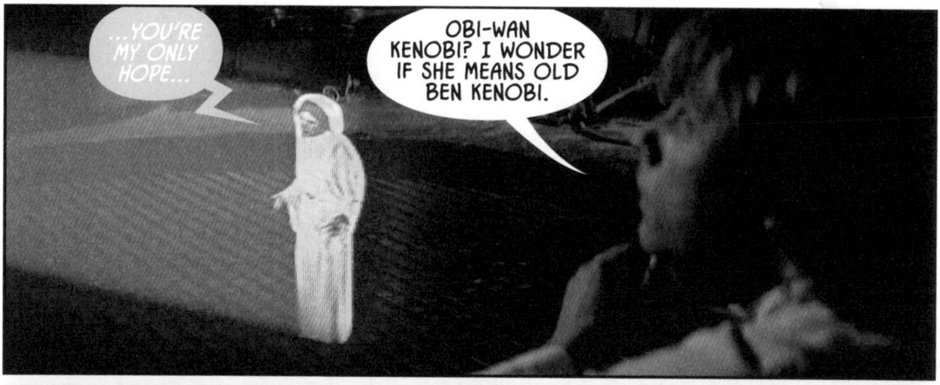
...YOU'RE MY ONLY HOPE...
OBI-WAN KENOBI? I WONDER IF SHE MEANS OLD BEN KENOBI.

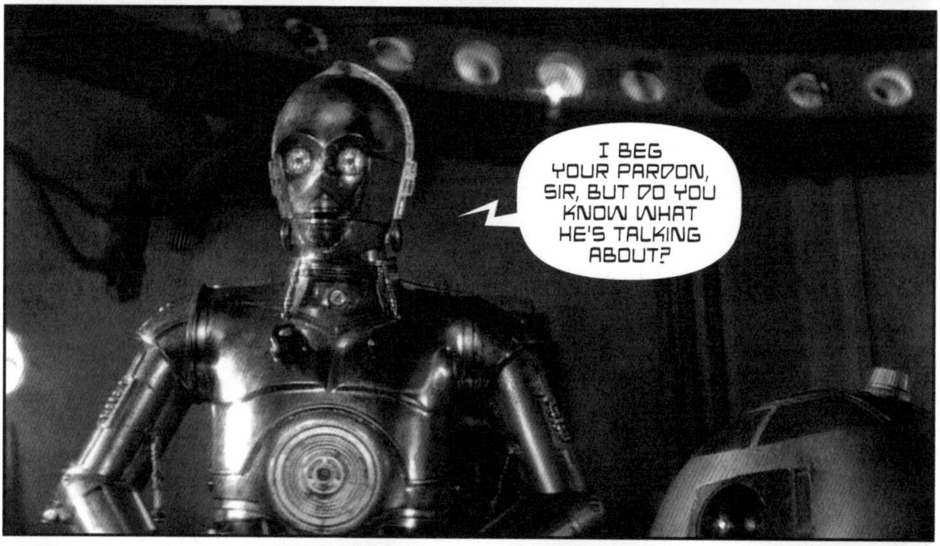
I BEG YOUR PARDON, SIR, BUT DO YOU KNOW WHAT HE'S TALKING ABOUT?

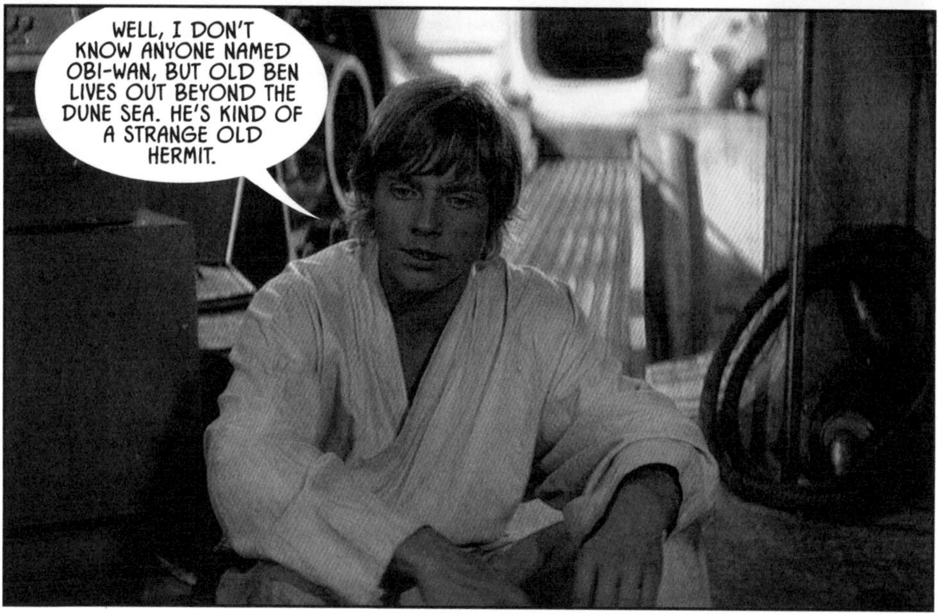
WELL, I DON'T KNOW ANYONE NAMED OBI-WAN, BUT OLD BEN LIVES OUT BEYOND THE DUNE SEA. HE'S KIND OF A STRANGE OLD HERMIT.

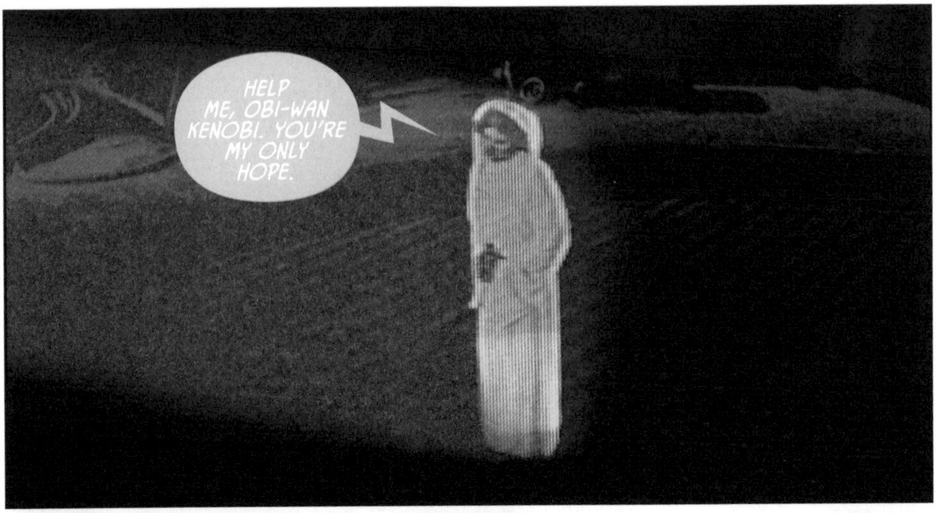
HELP ME, OBI-WAN KENOBI. YOU'RE MY ONLY HOPE.

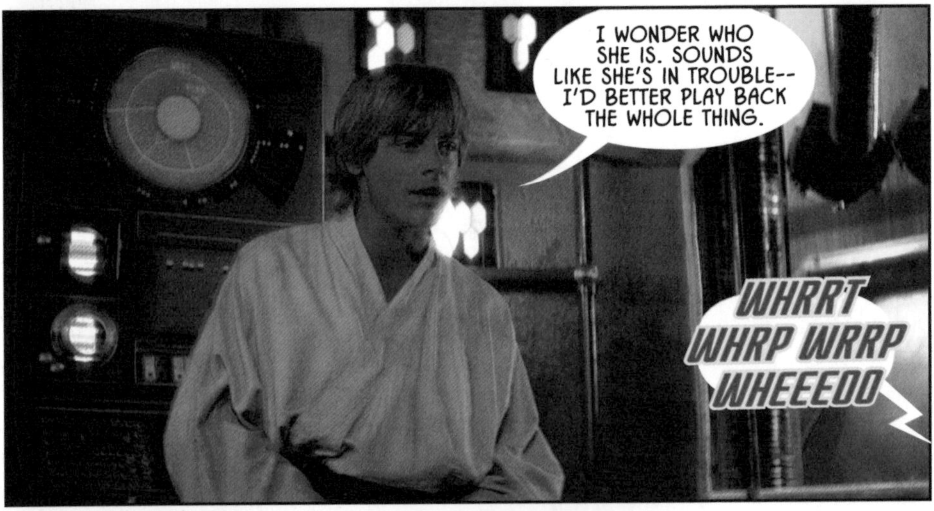
I WONDER WHO SHE IS. SOUNDS LIKE SHE'S IN TROUBLE-- I'D BETTER PLAY BACK THE WHOLE THING.
WHRRT WHRP WRRP WHEEEDO

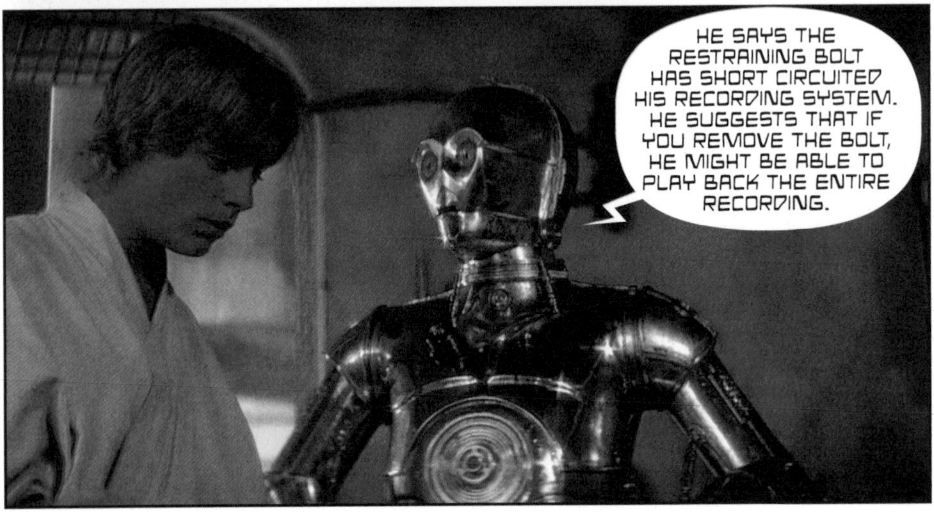
HE SAYS THE RESTRAINING BOLT HAS SHORT CIRCUITED HIS RECORDING SYSTEM. HE SUGGESTS THAT IF YOU REMOVE THE BOLT, HE MIGHT BE ABLE TO PLAY BACK THE ENTIRE RECORDING.

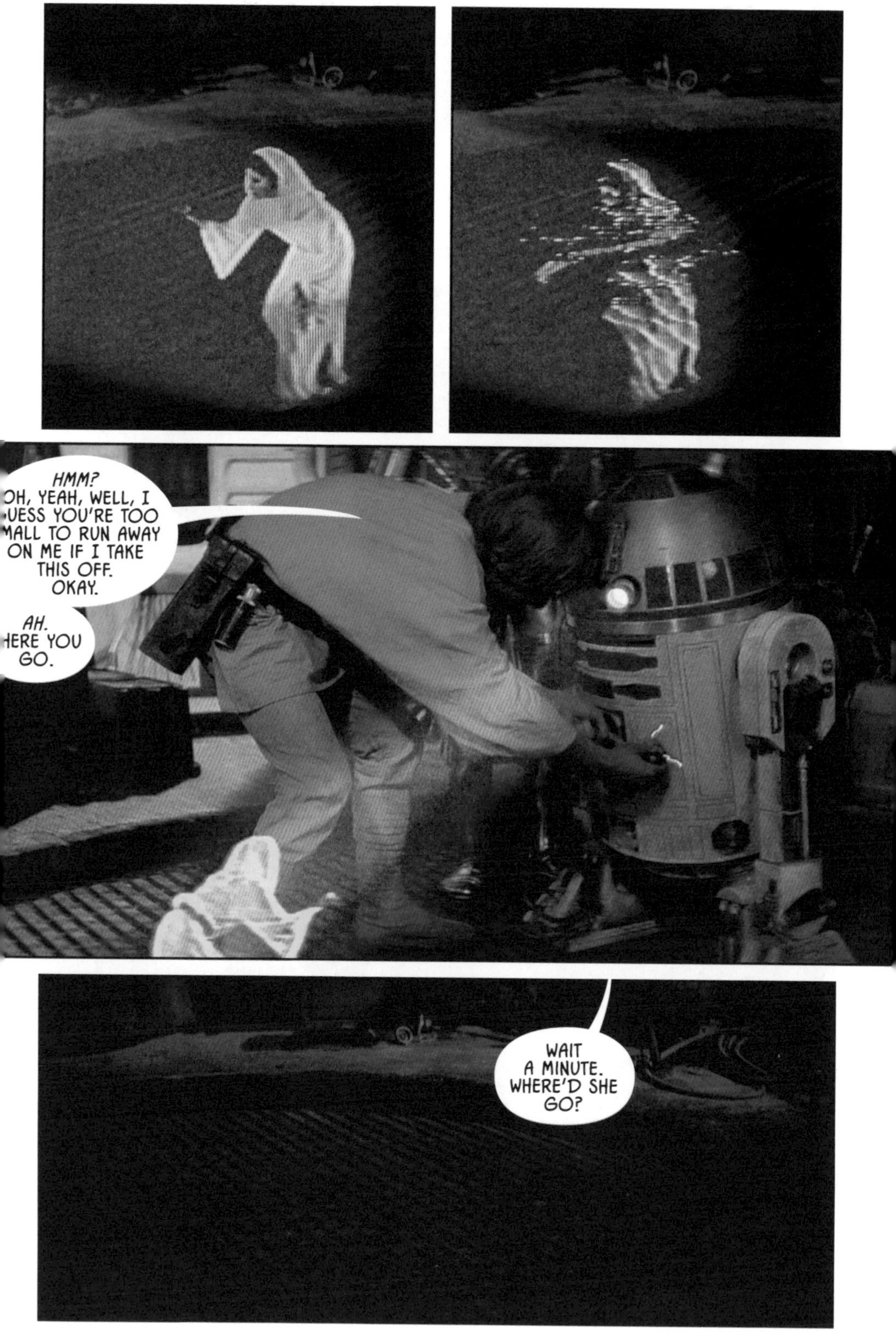

HMM?
OH, YEAH, WELL, I
UESS YOU'RE TOO
MALL TO RUN AWAY
ON ME IF I TAKE
THIS OFF.
OKAY.
AH.
HERE YOU
GO.
WAIT
A MINUTE.
WHERE'D SHE
GO?

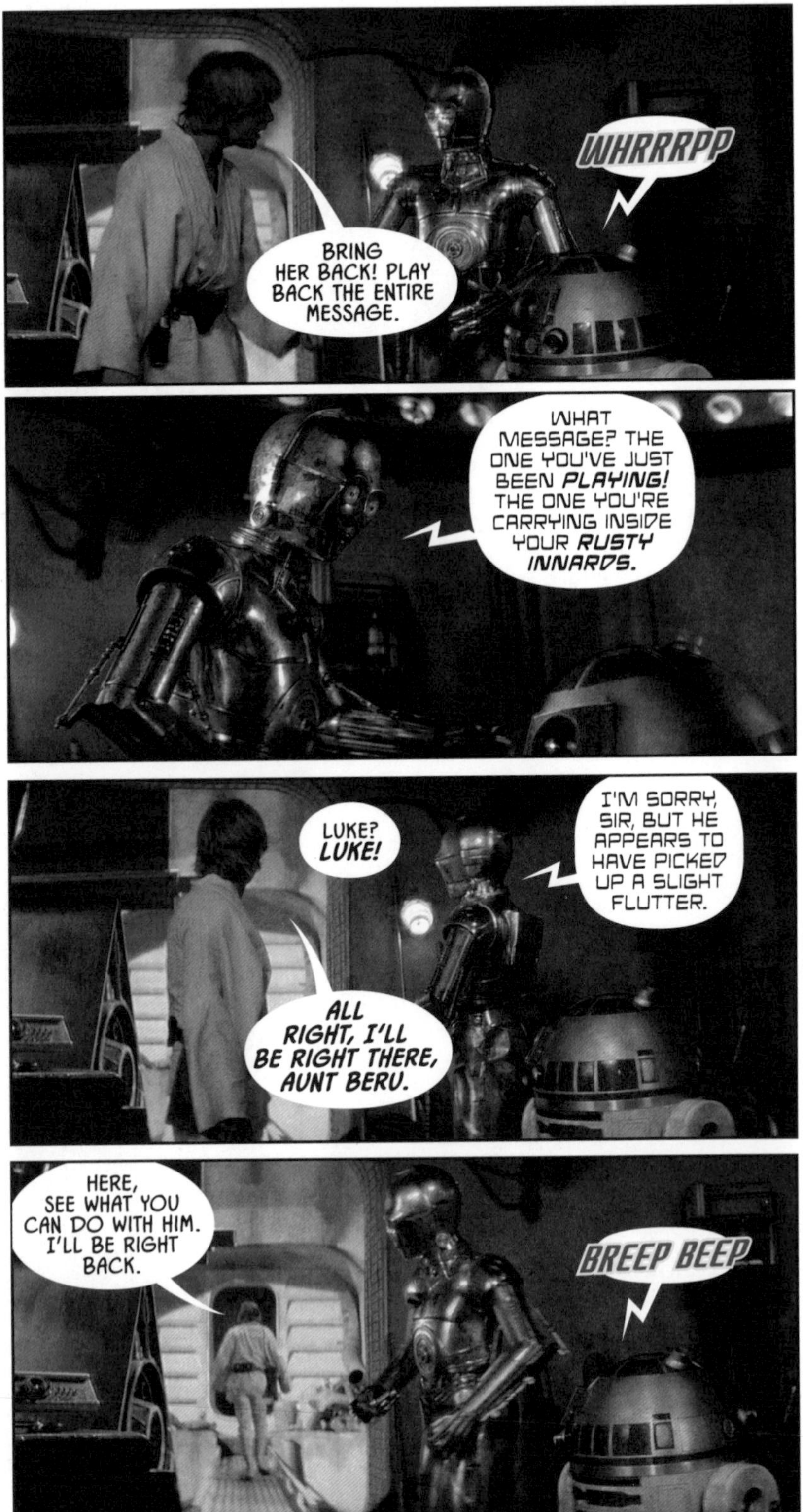
WHRRRPP
BRING HER BACK! PLAY BACK THE ENTIRE MESSAGE.
WHAT MESSAGE? THE ONE YOU'VE JUST BEEN PLAYING! THE ONE YOU'RE CARRYING INSIDE YOUR RUSTY INNARDS.
LUKE? LUKE!
I'M SORRY, SIR, BUT HE APPEARS TO HAVE PICKED UP A SLIGHT FLUTTER.
ALL RIGHT, I'LL BE RIGHT THERE, AUNT BERU.
HERE, SEE WHAT YOU CAN DO WITH HIM. I'LL BE RIGHT BACK.
BREEP BEEP

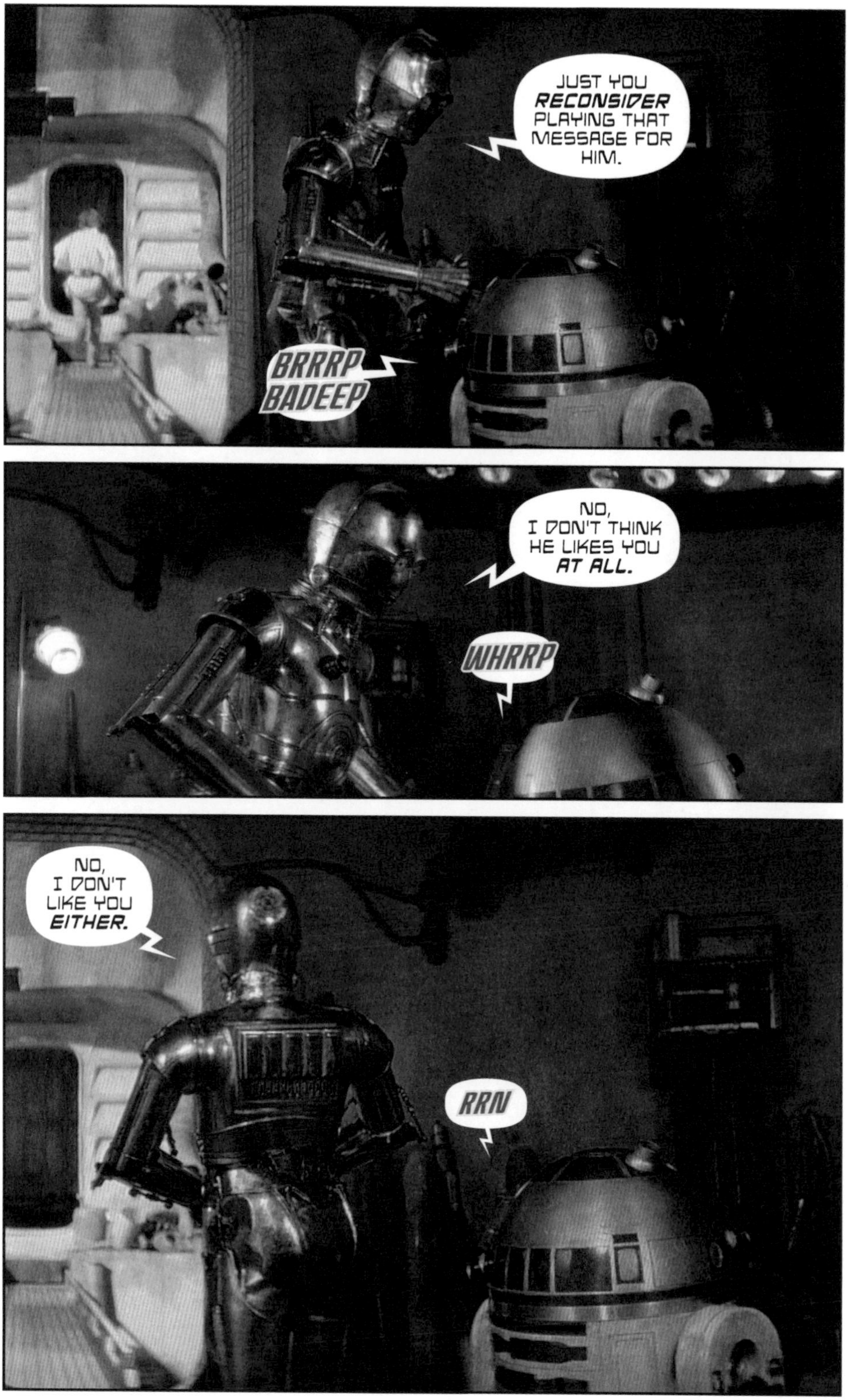
JUST YOU RECONSIDER PLAYING THAT MESSAGE FOR HIM.
BRRRP BADEEP
NO, I DON'T THINK HE LIKES YOU AT ALL.
WHRRP
NO, I DON'T LIKE YOU EITHER.
RRN

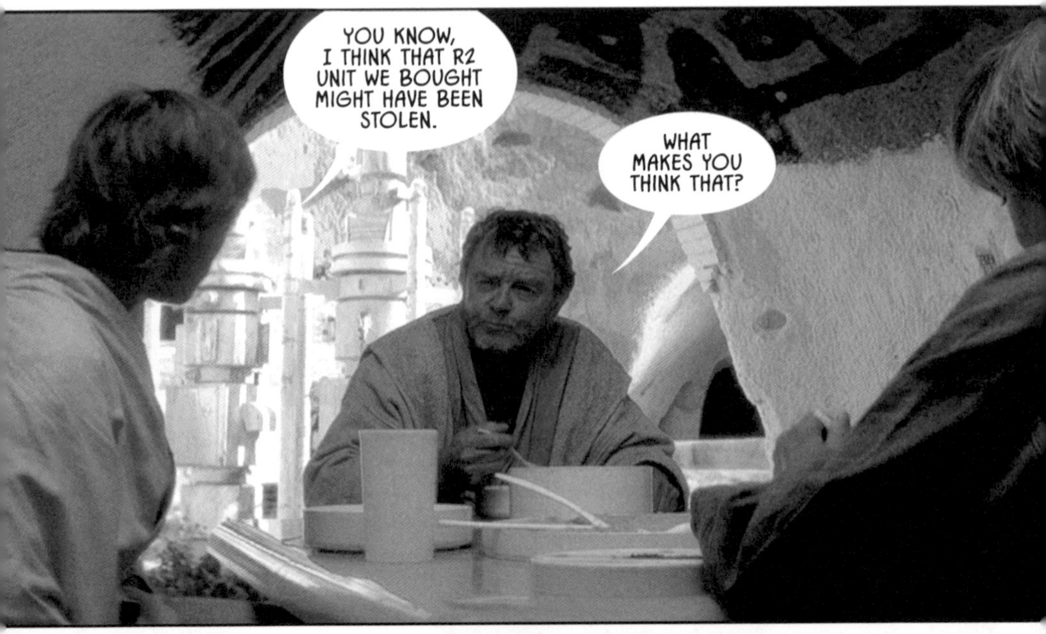
YOU KNOW, I THINK THAT R2 UNIT WE BOUGHT MIGHT HAVE BEEN STOLEN.
WHAT MAKES YOU THINK THAT?

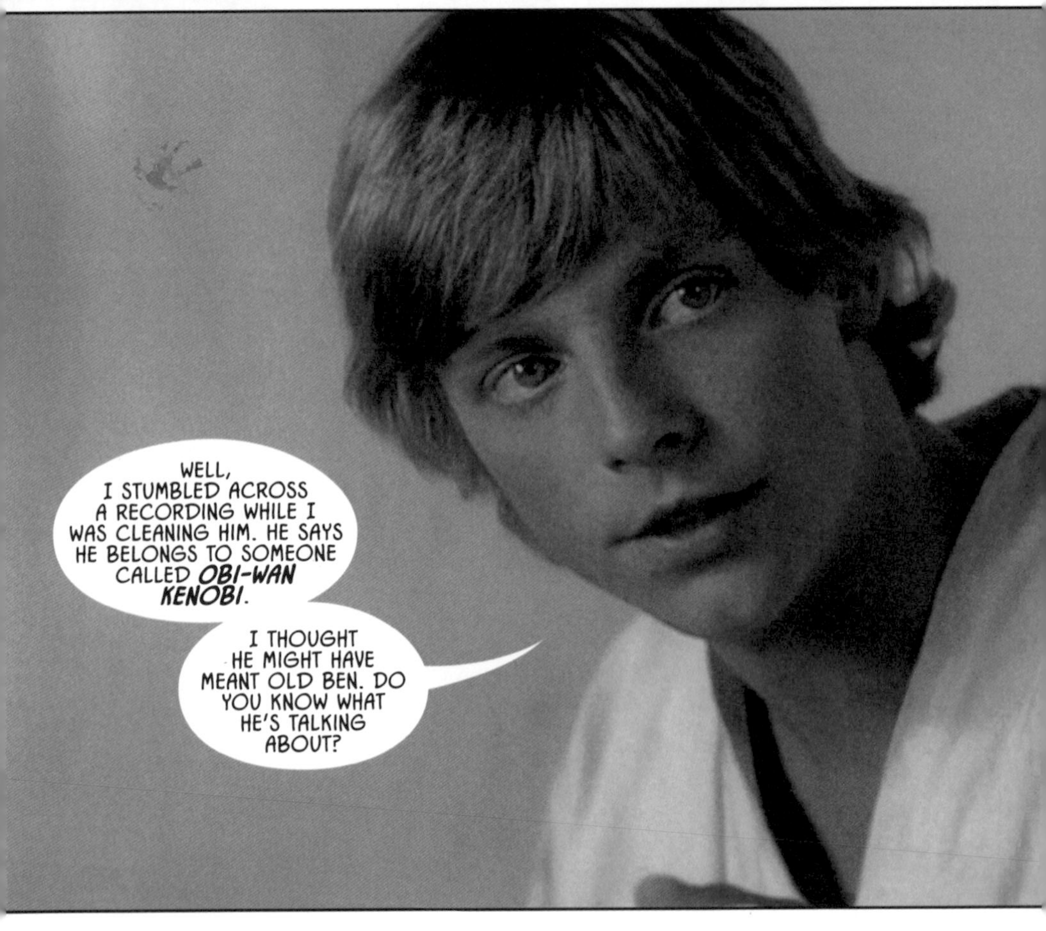
WELL, I STUMBLED ACROSS A RECORDING WHILE I WAS CLEANING HIM. HE SAYS HE BELONGS TO SOMEONE CALLED *OBI-WAN KENOBI*.
I THOUGHT HE MIGHT HAVE MEANT OLD BEN. DO YOU KNOW WHAT HE'S TALKING ABOUT?

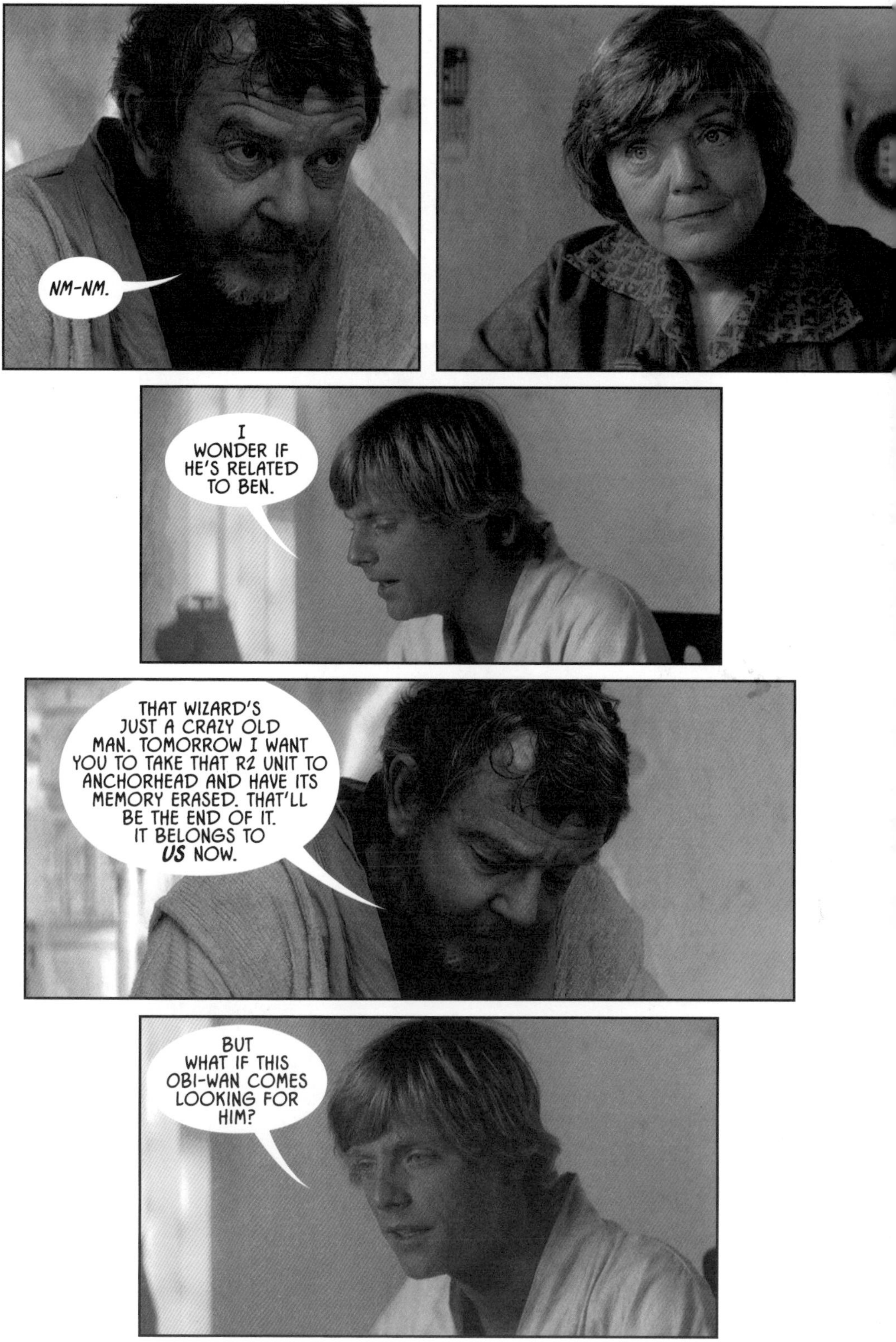
NM-NM.
I WONDER IF HE'S RELATED TO BEN.
THAT WIZARD'S JUST A CRAZY OLD MAN. TOMORROW I WANT YOU TO TAKE THAT R2 UNIT TO ANCHORHEAD AND HAVE ITS MEMORY ERASED. THAT'LL BE THE END OF IT. IT BELONGS TO *US* NOW.
BUT WHAT IF THIS OBI-WAN COMES LOOKING FOR HIM?

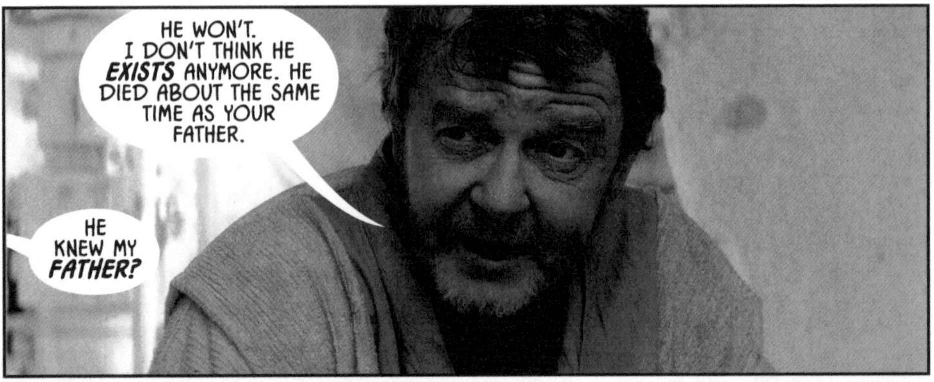
HE WON'T. I DON'T THINK HE EXISTS ANYMORE. HE DIED ABOUT THE SAME TIME AS YOUR FATHER.
HE KNEW MY FATHER?

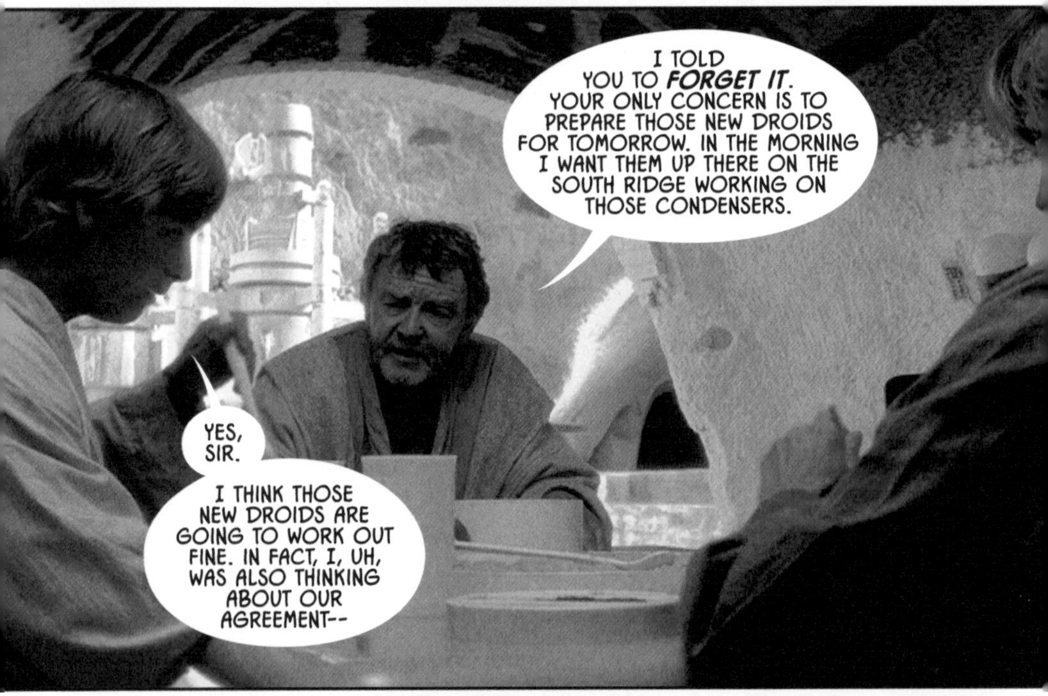
I TOLD YOU TO FORGET IT. YOUR ONLY CONCERN IS TO PREPARE THOSE NEW DROIDS FOR TOMORROW. IN THE MORNING I WANT THEM UP THERE ON THE SOUTH RIDGE WORKING ON THOSE CONDENSERS.
YES, SIR.
I THINK THOSE NEW DROIDS ARE GOING TO WORK OUT FINE. IN FACT, I, UH, WAS ALSO THINKING ABOUT OUR AGREEMENT--

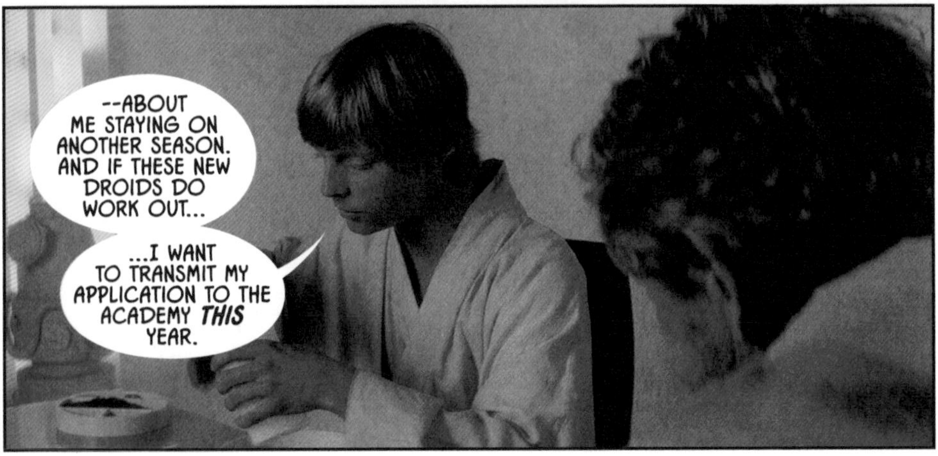
--ABOUT ME STAYING ON ANOTHER SEASON. AND IF THESE NEW DROIDS DO WORK OUT...
...I WANT TO TRANSMIT MY APPLICATION TO THE ACADEMY THIS YEAR.

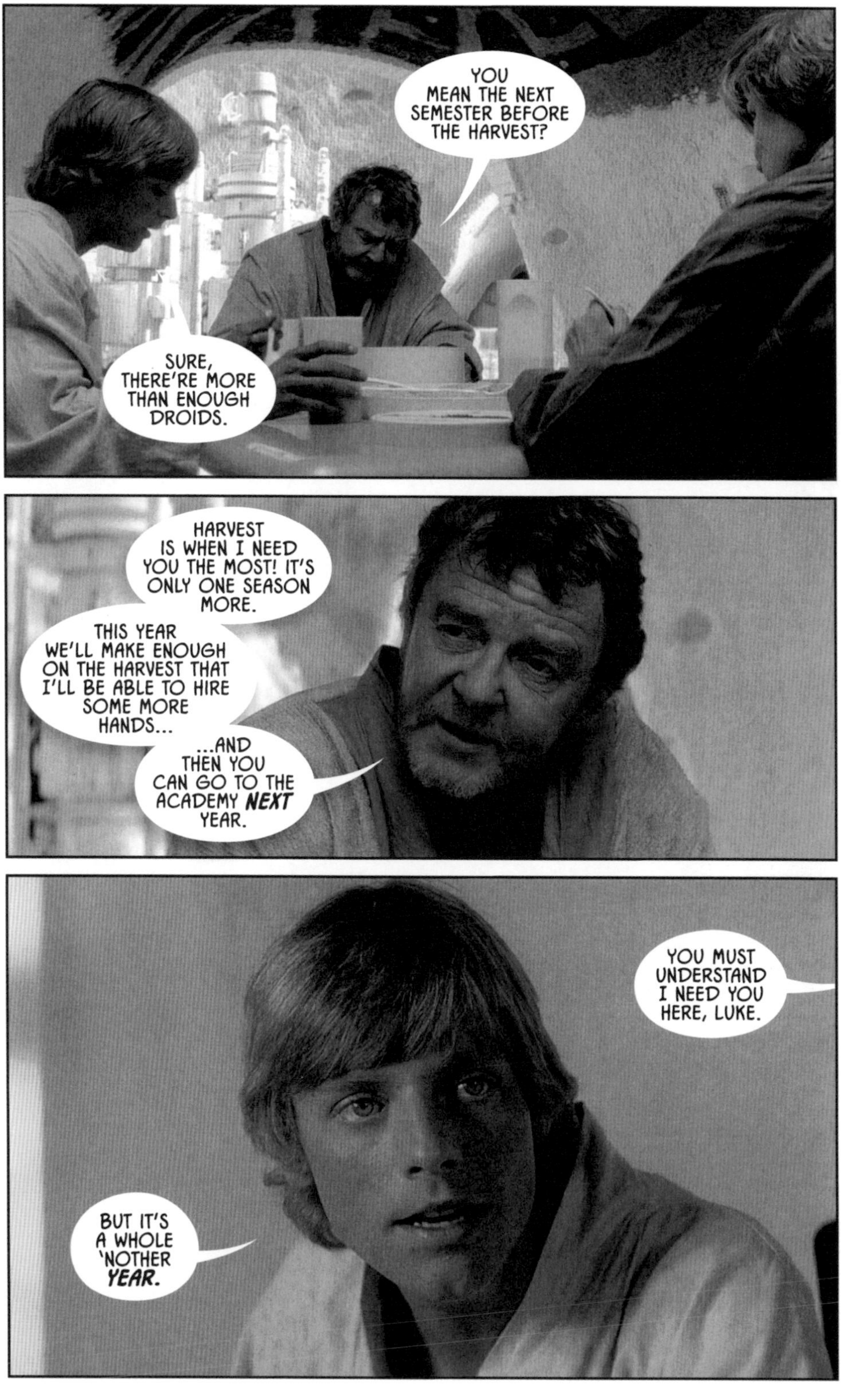
YOU MEAN THE NEXT SEMESTER BEFORE THE HARVEST?
SURE, THERE'RE MORE THAN ENOUGH DROIDS.
HARVEST IS WHEN I NEED YOU THE MOST! IT'S ONLY ONE SEASON MORE.
THIS YEAR WE'LL MAKE ENOUGH ON THE HARVEST THAT I'LL BE ABLE TO HIRE SOME MORE HANDS...
...AND THEN YOU CAN GO TO THE ACADEMY ***NEXT*** YEAR.
YOU MUST UNDERSTAND I NEED YOU HERE, LUKE.
BUT IT'S A WHOLE 'NOTHER ***YEAR.***

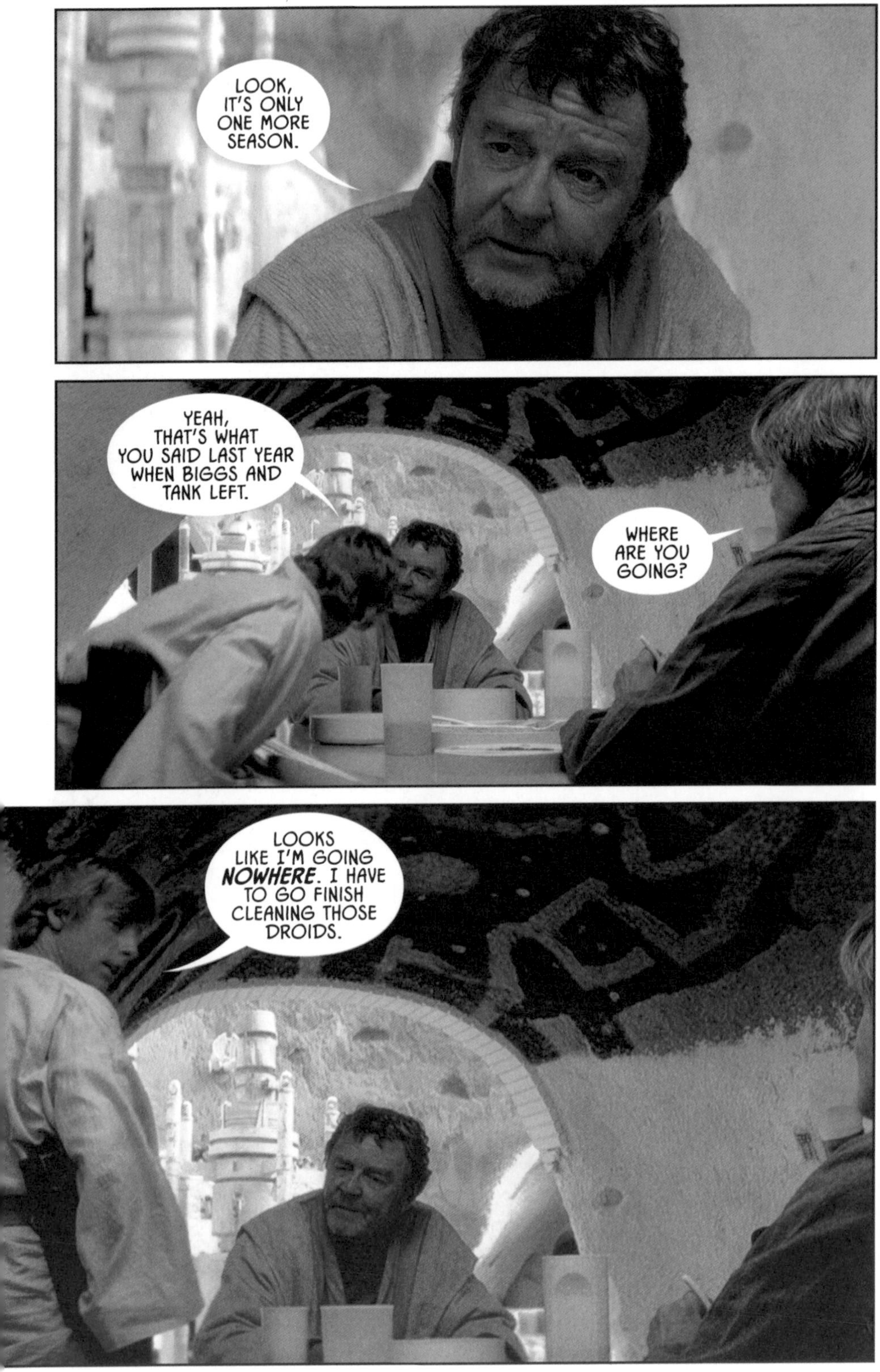
LOOK, IT'S ONLY ONE MORE SEASON.
YEAH, THAT'S WHAT YOU SAID LAST YEAR WHEN BIGGS AND TANK LEFT.
WHERE ARE YOU GOING?
LOOKS LIKE I'M GOING ***NOWHERE***. I HAVE TO GO FINISH CLEANING THOSE DROIDS.

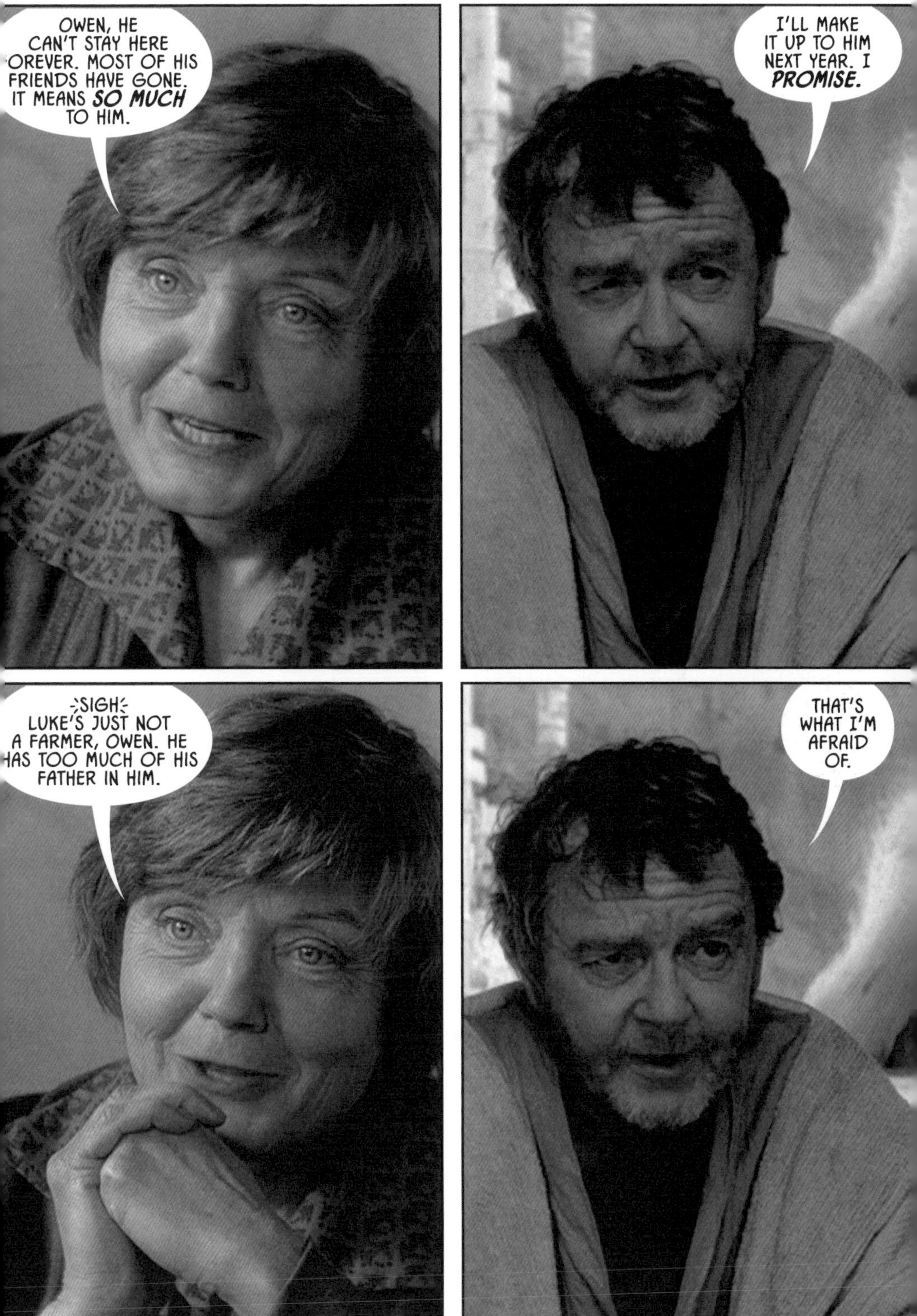
OWEN, HE CAN'T STAY HERE OREVER. MOST OF HIS FRIENDS HAVE GONE. IT MEANS **SO MUCH** TO HIM.
I'LL MAKE IT UP TO HIM NEXT YEAR. I **PROMISE.**
SIGH
LUKE'S JUST NOT A FARMER, OWEN. HE HAS TOO MUCH OF HIS FATHER IN HIM.
THAT'S WHAT I'M AFRAID OF.

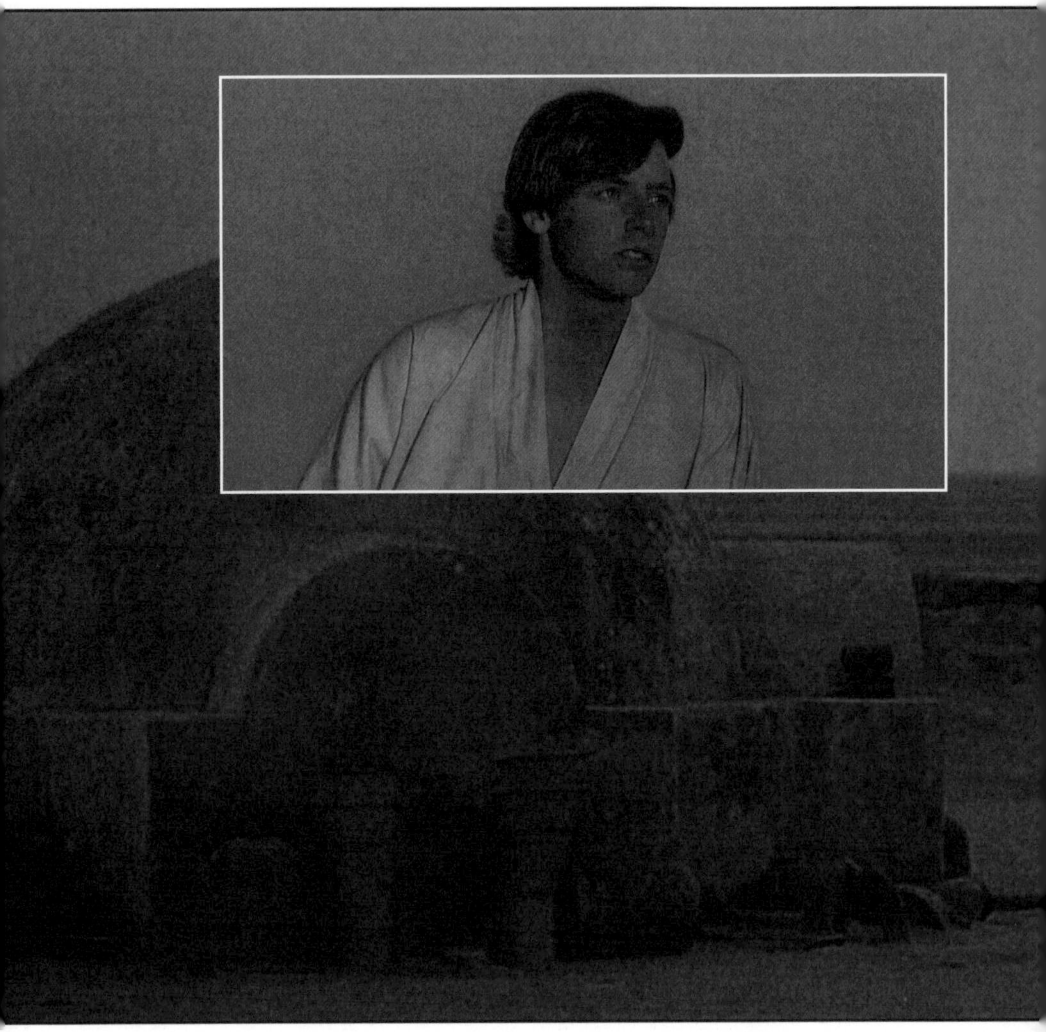

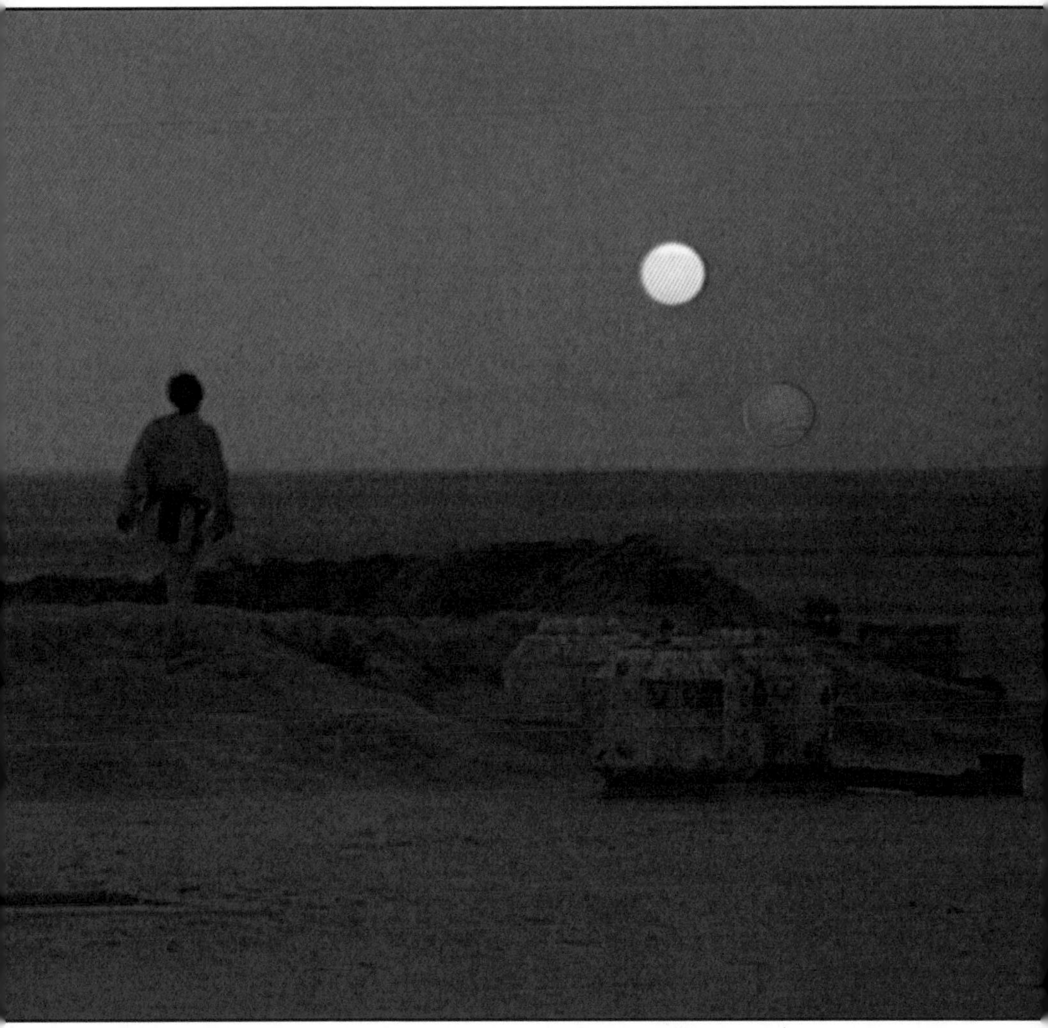

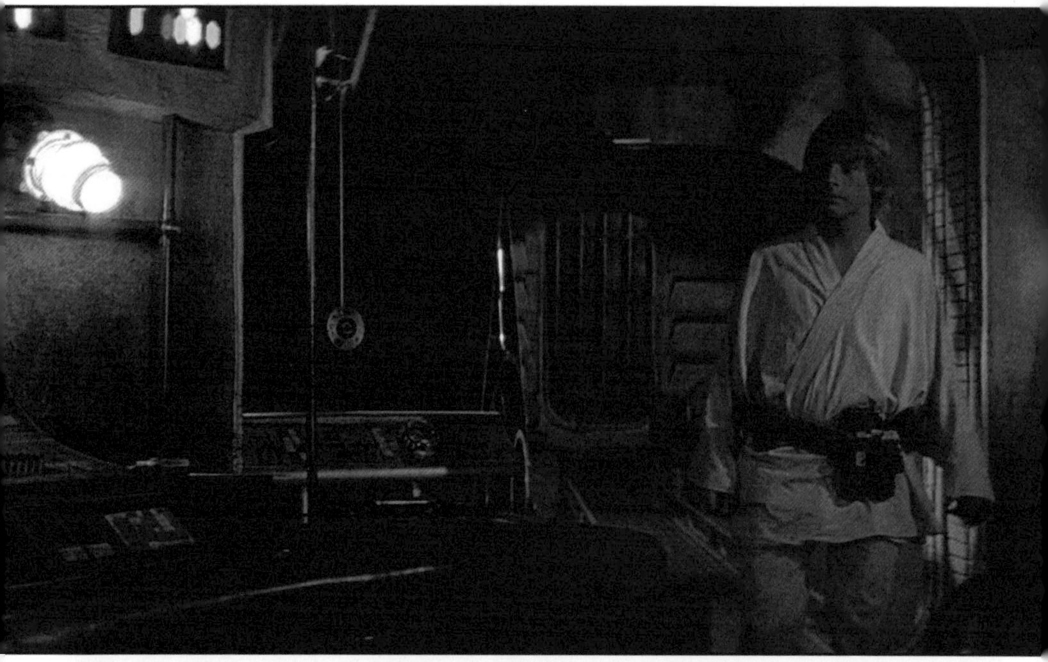

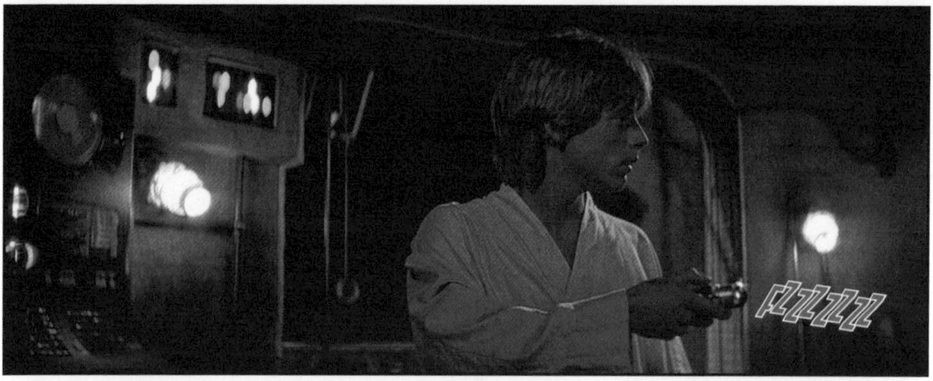
FZZZZZZ

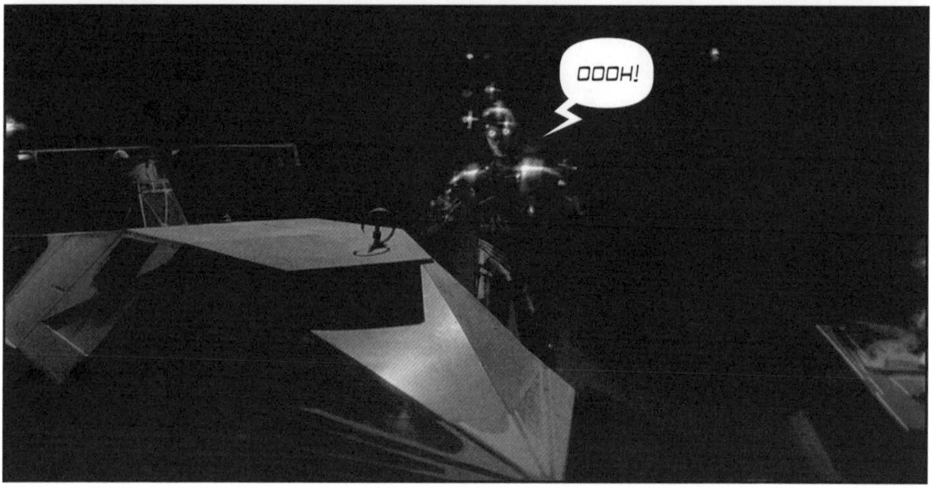
OOOH!

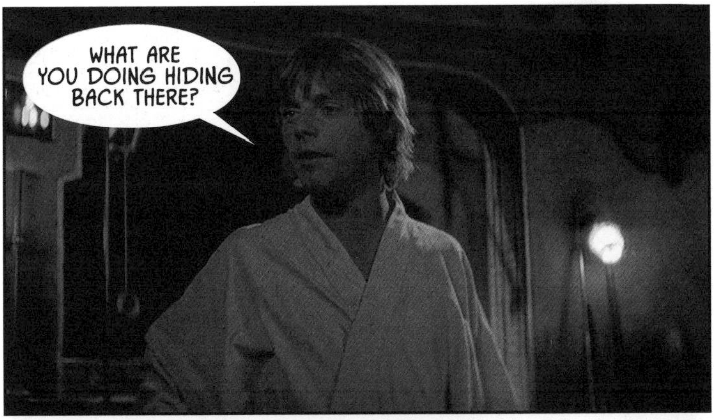
WHAT ARE YOU DOING HIDING BACK THERE?

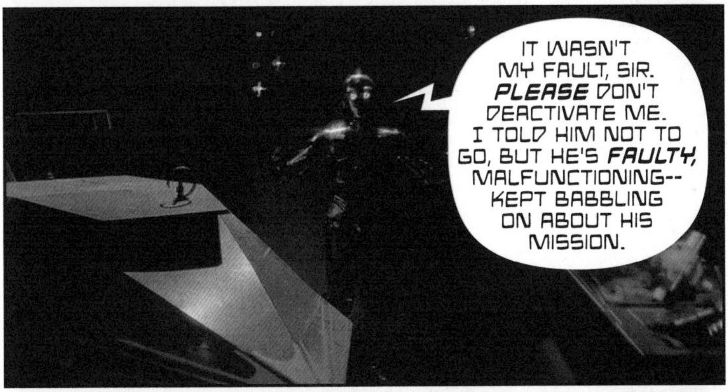
IT WASN'T MY FAULT, SIR. PLEASE DON'T DEACTIVATE ME. I TOLD HIM NOT TO GO, BUT HE'S FAULTY, MALFUNCTIONING--KEPT BABBLING ON ABOUT HIS MISSION.

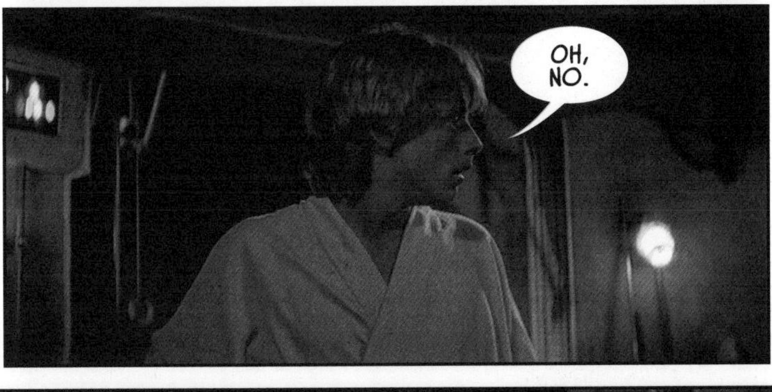
OH, NO.

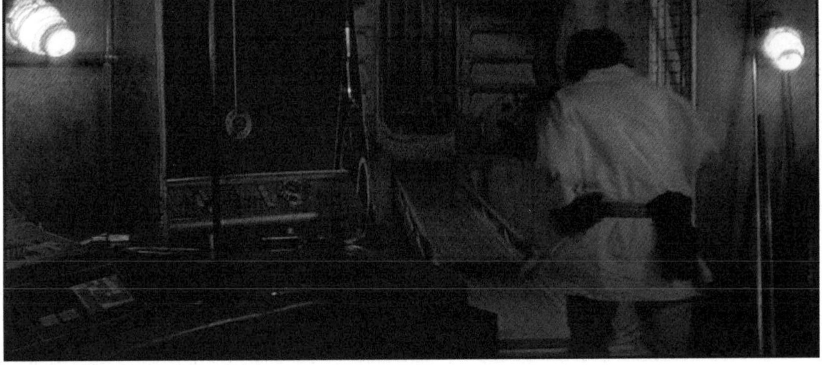

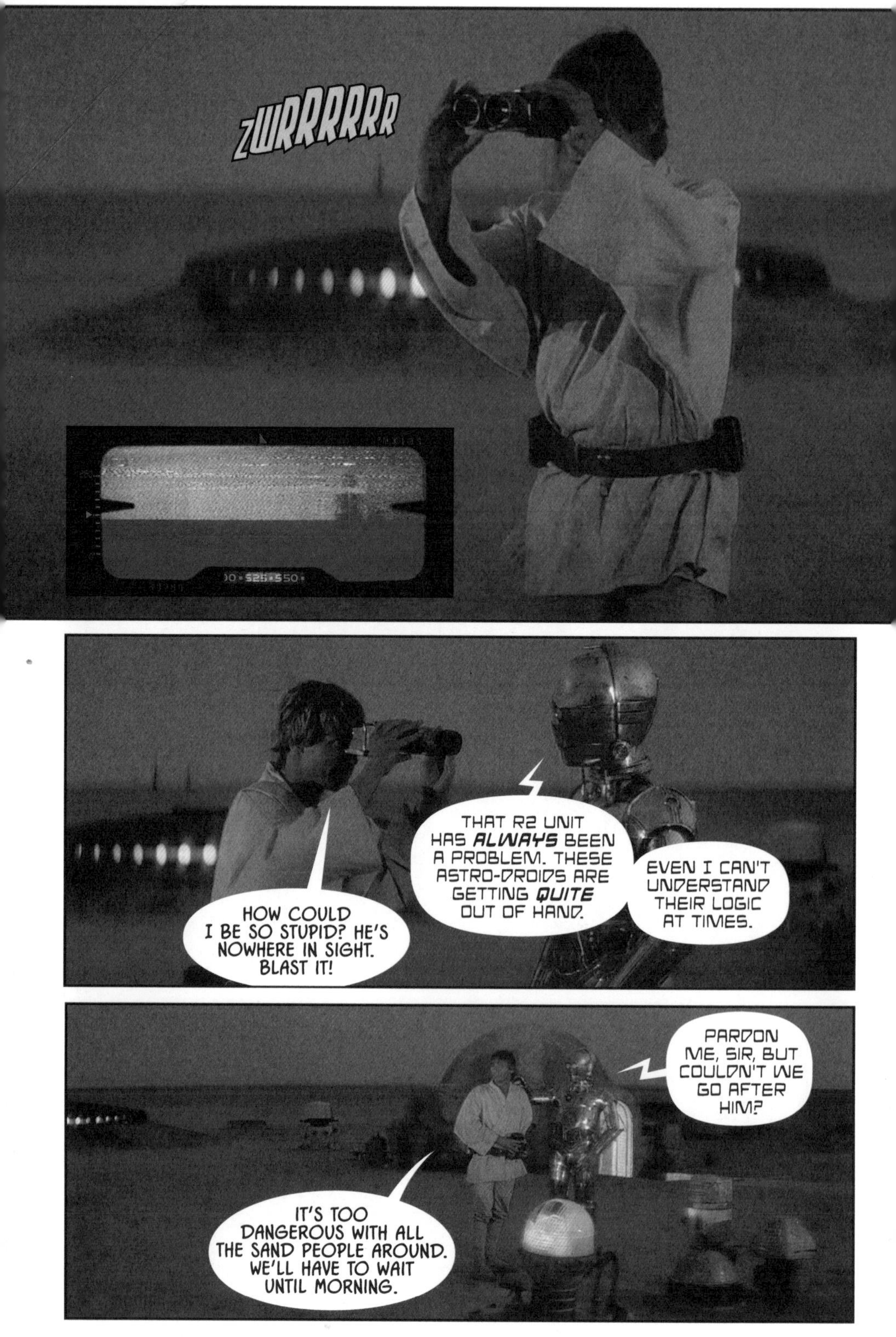
ZWRRRRRR
HOW COULD I BE SO STUPID? HE'S NOWHERE IN SIGHT. BLAST IT!
THAT R2 UNIT HAS **ALWAYS** BEEN A PROBLEM. THESE ASTRO-DROIDS ARE GETTING **QUITE** OUT OF HAND.
EVEN I CAN'T UNDERSTAND THEIR LOGIC AT TIMES.
PARDON ME, SIR, BUT COULDN'T WE GO AFTER HIM?
IT'S TOO DANGEROUS WITH ALL THE SAND PEOPLE AROUND. WE'LL HAVE TO WAIT UNTIL MORNING.

LUKE, I'M SHUTTING THE POWER DOWN.

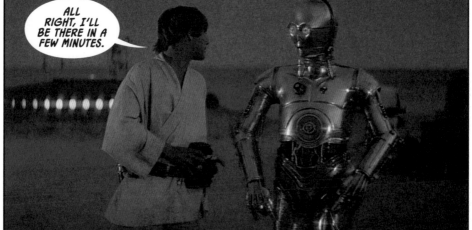

ALL RIGHT, I'LL BE THERE IN A FEW MINUTES.

BOY, AM I GONNA GET IT.

YOU KNOW, THAT LITTLE DROID IS GOING TO CAUSE ME A LOT OF TROUBLE.

OH, HE *EXCELS* AT THAT, SIR.

÷SIGH÷ COME ON.

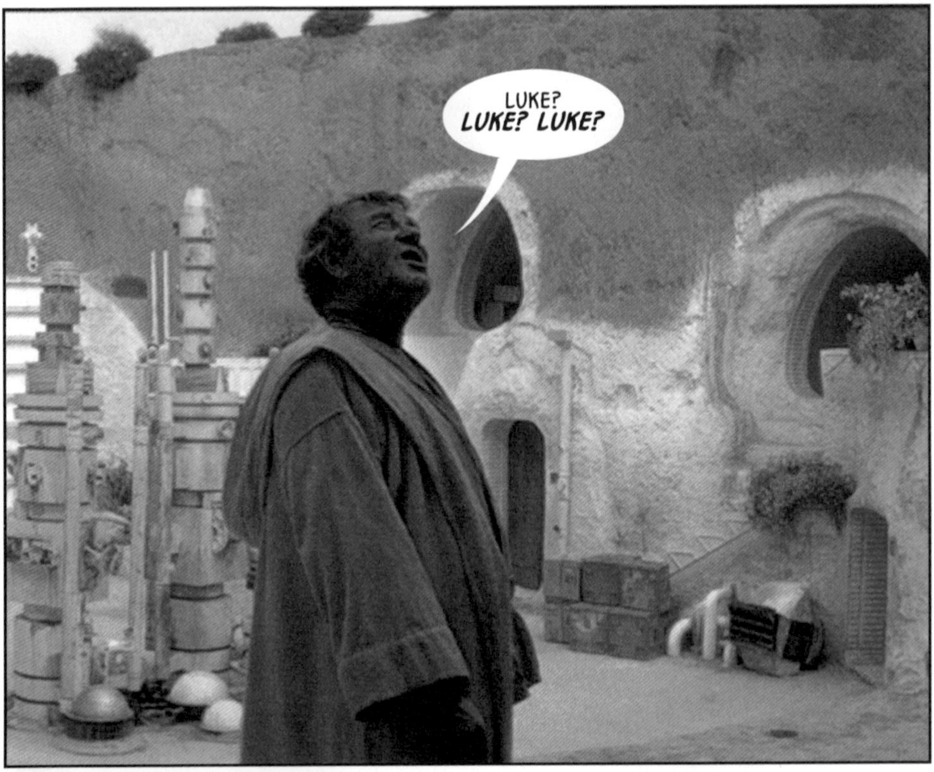
LUKE?
LUKE? LUKE?

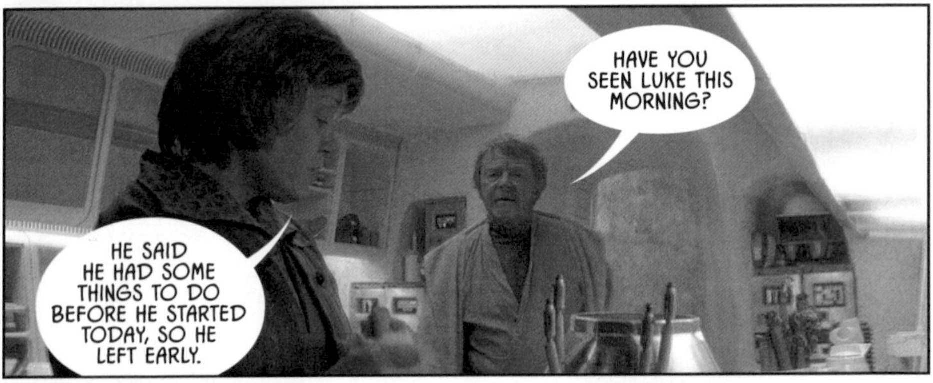
HAVE YOU SEEN LUKE THIS MORNING?
HE SAID HE HAD SOME THINGS TO DO BEFORE HE STARTED TODAY, SO HE LEFT EARLY.

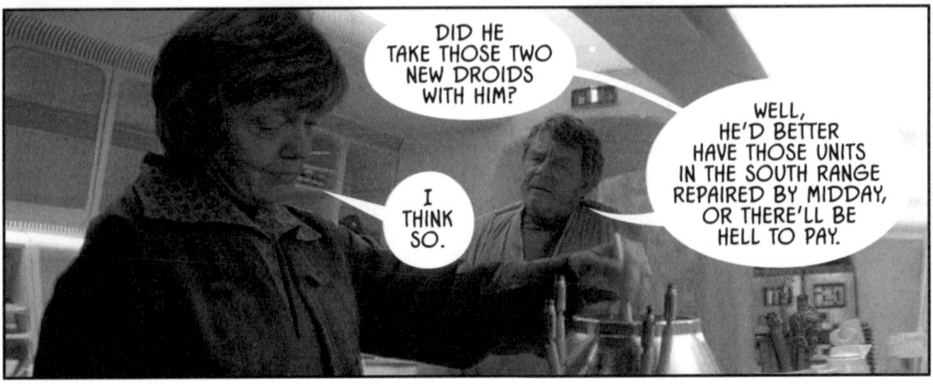
DID HE TAKE THOSE TWO NEW DROIDS WITH HIM?
I THINK SO.
WELL, HE'D BETTER HAVE THOSE UNITS IN THE SOUTH RANGE REPAIRED BY MIDDAY, OR THERE'LL BE HELL TO PAY.

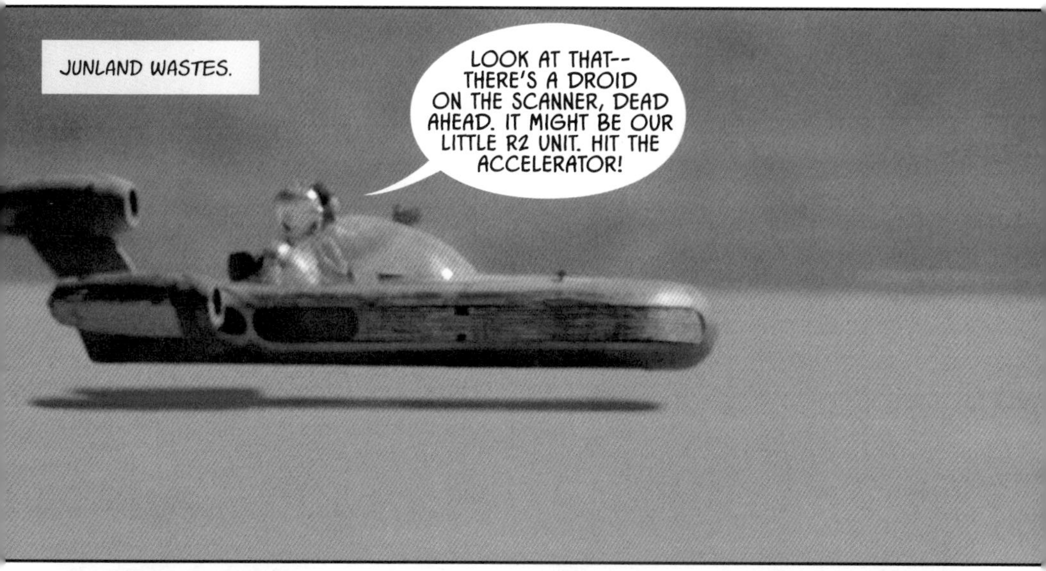
JUNLAND WASTES.
LOOK AT THAT-- THERE'S A DROID ON THE SCANNER, DEAD AHEAD. IT MIGHT BE OUR LITTLE R2 UNIT. HIT THE ACCELERATOR!

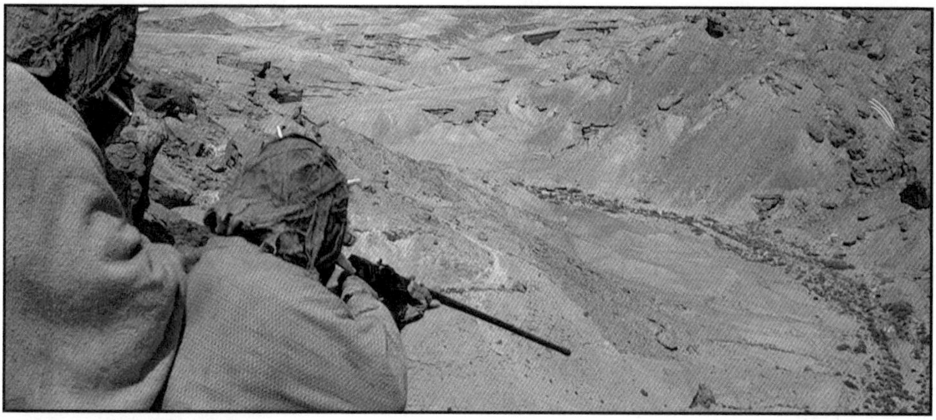

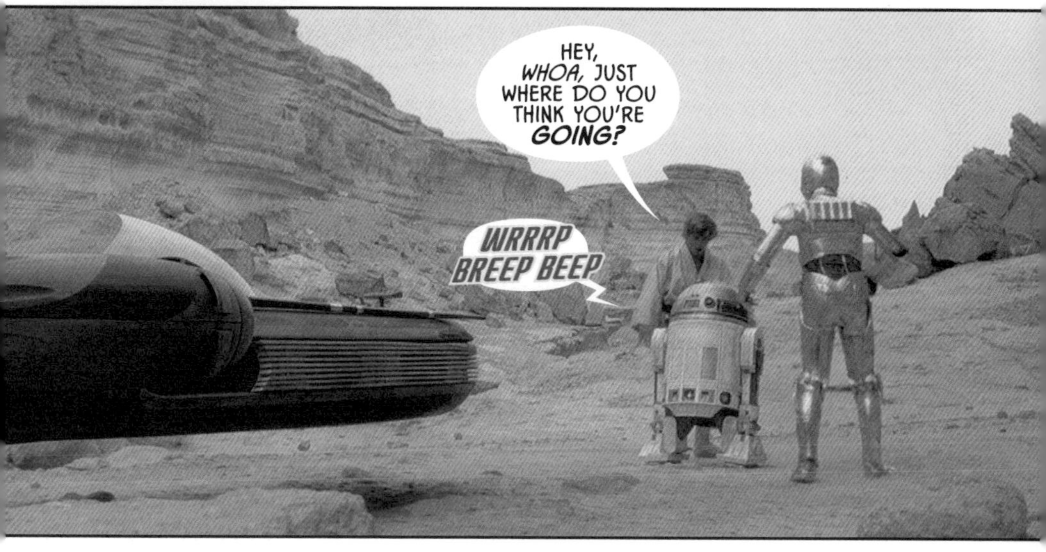
HEY, WHOA, JUST WHERE DO YOU THINK YOU'RE GOING?
WRRRP BREEP BEEP

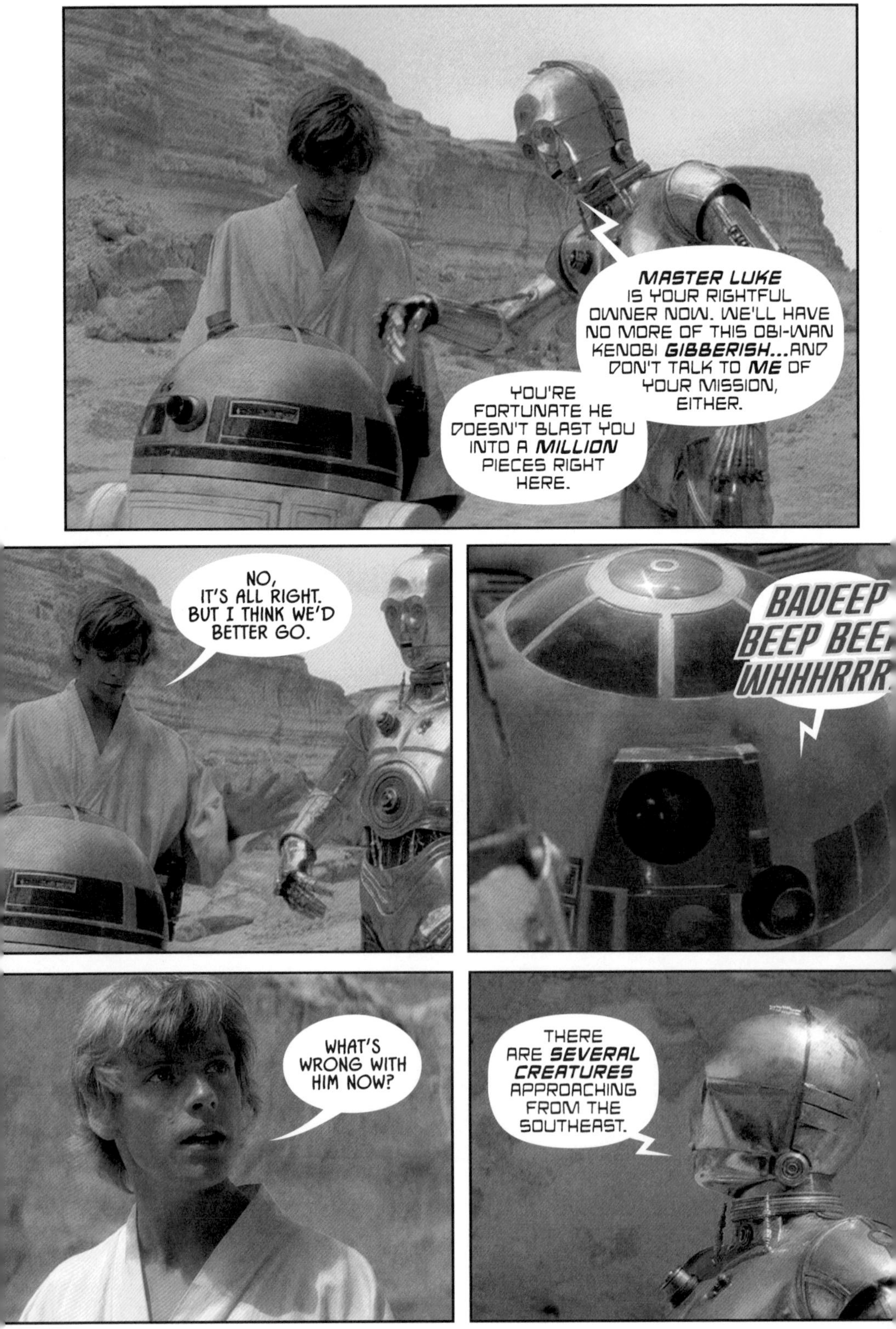
MASTER LUKE IS YOUR RIGHTFUL OWNER NOW. WE'LL HAVE NO MORE OF THIS OBI-WAN KENOBI GIBBERISH...AND DON'T TALK TO ME OF YOUR MISSION, EITHER.
YOU'RE FORTUNATE HE DOESN'T BLAST YOU INTO A MILLION PIECES RIGHT HERE.
NO, IT'S ALL RIGHT. BUT I THINK WE'D BETTER GO.
BADEEP BEEP BEE WHHHRRR
WHAT'S WRONG WITH HIM NOW?
THERE ARE SEVERAL CREATURES APPROACHING FROM THE SOUTHEAST.

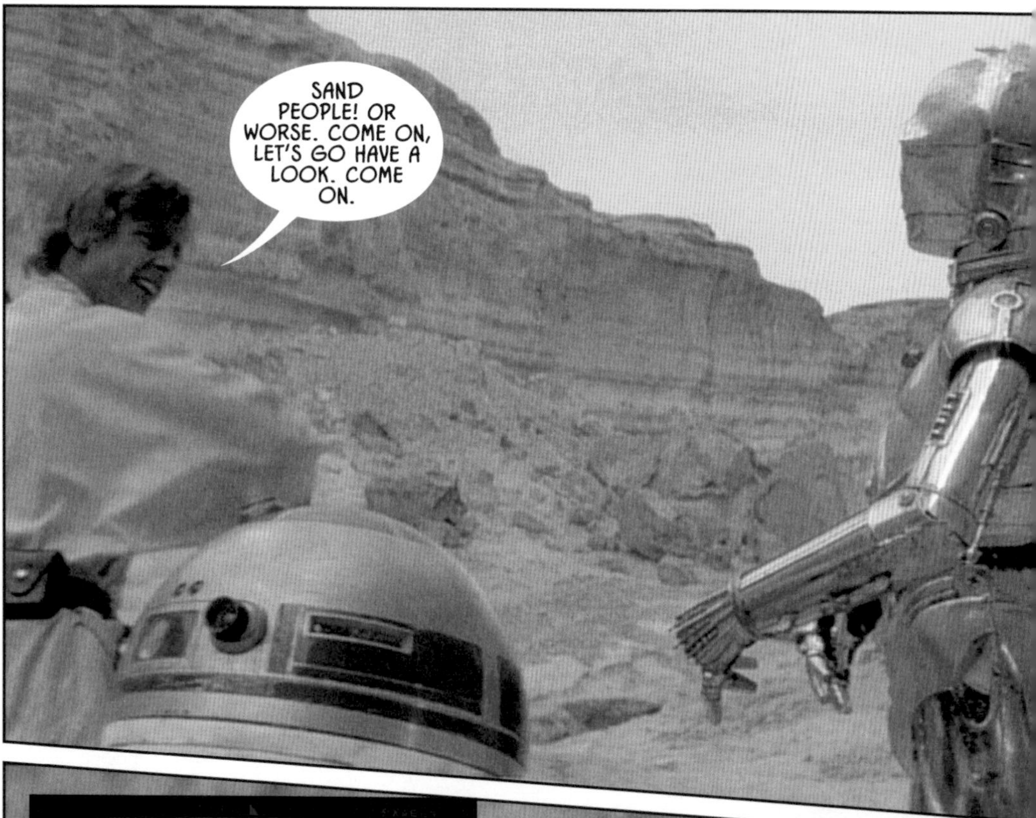
SAND PEOPLE! OR WORSE. COME ON, LET'S GO HAVE A LOOK. COME ON.

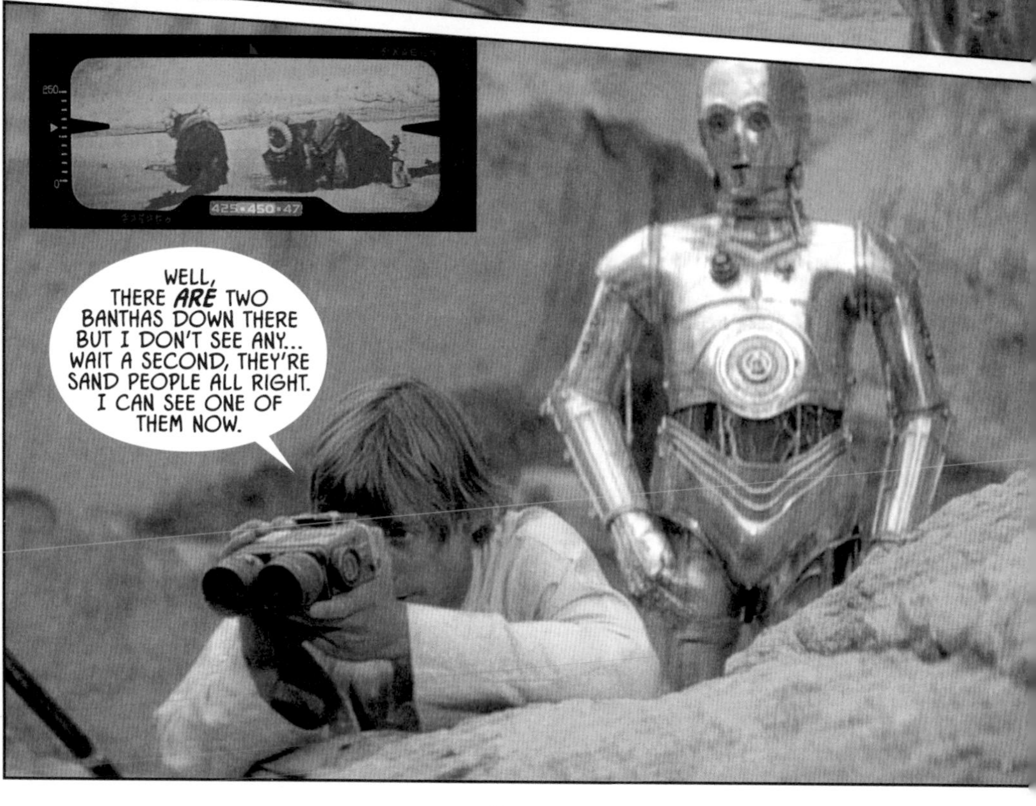
WELL, THERE *ARE* TWO BANTHAS DOWN THERE BUT I DON'T SEE ANY... WAIT A SECOND, THEY'RE SAND PEOPLE ALL RIGHT. I CAN SEE ONE OF THEM NOW.

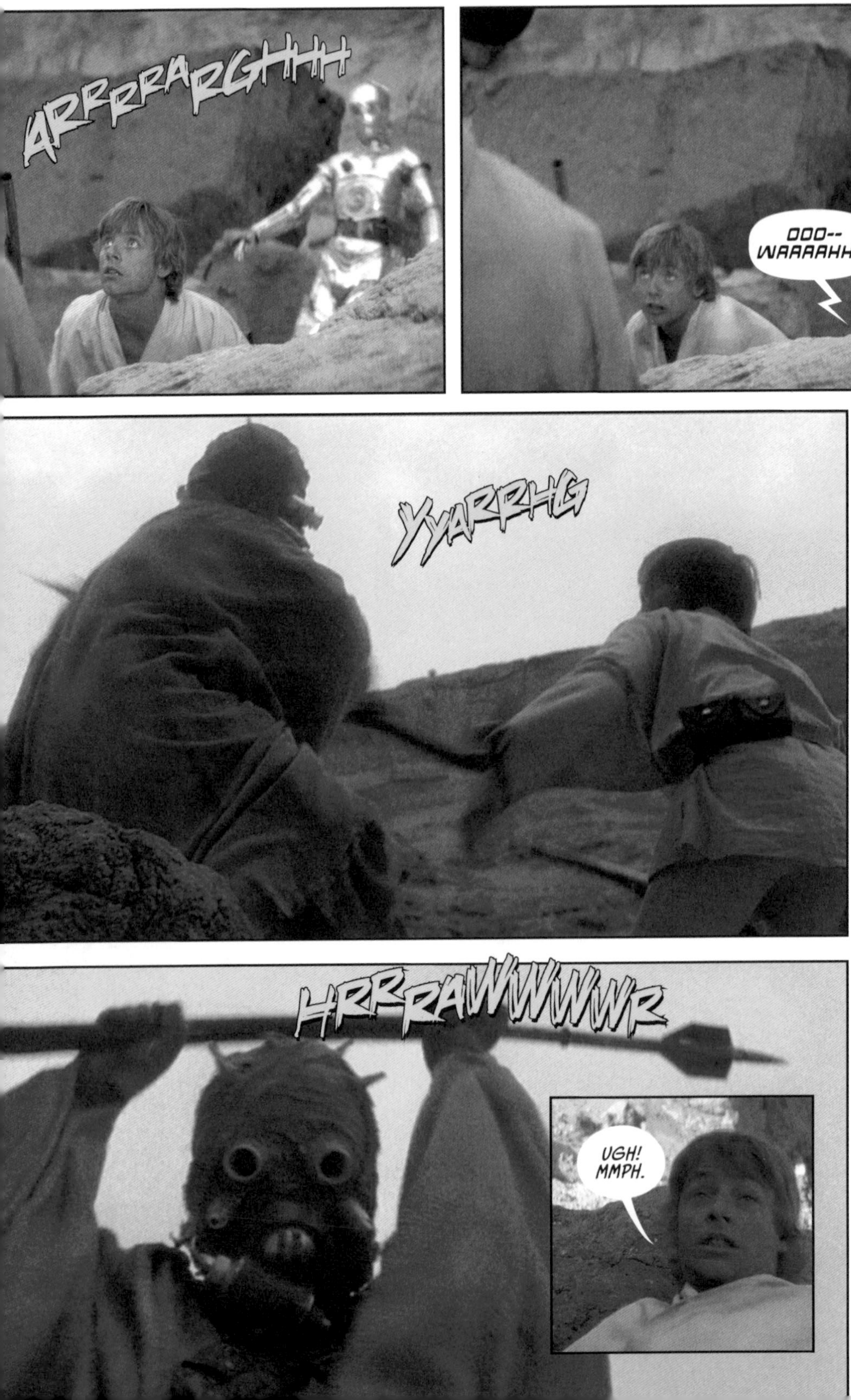
ARRRRARGHHH
OOO--
WAAAAHHH!
YYARRHG
HRRRAWWWWR
UGH!
MMPH.

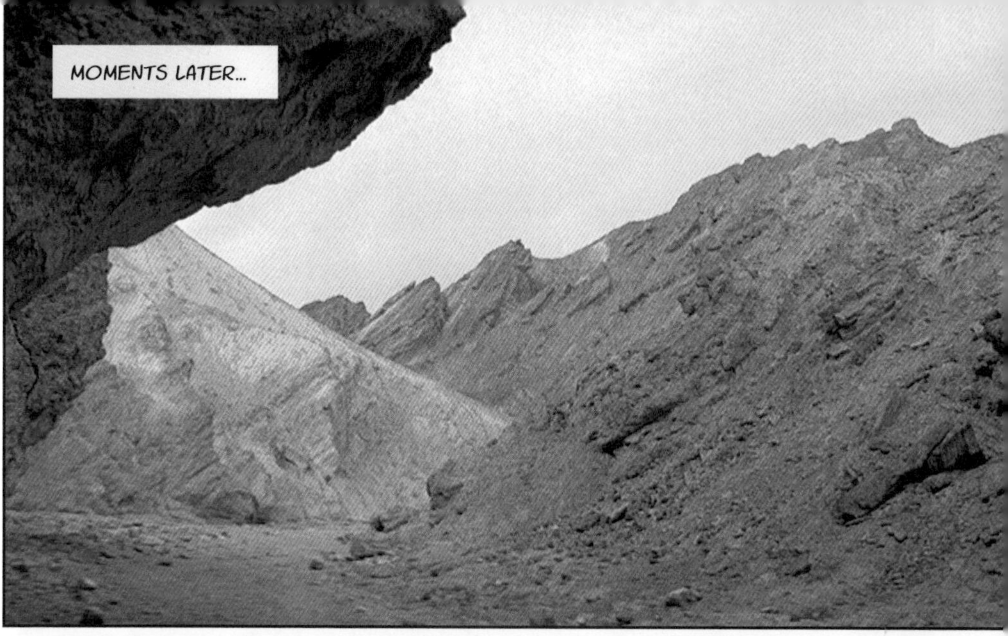
MOMENTS LATER...

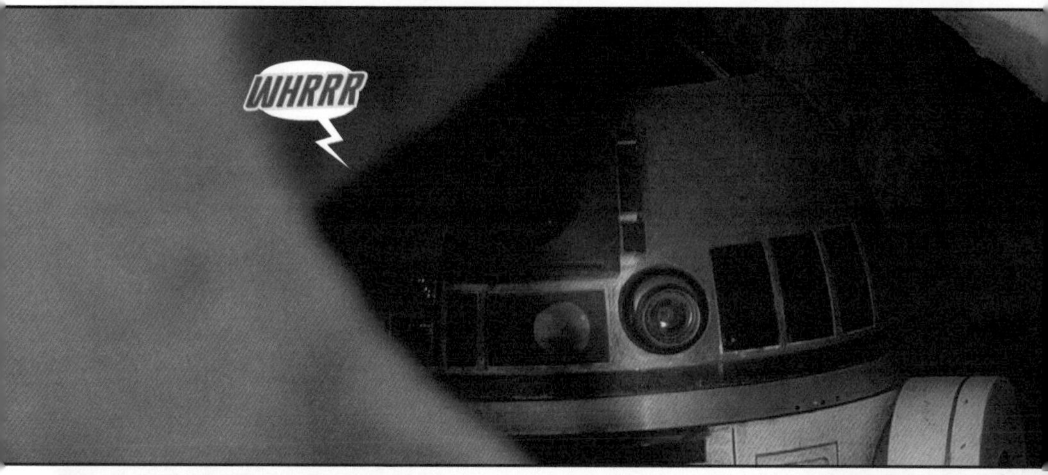
WHRRR

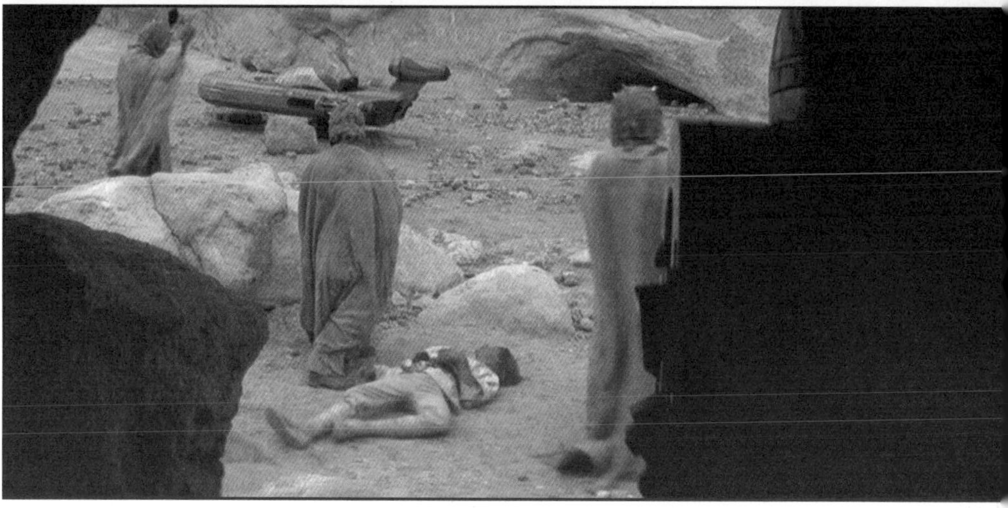

WHIIIRRP
BEEEEP

RRRWAINWOOOOOOOOWOO

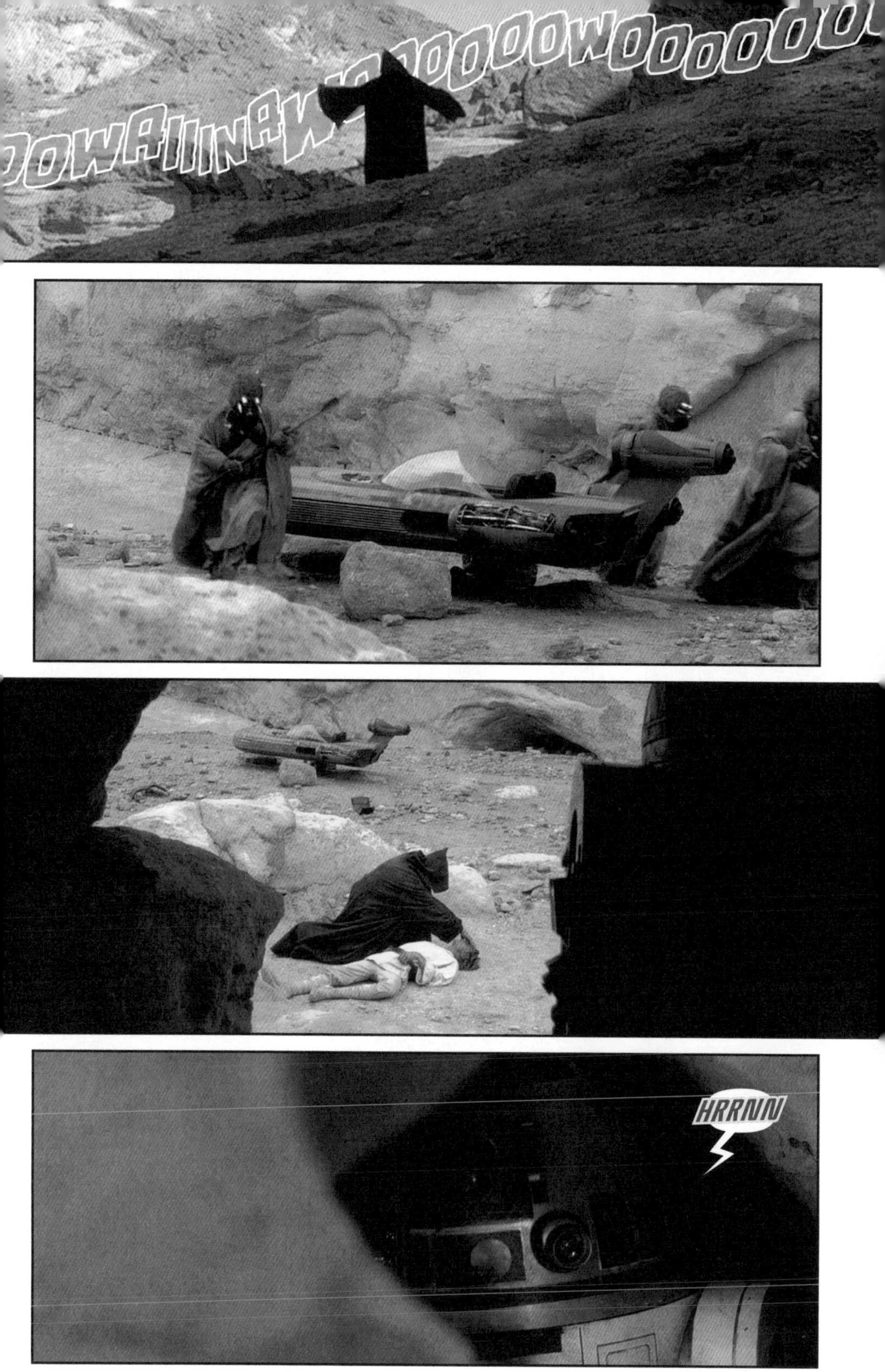
OWAIIINAW
OOOOOWOOOOO
HRRNN

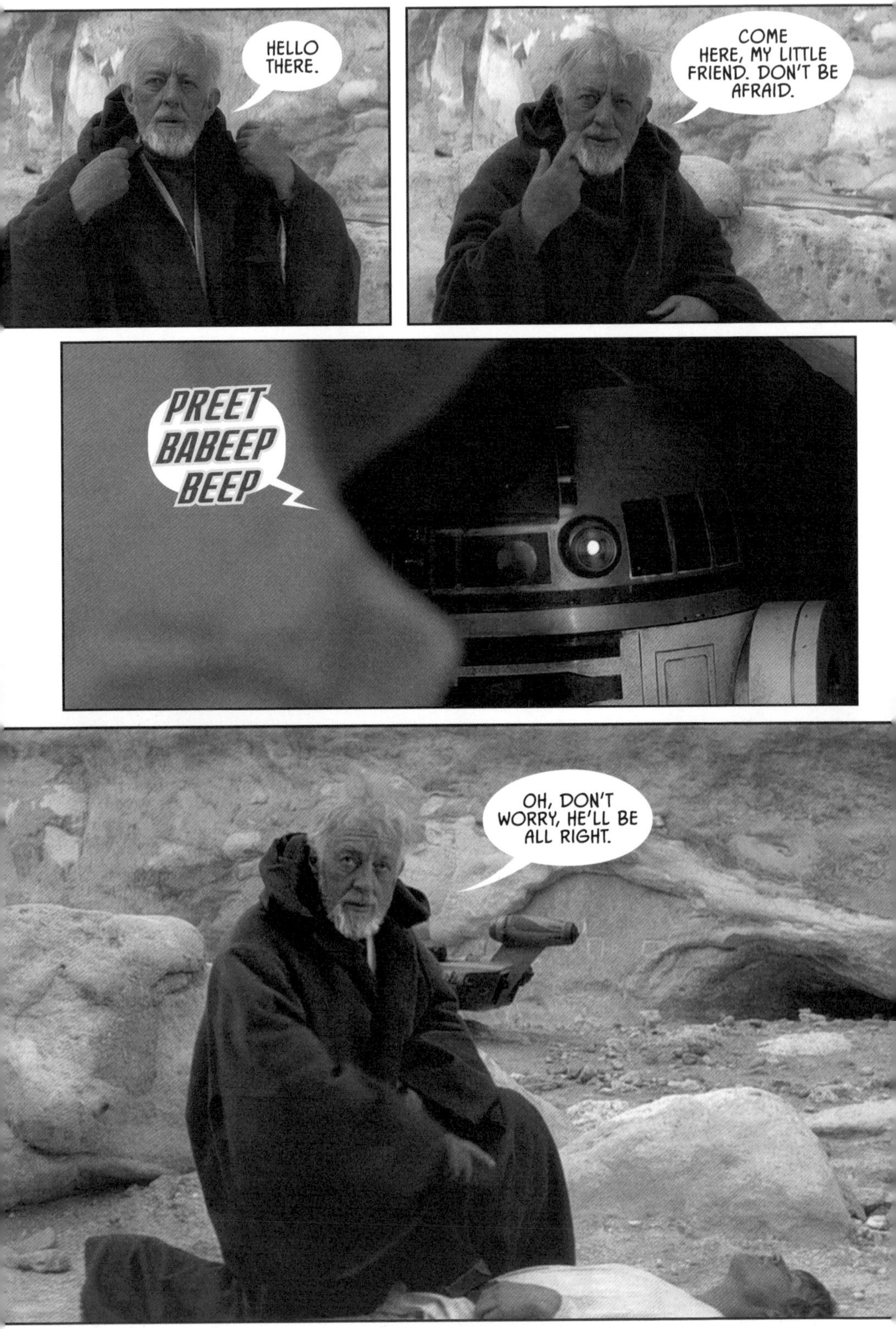
HELLO THERE.
COME HERE, MY LITTLE FRIEND. DON'T BE AFRAID.
PREET BABEEP BEEP
OH, DON'T WORRY, HE'LL BE ALL RIGHT.

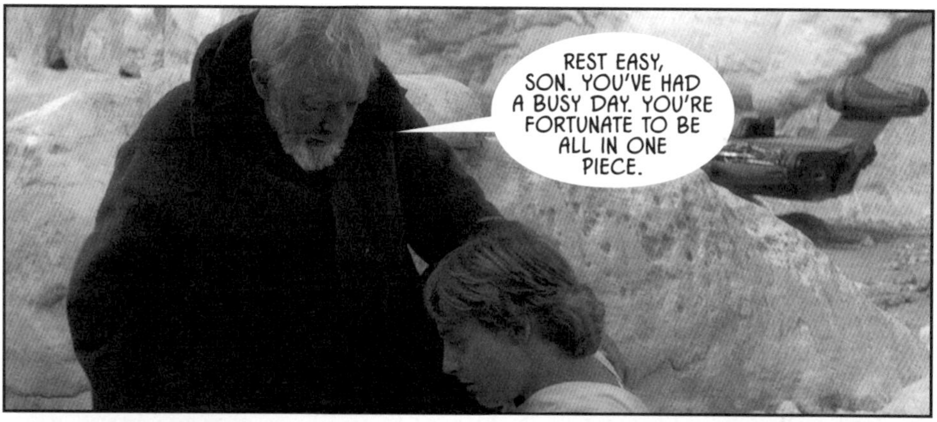
REST EASY, SON. YOU'VE HAD A BUSY DAY. YOU'RE FORTUNATE TO BE ALL IN ONE PIECE.

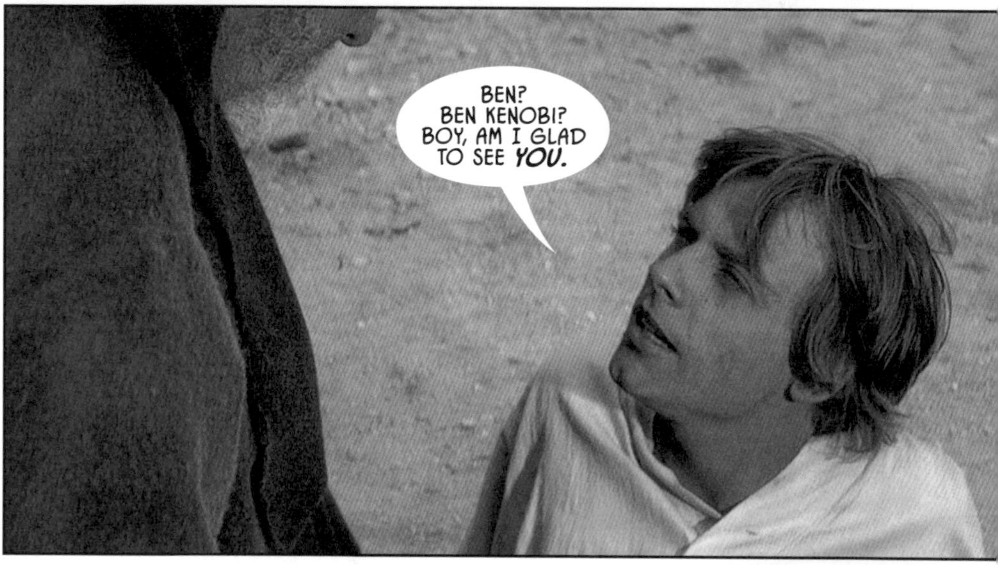
BEN? BEN KENOBI? BOY, AM I GLAD TO SEE *YOU.*

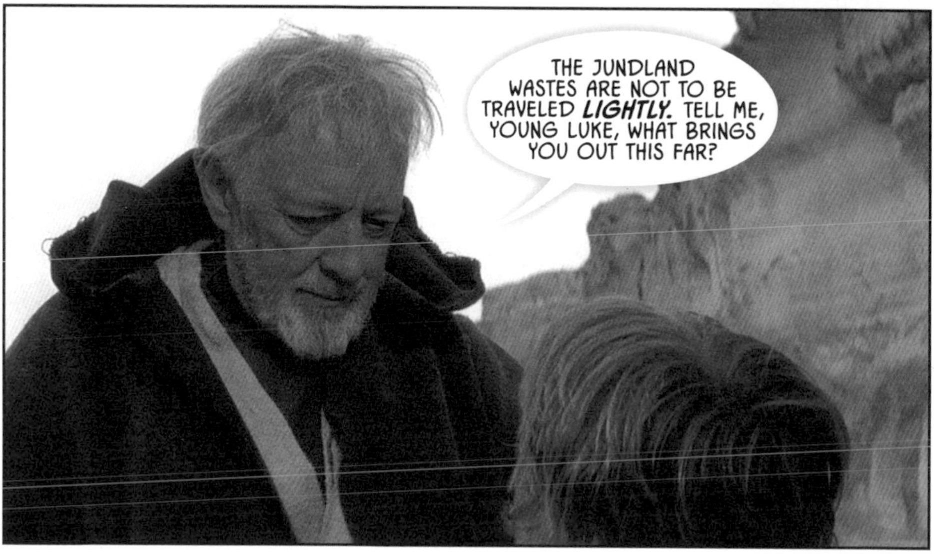
THE JUNDLAND WASTES ARE NOT TO BE TRAVELED *LIGHTLY.* TELL ME, YOUNG LUKE, WHAT BRINGS YOU OUT THIS FAR?

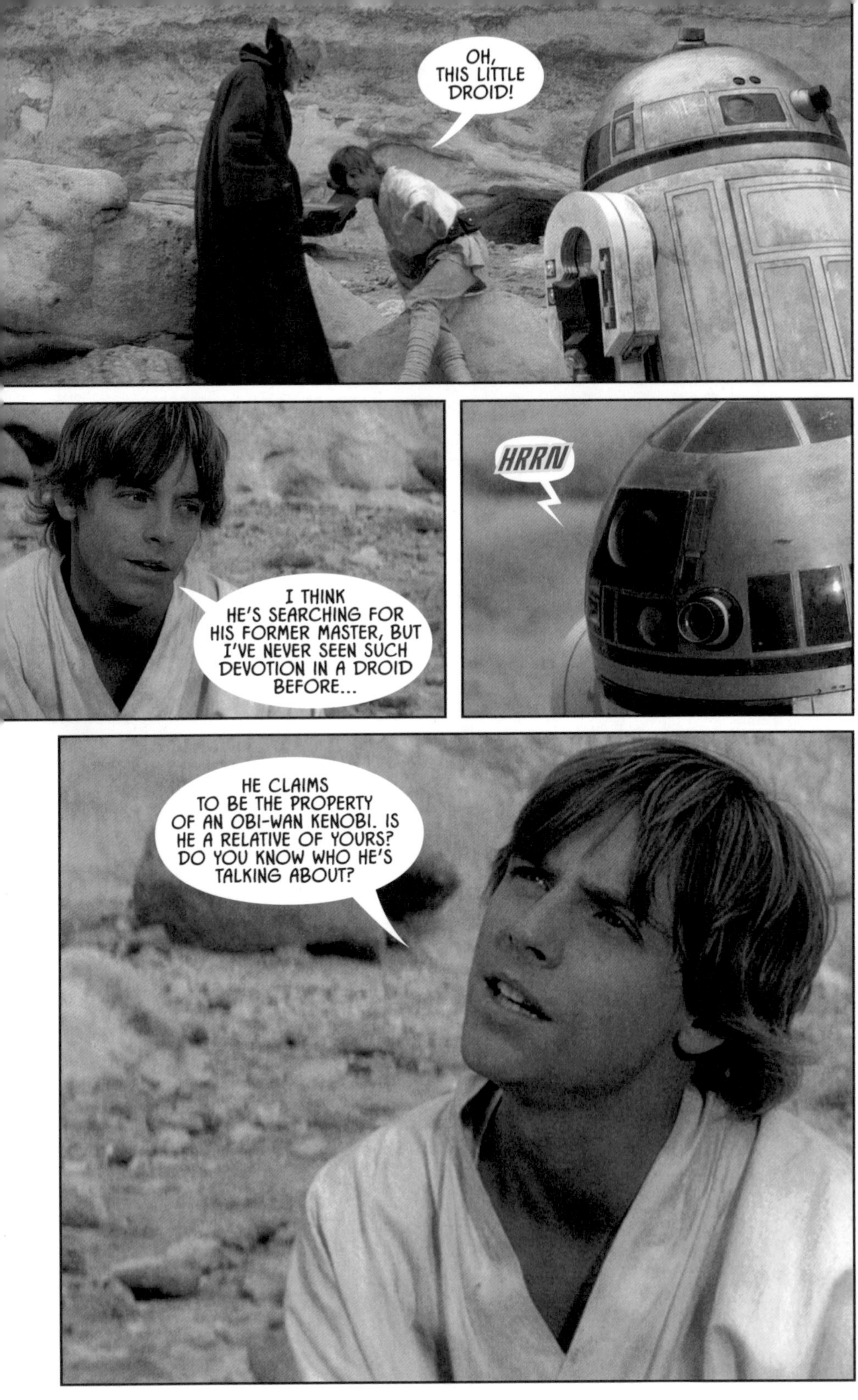
OH, THIS LITTLE DROID!
I THINK HE'S SEARCHING FOR HIS FORMER MASTER, BUT I'VE NEVER SEEN SUCH DEVOTION IN A DROID BEFORE...
HRRN
HE CLAIMS TO BE THE PROPERTY OF AN OBI-WAN KENOBI. IS HE A RELATIVE OF YOURS? DO YOU KNOW WHO HE'S TALKING ABOUT?

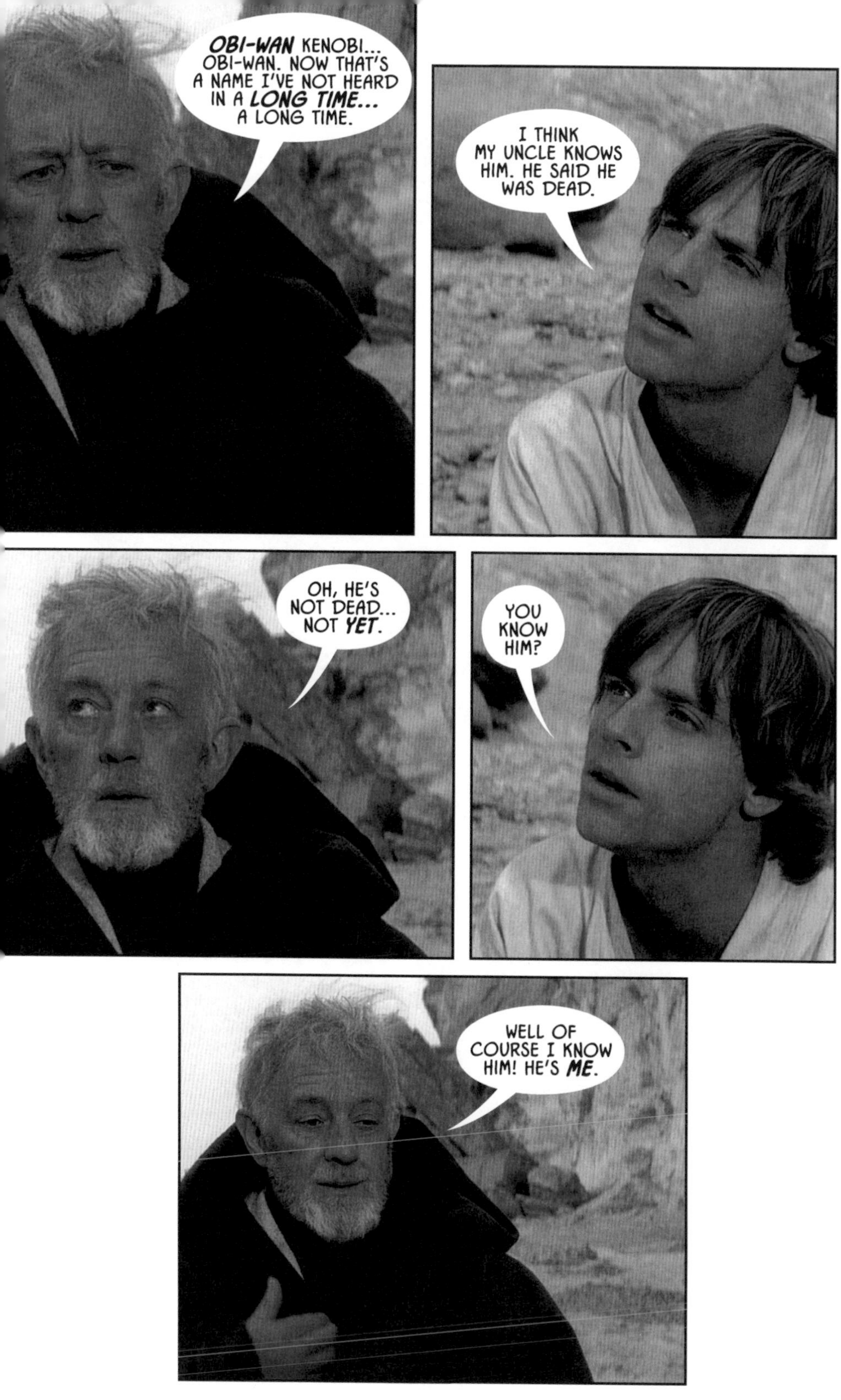
OBI-WAN KENOBI... OBI-WAN. NOW THAT'S A NAME I'VE NOT HEARD IN A LONG TIME... A LONG TIME.
I THINK MY UNCLE KNOWS HIM. HE SAID HE WAS DEAD.
OH, HE'S NOT DEAD... NOT YET.
YOU KNOW HIM?
WELL OF COURSE I KNOW HIM! HE'S ME.

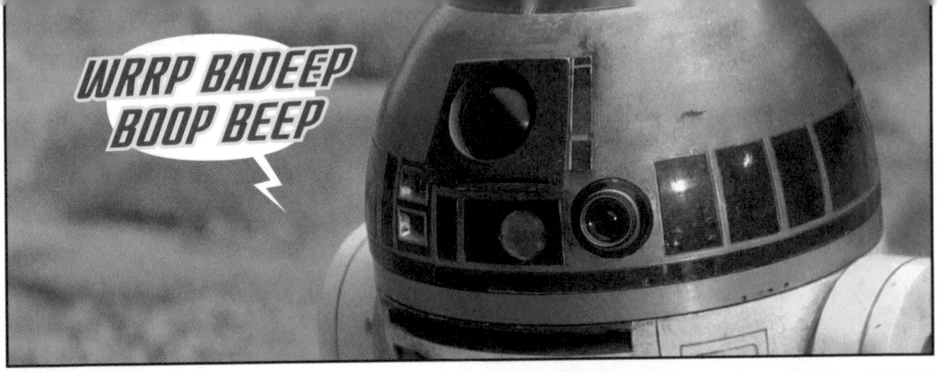
WRRP BADEEP BOOP BEEP

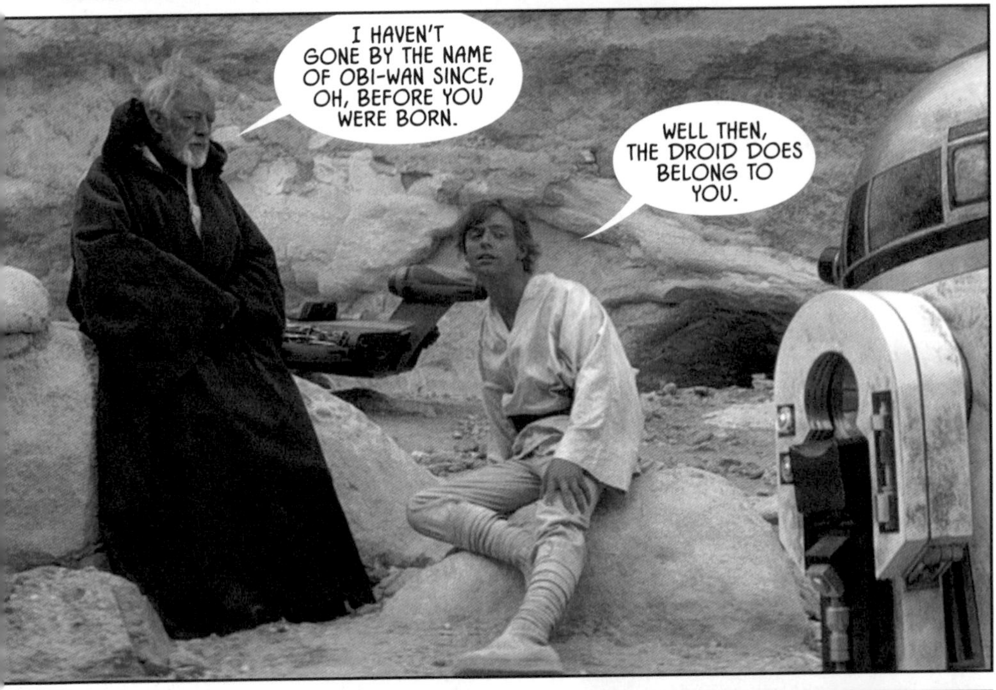
I HAVEN'T GONE BY THE NAME OF OBI-WAN SINCE, OH, BEFORE YOU WERE BORN.
WELL THEN, THE DROID DOES BELONG TO YOU.

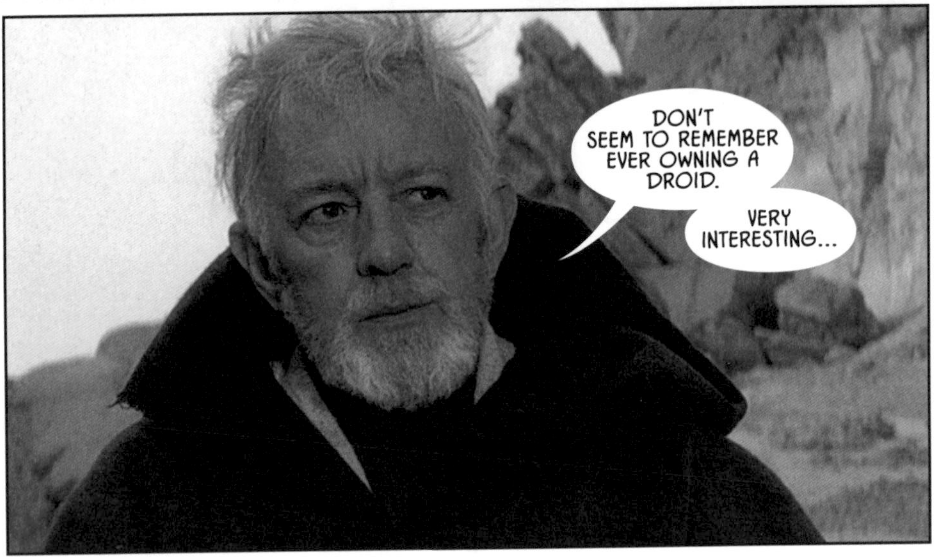
DON'T SEEM TO REMEMBER EVER OWNING A DROID.
VERY INTERESTING...

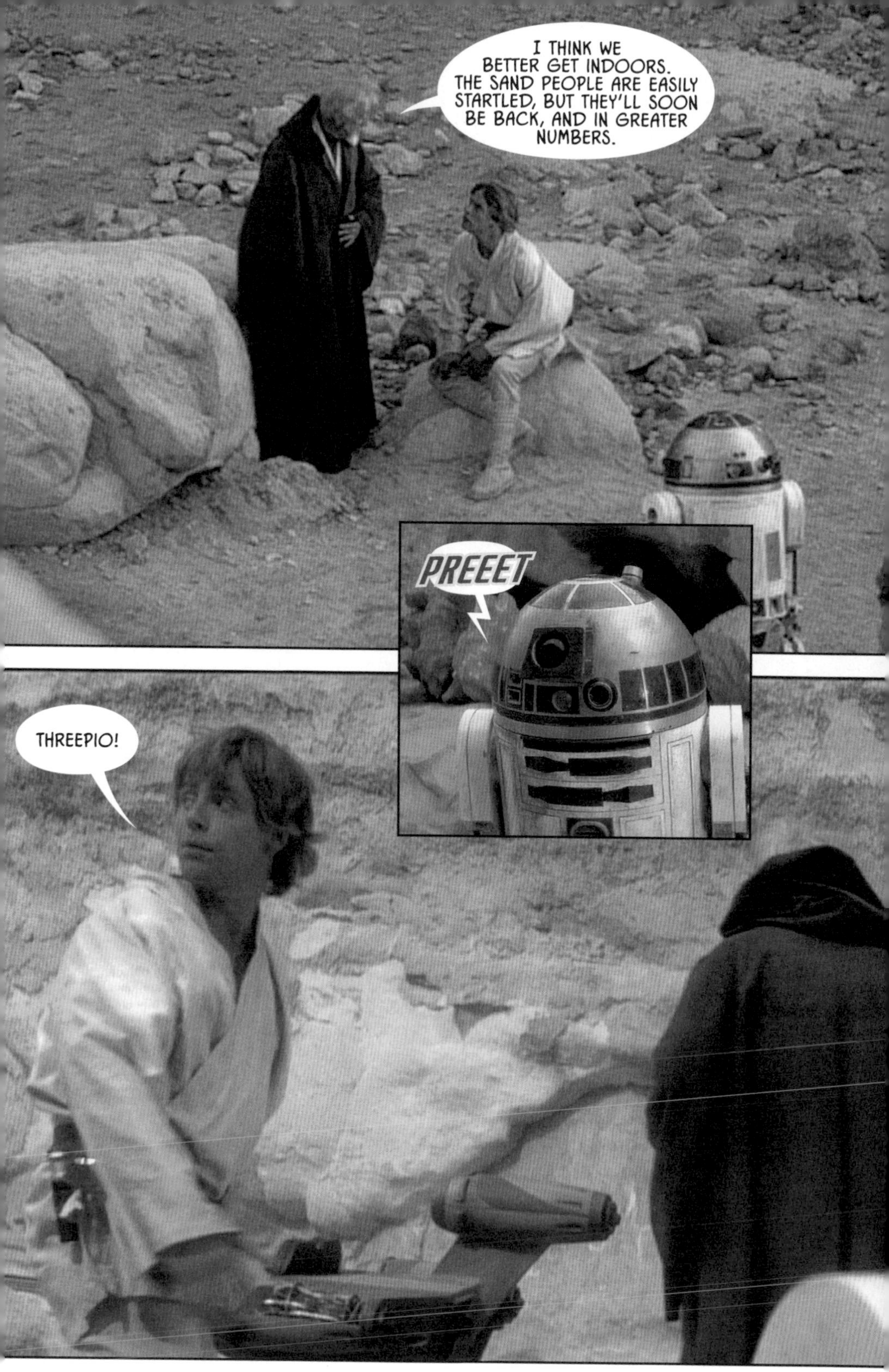
I THINK WE BETTER GET INDOORS. THE SAND PEOPLE ARE EASILY STARTLED, BUT THEY'LL SOON BE BACK, AND IN GREATER NUMBERS.
PREEET
THREEPIO!

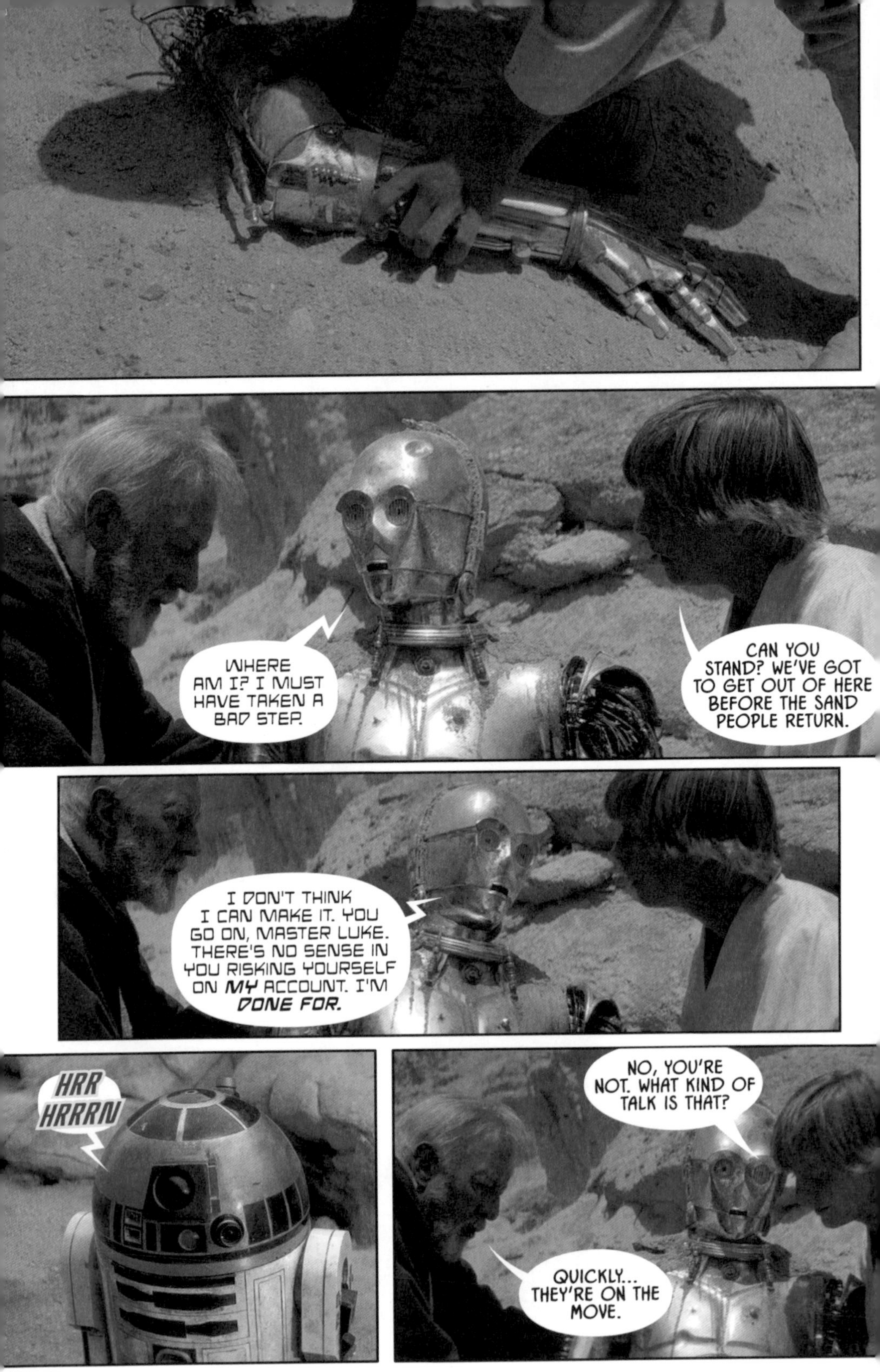
WHERE AM I? I MUST HAVE TAKEN A BAD STEP.
CAN YOU STAND? WE'VE GOT TO GET OUT OF HERE BEFORE THE SAND PEOPLE RETURN.
I DON'T THINK I CAN MAKE IT. YOU GO ON, MASTER LUKE. THERE'S NO SENSE IN YOU RISKING YOURSELF ON *MY* ACCOUNT. I'M ***DONE FOR.***
HRR HRRRN
NO, YOU'RE NOT. WHAT KIND OF TALK IS THAT?
QUICKLY... THEY'RE ON THE MOVE.

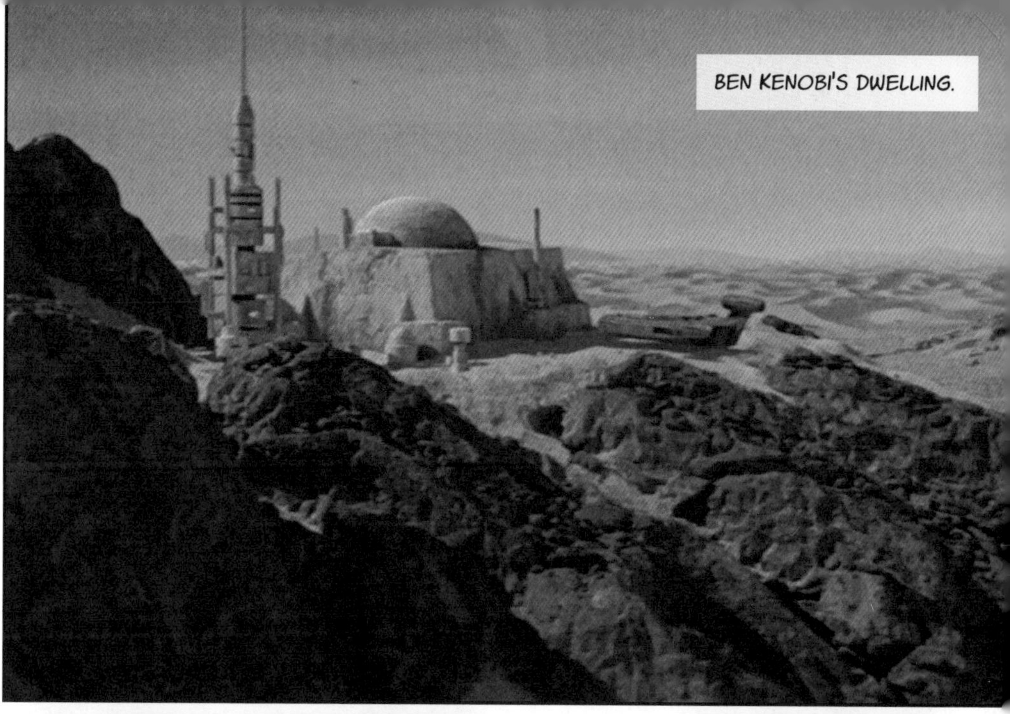
BEN KENOBI'S DWELLING.

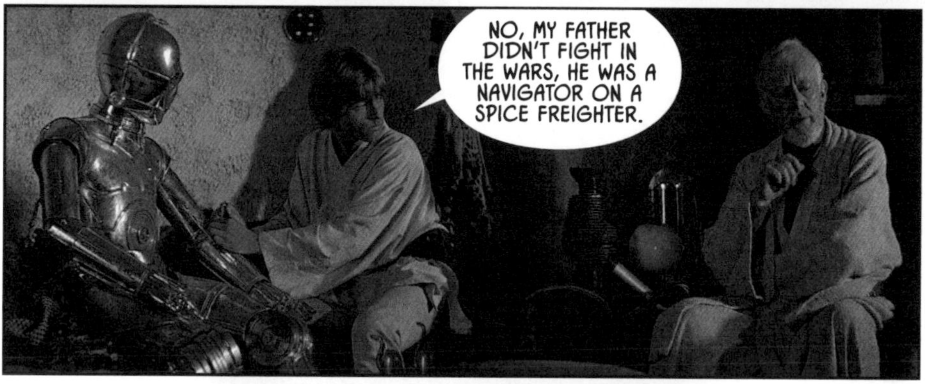
NO, MY FATHER DIDN'T FIGHT IN THE WARS, HE WAS A NAVIGATOR ON A SPICE FREIGHTER.

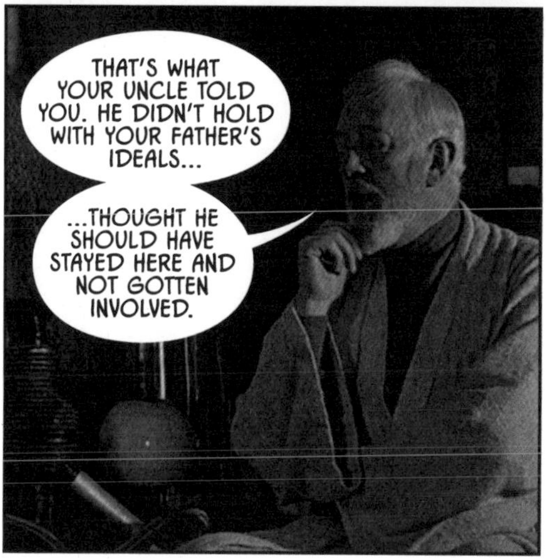
THAT'S WHAT YOUR UNCLE TOLD YOU. HE DIDN'T HOLD WITH YOUR FATHER'S IDEALS...
...THOUGHT HE SHOULD HAVE STAYED HERE AND NOT GOTTEN INVOLVED.

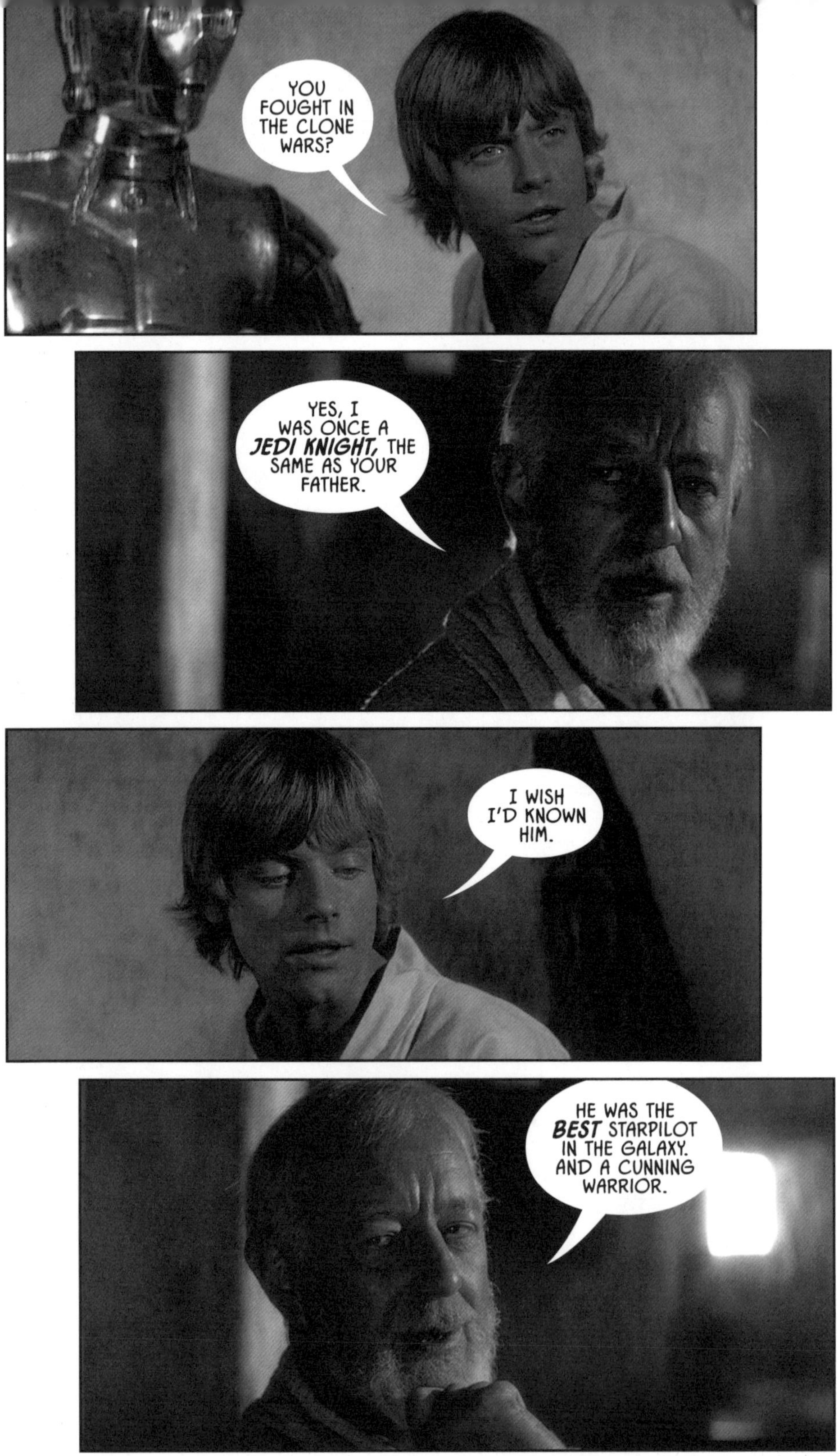
YOU FOUGHT IN THE CLONE WARS?
YES, I WAS ONCE A **JEDI KNIGHT,** THE SAME AS YOUR FATHER.
I WISH I'D KNOWN HIM.
HE WAS THE **BEST** STARPILOT IN THE GALAXY. AND A CUNNING WARRIOR.

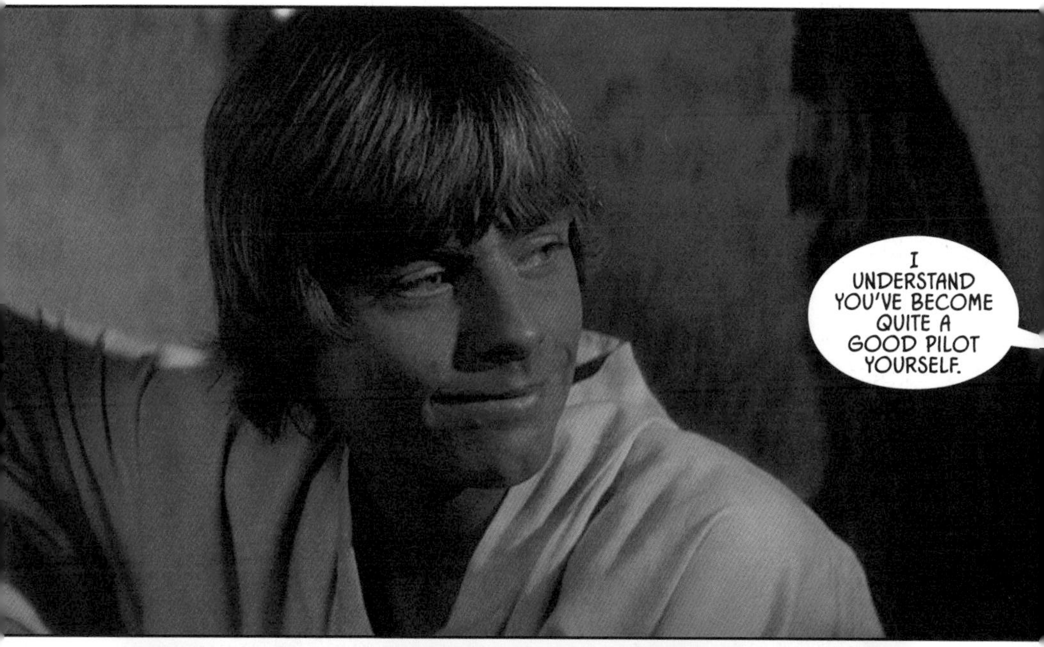
I UNDERSTAND YOU'VE BECOME QUITE A GOOD PILOT YOURSELF.

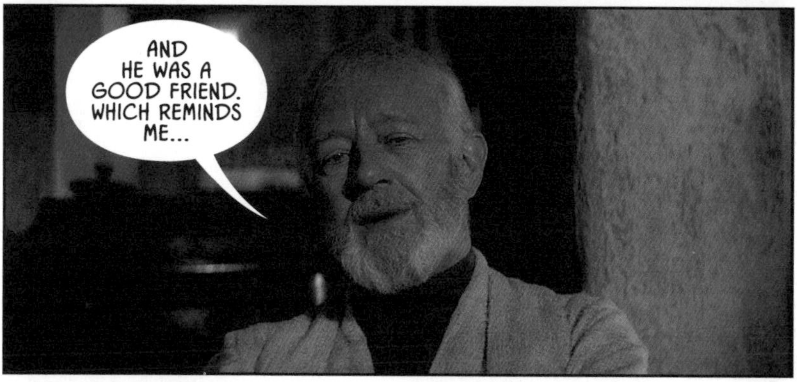
AND HE WAS A GOOD FRIEND. WHICH REMINDS ME...

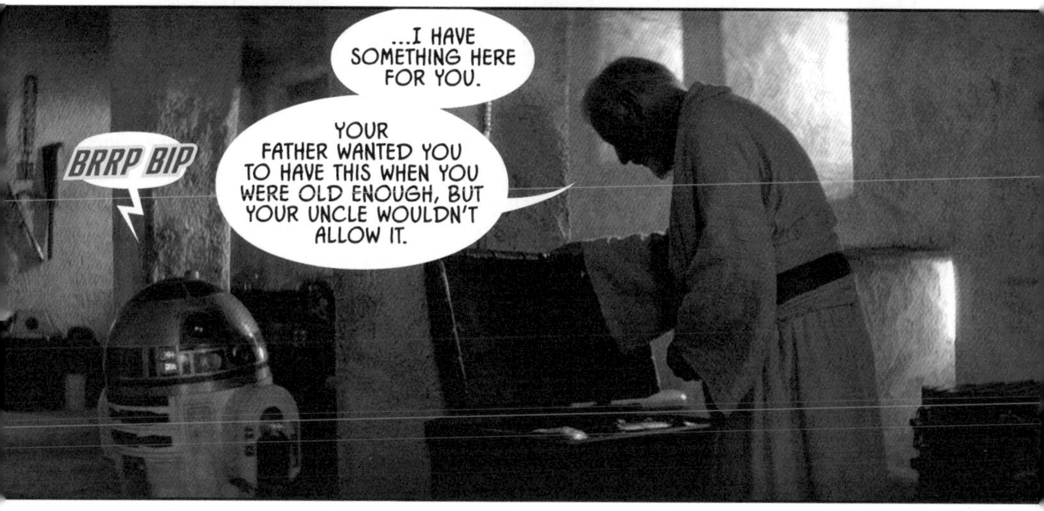
...I HAVE SOMETHING HERE FOR YOU.
YOUR FATHER WANTED YOU TO HAVE THIS WHEN YOU WERE OLD ENOUGH, BUT YOUR UNCLE WOULDN'T ALLOW IT.
BRRP BIP

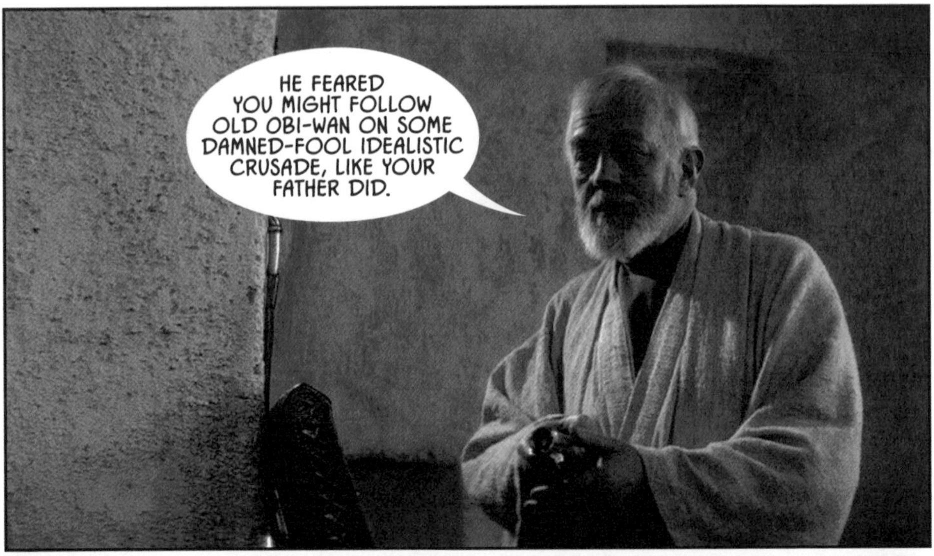
HE FEARED YOU MIGHT FOLLOW OLD OBI-WAN ON SOME DAMNED-FOOL IDEALISTIC CRUSADE, LIKE YOUR FATHER DID.

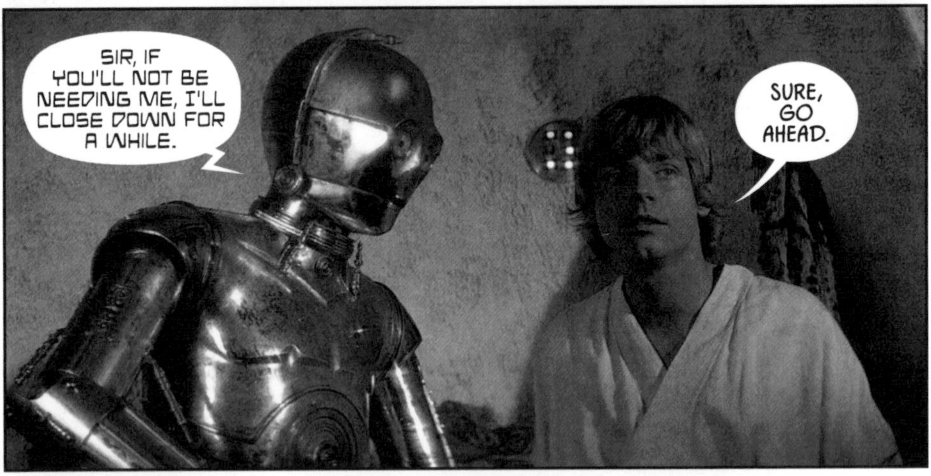
SIR, IF YOU'LL NOT BE NEEDING ME, I'LL CLOSE DOWN FOR A WHILE.
SURE, GO AHEAD.

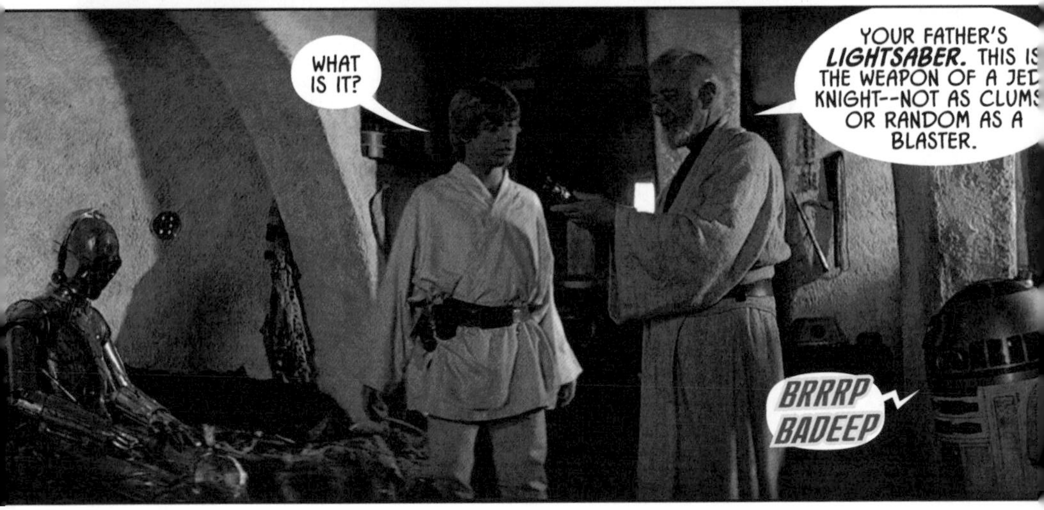
WHAT IS IT?
YOUR FATHER'S LIGHTSABER. THIS IS THE WEAPON OF A JED KNIGHT--NOT AS CLUMS OR RANDOM AS A BLASTER.
BRRRP BADEEP

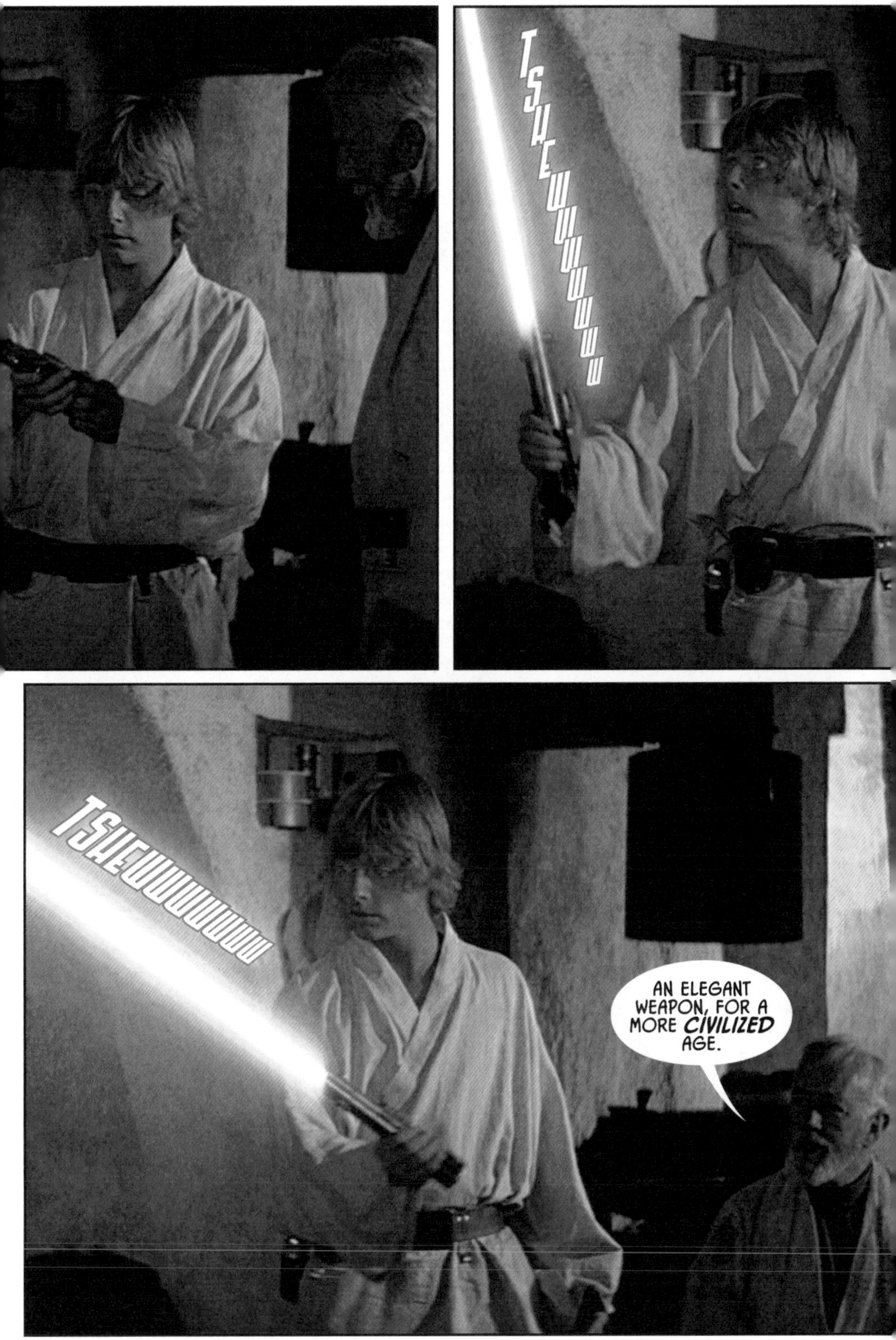
TSHEWWWWWWW
TSHEWWWWWWW
AN ELEGANT WEAPON, FOR A MORE *CIVILIZED* AGE.

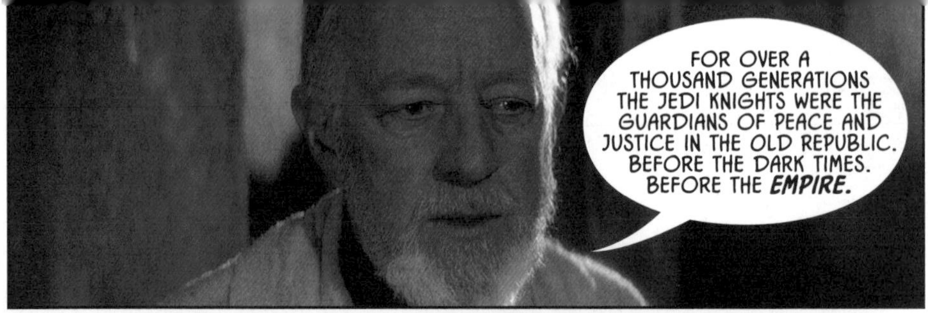
FOR OVER A THOUSAND GENERATIONS THE JEDI KNIGHTS WERE THE GUARDIANS OF PEACE AND JUSTICE IN THE OLD REPUBLIC. BEFORE THE DARK TIMES. BEFORE THE *EMPIRE.*

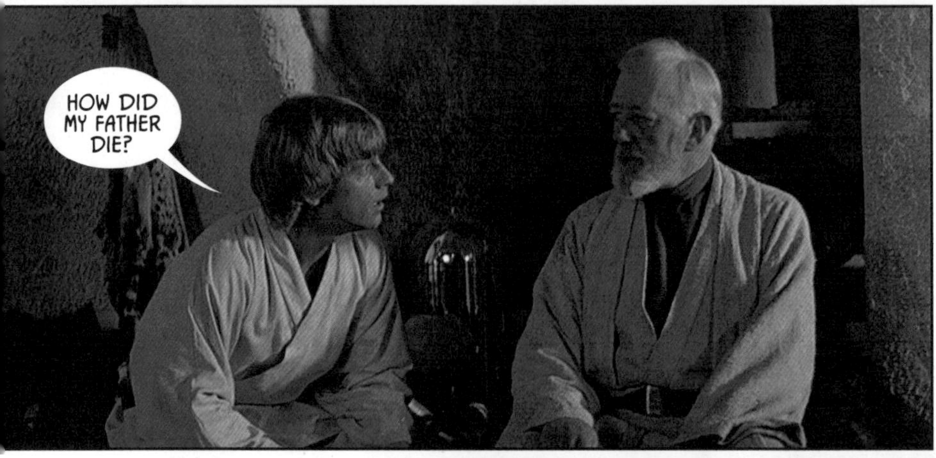
HOW DID MY FATHER DIE?

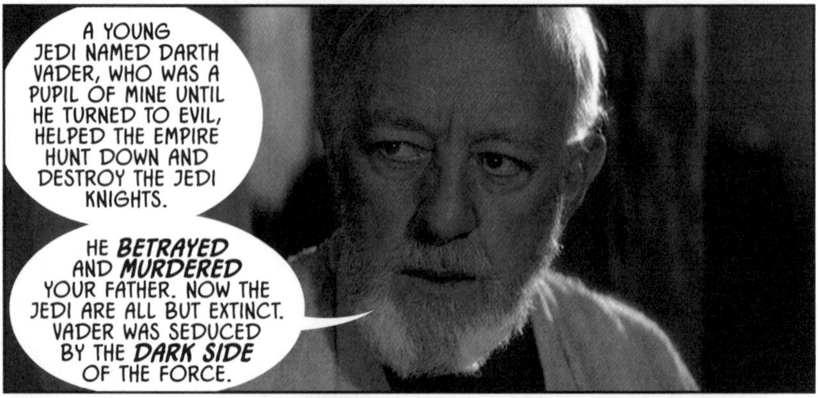
A YOUNG JEDI NAMED DARTH VADER, WHO WAS A PUPIL OF MINE UNTIL HE TURNED TO EVIL, HELPED THE EMPIRE HUNT DOWN AND DESTROY THE JEDI KNIGHTS.
HE *BETRAYED* AND *MURDERED* YOUR FATHER. NOW THE JEDI ARE ALL BUT EXTINCT. VADER WAS SEDUCED BY THE *DARK SIDE* OF THE FORCE.

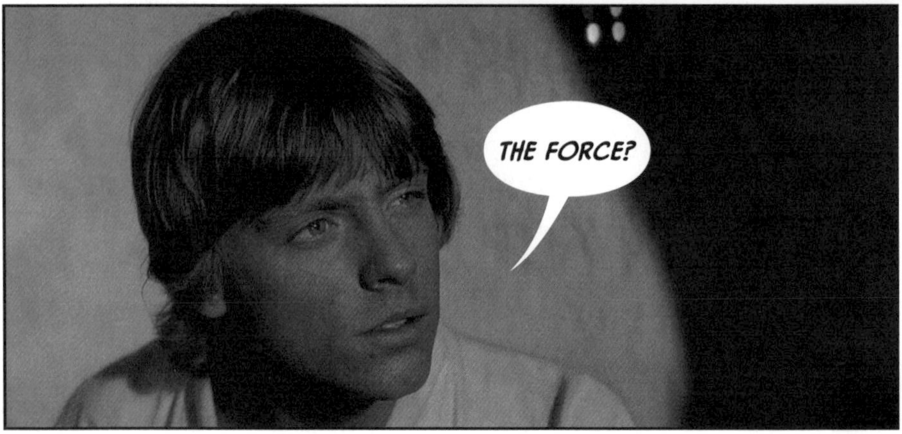
THE FORCE?

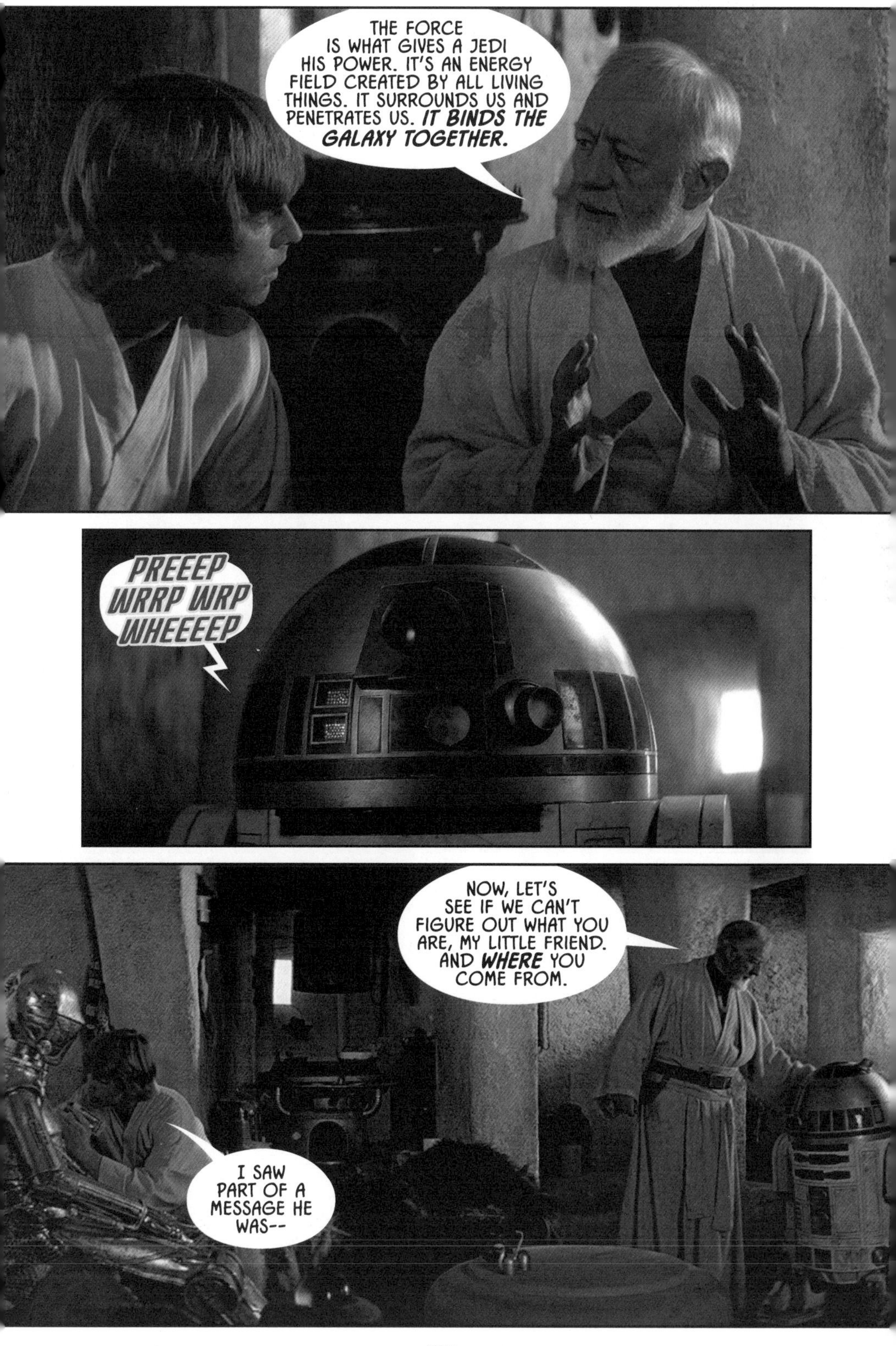
THE FORCE IS WHAT GIVES A JEDI HIS POWER. IT'S AN ENERGY FIELD CREATED BY ALL LIVING THINGS. IT SURROUNDS US AND PENETRATES US. *IT BINDS THE GALAXY TOGETHER.*
PREEEP WRRP WRP WHEEEEP
NOW, LET'S SEE IF WE CAN'T FIGURE OUT WHAT YOU ARE, MY LITTLE FRIEND. AND ***WHERE*** YOU COME FROM.
I SAW PART OF A MESSAGE HE WAS--

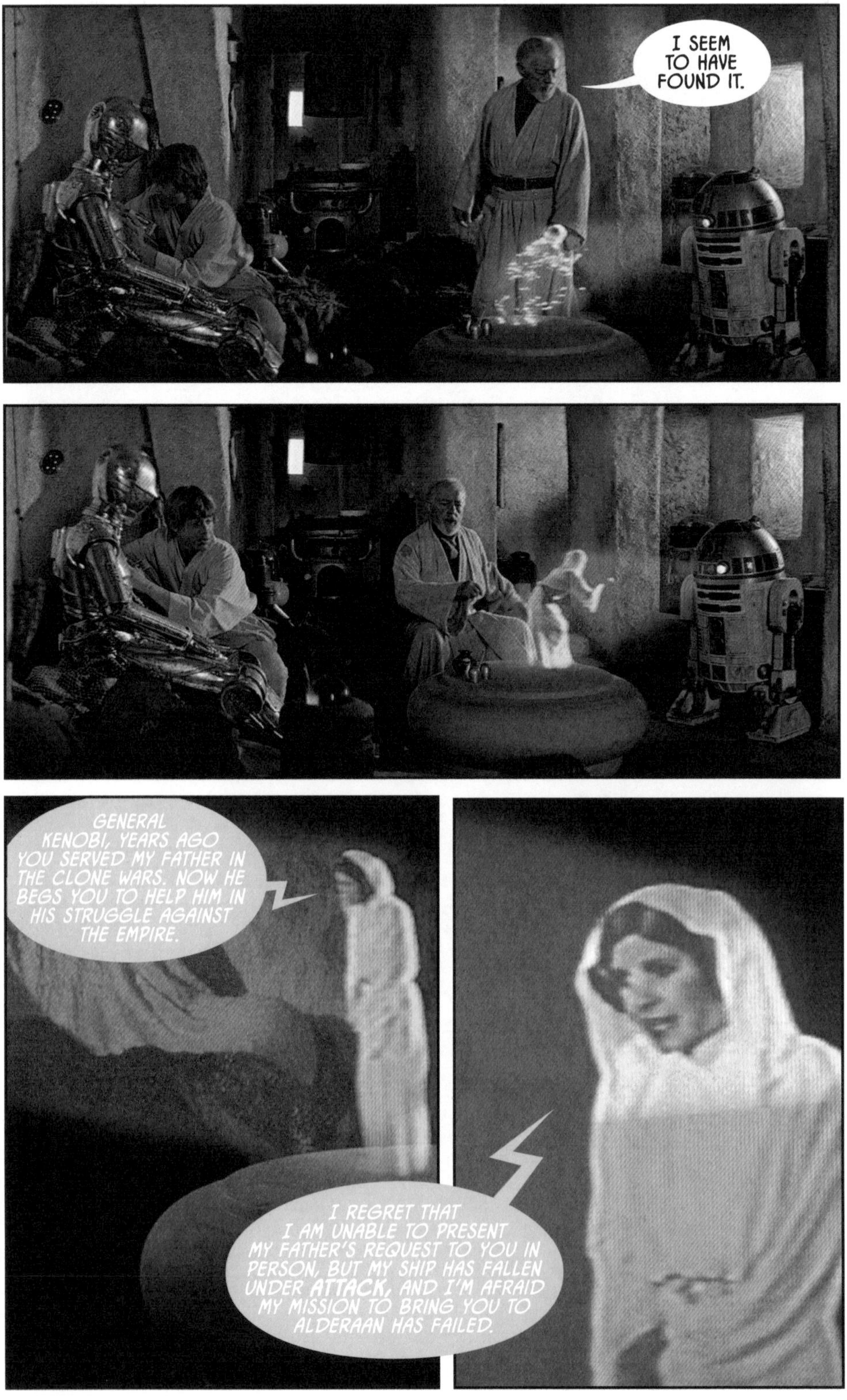
I SEEM TO HAVE FOUND IT.
GENERAL KENOBI, YEARS AGO YOU SERVED MY FATHER IN THE CLONE WARS. NOW HE BEGS YOU TO HELP HIM IN HIS STRUGGLE AGAINST THE EMPIRE.
I REGRET THAT I AM UNABLE TO PRESENT MY FATHER'S REQUEST TO YOU IN PERSON, BUT MY SHIP HAS FALLEN UNDER ATTACK, AND I'M AFRAID MY MISSION TO BRING YOU TO ALDERAAN HAS FAILED.

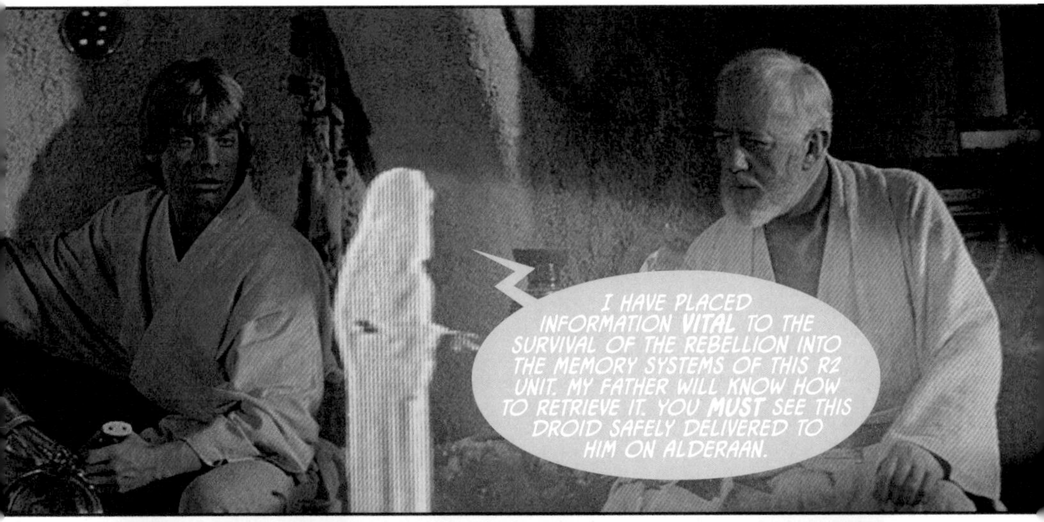
I HAVE PLACED INFORMATION VITAL TO THE SURVIVAL OF THE REBELLION INTO THE MEMORY SYSTEMS OF THIS R2 UNIT. MY FATHER WILL KNOW HOW TO RETRIEVE IT. YOU MUST SEE THIS DROID SAFELY DELIVERED TO HIM ON ALDERAAN.

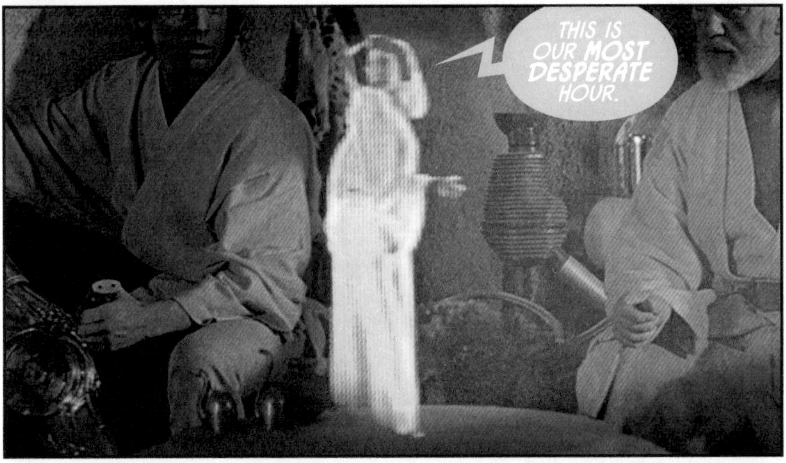
THIS IS OUR MOST DESPERATE HOUR.

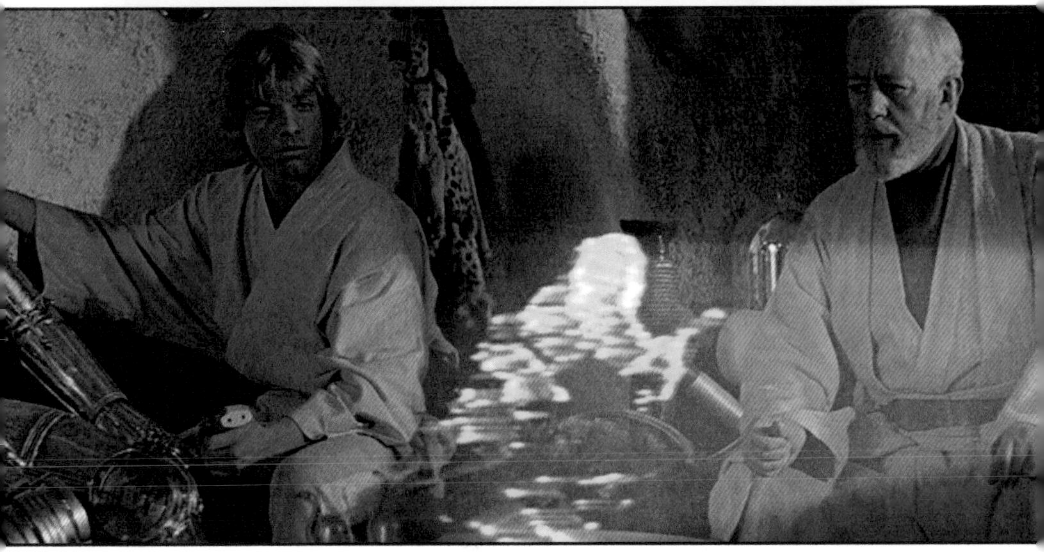

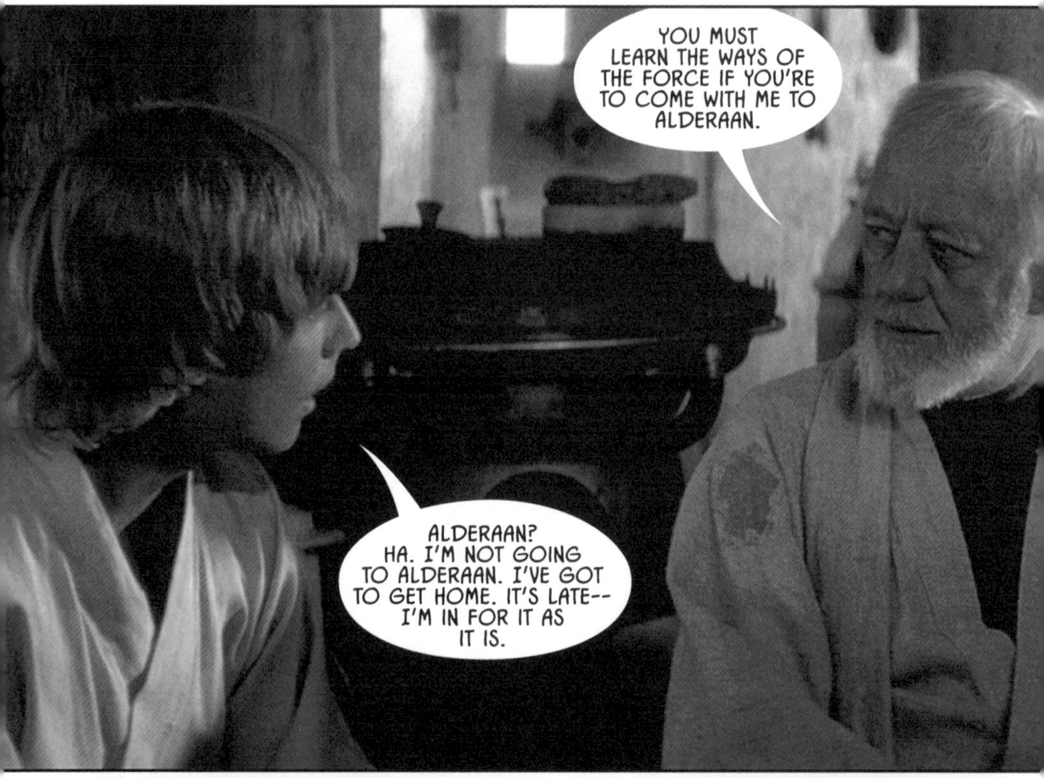
YOU MUST LEARN THE WAYS OF THE FORCE IF YOU'RE TO COME WITH ME TO ALDERAAN.
ALDERAAN? HA. I'M NOT GOING TO ALDERAAN. I'VE GOT TO GET HOME. IT'S LATE-- I'M IN FOR IT AS IT IS.

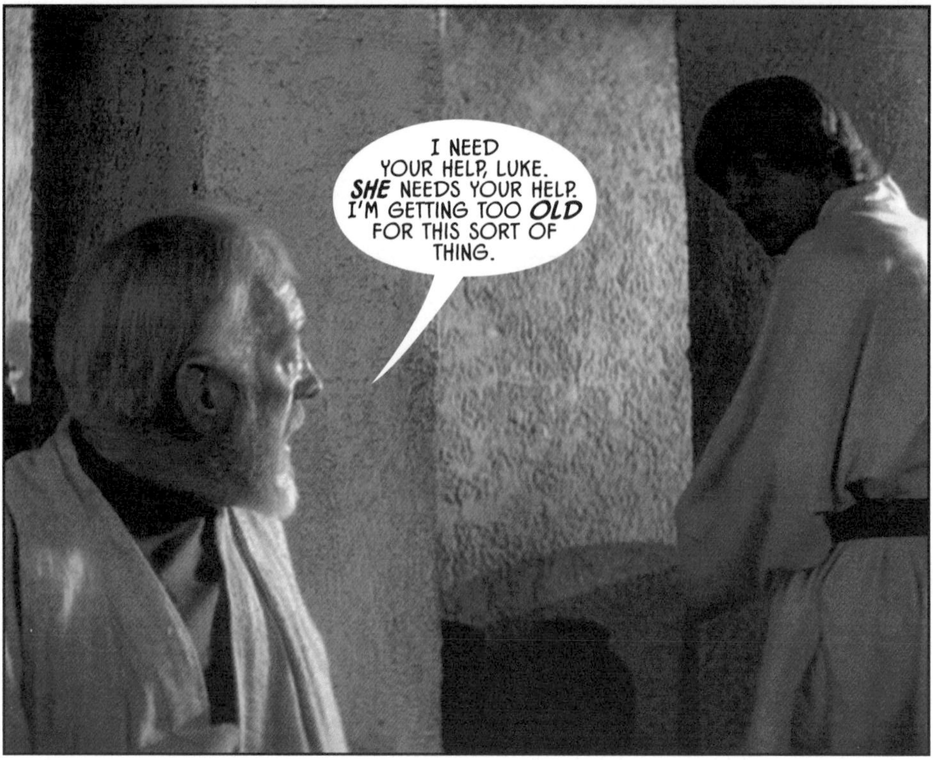
I NEED YOUR HELP, LUKE. ***SHE*** NEEDS YOUR HELP. I'M GETTING TOO ***OLD*** FOR THIS SORT OF THING.

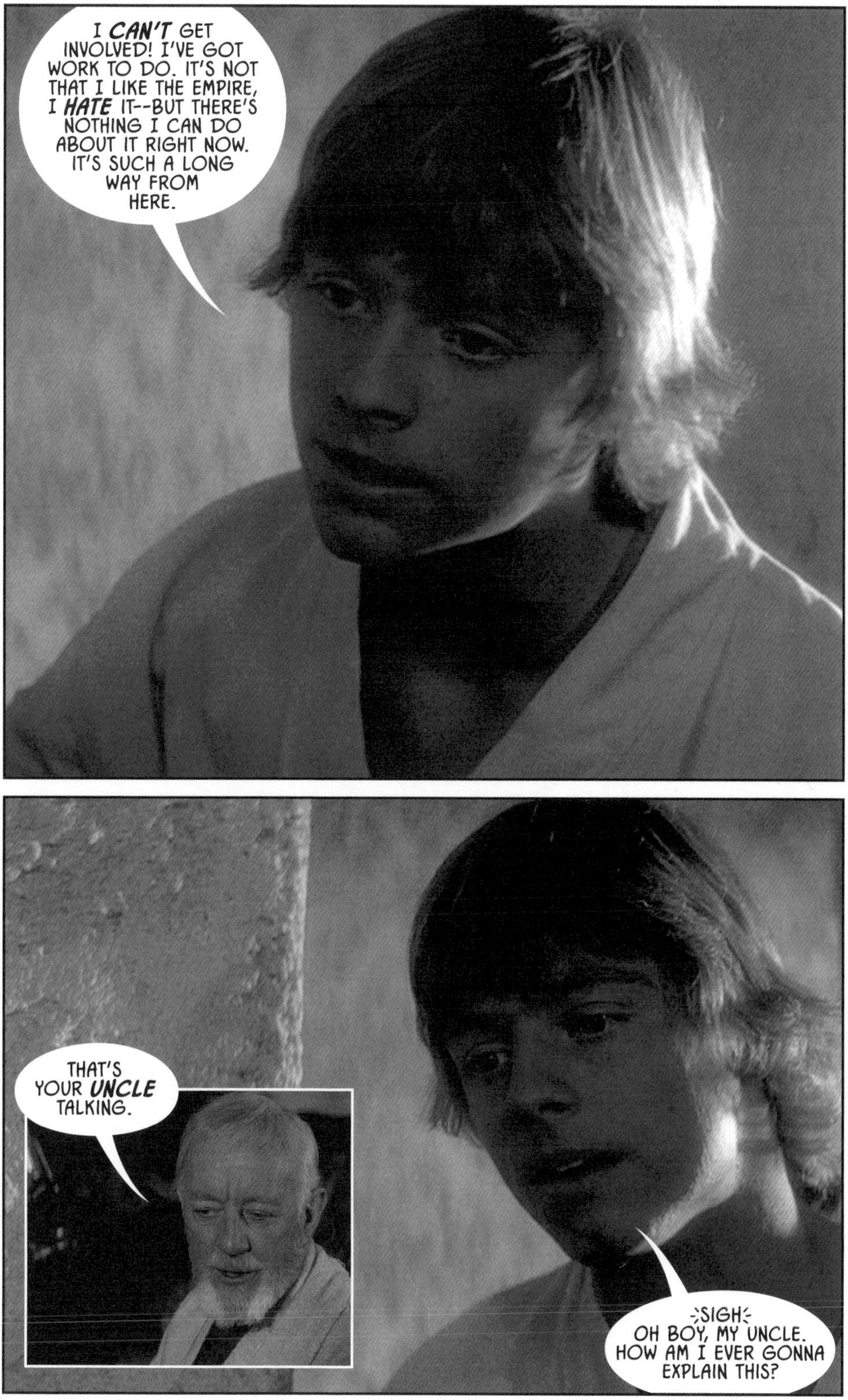
I CAN'T GET INVOLVED! I'VE GOT WORK TO DO. IT'S NOT THAT I LIKE THE EMPIRE, I HATE IT--BUT THERE'S NOTHING I CAN DO ABOUT IT RIGHT NOW. IT'S SUCH A LONG WAY FROM HERE.
THAT'S YOUR UNCLE TALKING.
SIGH
OH BOY, MY UNCLE. HOW AM I EVER GONNA EXPLAIN THIS?

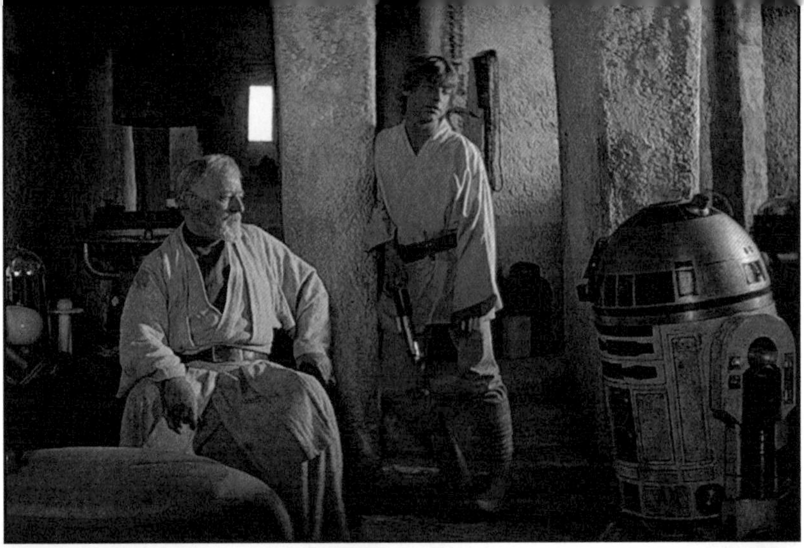

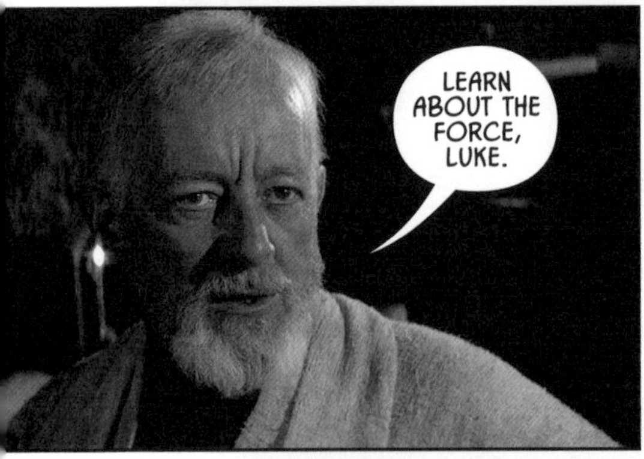
LEARN ABOUT THE FORCE, LUKE.

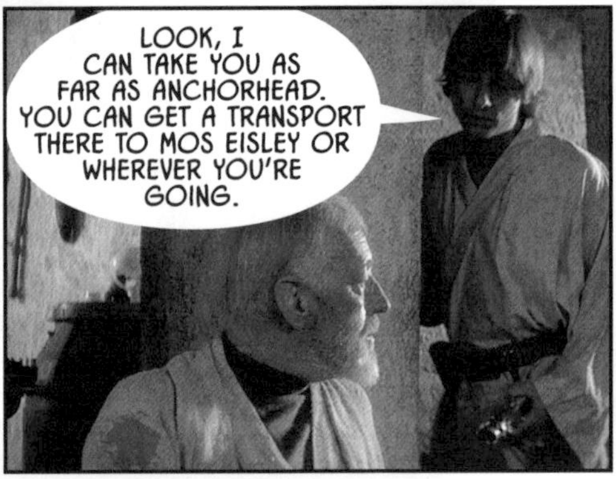
LOOK, I CAN TAKE YOU AS FAR AS ANCHORHEAD. YOU CAN GET A TRANSPORT THERE TO MOS EISLEY OR WHEREVER YOU'RE GOING.

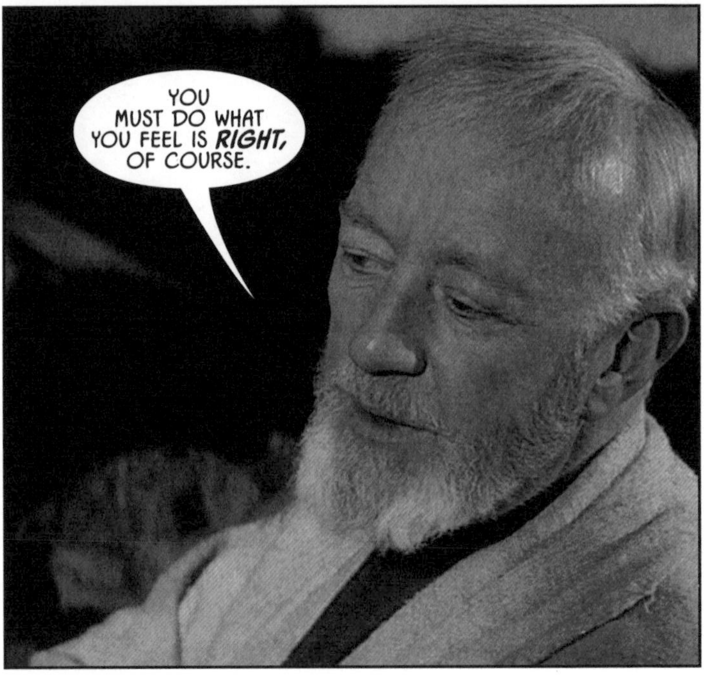
YOU MUST DO WHAT YOU FEEL IS ***RIGHT,*** OF COURSE.

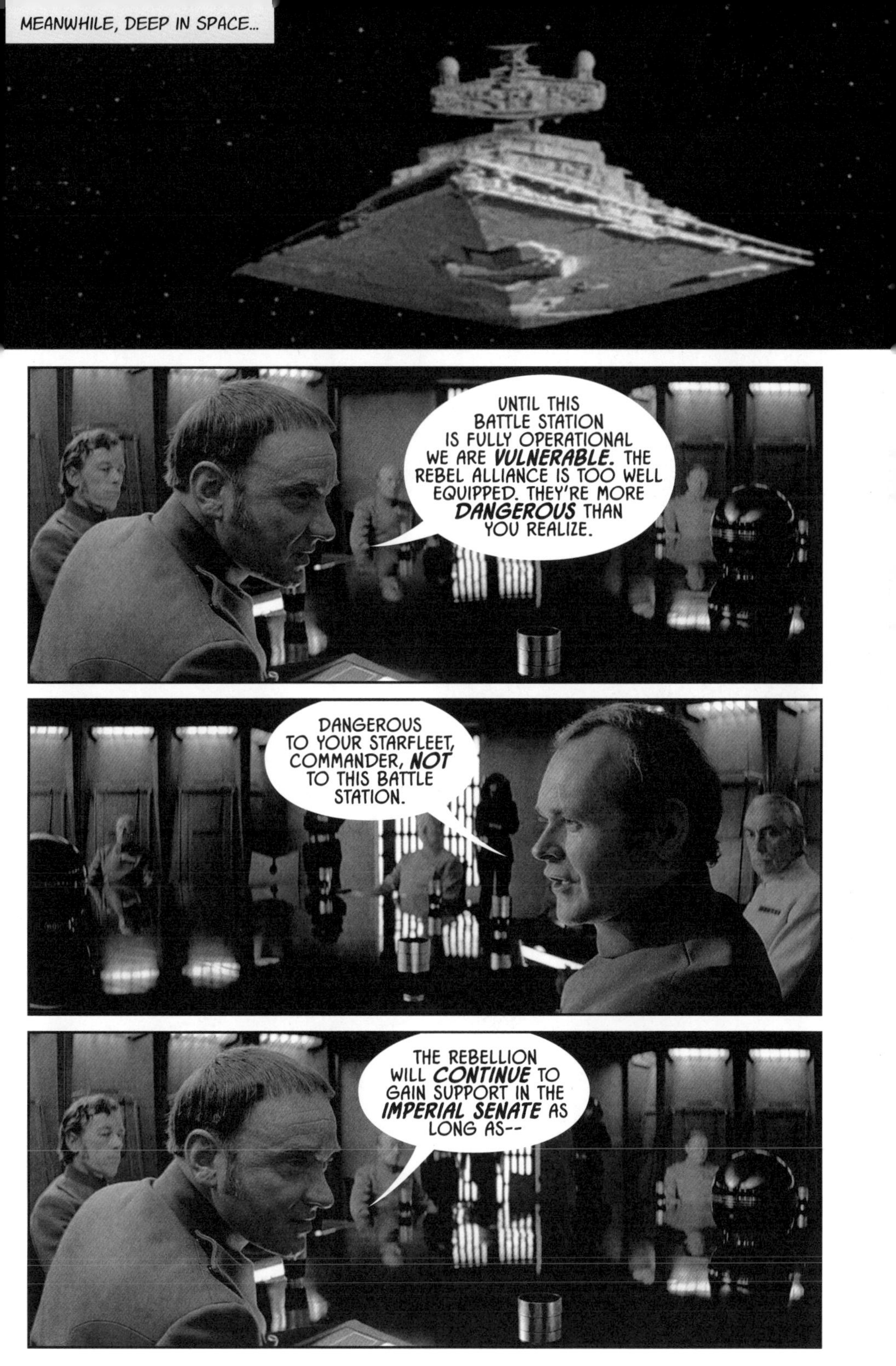
MEANWHILE, DEEP IN SPACE...
UNTIL THIS BATTLE STATION IS FULLY OPERATIONAL WE ARE VULNERABLE. THE REBEL ALLIANCE IS TOO WELL EQUIPPED. THEY'RE MORE DANGEROUS THAN YOU REALIZE.
DANGEROUS TO YOUR STARFLEET, COMMANDER, NOT TO THIS BATTLE STATION.
THE REBELLION WILL CONTINUE TO GAIN SUPPORT IN THE IMPERIAL SENATE AS LONG AS--

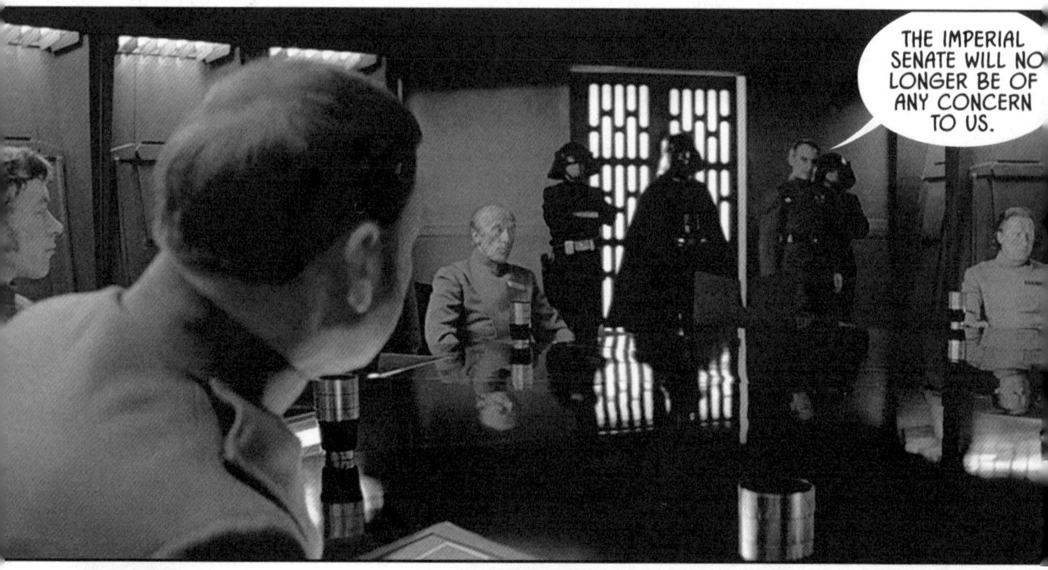
THE IMPERIAL SENATE WILL NO LONGER BE OF ANY CONCERN TO US.

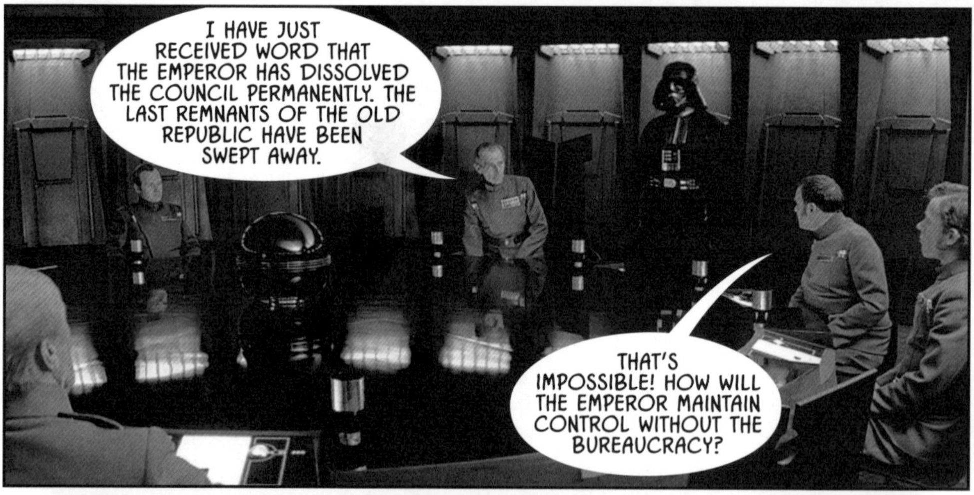
I HAVE JUST RECEIVED WORD THAT THE EMPEROR HAS DISSOLVED THE COUNCIL PERMANENTLY. THE LAST REMNANTS OF THE OLD REPUBLIC HAVE BEEN SWEPT AWAY.
THAT'S IMPOSSIBLE! HOW WILL THE EMPEROR MAINTAIN CONTROL WITHOUT THE BUREAUCRACY?

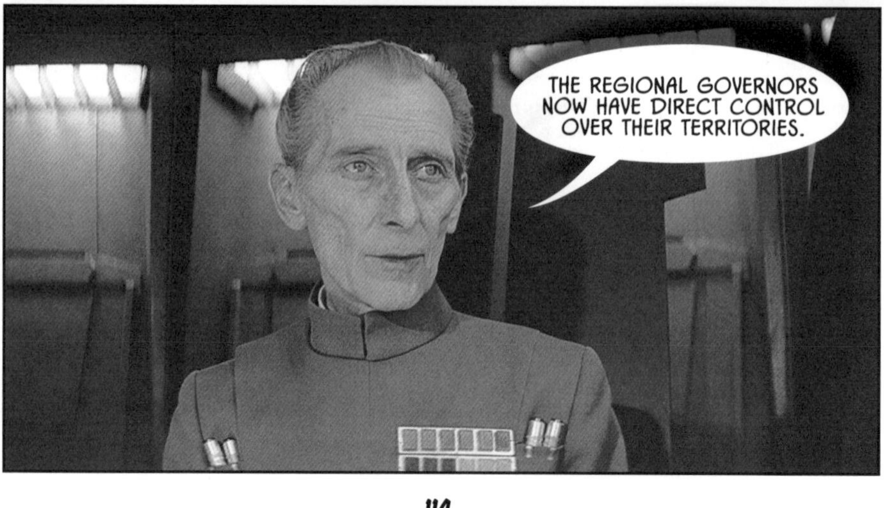
THE REGIONAL GOVERNORS NOW HAVE DIRECT CONTROL OVER THEIR TERRITORIES.

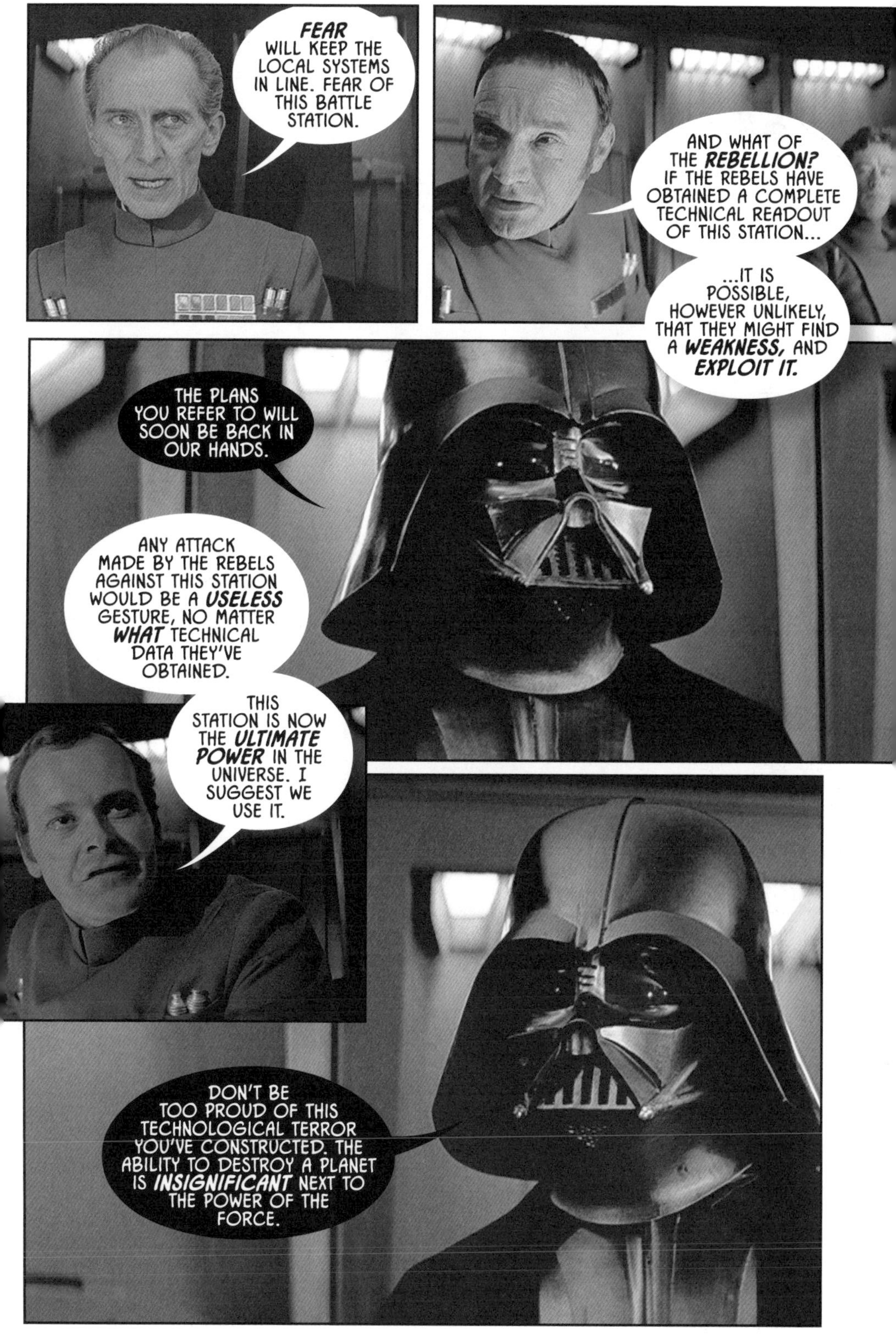
FEAR WILL KEEP THE LOCAL SYSTEMS IN LINE. FEAR OF THIS BATTLE STATION.
AND WHAT OF THE REBELLION? IF THE REBELS HAVE OBTAINED A COMPLETE TECHNICAL READOUT OF THIS STATION...
...IT IS POSSIBLE, HOWEVER UNLIKELY, THAT THEY MIGHT FIND A WEAKNESS, AND EXPLOIT IT.
THE PLANS YOU REFER TO WILL SOON BE BACK IN OUR HANDS.
ANY ATTACK MADE BY THE REBELS AGAINST THIS STATION WOULD BE A USELESS GESTURE, NO MATTER WHAT TECHNICAL DATA THEY'VE OBTAINED.
THIS STATION IS NOW THE ULTIMATE POWER IN THE UNIVERSE. I SUGGEST WE USE IT.
DON'T BE TOO PROUD OF THIS TECHNOLOGICAL TERROR YOU'VE CONSTRUCTED. THE ABILITY TO DESTROY A PLANET IS INSIGNIFICANT NEXT TO THE POWER OF THE FORCE.

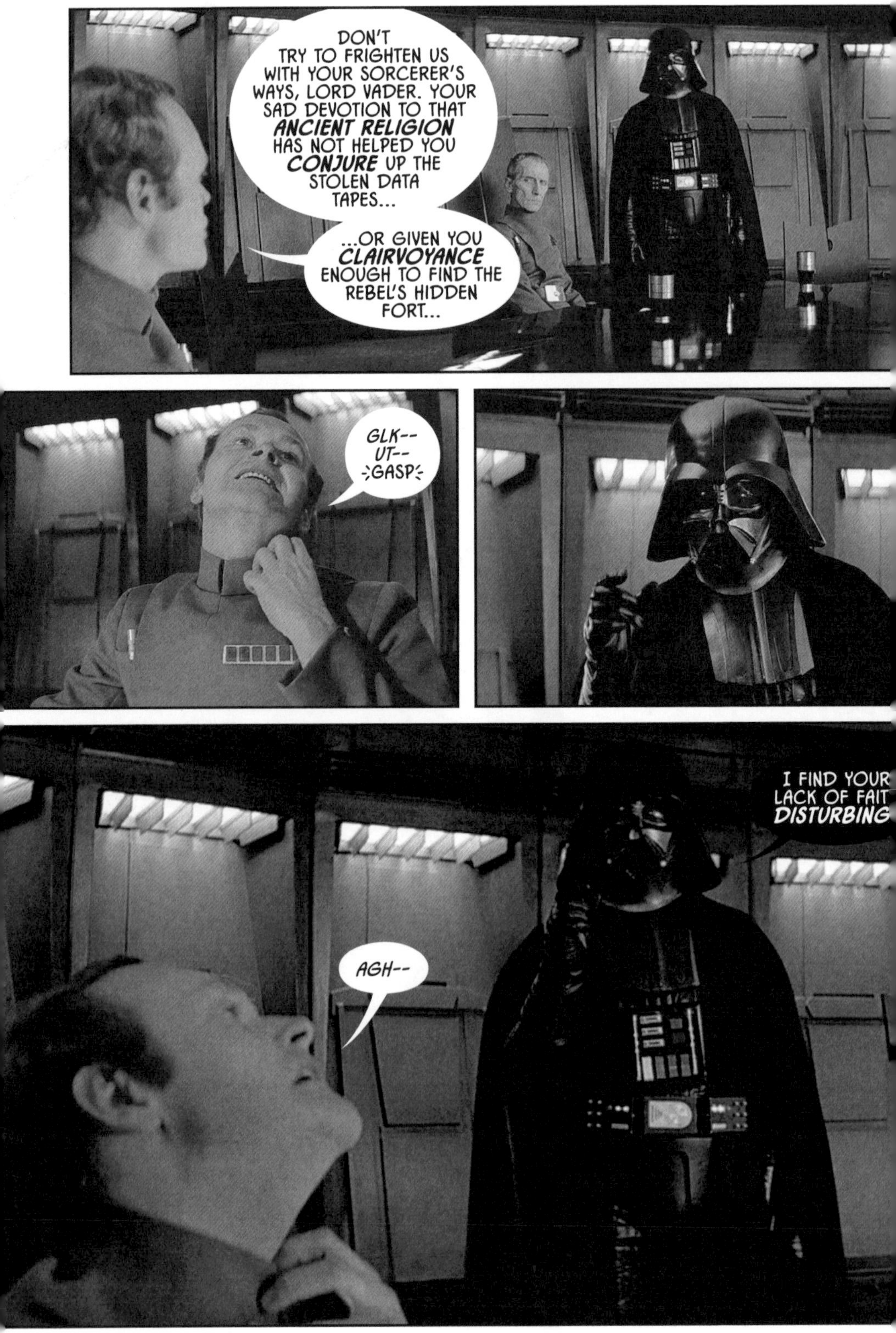
DON'T TRY TO FRIGHTEN US WITH YOUR SORCERER'S WAYS, LORD VADER. YOUR SAD DEVOTION TO THAT ANCIENT RELIGION HAS NOT HELPED YOU CONJURE UP THE STOLEN DATA TAPES...
...OR GIVEN YOU CLAIRVOYANCE ENOUGH TO FIND THE REBEL'S HIDDEN FORT...
GLK-- UT-- GASP
I FIND YOUR LACK OF FAIT DISTURBING
AGH--

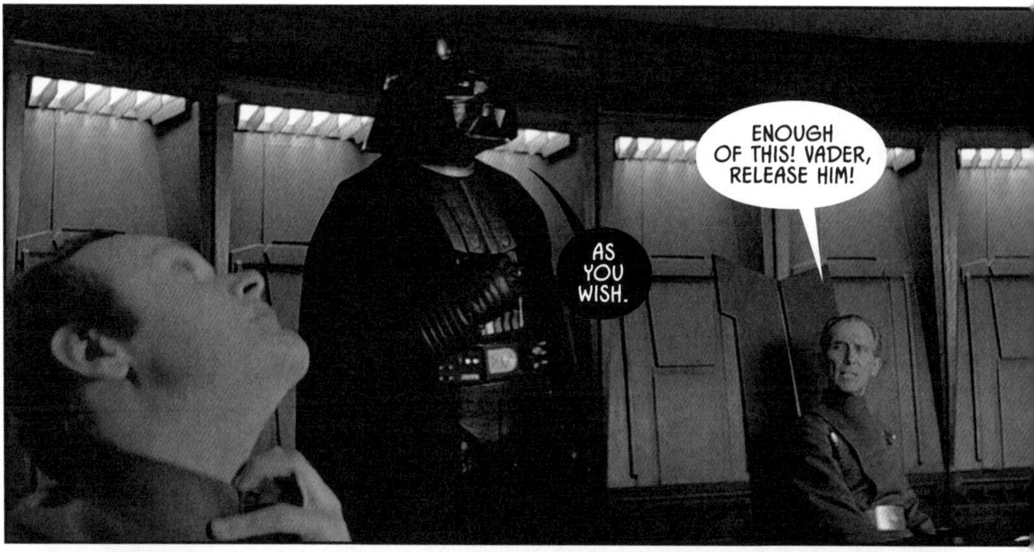
ENOUGH OF THIS! VADER, RELEASE HIM!
AS YOU WISH.

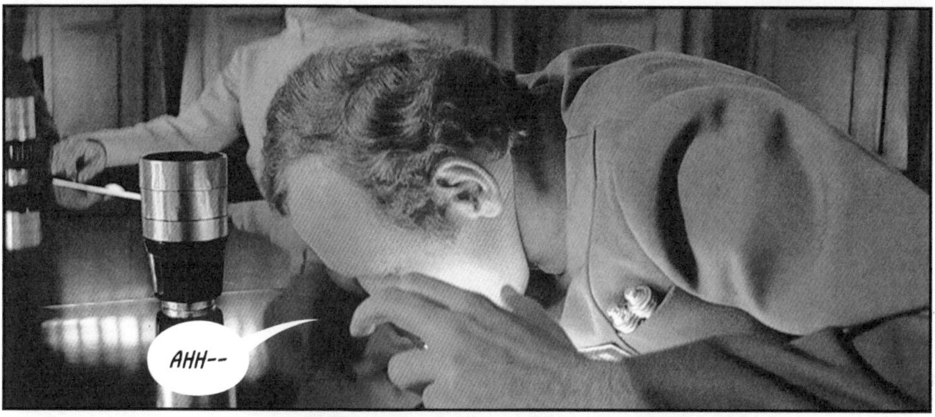
AHH--

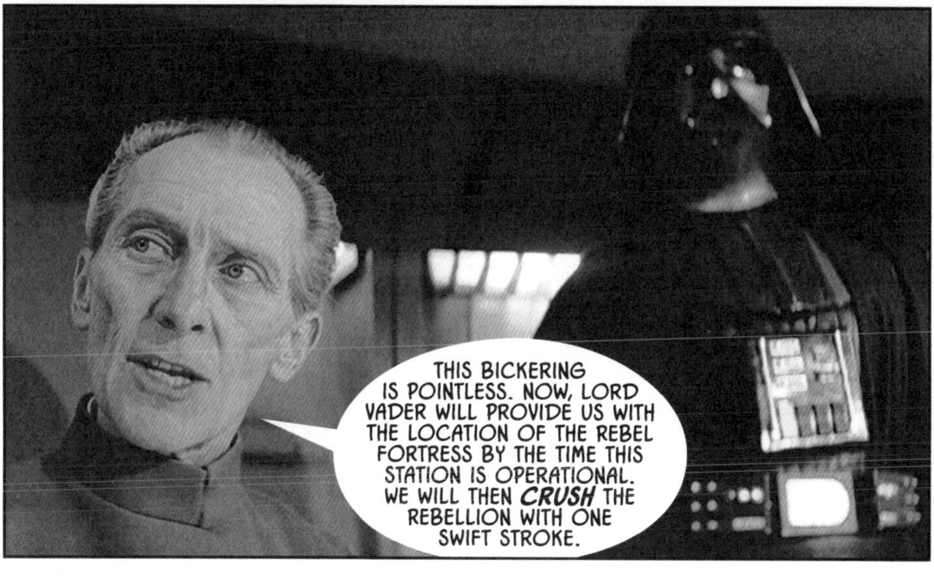
THIS BICKERING IS POINTLESS. NOW, LORD VADER WILL PROVIDE US WITH THE LOCATION OF THE REBEL FORTRESS BY THE TIME THIS STATION IS OPERATIONAL. WE WILL THEN CRUSH THE REBELLION WITH ONE SWIFT STROKE.

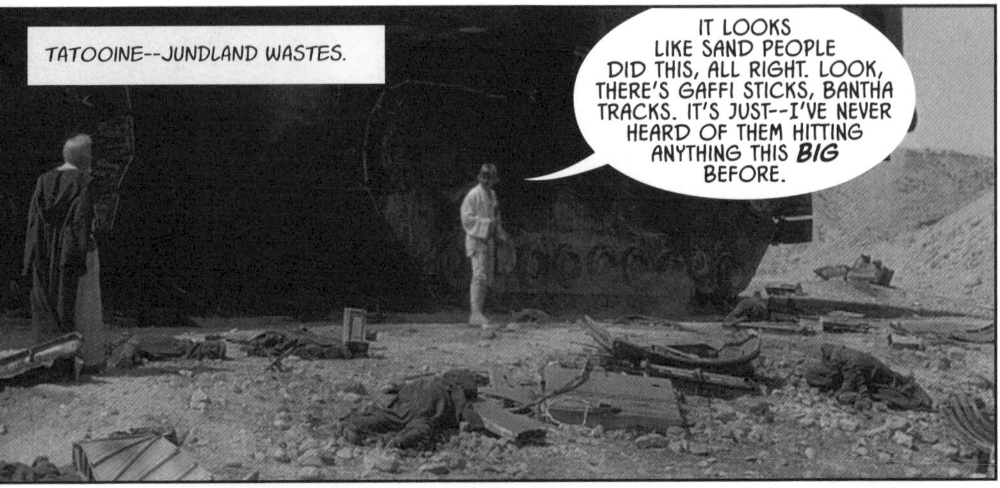
TATOOINE--JUNDLAND WASTES.
IT LOOKS LIKE SAND PEOPLE DID THIS, ALL RIGHT. LOOK, THERE'S GAFFI STICKS, BANTHA TRACKS. IT'S JUST--I'VE NEVER HEARD OF THEM HITTING ANYTHING THIS BIG BEFORE.

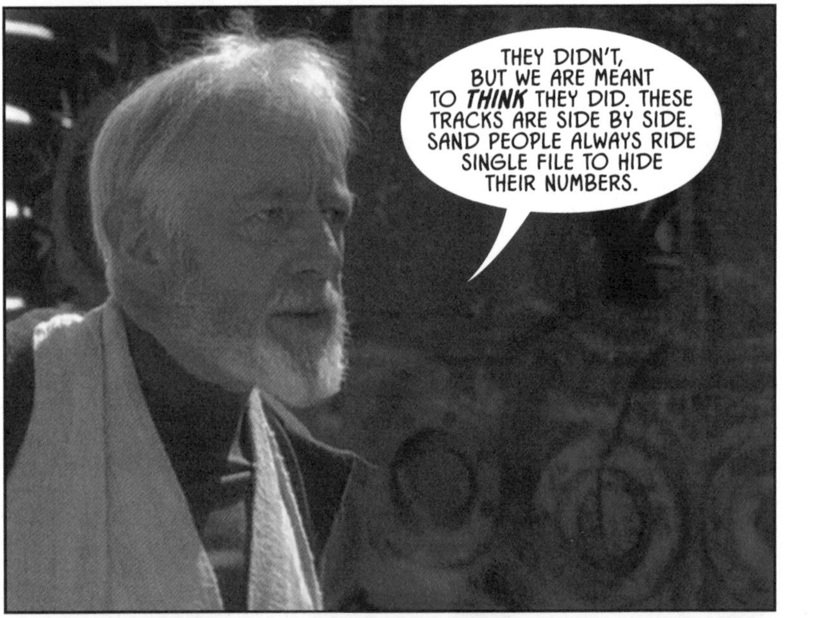
THEY DIDN'T, BUT WE ARE MEANT TO THINK THEY DID. THESE TRACKS ARE SIDE BY SIDE. SAND PEOPLE ALWAYS RIDE SINGLE FILE TO HIDE THEIR NUMBERS.

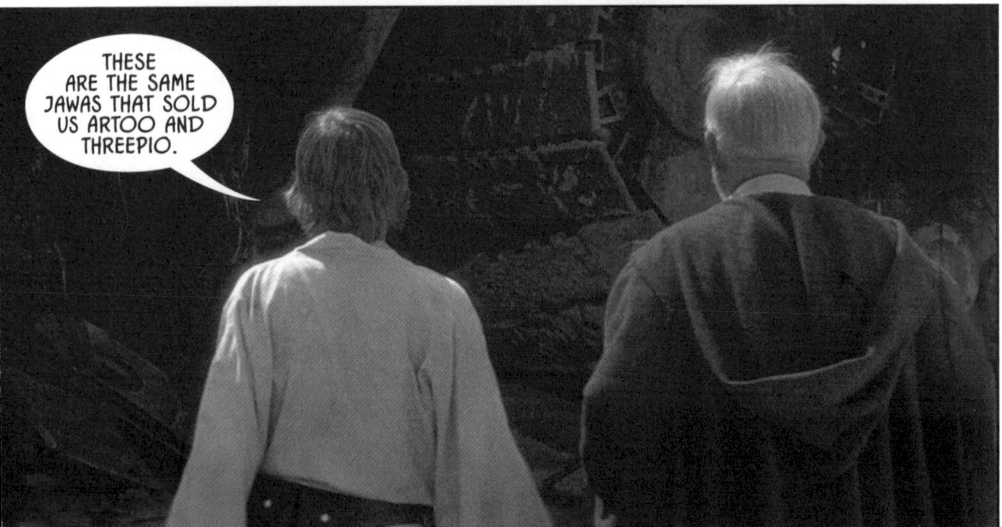
THESE ARE THE SAME JAWAS THAT SOLD US ARTOO AND THREEPIO.

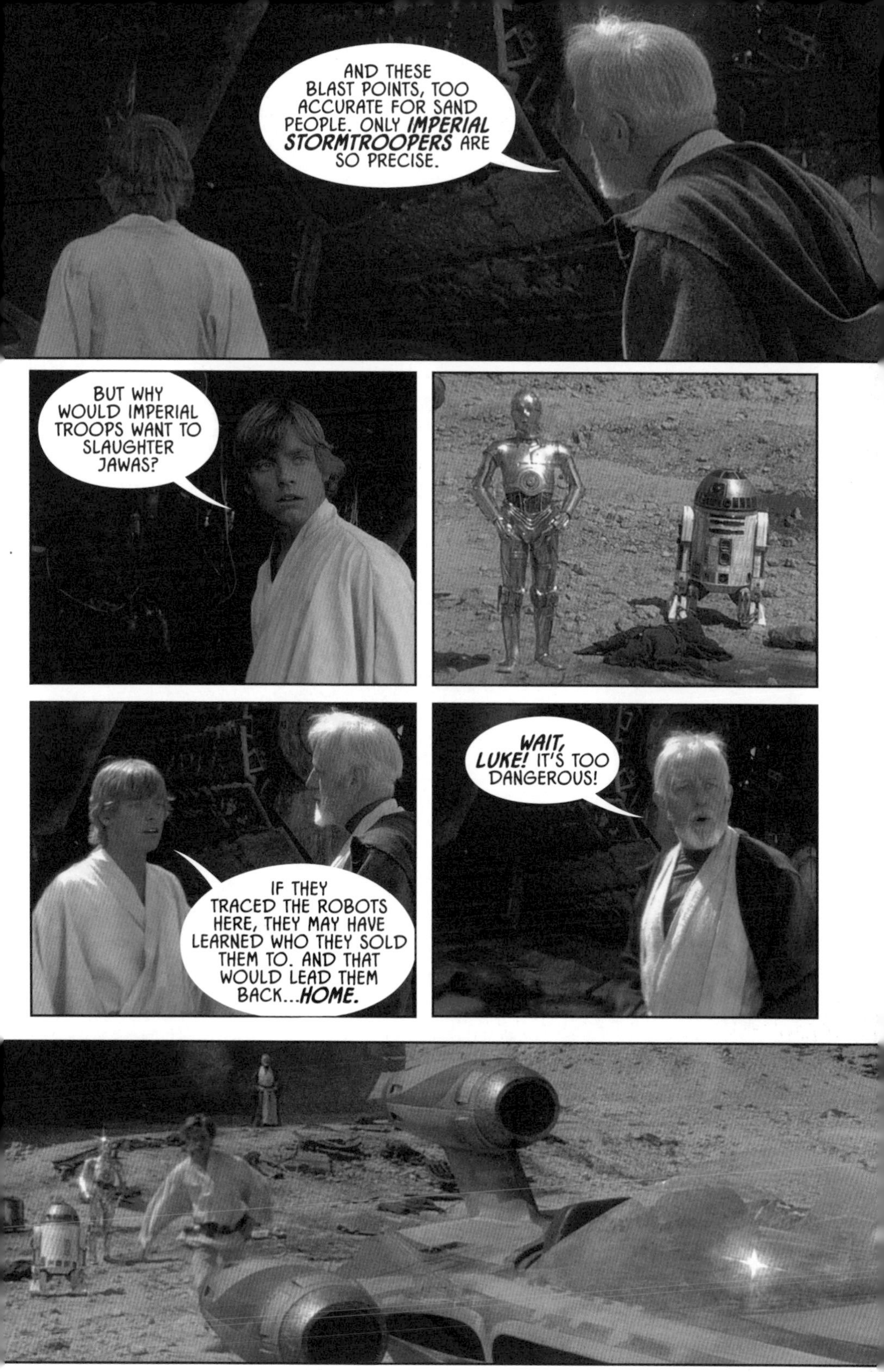
AND THESE BLAST POINTS, TOO ACCURATE FOR SAND PEOPLE. ONLY IMPERIAL STORMTROOPERS ARE SO PRECISE.
BUT WHY WOULD IMPERIAL TROOPS WANT TO SLAUGHTER JAWAS?
IF THEY TRACED THE ROBOTS HERE, THEY MAY HAVE LEARNED WHO THEY SOLD THEM TO. AND THAT WOULD LEAD THEM BACK...HOME.
WAIT, LUKE! IT'S TOO DANGEROUS!

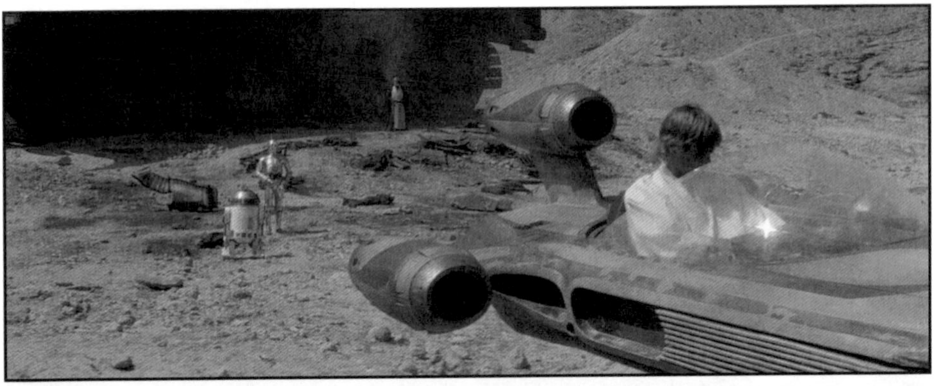

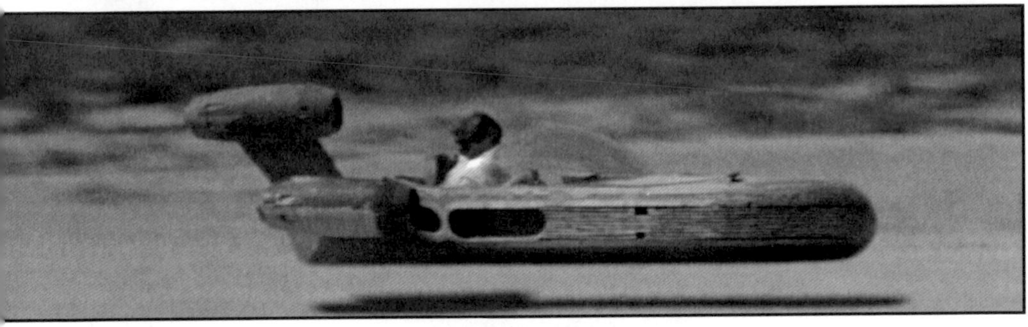

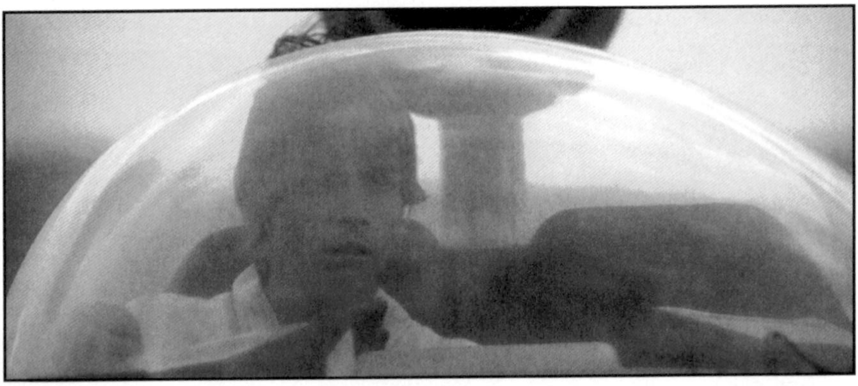

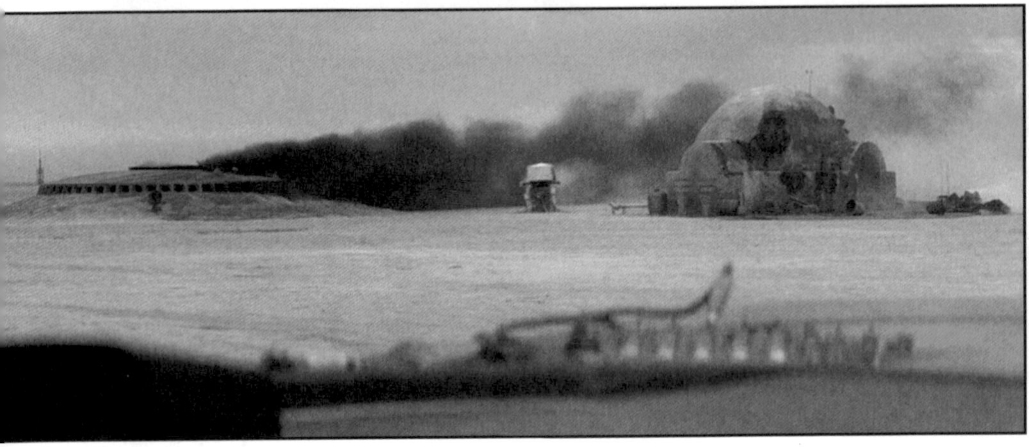

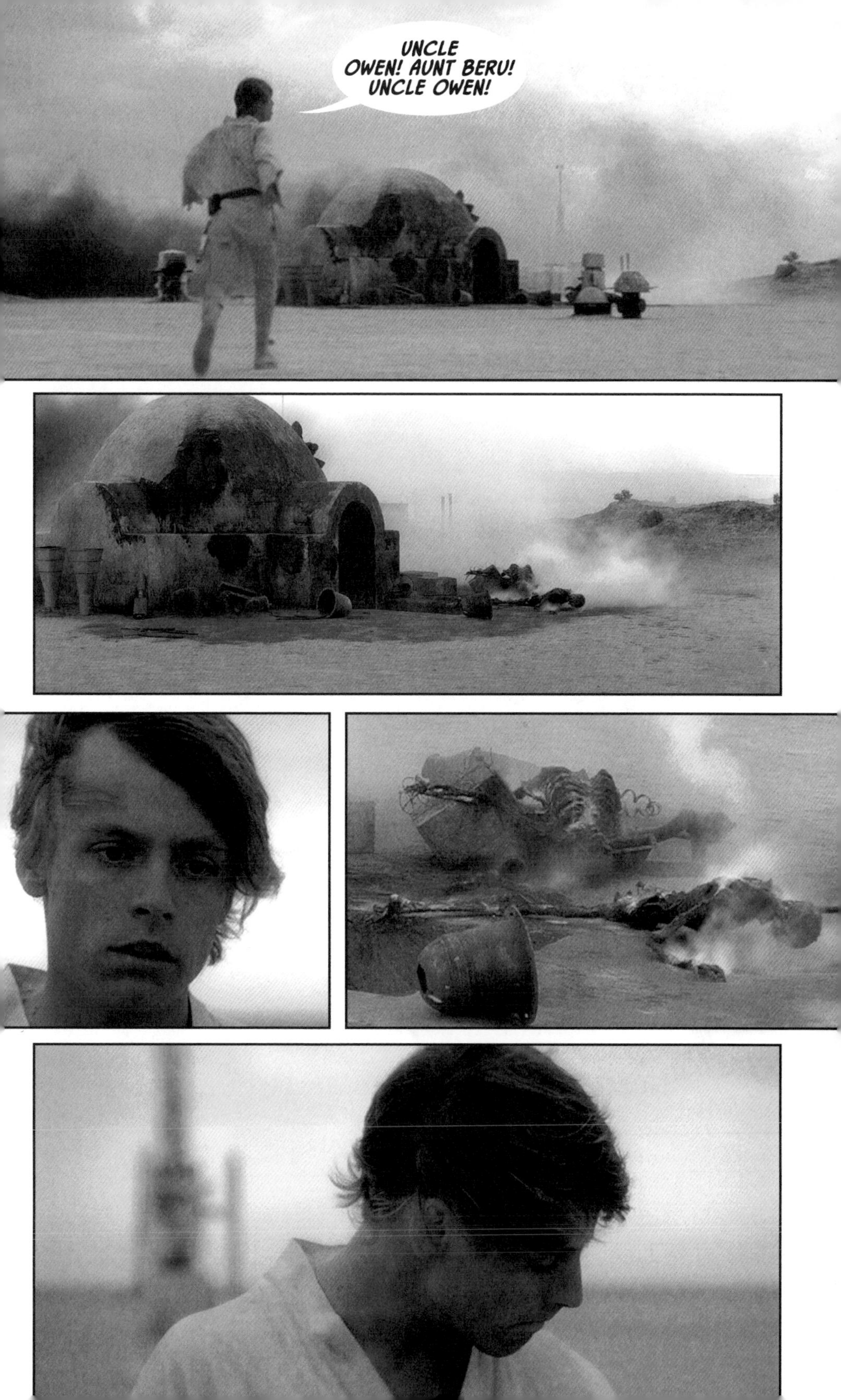
UNCLE OWEN! AUNT BERU! UNCLE OWEN!

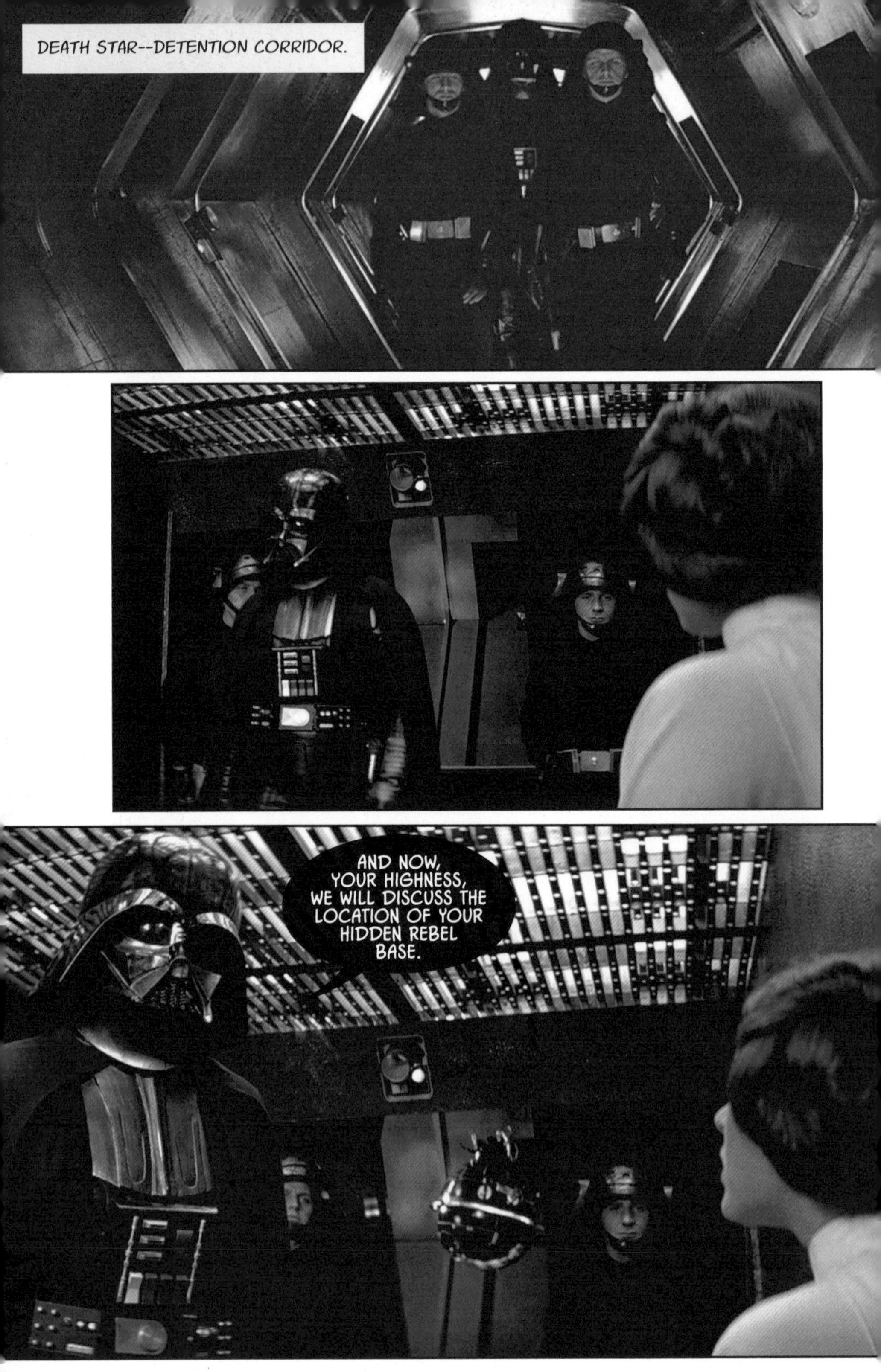
DEATH STAR--DETENTION CORRIDOR.
AND NOW, YOUR HIGHNESS, WE WILL DISCUSS THE LOCATION OF YOUR HIDDEN REBEL BASE.

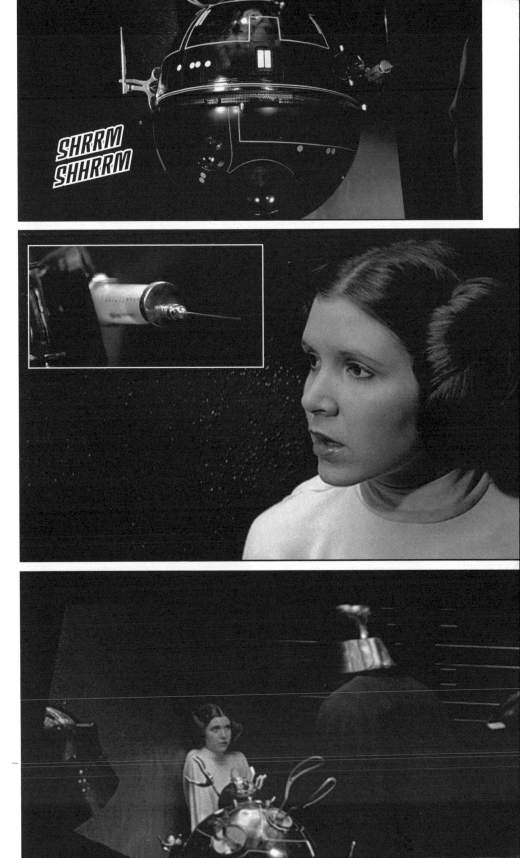

SHRRM
SHHRRM

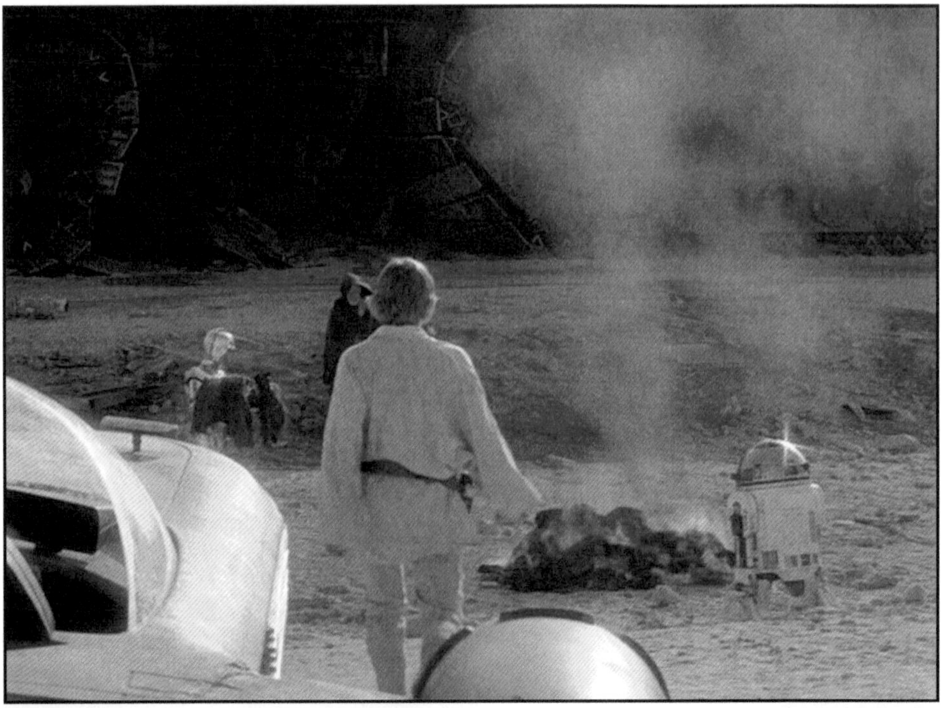

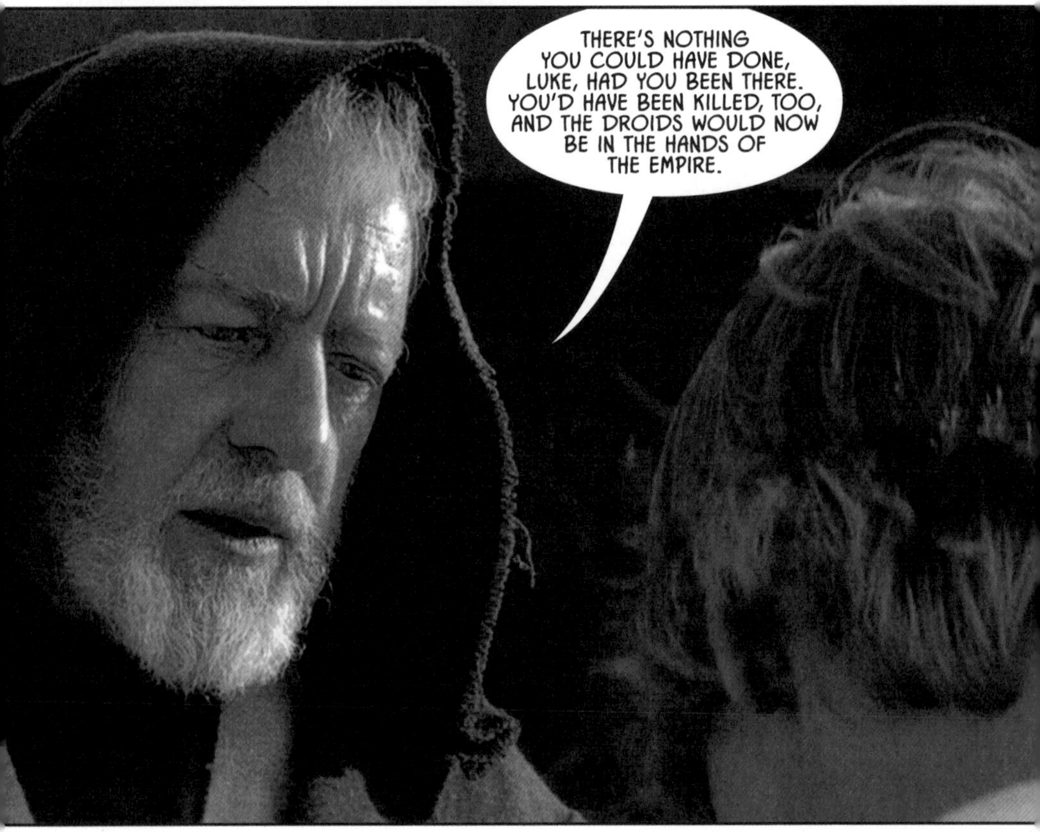
THERE'S NOTHING YOU COULD HAVE DONE, LUKE, HAD YOU BEEN THERE. YOU'D HAVE BEEN KILLED, TOO, AND THE DROIDS WOULD NOW BE IN THE HANDS OF THE EMPIRE.

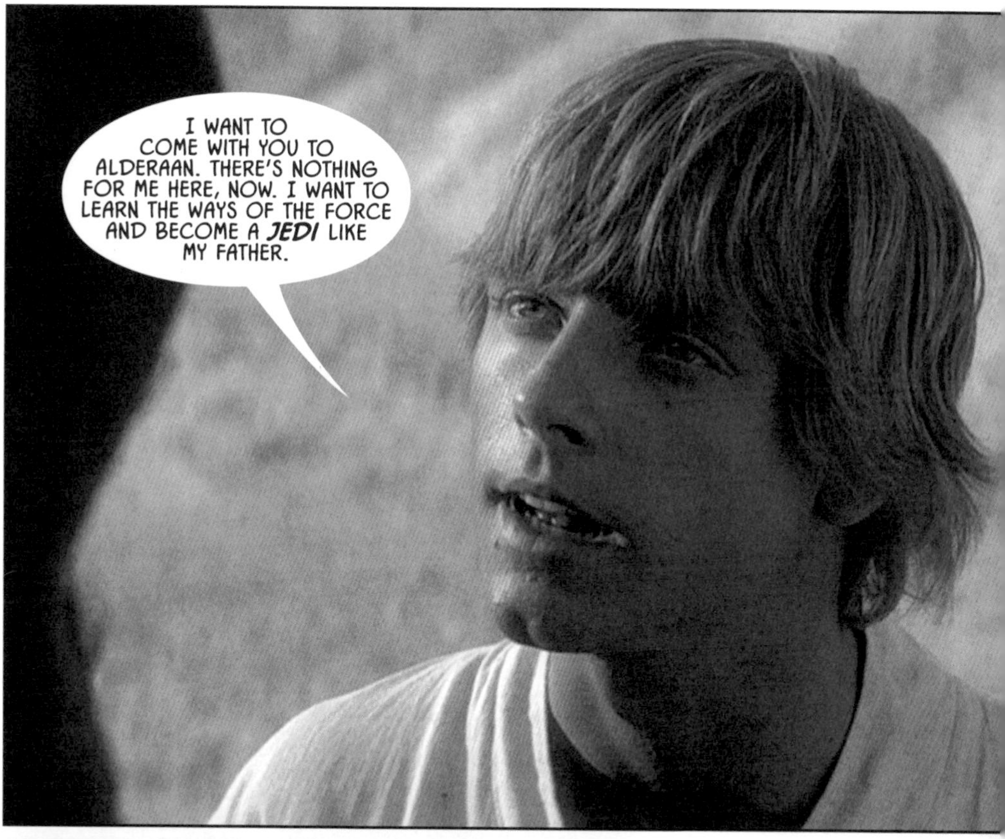
I WANT TO COME WITH YOU TO ALDERAAN. THERE'S NOTHING FOR ME HERE, NOW. I WANT TO LEARN THE WAYS OF THE FORCE AND BECOME A JEDI LIKE MY FATHER.

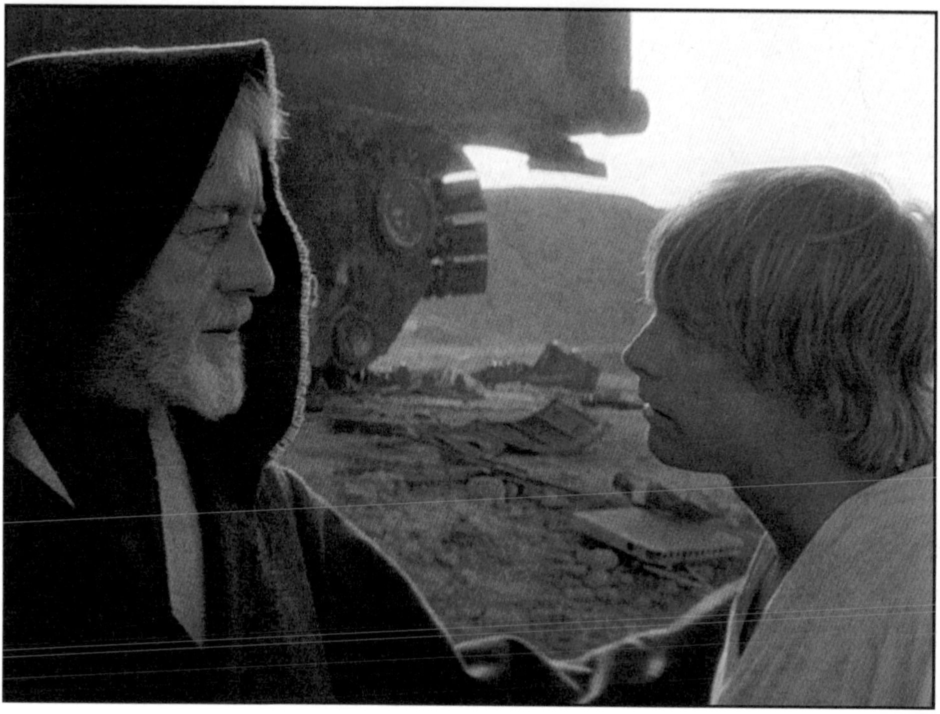

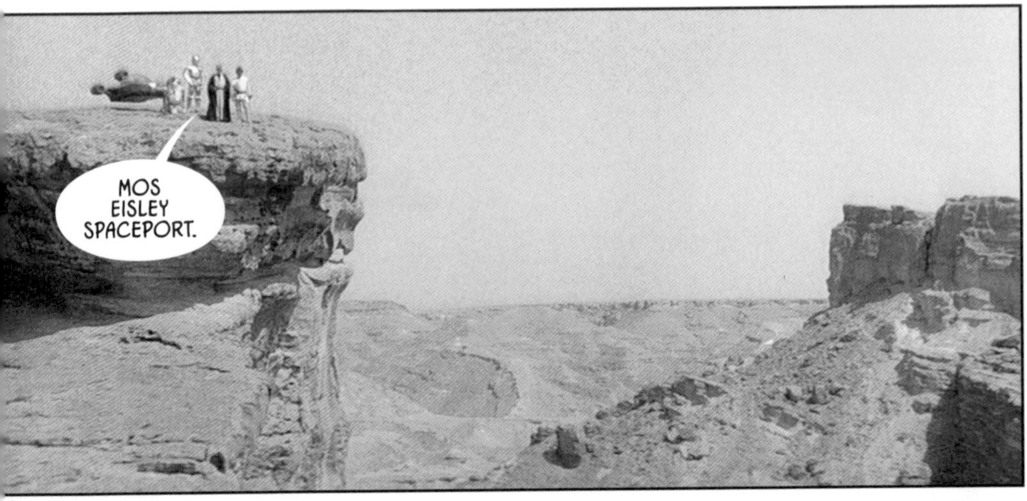
MOS EISLEY SPACEPORT.

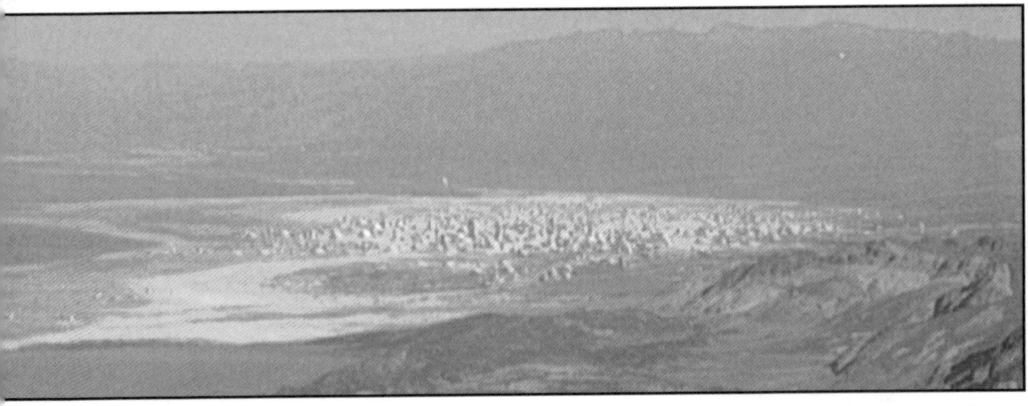

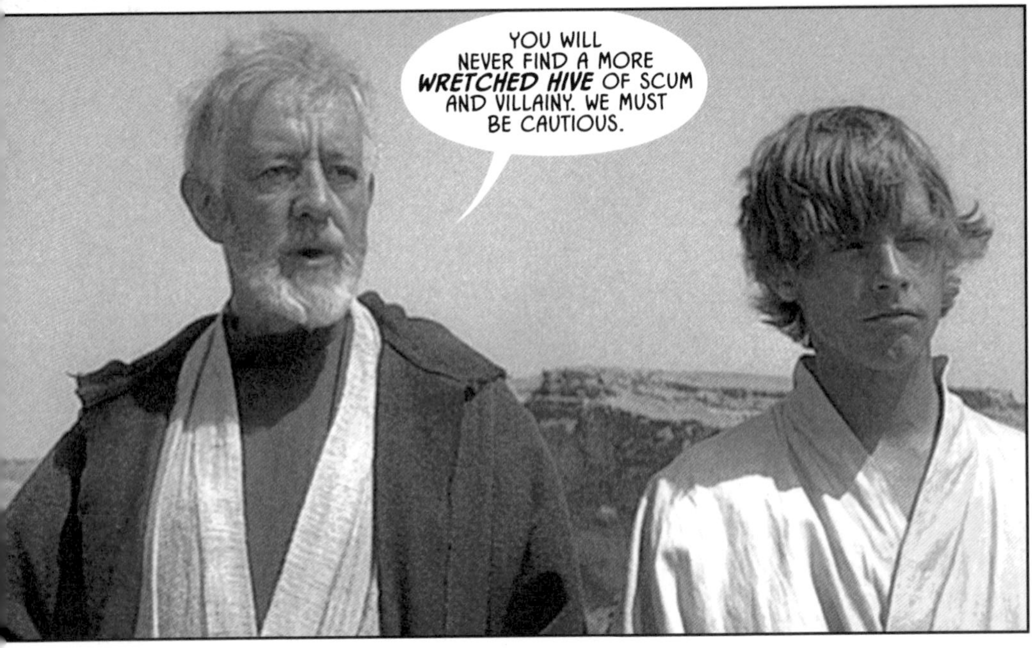
YOU WILL NEVER FIND A MORE WRETCHED HIVE OF SCUM AND VILLAINY. WE MUST BE CAUTIOUS.

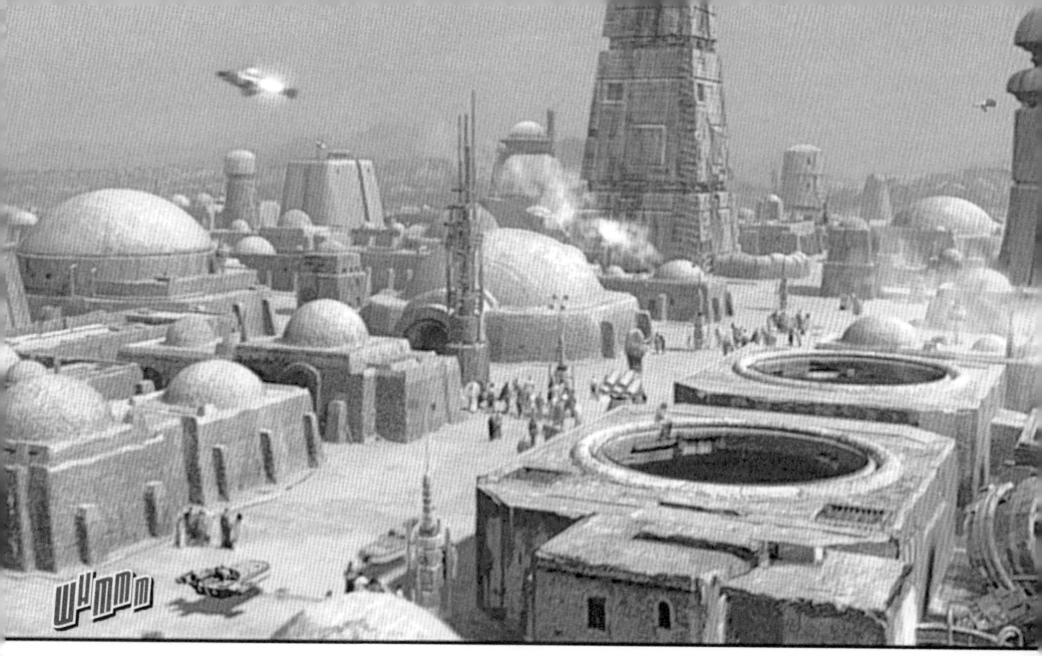
WHMMM

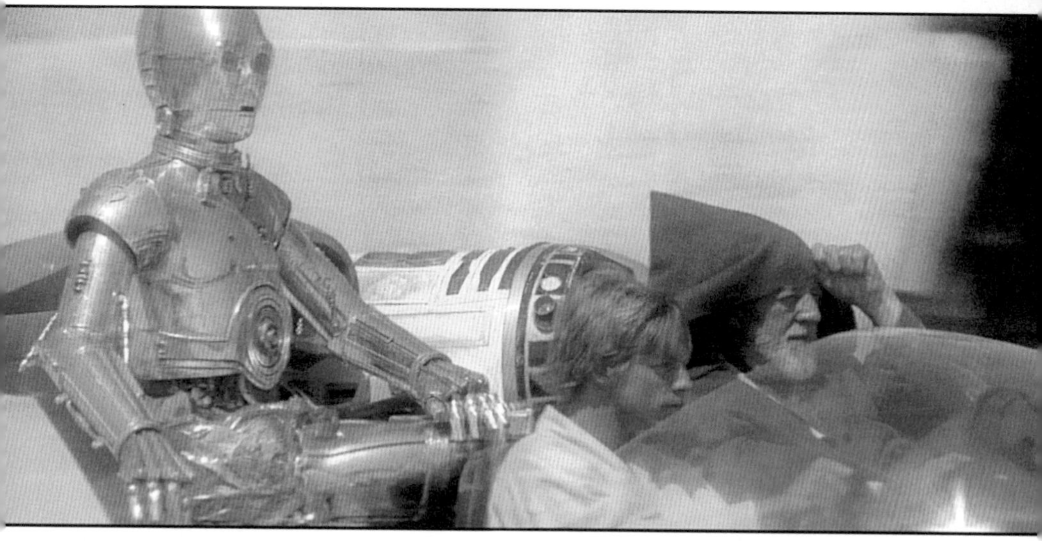

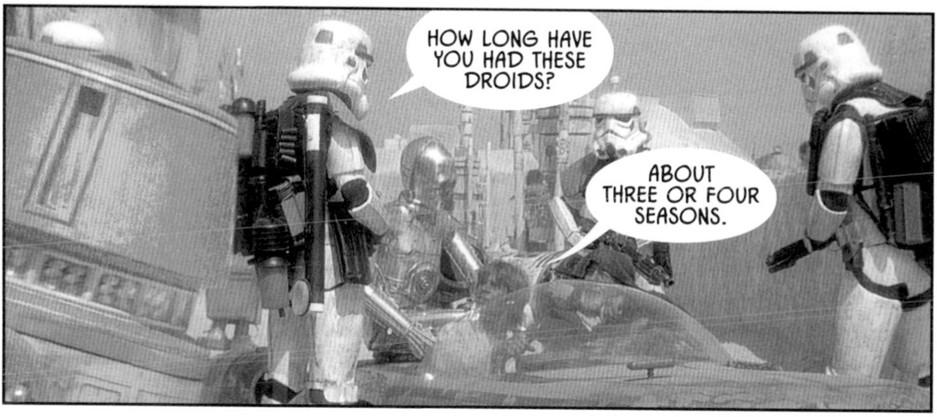
HOW LONG HAVE YOU HAD THESE DROIDS?
ABOUT THREE OR FOUR SEASONS.

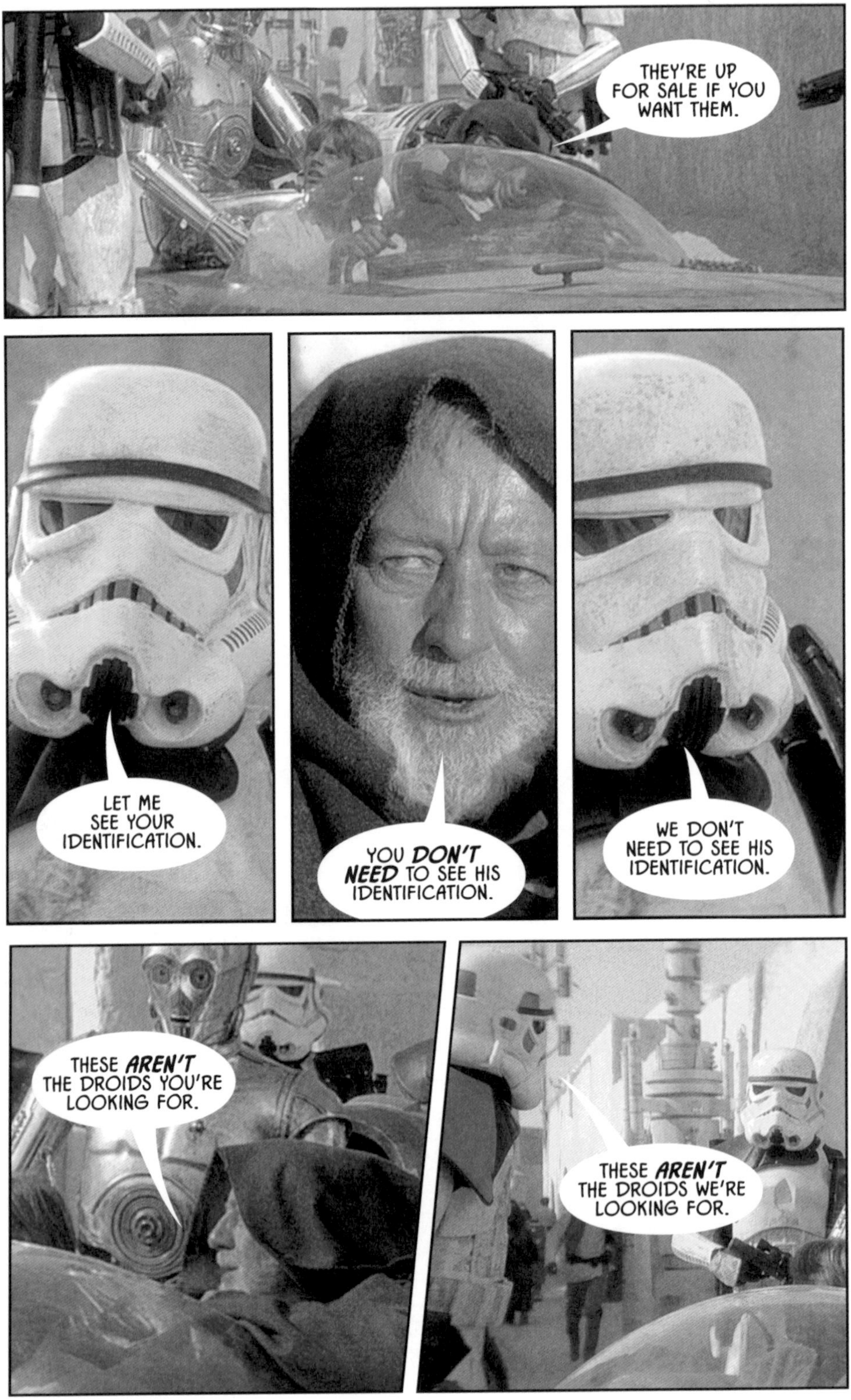
THEY'RE UP FOR SALE IF YOU WANT THEM.
LET ME SEE YOUR IDENTIFICATION.
YOU DON'T NEED TO SEE HIS IDENTIFICATION.
WE DON'T NEED TO SEE HIS IDENTIFICATION.
THESE AREN'T THE DROIDS YOU'RE LOOKING FOR.
THESE AREN'T THE DROIDS WE'RE LOOKING FOR.

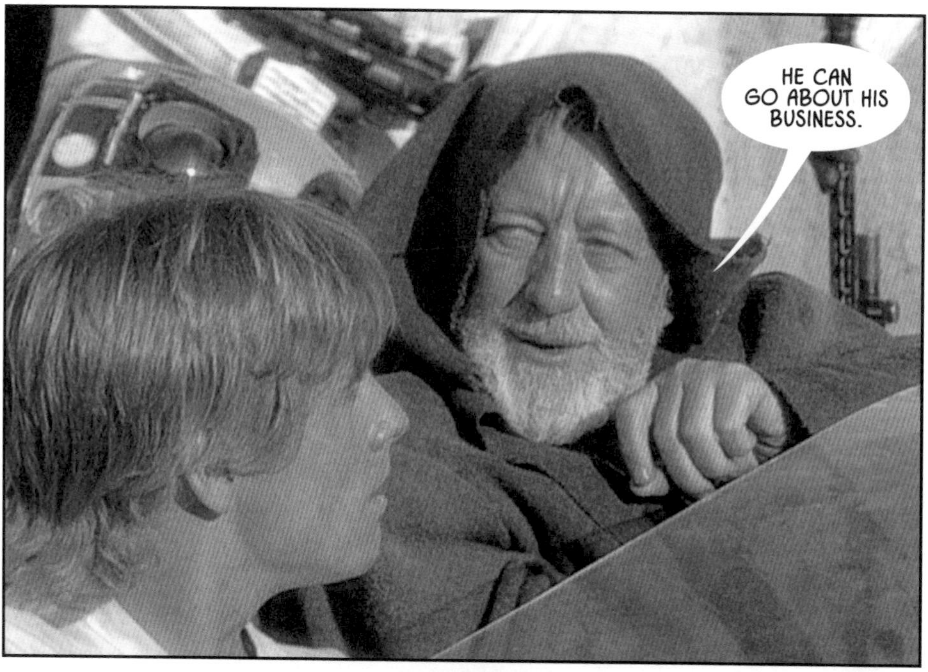
HE CAN GO ABOUT HIS BUSINESS.

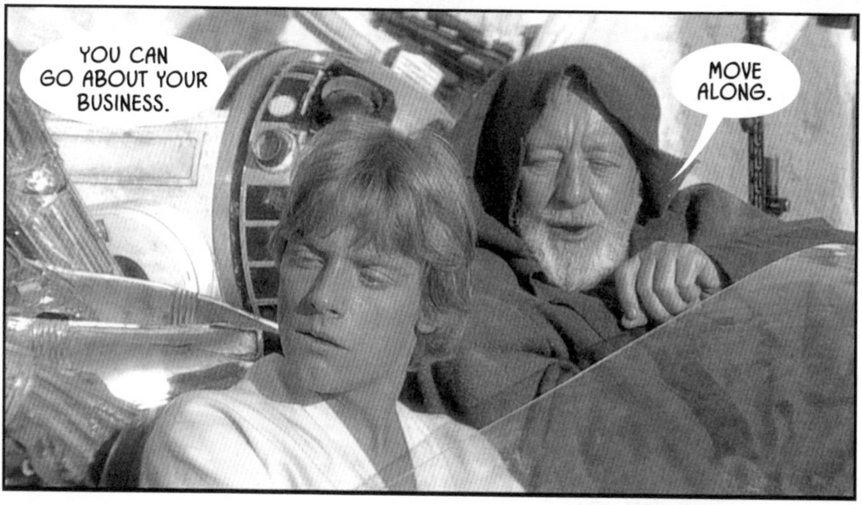
YOU CAN GO ABOUT YOUR BUSINESS.
MOVE ALONG.

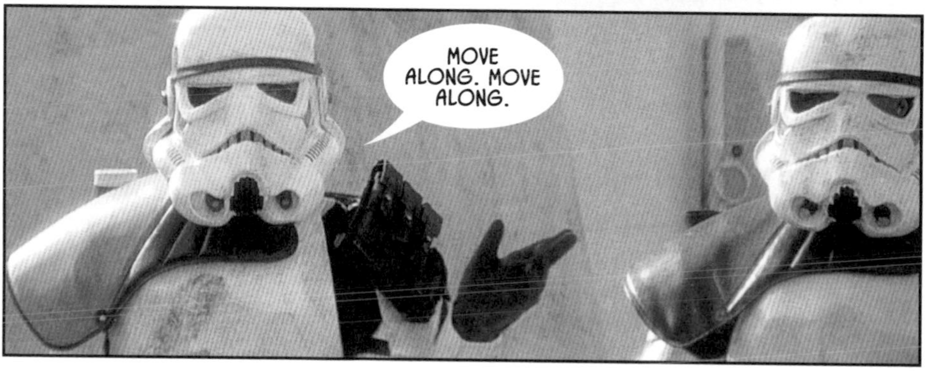
MOVE ALONG. MOVE ALONG.

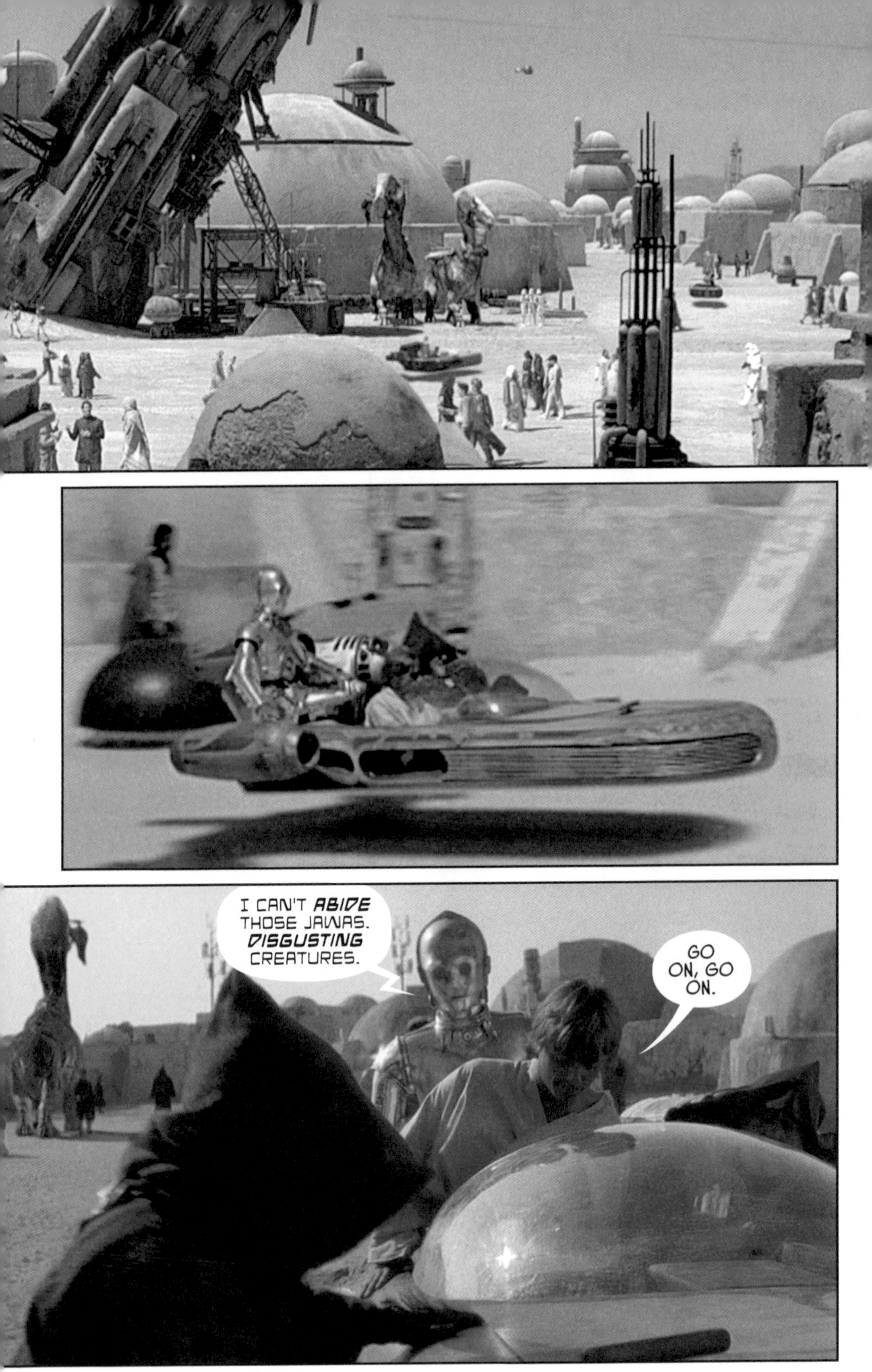
I CAN'T ABIDE THOSE JAWAS. DISGUSTING CREATURES.
GO ON, GO ON.

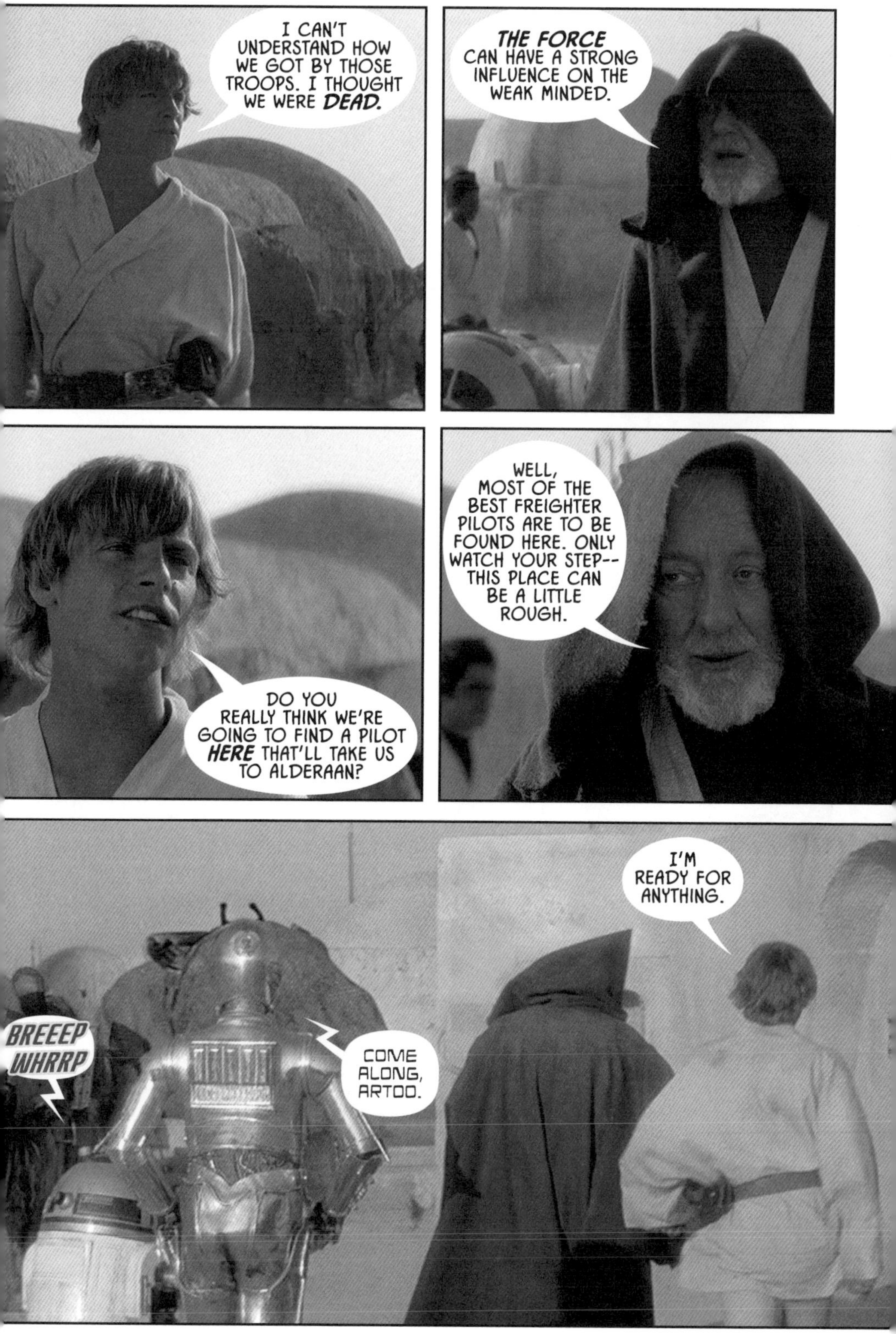
I CAN'T UNDERSTAND HOW WE GOT BY THOSE TROOPS. I THOUGHT WE WERE *DEAD.*
THE FORCE CAN HAVE A STRONG INFLUENCE ON THE WEAK MINDED.
DO YOU REALLY THINK WE'RE GOING TO FIND A PILOT *HERE* THAT'LL TAKE US TO ALDERAAN?
WELL, MOST OF THE BEST FREIGHTER PILOTS ARE TO BE FOUND HERE. ONLY WATCH YOUR STEP-- THIS PLACE CAN BE A LITTLE ROUGH.
I'M READY FOR ANYTHING.
COME ALONG, ARTOO.
BREEEP WHRRP

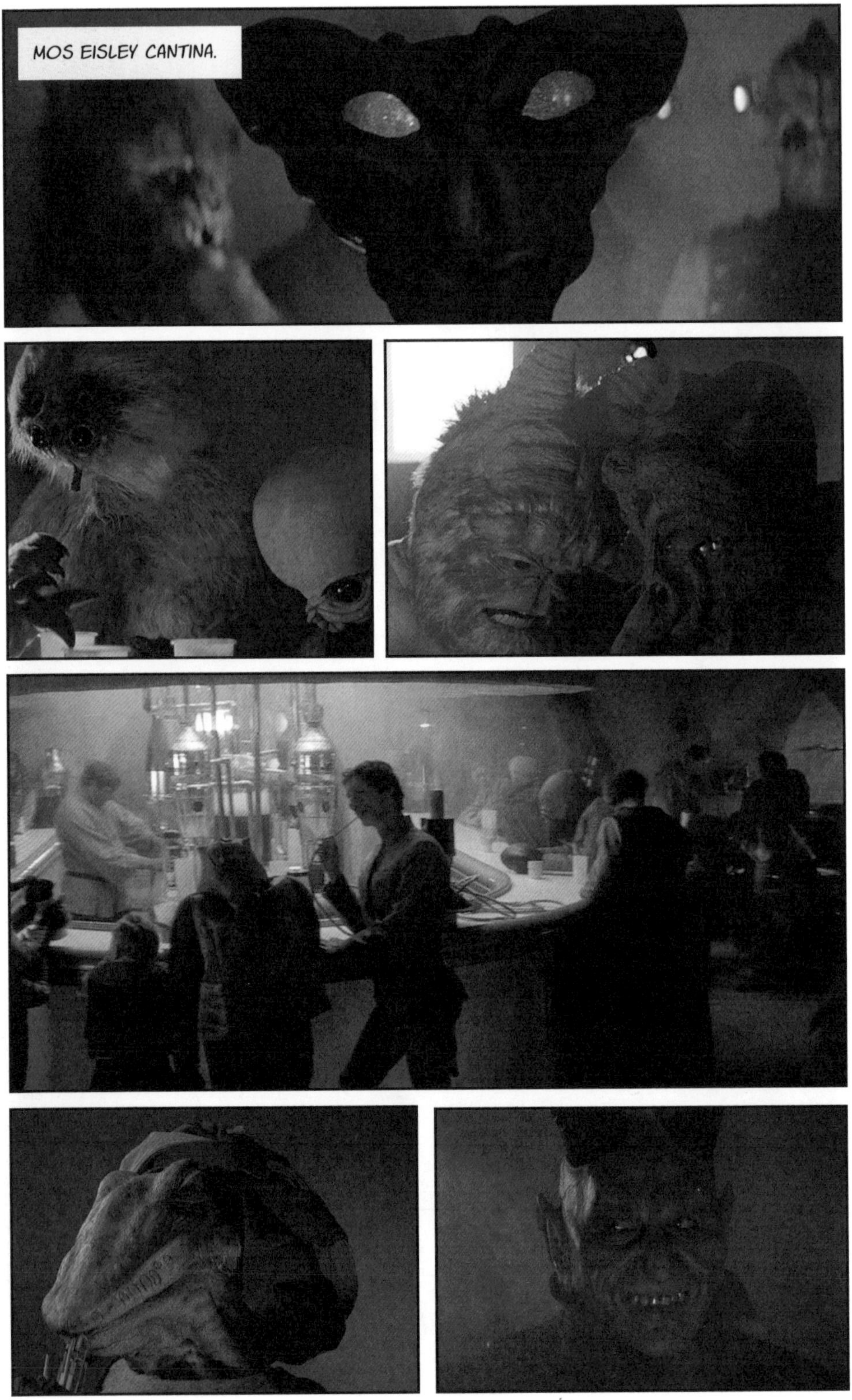
MOS EISLEY CANTINA.

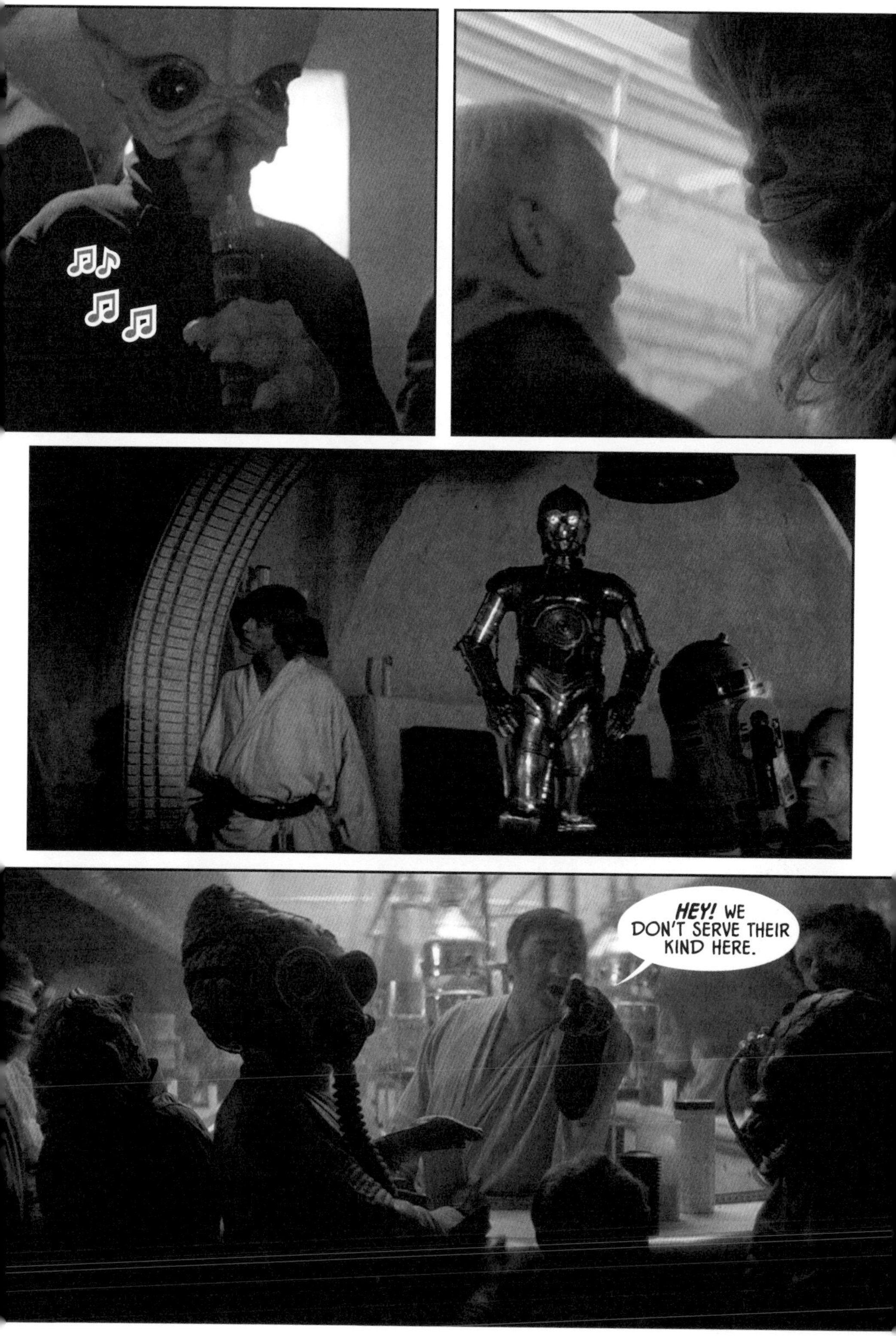
HEY! WE DON'T SERVE THEIR KIND HERE.

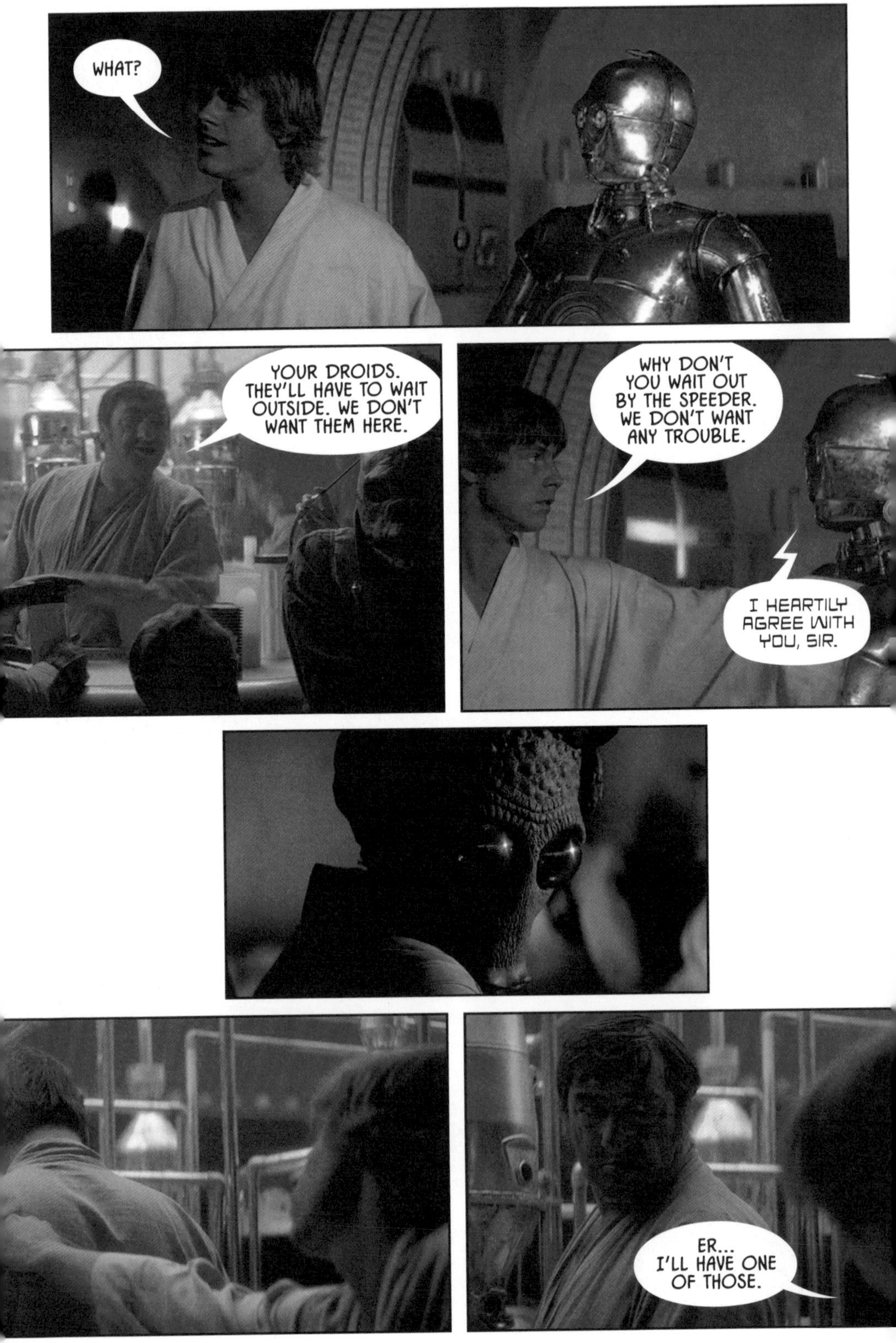
WHAT?
YOUR DROIDS. THEY'LL HAVE TO WAIT OUTSIDE. WE DON'T WANT THEM HERE.
WHY DON'T YOU WAIT OUT BY THE SPEEDER. WE DON'T WANT ANY TROUBLE.
I HEARTILY AGREE WITH YOU, SIR.
ER... I'LL HAVE ONE OF THOSE.

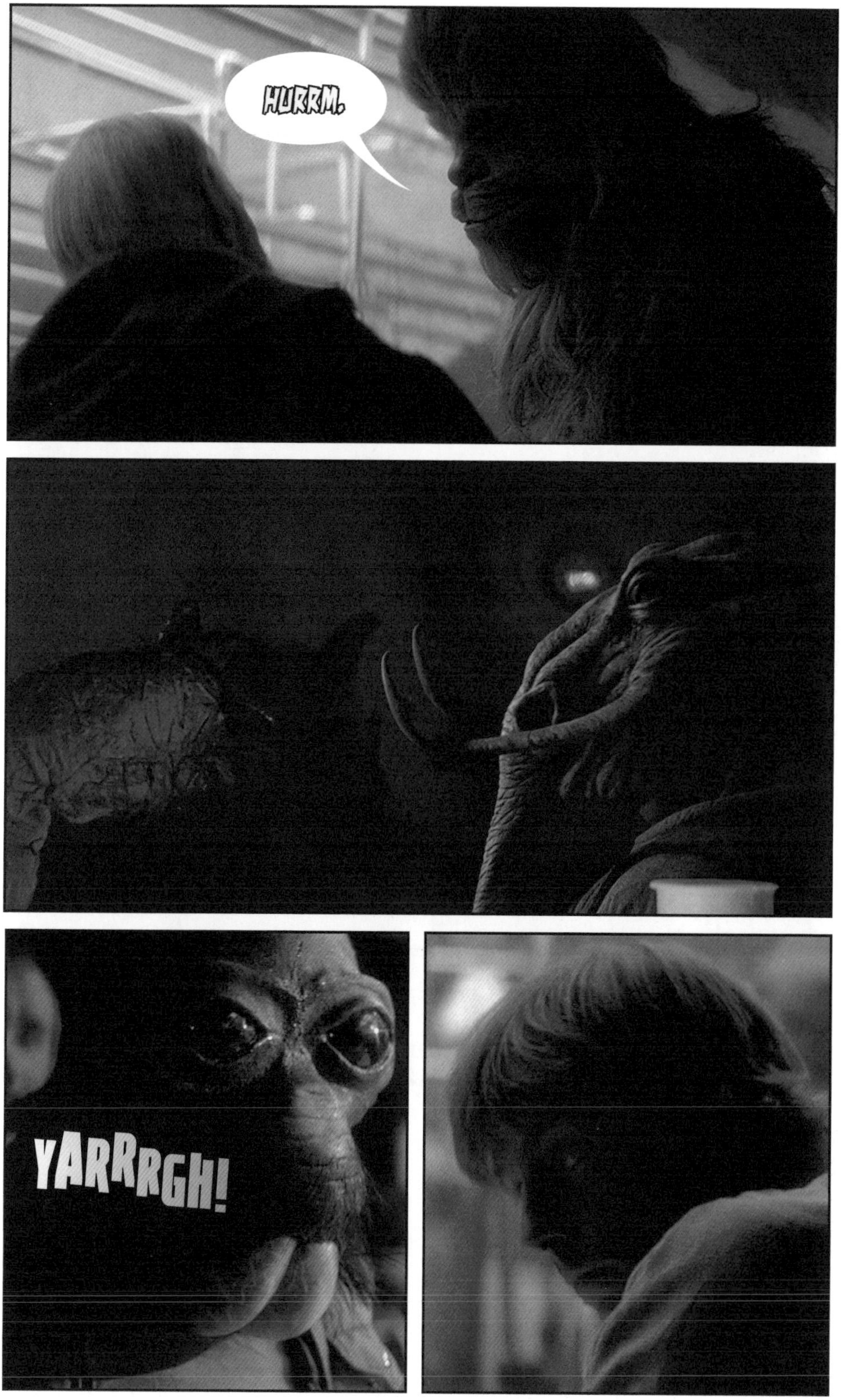
HURRM.
YARRRGH!

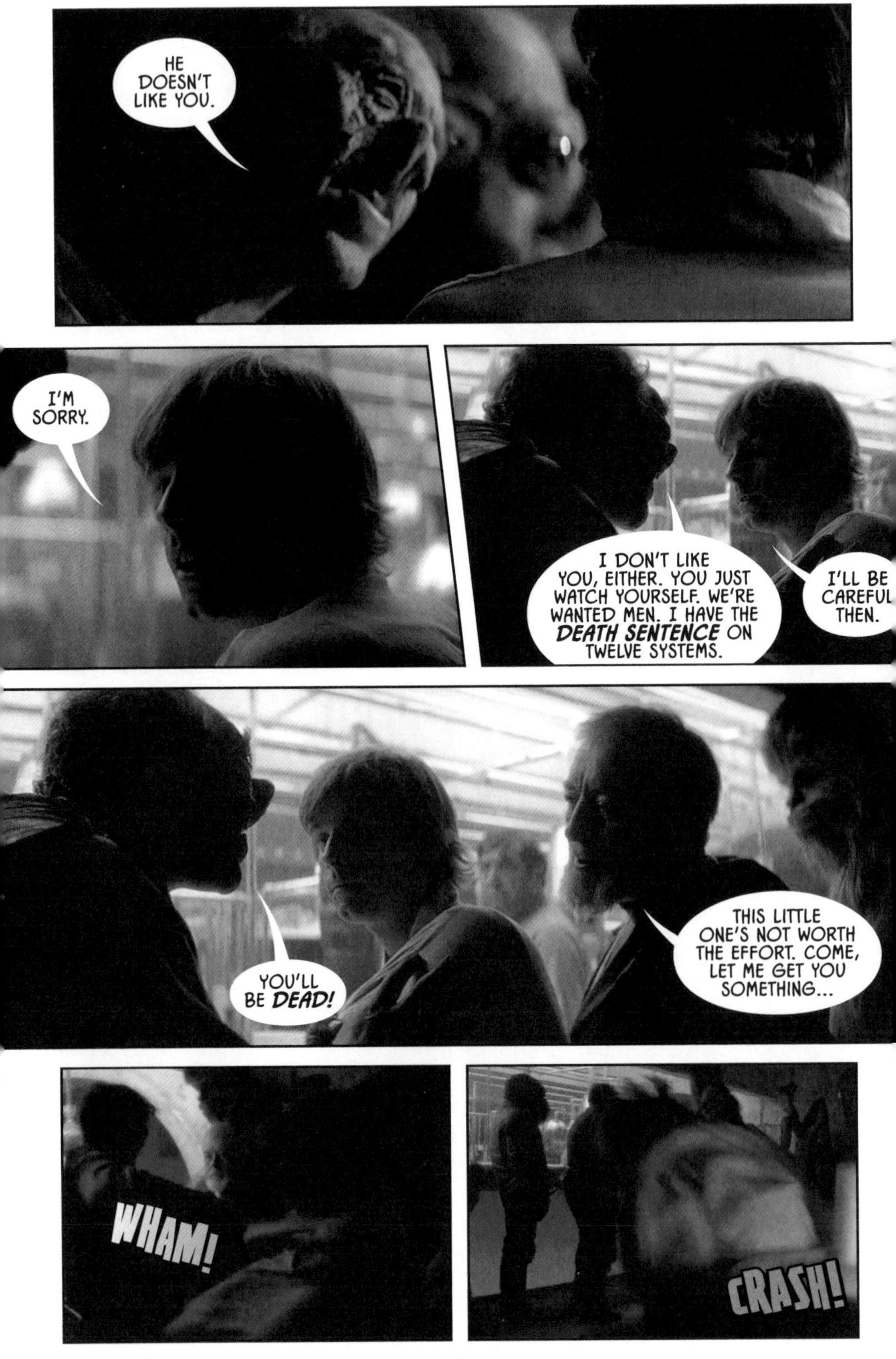
HE DOESN'T LIKE YOU.
I'M SORRY.
I DON'T LIKE YOU, EITHER. YOU JUST WATCH YOURSELF. WE'RE WANTED MEN. I HAVE THE DEATH SENTENCE ON TWELVE SYSTEMS.
I'LL BE CAREFUL THEN.
YOU'LL BE DEAD!
THIS LITTLE ONE'S NOT WORTH THE EFFORT. COME, LET ME GET YOU SOMETHING...
WHAM!
CRASH!

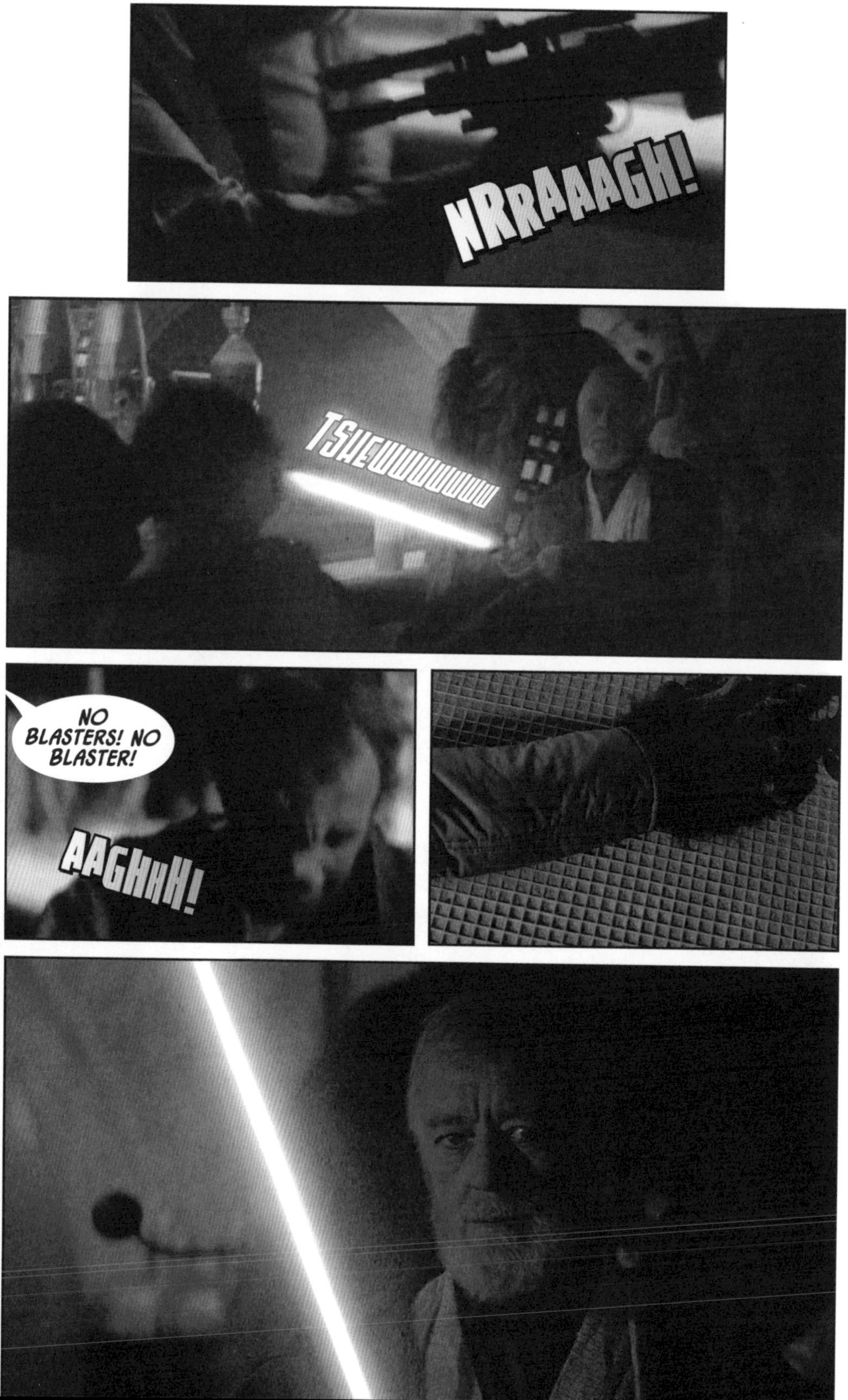
NRRAAAGH!
TSHEWWWWWWW
NO BLASTERS! NO BLASTER!
AAGHHH!

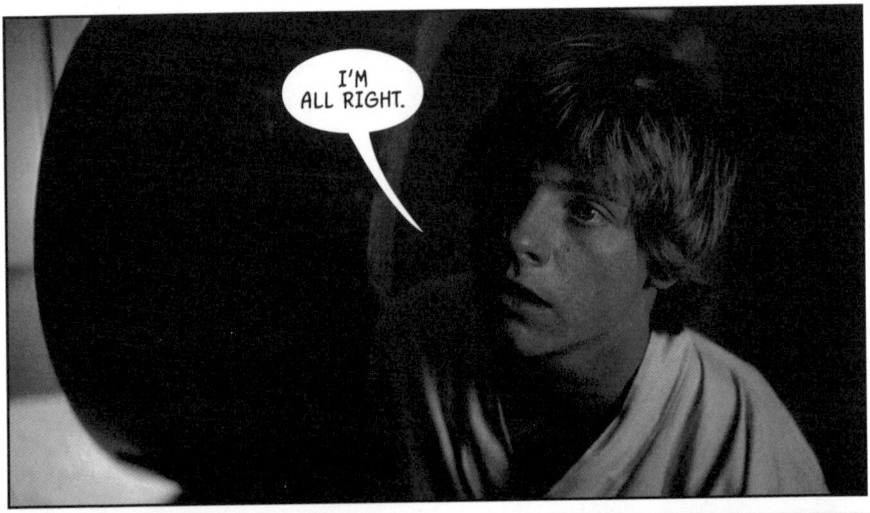
I'M ALL RIGHT.

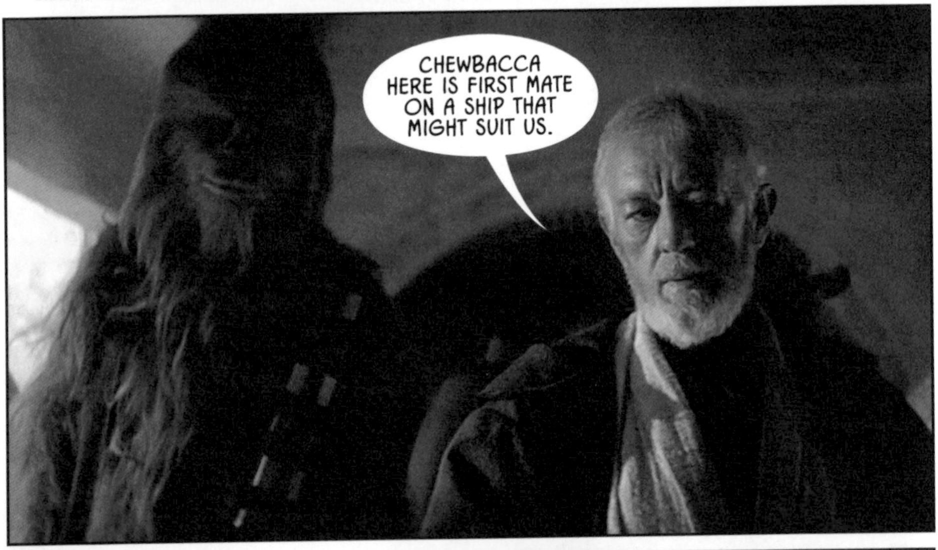
CHEWBACCA HERE IS FIRST MATE ON A SHIP THAT MIGHT SUIT US.

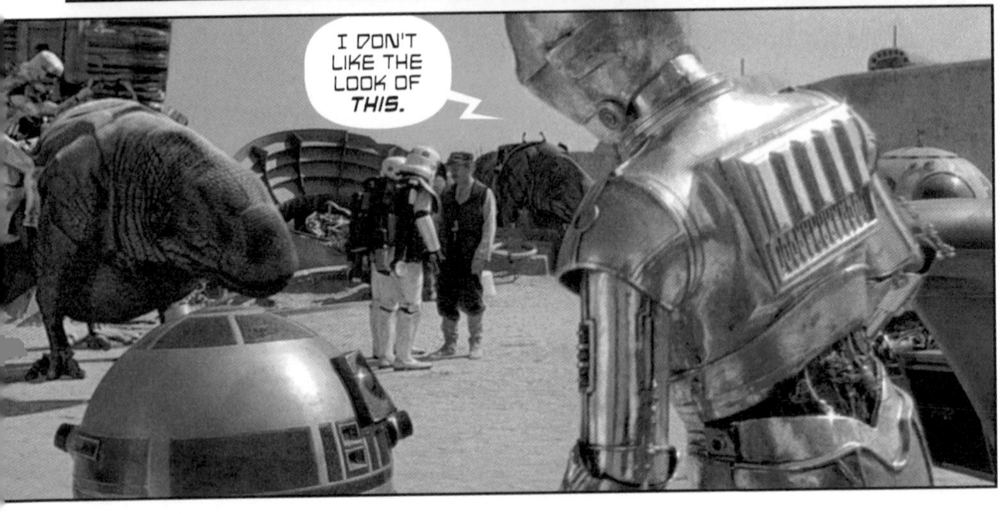
I DON'T LIKE THE LOOK OF *THIS.*

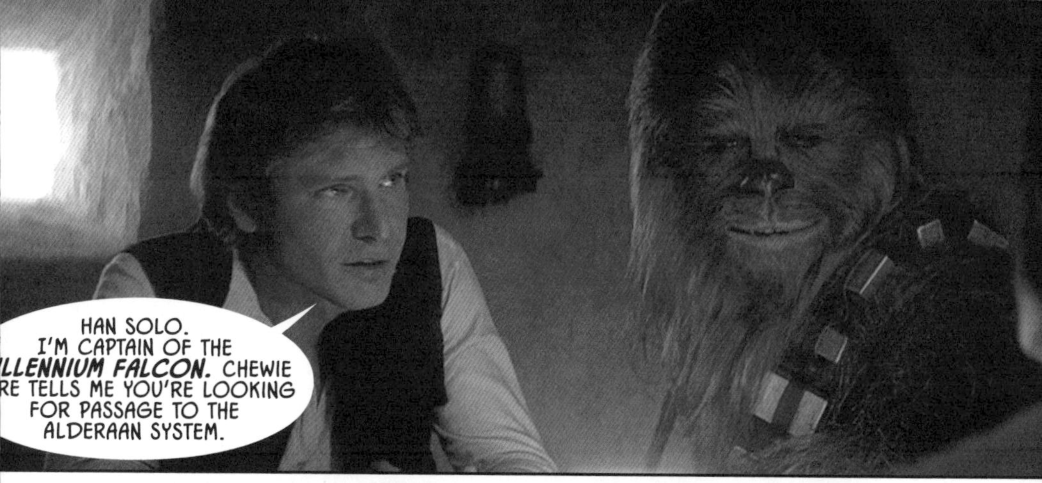
HAN SOLO.
I'M CAPTAIN OF THE
ILLENNIUM FALCON. CHEWIE
RE TELLS ME YOU'RE LOOKING
FOR PASSAGE TO THE
ALDERAAN SYSTEM.

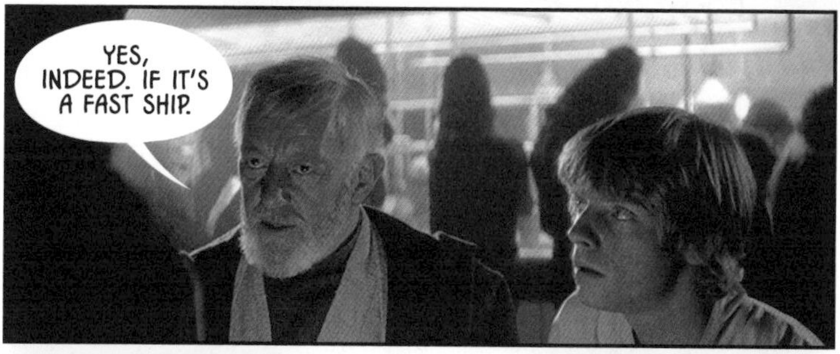
YES, INDEED. IF IT'S A FAST SHIP.

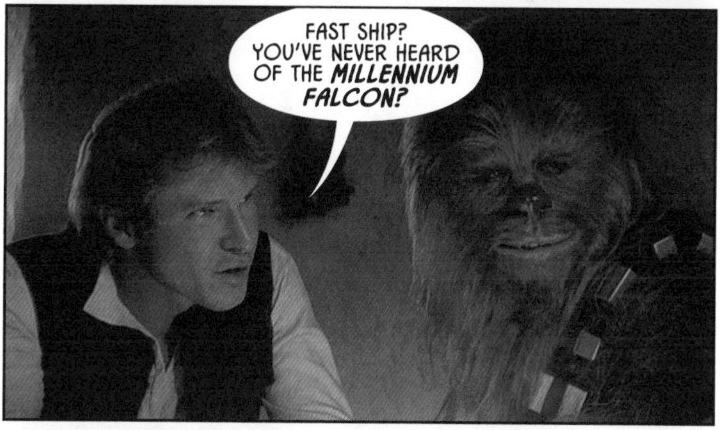
FAST SHIP? YOU'VE NEVER HEARD OF THE *MILLENNIUM FALCON?*

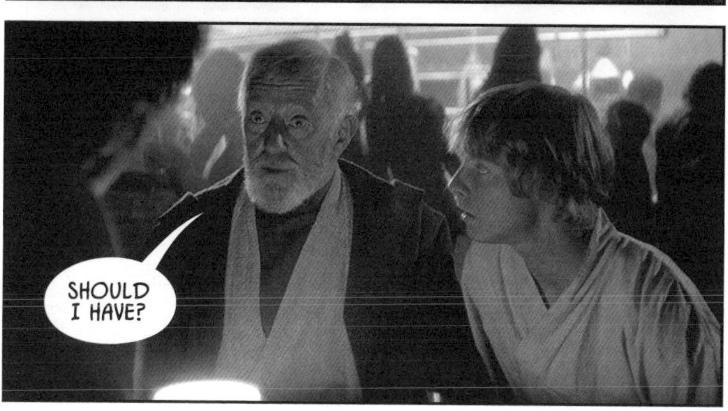
SHOULD I HAVE?

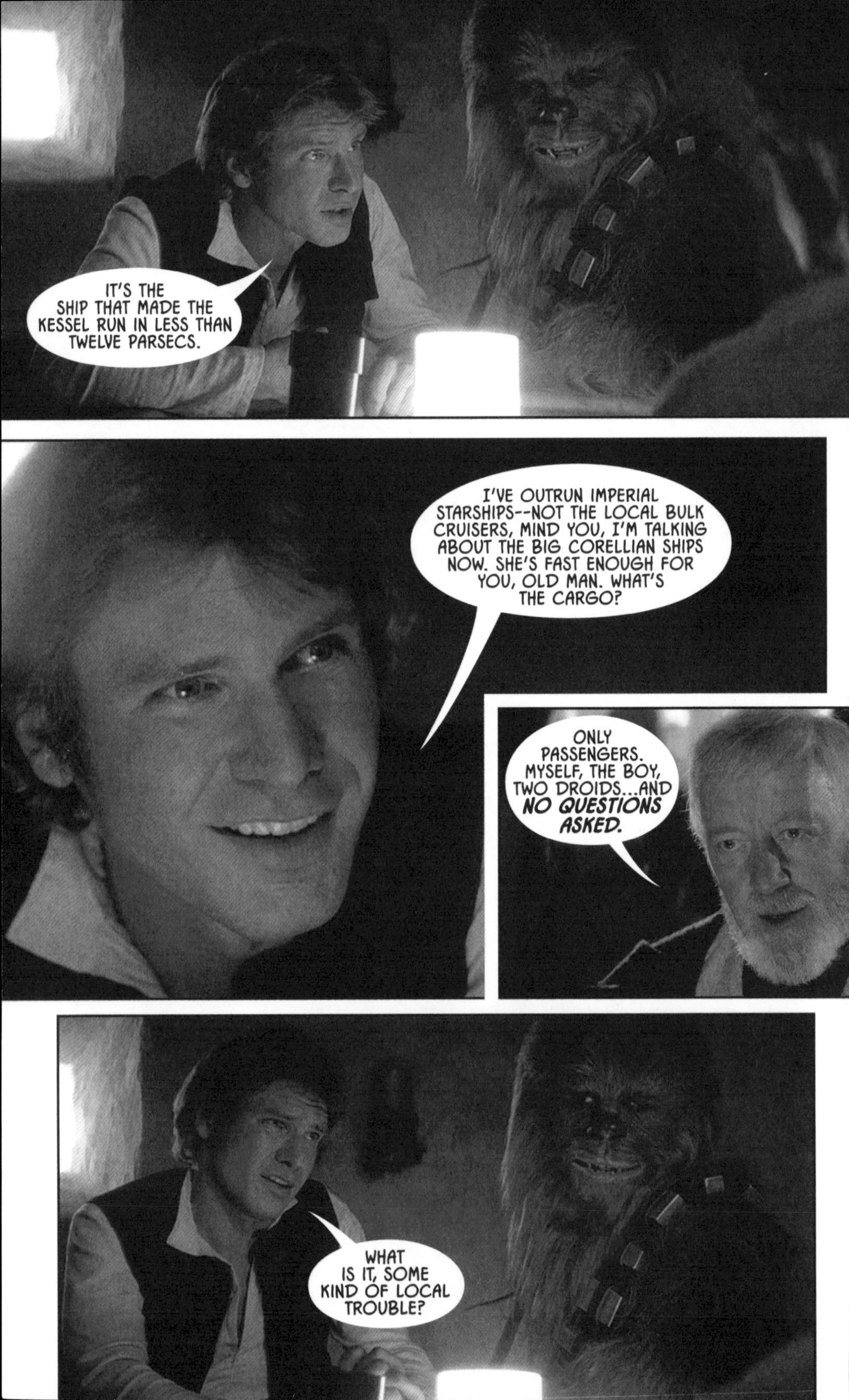
IT'S THE SHIP THAT MADE THE KESSEL RUN IN LESS THAN TWELVE PARSECS.
I'VE OUTRUN IMPERIAL STARSHIPS--NOT THE LOCAL BULK CRUISERS, MIND YOU, I'M TALKING ABOUT THE BIG CORELLIAN SHIPS NOW. SHE'S FAST ENOUGH FOR YOU, OLD MAN. WHAT'S THE CARGO?
ONLY PASSENGERS. MYSELF, THE BOY, TWO DROIDS...AND ***NO QUESTIONS ASKED.***
WHAT IS IT, SOME KIND OF LOCAL TROUBLE?

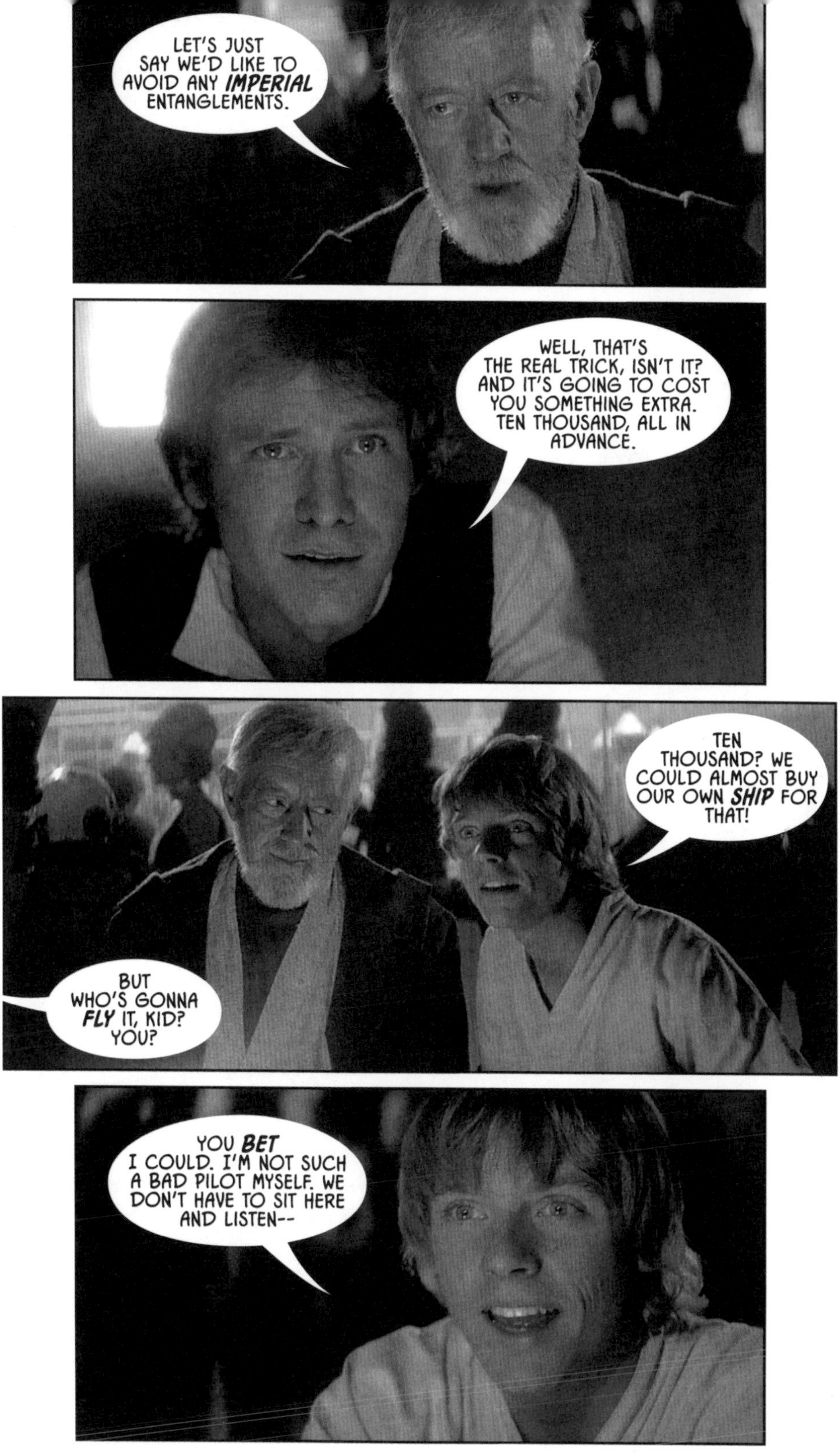
LET'S JUST SAY WE'D LIKE TO AVOID ANY IMPERIAL ENTANGLEMENTS.
WELL, THAT'S THE REAL TRICK, ISN'T IT? AND IT'S GOING TO COST YOU SOMETHING EXTRA. TEN THOUSAND, ALL IN ADVANCE.
TEN THOUSAND? WE COULD ALMOST BUY OUR OWN SHIP FOR THAT!
BUT WHO'S GONNA FLY IT, KID? YOU?
YOU BET I COULD. I'M NOT SUCH A BAD PILOT MYSELF. WE DON'T HAVE TO SIT HERE AND LISTEN--

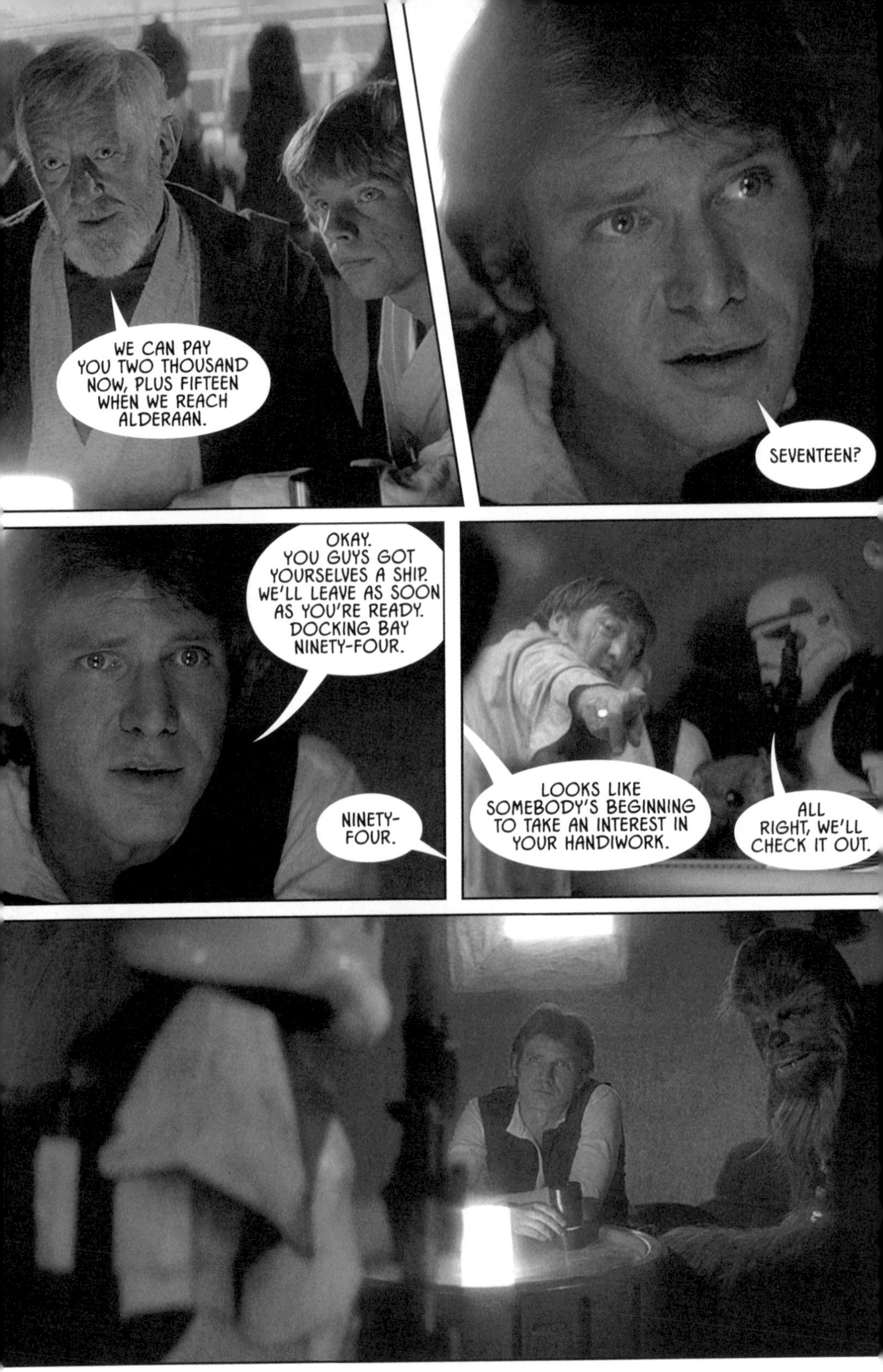
WE CAN PAY YOU TWO THOUSAND NOW, PLUS FIFTEEN WHEN WE REACH ALDERAAN.
SEVENTEEN?
OKAY. YOU GUYS GOT YOURSELVES A SHIP. WE'LL LEAVE AS SOON AS YOU'RE READY. DOCKING BAY NINETY-FOUR.
NINETY-FOUR.
LOOKS LIKE SOMEBODY'S BEGINNING TO TAKE AN INTEREST IN YOUR HANDIWORK.
ALL RIGHT, WE'LL CHECK IT OUT.

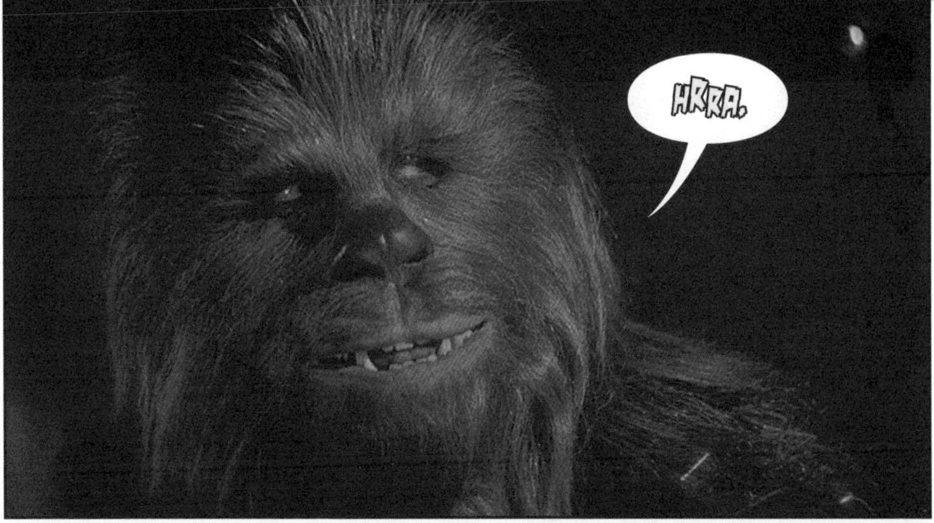
HRRA.

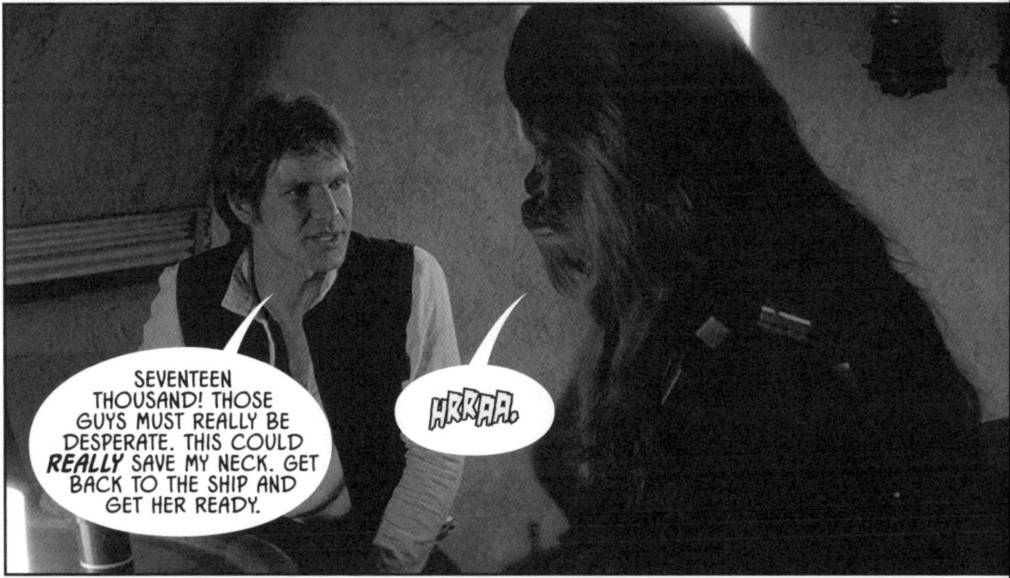
SEVENTEEN THOUSAND! THOSE GUYS MUST REALLY BE DESPERATE. THIS COULD ***REALLY*** SAVE MY NECK. GET BACK TO THE SHIP AND GET HER READY.
HRRAA.

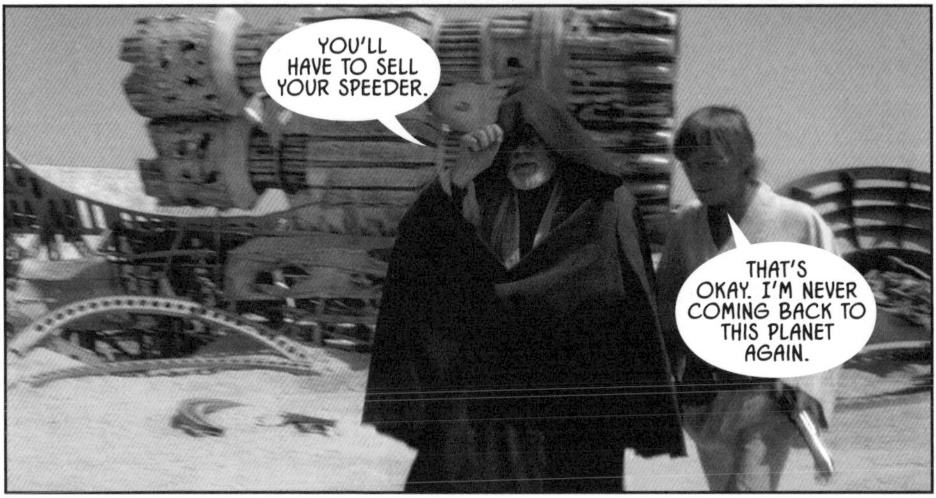
YOU'LL HAVE TO SELL YOUR SPEEDER.
THAT'S OKAY. I'M NEVER COMING BACK TO THIS PLANET AGAIN.

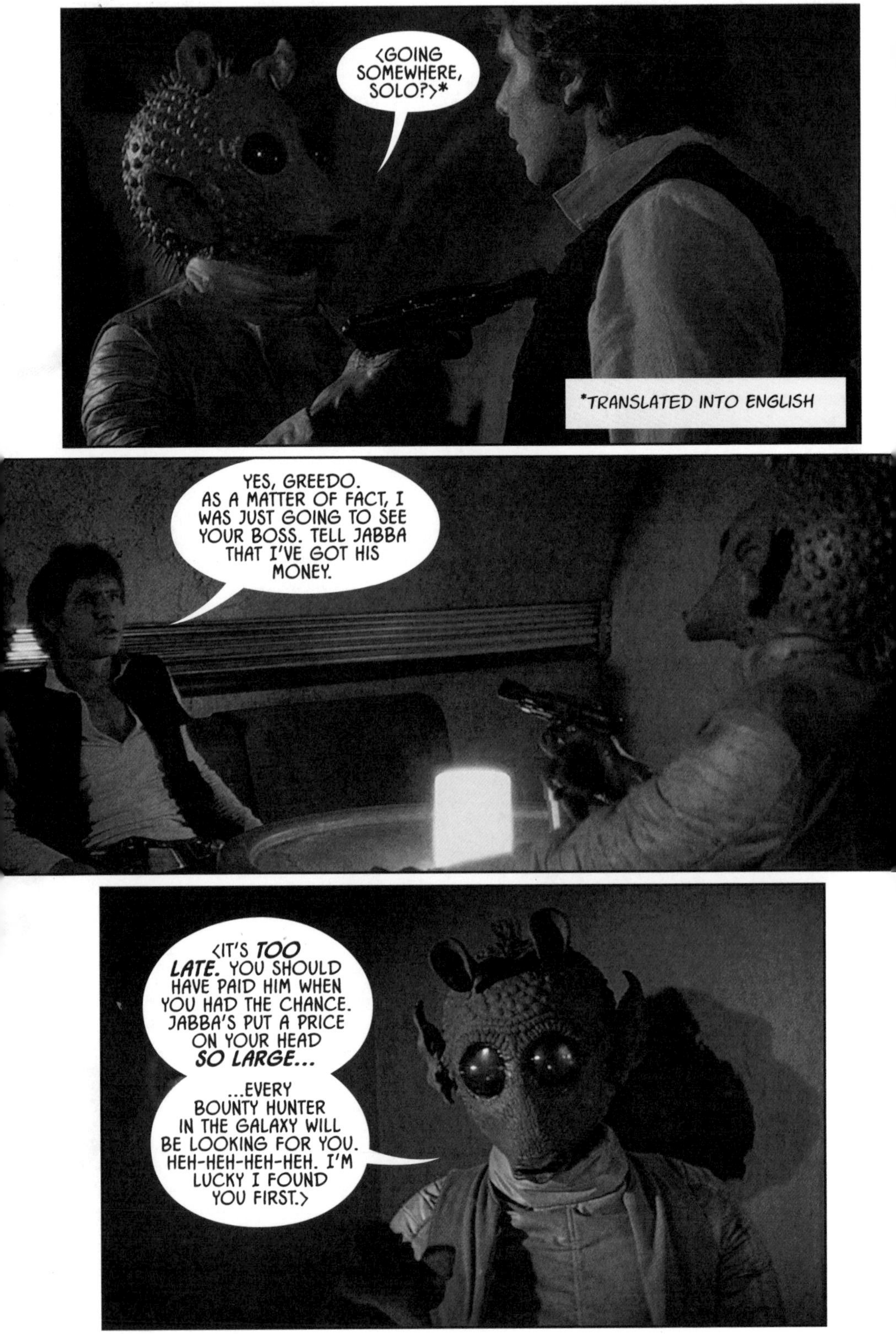
<GOING SOMEWHERE, SOLO?>*
*TRANSLATED INTO ENGLISH
YES, GREEDO. AS A MATTER OF FACT, I WAS JUST GOING TO SEE YOUR BOSS. TELL JABBA THAT I'VE GOT HIS MONEY.
<IT'S **TOO LATE.** YOU SHOULD HAVE PAID HIM WHEN YOU HAD THE CHANCE. JABBA'S PUT A PRICE ON YOUR HEAD **SO LARGE...**
...EVERY BOUNTY HUNTER IN THE GALAXY WILL BE LOOKING FOR YOU. HEH-HEH-HEH-HEH. I'M LUCKY I FOUND YOU FIRST.>

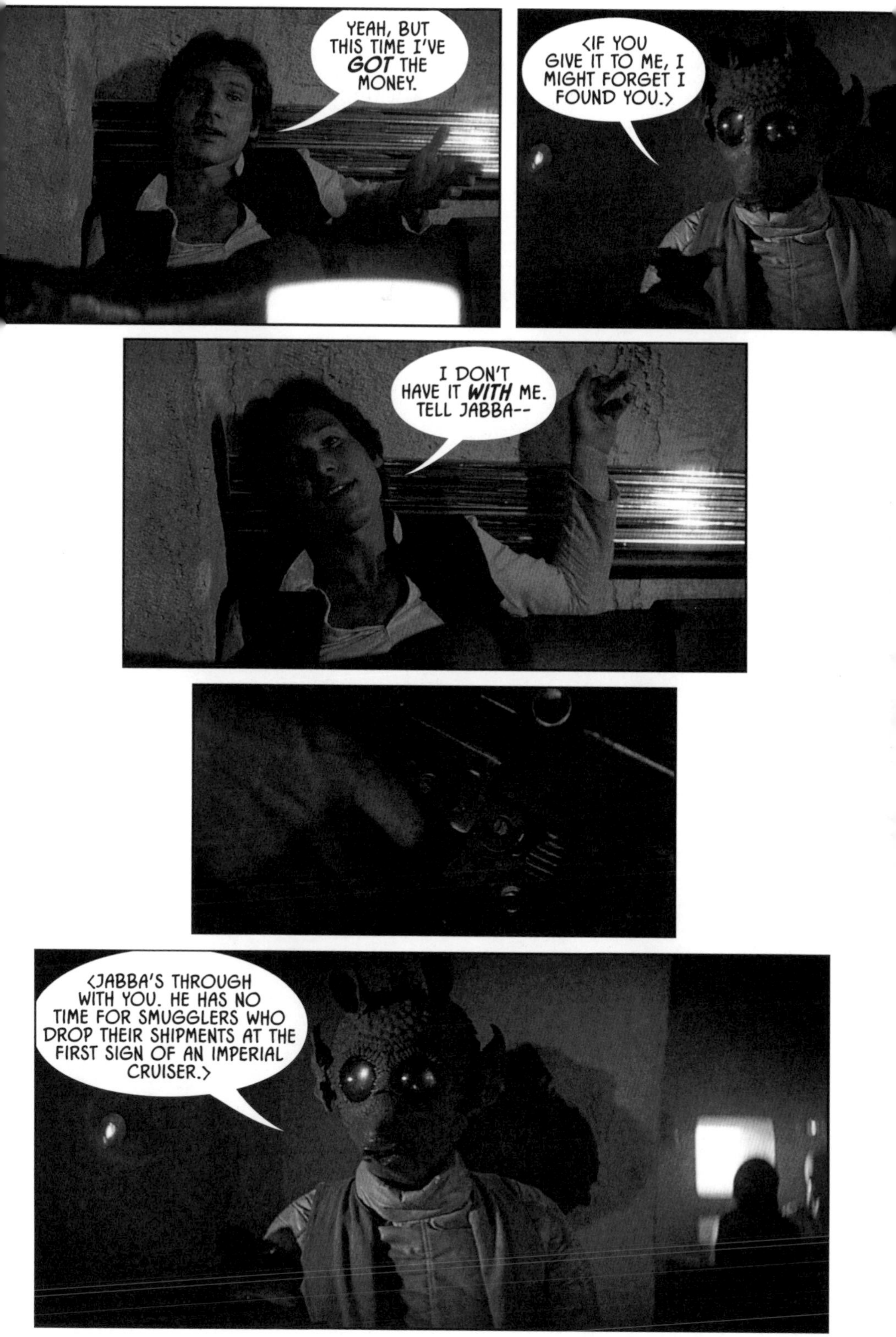
YEAH, BUT THIS TIME I'VE **GOT** THE MONEY.
<IF YOU GIVE IT TO ME, I MIGHT FORGET I FOUND YOU.>
I DON'T HAVE IT **WITH** ME. TELL JABBA--
<JABBA'S THROUGH WITH YOU. HE HAS NO TIME FOR SMUGGLERS WHO DROP THEIR SHIPMENTS AT THE FIRST SIGN OF AN IMPERIAL CRUISER.>

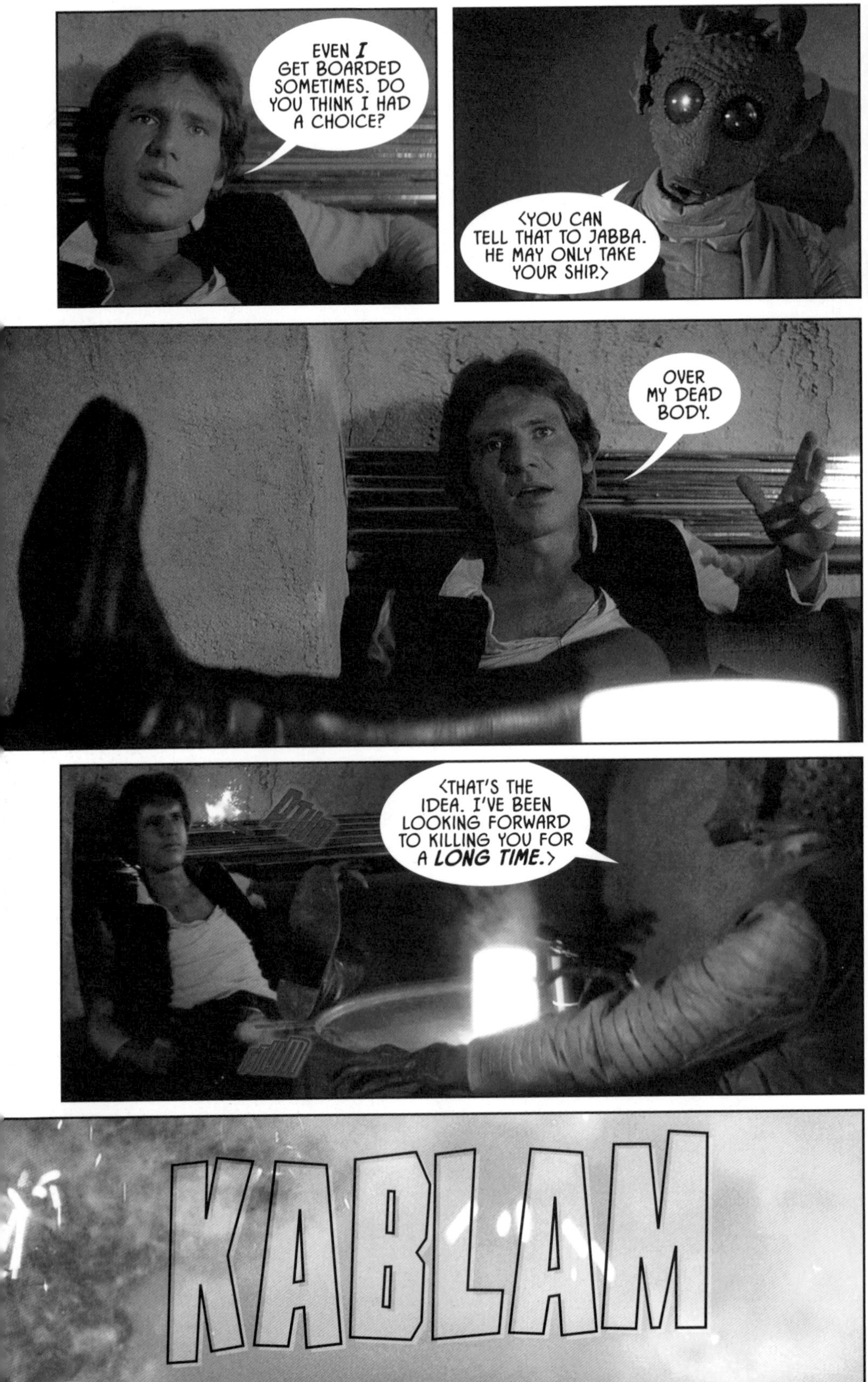
EVEN *I* GET BOARDED SOMETIMES. DO YOU THINK I HAD A CHOICE?
<YOU CAN TELL THAT TO JABBA. HE MAY ONLY TAKE YOUR SHIP.>
OVER MY DEAD BODY.
<THAT'S THE IDEA. I'VE BEEN LOOKING FORWARD TO KILLING YOU FOR A ***LONG TIME.***>
KABLAM

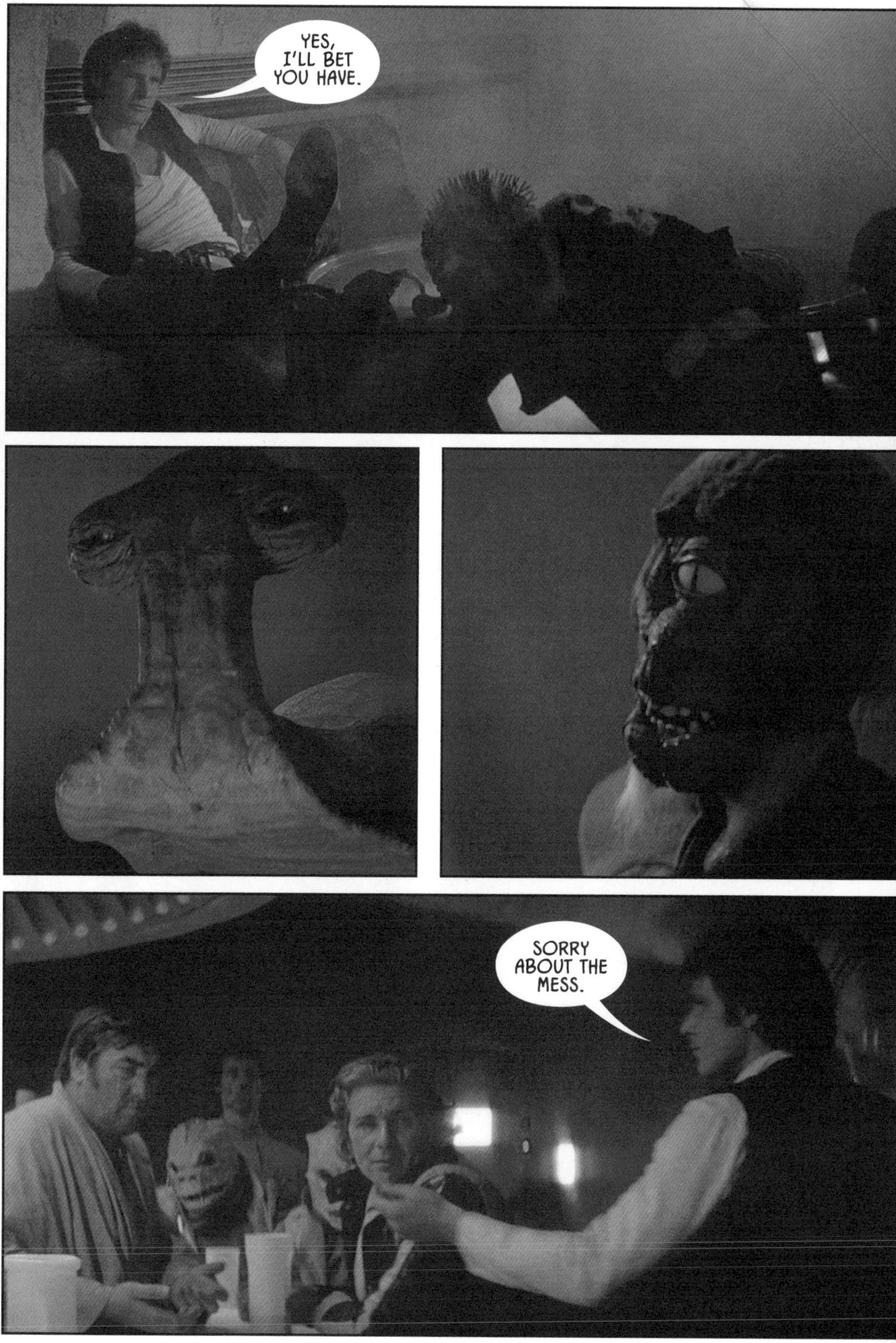
YES, I'LL BET YOU HAVE.
SORRY ABOUT THE MESS.

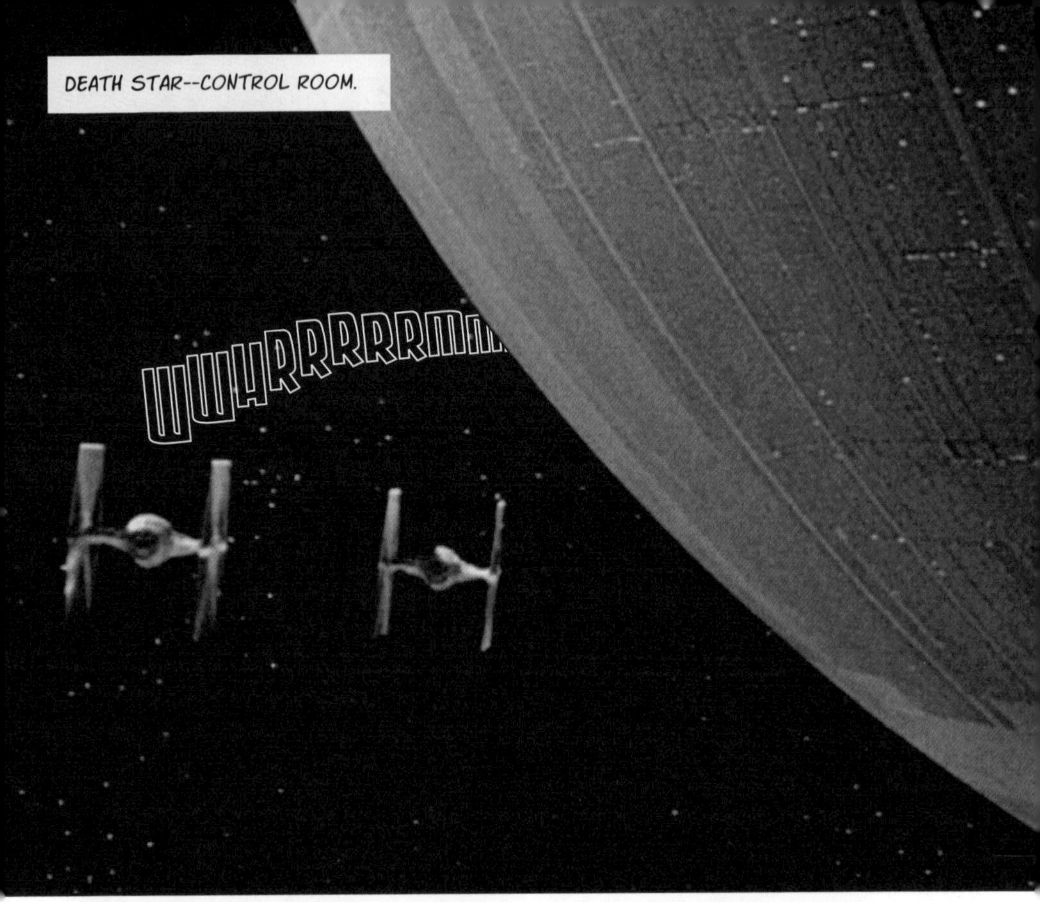
DEATH STAR--CONTROL ROOM.
WWHRRRRRMM

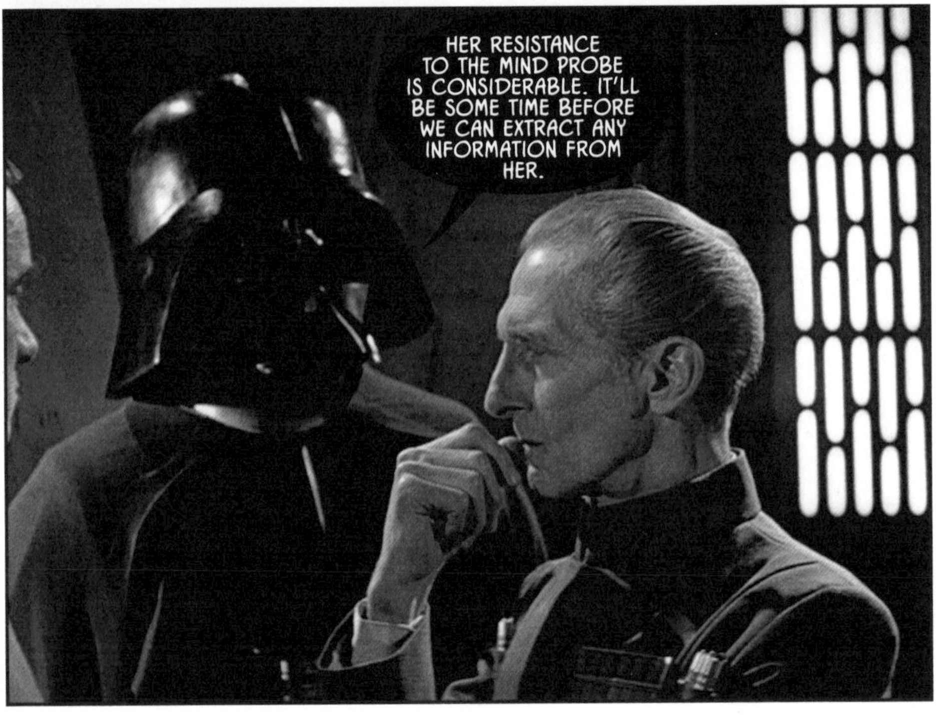
HER RESISTANCE TO THE MIND PROBE IS CONSIDERABLE. IT'LL BE SOME TIME BEFORE WE CAN EXTRACT ANY INFORMATION FROM HER.

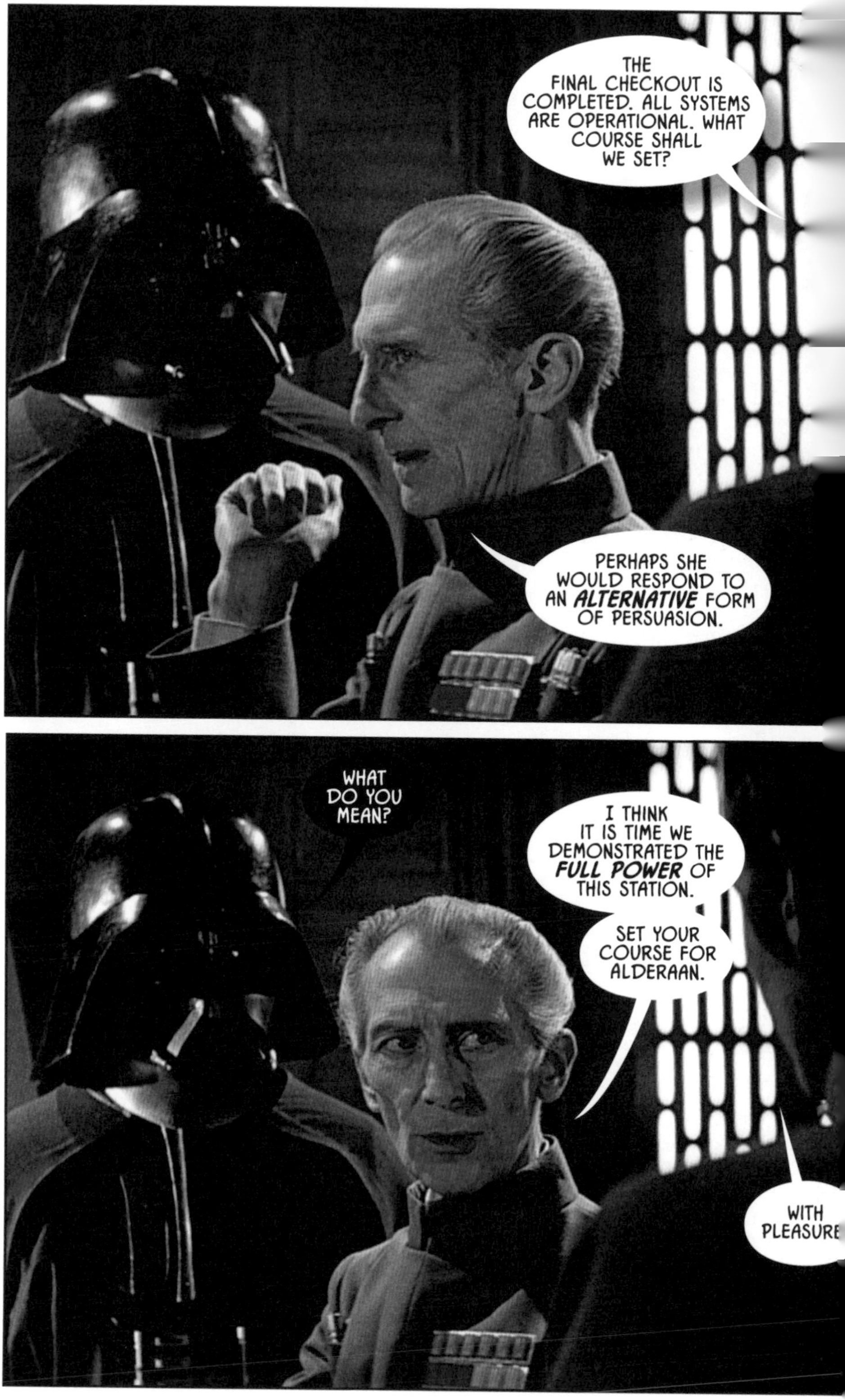
THE FINAL CHECKOUT IS COMPLETED. ALL SYSTEMS ARE OPERATIONAL. WHAT COURSE SHALL WE SET?
PERHAPS SHE WOULD RESPOND TO AN ALTERNATIVE FORM OF PERSUASION.
WHAT DO YOU MEAN?
I THINK IT IS TIME WE DEMONSTRATED THE FULL POWER OF THIS STATION.
SET YOUR COURSE FOR ALDERAAN.
WITH PLEASURE

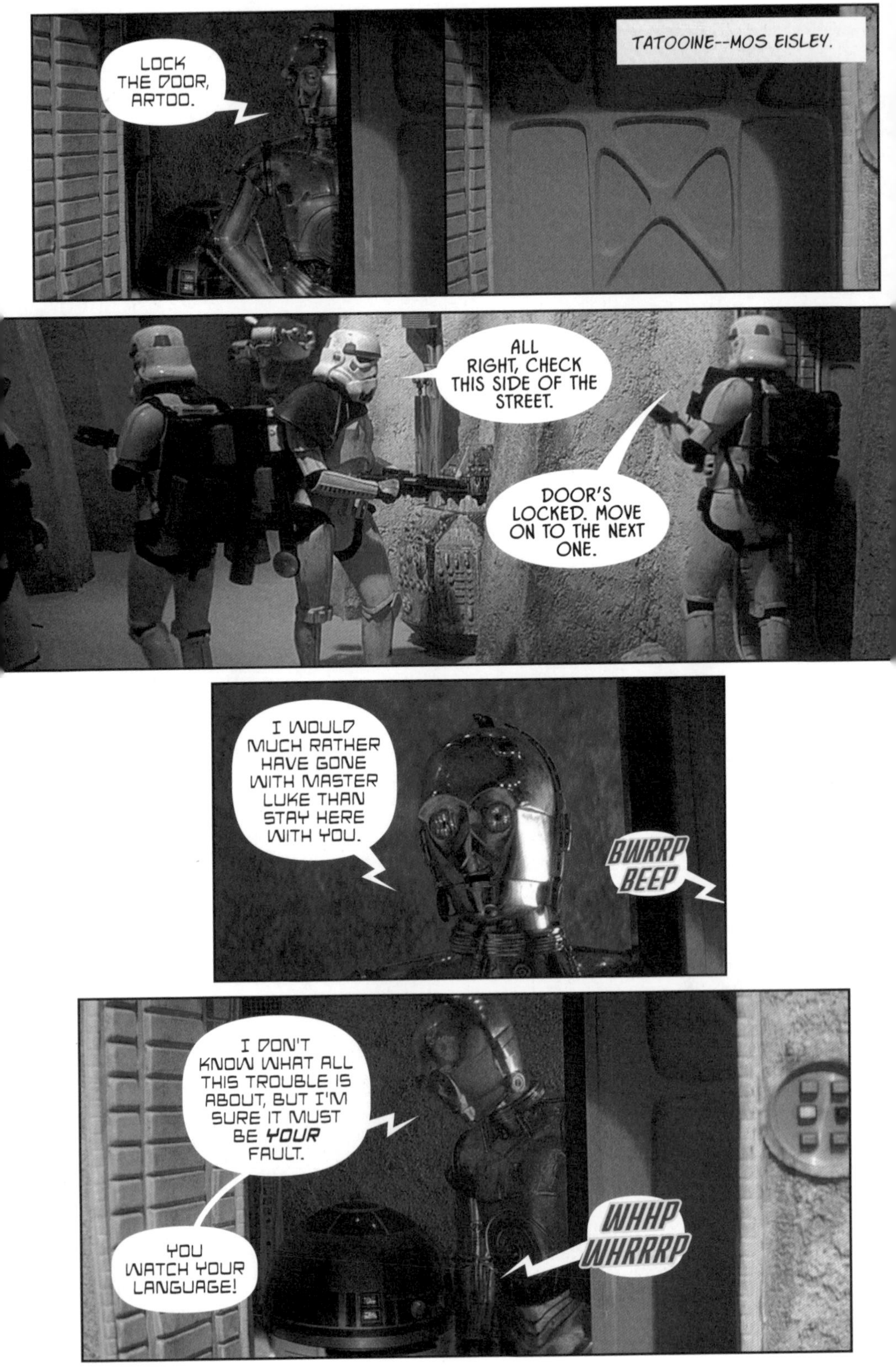
TATOOINE--MOS EISLEY.
LOCK THE DOOR, ARTOO.
ALL RIGHT, CHECK THIS SIDE OF THE STREET.
DOOR'S LOCKED. MOVE ON TO THE NEXT ONE.
I WOULD MUCH RATHER HAVE GONE WITH MASTER LUKE THAN STAY HERE WITH YOU.
BWRRP BEEP
I DON'T KNOW WHAT ALL THIS TROUBLE IS ABOUT, BUT I'M SURE IT MUST BE *YOUR* FAULT.
WHHP WHRRRP
YOU WATCH YOUR LANGUAGE!

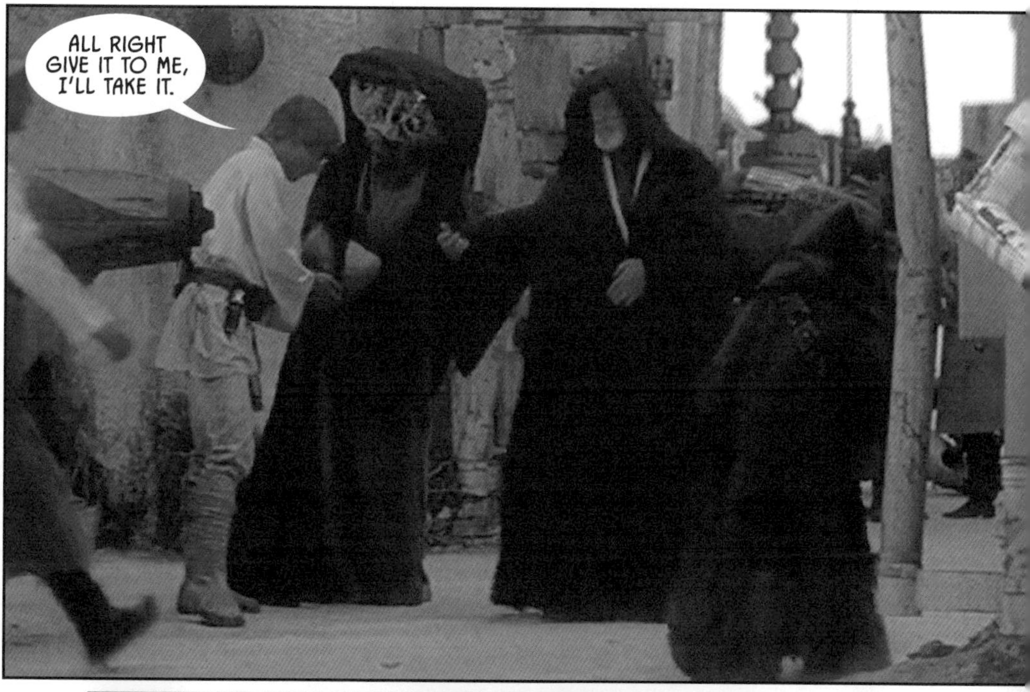
ALL RIGHT GIVE IT TO ME, I'LL TAKE IT.

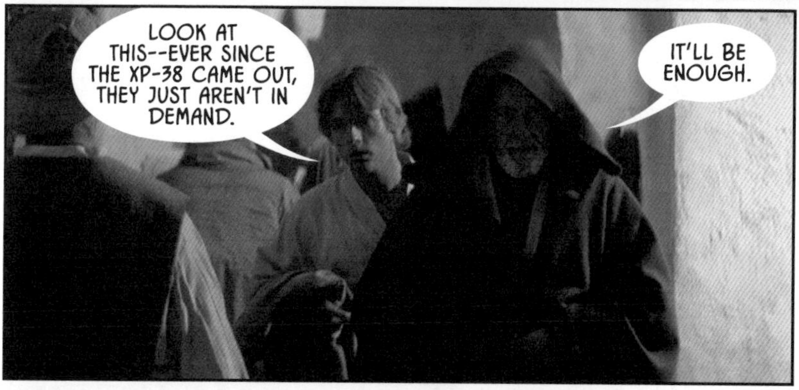
LOOK AT THIS--EVER SINCE THE XP-38 CAME OUT, THEY JUST AREN'T IN DEMAND.
IT'LL BE ENOUGH.

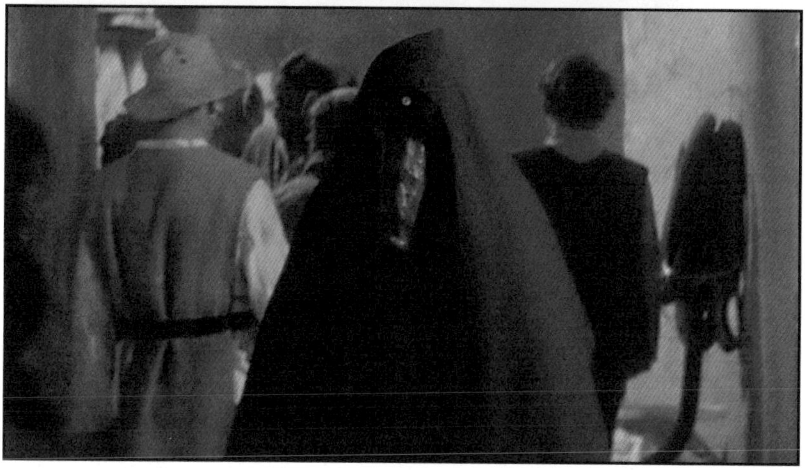

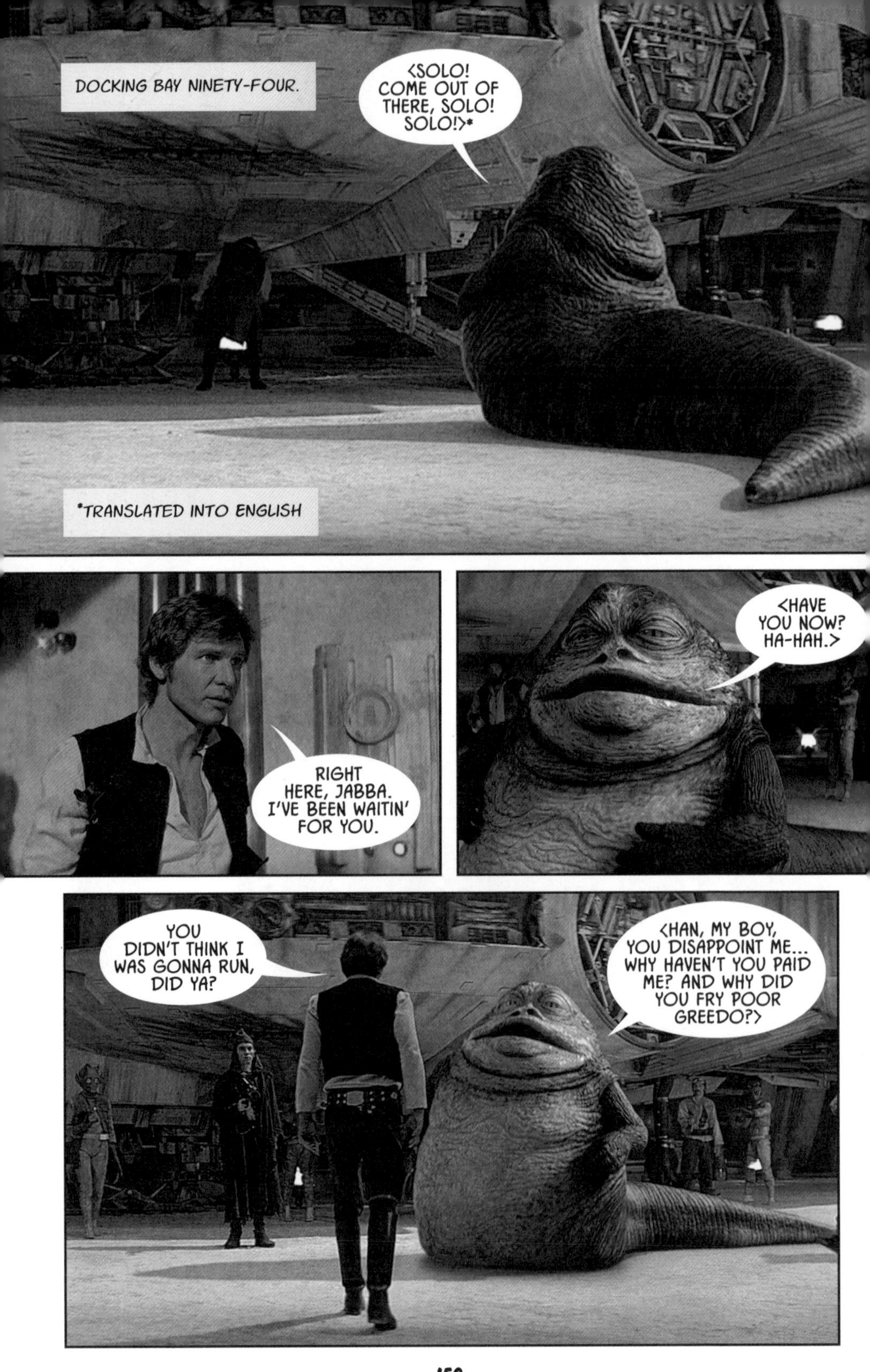
DOCKING BAY NINETY-FOUR.
<SOLO! COME OUT OF THERE, SOLO! SOLO!>*
*TRANSLATED INTO ENGLISH
RIGHT HERE, JABBA. I'VE BEEN WAITIN' FOR YOU.
<HAVE YOU NOW? HA-HAH.>
YOU DIDN'T THINK I WAS GONNA RUN, DID YA?
<HAN, MY BOY, YOU DISAPPOINT ME... WHY HAVEN'T YOU PAID ME? AND WHY DID YOU FRY POOR GREEDO?>

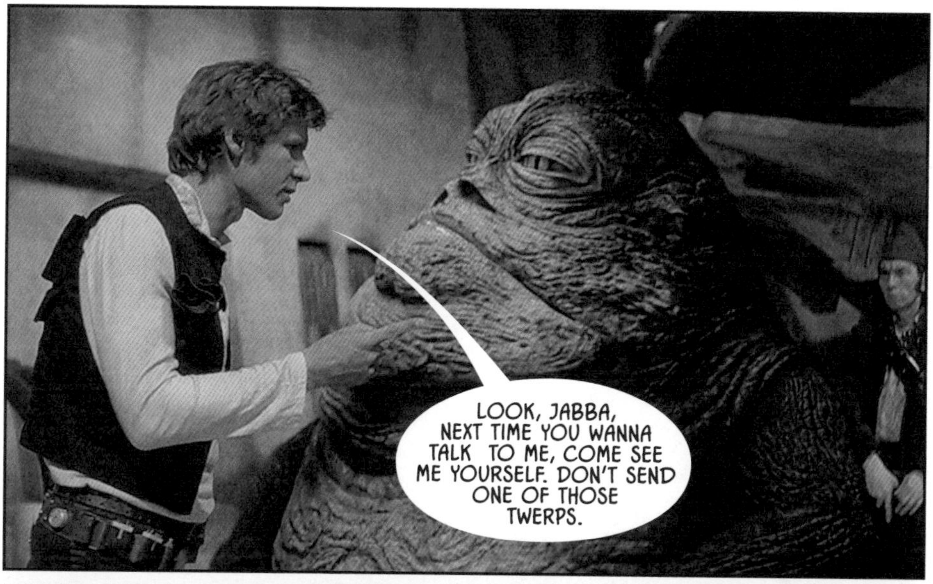
LOOK, JABBA, NEXT TIME YOU WANNA TALK TO ME, COME SEE ME YOURSELF. DON'T SEND ONE OF THOSE TWERPS.

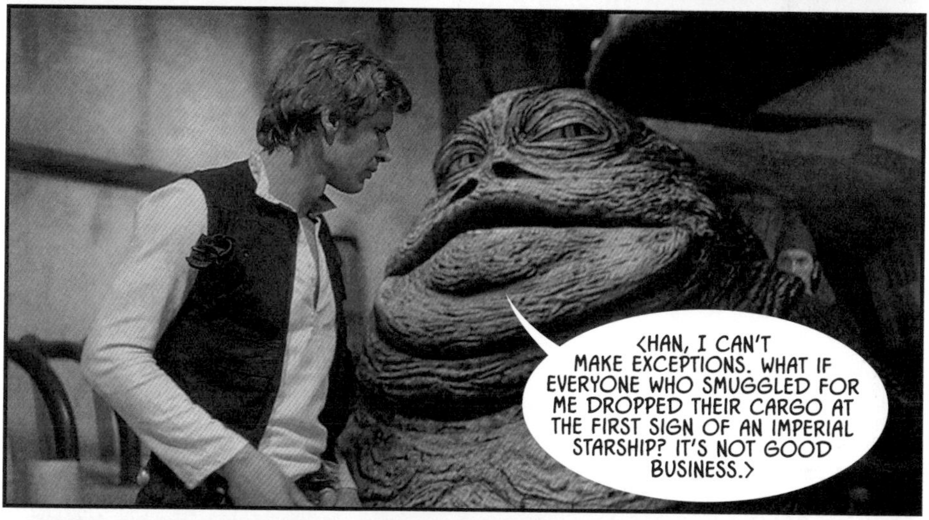
<HAN, I CAN'T MAKE EXCEPTIONS. WHAT IF EVERYONE WHO SMUGGLED FOR ME DROPPED THEIR CARGO AT THE FIRST SIGN OF AN IMPERIAL STARSHIP? IT'S NOT GOOD BUSINESS.>

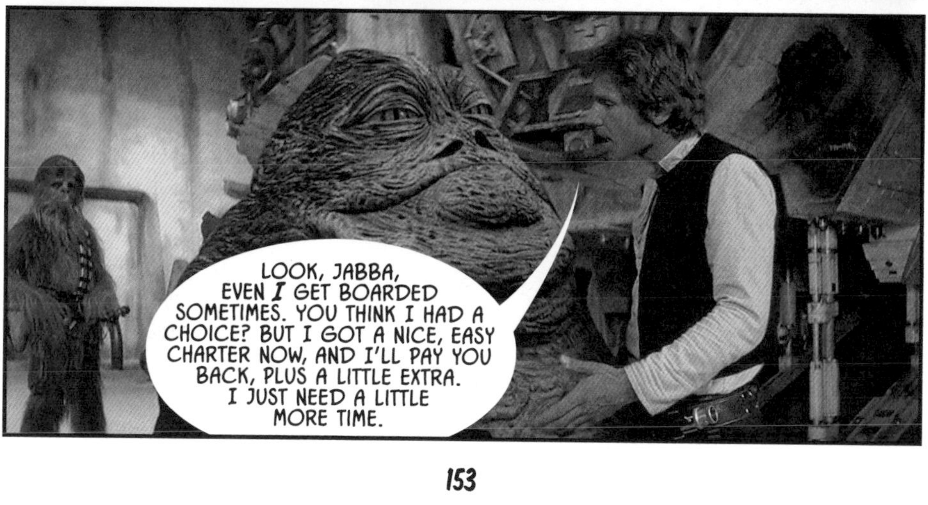
LOOK, JABBA, EVEN *I* GET BOARDED SOMETIMES. YOU THINK I HAD A CHOICE? BUT I GOT A NICE, EASY CHARTER NOW, AND I'LL PAY YOU BACK, PLUS A LITTLE EXTRA. I JUST NEED A LITTLE MORE TIME.

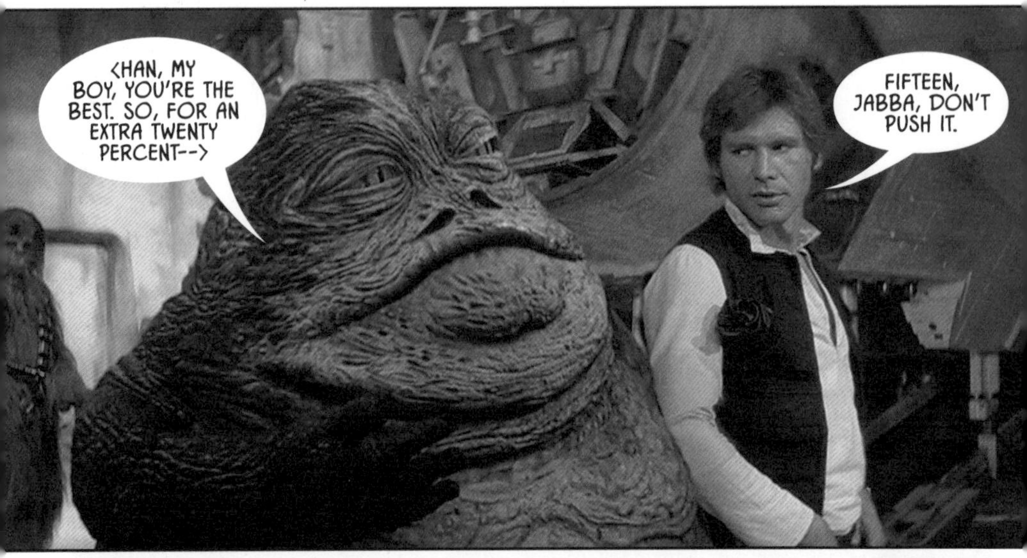
<HAN, MY BOY, YOU'RE THE BEST. SO, FOR AN EXTRA TWENTY PERCENT-->
FIFTEEN, JABBA, DON'T PUSH IT.

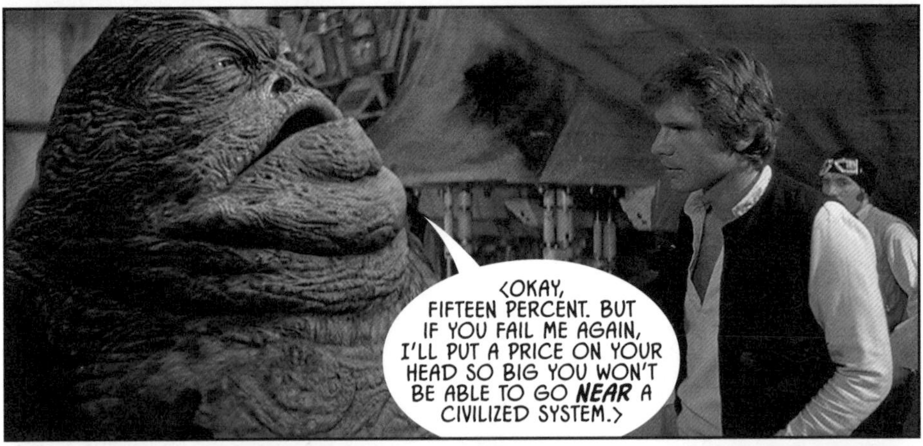
<OKAY, FIFTEEN PERCENT. BUT IF YOU FAIL ME AGAIN, I'LL PUT A PRICE ON YOUR HEAD SO BIG YOU WON'T BE ABLE TO GO ***NEAR*** A CIVILIZED SYSTEM.>

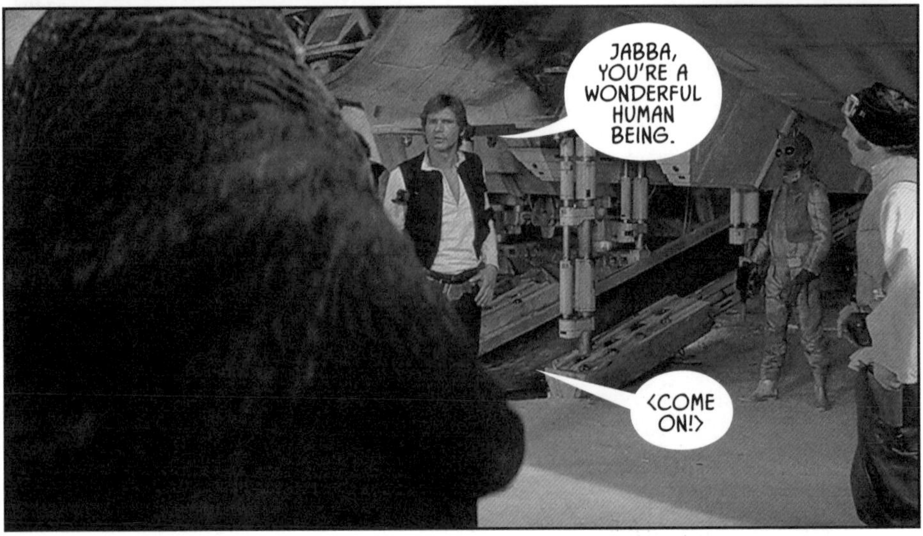
JABBA, YOU'RE A WONDERFUL HUMAN BEING.
<COME ON!>

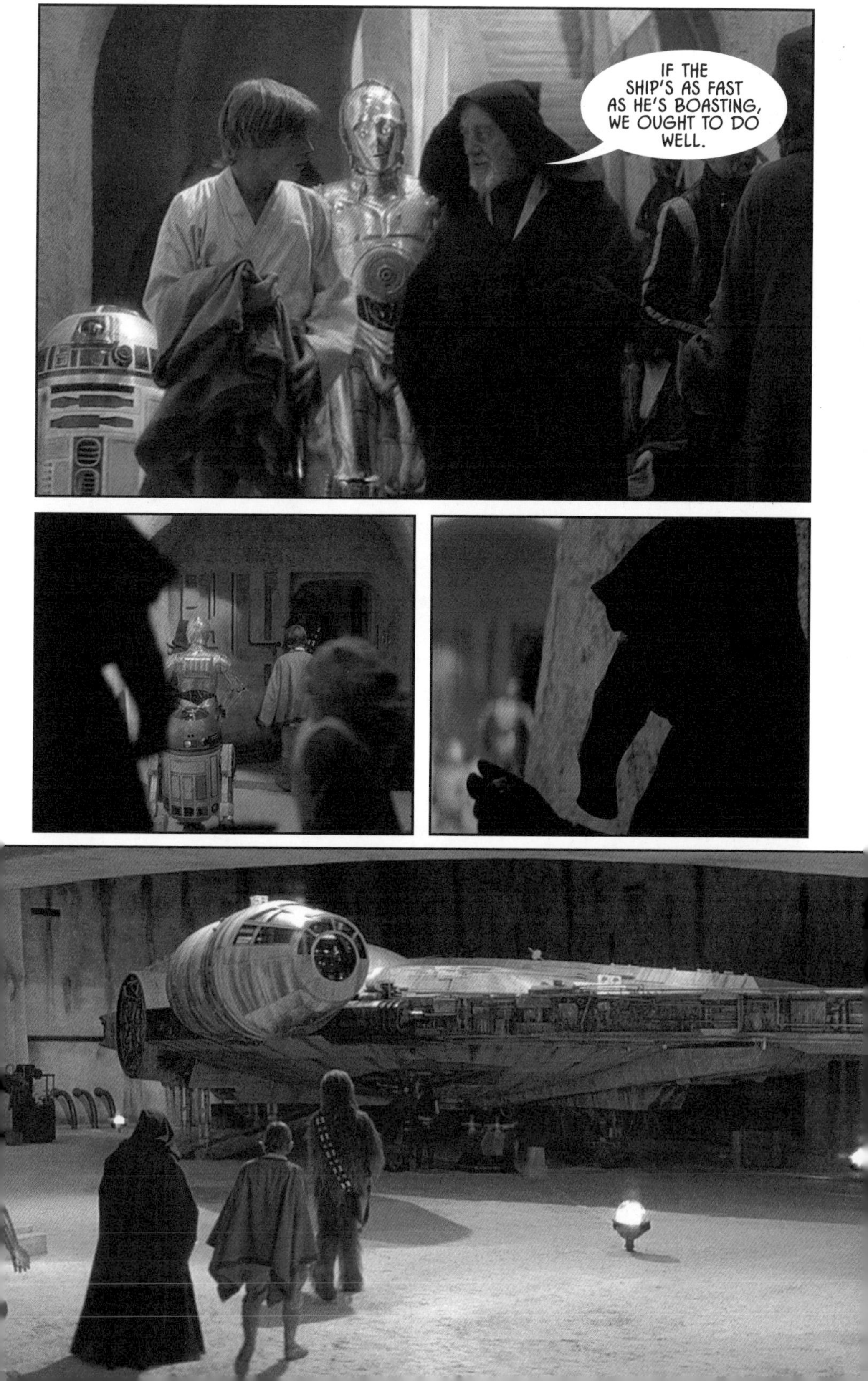
IF THE SHIP'S AS FAST AS HE'S BOASTING, WE OUGHT TO DO WELL.

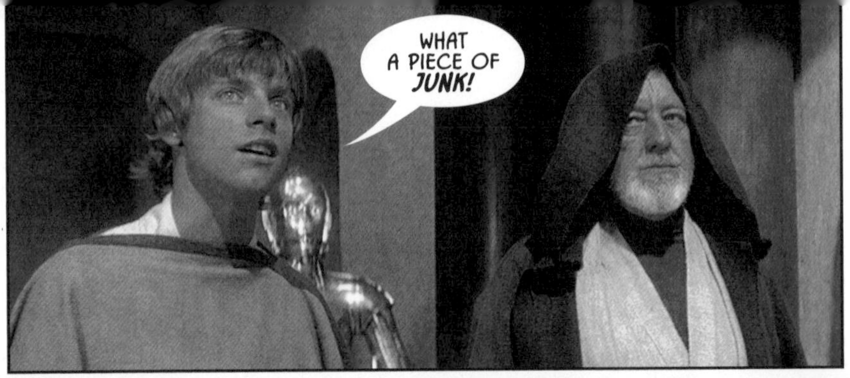
WHAT A PIECE OF *JUNK!*

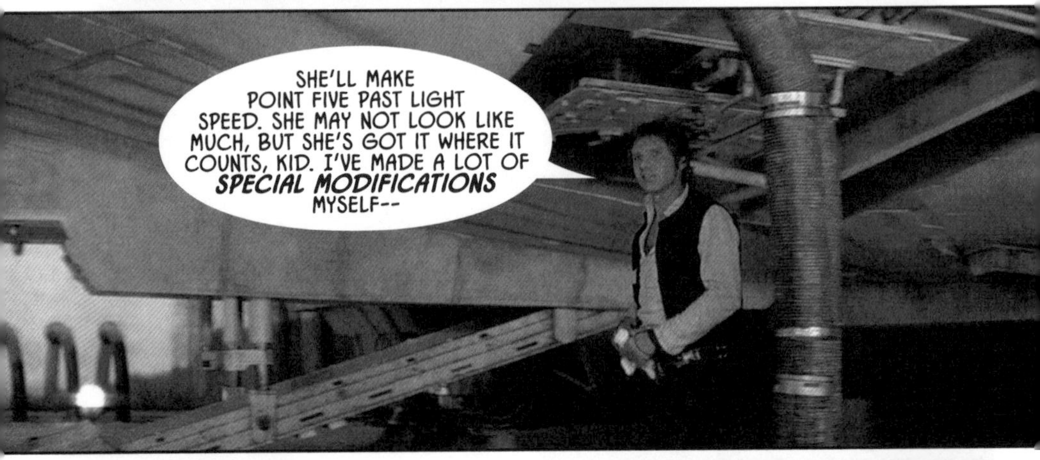
SHE'LL MAKE POINT FIVE PAST LIGHT SPEED. SHE MAY NOT LOOK LIKE MUCH, BUT SHE'S GOT IT WHERE IT COUNTS, KID. I'VE MADE A LOT OF ***SPECIAL MODIFICATIONS*** MYSELF--

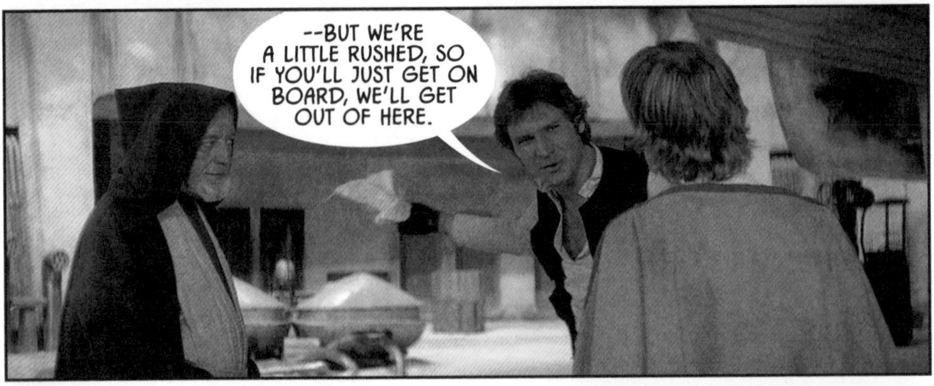
--BUT WE'RE A LITTLE RUSHED, SO IF YOU'LL JUST GET ON BOARD, WE'LL GET OUT OF HERE.

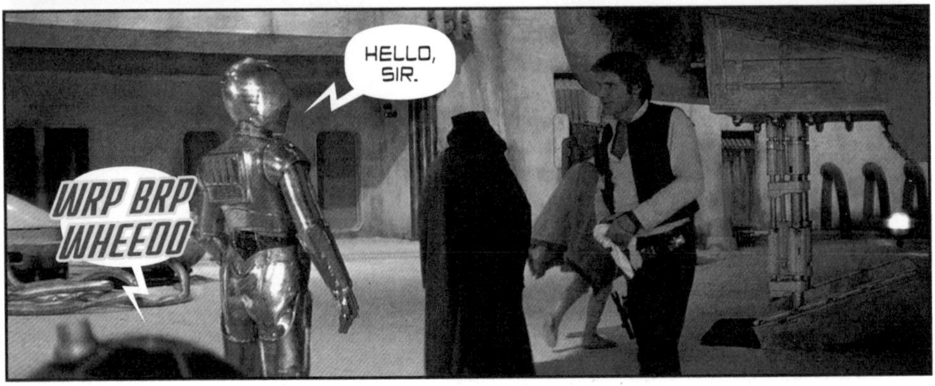
HELLO, SIR.
WRP BRP WHEEDO

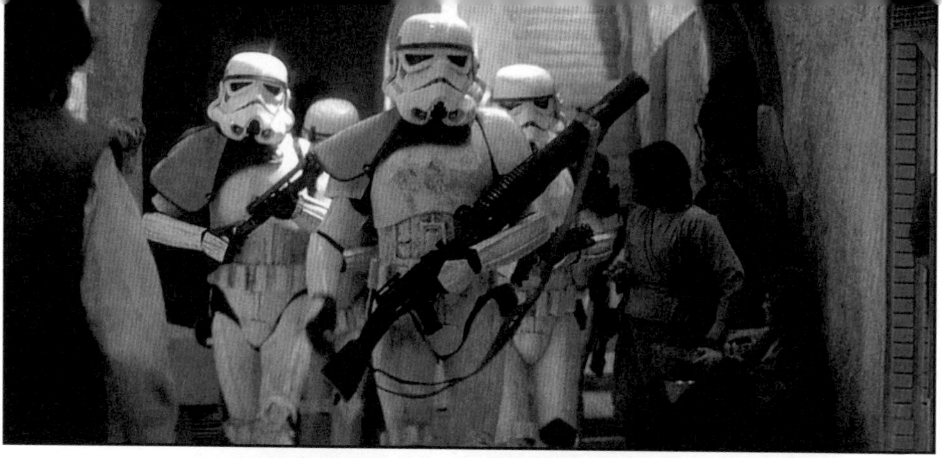

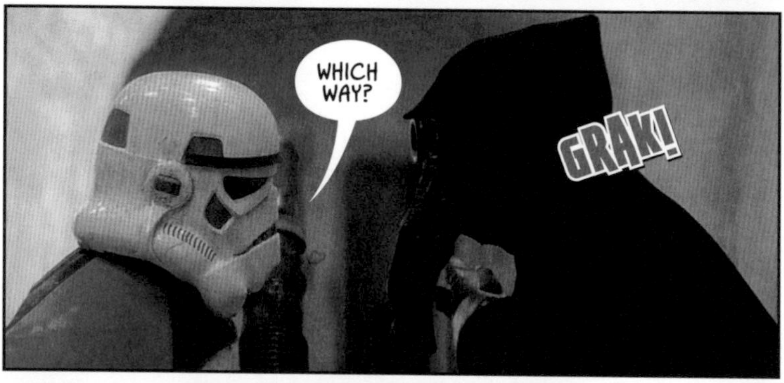
WHICH WAY?
GRAK!

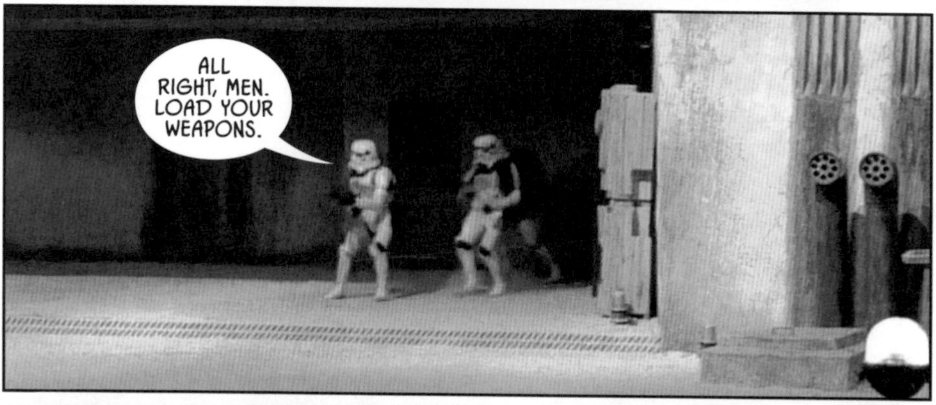
ALL RIGHT, MEN. LOAD YOUR WEAPONS.

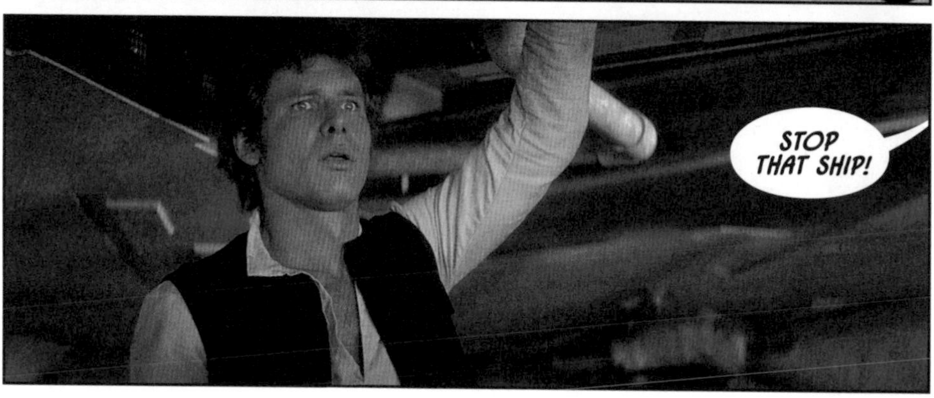
STOP THAT SHIP!

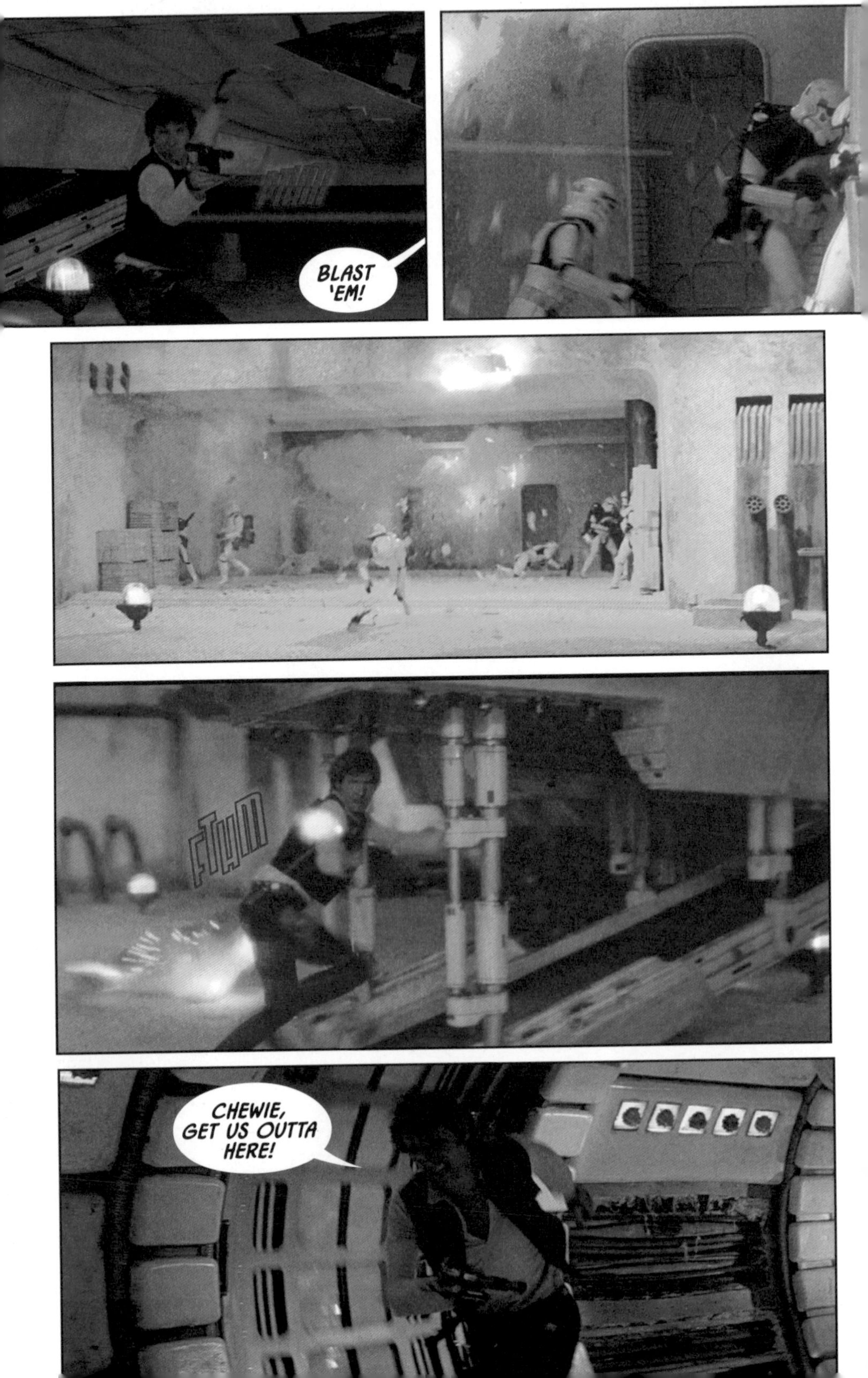
BLAST 'EM!
FTUM
CHEWIE, GET US OUTTA HERE!

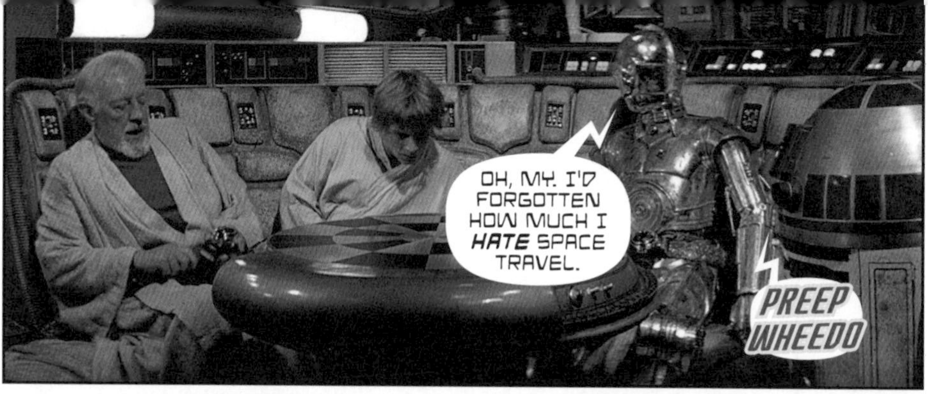
OH, MY. I'D FORGOTTEN HOW MUCH I *HATE* SPACE TRAVEL.
PREEP WHEEDO

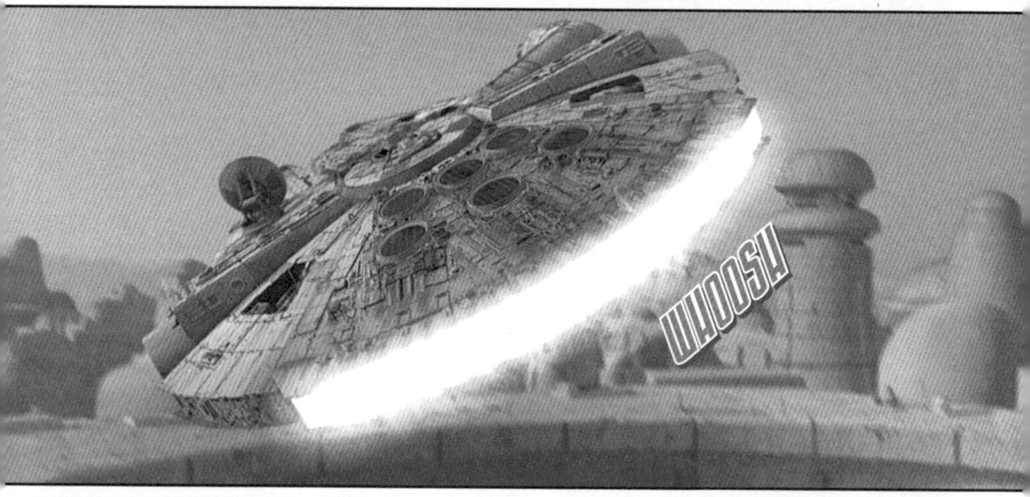
WHOOSH

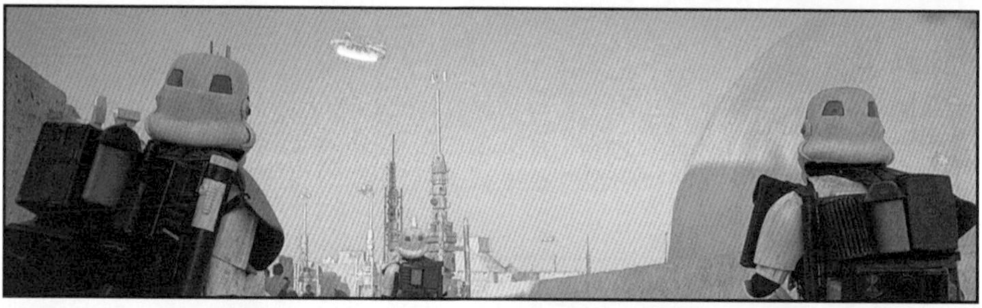

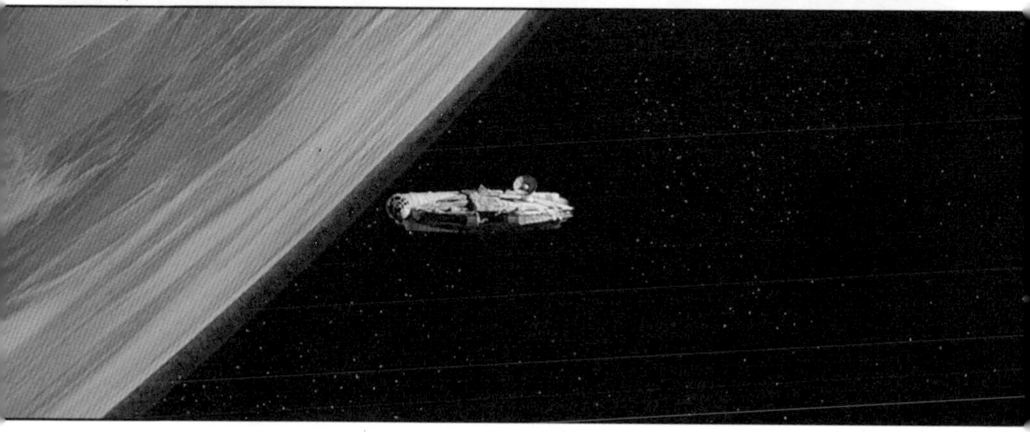

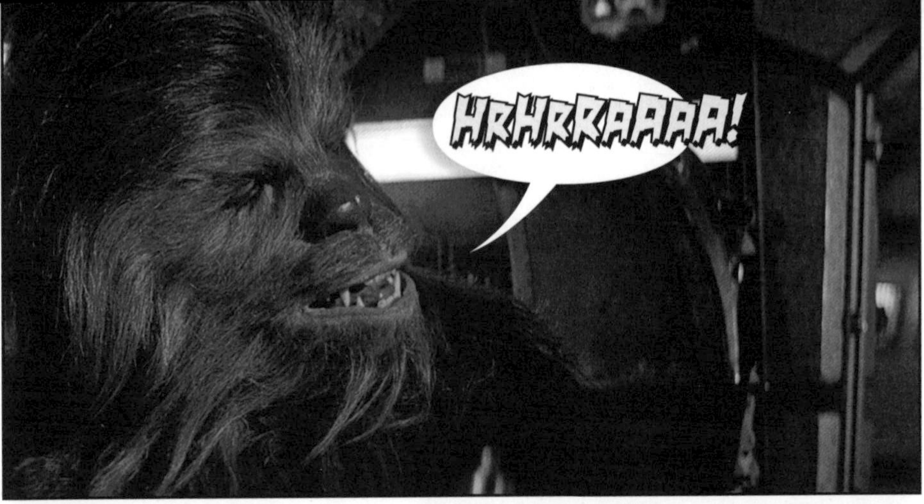
HRHRRAAAAA!

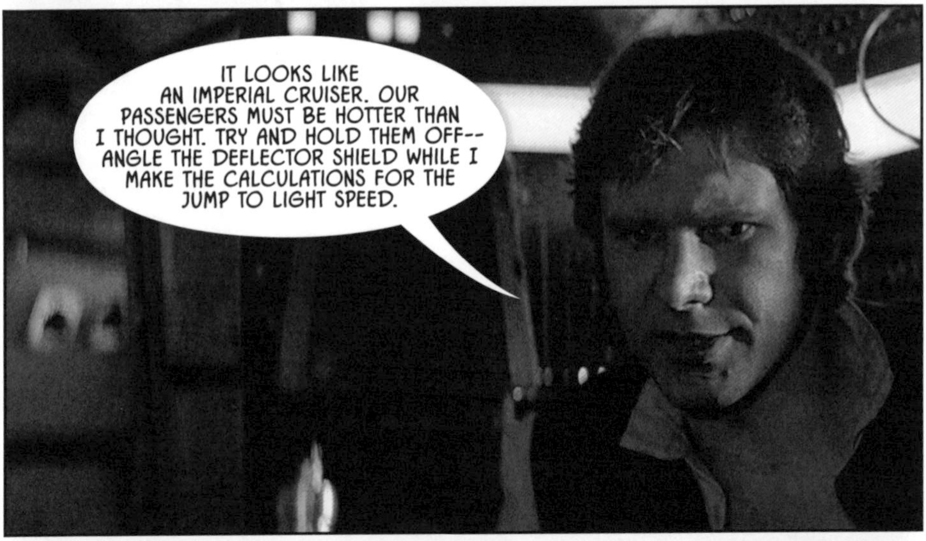
IT LOOKS LIKE AN IMPERIAL CRUISER. OUR PASSENGERS MUST BE HOTTER THAN I THOUGHT. TRY AND HOLD THEM OFF-- ANGLE THE DEFLECTOR SHIELD WHILE I MAKE THE CALCULATIONS FOR THE JUMP TO LIGHT SPEED.

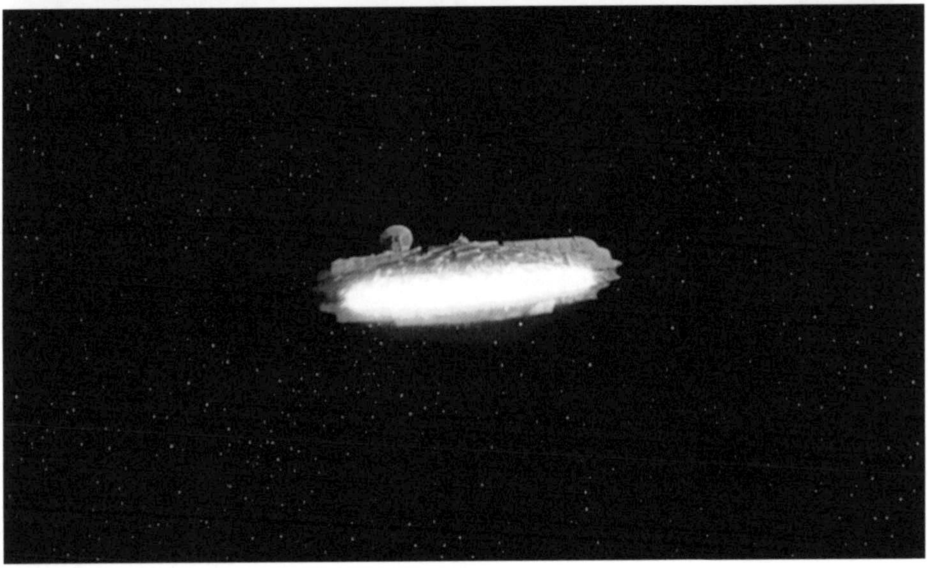

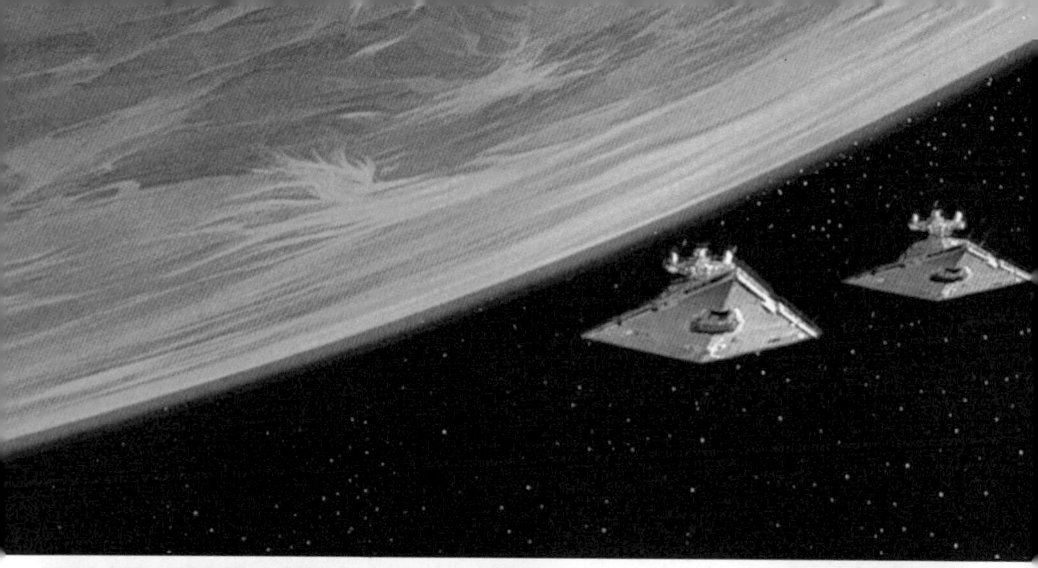

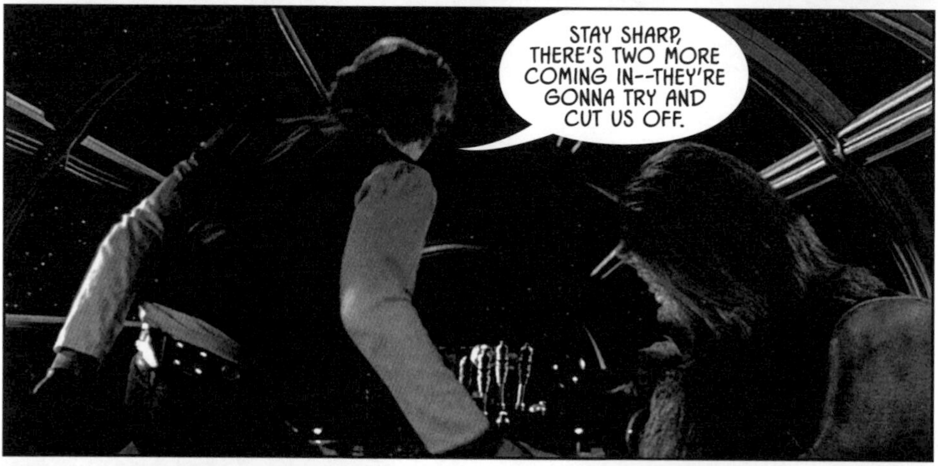
STAY SHARP, THERE'S TWO MORE COMING IN--THEY'RE GONNA TRY AND CUT US OFF.

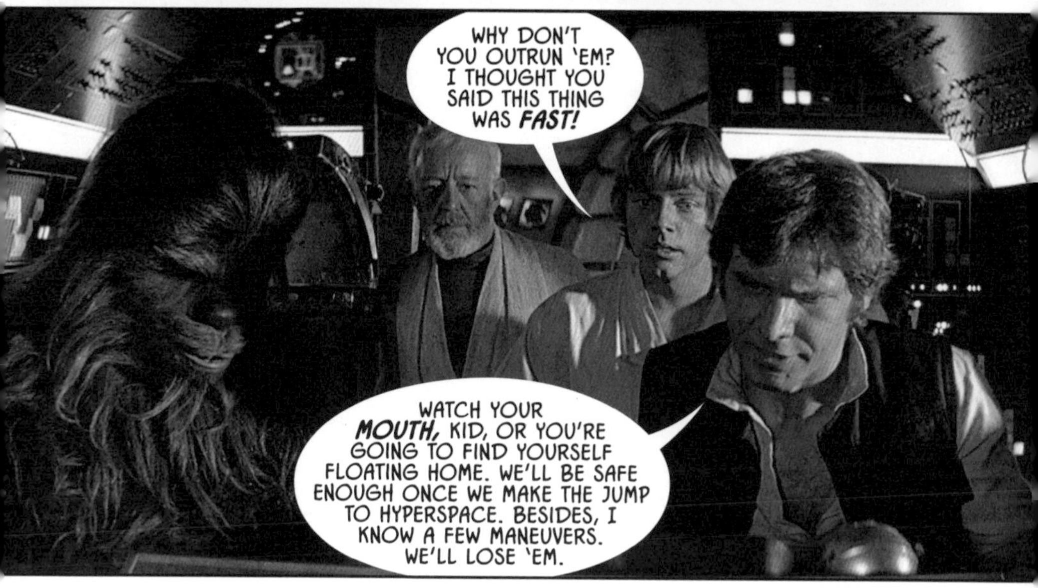
WHY DON'T YOU OUTRUN 'EM? I THOUGHT YOU SAID THIS THING WAS FAST!
WATCH YOUR MOUTH, KID, OR YOU'RE GOING TO FIND YOURSELF FLOATING HOME. WE'LL BE SAFE ENOUGH ONCE WE MAKE THE JUMP TO HYPERSPACE. BESIDES, I KNOW A FEW MANEUVERS. WE'LL LOSE 'EM.

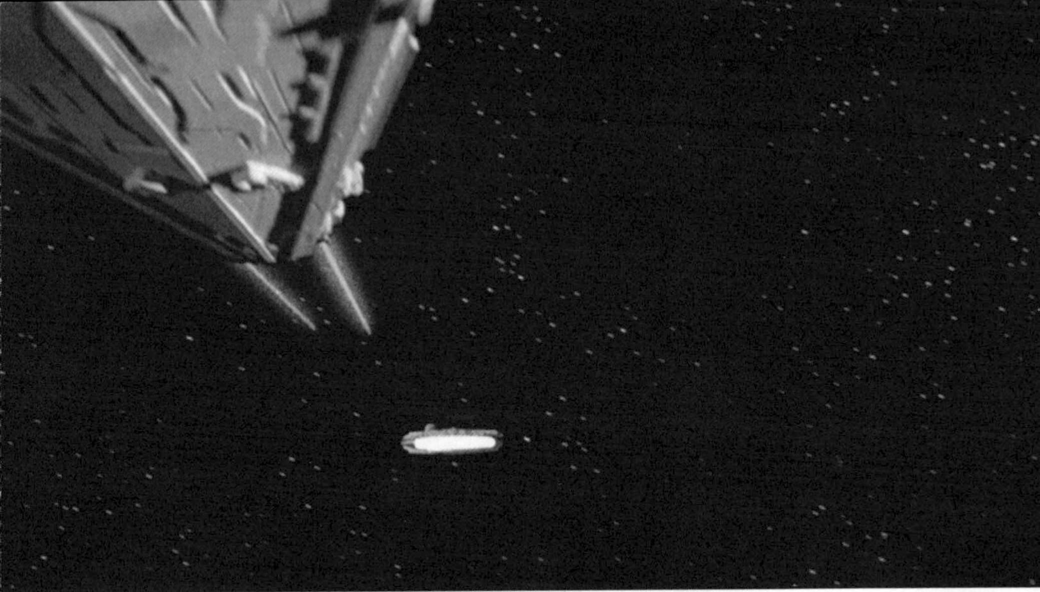

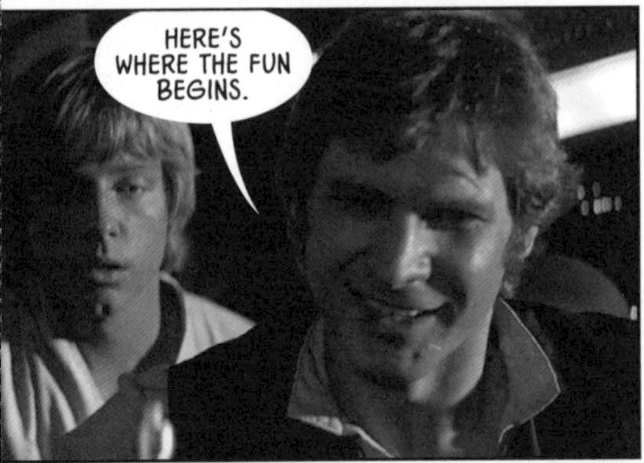
HERE'S WHERE THE FUN BEGINS.

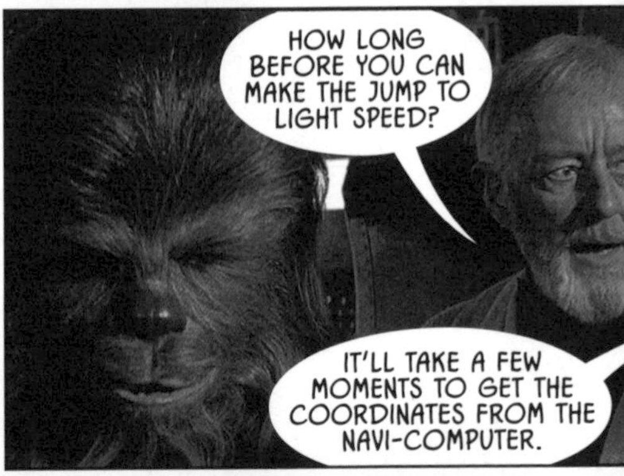
HOW LONG BEFORE YOU CAN MAKE THE JUMP TO LIGHT SPEED?
IT'LL TAKE A FEW MOMENTS TO GET THE COORDINATES FROM THE NAVI-COMPUTER.

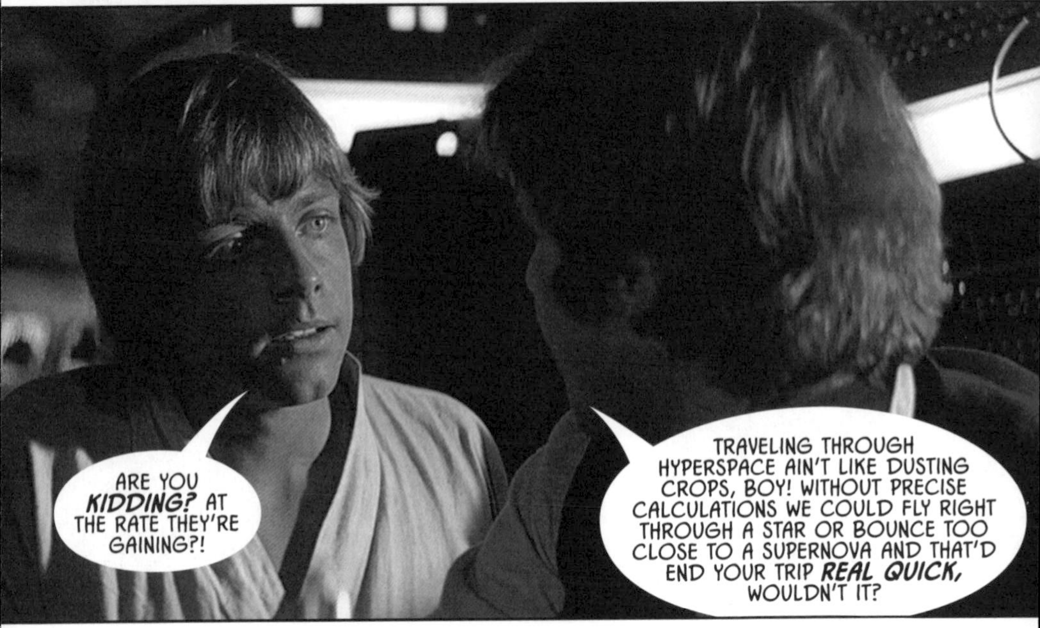
ARE YOU *KIDDING?* AT THE RATE THEY'RE GAINING?!
TRAVELING THROUGH HYPERSPACE AIN'T LIKE DUSTING CROPS, BOY! WITHOUT PRECISE CALCULATIONS WE COULD FLY RIGHT THROUGH A STAR OR BOUNCE TOO CLOSE TO A SUPERNOVA AND THAT'D END YOUR TRIP *REAL QUICK,* WOULDN'T IT?

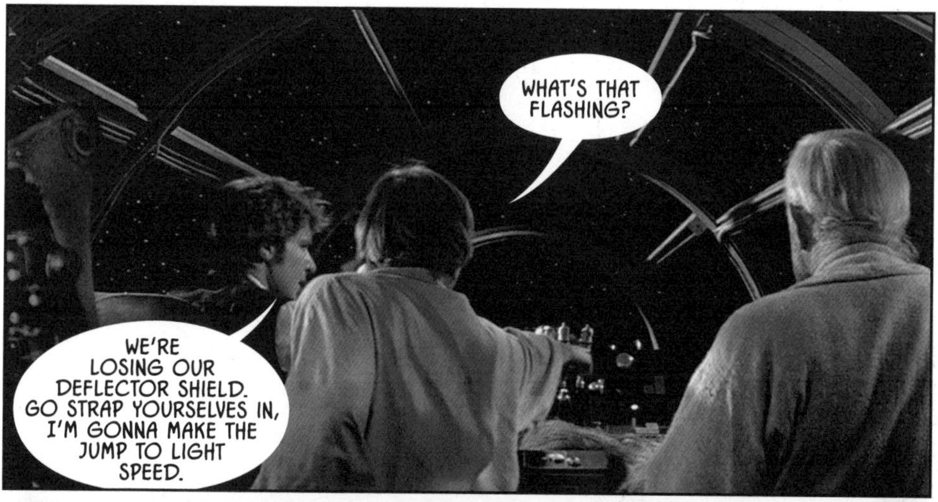
WHAT'S THAT FLASHING?
WE'RE LOSING OUR DEFLECTOR SHIELD. GO STRAP YOURSELVES IN, I'M GONNA MAKE THE JUMP TO LIGHT SPEED.

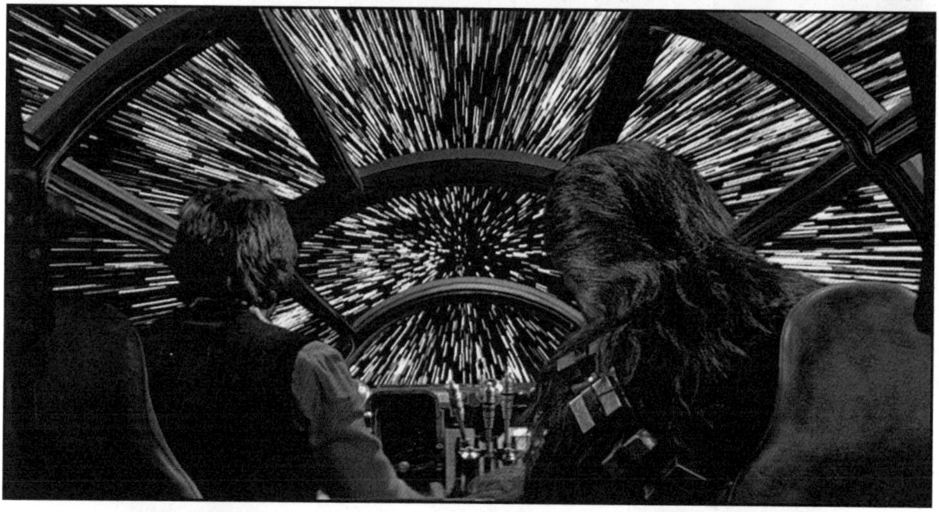

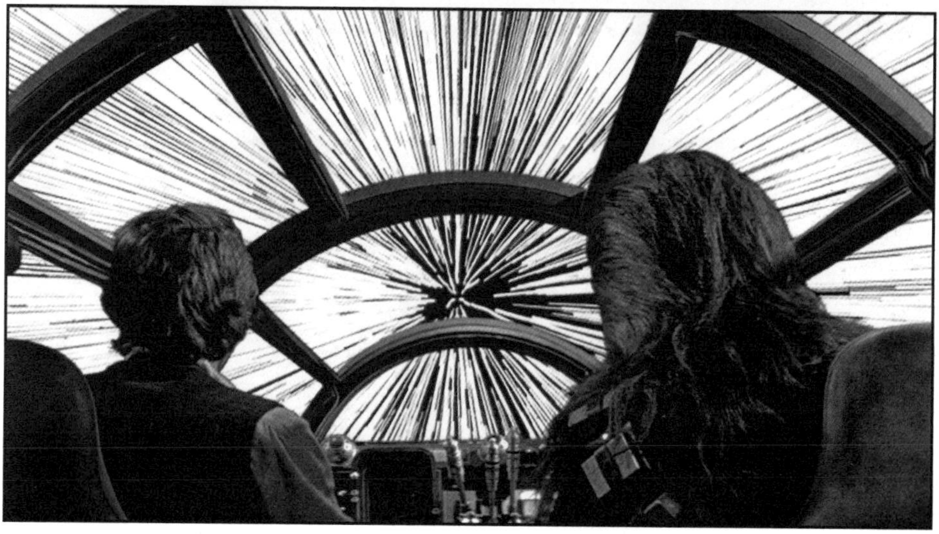

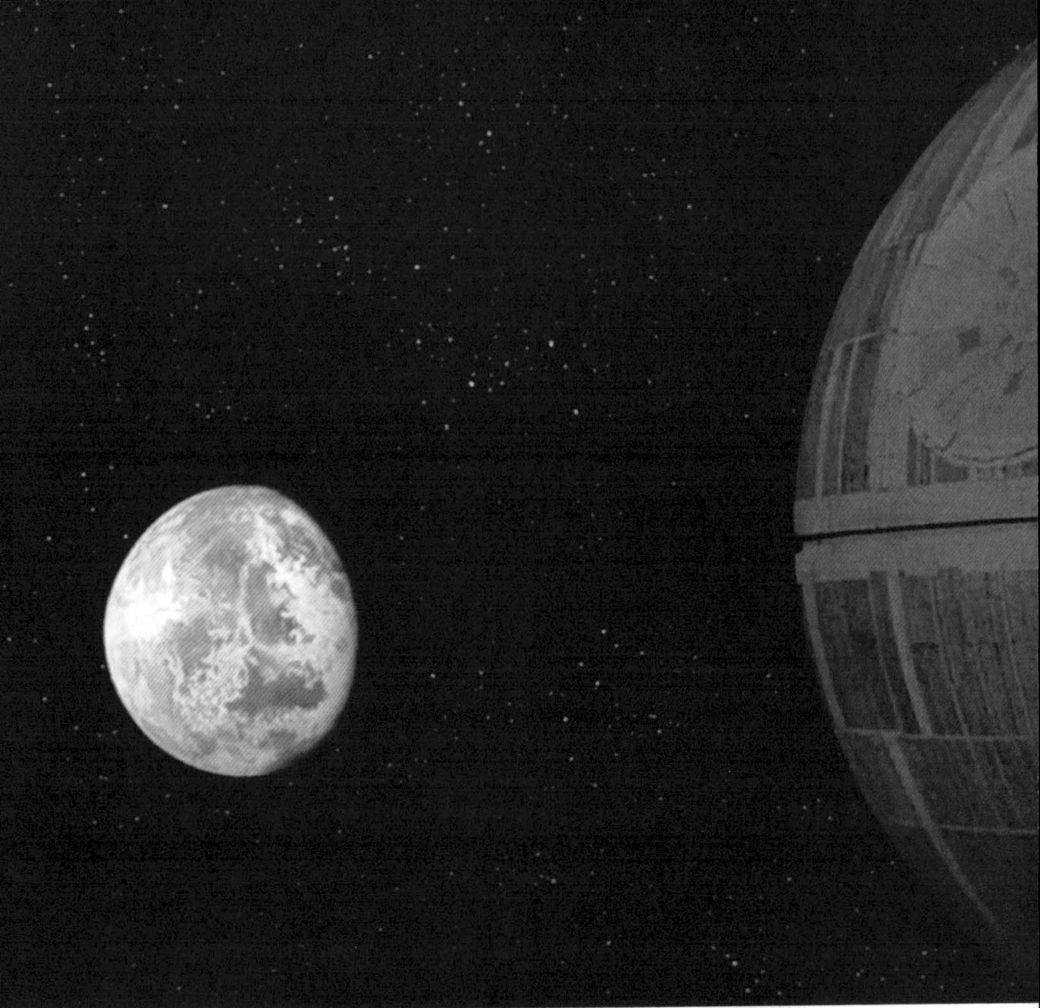

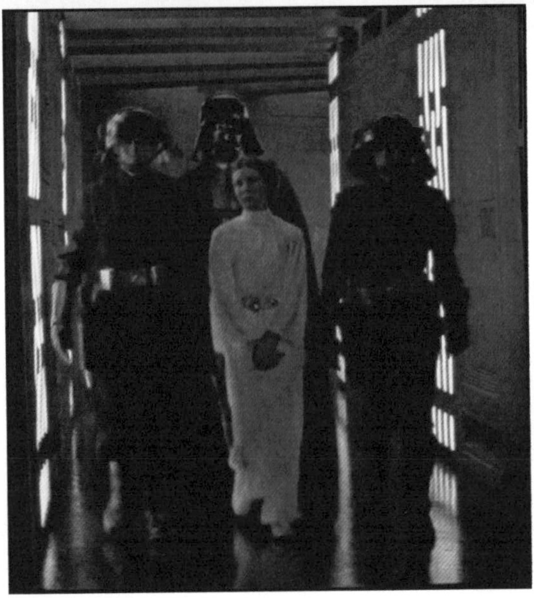

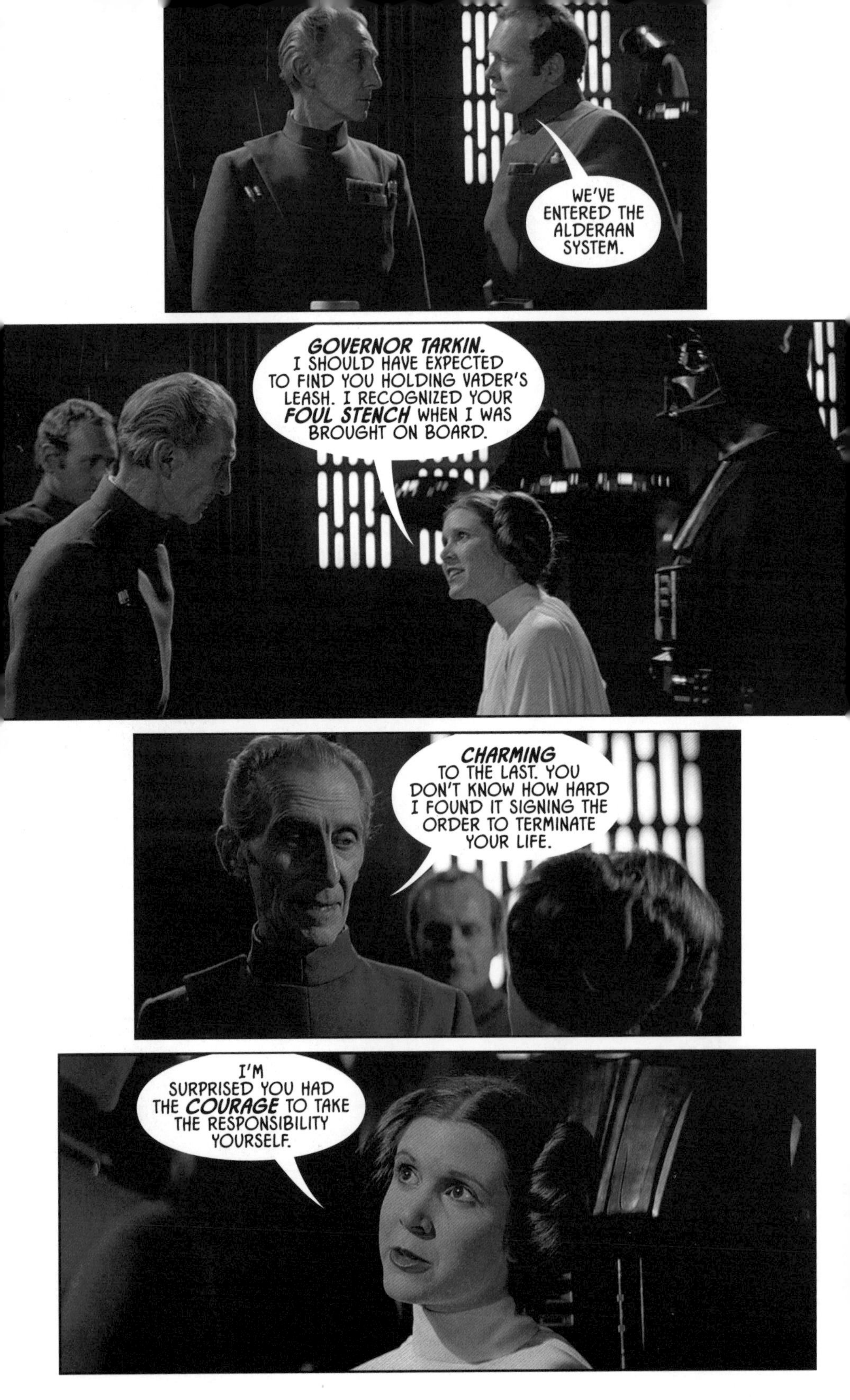
WE'VE ENTERED THE ALDERAAN SYSTEM.
GOVERNOR TARKIN. I SHOULD HAVE EXPECTED TO FIND YOU HOLDING VADER'S LEASH. I RECOGNIZED YOUR FOUL STENCH WHEN I WAS BROUGHT ON BOARD.
CHARMING TO THE LAST. YOU DON'T KNOW HOW HARD I FOUND IT SIGNING THE ORDER TO TERMINATE YOUR LIFE.
I'M SURPRISED YOU HAD THE COURAGE TO TAKE THE RESPONSIBILITY YOURSELF.

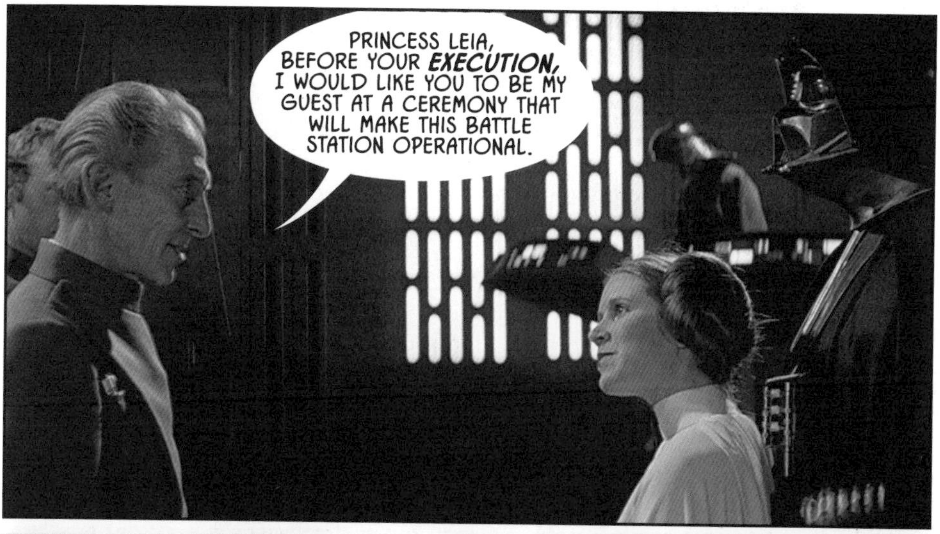
PRINCESS LEIA, BEFORE YOUR *EXECUTION,* I WOULD LIKE YOU TO BE MY GUEST AT A CEREMONY THAT WILL MAKE THIS BATTLE STATION OPERATIONAL.

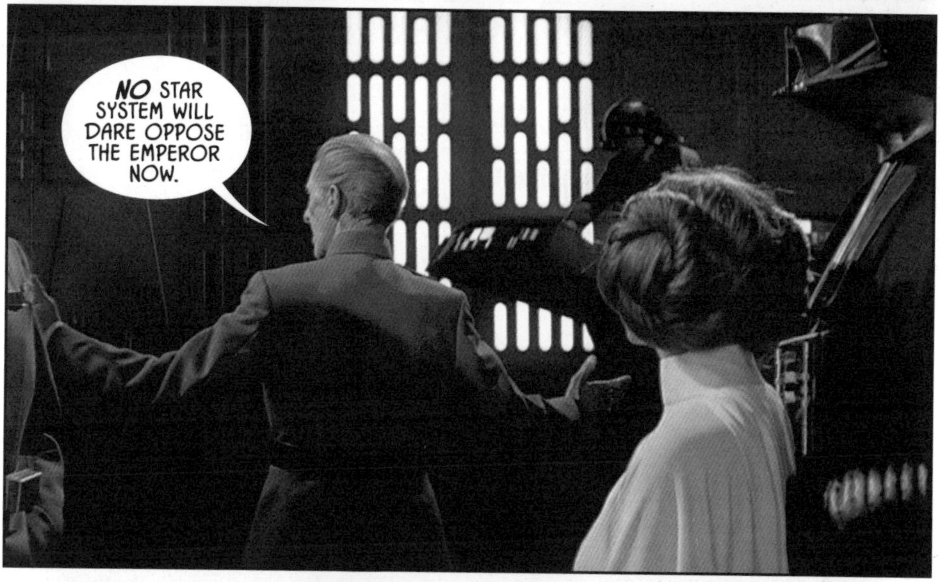
NO STAR SYSTEM WILL DARE OPPOSE THE EMPEROR NOW.

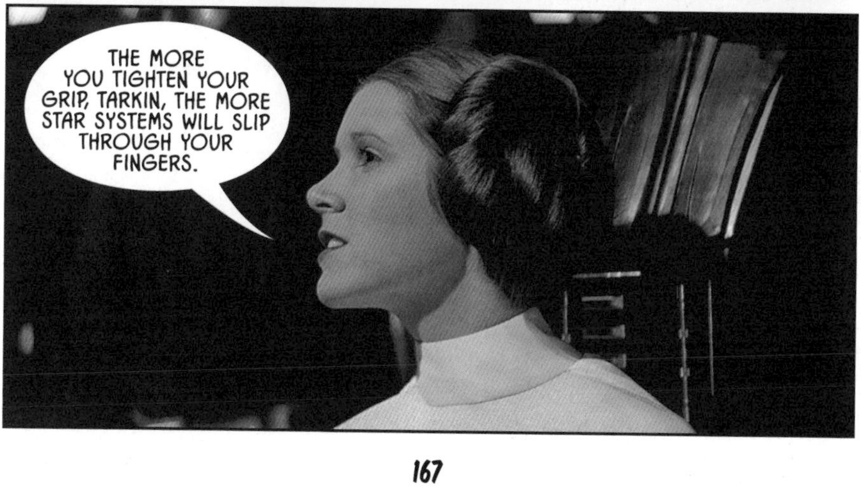
THE MORE YOU TIGHTEN YOUR GRIP, TARKIN, THE MORE STAR SYSTEMS WILL SLIP THROUGH YOUR FINGERS.

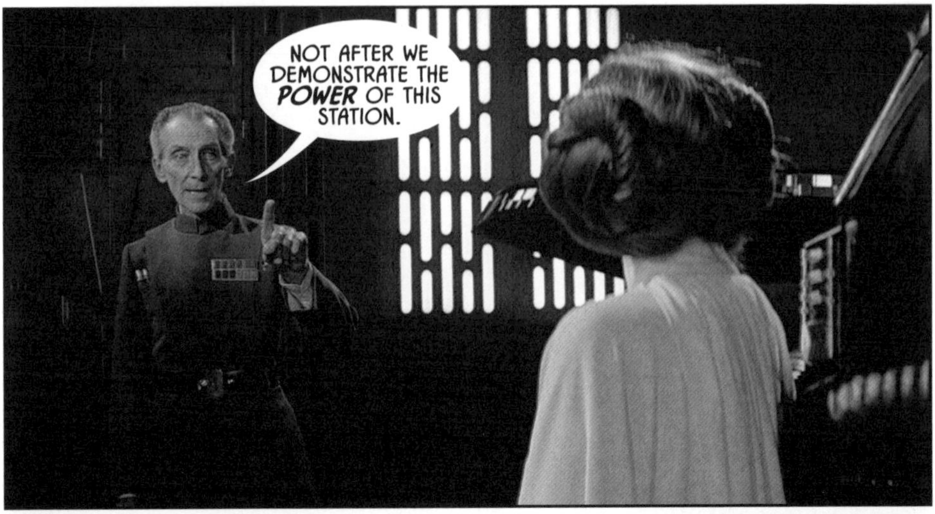
NOT AFTER WE DEMONSTRATE THE POWER OF THIS STATION.

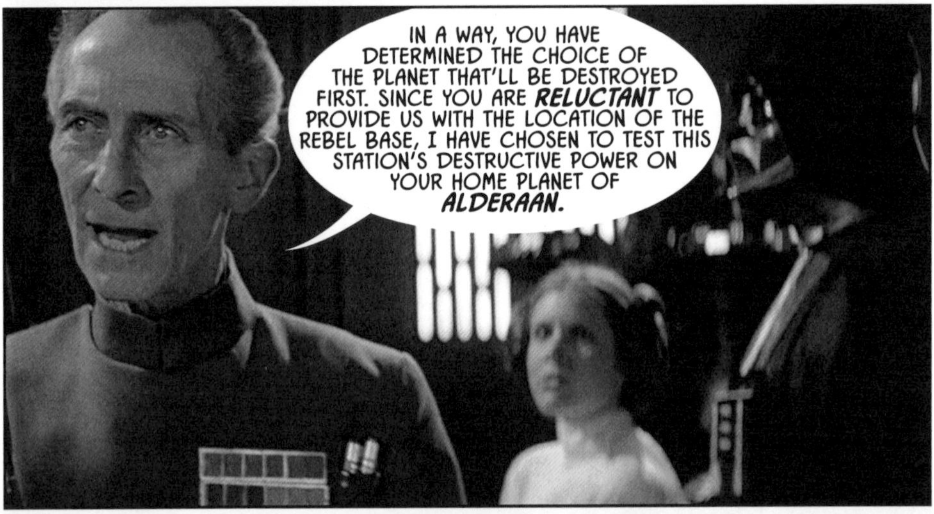
IN A WAY, YOU HAVE DETERMINED THE CHOICE OF THE PLANET THAT'LL BE DESTROYED FIRST. SINCE YOU ARE RELUCTANT TO PROVIDE US WITH THE LOCATION OF THE REBEL BASE, I HAVE CHOSEN TO TEST THIS STATION'S DESTRUCTIVE POWER ON YOUR HOME PLANET OF ALDERAAN.

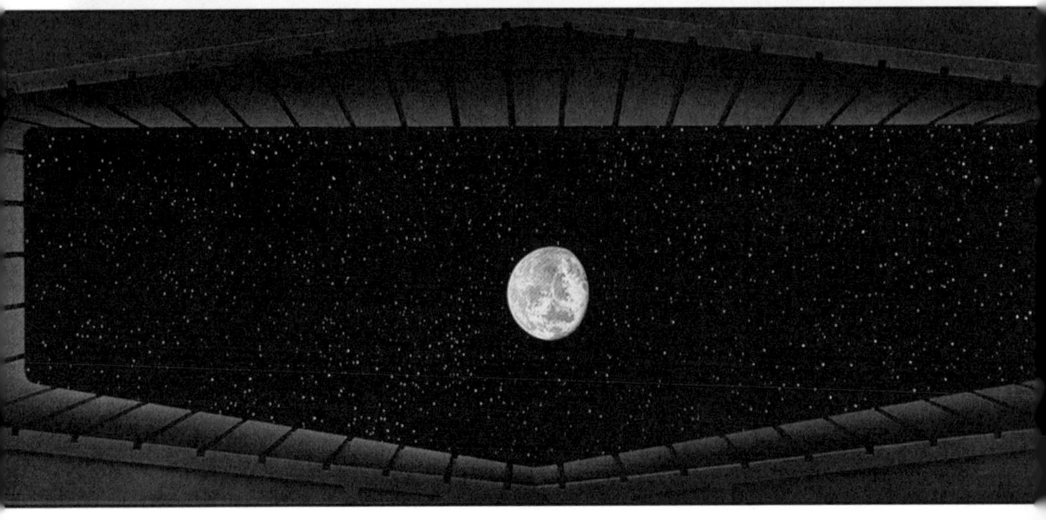

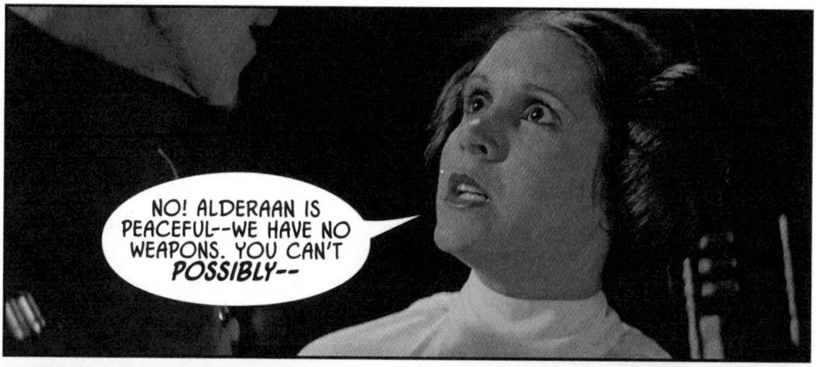
NO! ALDERAAN IS PEACEFUL--WE HAVE NO WEAPONS. YOU CAN'T *POSSIBLY--*

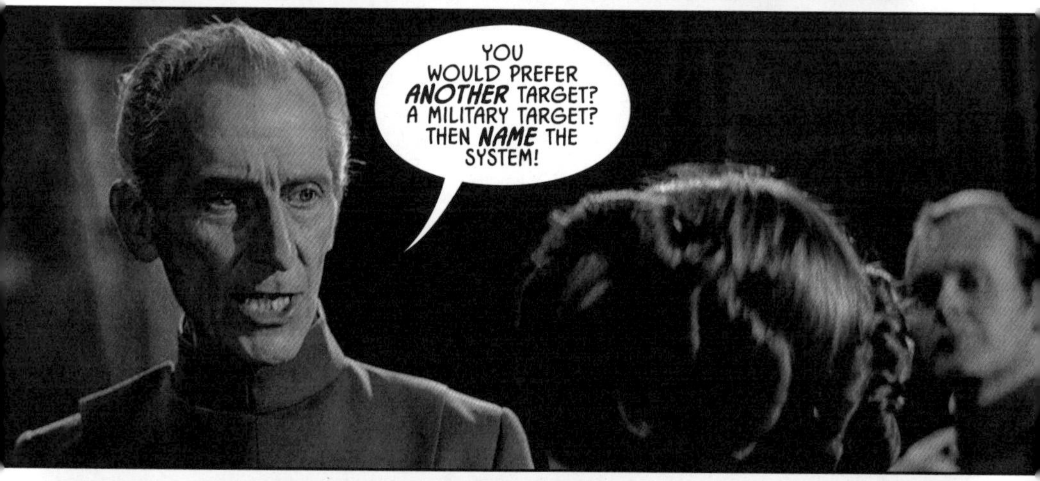
YOU WOULD PREFER *ANOTHER* TARGET? A MILITARY TARGET? THEN *NAME* THE SYSTEM!

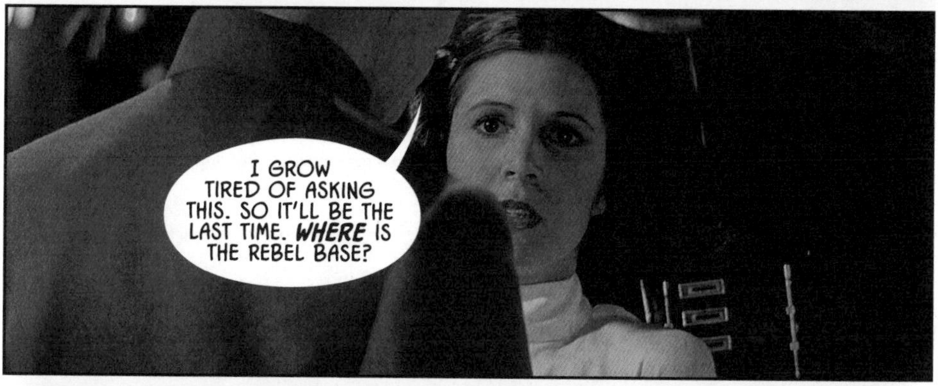
I GROW TIRED OF ASKING THIS. SO IT'LL BE THE LAST TIME. *WHERE* IS THE REBEL BASE?

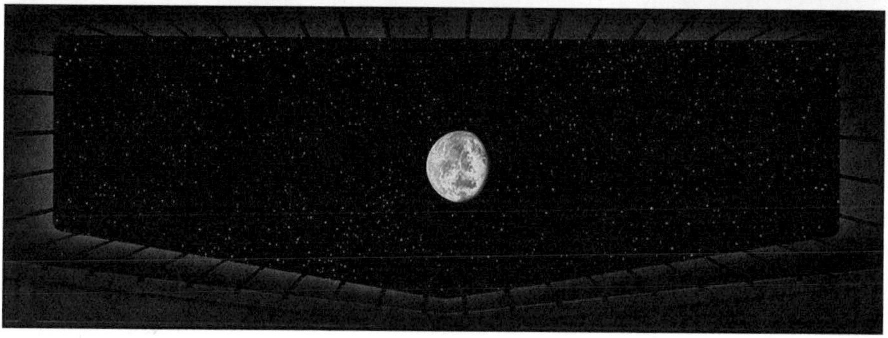

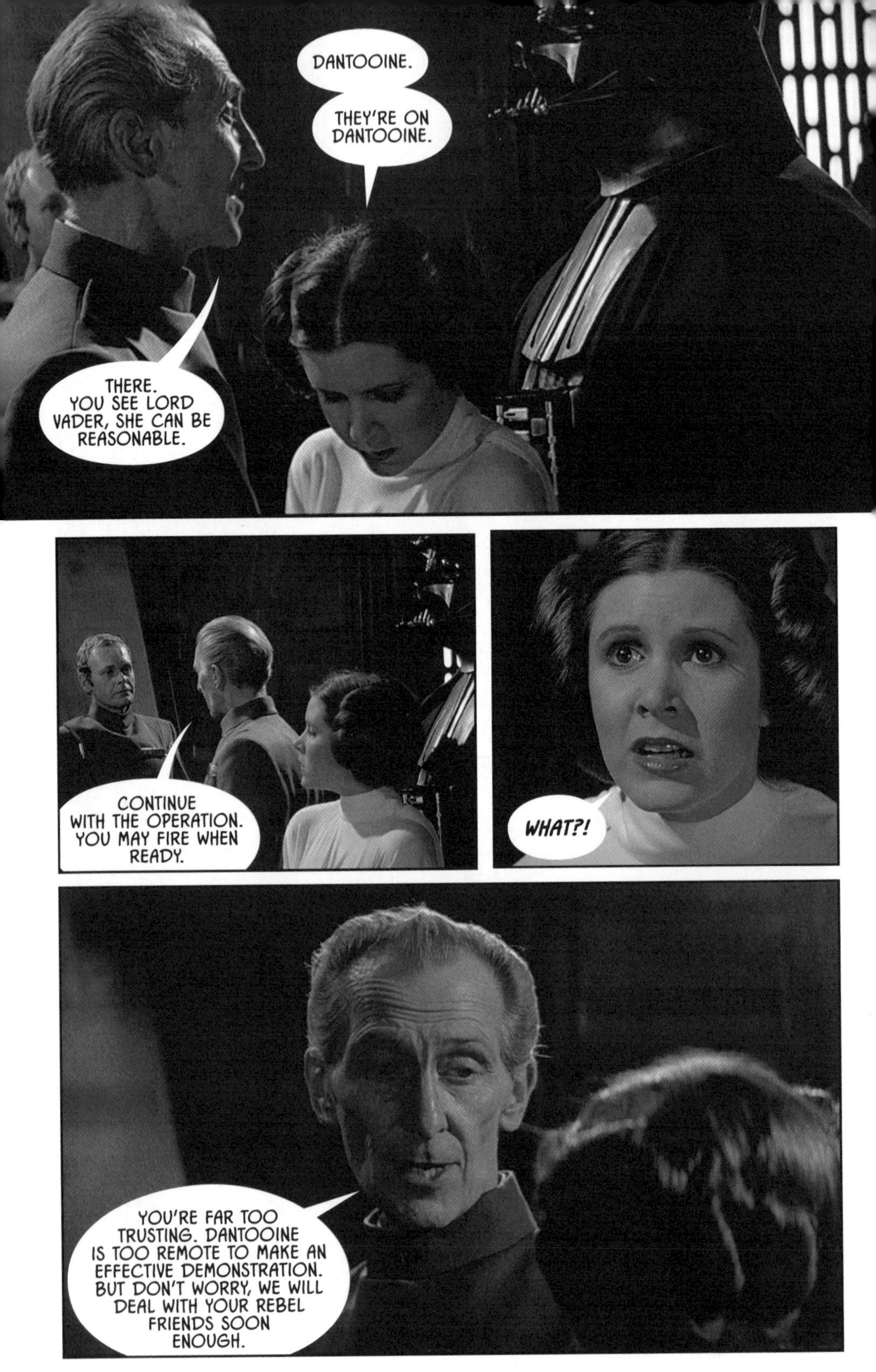
DANTOOINE.
THEY'RE ON DANTOOINE.
THERE. YOU SEE LORD VADER, SHE CAN BE REASONABLE.
CONTINUE WITH THE OPERATION. YOU MAY FIRE WHEN READY.
WHAT?!
YOU'RE FAR TOO TRUSTING. DANTOOINE IS TOO REMOTE TO MAKE AN EFFECTIVE DEMONSTRATION. BUT DON'T WORRY, WE WILL DEAL WITH YOUR REBEL FRIENDS SOON ENOUGH.

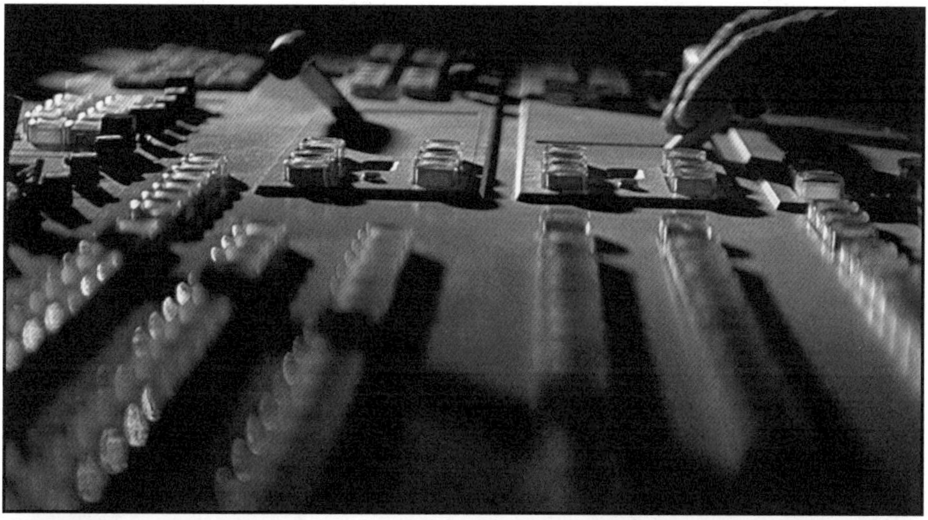

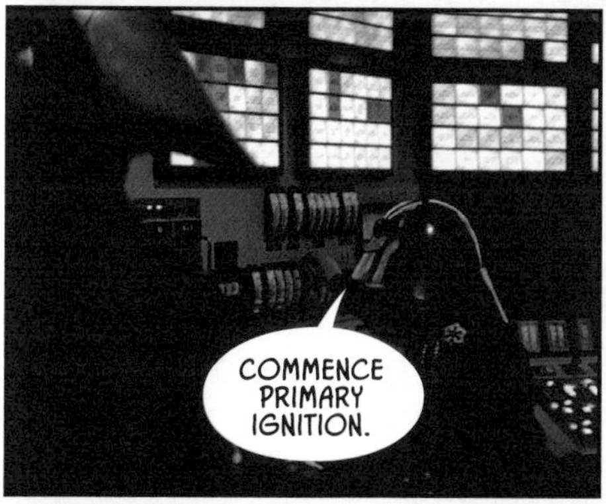
COMMENCE PRIMARY IGNITION.

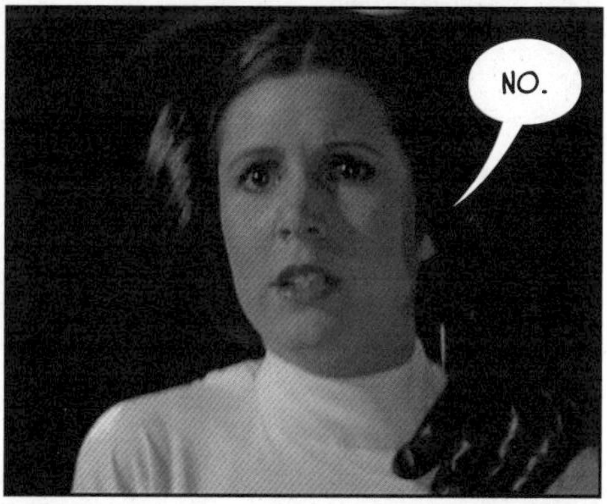
NO.

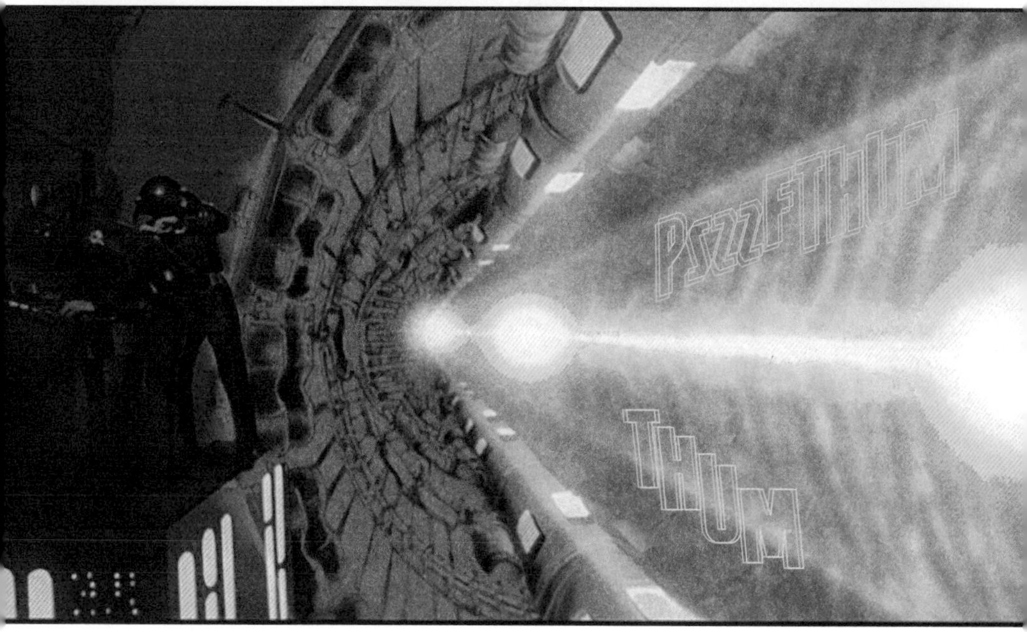
PSZZFTHUM
THUM

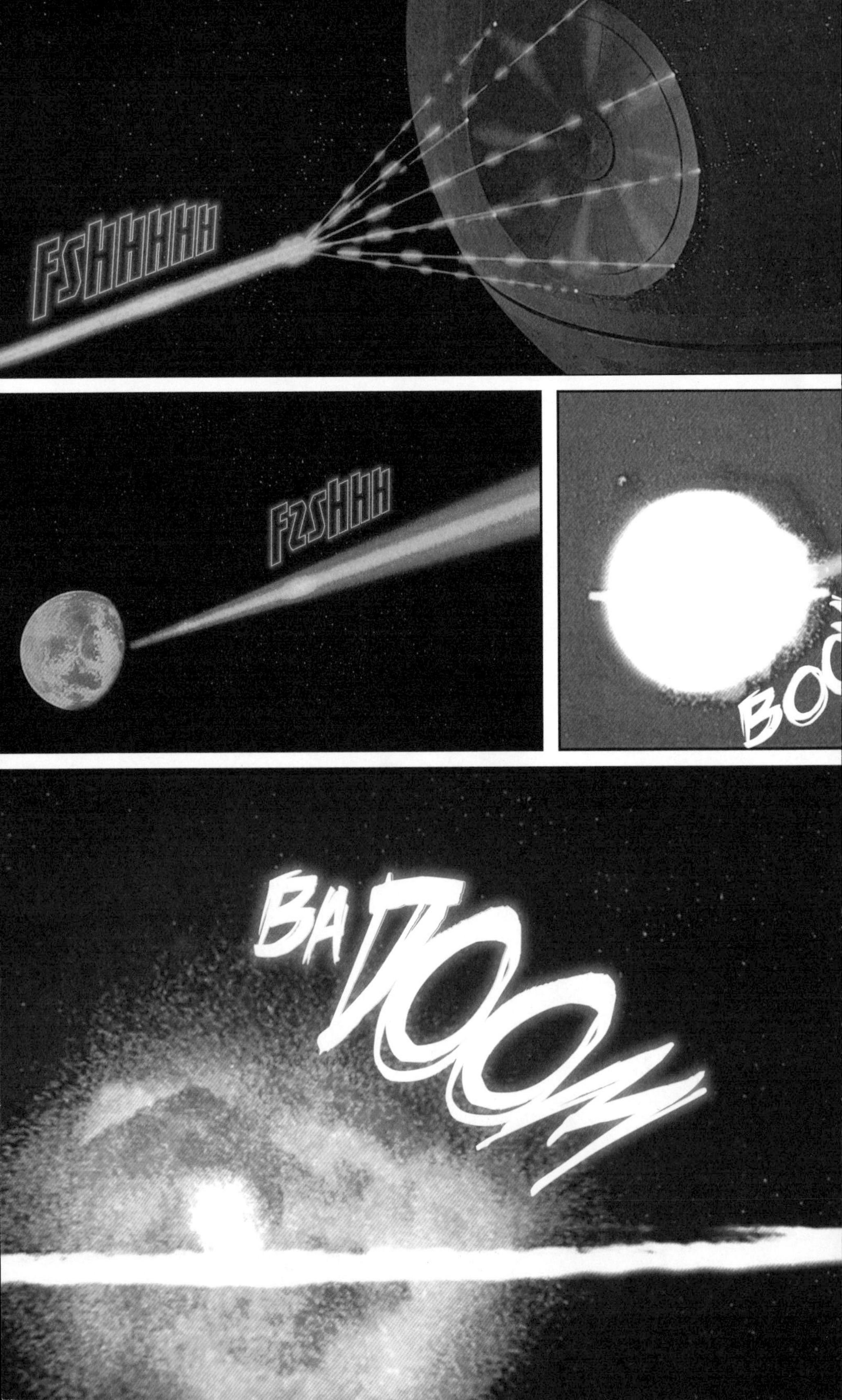
FSHHHHH
FZSHHH
BOO
BA DOOM

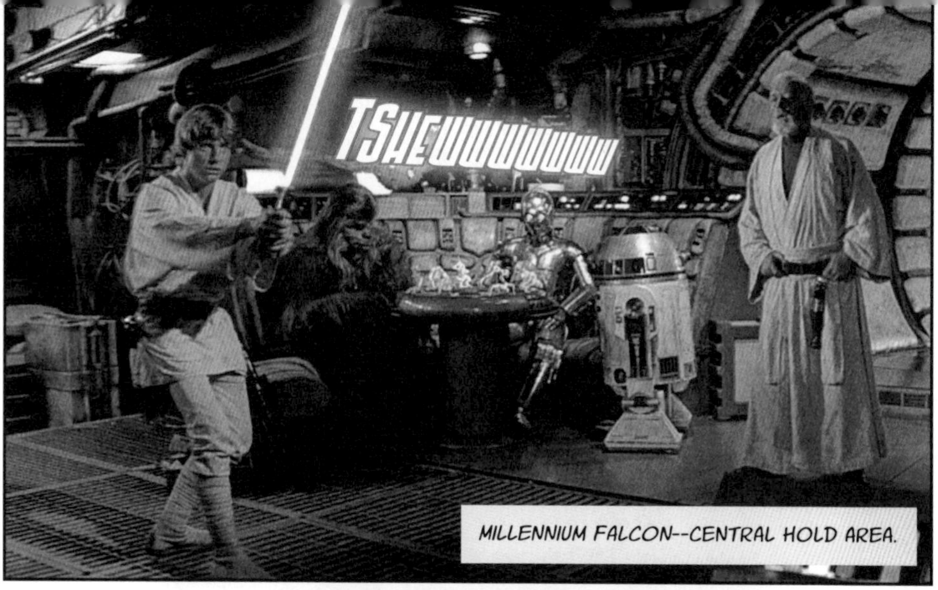
TSHEWWWWWWW
MILLENNIUM FALCON--CENTRAL HOLD AREA.

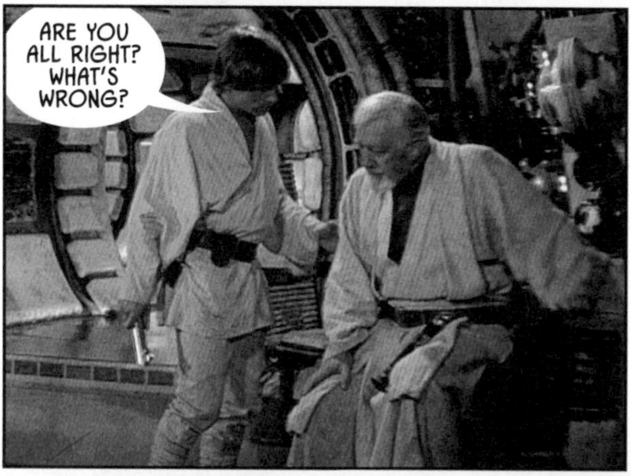
ARE YOU ALL RIGHT? WHAT'S WRONG?

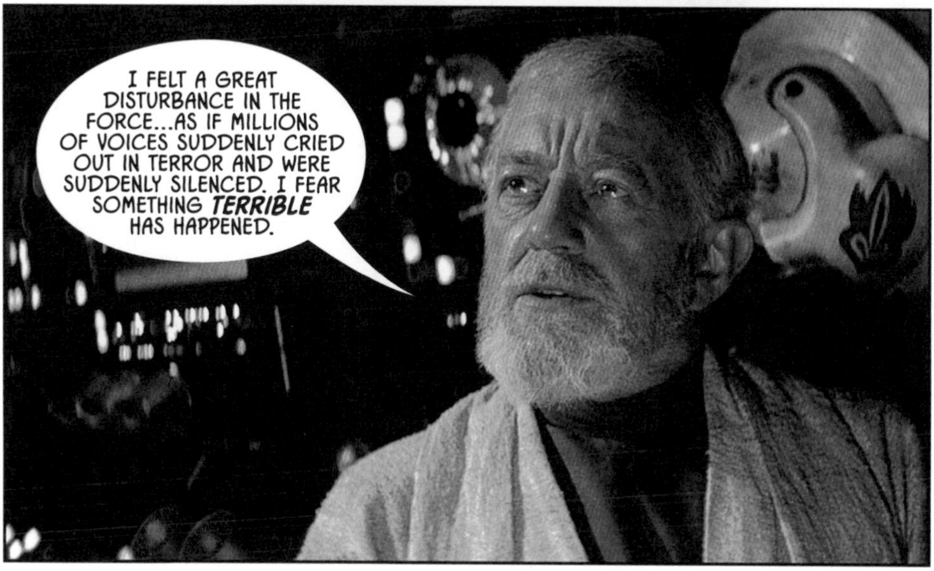
I FELT A GREAT DISTURBANCE IN THE FORCE...AS IF MILLIONS OF VOICES SUDDENLY CRIED OUT IN TERROR AND WERE SUDDENLY SILENCED. I FEAR SOMETHING ***TERRIBLE*** HAS HAPPENED.

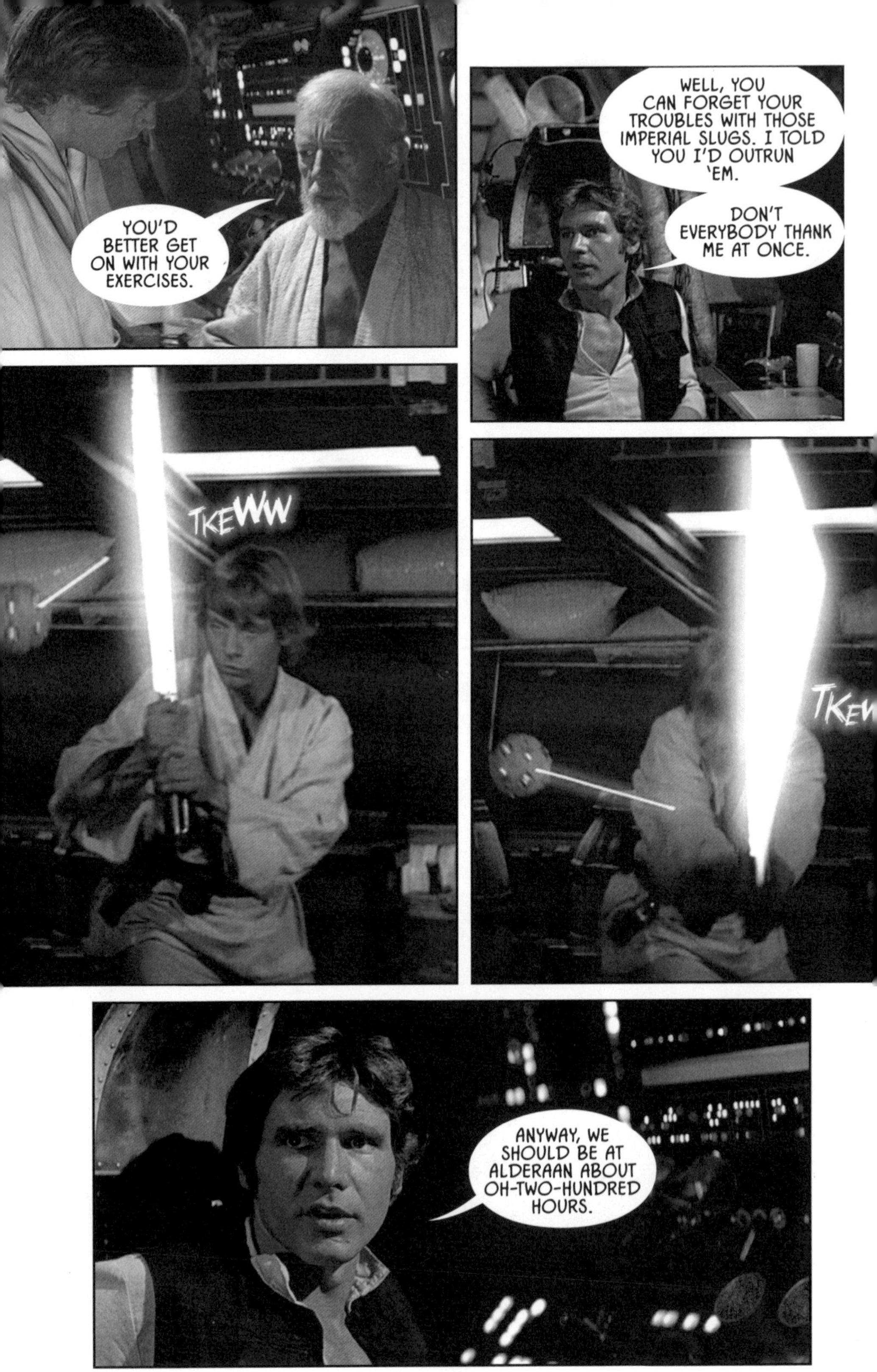
YOU'D BETTER GET ON WITH YOUR EXERCISES.
WELL, YOU CAN FORGET YOUR TROUBLES WITH THOSE IMPERIAL SLUGS. I TOLD YOU I'D OUTRUN 'EM.
DON'T EVERYBODY THANK ME AT ONCE.
TKEWW
TKEW
ANYWAY, WE SHOULD BE AT ALDERAAN ABOUT OH-TWO-HUNDRED HOURS.

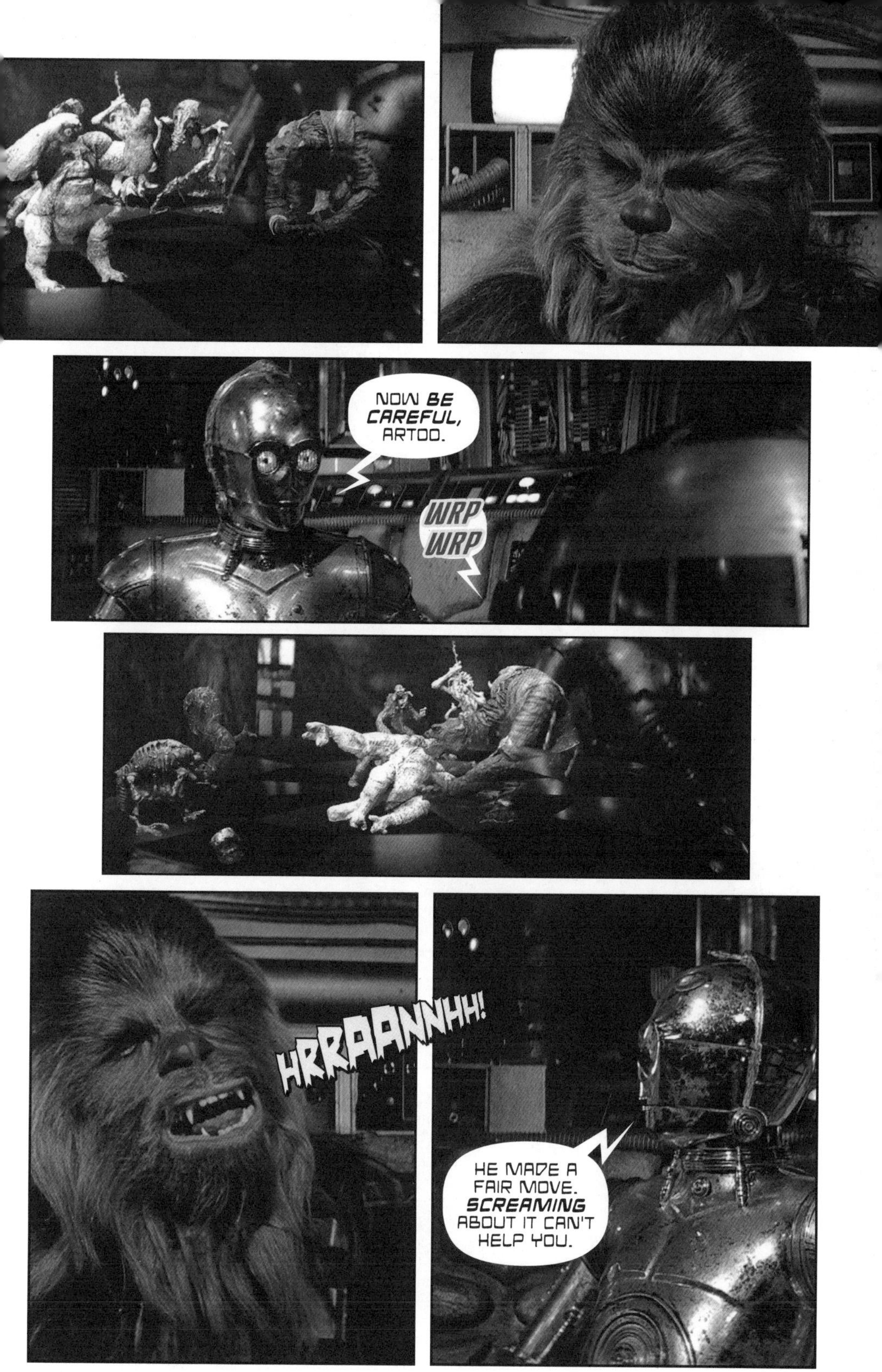

NOW *BE CAREFUL,* ARTOO.
WRP WRP
HRRAANNHH!
HE MADE A FAIR MOVE. ***SCREAMING*** ABOUT IT CAN'T HELP YOU.

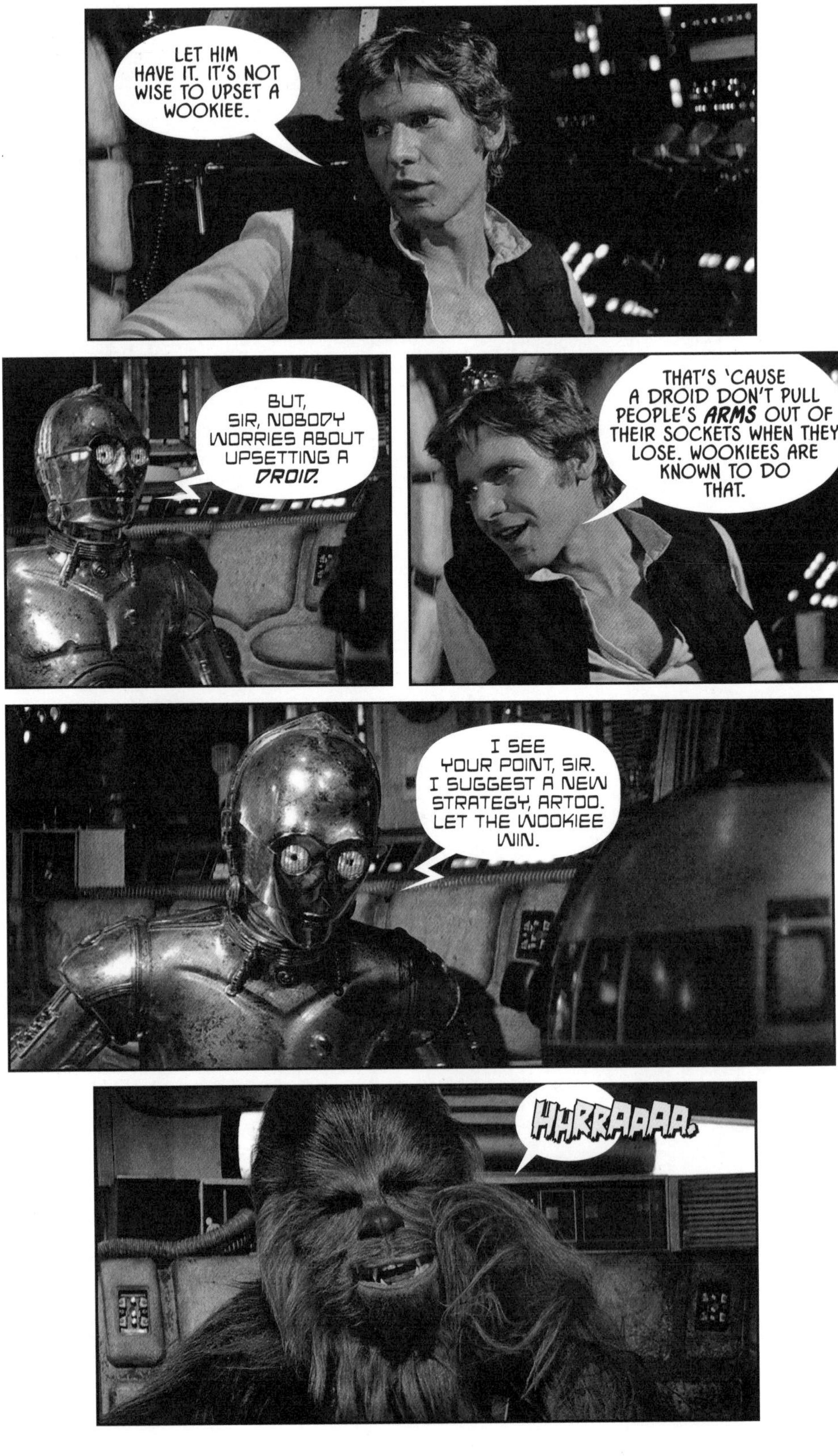
LET HIM HAVE IT. IT'S NOT WISE TO UPSET A WOOKIEE.
BUT, SIR, NOBODY WORRIES ABOUT UPSETTING A *DROID.*
THAT'S 'CAUSE A DROID DON'T PULL PEOPLE'S ***ARMS*** OUT OF THEIR SOCKETS WHEN THEY LOSE. WOOKIEES ARE KNOWN TO DO THAT.
I SEE YOUR POINT, SIR. I SUGGEST A NEW STRATEGY, ARTOO. LET THE WOOKIEE WIN.
HHRRAAAA.

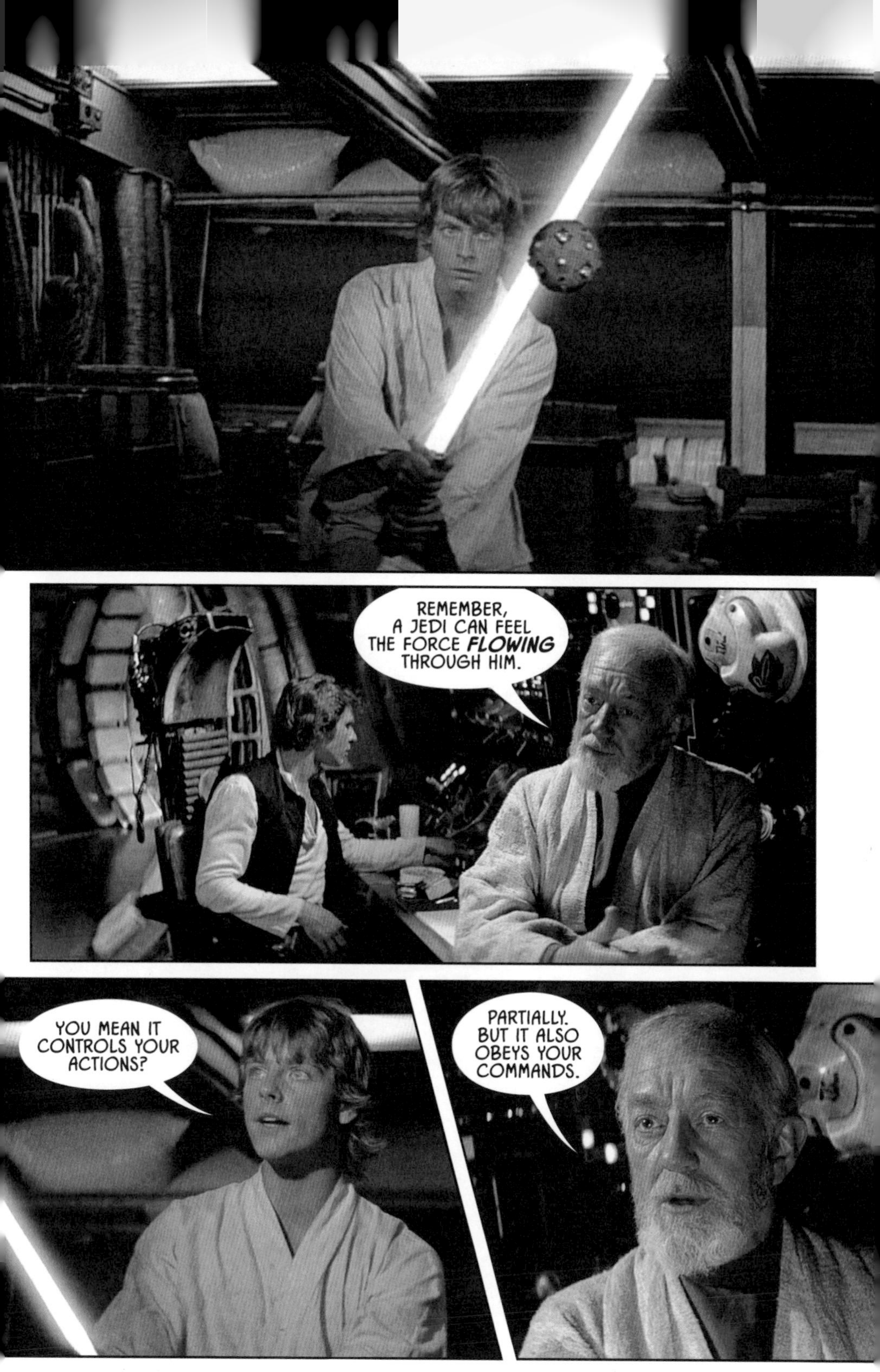
REMEMBER, A JEDI CAN FEEL THE FORCE FLOWING THROUGH HIM.
YOU MEAN IT CONTROLS YOUR ACTIONS?
PARTIALLY. BUT IT ALSO OBEYS YOUR COMMANDS.

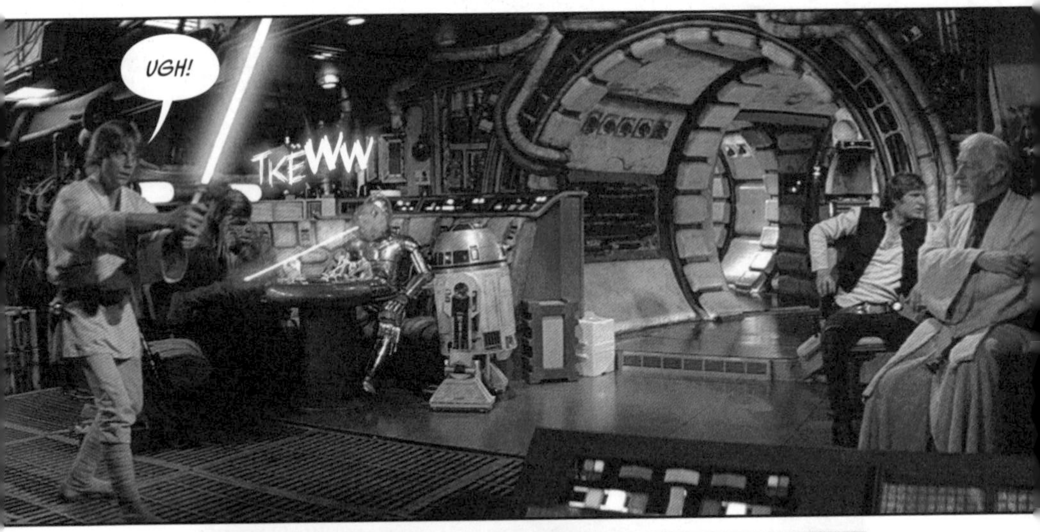
UGH!
TKEWW

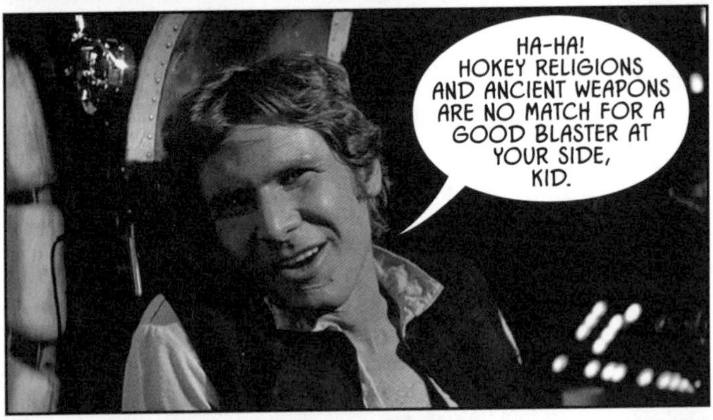
HA-HA! HOKEY RELIGIONS AND ANCIENT WEAPONS ARE NO MATCH FOR A GOOD BLASTER AT YOUR SIDE, KID.

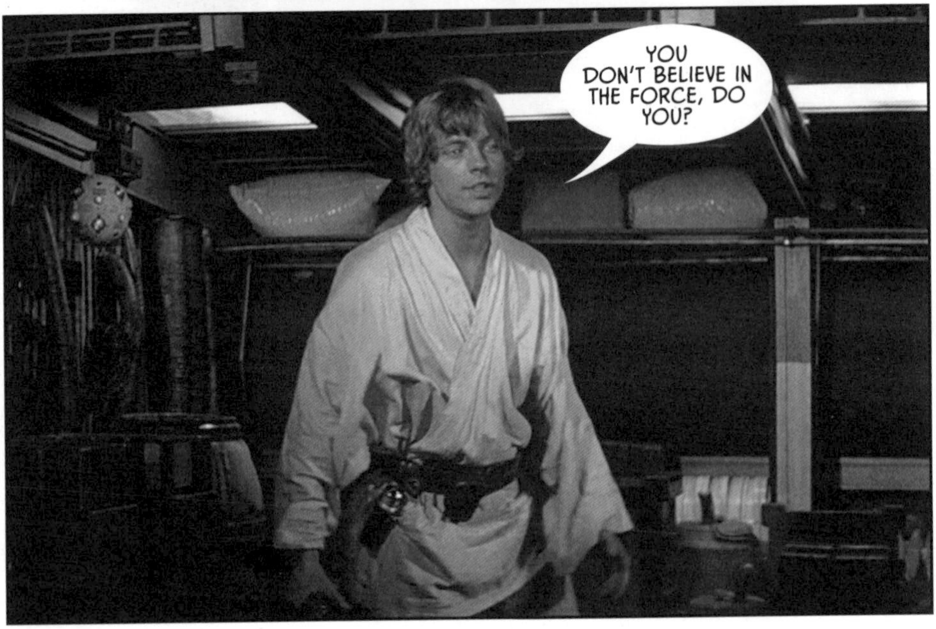
YOU DON'T BELIEVE IN THE FORCE, DO YOU?

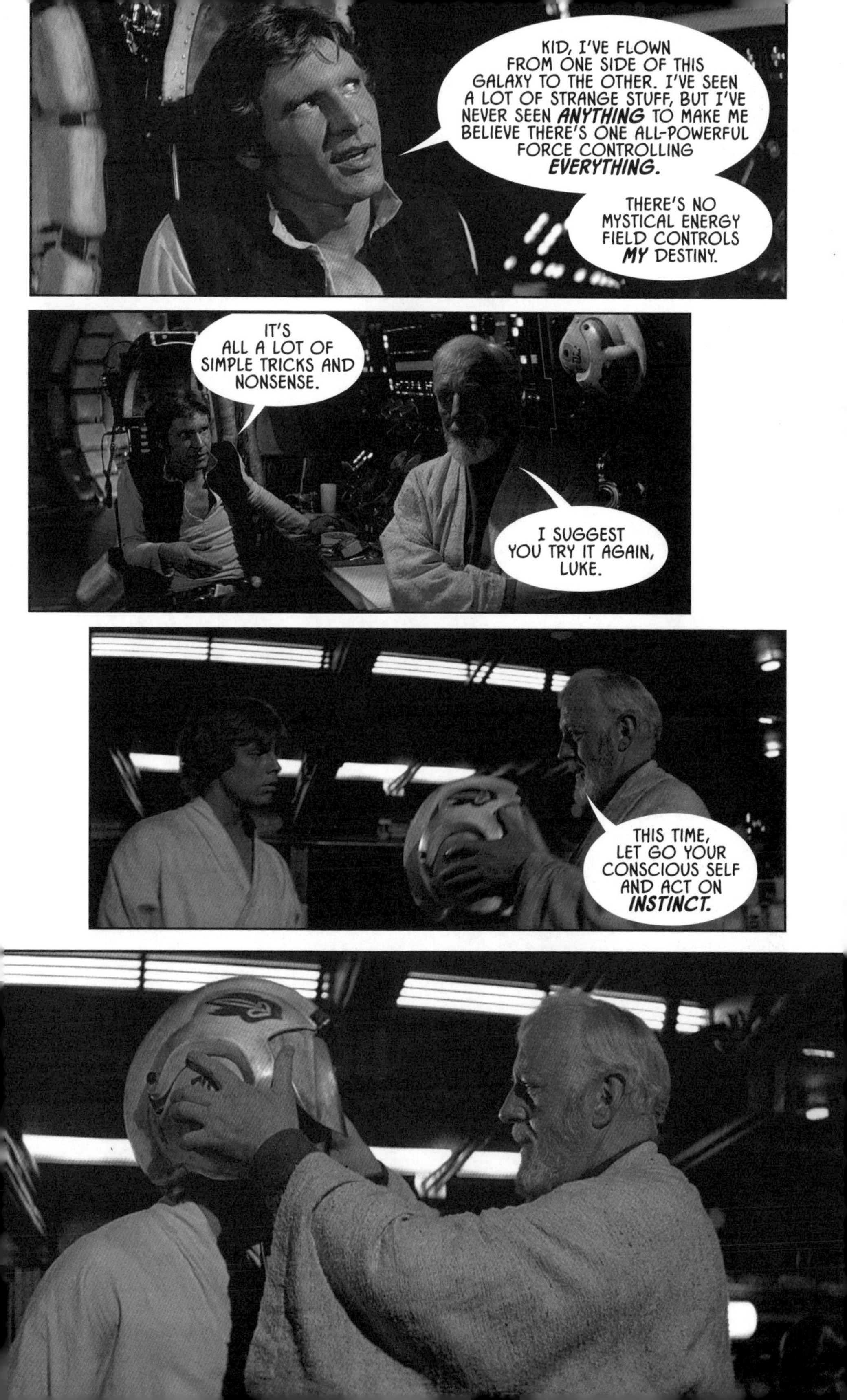
KID, I'VE FLOWN FROM ONE SIDE OF THIS GALAXY TO THE OTHER. I'VE SEEN A LOT OF STRANGE STUFF, BUT I'VE NEVER SEEN **ANYTHING** TO MAKE ME BELIEVE THERE'S ONE ALL-POWERFUL FORCE CONTROLLING **EVERYTHING.**
THERE'S NO MYSTICAL ENERGY FIELD CONTROLS **MY** DESTINY.
IT'S ALL A LOT OF SIMPLE TRICKS AND NONSENSE.
I SUGGEST YOU TRY IT AGAIN, LUKE.
THIS TIME, LET GO YOUR CONSCIOUS SELF AND ACT ON **INSTINCT.**

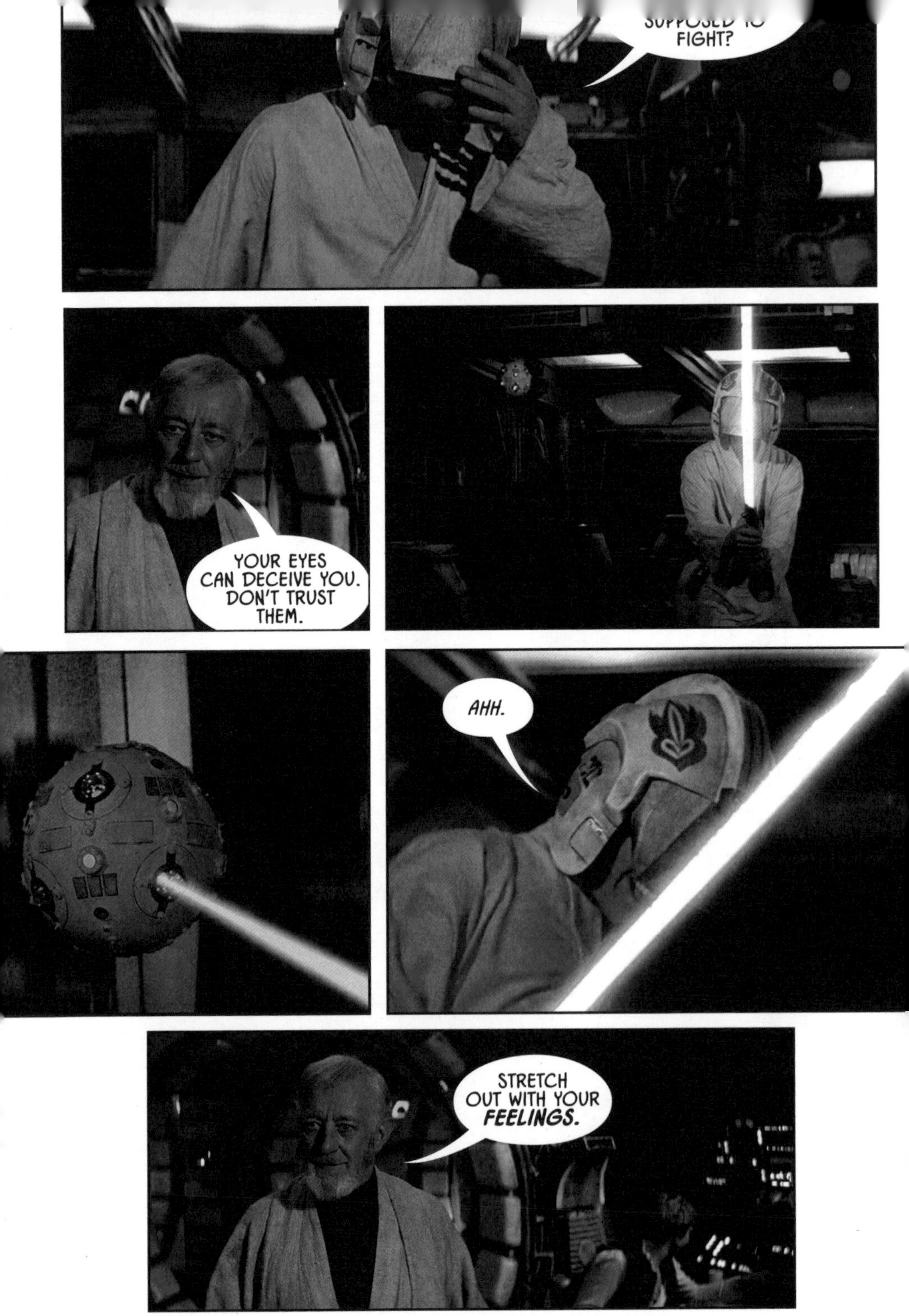
FIGHT?
YOUR EYES CAN DECEIVE YOU. DON'T TRUST THEM.
AHH.
STRETCH OUT WITH YOUR *FEELINGS.*

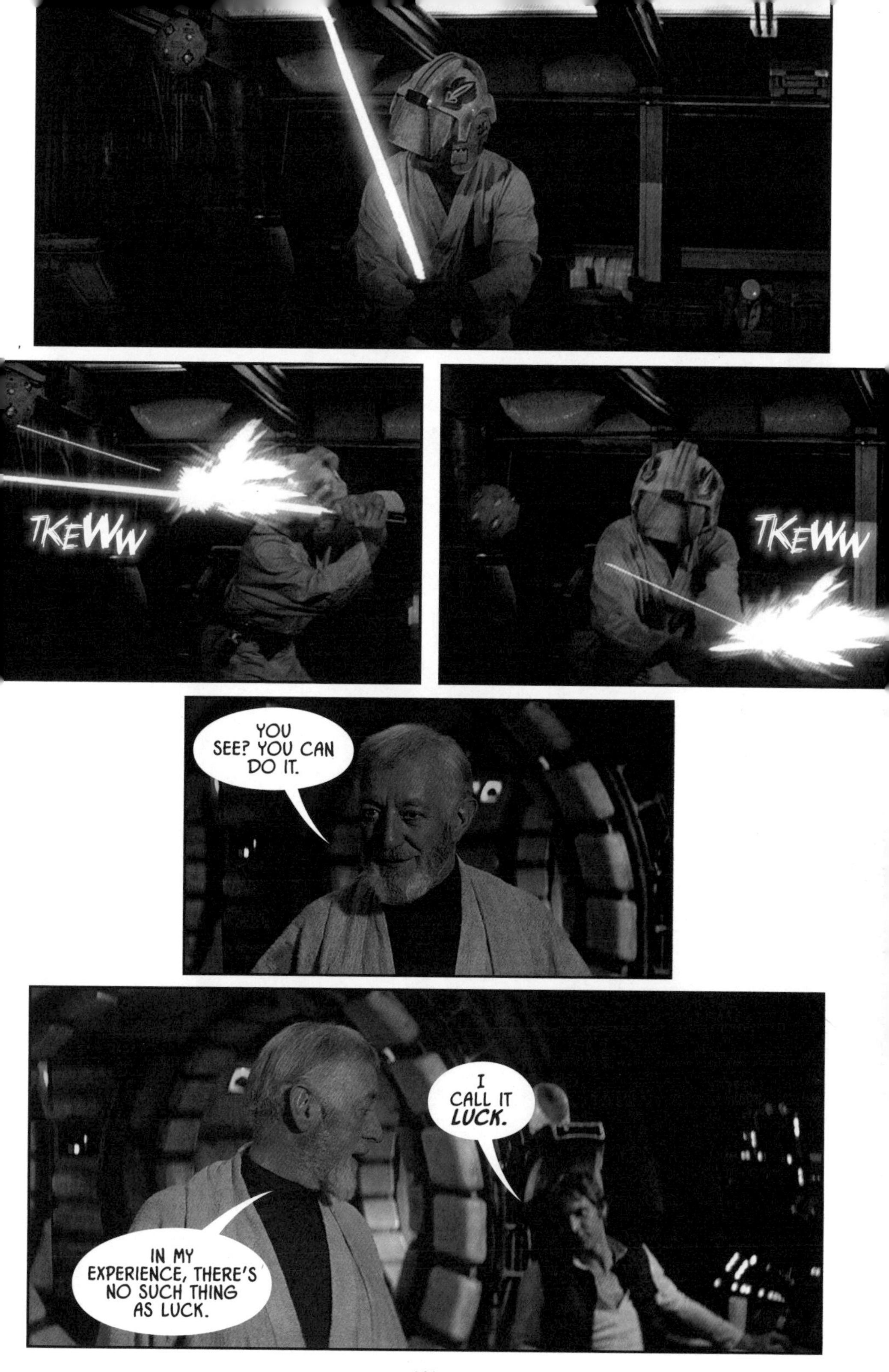
TKEWW
TKEWW
YOU SEE? YOU CAN DO IT.
I CALL IT LUCK.
IN MY EXPERIENCE, THERE'S NO SUCH THING AS LUCK.

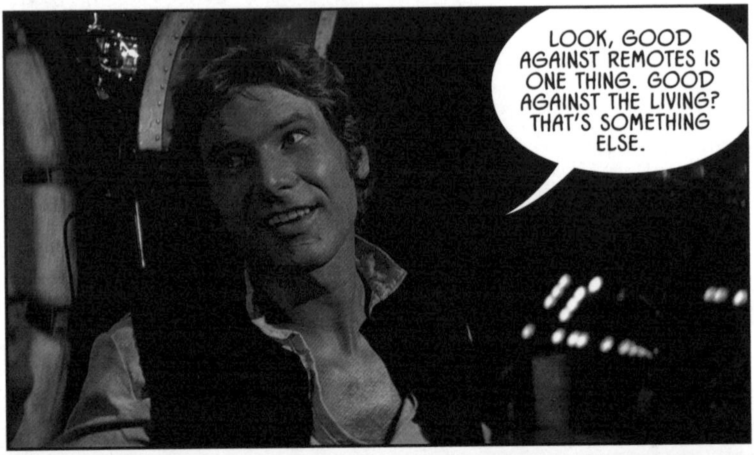
LOOK, GOOD AGAINST REMOTES IS ONE THING. GOOD AGAINST THE LIVING? THAT'S SOMETHING ELSE.

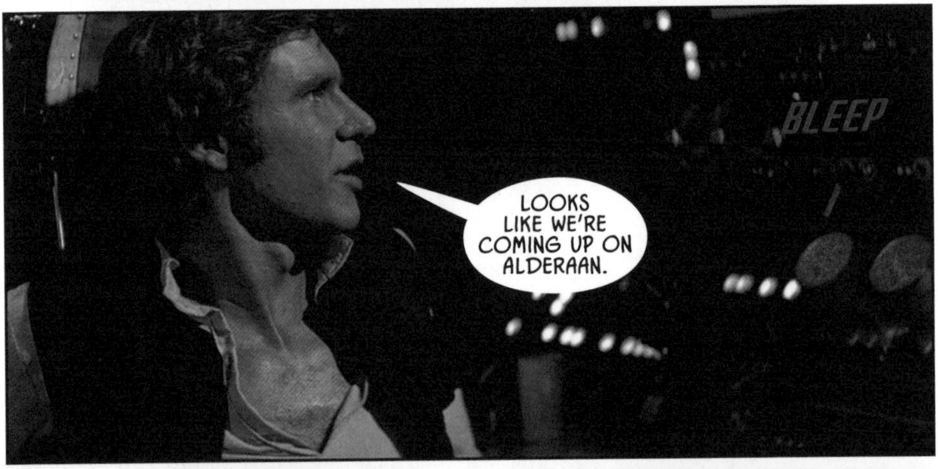
BLEEP
LOOKS LIKE WE'RE COMING UP ON ALDERAAN.

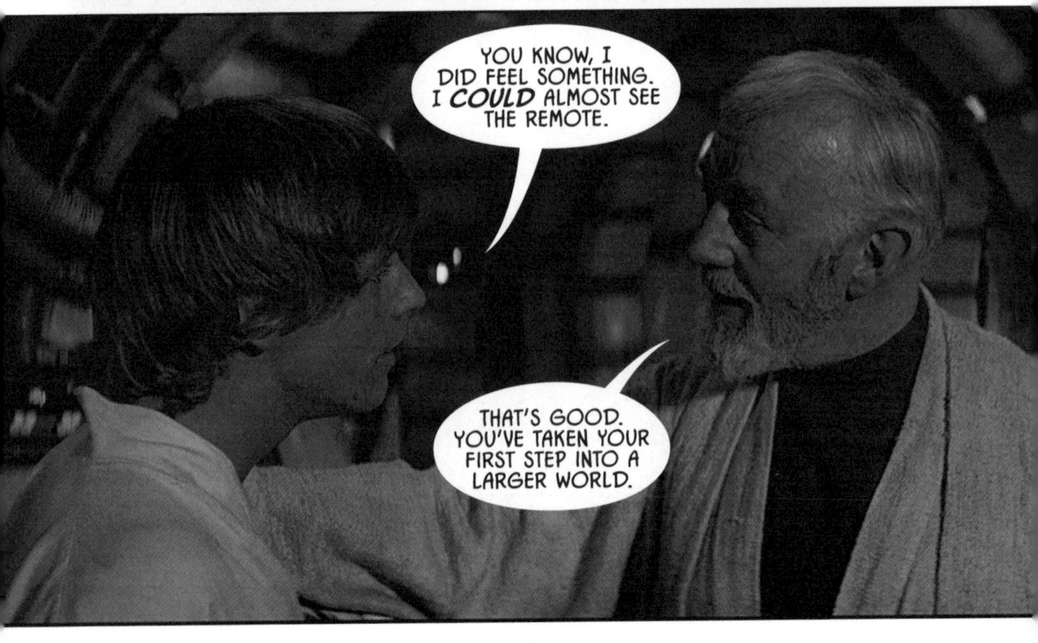
YOU KNOW, I DID FEEL SOMETHING. I COULD ALMOST SEE THE REMOTE.
THAT'S GOOD. YOU'VE TAKEN YOUR FIRST STEP INTO A LARGER WORLD.

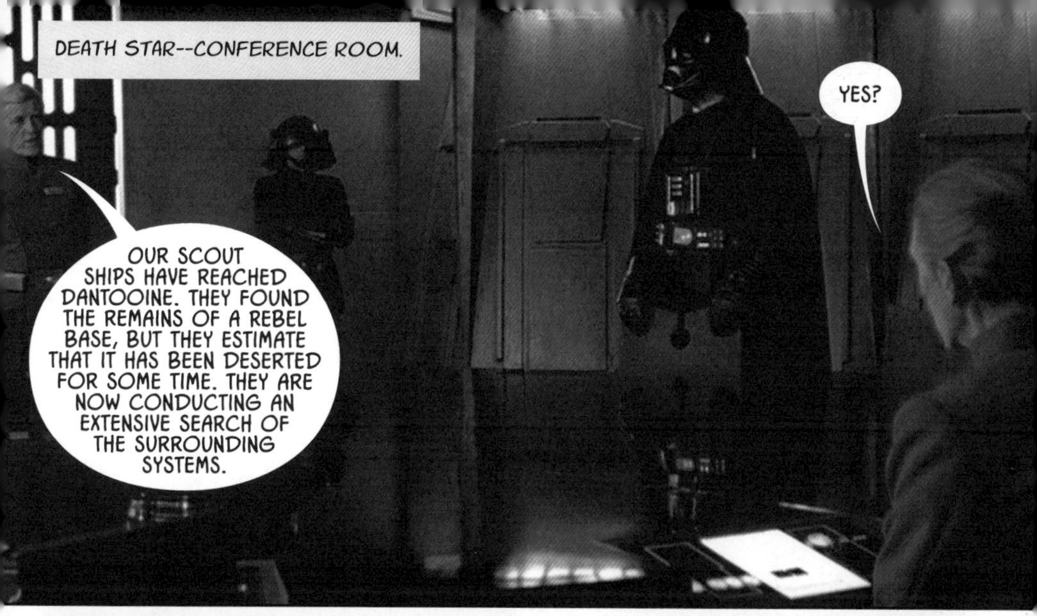
DEATH STAR--CONFERENCE ROOM.
OUR SCOUT SHIPS HAVE REACHED DANTOOINE. THEY FOUND THE REMAINS OF A REBEL BASE, BUT THEY ESTIMATE THAT IT HAS BEEN DESERTED FOR SOME TIME. THEY ARE NOW CONDUCTING AN EXTENSIVE SEARCH OF THE SURROUNDING SYSTEMS.
YES?

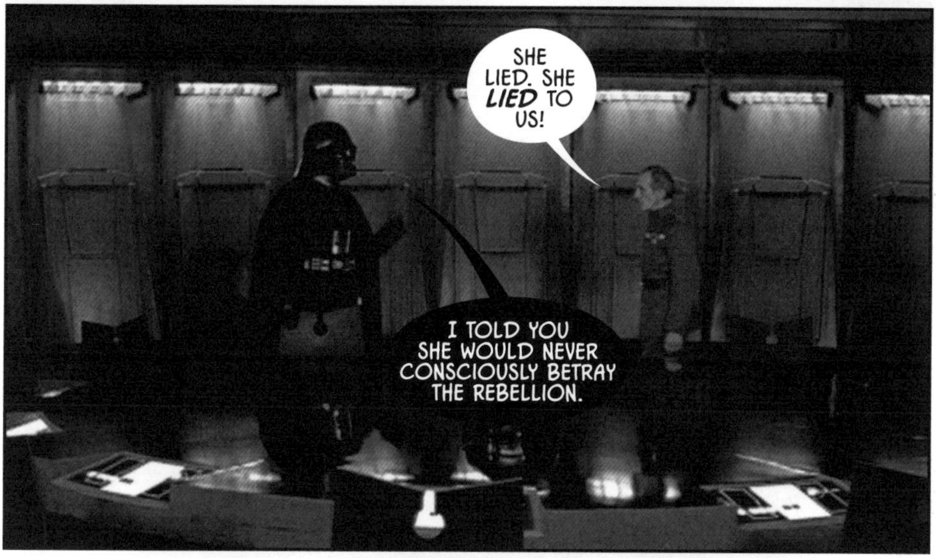
SHE LIED. SHE *LIED* TO US!
I TOLD YOU SHE WOULD NEVER CONSCIOUSLY BETRAY THE REBELLION.

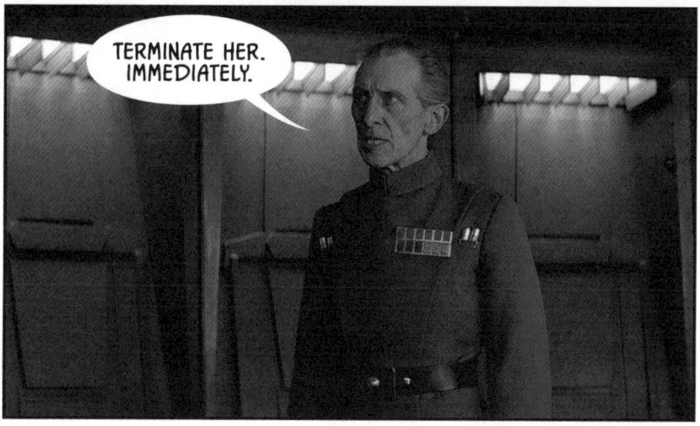
TERMINATE HER. IMMEDIATELY.

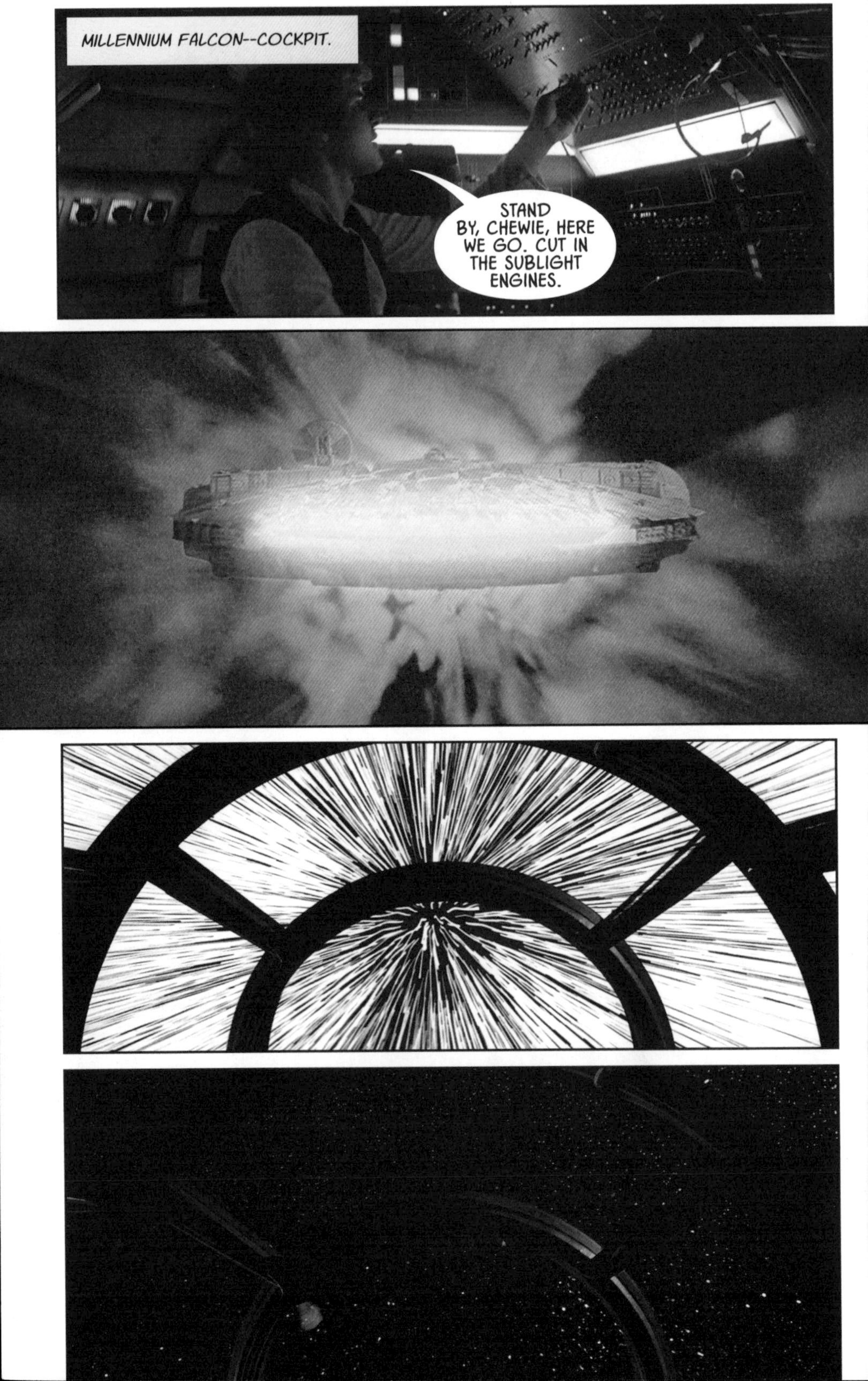
MILLENNIUM FALCON--COCKPIT.
STAND BY, CHEWIE, HERE WE GO. CUT IN THE SUBLIGHT ENGINES.

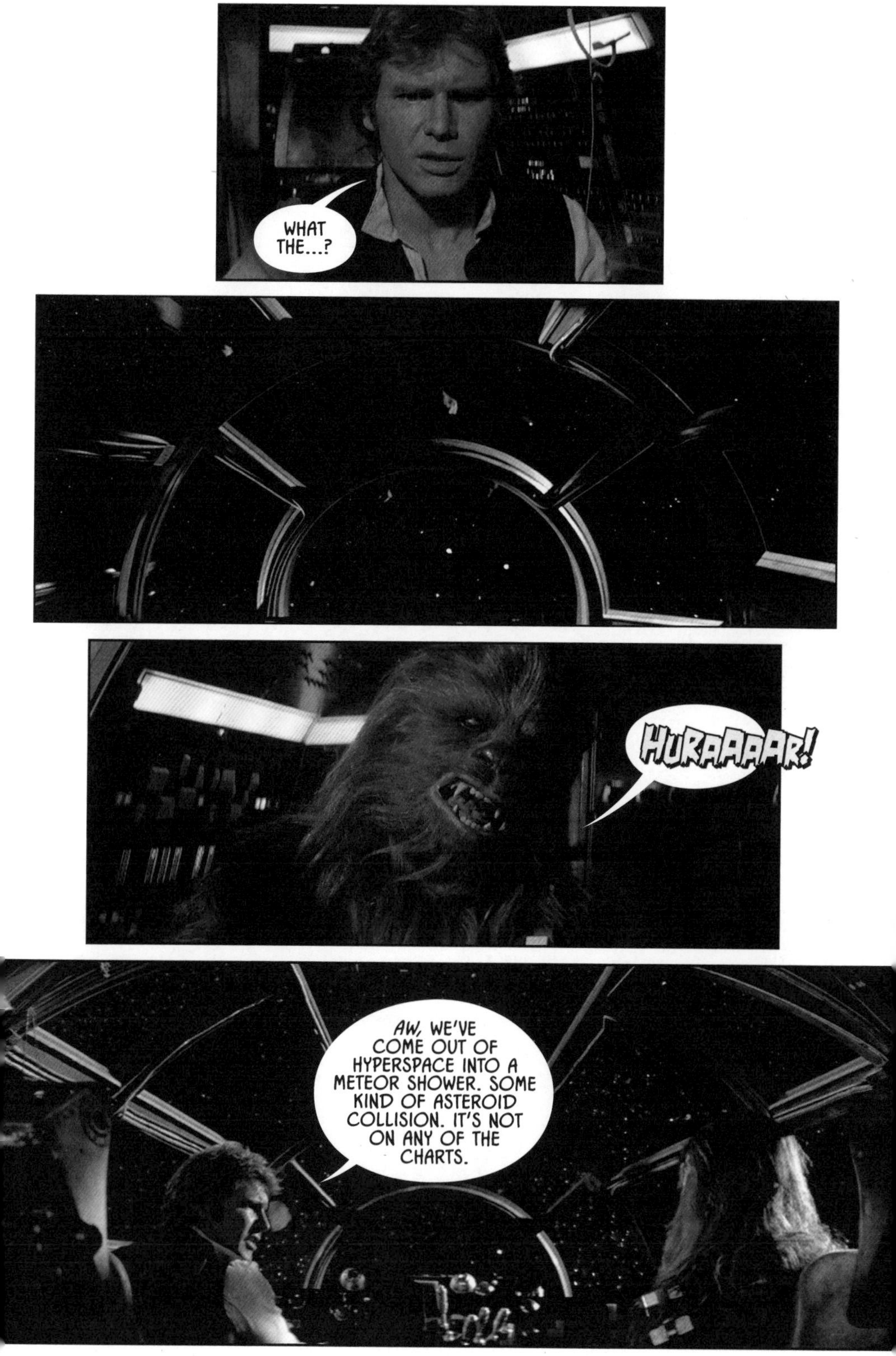
WHAT THE...?
HURAAAAR!
AW, WE'VE COME OUT OF HYPERSPACE INTO A METEOR SHOWER. SOME KIND OF ASTEROID COLLISION. IT'S NOT ON ANY OF THE CHARTS.

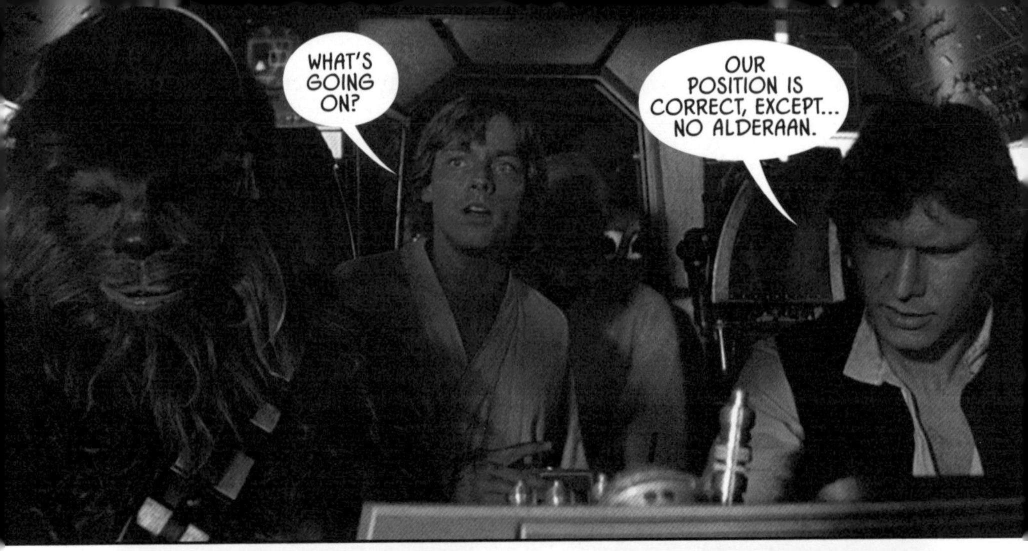
WHAT'S GOING ON?
OUR POSITION IS CORRECT, EXCEPT... NO ALDERAAN.

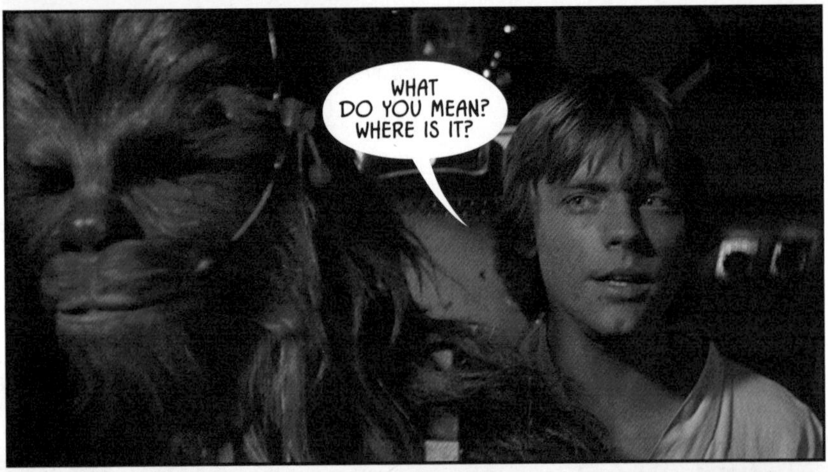
WHAT DO YOU MEAN? WHERE IS IT?

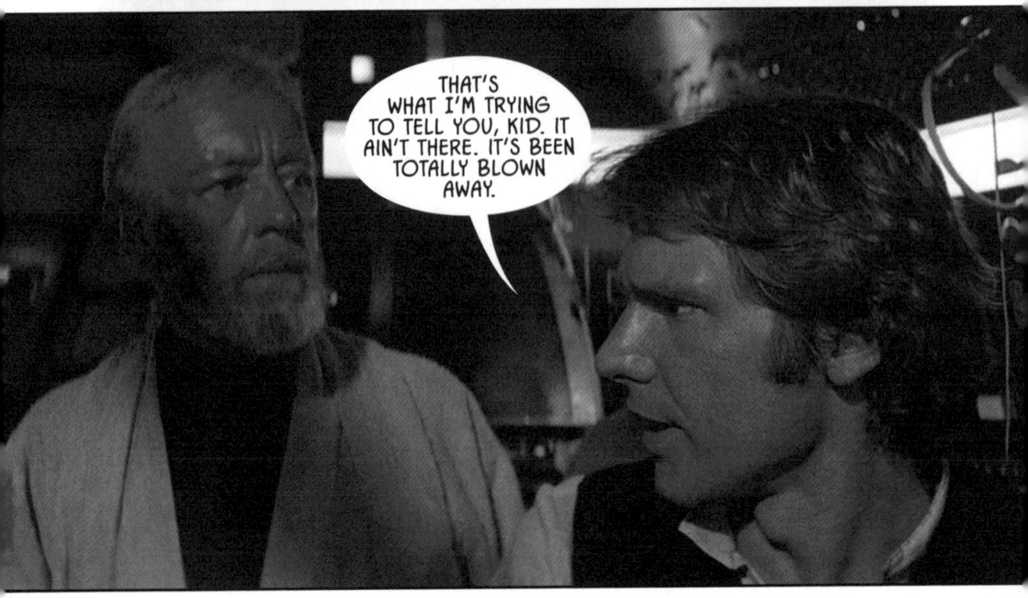
THAT'S WHAT I'M TRYING TO TELL YOU, KID. IT AIN'T THERE. IT'S BEEN TOTALLY BLOWN AWAY.

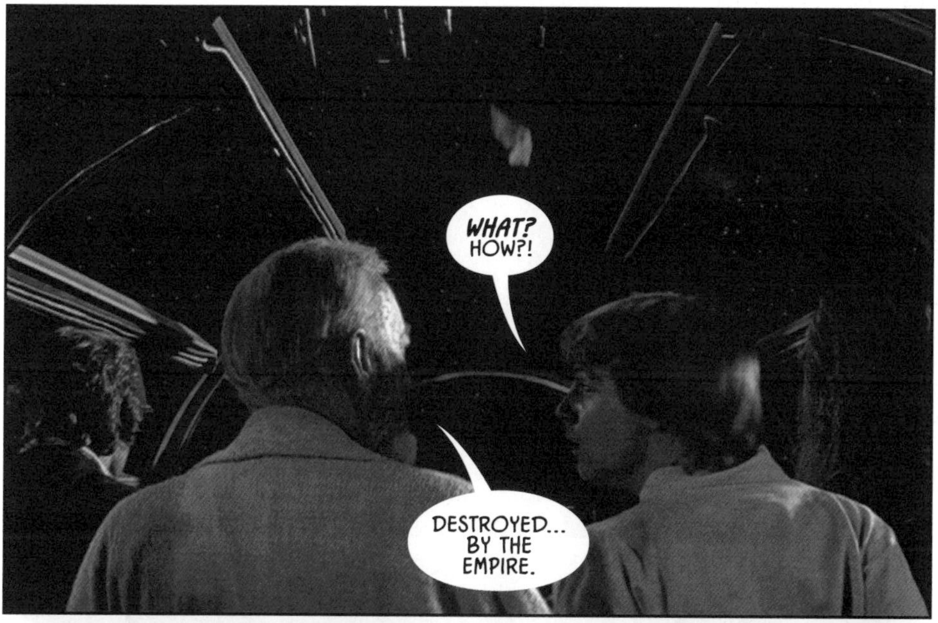
WHAT? HOW?!
DESTROYED... BY THE EMPIRE.

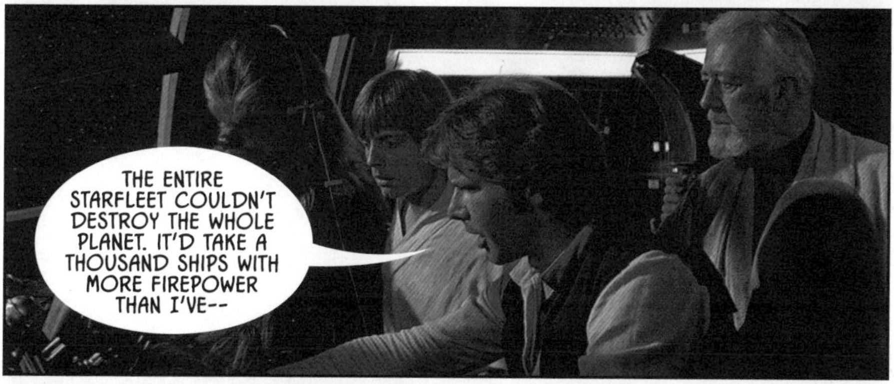
THE ENTIRE STARFLEET COULDN'T DESTROY THE WHOLE PLANET. IT'D TAKE A THOUSAND SHIPS WITH MORE FIREPOWER THAN I'VE--

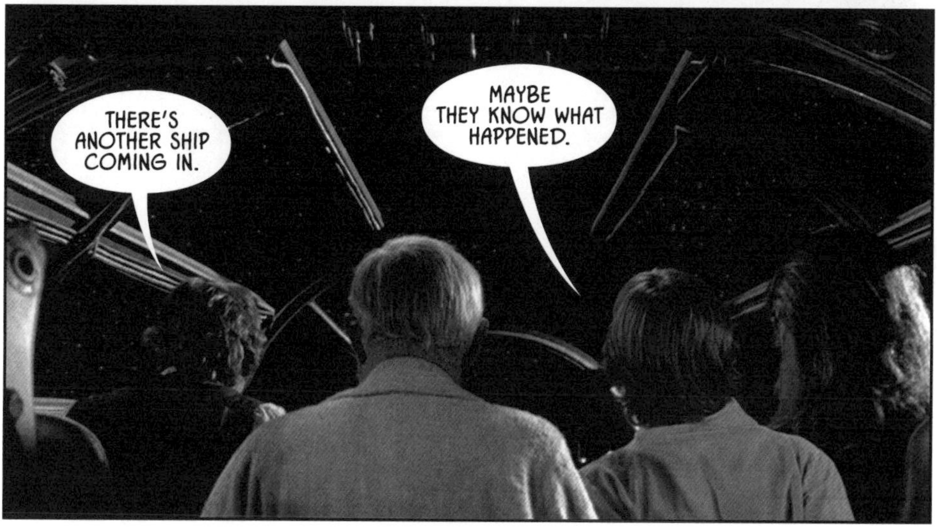
THERE'S ANOTHER SHIP COMING IN.
MAYBE THEY KNOW WHAT HAPPENED.

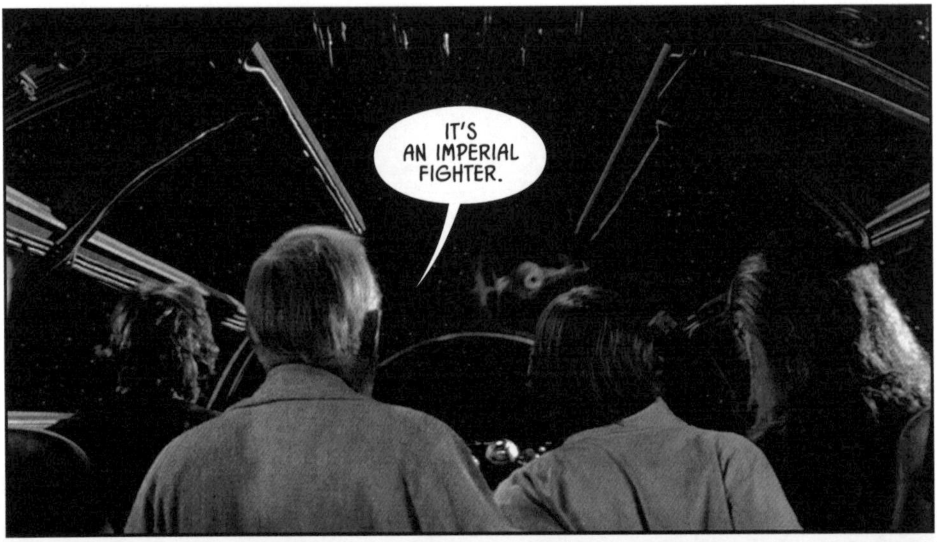
IT'S AN IMPERIAL FIGHTER.

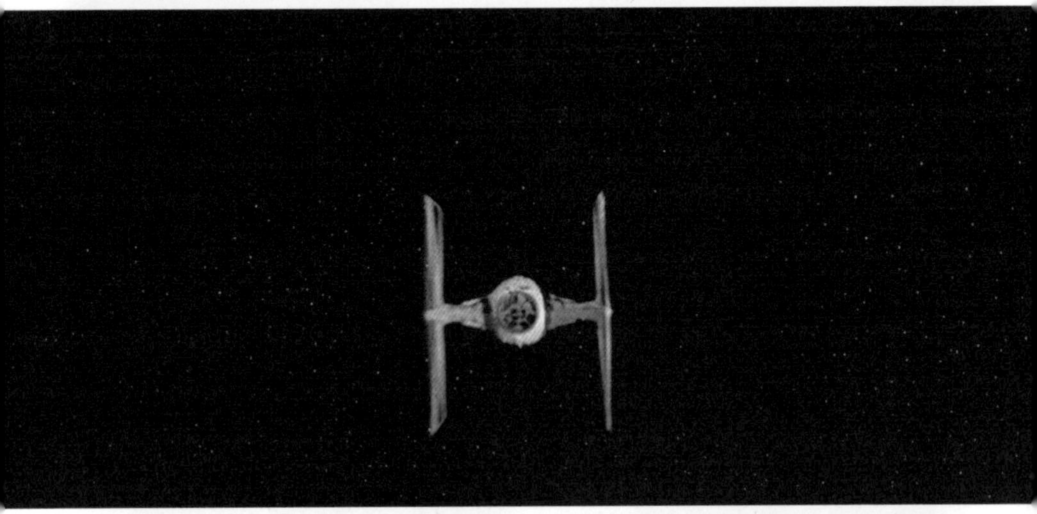

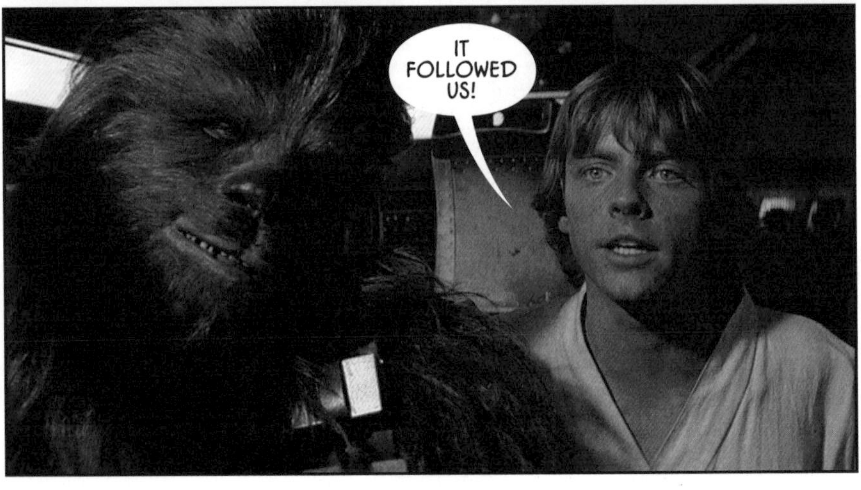
IT FOLLOWED US!

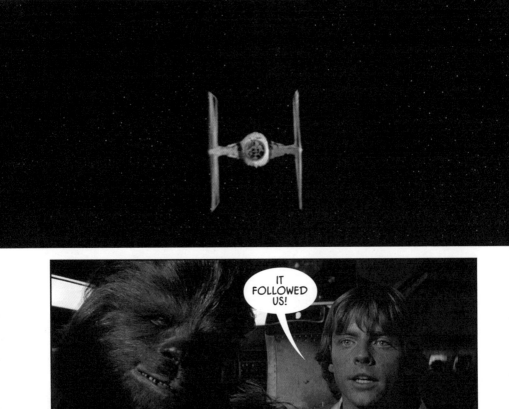

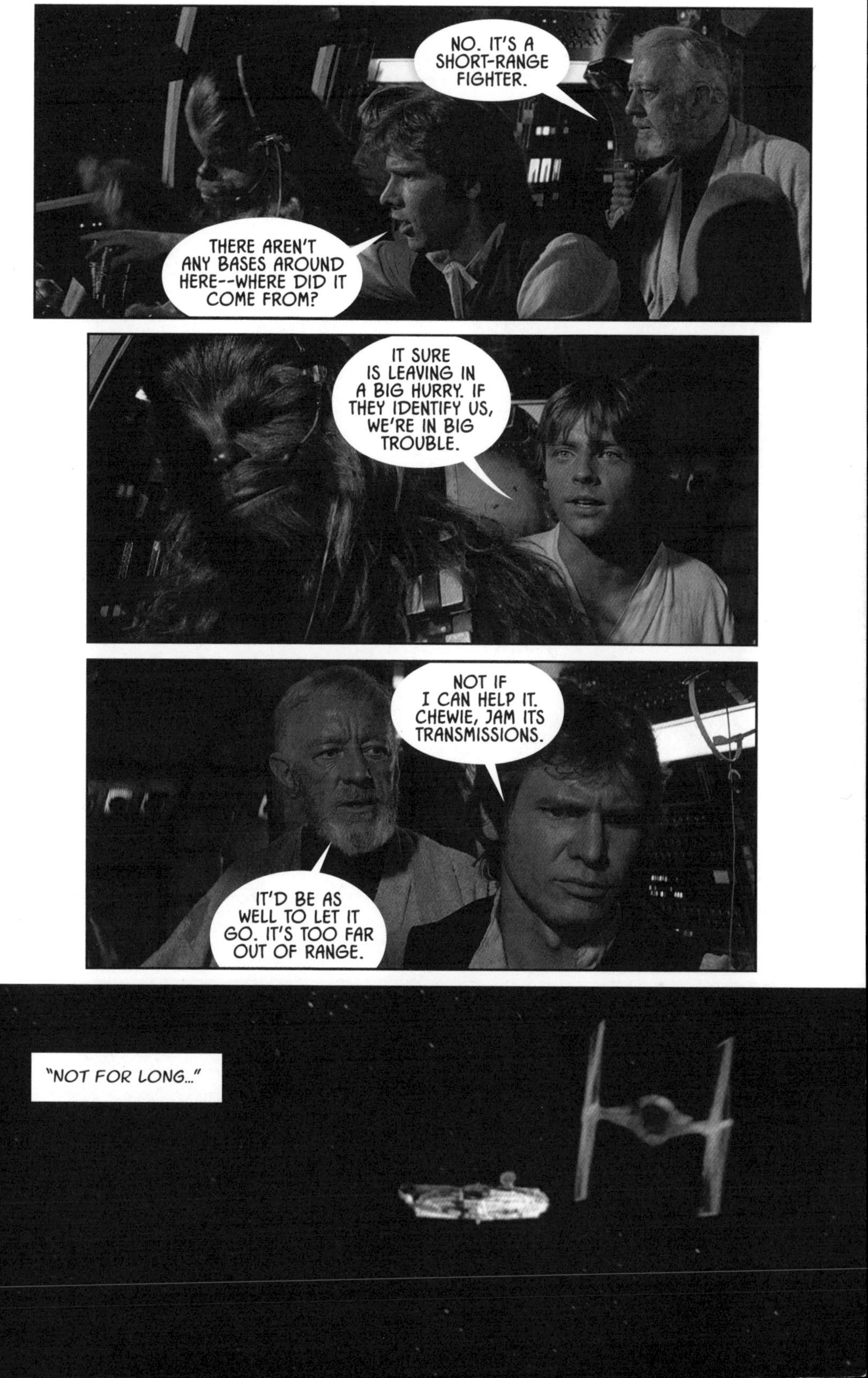
NO. IT'S A SHORT-RANGE FIGHTER.
THERE AREN'T ANY BASES AROUND HERE--WHERE DID IT COME FROM?
IT SURE IS LEAVING IN A BIG HURRY. IF THEY IDENTIFY US, WE'RE IN BIG TROUBLE.
NOT IF I CAN HELP IT. CHEWIE, JAM ITS TRANSMISSIONS.
IT'D BE AS WELL TO LET IT GO. IT'S TOO FAR OUT OF RANGE.
"NOT FOR LONG..."

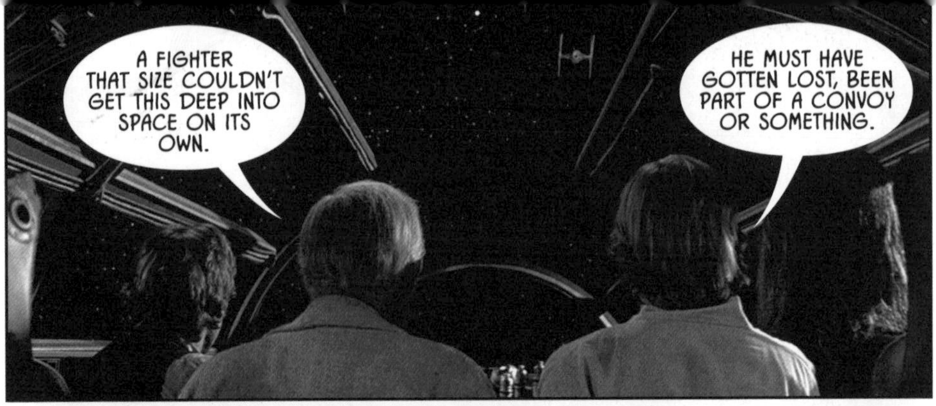
A FIGHTER THAT SIZE COULDN'T GET THIS DEEP INTO SPACE ON ITS OWN.
HE MUST HAVE GOTTEN LOST, BEEN PART OF A CONVOY OR SOMETHING.

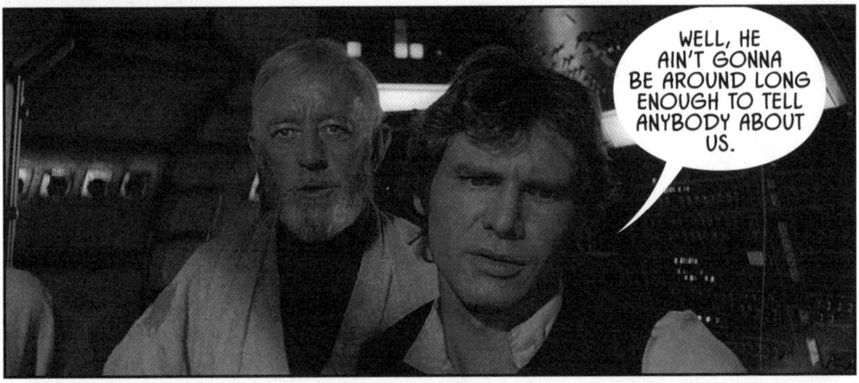
WELL, HE AIN'T GONNA BE AROUND LONG ENOUGH TO TELL ANYBODY ABOUT US.

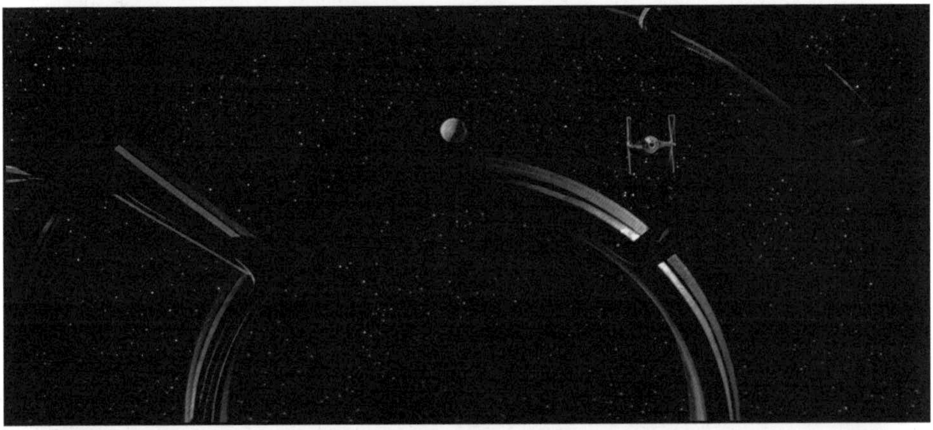

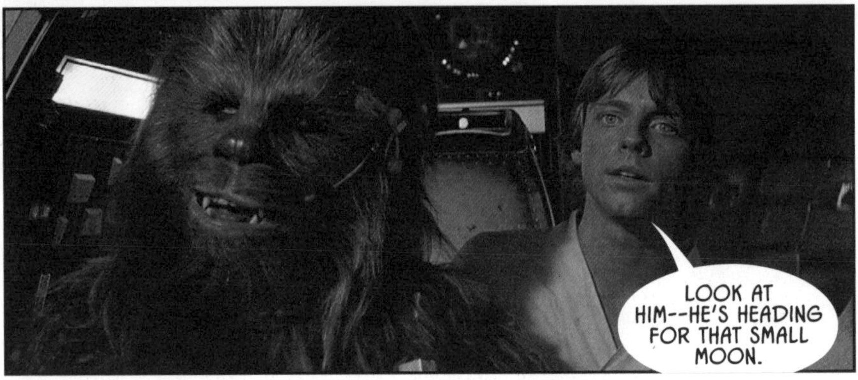
LOOK AT HIM--HE'S HEADING FOR THAT SMALL MOON.

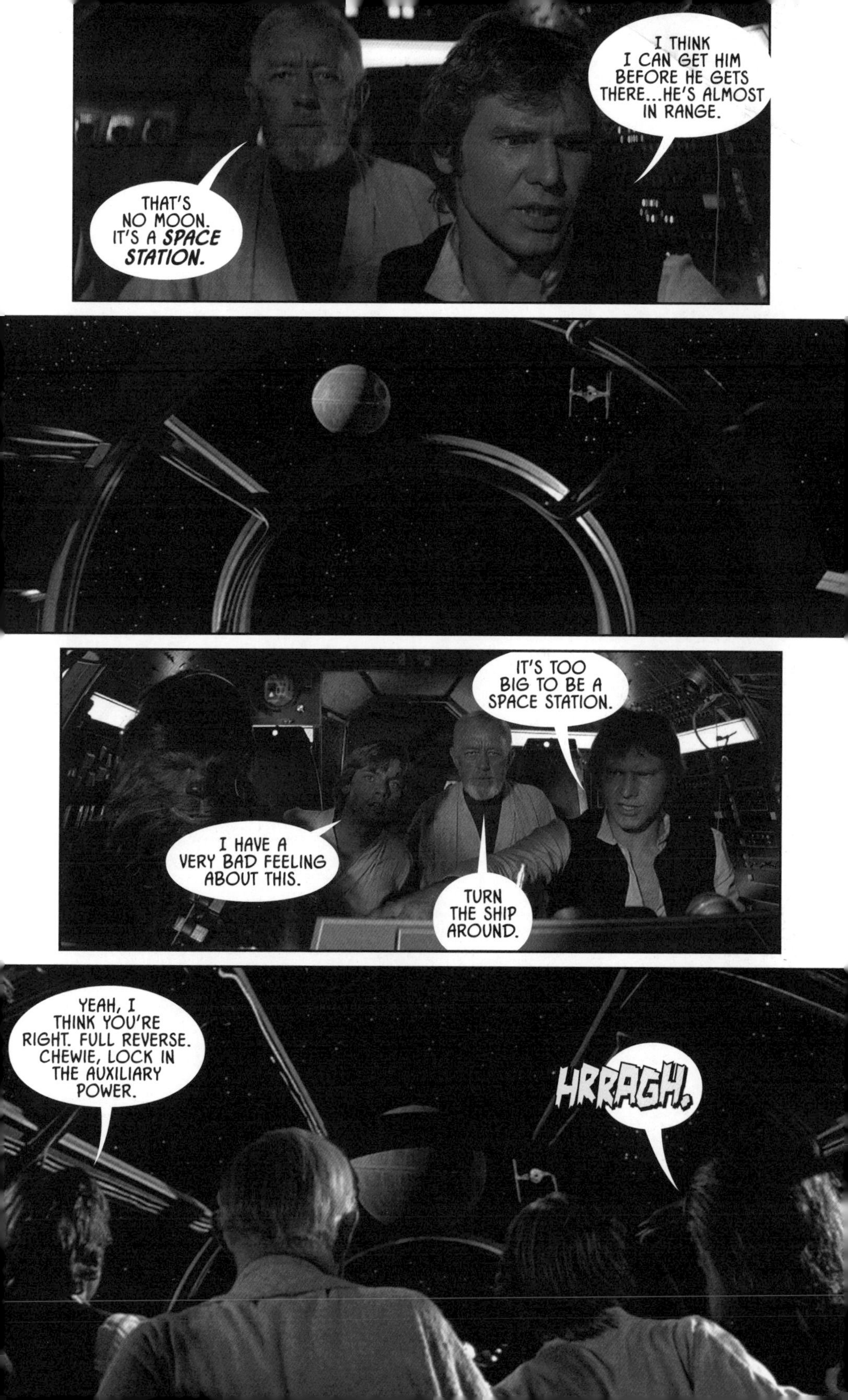
THAT'S NO MOON. IT'S A *SPACE STATION.*
I THINK I CAN GET HIM BEFORE HE GETS THERE...HE'S ALMOST IN RANGE.
IT'S TOO BIG TO BE A SPACE STATION.
I HAVE A VERY BAD FEELING ABOUT THIS.
TURN THE SHIP AROUND.
YEAH, I THINK YOU'RE RIGHT. FULL REVERSE. CHEWIE, LOCK IN THE AUXILIARY POWER.
HRRAGH!

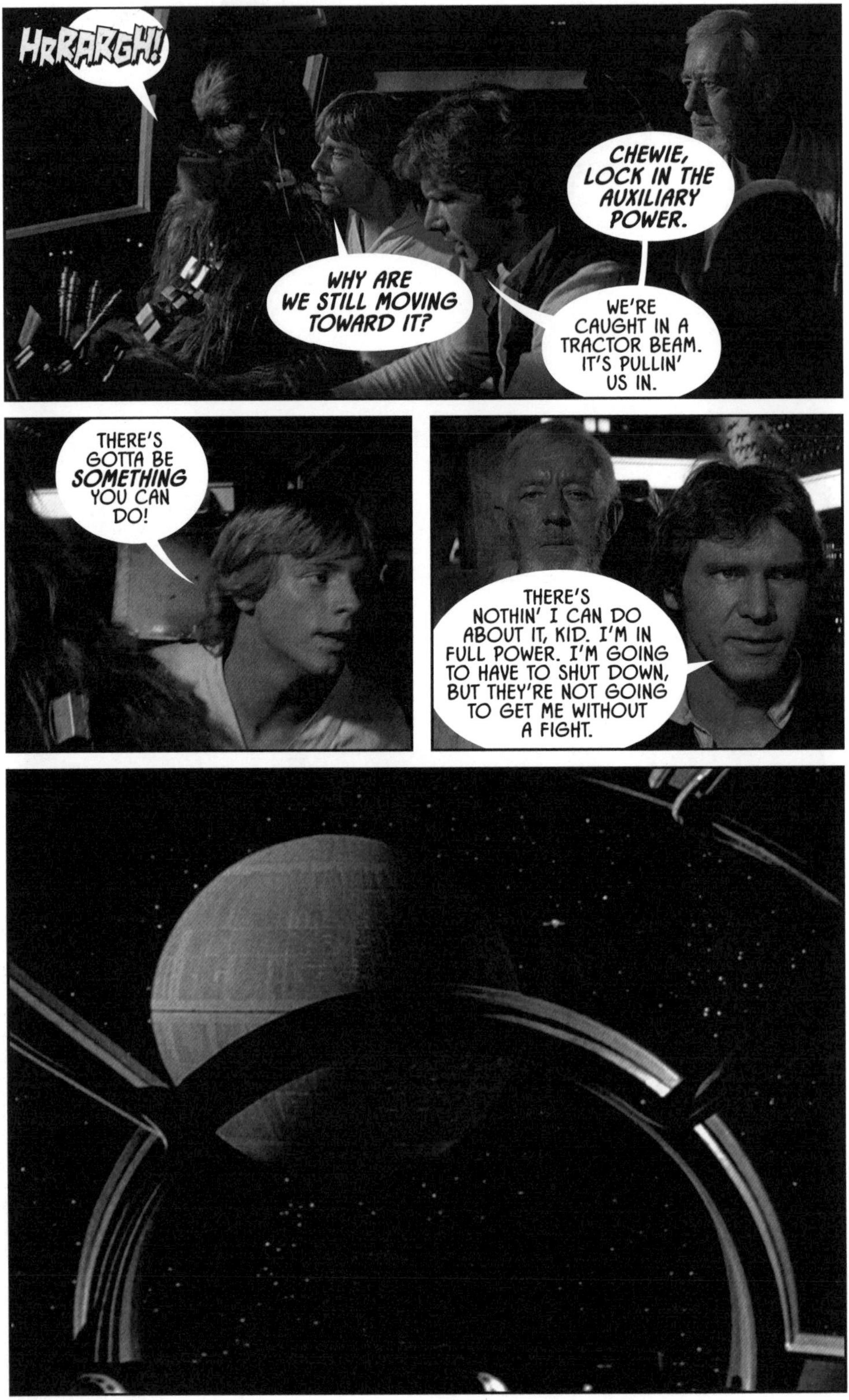
HRRARGH!
WHY ARE WE STILL MOVING TOWARD IT?
CHEWIE, LOCK IN THE AUXILIARY POWER.
WE'RE CAUGHT IN A TRACTOR BEAM. IT'S PULLIN' US IN.
THERE'S GOTTA BE SOMETHING YOU CAN DO!
THERE'S NOTHIN' I CAN DO ABOUT IT, KID. I'M IN FULL POWER. I'M GOING TO HAVE TO SHUT DOWN, BUT THEY'RE NOT GOING TO GET ME WITHOUT A FIGHT.

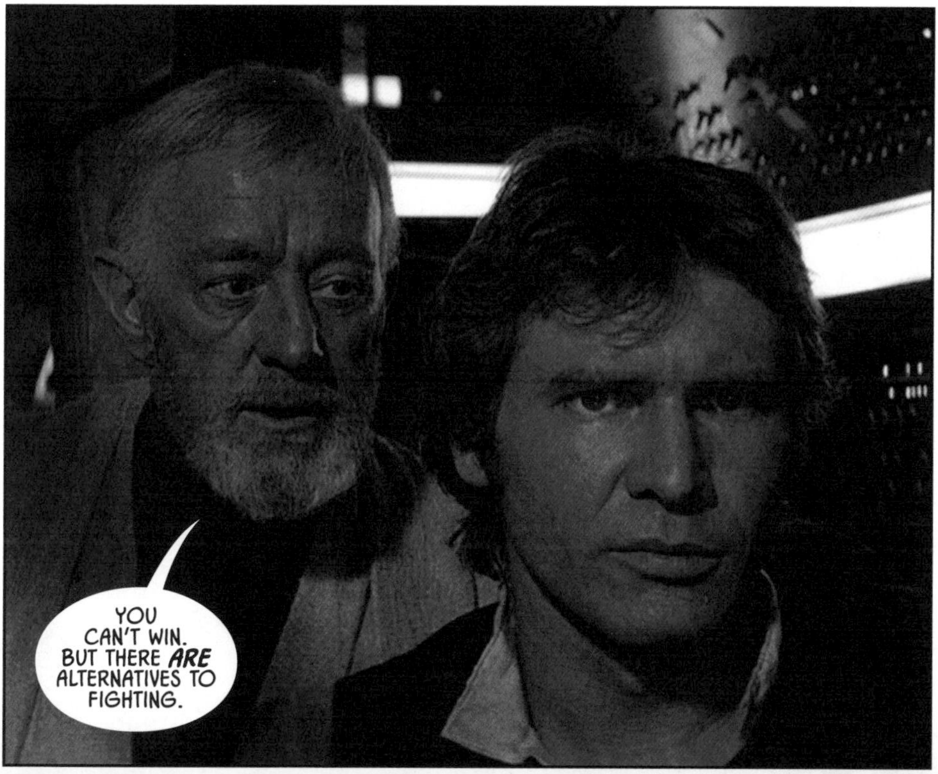
YOU CAN'T WIN. BUT THERE ***ARE*** ALTERNATIVES TO FIGHTING.

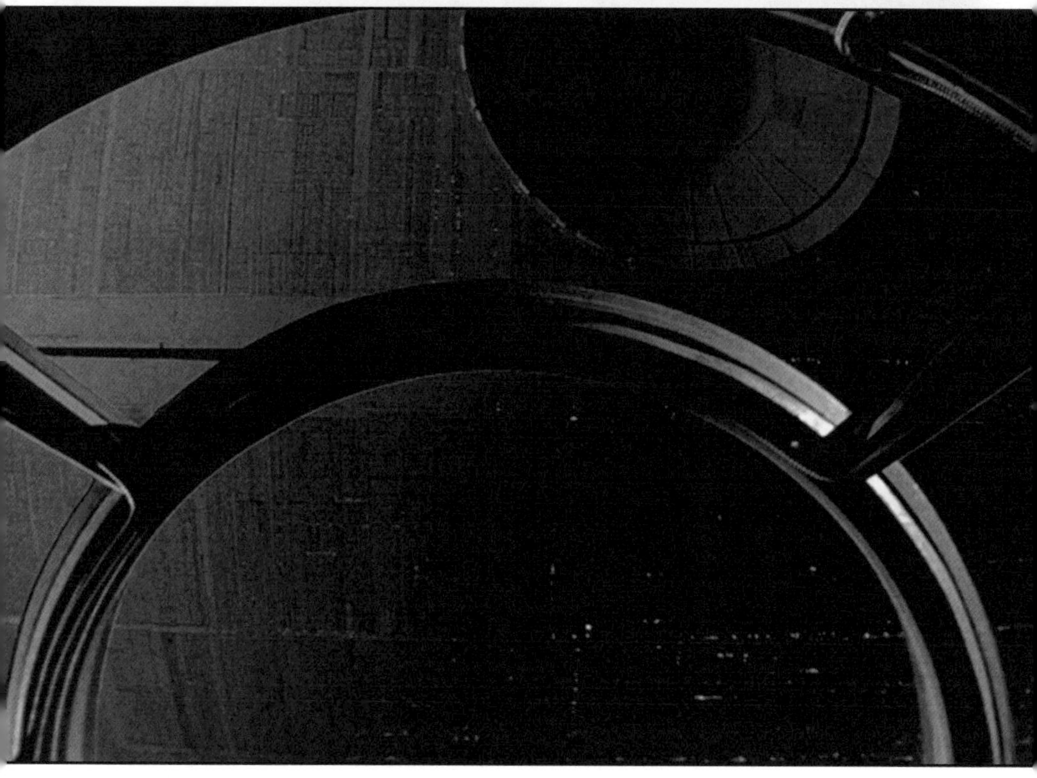

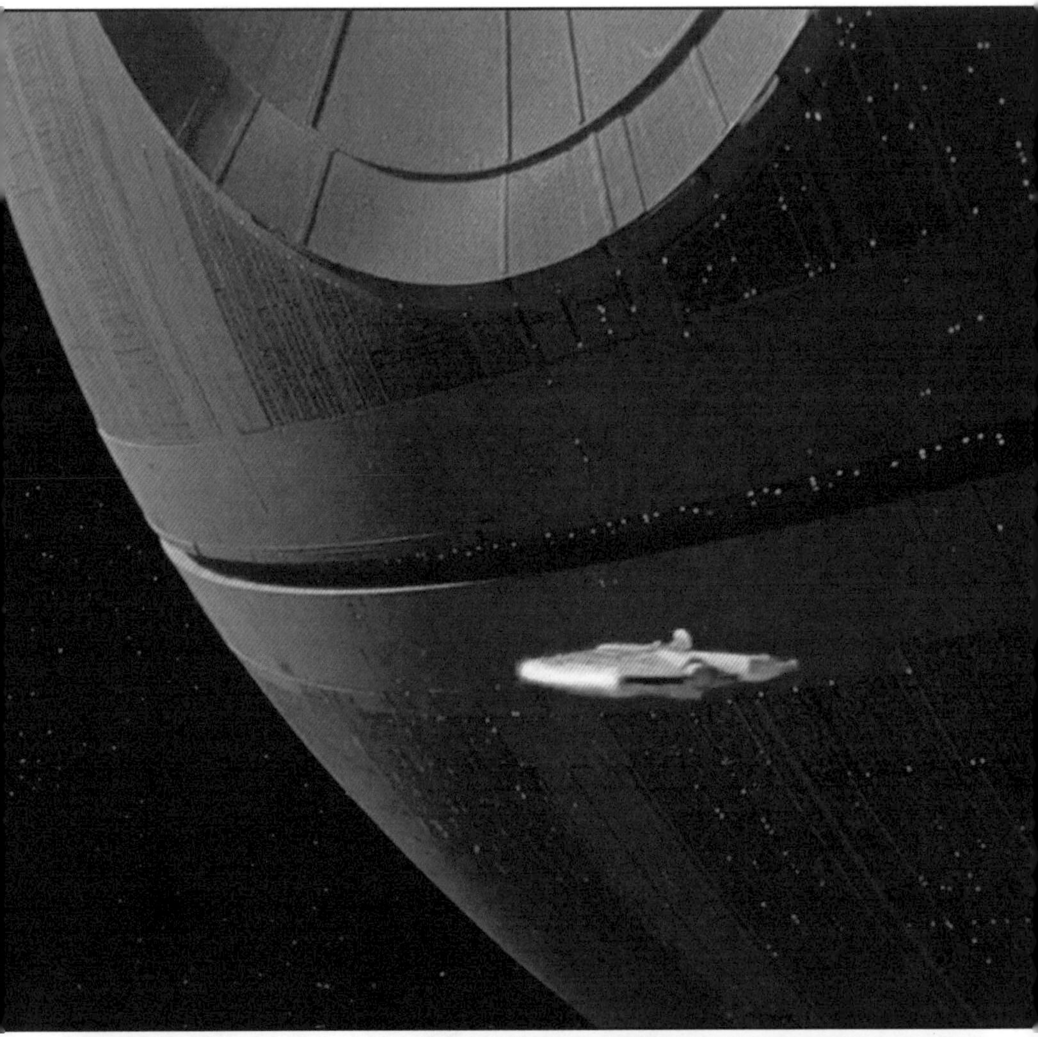

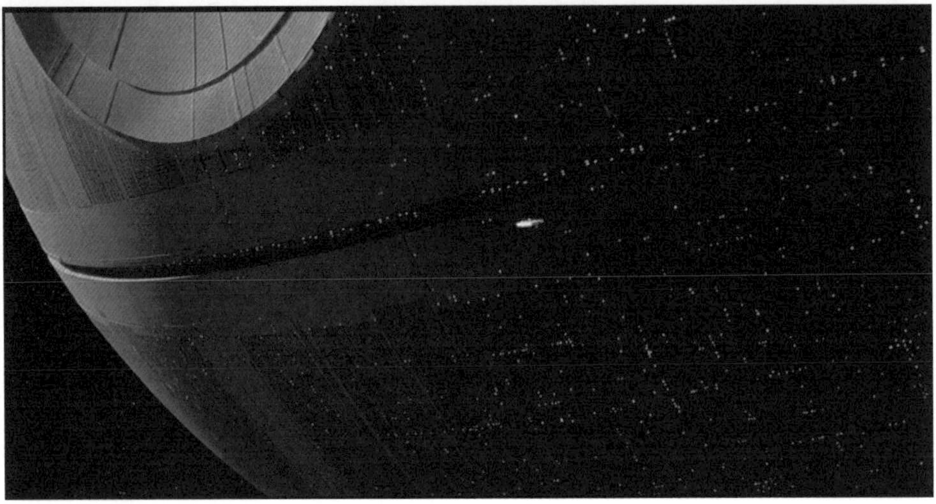

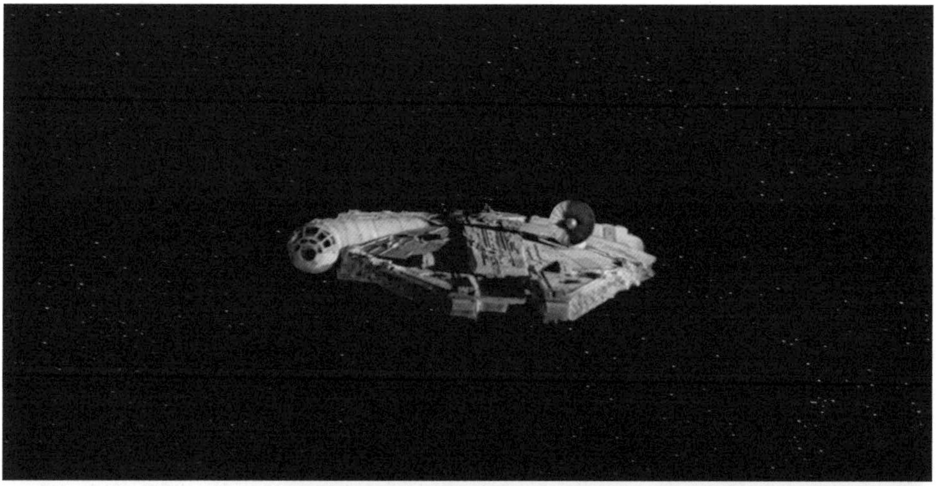

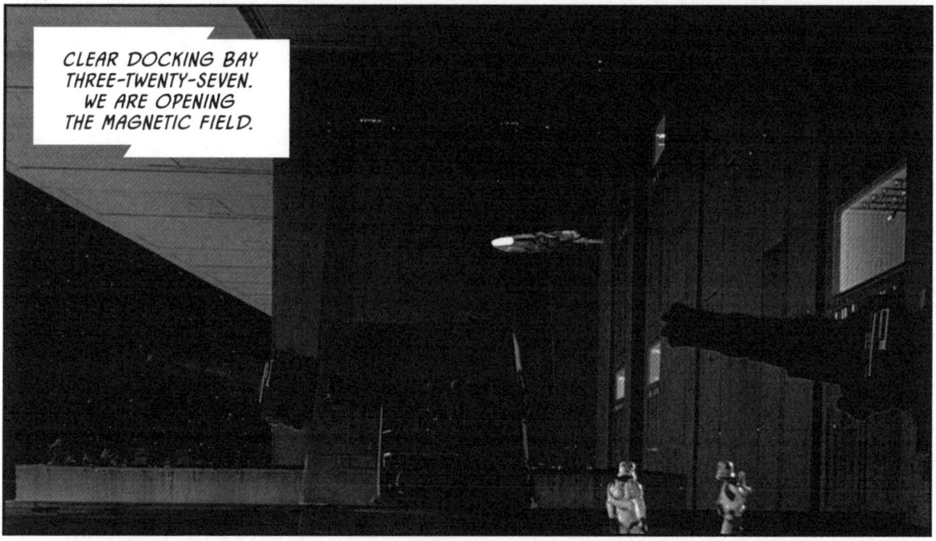
CLEAR DOCKING BAY THREE-TWENTY-SEVEN. WE ARE OPENING THE MAGNETIC FIELD.

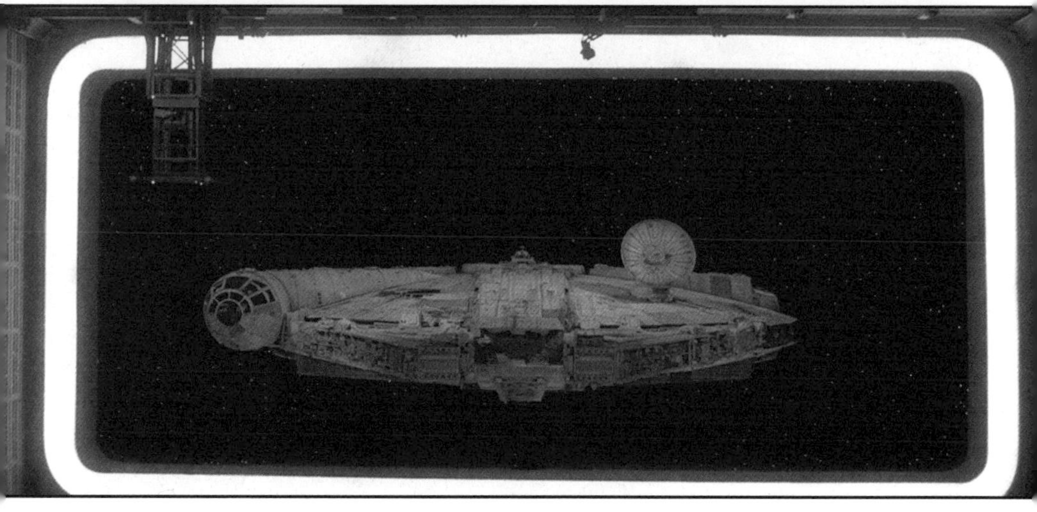

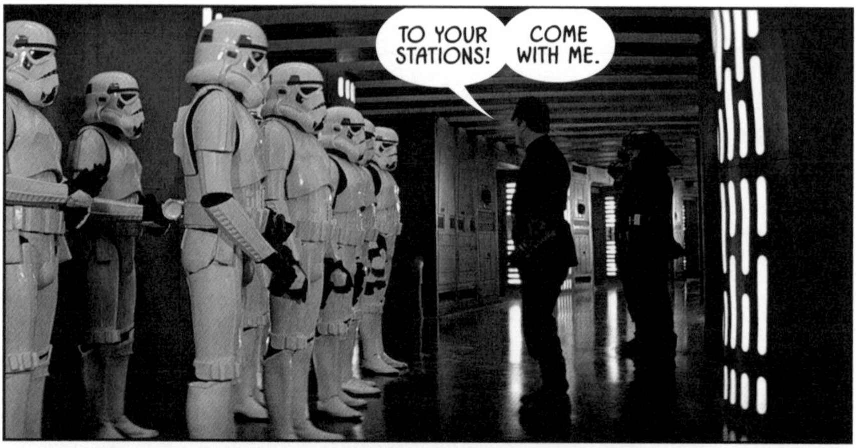
TO YOUR STATIONS!
COME WITH ME.

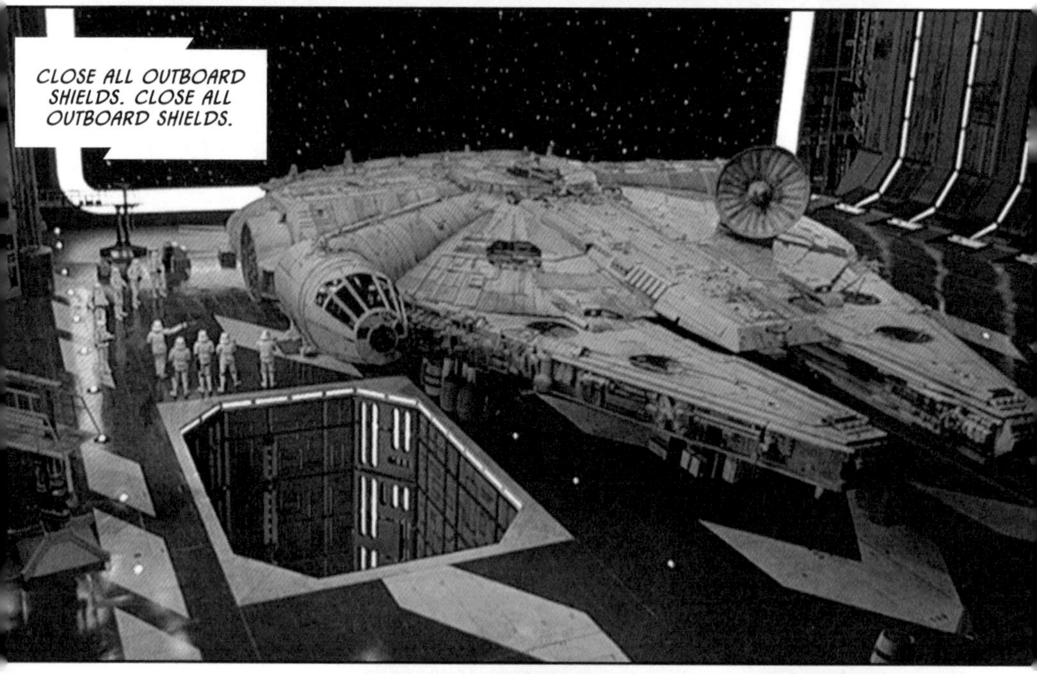
CLOSE ALL OUTBOARD SHIELDS. CLOSE ALL OUTBOARD SHIELDS.

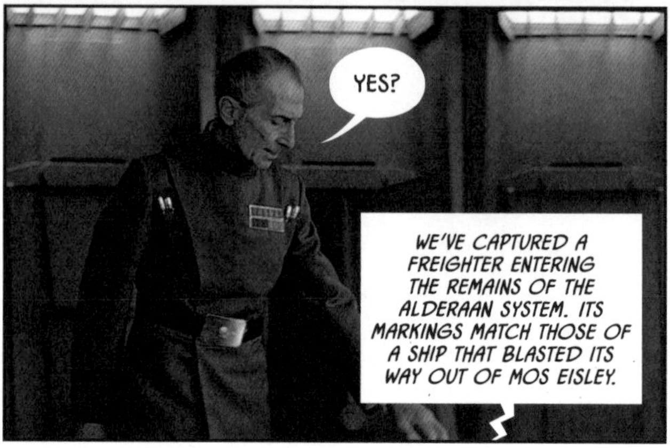
YES?
WE'VE CAPTURED A FREIGHTER ENTERING THE REMAINS OF THE ALDERAAN SYSTEM. ITS MARKINGS MATCH THOSE OF A SHIP THAT BLASTED ITS WAY OUT OF MOS EISLEY.

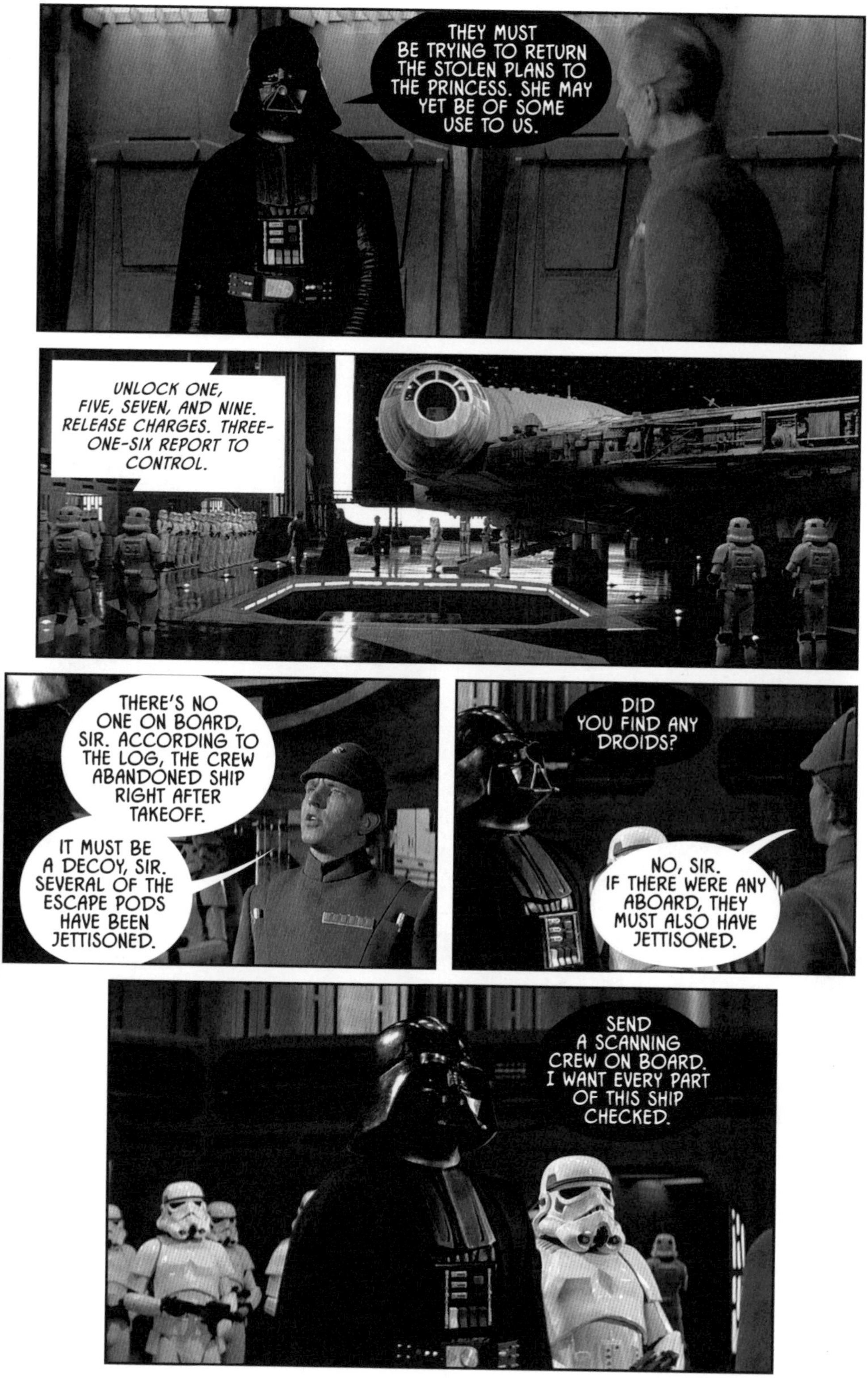
THEY MUST BE TRYING TO RETURN THE STOLEN PLANS TO THE PRINCESS. SHE MAY YET BE OF SOME USE TO US.
UNLOCK ONE, FIVE, SEVEN, AND NINE. RELEASE CHARGES. THREE-ONE-SIX REPORT TO CONTROL.
THERE'S NO ONE ON BOARD, SIR. ACCORDING TO THE LOG, THE CREW ABANDONED SHIP RIGHT AFTER TAKEOFF.
IT MUST BE A DECOY, SIR. SEVERAL OF THE ESCAPE PODS HAVE BEEN JETTISONED.
DID YOU FIND ANY DROIDS?
NO, SIR. IF THERE WERE ANY ABOARD, THEY MUST ALSO HAVE JETTISONED.
SEND A SCANNING CREW ON BOARD. I WANT EVERY PART OF THIS SHIP CHECKED.

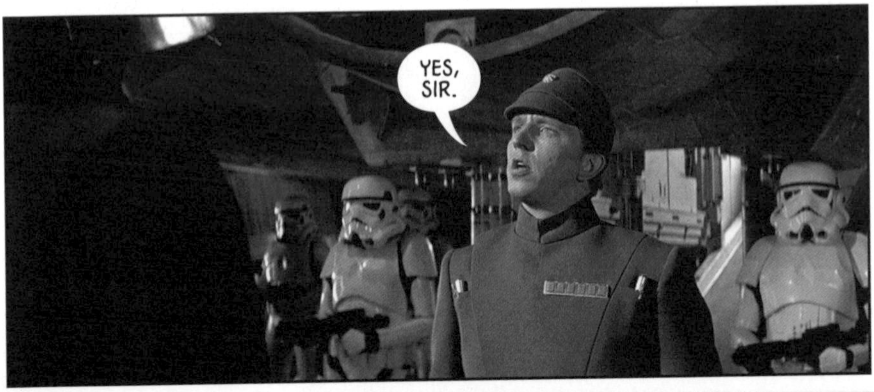
YES, SIR.

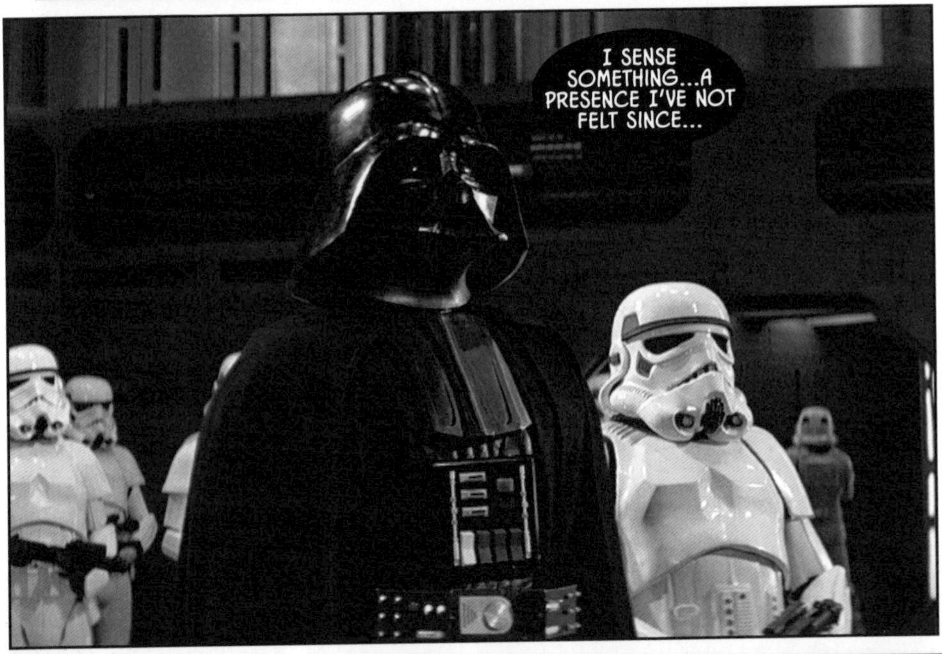
I SENSE SOMETHING...A PRESENCE I'VE NOT FELT SINCE...

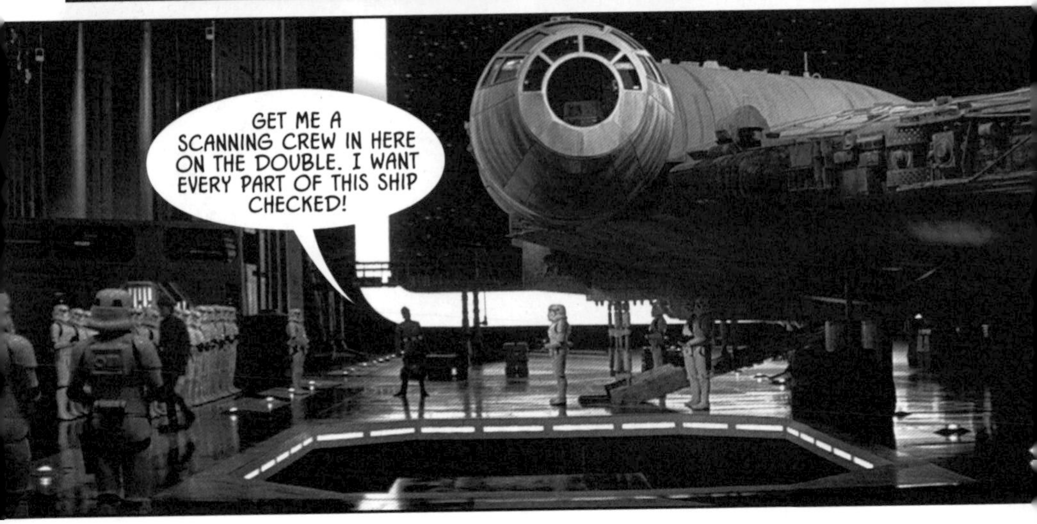
GET ME A SCANNING CREW IN HERE ON THE DOUBLE. I WANT EVERY PART OF THIS SHIP CHECKED!

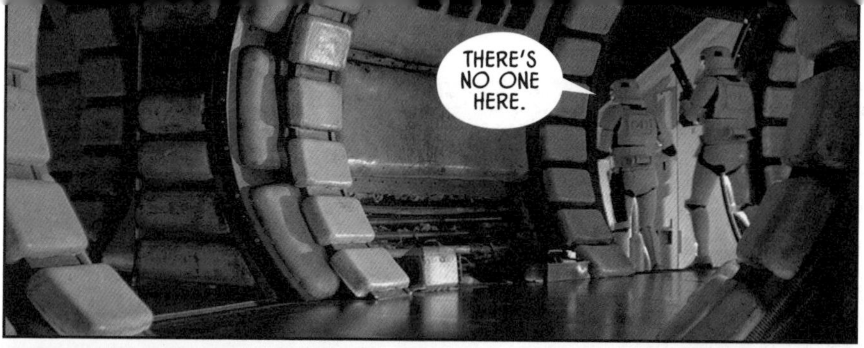
THERE'S NO ONE HERE.

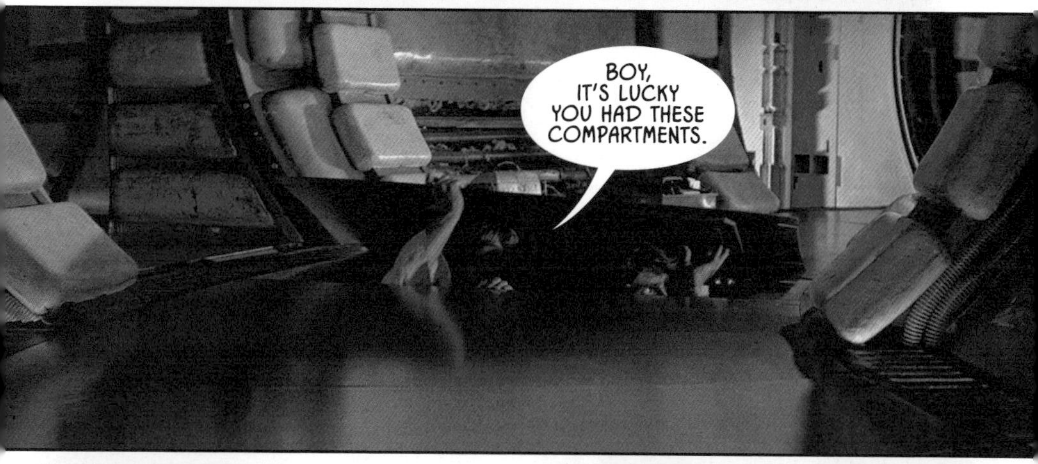
BOY, IT'S LUCKY YOU HAD THESE COMPARTMENTS.

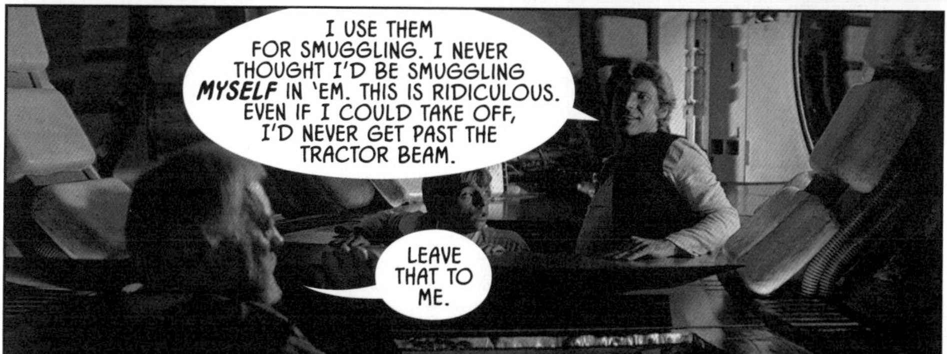
I USE THEM FOR SMUGGLING. I NEVER THOUGHT I'D BE SMUGGLING ***MYSELF*** IN 'EM. THIS IS RIDICULOUS. EVEN IF I COULD TAKE OFF, I'D NEVER GET PAST THE TRACTOR BEAM.
LEAVE THAT TO ME.

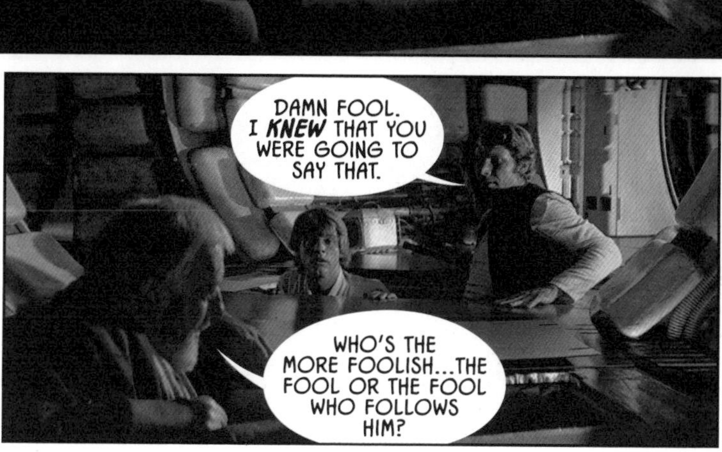
DAMN FOOL. I ***KNEW*** THAT YOU WERE GOING TO SAY THAT.
WHO'S THE MORE FOOLISH...THE FOOL OR THE FOOL WHO FOLLOWS HIM?

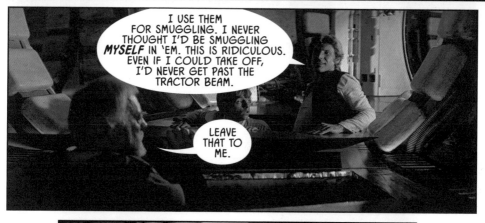

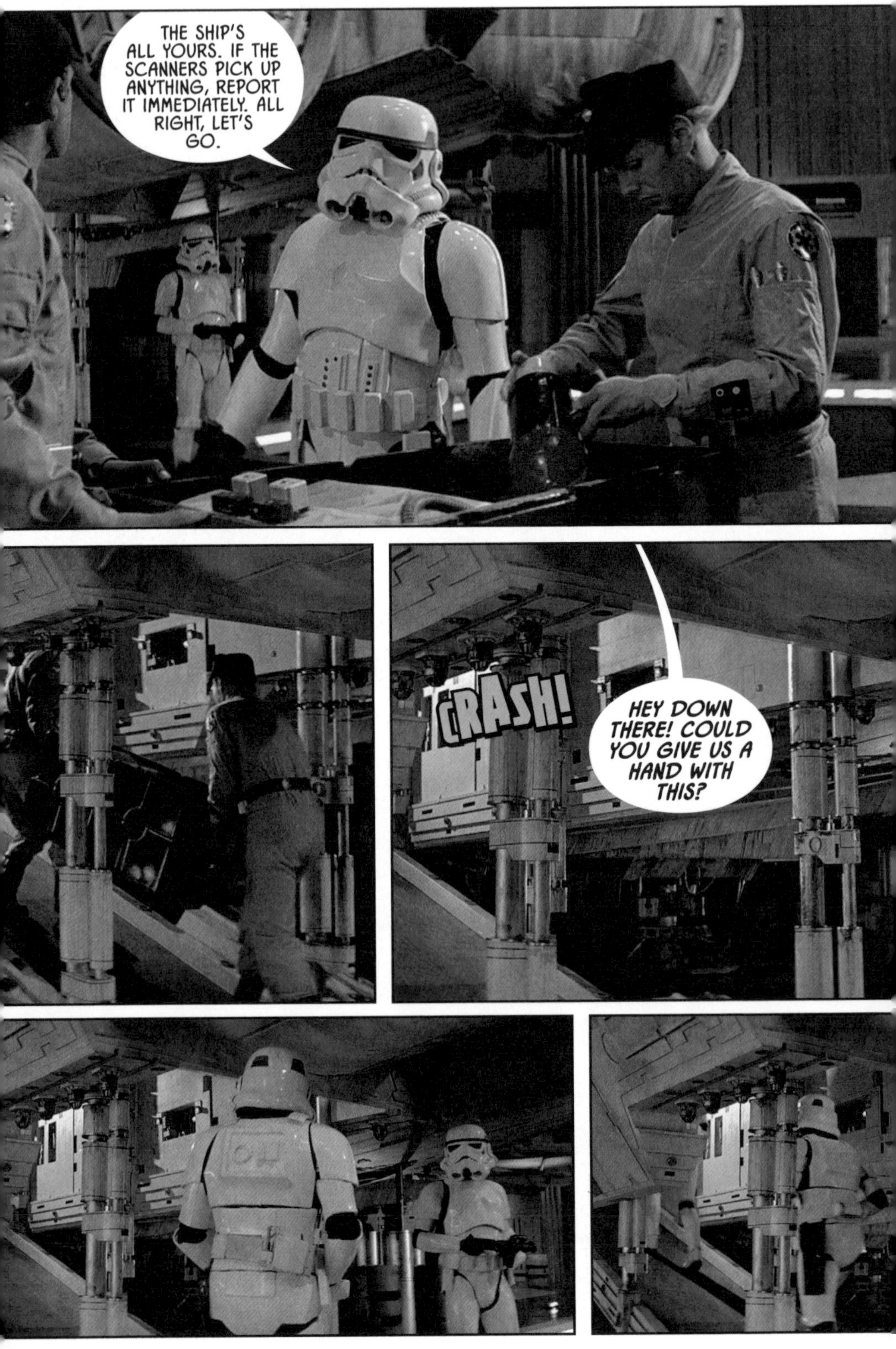
THE SHIP'S ALL YOURS. IF THE SCANNERS PICK UP ANYTHING, REPORT IT IMMEDIATELY. ALL RIGHT, LET'S GO.
CRASH!
HEY DOWN THERE! COULD YOU GIVE US A HAND WITH THIS?

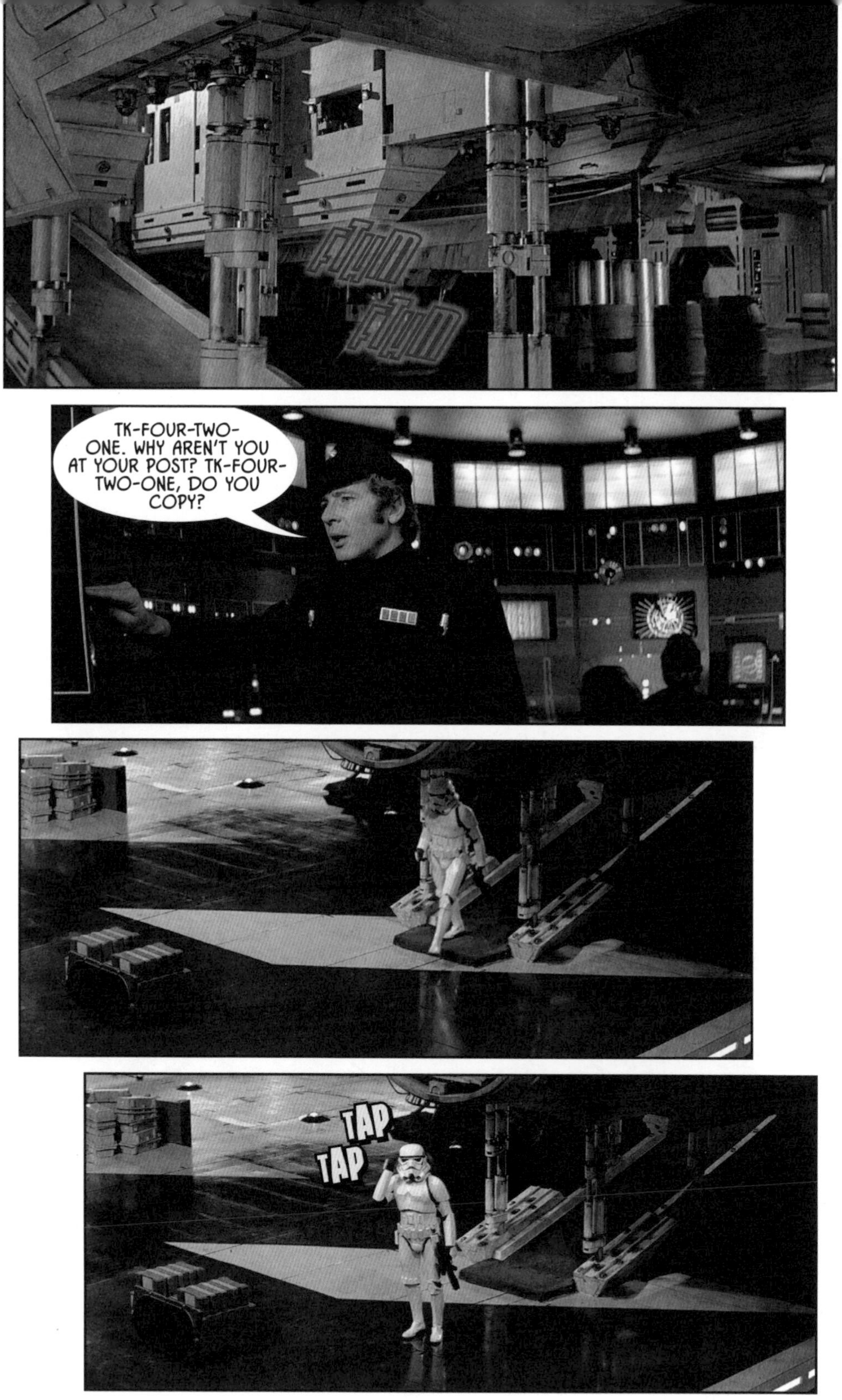
TK-FOUR-TWO-ONE. WHY AREN'T YOU AT YOUR POST? TK-FOUR-TWO-ONE, DO YOU COPY?
TAP
TAP

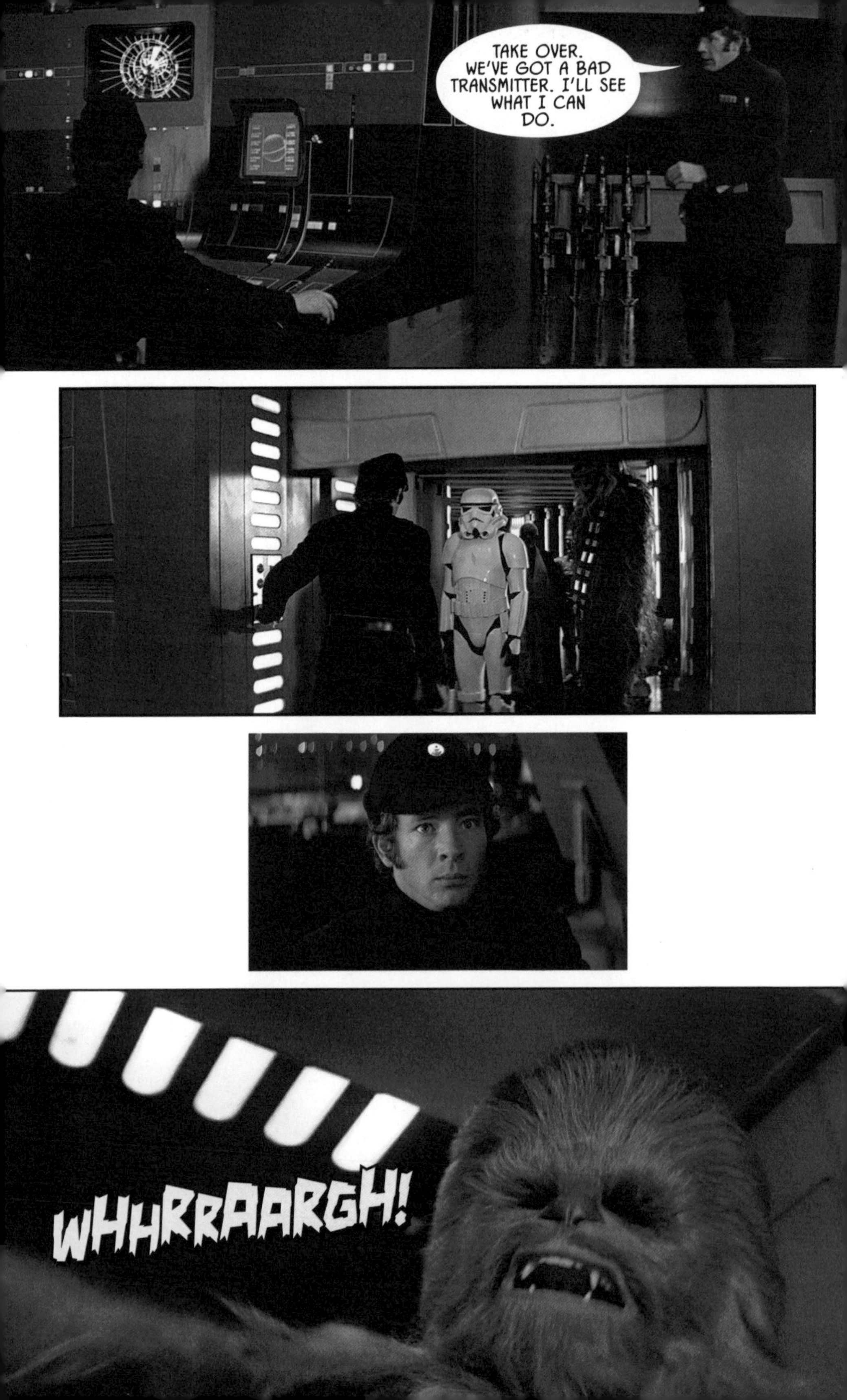
TAKE OVER. WE'VE GOT A BAD TRANSMITTER. I'LL SEE WHAT I CAN DO.
WHHRRAARGH!

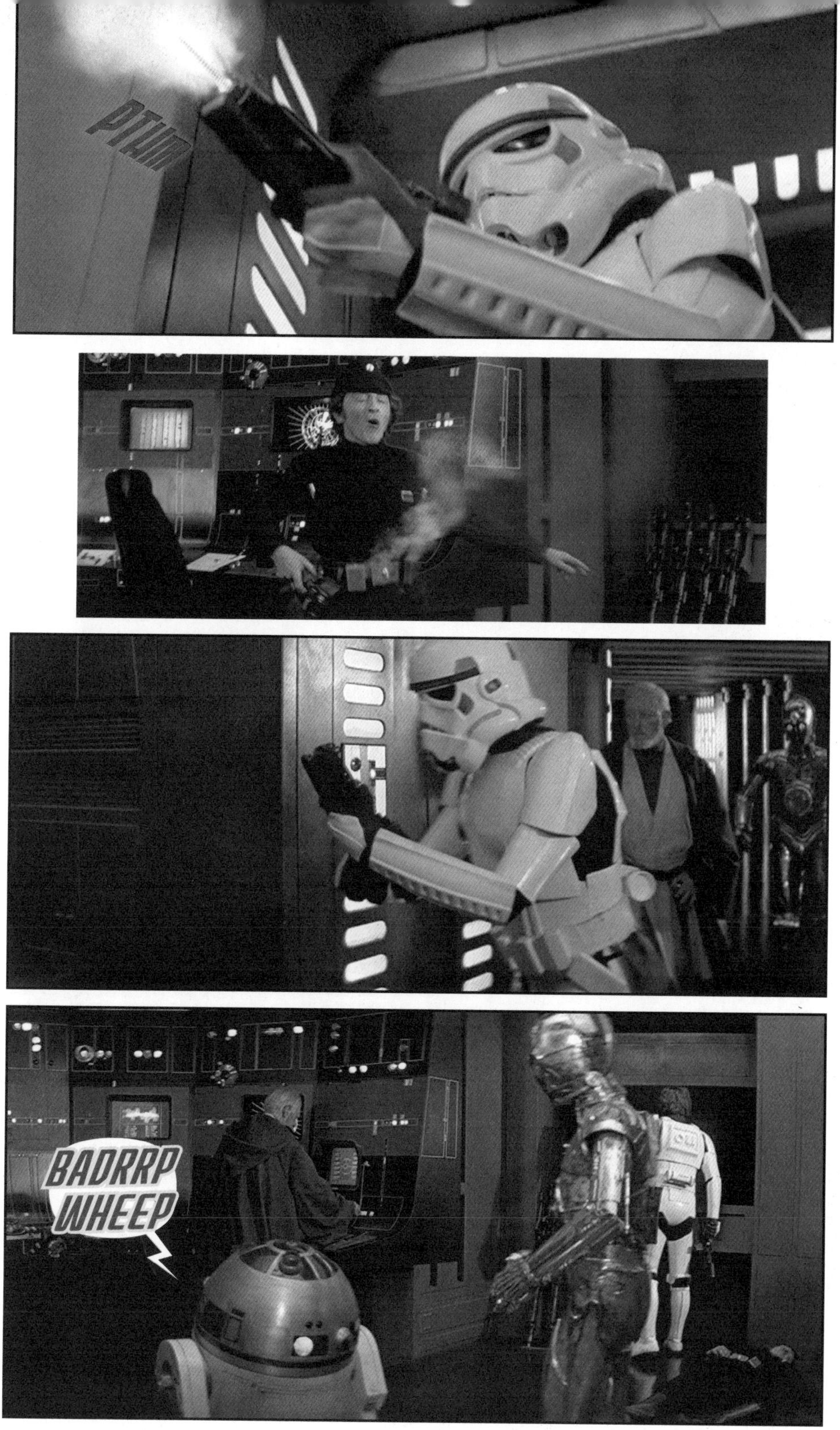
PTWM
BADRRP WHEEP

YOU KNOW, BETWEEN HIS *HOWLING* AND YOUR *BLASTING* EVERYTHING IN SIGHT, IT'S A WONDER THE *WHOLE STATION* DOESN'T KNOW WE'RE HERE.

BRING 'EM ON! I PREFER A STRAIGHT *FIGHT* TO ALL THIS *SNEAKING AROUND.*

WE FOUND T[...] COMPUT[...] OUTLE[...] SIR.

PLUG IN. HE SHOULD BE ABLE TO INTERPRET THE ENTIRE IMPERIAL NETWORK.

BABWEEP

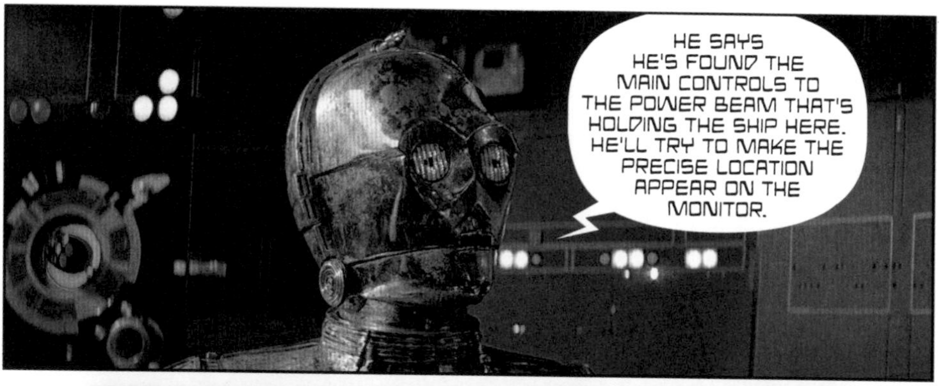
HE SAYS HE'S FOUND THE MAIN CONTROLS TO THE POWER BEAM THAT'S HOLDING THE SHIP HERE. HE'LL TRY TO MAKE THE PRECISE LOCATION APPEAR ON THE MONITOR.

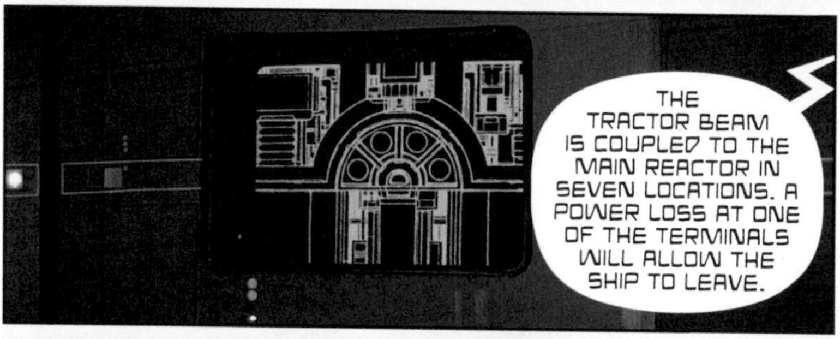
THE TRACTOR BEAM IS COUPLED TO THE MAIN REACTOR IN SEVEN LOCATIONS. A POWER LOSS AT ONE OF THE TERMINALS WILL ALLOW THE SHIP TO LEAVE.

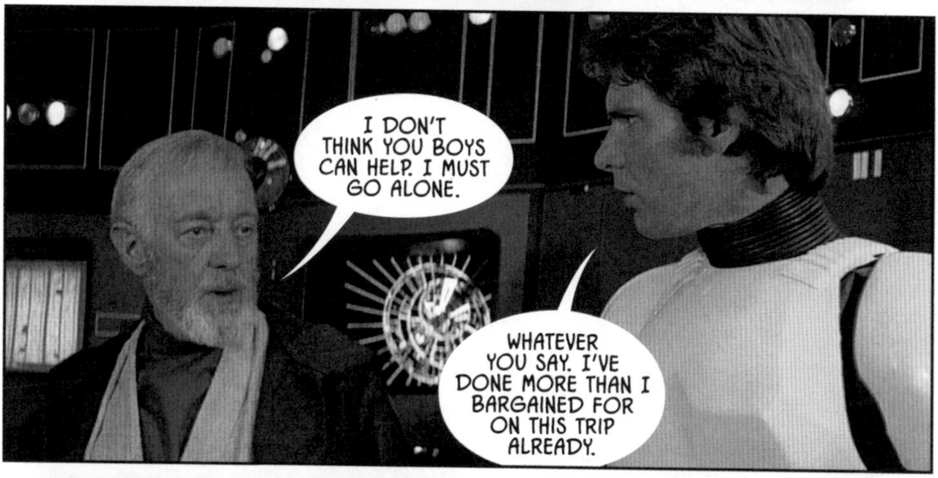
I DON'T THINK YOU BOYS CAN HELP. I MUST GO ALONE.
WHATEVER YOU SAY. I'VE DONE MORE THAN I BARGAINED FOR ON THIS TRIP ALREADY.

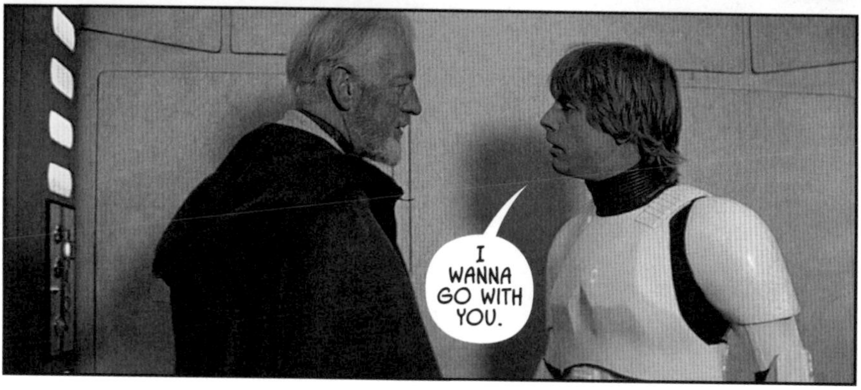
I WANNA GO WITH YOU.

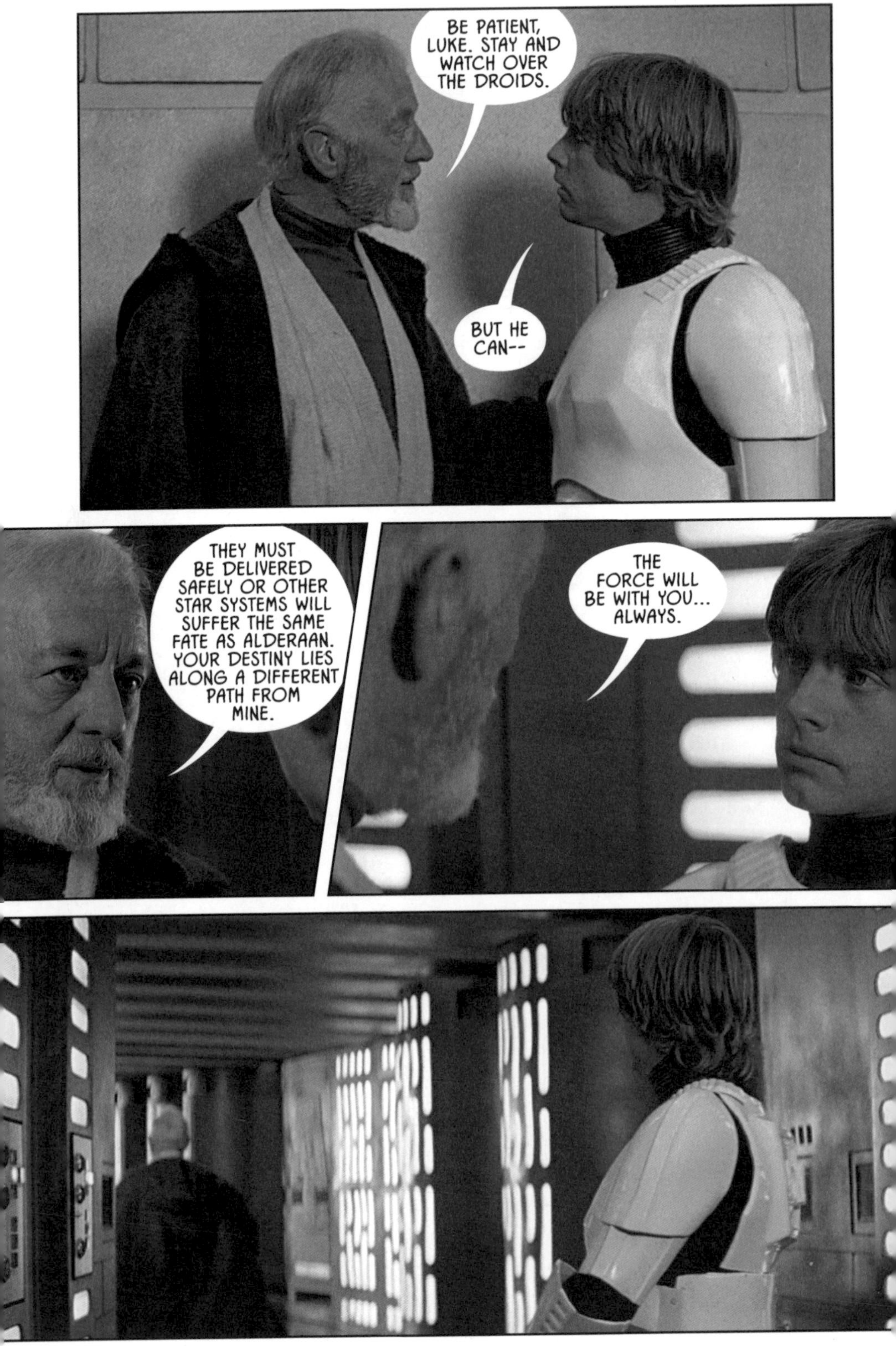
BE PATIENT, LUKE. STAY AND WATCH OVER THE DROIDS.
BUT HE CAN--
THEY MUST BE DELIVERED SAFELY OR OTHER STAR SYSTEMS WILL SUFFER THE SAME FATE AS ALDERAAN. YOUR DESTINY LIES ALONG A DIFFERENT PATH FROM MINE.
THE FORCE WILL BE WITH YOU... ALWAYS.

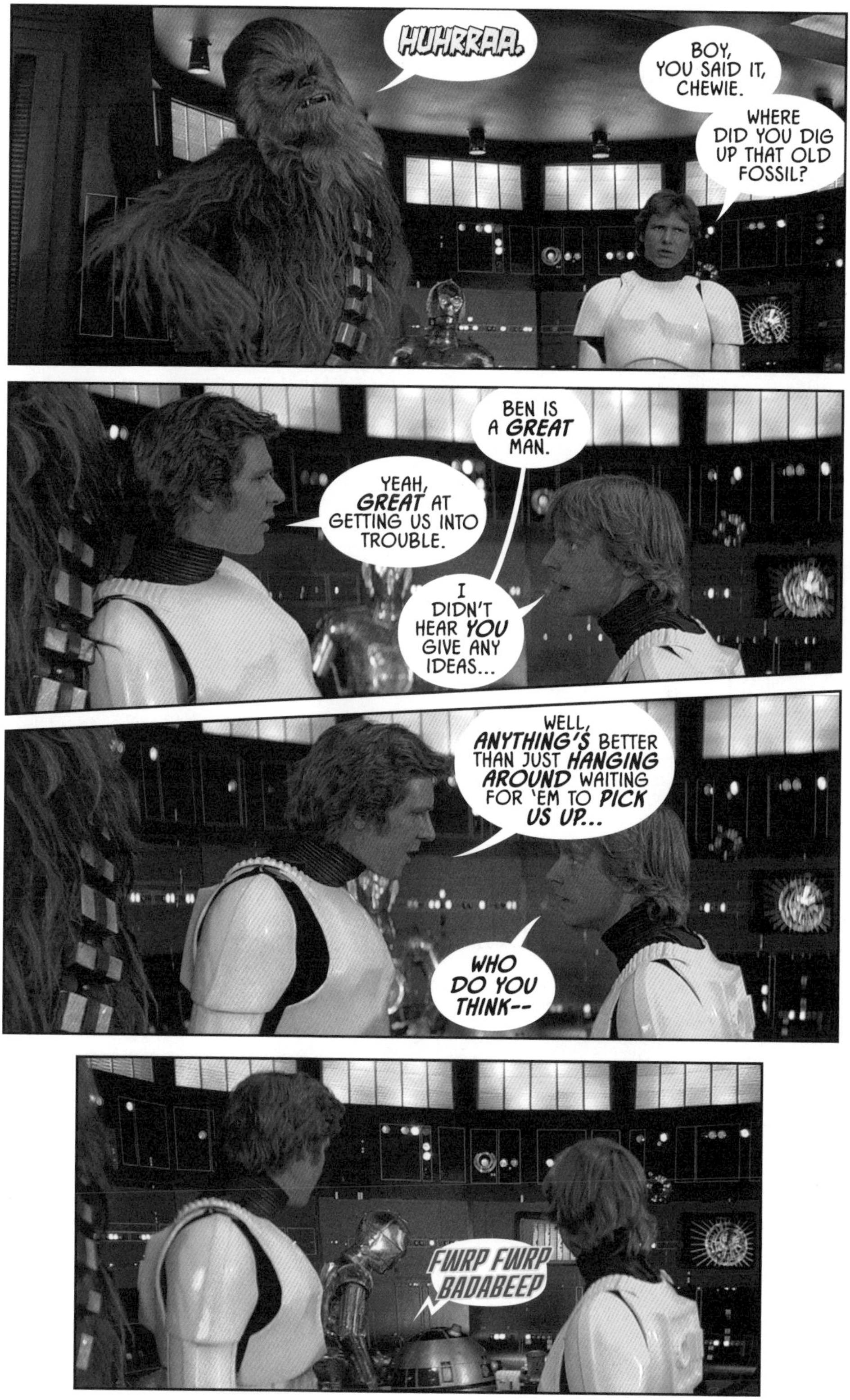
HUHRRAA.
BOY, YOU SAID IT, CHEWIE.
WHERE DID YOU DIG UP THAT OLD FOSSIL?
BEN IS A GREAT MAN.
YEAH, GREAT AT GETTING US INTO TROUBLE.
I DIDN'T HEAR YOU GIVE ANY IDEAS...
WELL, ANYTHING'S BETTER THAN JUST HANGING AROUND WAITING FOR 'EM TO PICK US UP...
WHO DO YOU THINK--
FWRP FWRP BADABEEP

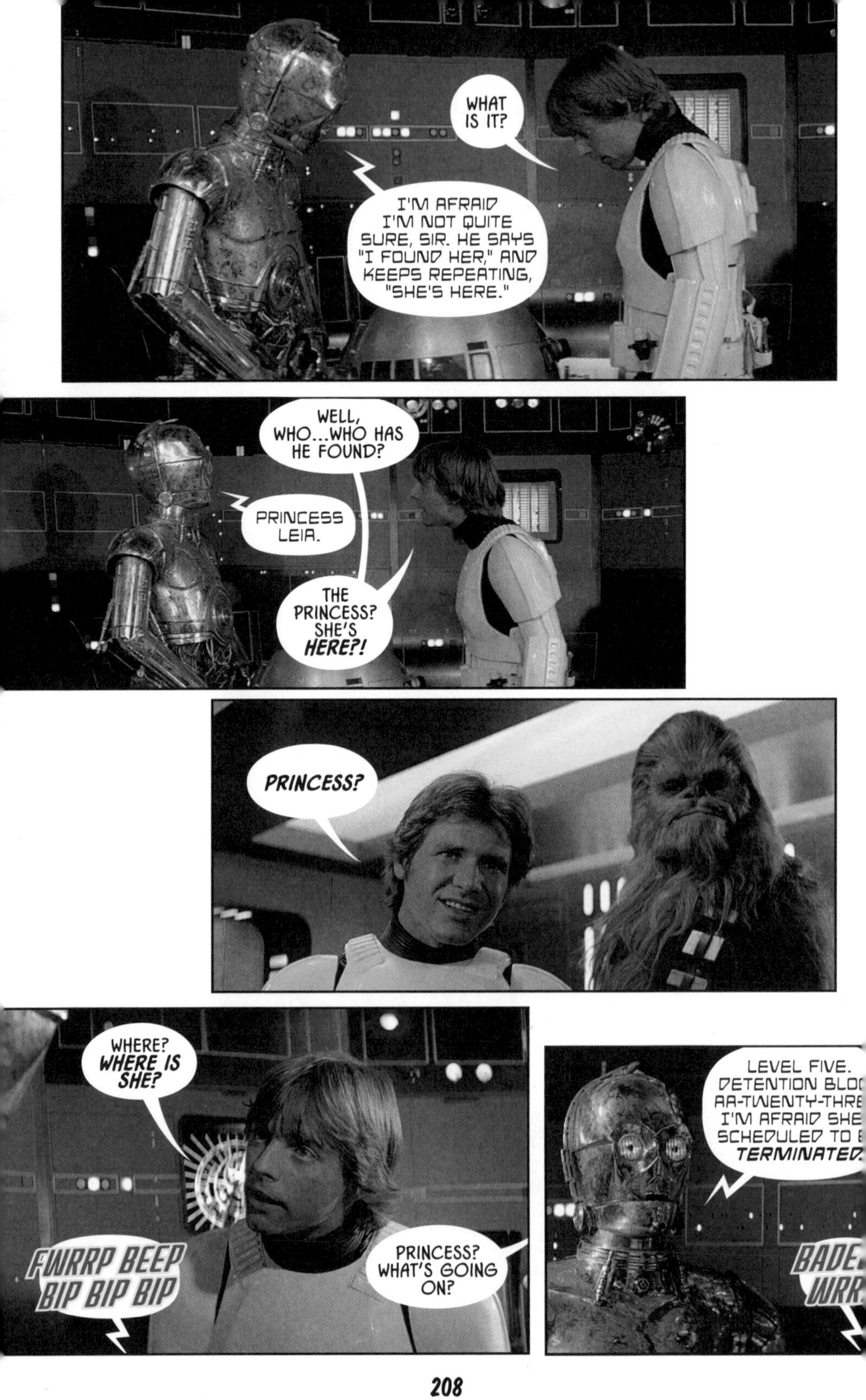
WHAT IS IT?
I'M AFRAID I'M NOT QUITE SURE, SIR. HE SAYS "I FOUND HER," AND KEEPS REPEATING, "SHE'S HERE."
WELL, WHO...WHO HAS HE FOUND?
PRINCESS LEIA.
THE PRINCESS? SHE'S *HERE?!*
PRINCESS?
WHERE? *WHERE IS SHE?*
FWRRP BEEP BIP BIP BIP
PRINCESS? WHAT'S GOING ON?
LEVEL FIVE. DETENTION BLOC
AA-TWENTY-THRE
I'M AFRAID SHE
SCHEDULED TO
TERMINATED
BADE
WRR

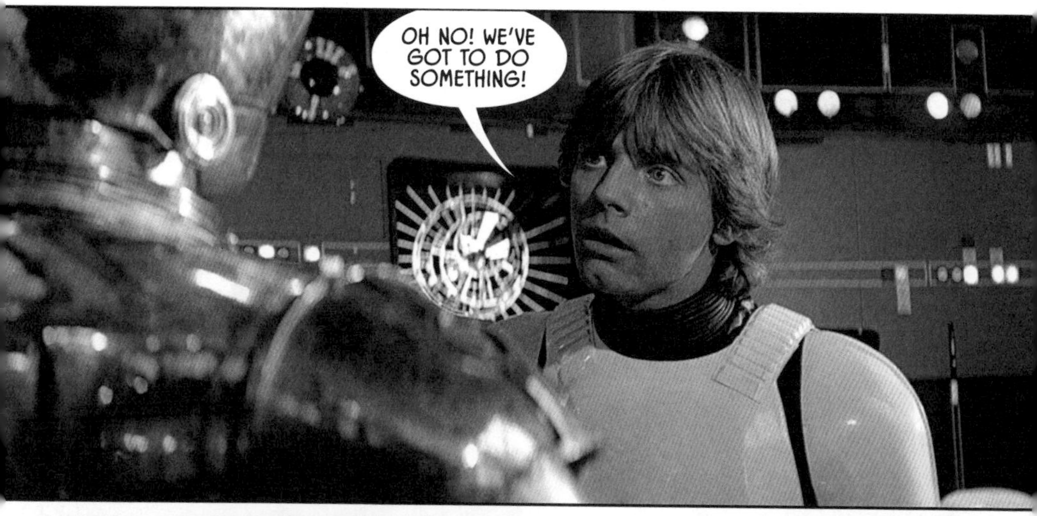
OH NO! WE'VE GOT TO DO SOMETHING!

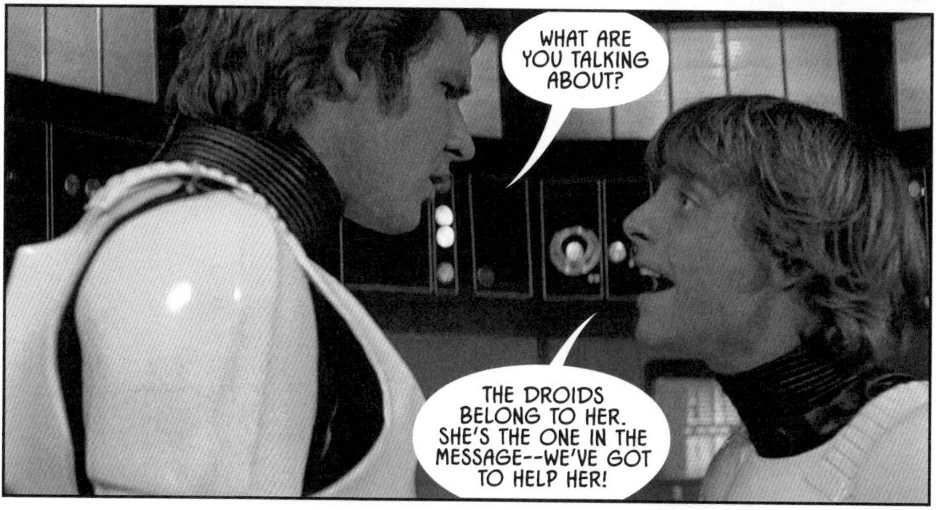
WHAT ARE YOU TALKING ABOUT?
THE DROIDS BELONG TO HER. SHE'S THE ONE IN THE MESSAGE--WE'VE GOT TO HELP HER!

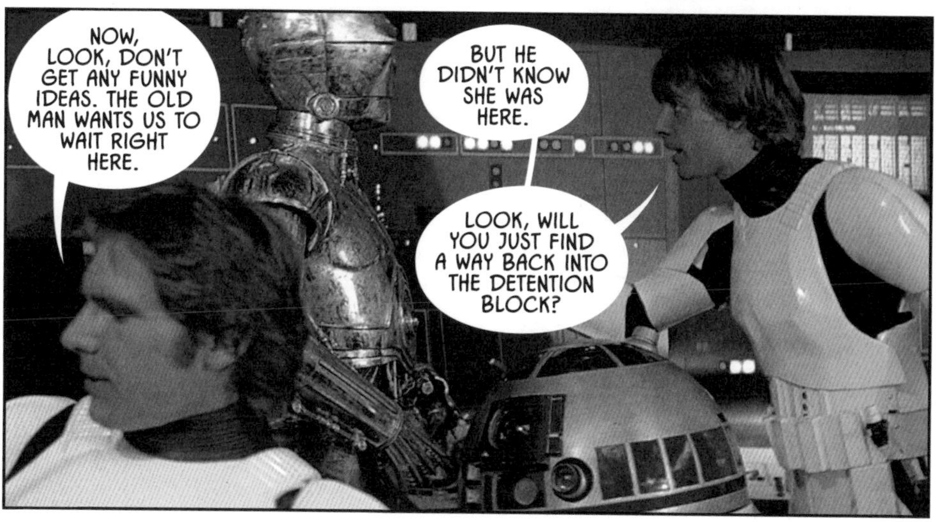
NOW, LOOK, DON'T GET ANY FUNNY IDEAS. THE OLD MAN WANTS US TO WAIT RIGHT HERE.
BUT HE DIDN'T KNOW SHE WAS HERE.
LOOK, WILL YOU JUST FIND A WAY BACK INTO THE DETENTION BLOCK?

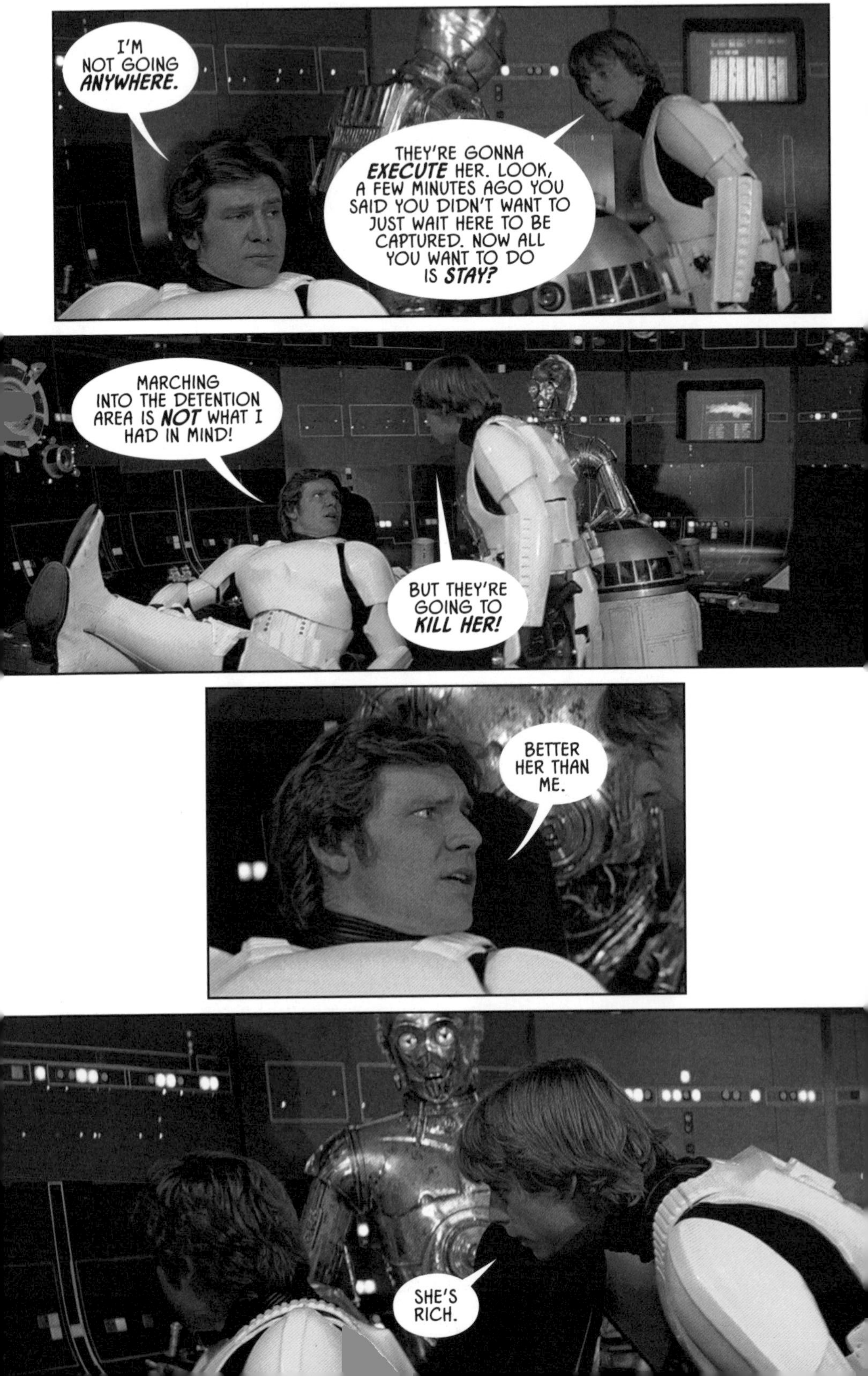
I'M NOT GOING ANYWHERE.
THEY'RE GONNA EXECUTE HER. LOOK, A FEW MINUTES AGO YOU SAID YOU DIDN'T WANT TO JUST WAIT HERE TO BE CAPTURED. NOW ALL YOU WANT TO DO IS STAY?
MARCHING INTO THE DETENTION AREA IS NOT WHAT I HAD IN MIND!
BUT THEY'RE GOING TO KILL HER!
BETTER HER THAN ME.
SHE'S RICH.

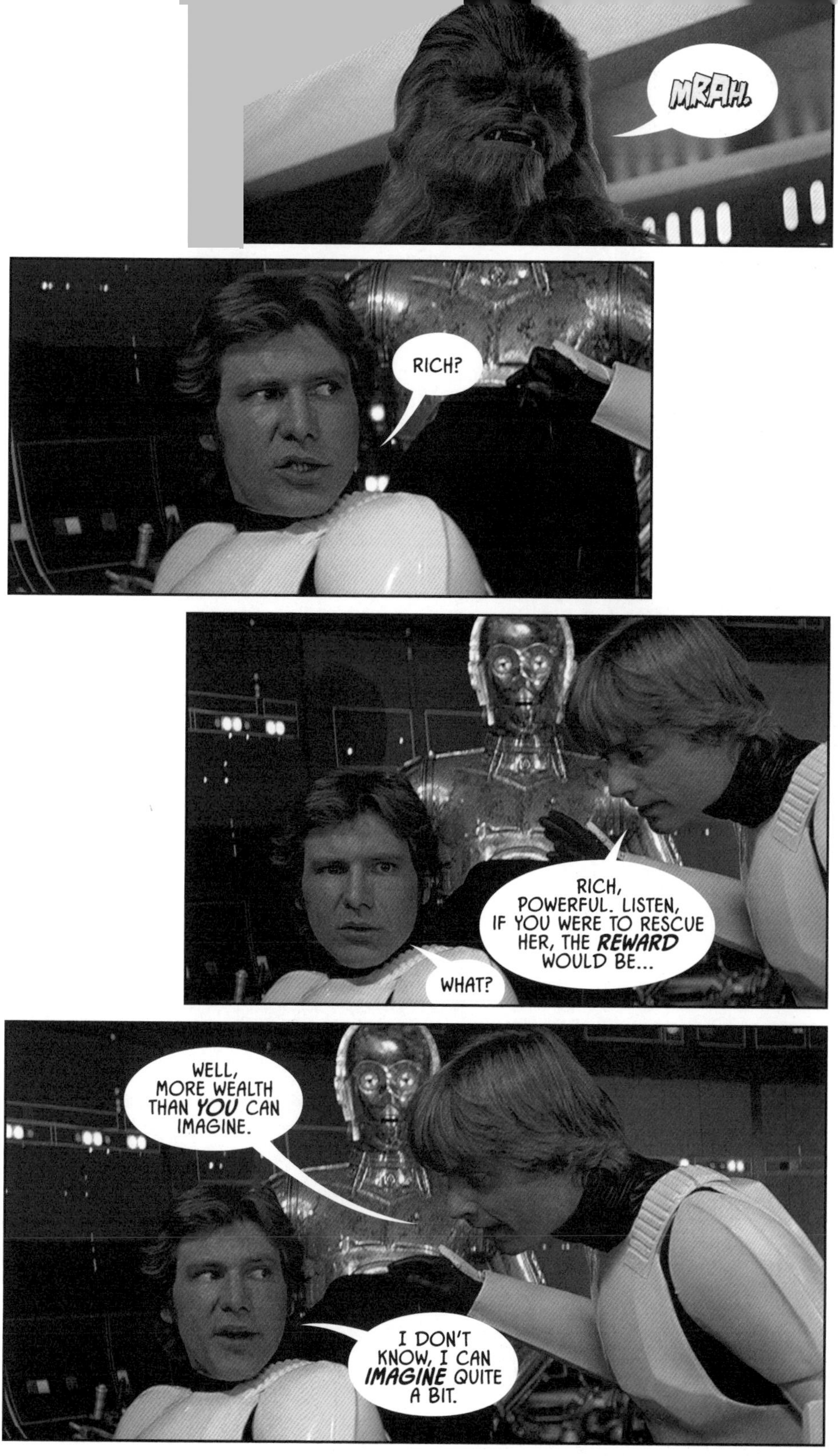
MRAH.
RICH?
RICH, POWERFUL. LISTEN, IF YOU WERE TO RESCUE HER, THE REWARD WOULD BE...
WHAT?
WELL, MORE WEALTH THAN YOU CAN IMAGINE.
I DON'T KNOW, I CAN IMAGINE QUITE A BIT.

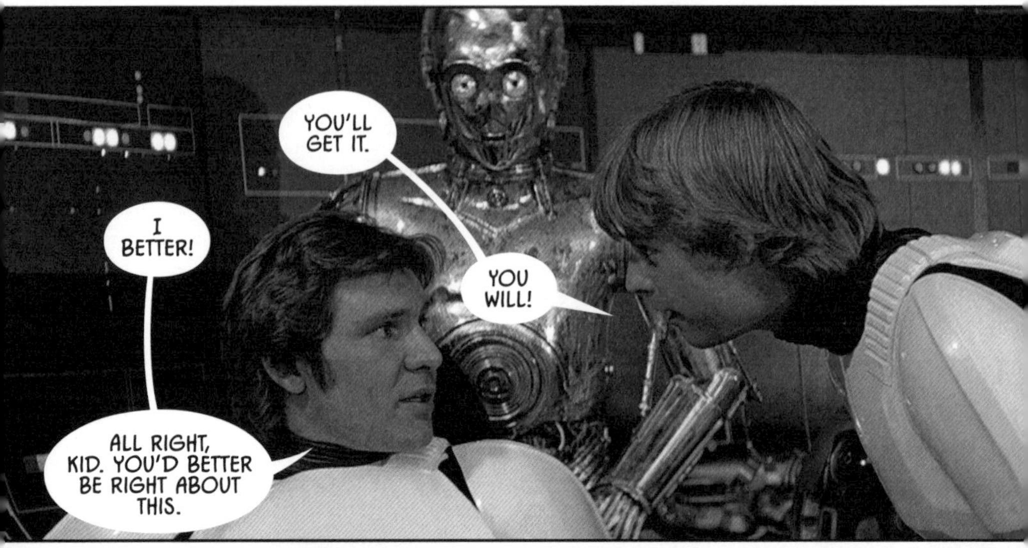
YOU'LL GET IT.
I BETTER!
YOU WILL!
ALL RIGHT, KID. YOU'D BETTER BE RIGHT ABOUT THIS.

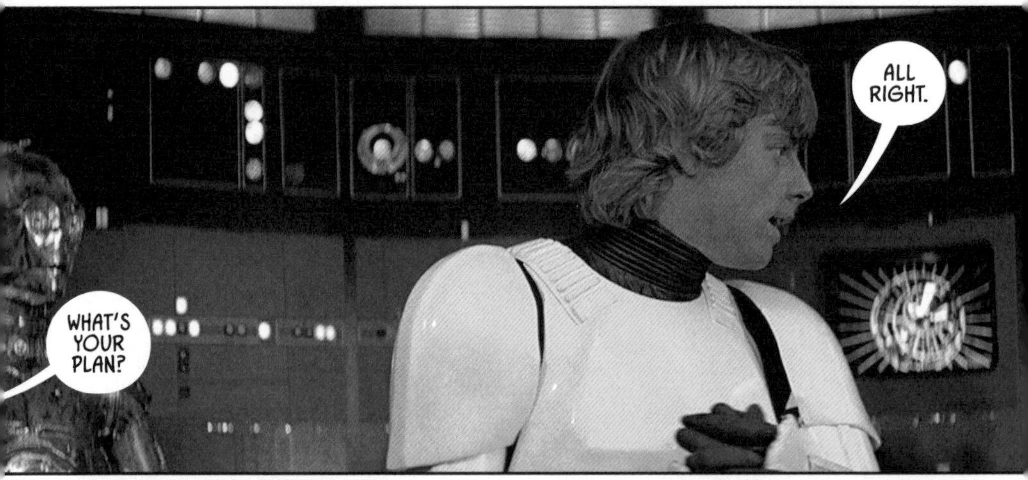
WHAT'S YOUR PLAN?
ALL RIGHT.

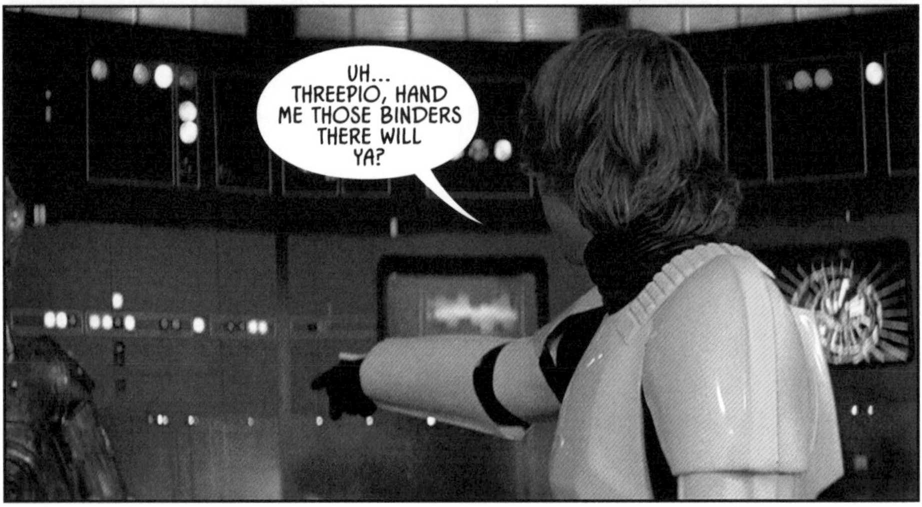
UH... THREEPIO, HAND ME THOSE BINDERS THERE WILL YA?

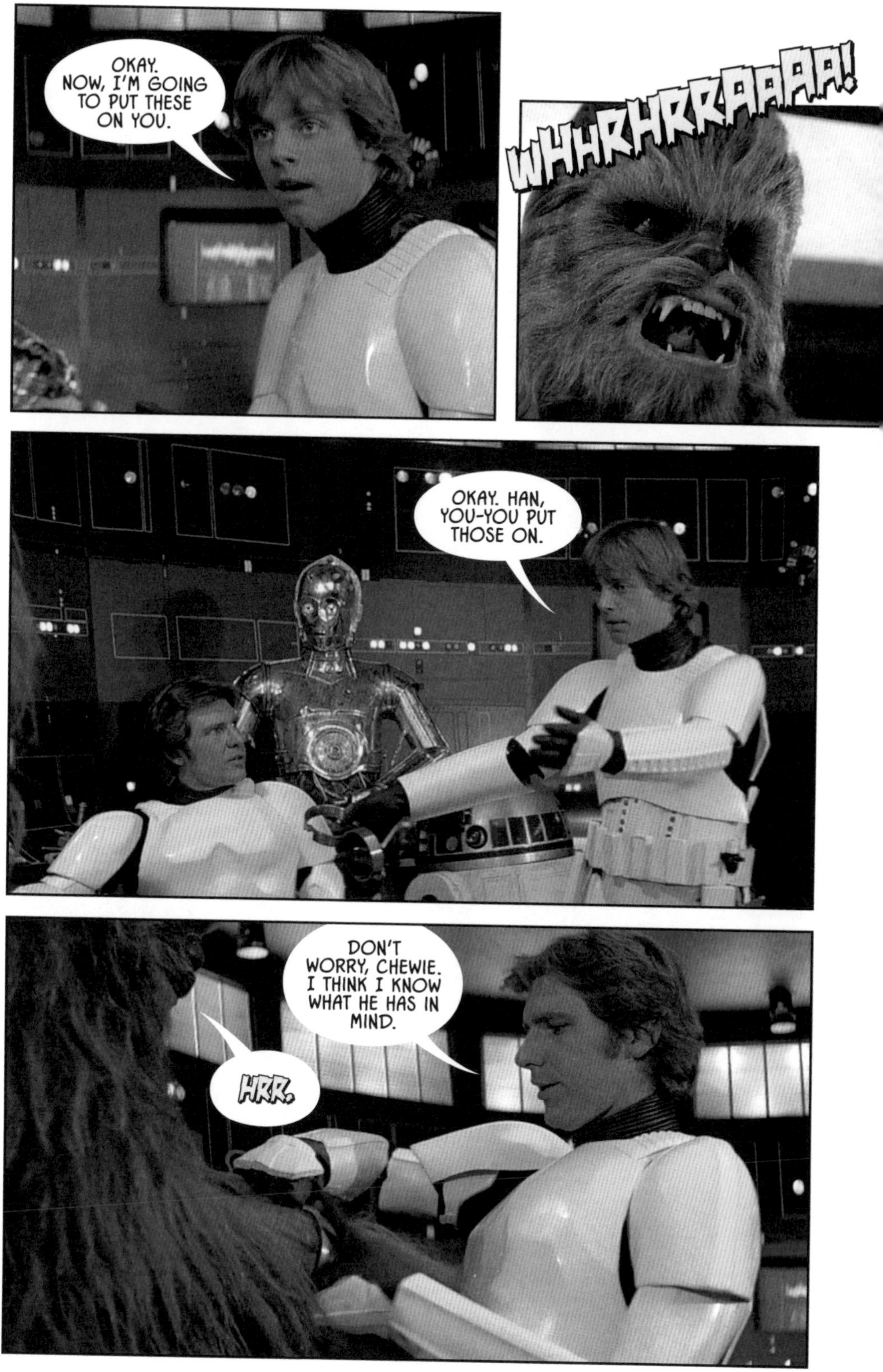
OKAY. NOW, I'M GOING TO PUT THESE ON YOU.
WHHRHRRAAAAA!
OKAY. HAN, YOU-YOU PUT THOSE ON.
DON'T WORRY, CHEWIE. I THINK I KNOW WHAT HE HAS IN MIND.
HRR.

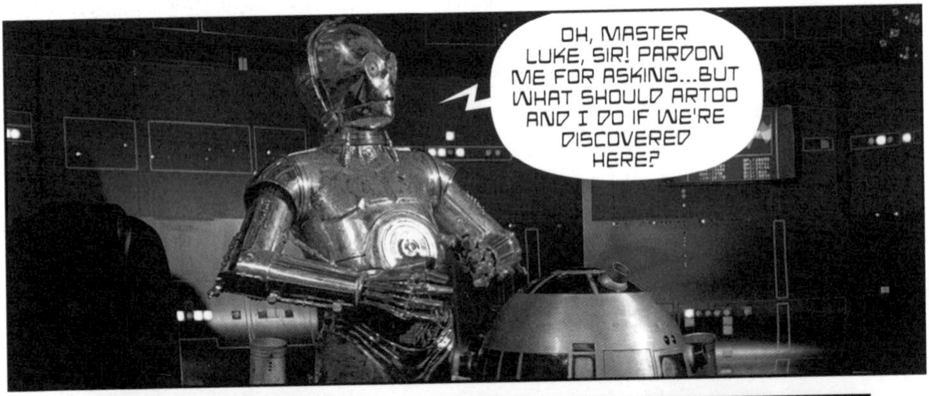
OH, MASTER LUKE, SIR! PARDON ME FOR ASKING...BUT WHAT SHOULD ARTOO AND I DO IF WE'RE DISCOVERED HERE?

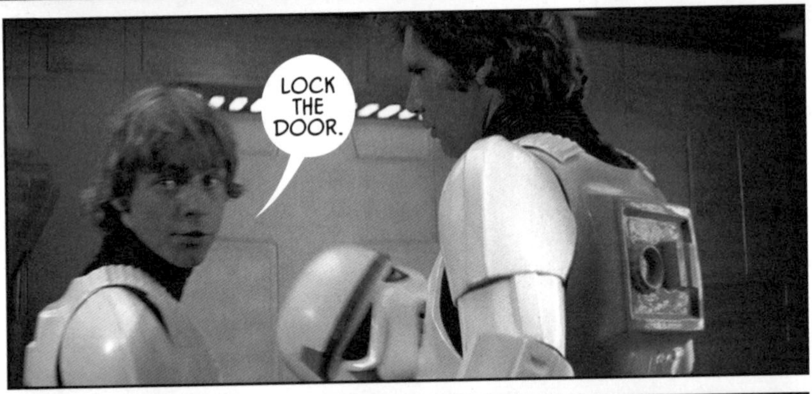
LOCK THE DOOR.

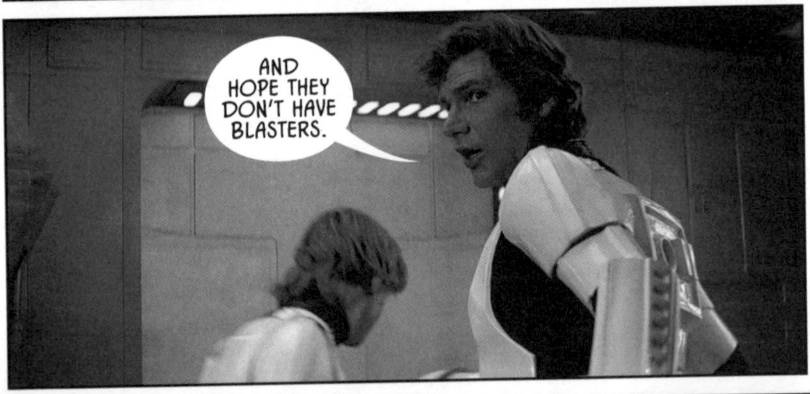
AND HOPE THEY DON'T HAVE BLASTERS.

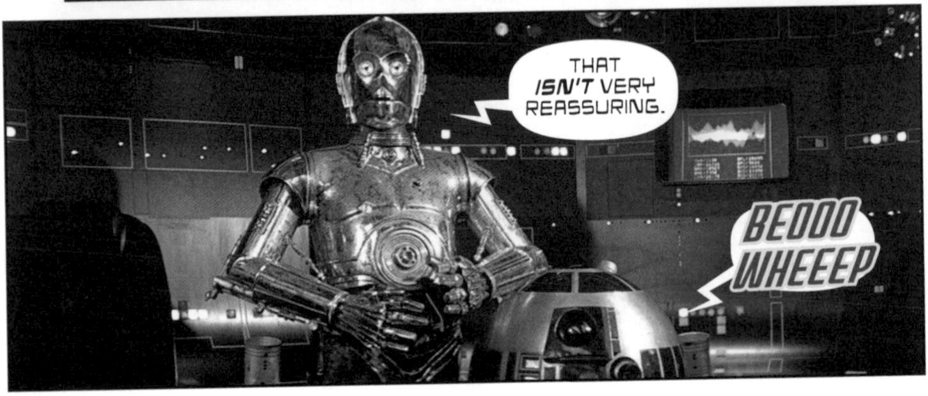
THAT *ISN'T* VERY REASSURING.
BEDOO WHEEEP

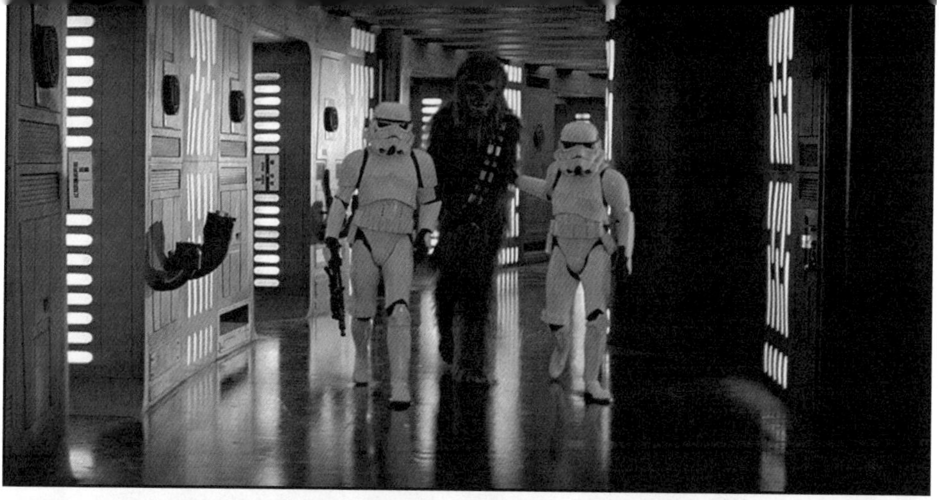

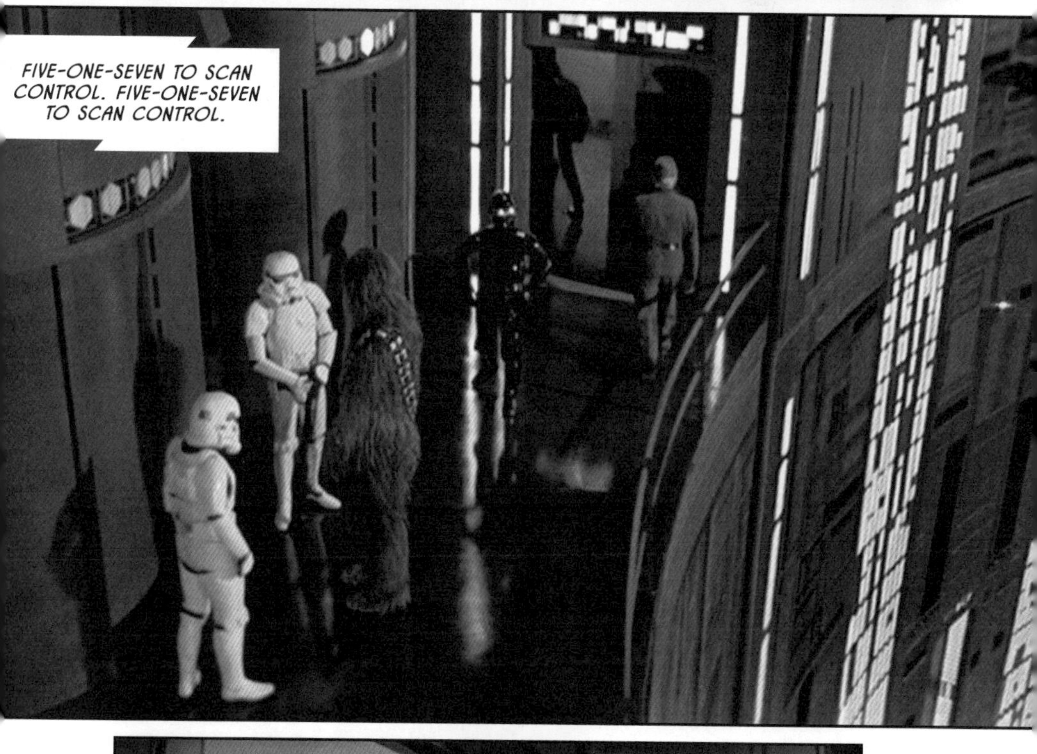
FIVE-ONE-SEVEN TO SCAN CONTROL. FIVE-ONE-SEVEN TO SCAN CONTROL.

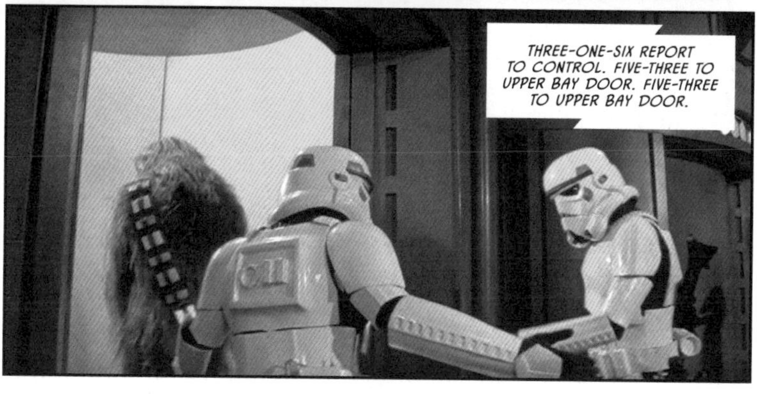
THREE-ONE-SIX REPORT TO CONTROL. FIVE-THREE TO UPPER BAY DOOR. FIVE-THREE TO UPPER BAY DOOR.

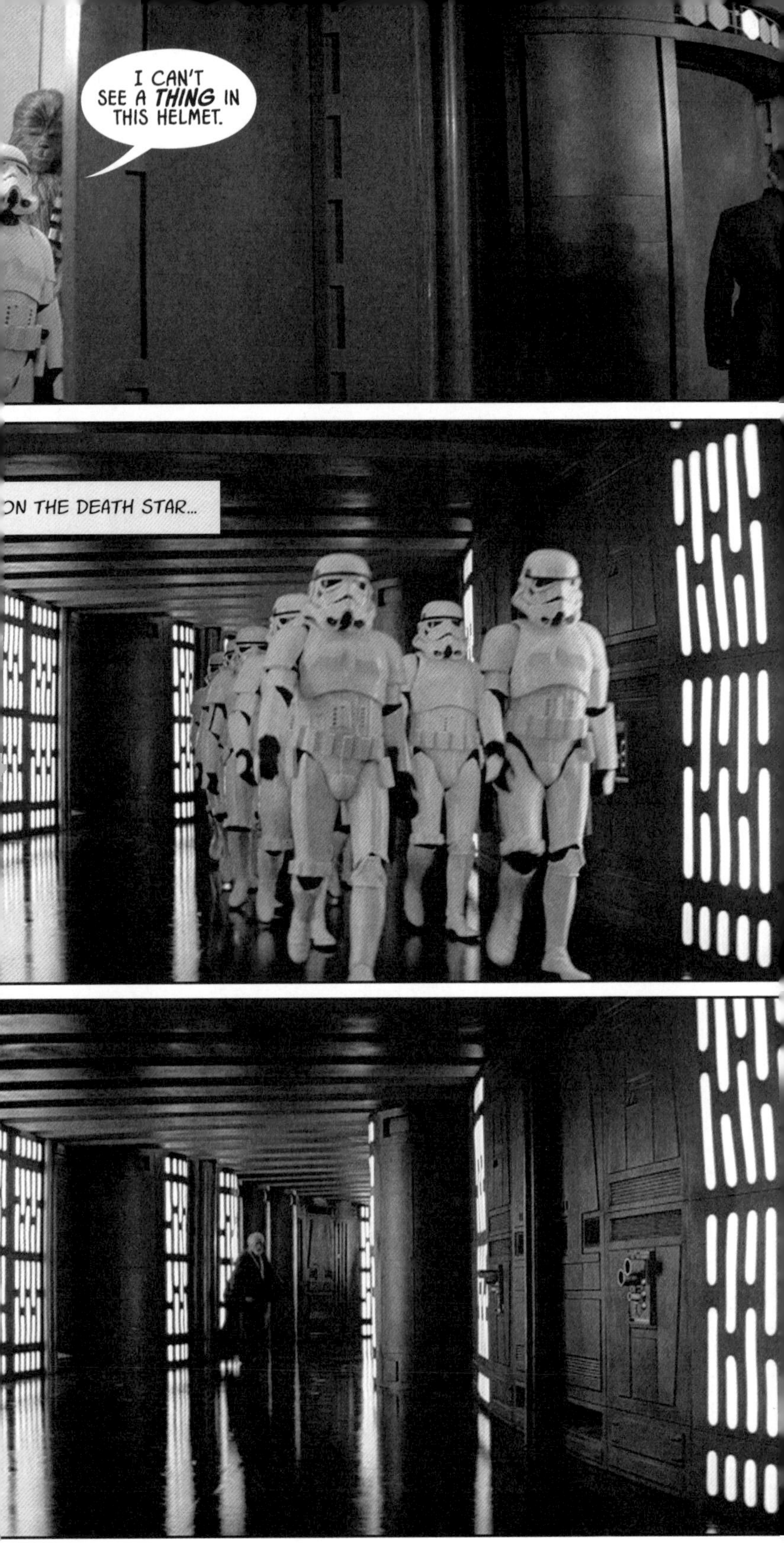
I CAN'T SEE A THING IN THIS HELMET.
ON THE DEATH STAR...

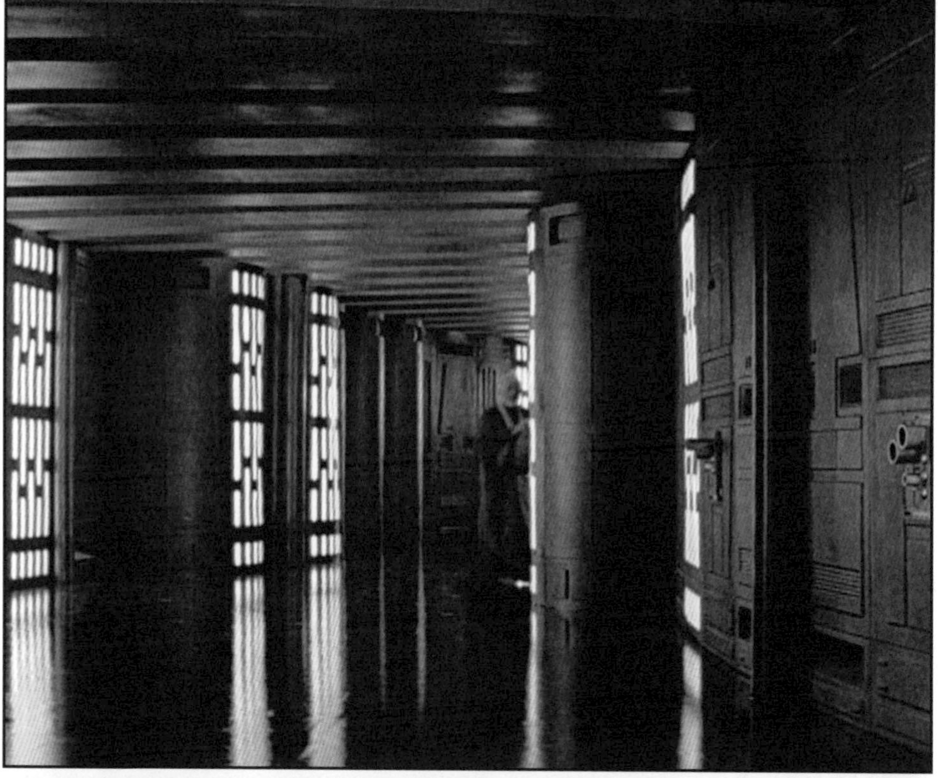

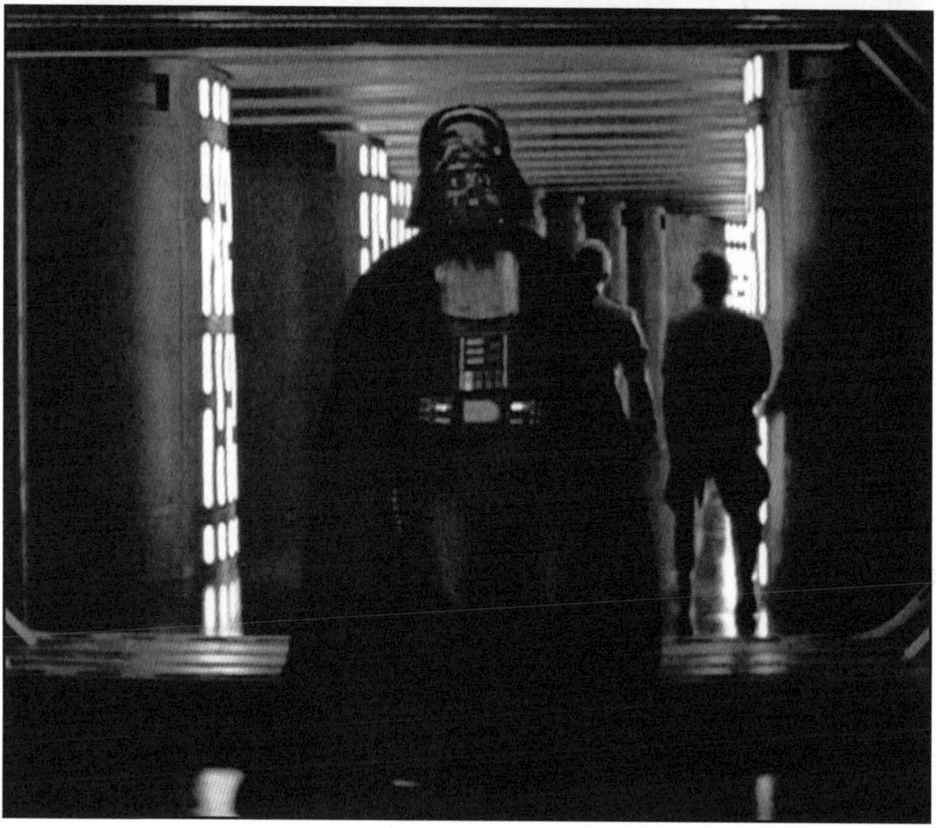

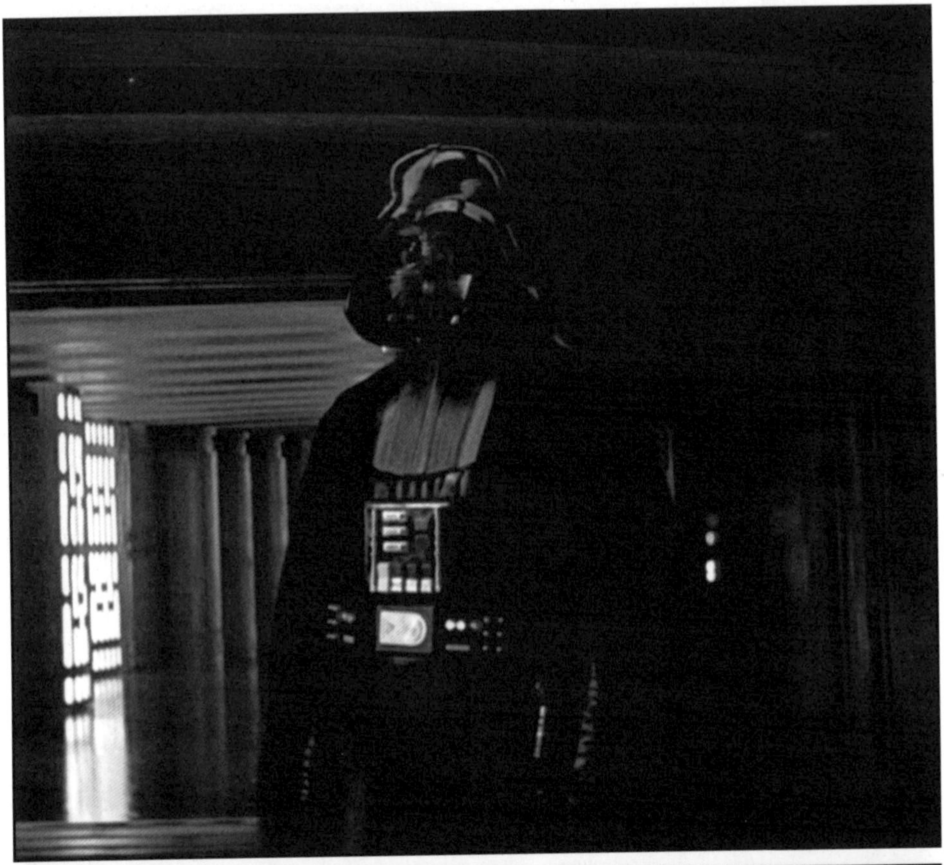

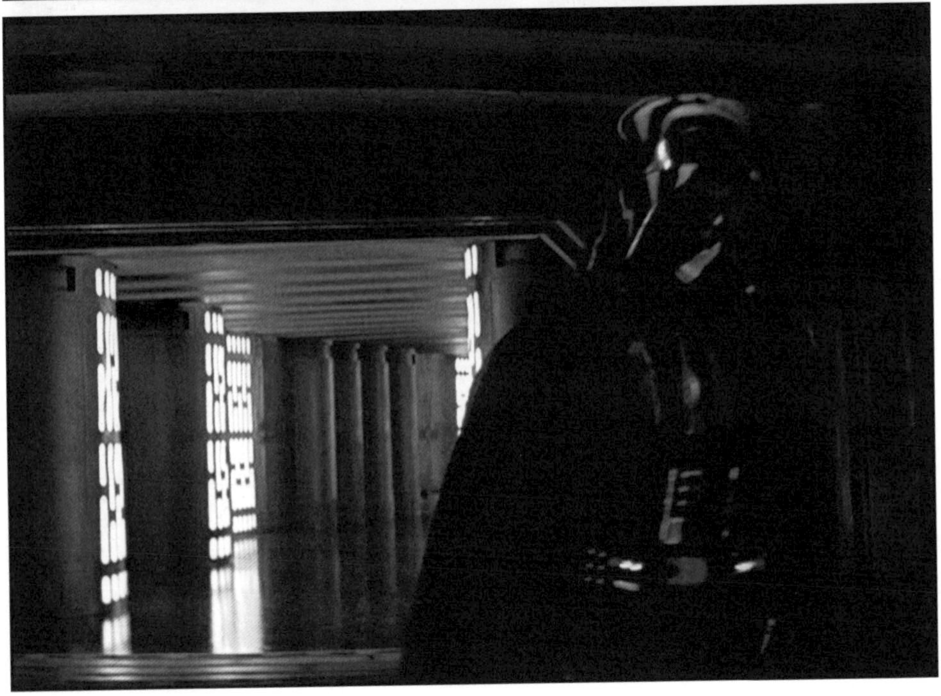

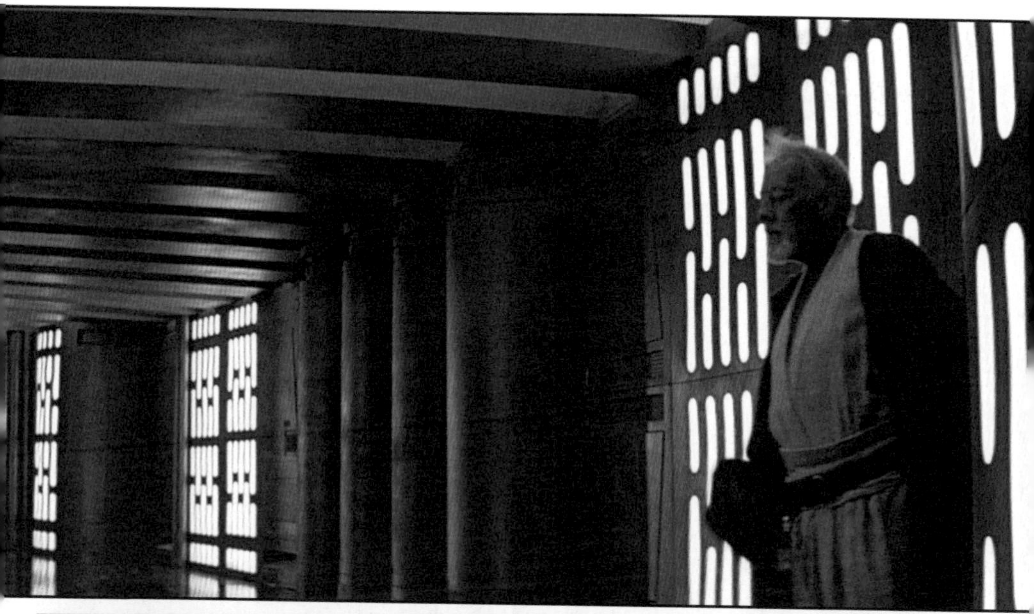

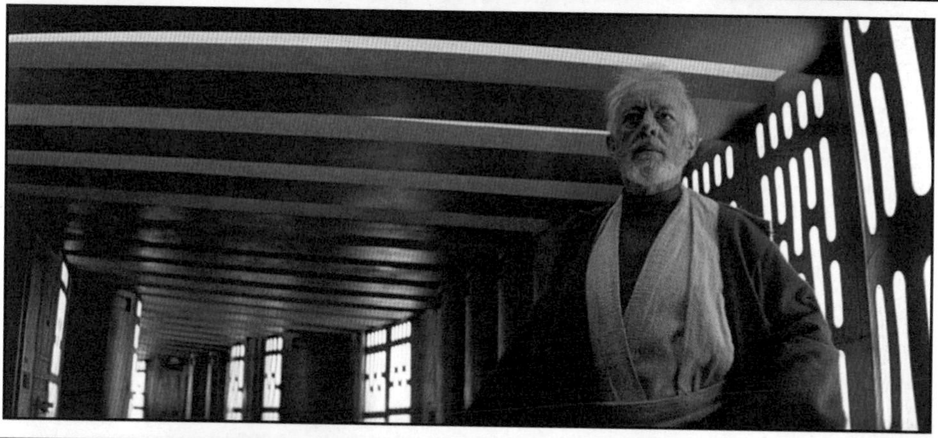

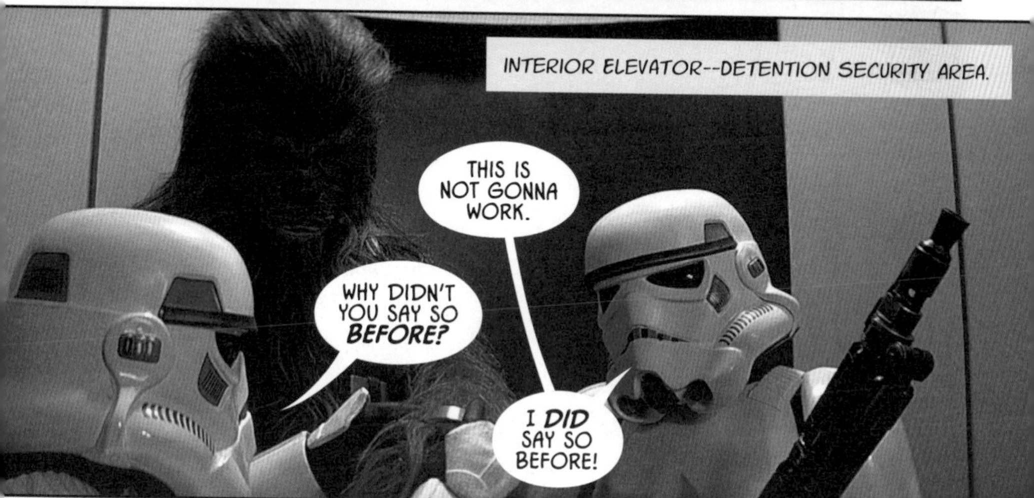
INTERIOR ELEVATOR--DETENTION SECURITY AREA.
THIS IS NOT GONNA WORK.
WHY DIDN'T YOU SAY SO BEFORE?
I DID SAY SO BEFORE!

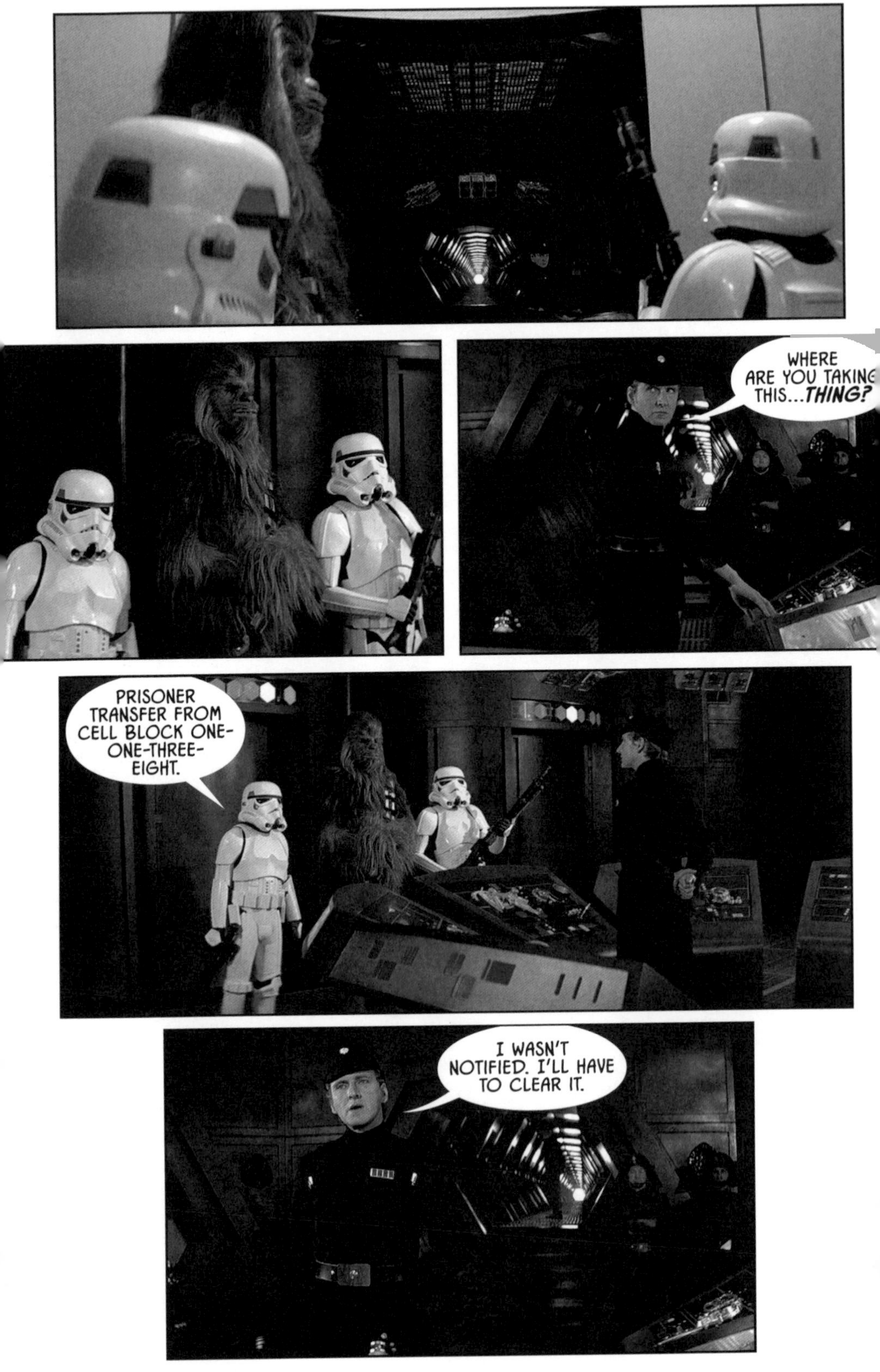
WHERE ARE YOU TAKING THIS...*THING?*
PRISONER TRANSFER FROM CELL BLOCK ONE-ONE-THREE-EIGHT.
I WASN'T NOTIFIED. I'LL HAVE TO CLEAR IT.

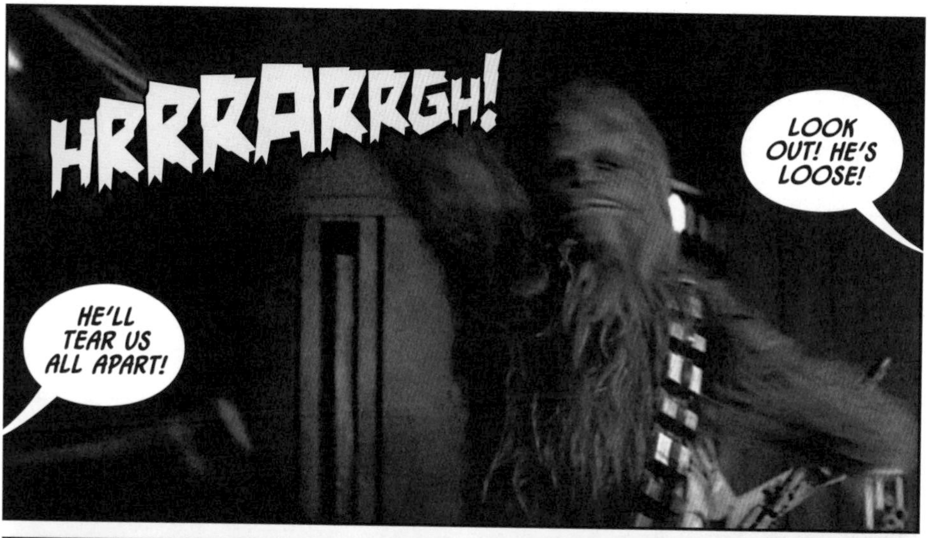
HRRRARRGH!
LOOK OUT! HE'S LOOSE!
HE'LL TEAR US ALL APART!

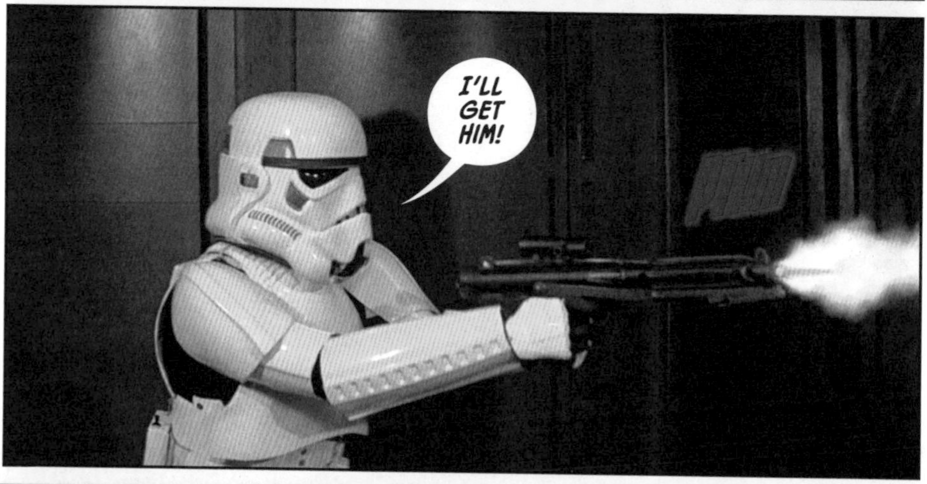
I'LL GET HIM!

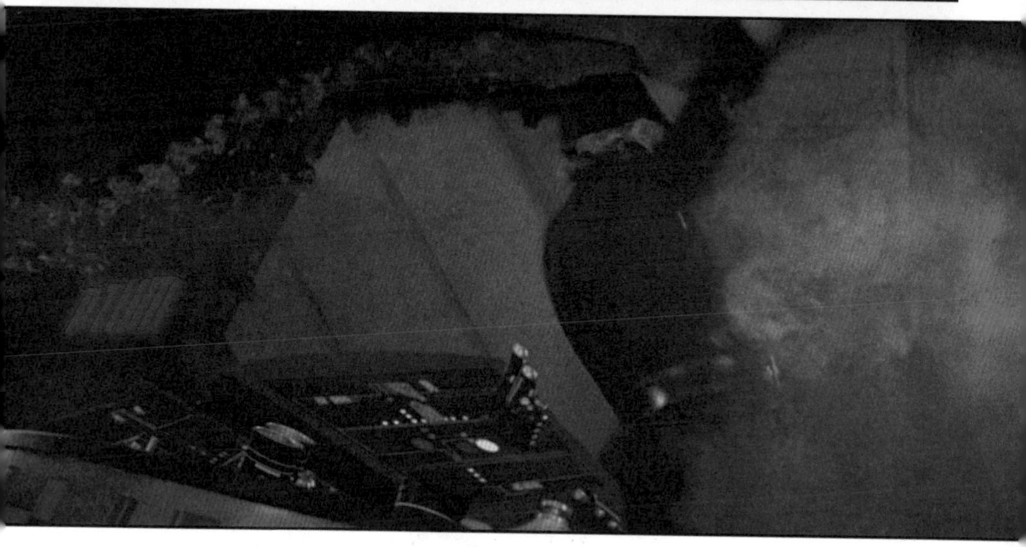

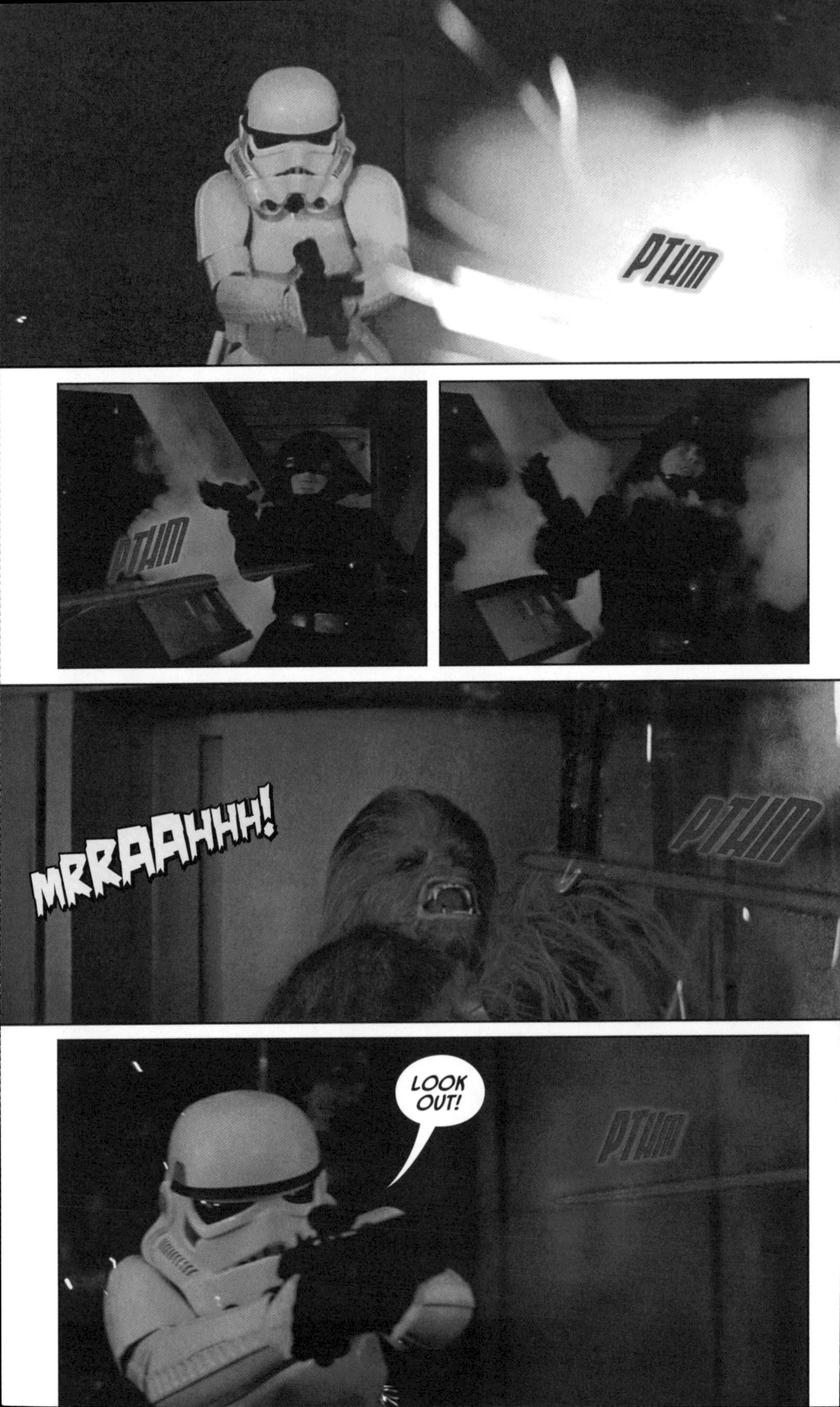
PTUM
PTUM
MRRAAHHH!
PTUM
LOOK OUT!
PTUM

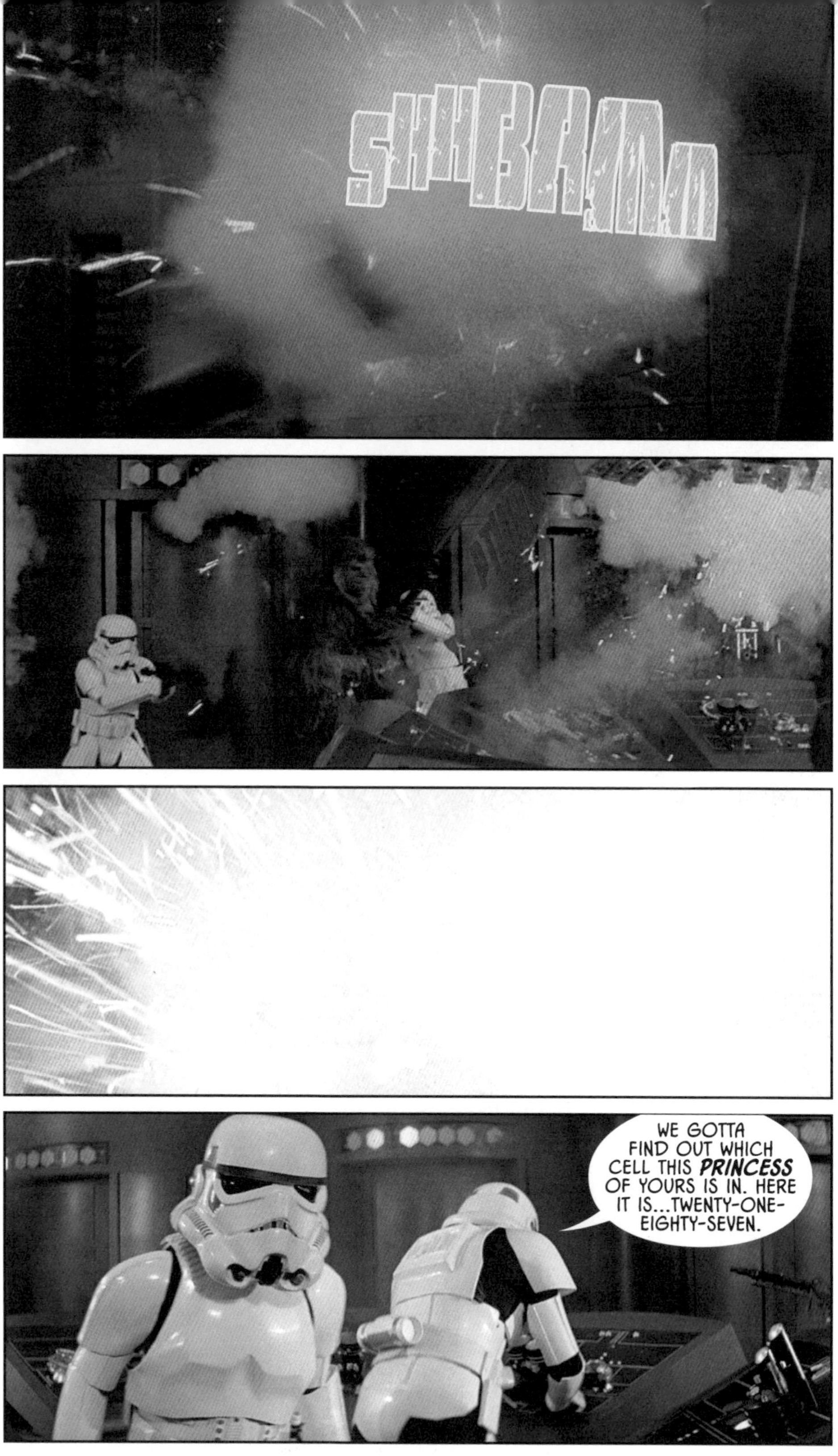
SHHBRAMM
WE GOTTA FIND OUT WHICH CELL THIS *PRINCESS* OF YOURS IS IN. HERE IT IS...TWENTY-ONE-EIGHTY-SEVEN.

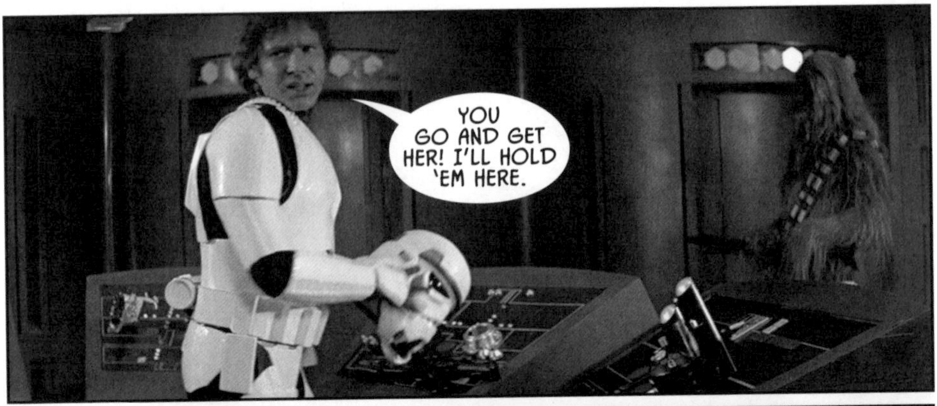
YOU GO AND GET HER! I'LL HOLD 'EM HERE.

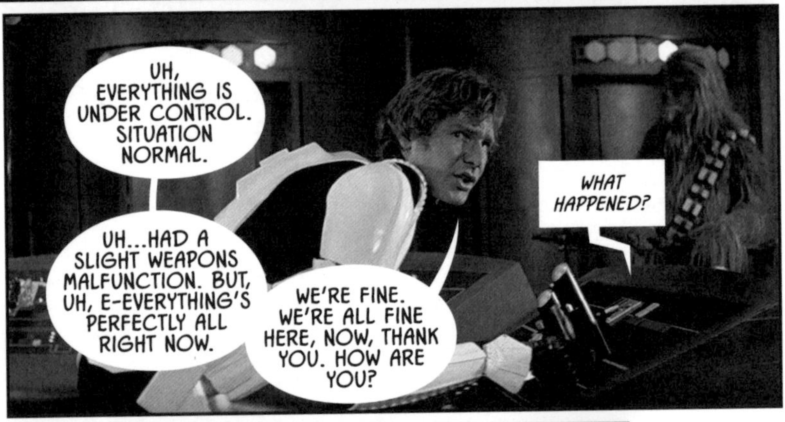
UH, EVERYTHING IS UNDER CONTROL. SITUATION NORMAL.
WHAT HAPPENED?
UH...HAD A SLIGHT WEAPONS MALFUNCTION. BUT, UH, E-EVERYTHING'S PERFECTLY ALL RIGHT NOW.
WE'RE FINE. WE'RE ALL FINE HERE, NOW, THANK YOU. HOW ARE YOU?

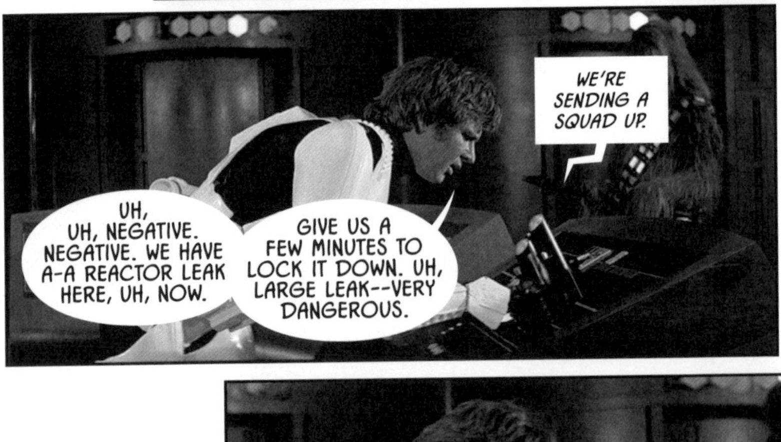
WE'RE SENDING A SQUAD UP.
UH, UH, NEGATIVE. NEGATIVE. WE HAVE A-A REACTOR LEAK HERE, UH, NOW.
GIVE US A FEW MINUTES TO LOCK IT DOWN. UH, LARGE LEAK--VERY DANGEROUS.

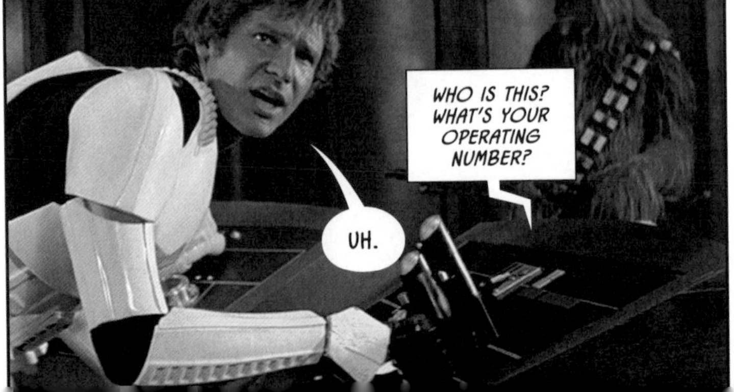
WHO IS THIS? WHAT'S YOUR OPERATING NUMBER?
UH.

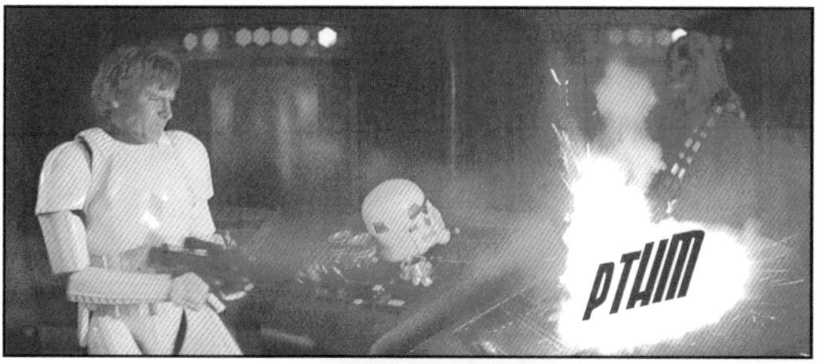
PTHIM

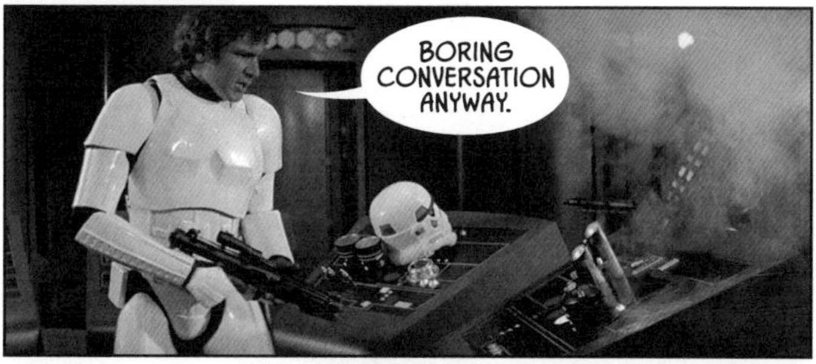
BORING CONVERSATION ANYWAY.

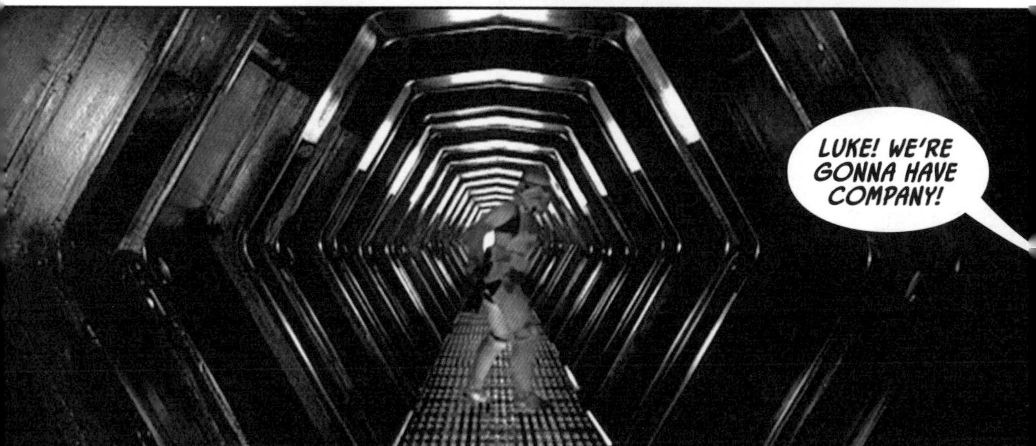
LUKE! WE'RE GONNA HAVE COMPANY!

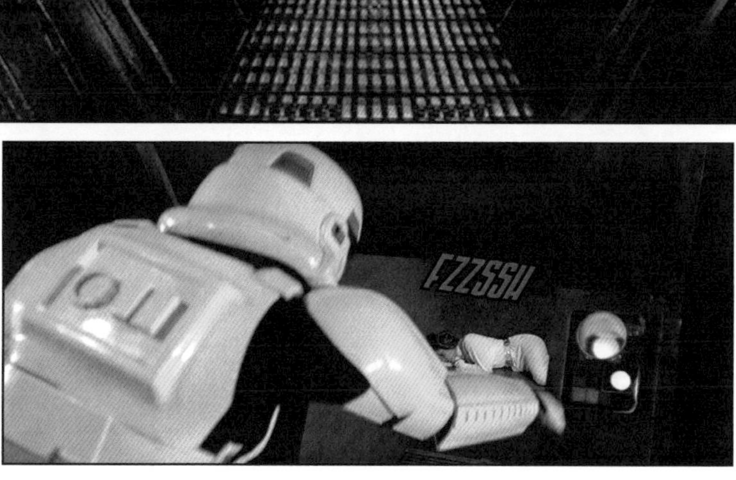
FZZSSH

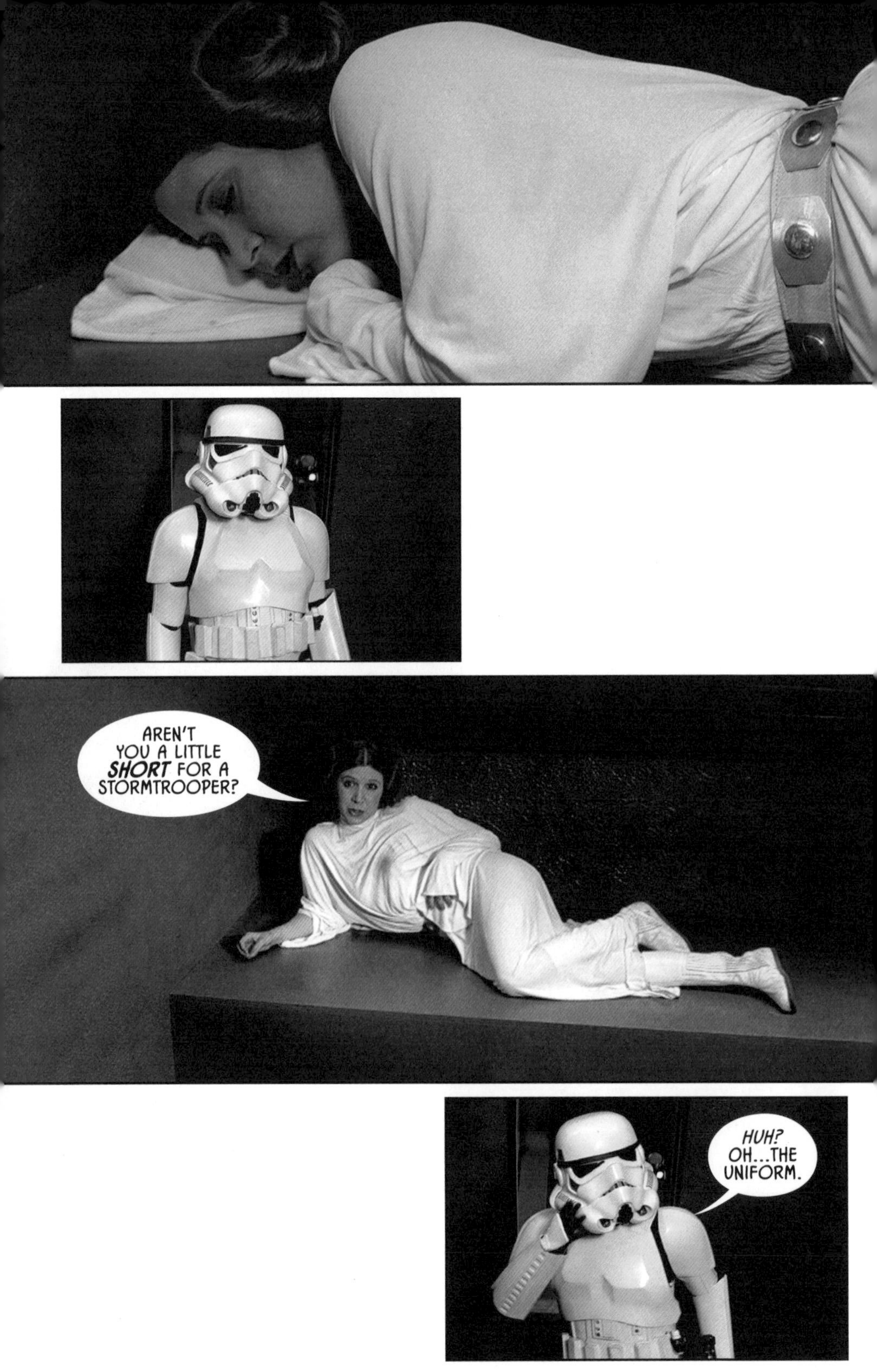
AREN'T YOU A LITTLE SHORT FOR A STORMTROOPER?
HUH? OH...THE UNIFORM.

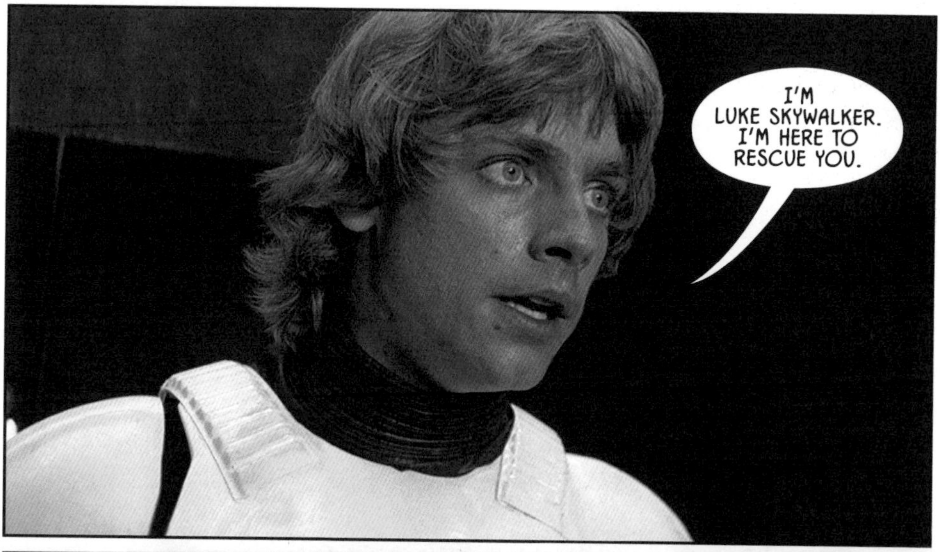
I'M LUKE SKYWALKER. I'M HERE TO RESCUE YOU.

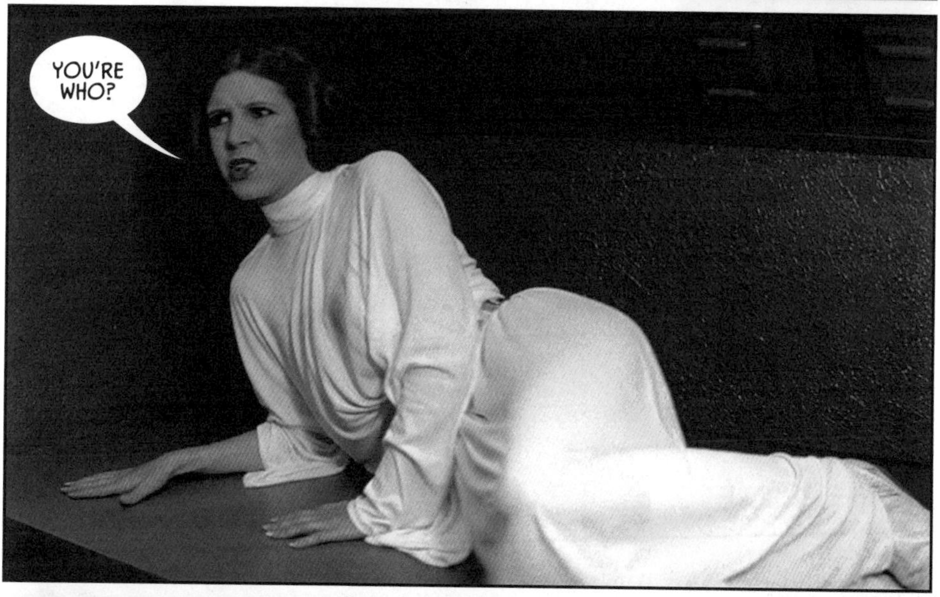
YOU'RE WHO?

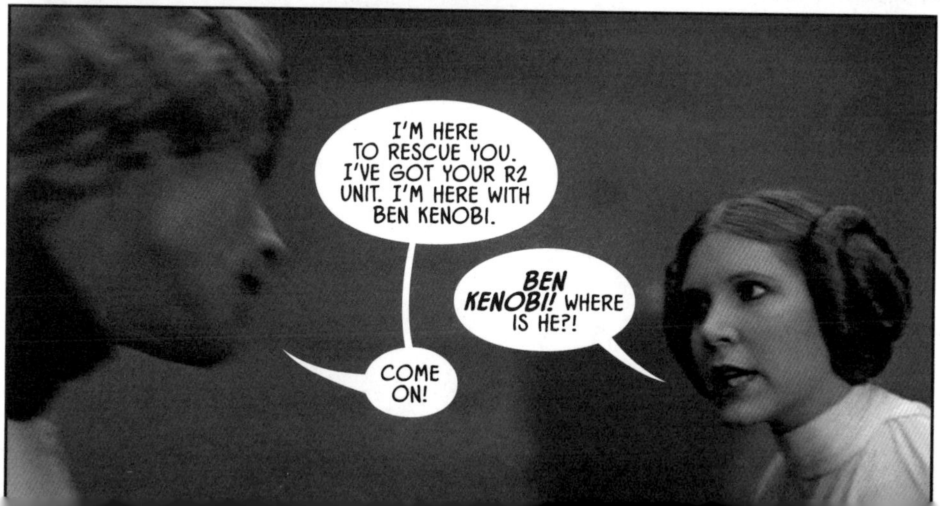
I'M HERE TO RESCUE YOU. I'VE GOT YOUR R2 UNIT. I'M HERE WITH BEN KENOBI.
BEN KENOBI! WHERE IS HE?!
COME ON!

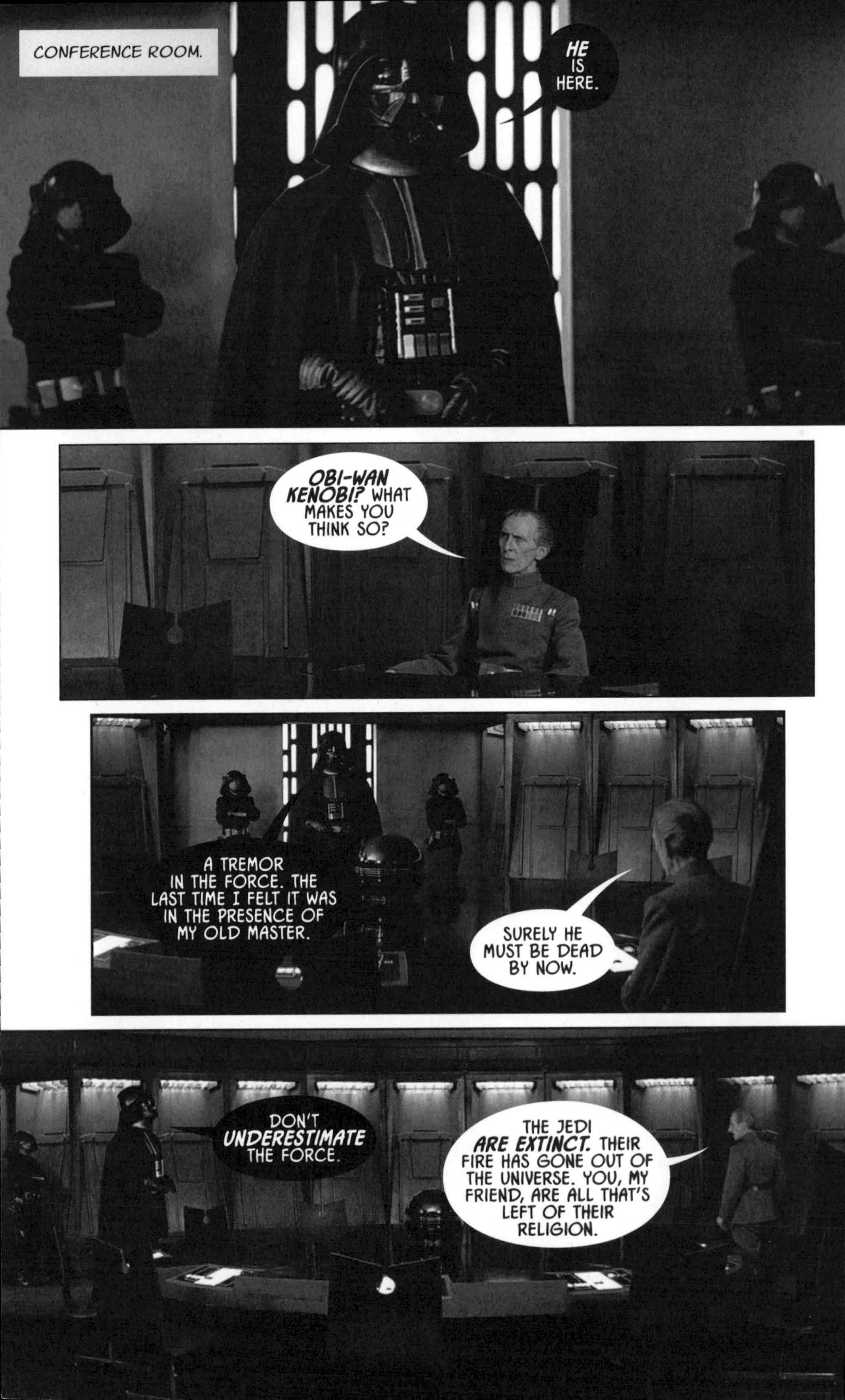
CONFERENCE ROOM.
HE IS HERE.
OBI-WAN KENOBI? WHAT MAKES YOU THINK SO?
A TREMOR IN THE FORCE. THE LAST TIME I FELT IT WAS IN THE PRESENCE OF MY OLD MASTER.
SURELY HE MUST BE DEAD BY NOW.
DON'T UNDERESTIMATE THE FORCE.
THE JEDI ARE EXTINCT. THEIR FIRE HAS GONE OUT OF THE UNIVERSE. YOU, MY FRIEND, ARE ALL THAT'S LEFT OF THEIR RELIGION.

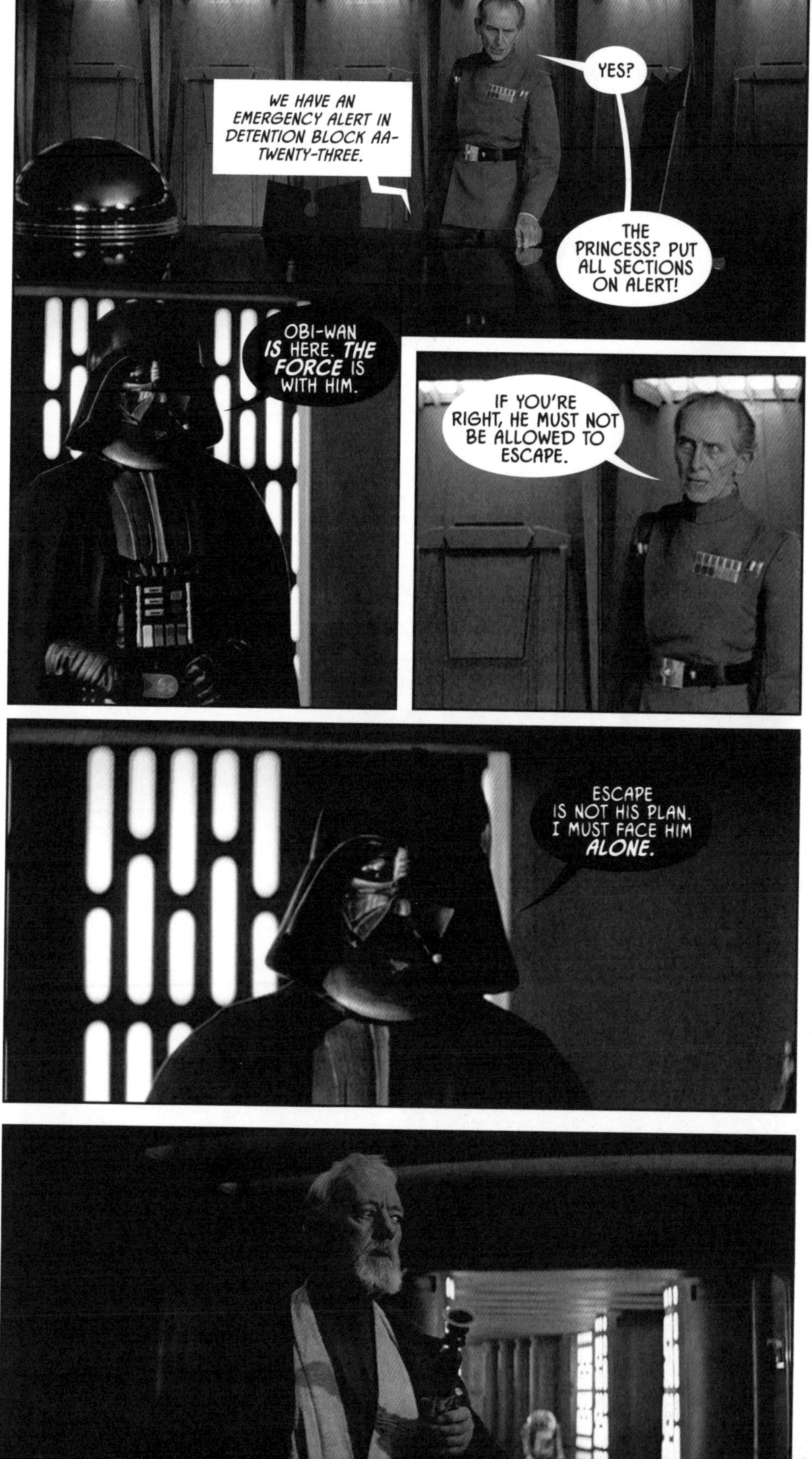
WE HAVE AN EMERGENCY ALERT IN DETENTION BLOCK AA-TWENTY-THREE.
YES?
THE PRINCESS? PUT ALL SECTIONS ON ALERT!
OBI-WAN IS HERE. THE FORCE IS WITH HIM.
IF YOU'RE RIGHT, HE MUST NOT BE ALLOWED TO ESCAPE.
ESCAPE IS NOT HIS PLAN. I MUST FACE HIM ALONE.

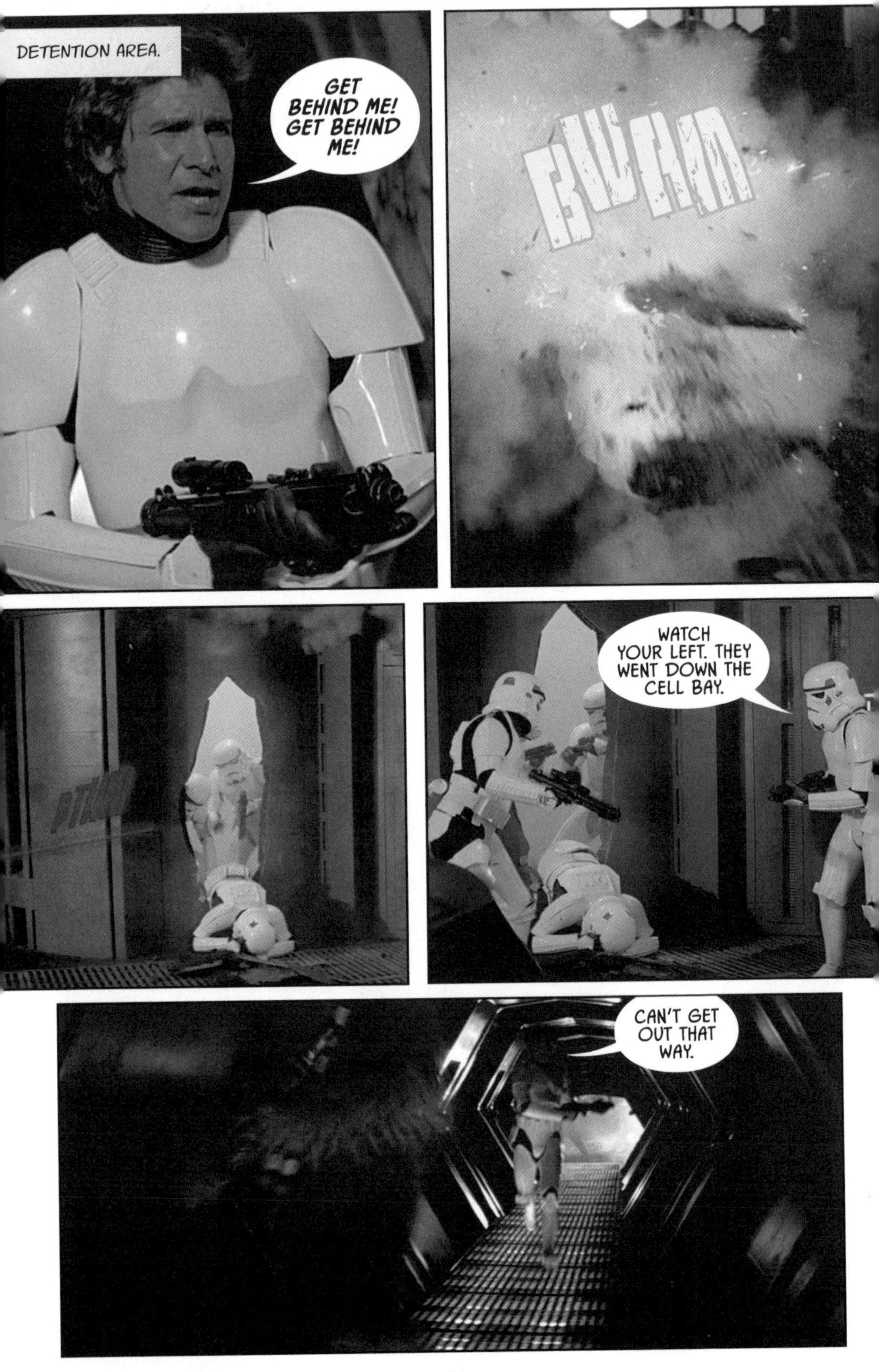
DETENTION AREA.
GET BEHIND ME! GET BEHIND ME!
WATCH YOUR LEFT. THEY WENT DOWN THE CELL BAY.
CAN'T GET OUT THAT WAY.

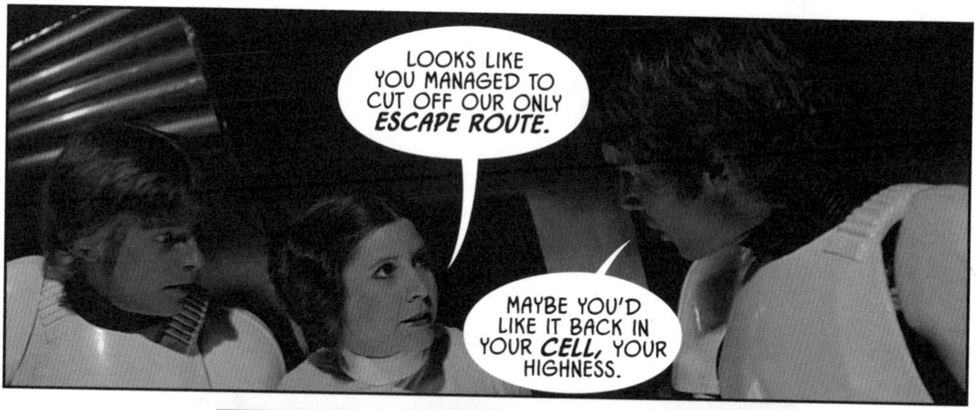
LOOKS LIKE YOU MANAGED TO CUT OFF OUR ONLY ESCAPE ROUTE.
MAYBE YOU'D LIKE IT BACK IN YOUR CELL, YOUR HIGHNESS.

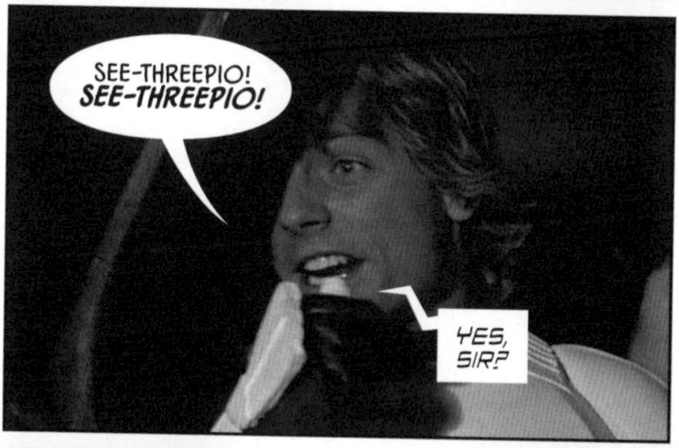
SEE-THREEPIO! SEE-THREEPIO!
YES, SIR?

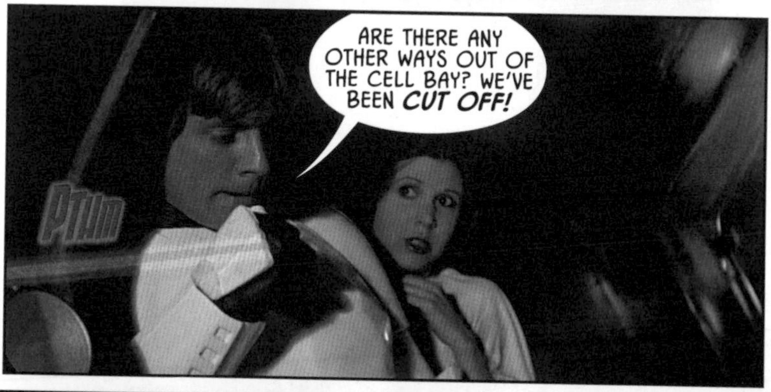
ARE THERE ANY OTHER WAYS OUT OF THE CELL BAY? WE'VE BEEN CUT OFF!
PTUM

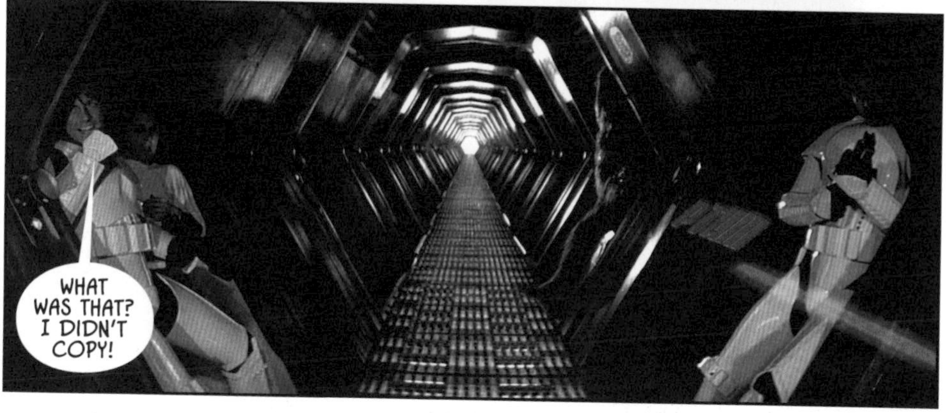
WHAT WAS THAT? I DIDN'T COPY!

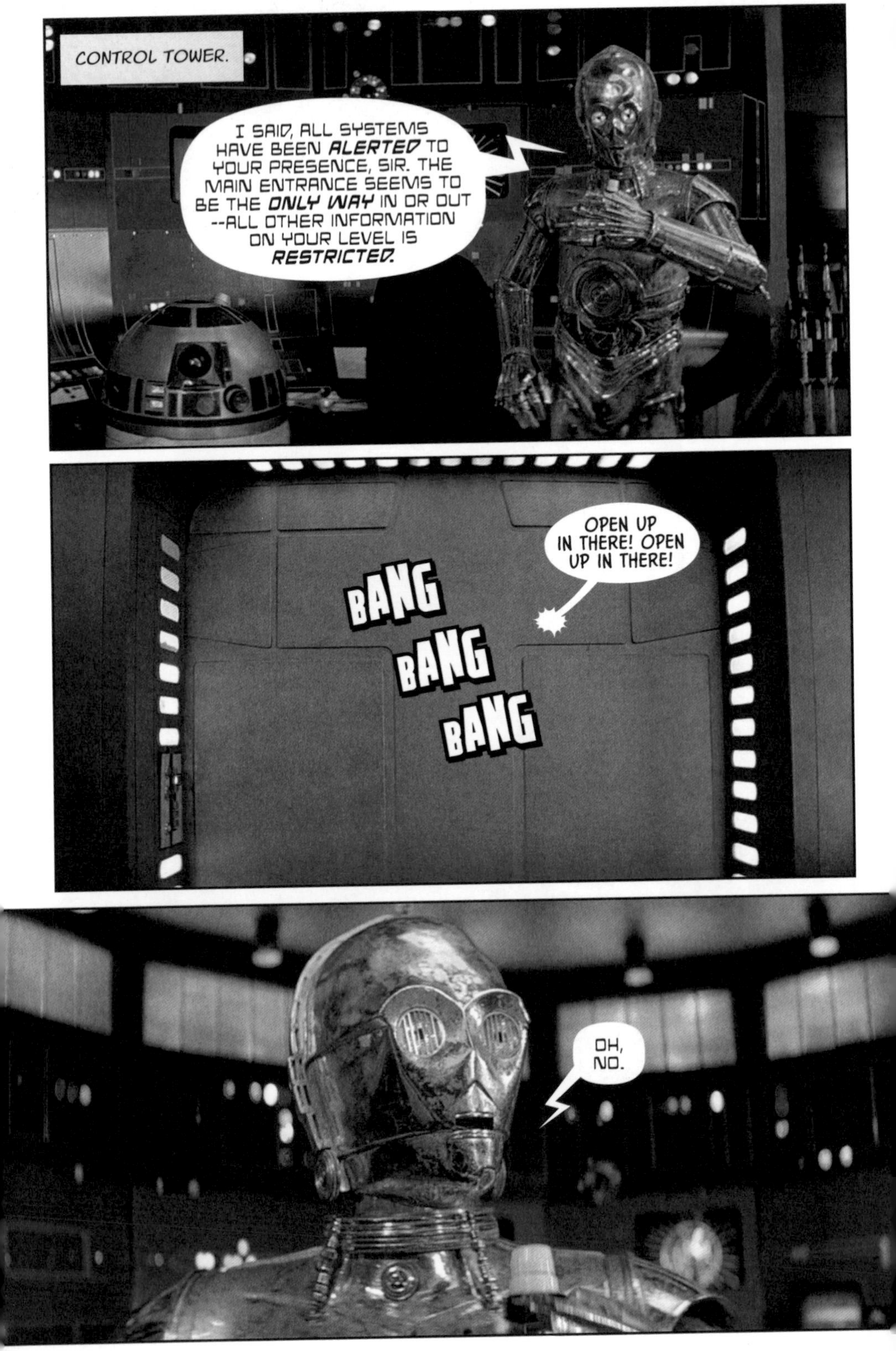
CONTROL TOWER.
I SAID, ALL SYSTEMS HAVE BEEN ALERTED TO YOUR PRESENCE, SIR. THE MAIN ENTRANCE SEEMS TO BE THE ONLY WAY IN OR OUT --ALL OTHER INFORMATION ON YOUR LEVEL IS RESTRICTED.
BANG
BANG
BANG
OPEN UP IN THERE! OPEN UP IN THERE!
OH, NO.

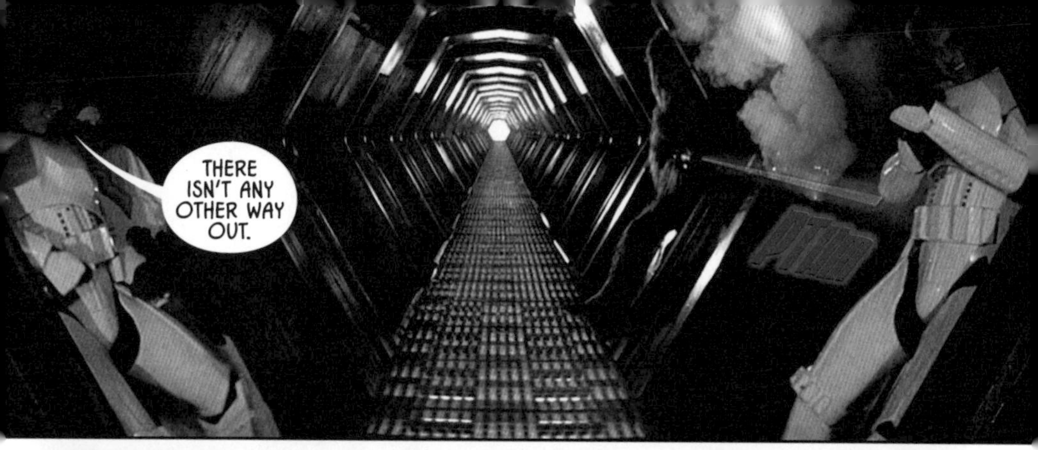
THERE ISN'T ANY OTHER WAY OUT.

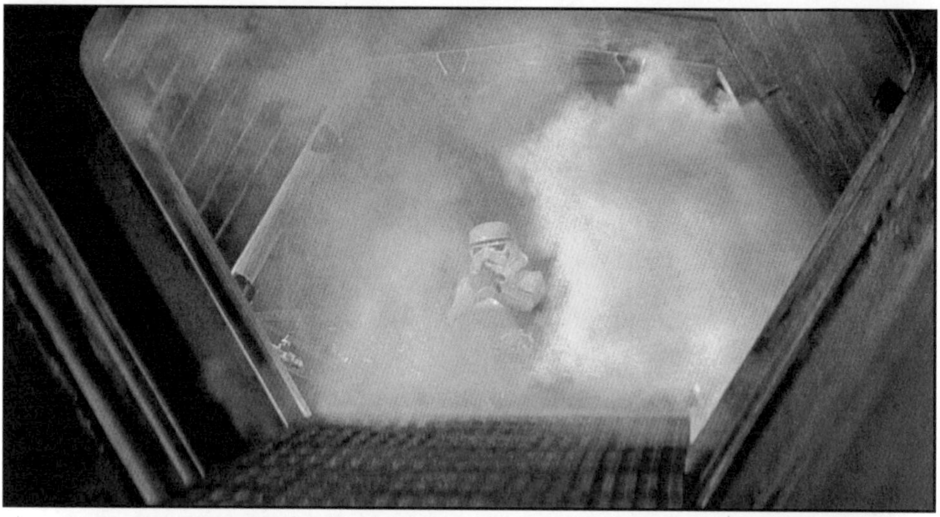

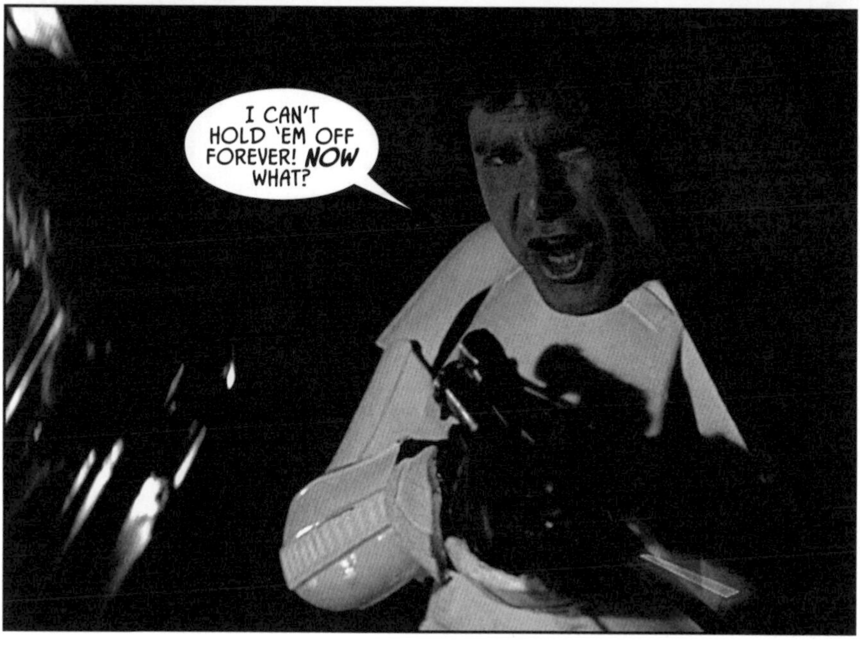
I CAN'T HOLD 'EM OFF FOREVER! ***NOW*** WHAT?

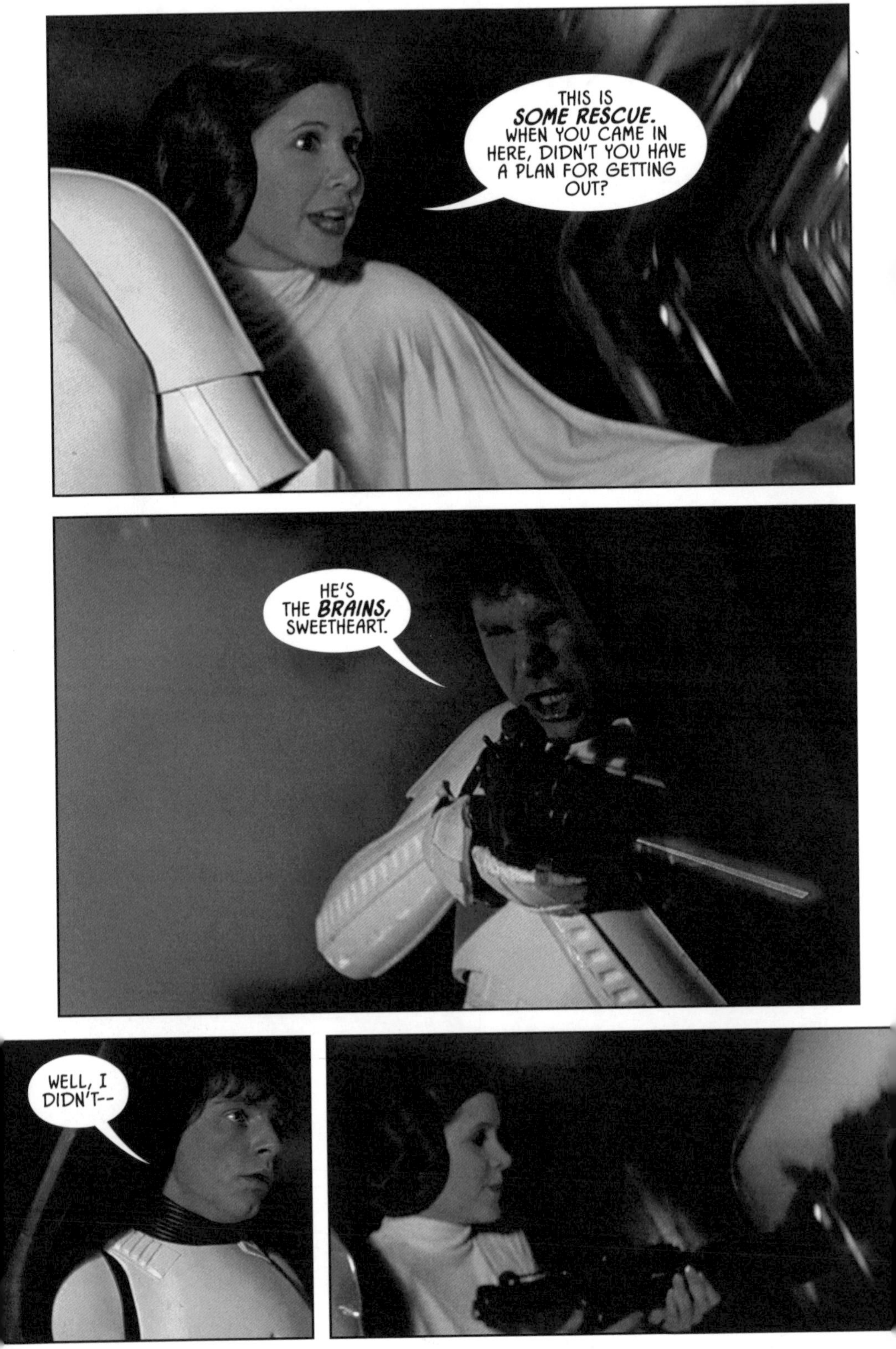
THIS IS **SOME RESCUE.** WHEN YOU CAME IN HERE, DIDN'T YOU HAVE A PLAN FOR GETTING OUT?
HE'S THE **BRAINS,** SWEETHEART.
WELL, I DIDN'T--

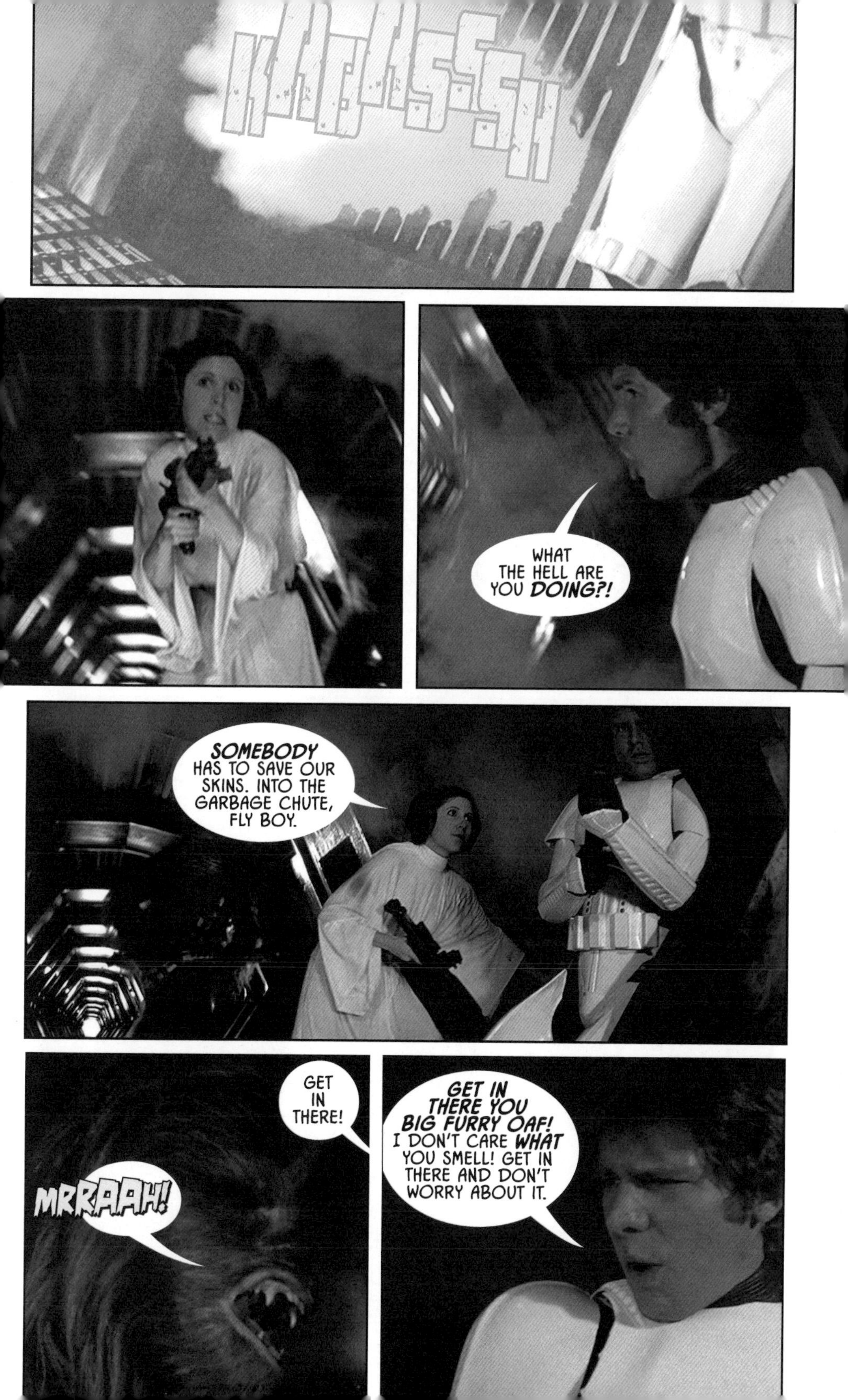

WHAT THE HELL ARE YOU DOING?!
SOMEBODY HAS TO SAVE OUR SKINS. INTO THE GARBAGE CHUTE, FLY BOY.
GET IN THERE!
MRRAAH!
GET IN THERE YOU BIG FURRY OAF! I DON'T CARE WHAT YOU SMELL! GET IN THERE AND DON'T WORRY ABOUT IT.

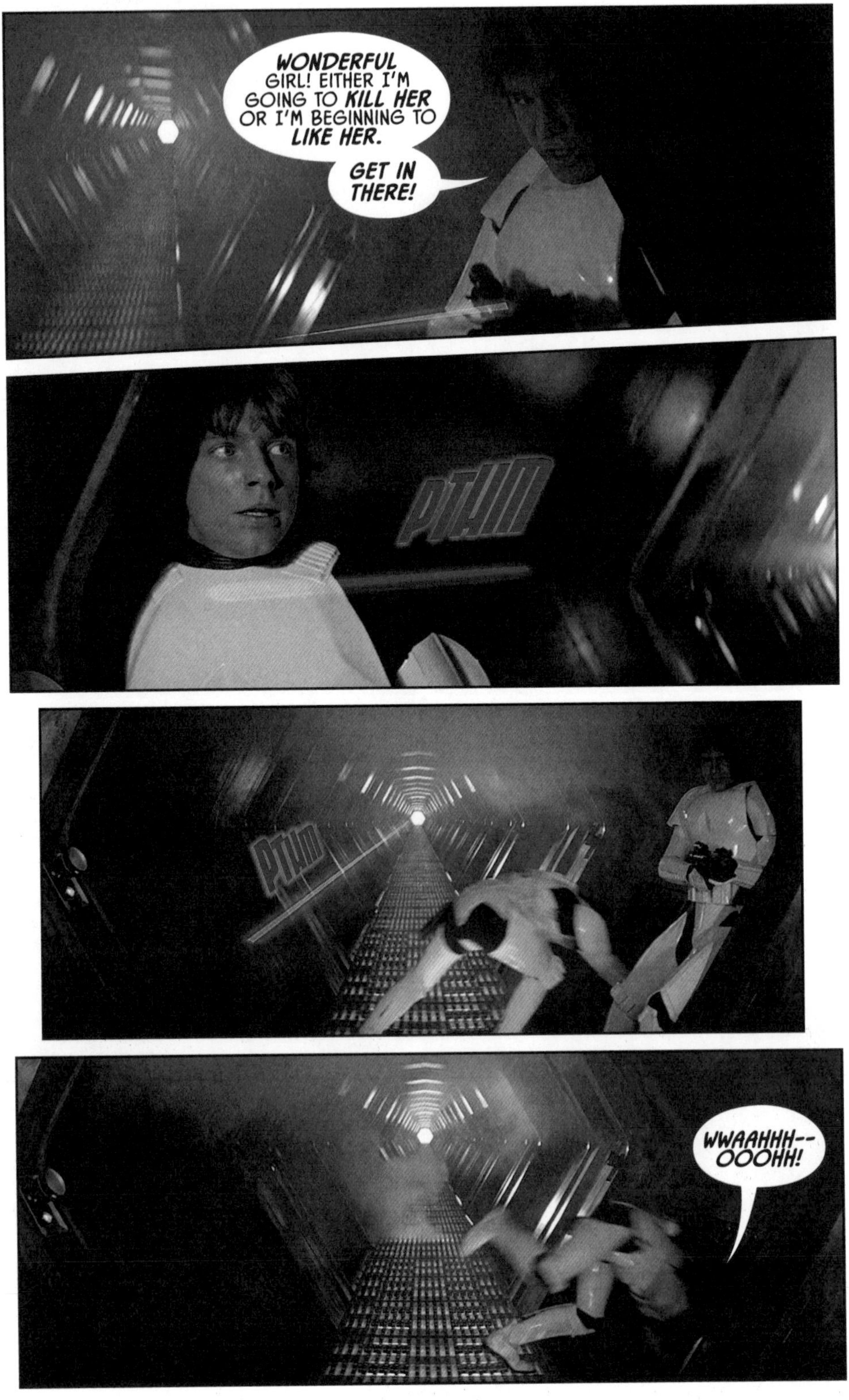
WONDERFUL GIRL! EITHER I'M GOING TO KILL HER OR I'M BEGINNING TO LIKE HER.
GET IN THERE!
WWAAHHH--OOOHH!

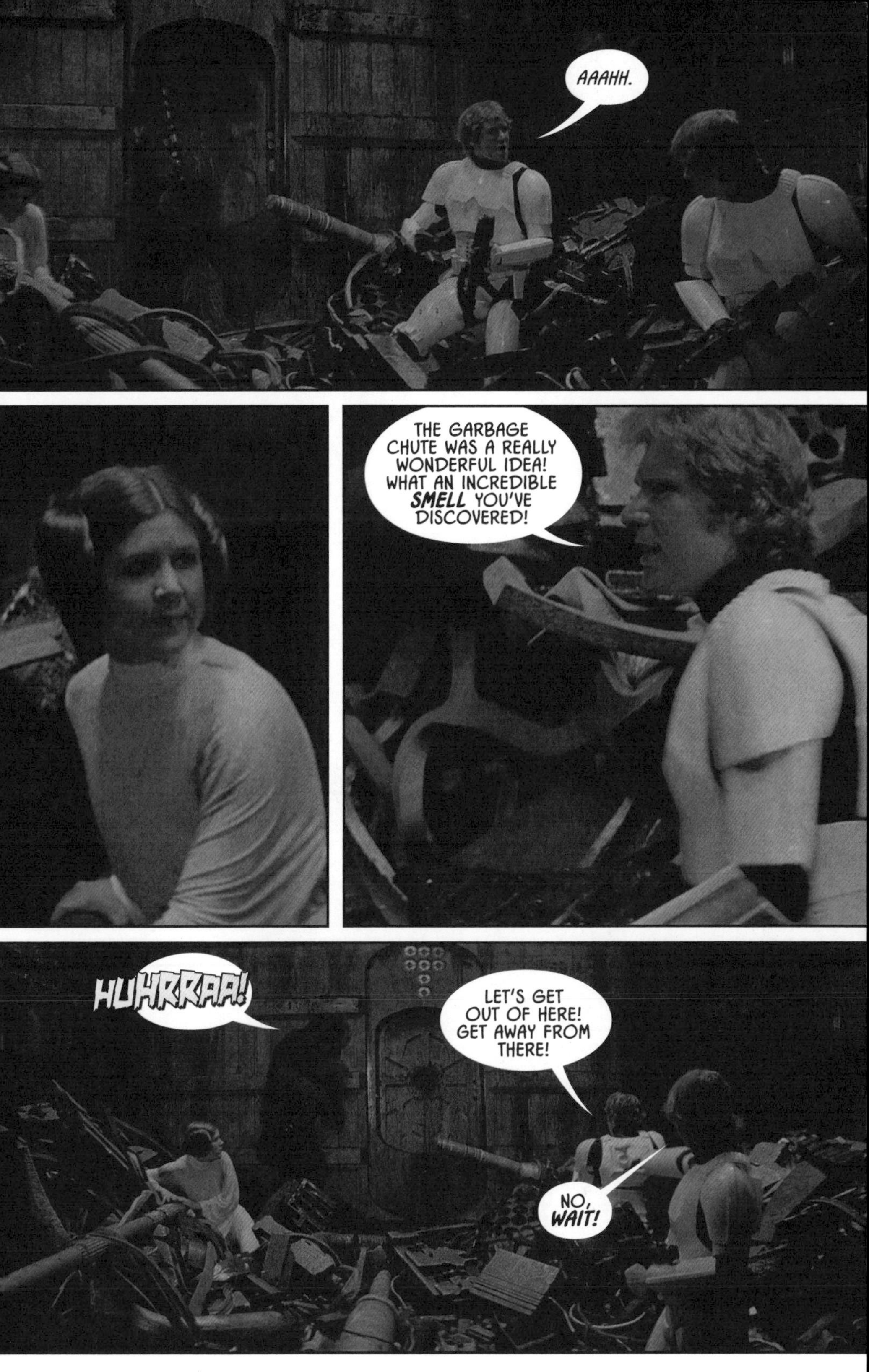
AAAHH.
THE GARBAGE CHUTE WAS A REALLY WONDERFUL IDEA! WHAT AN INCREDIBLE SMELL YOU'VE DISCOVERED!
HUHRRAA!
LET'S GET OUT OF HERE! GET AWAY FROM THERE!
NO, WAIT!

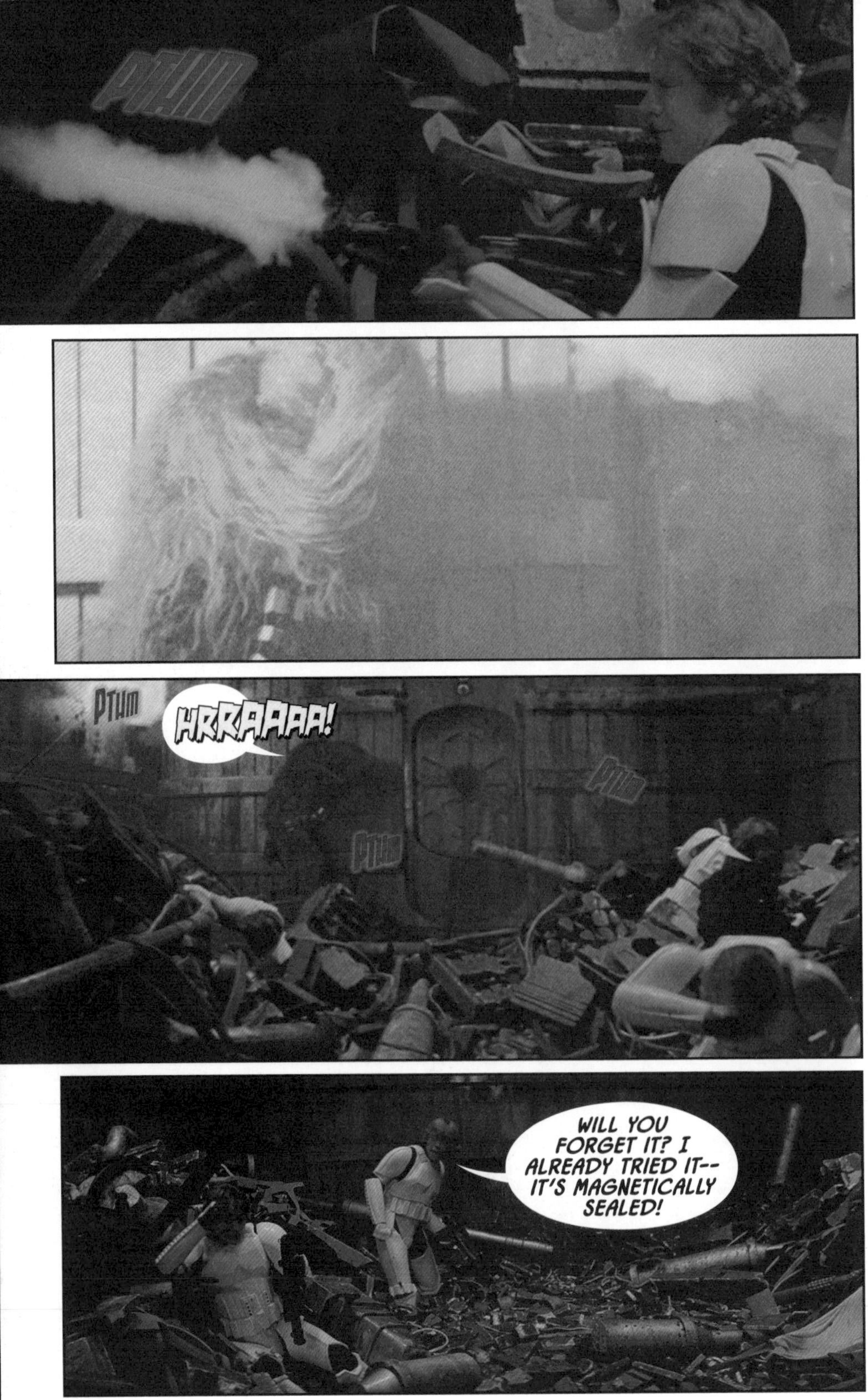
PTHM
PTHM
HRRAAAAA!
PTHM
PTHM
WILL YOU FORGET IT? I ALREADY TRIED IT-- IT'S MAGNETICALLY SEALED!

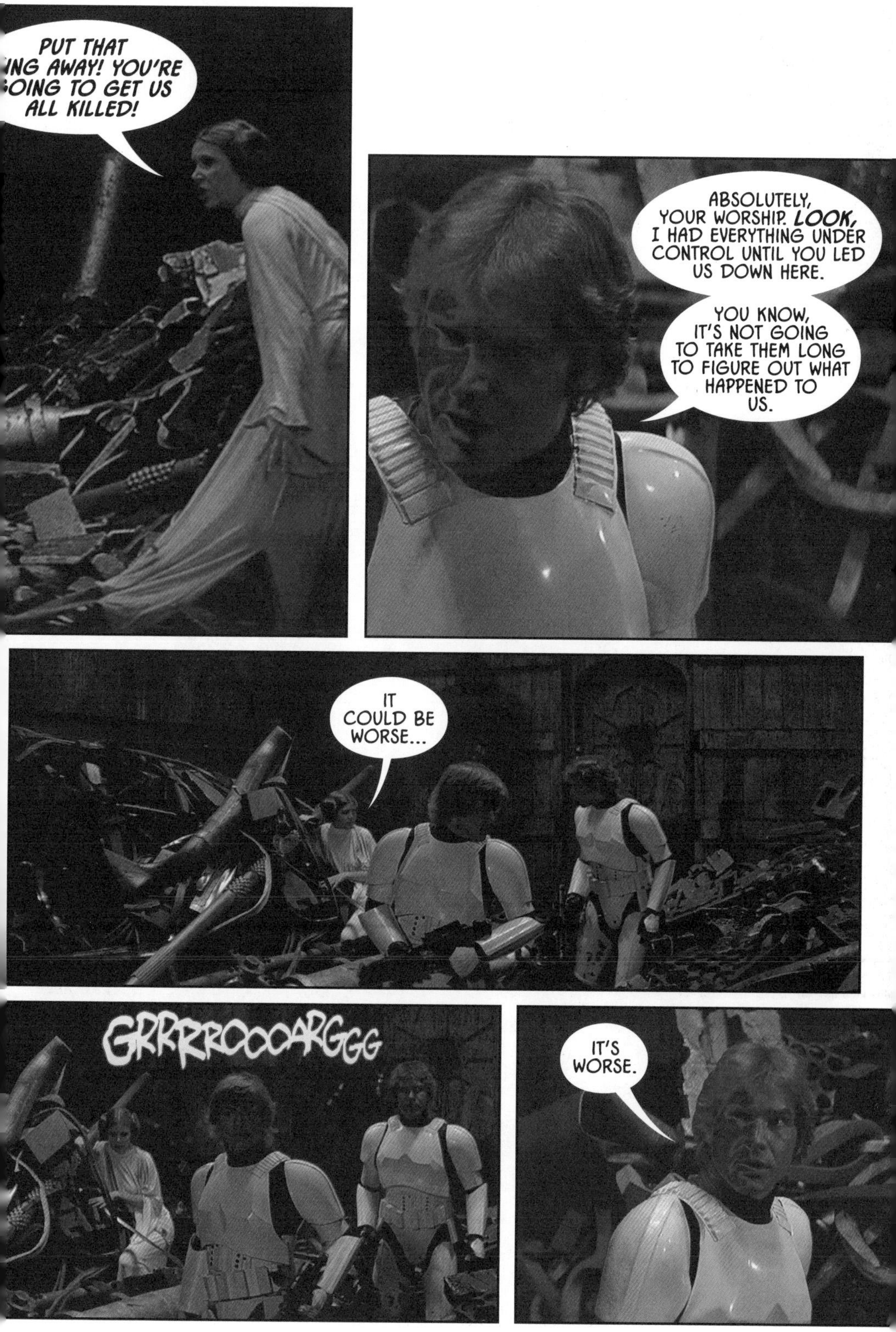
PUT THAT ING AWAY! YOU'RE OING TO GET US ALL KILLED!
ABSOLUTELY, YOUR WORSHIP. **LOOK,** I HAD EVERYTHING UNDER CONTROL UNTIL YOU LED US DOWN HERE.
YOU KNOW, IT'S NOT GOING TO TAKE THEM LONG TO FIGURE OUT WHAT HAPPENED TO US.
IT COULD BE WORSE...
GRRRROOOARGGG
IT'S WORSE.

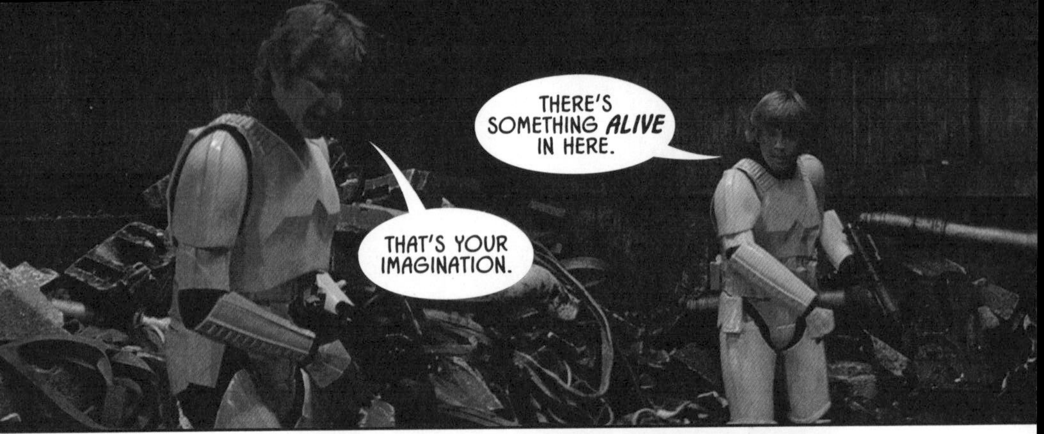
THERE'S SOMETHING ALIVE IN HERE.
THAT'S YOUR IMAGINATION.

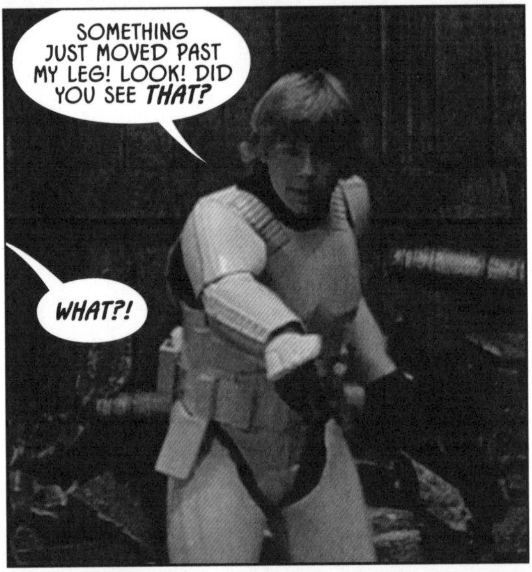
SOMETHING JUST MOVED PAST MY LEG! LOOK! DID YOU SEE THAT?
WHAT?!

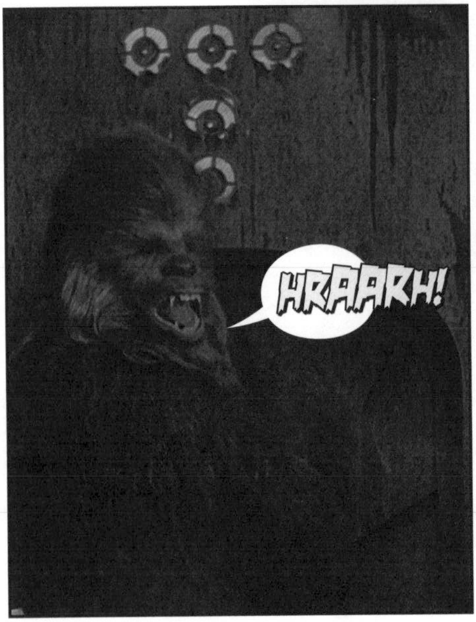
HRAARH!

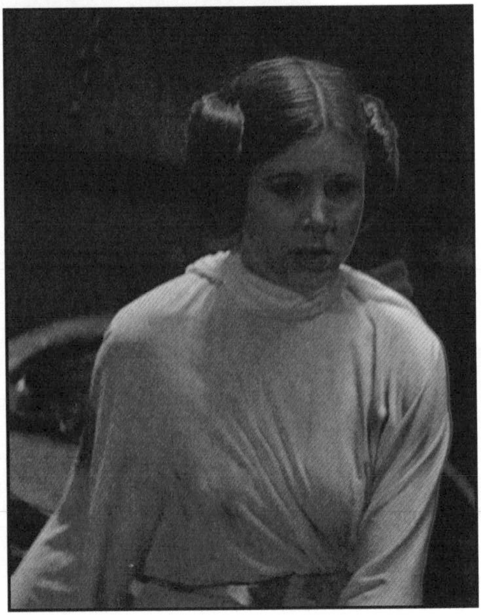

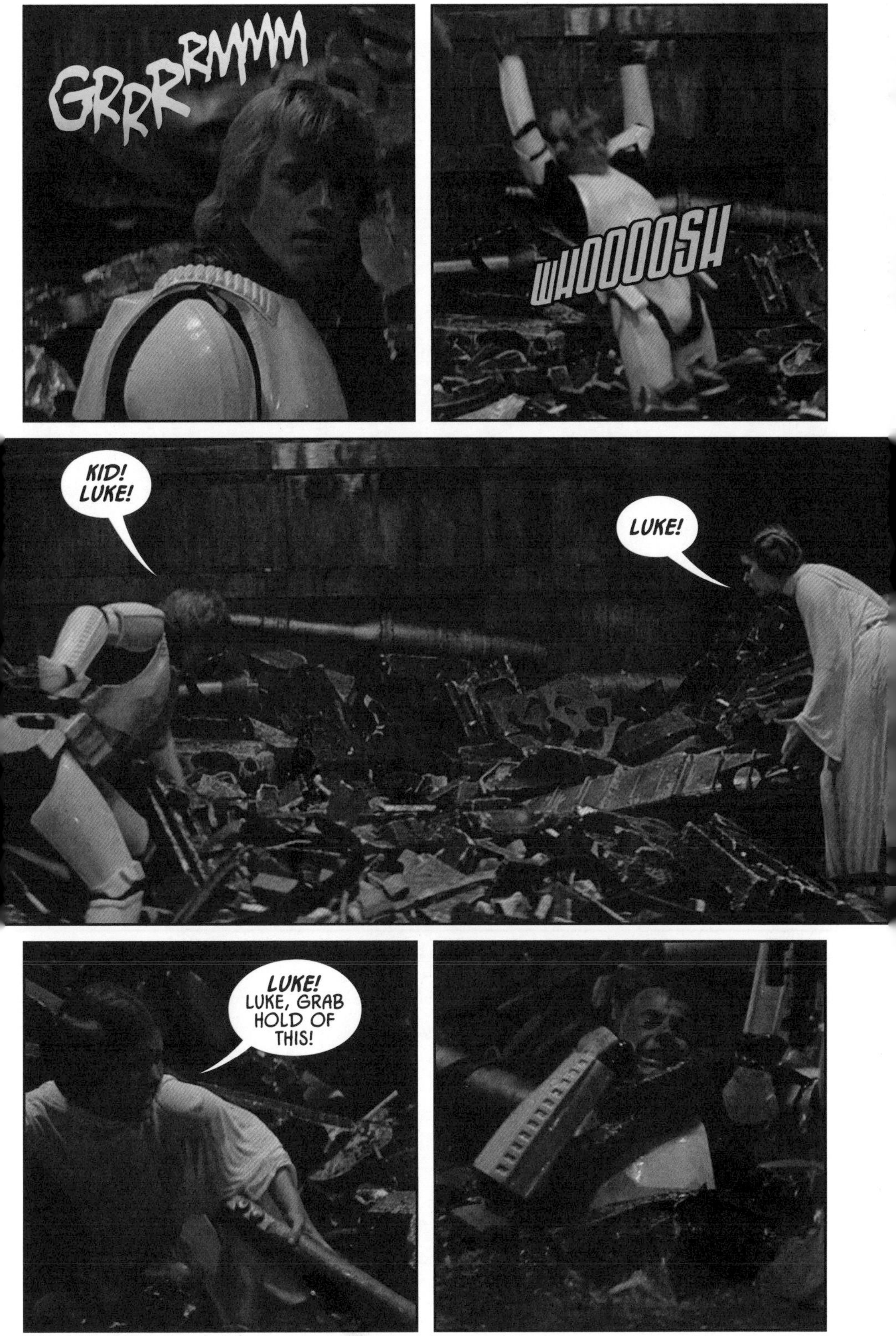
GRRRRMMM
WHOOOOSH
KID! LUKE!
LUKE!
LUKE! LUKE, GRAB HOLD OF THIS!

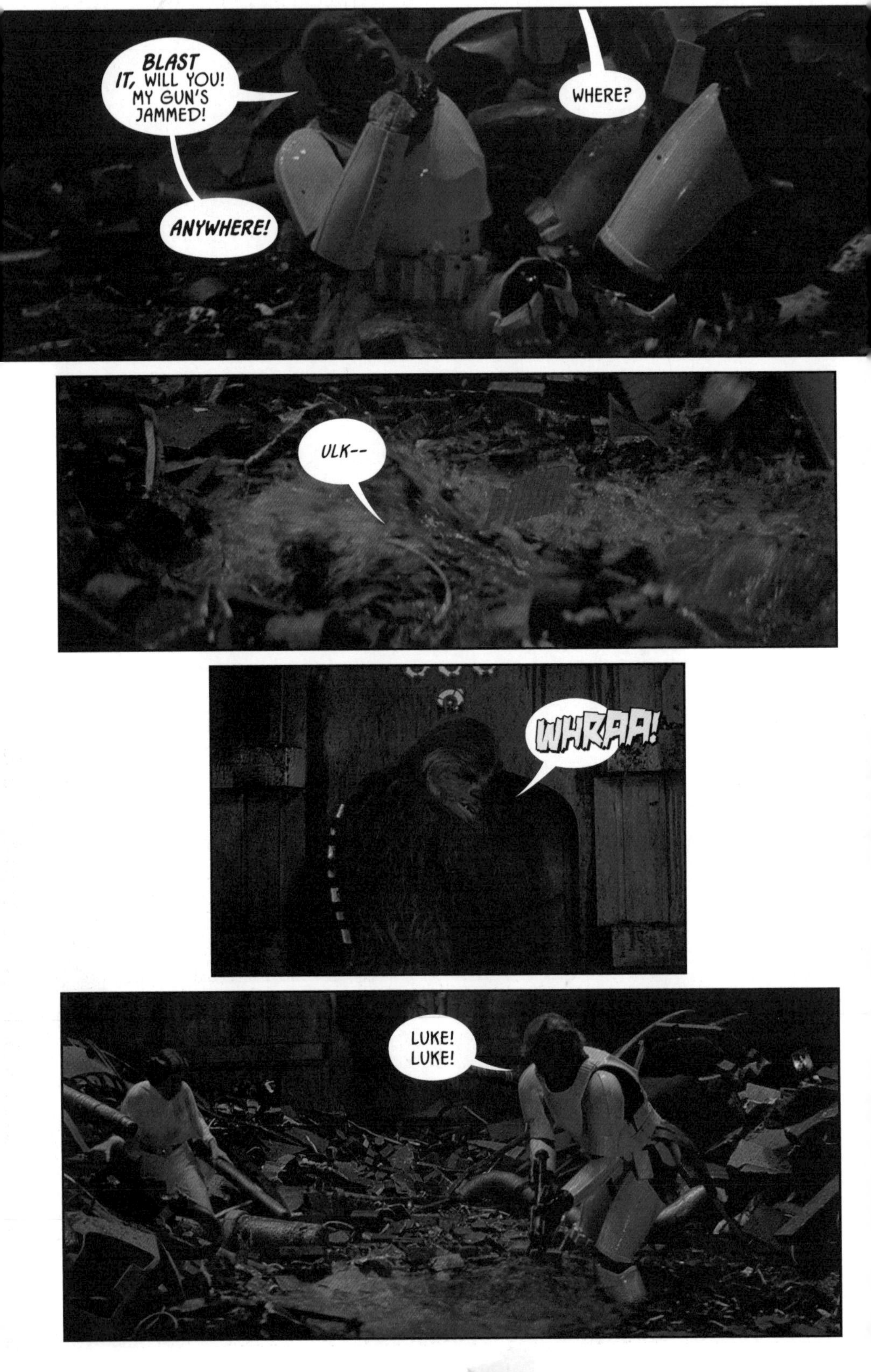
BLAST IT, WILL YOU! MY GUN'S JAMMED!
WHERE?
ANYWHERE!
ULK--
WHRAA!
LUKE! LUKE!

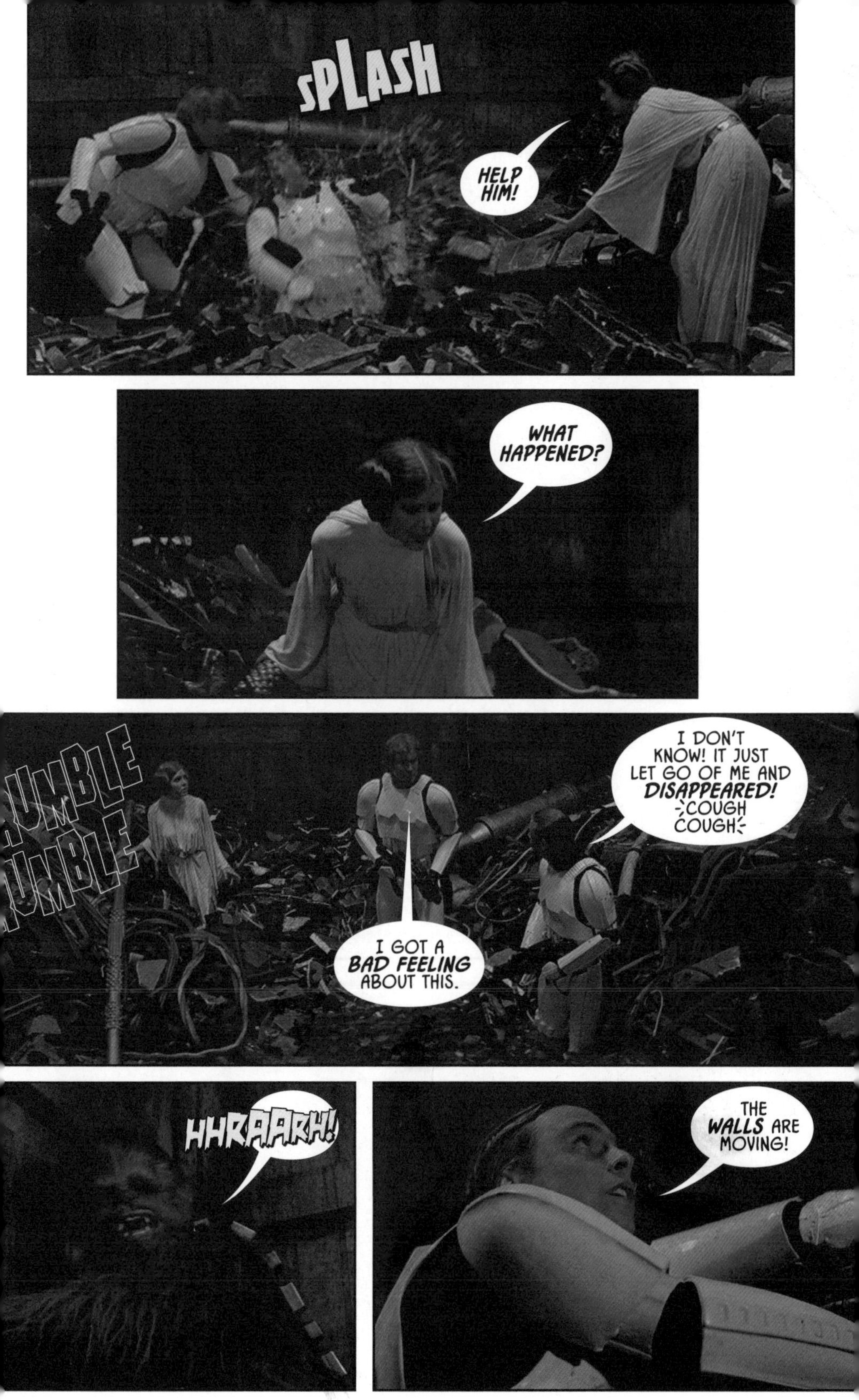

SPLASH
HELP HIM!
WHAT HAPPENED?
RUMBLE RUMBLE
I DON'T KNOW! IT JUST LET GO OF ME AND DISAPPEARED! COUGH COUGH
I GOT A BAD FEELING ABOUT THIS.
HHRAAARH!
THE WALLS ARE MOVING!

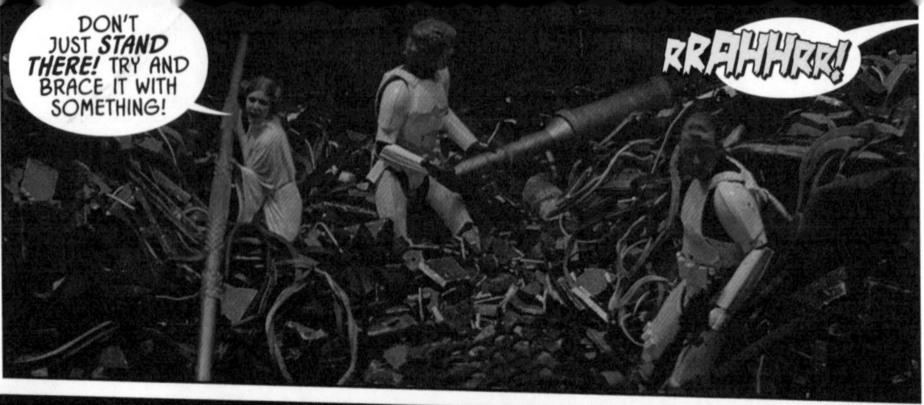
DON'T JUST **STAND THERE!** TRY AND BRACE IT WITH SOMETHING!
RRAHHRR!

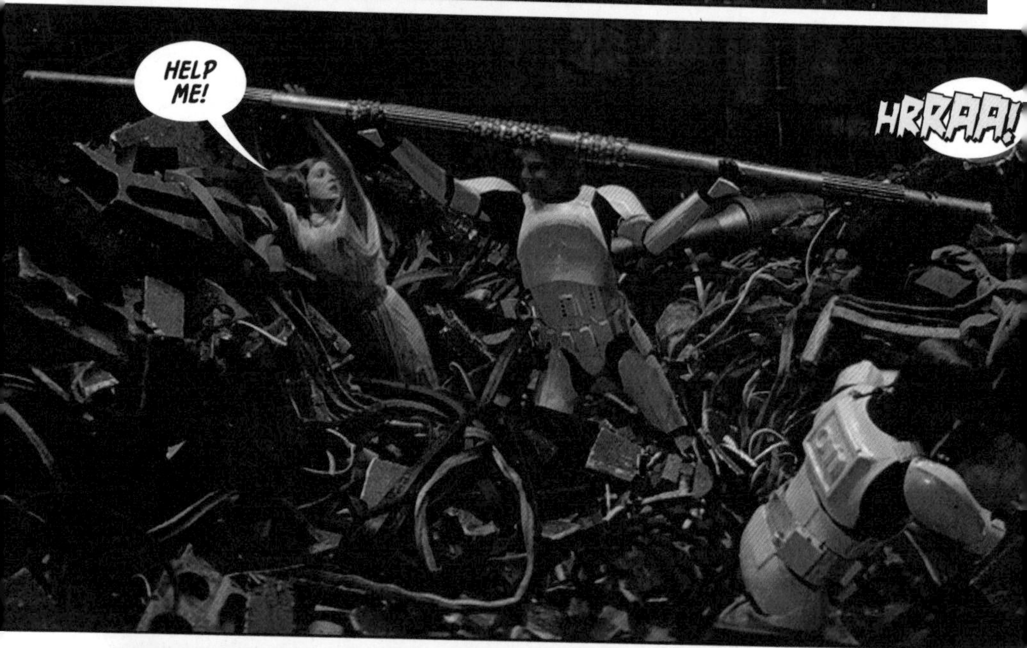
HELP ME!
HRRAA!

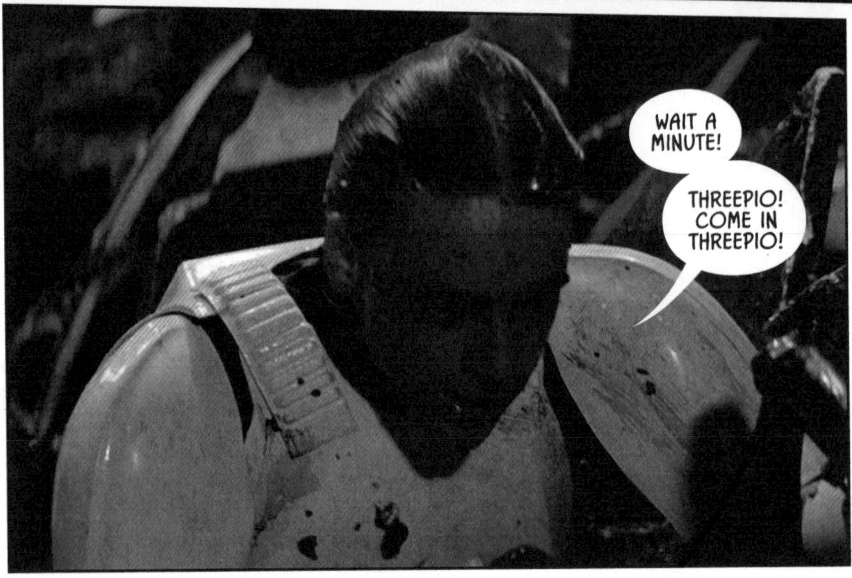
WAIT A MINUTE!
THREEPIO! COME IN THREEPIO!

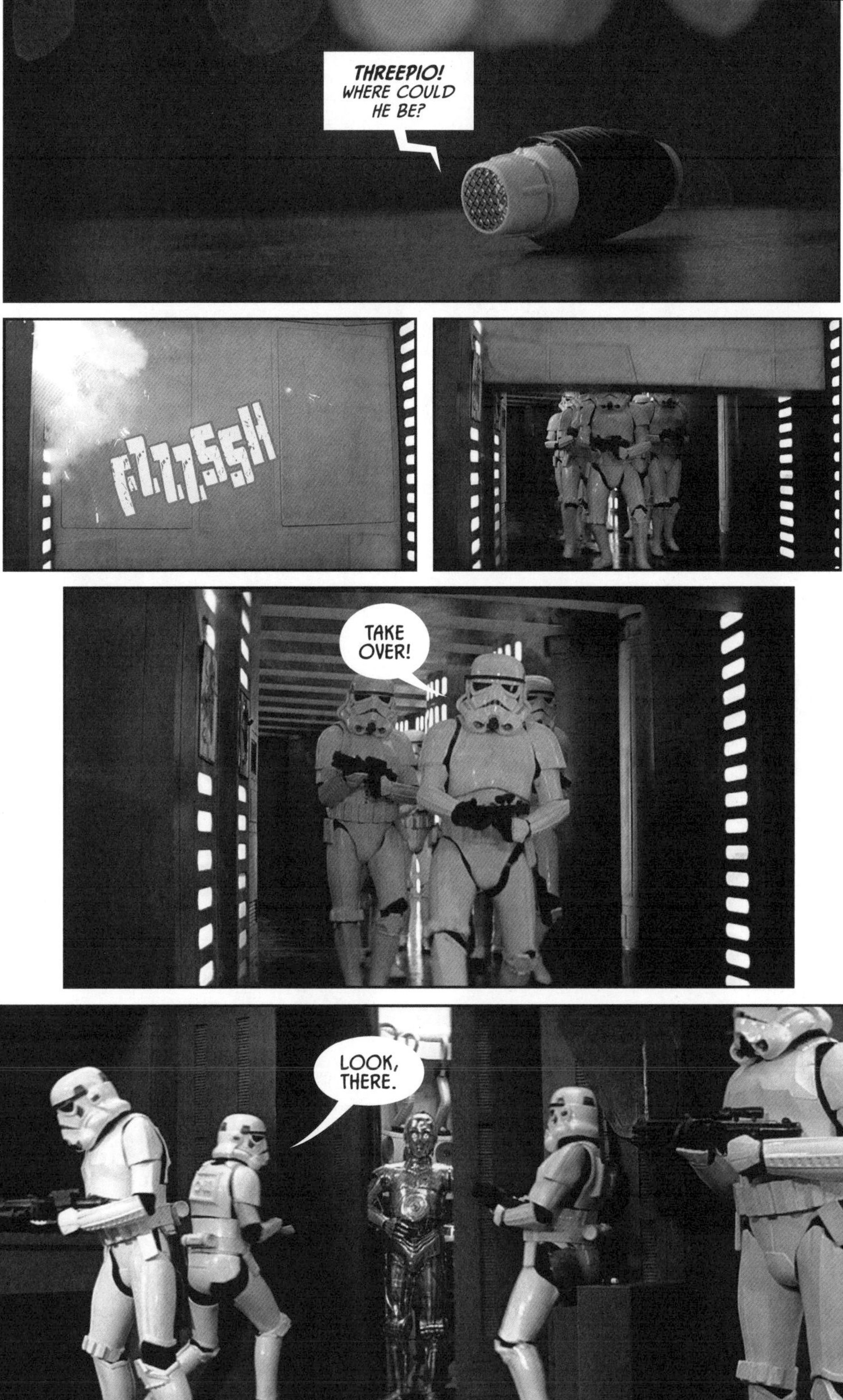
THREEPIO! WHERE COULD HE BE?
FZZZSSH
TAKE OVER!
LOOK, THERE.

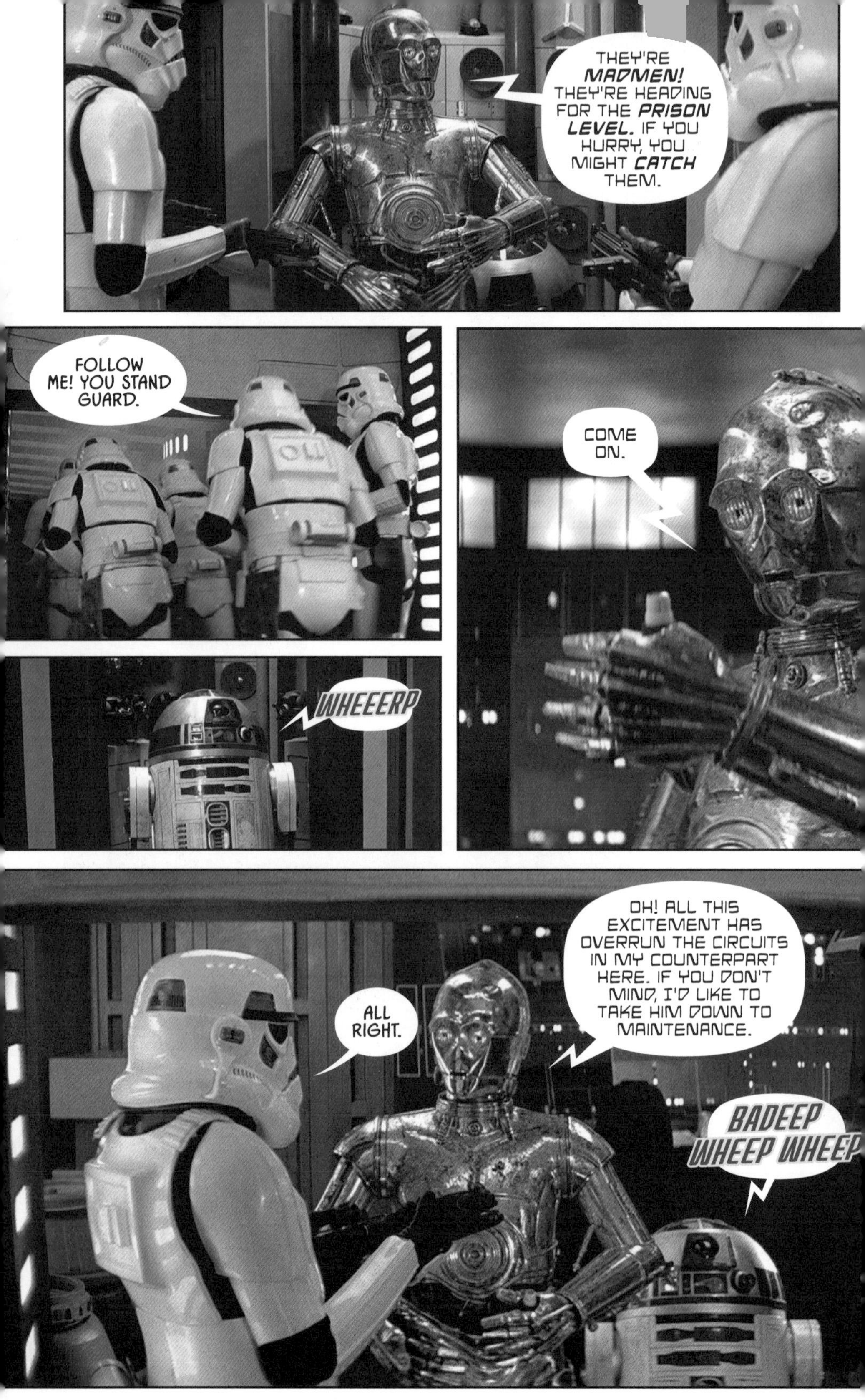
THEY'RE MADMEN! THEY'RE HEADING FOR THE PRISON LEVEL. IF YOU HURRY, YOU MIGHT CATCH THEM.
FOLLOW ME! YOU STAND GUARD.
WHEEERP
COME ON.
ALL RIGHT.
OH! ALL THIS EXCITEMENT HAS OVERRUN THE CIRCUITS IN MY COUNTERPART HERE. IF YOU DON'T MIND, I'D LIKE TO TAKE HIM DOWN TO MAINTENANCE.
BADEEP WHEEP WHEEP

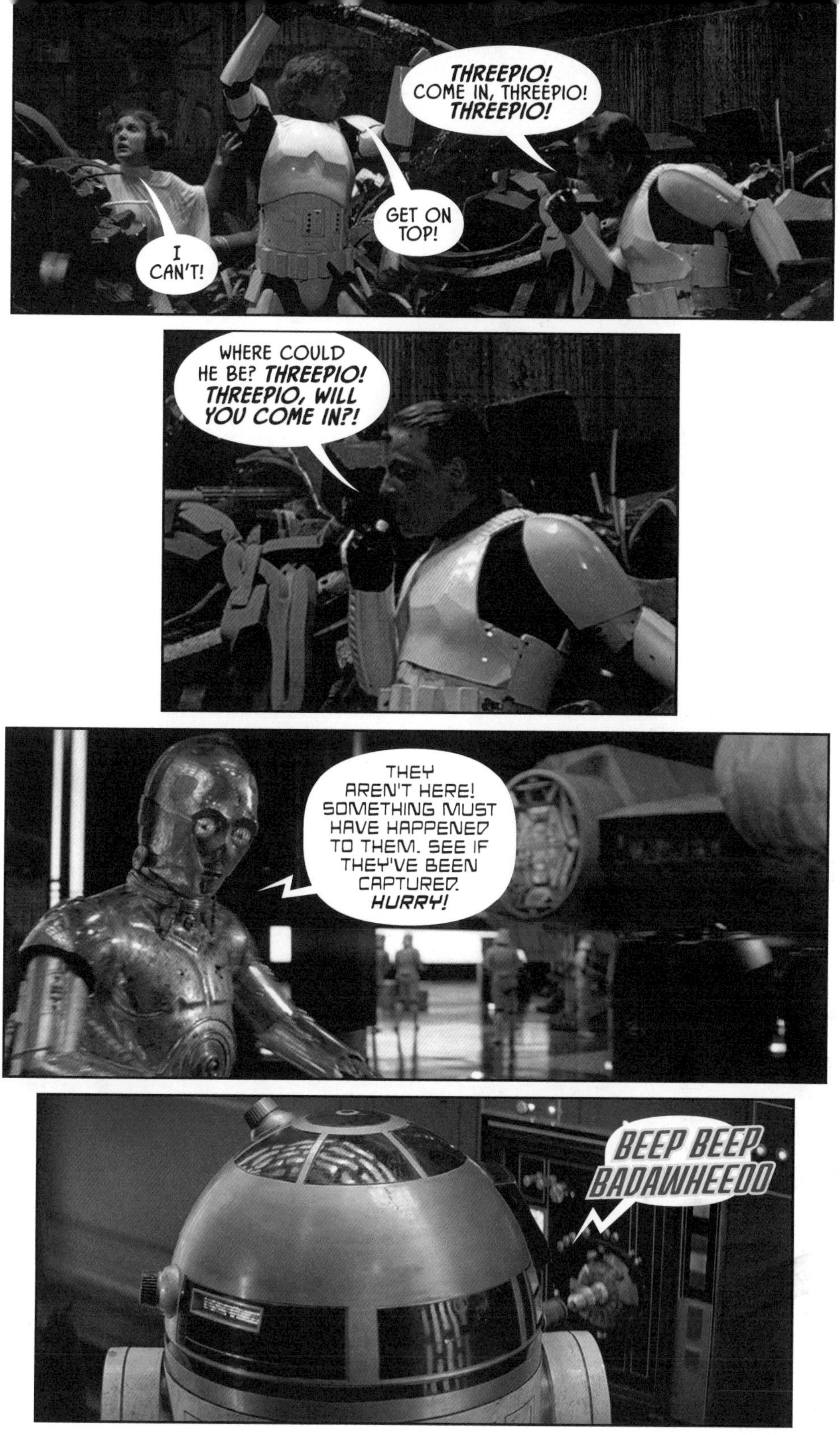
THREEPIO! COME IN, THREEPIO! THREEPIO!
GET ON TOP!
I CAN'T!
WHERE COULD HE BE? THREEPIO! THREEPIO, WILL YOU COME IN?!
THEY AREN'T HERE! SOMETHING MUST HAVE HAPPENED TO THEM. SEE IF THEY'VE BEEN CAPTURED. HURRY!
BEEP BEEP BADAWHEEDO

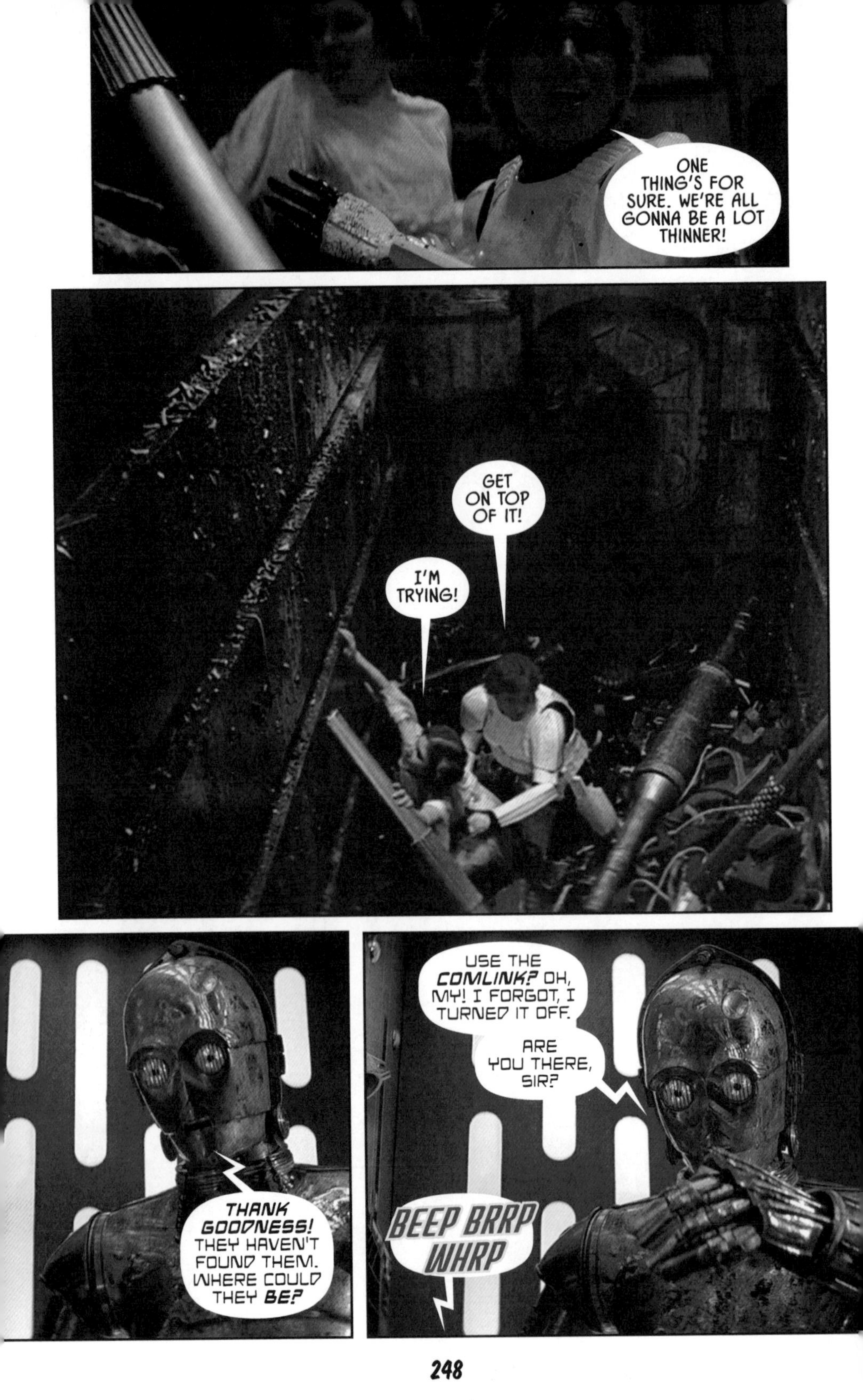
ONE THING'S FOR SURE. WE'RE ALL GONNA BE A LOT THINNER!
GET ON TOP OF IT!
I'M TRYING!
THANK GOODNESS! THEY HAVEN'T FOUND THEM. WHERE COULD THEY BE?
USE THE COMLINK? OH, MY! I FORGOT, I TURNED IT OFF.
ARE YOU THERE, SIR?
BEEP BRRP WHRP

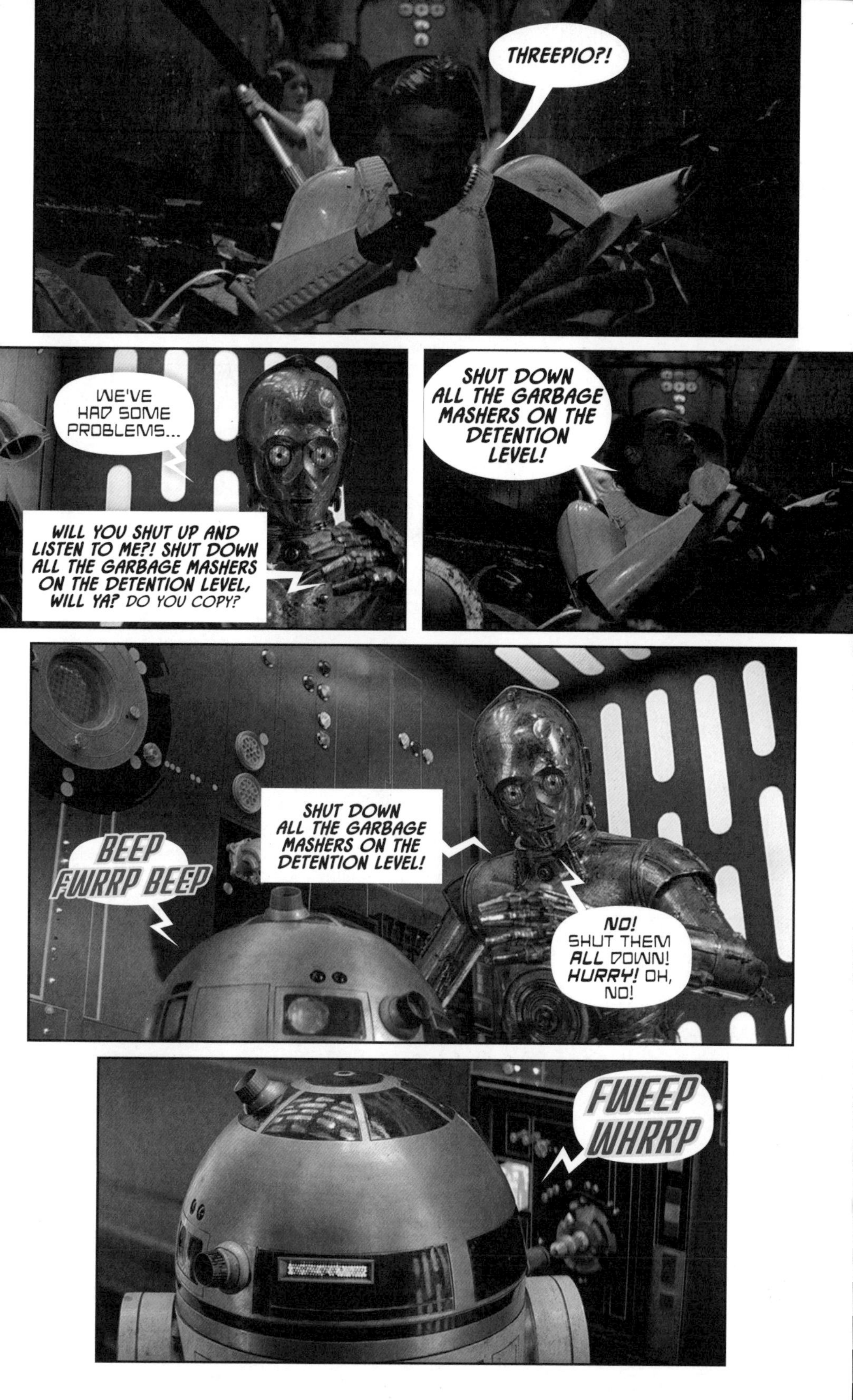
THREEPIO?!
WE'VE HAD SOME PROBLEMS...
WILL YOU SHUT UP AND LISTEN TO ME?! SHUT DOWN ALL THE GARBAGE MASHERS ON THE DETENTION LEVEL, WILL YA? DO YOU COPY?
SHUT DOWN ALL THE GARBAGE MASHERS ON THE DETENTION LEVEL!
BEEP FWRRP BEEP
SHUT DOWN ALL THE GARBAGE MASHERS ON THE DETENTION LEVEL!
NO! SHUT THEM ALL DOWN! HURRY! OH, NO!
FWEEP WHRRP

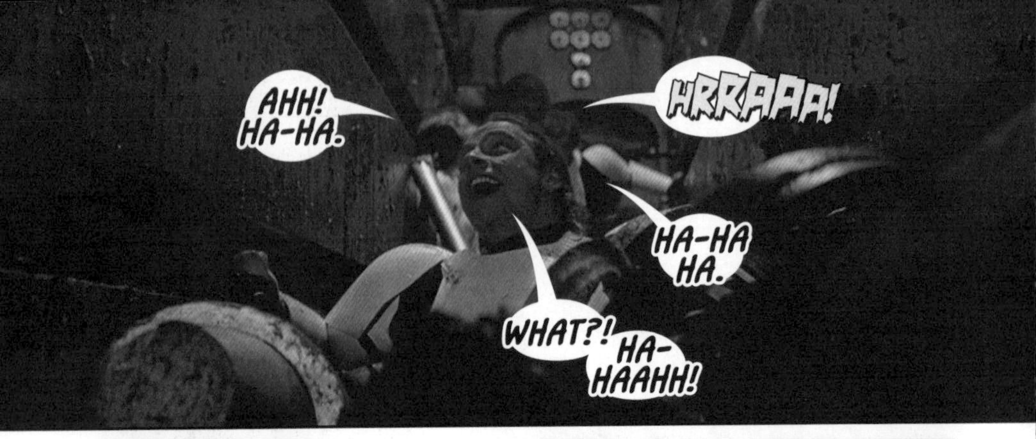
AHH! HA-HA.
HRRAAAA!
HA-HA HA.
WHAT?! HA-HAAAHH!

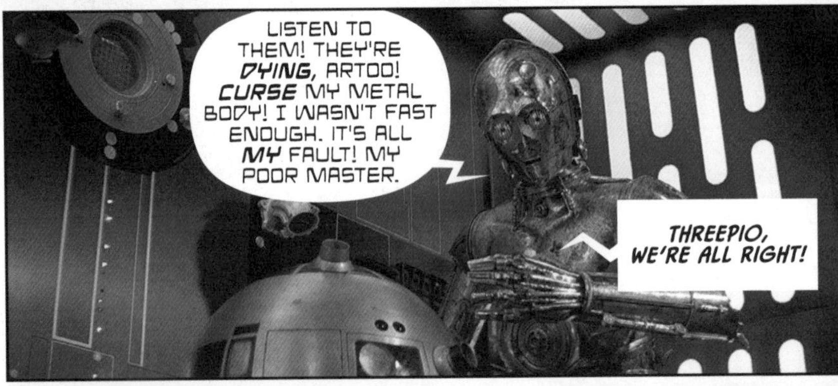
LISTEN TO THEM! THEY'RE DYING, ARTOO! CURSE MY METAL BODY! I WASN'T FAST ENOUGH. IT'S ALL MY FAULT! MY POOR MASTER.
THREEPIO, WE'RE ALL RIGHT!

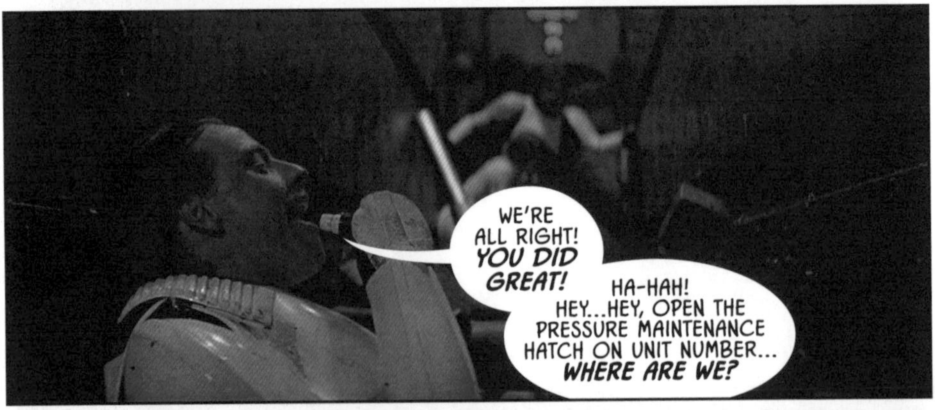
WE'RE ALL RIGHT! YOU DID GREAT!
HA-HAH! HEY...HEY, OPEN THE PRESSURE MAINTENANCE HATCH ON UNIT NUMBER... WHERE ARE WE?

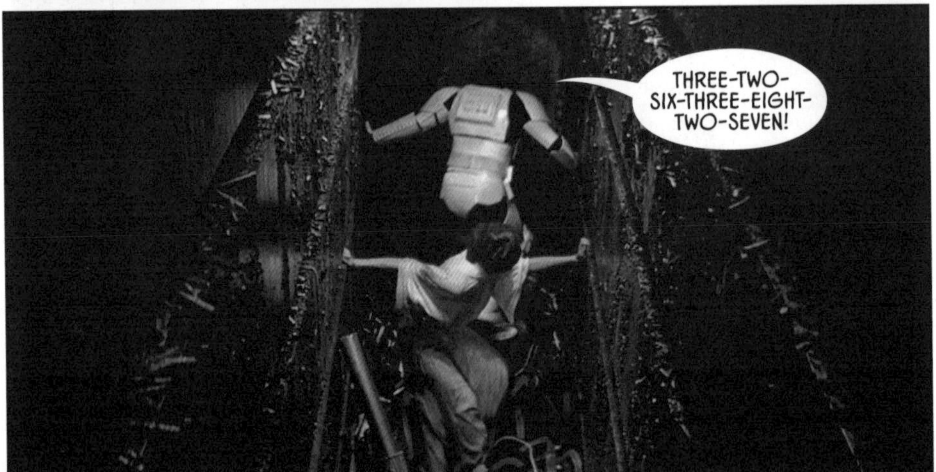
THREE-TWO-SIX-THREE-EIGHT-TWO-SEVEN!

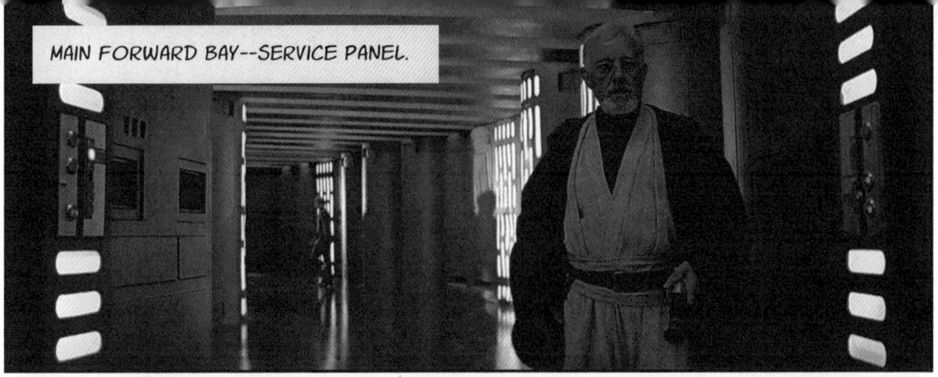
MAIN FORWARD BAY--SERVICE PANEL.

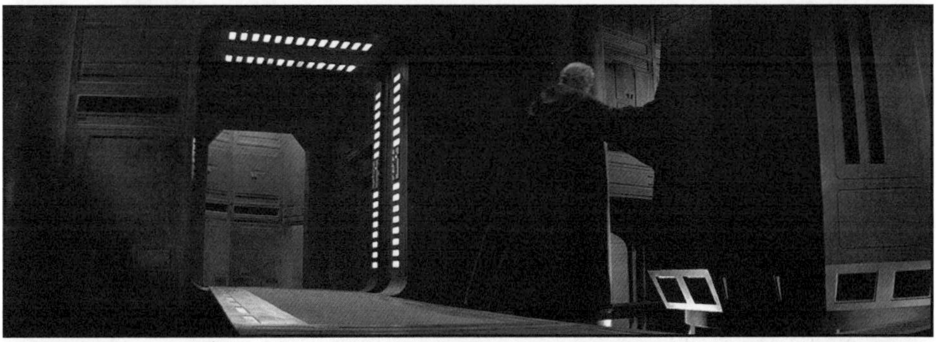

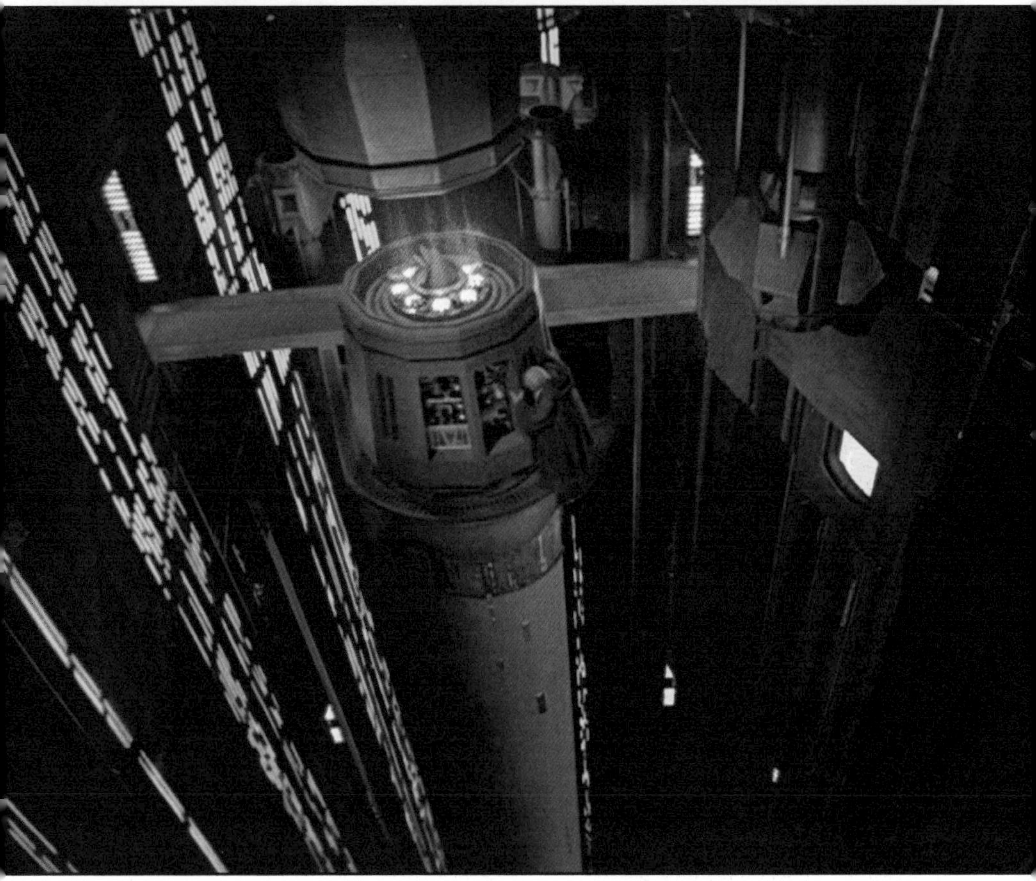

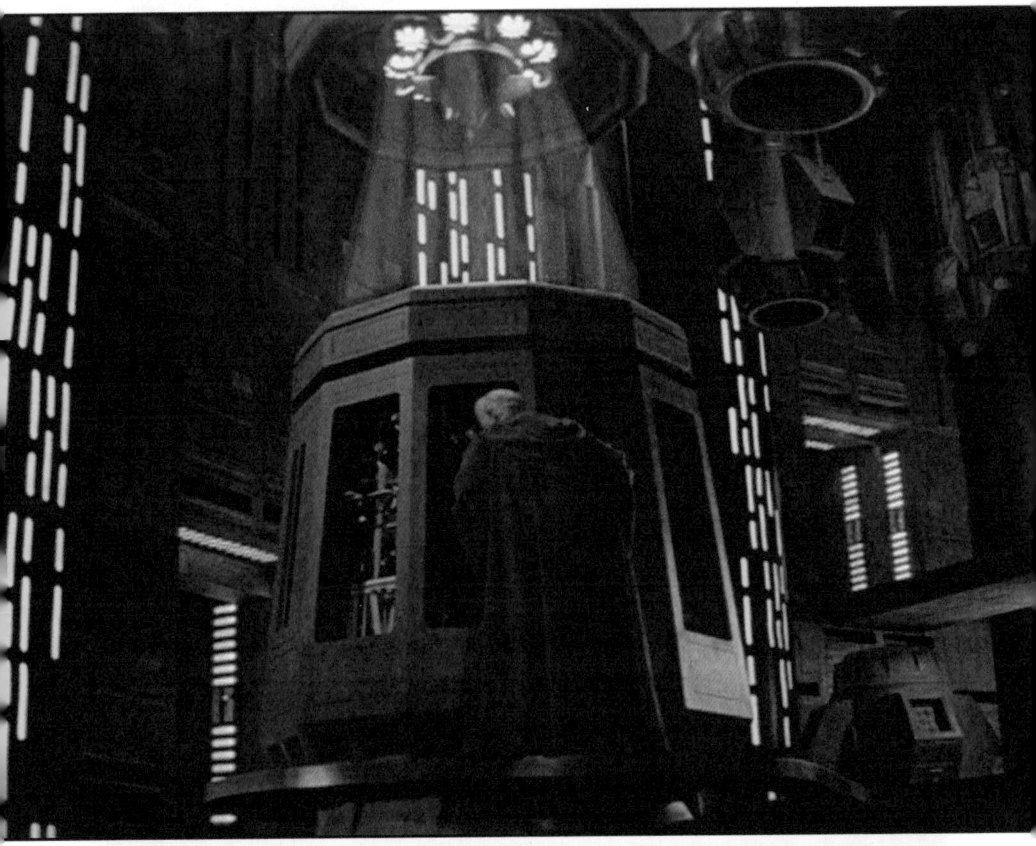

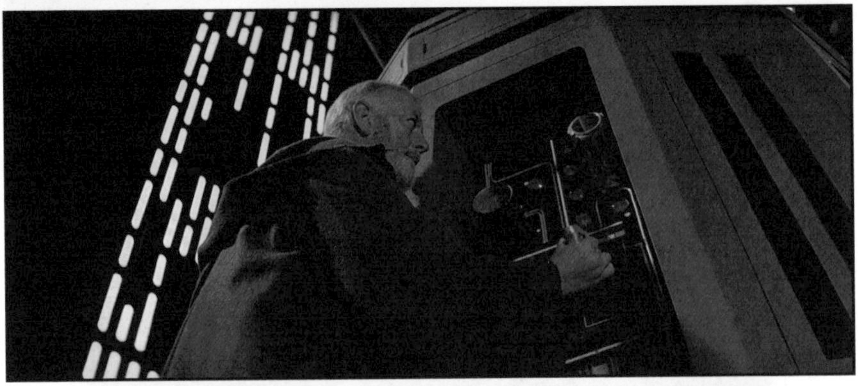

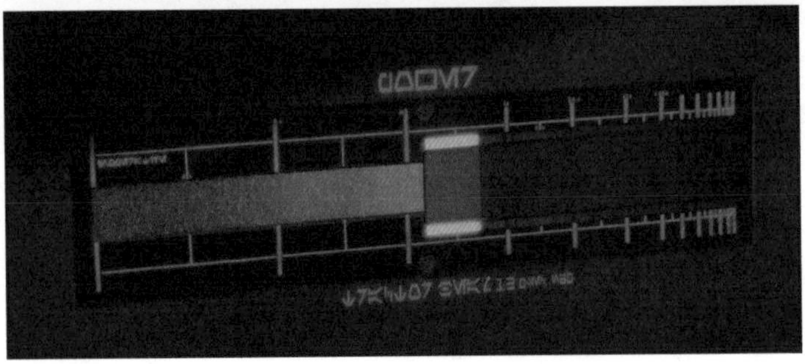

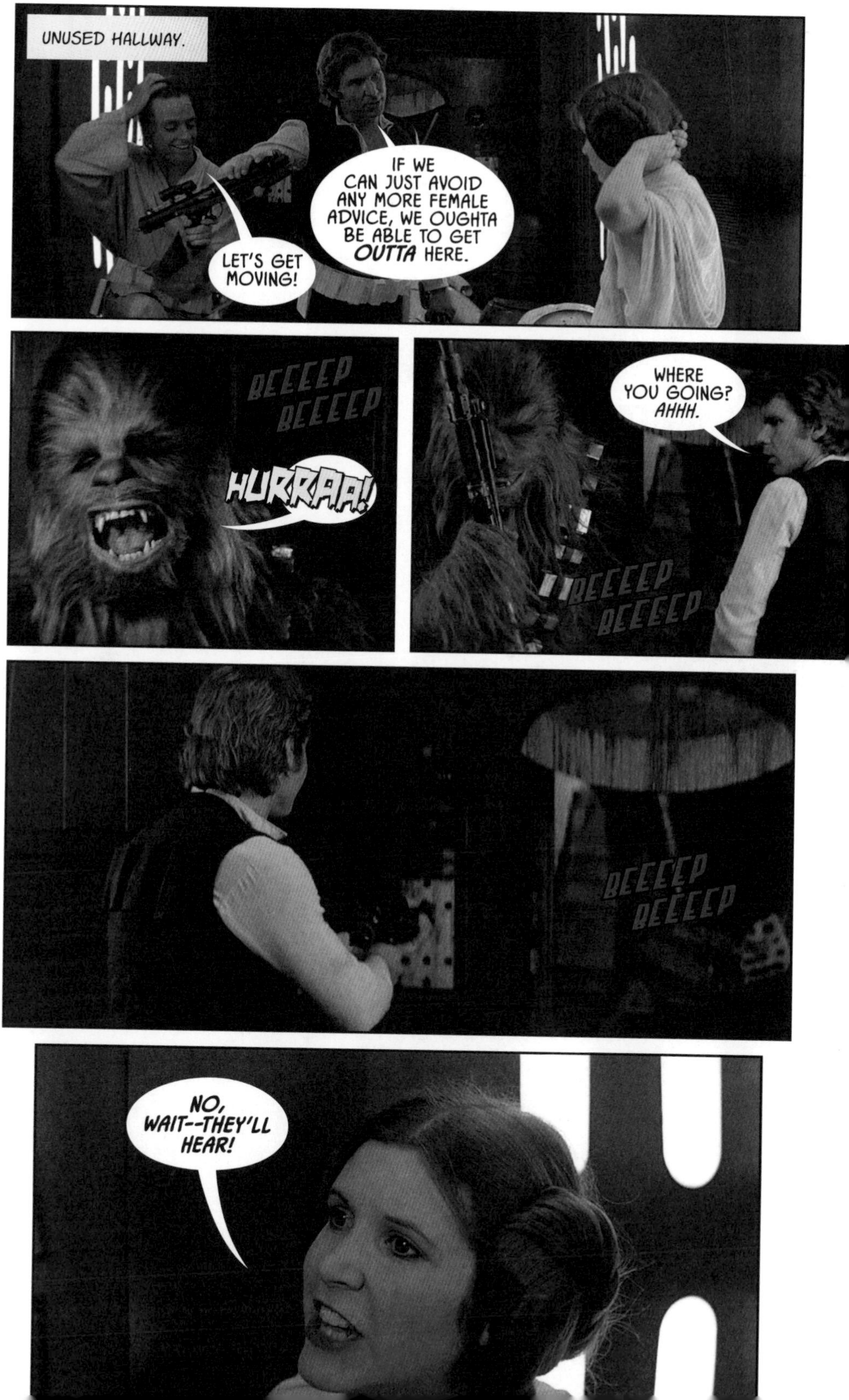
UNUSED HALLWAY.
LET'S GET MOVING!
IF WE CAN JUST AVOID ANY MORE FEMALE ADVICE, WE OUGHTA BE ABLE TO GET OUTTA HERE.
BEEEEP BEEEEP
HURRAA!
WHERE YOU GOING? AHHH.
BEEEEP BEEEEP
BEEEEP BEEEEP
NO, WAIT--THEY'LL HEAR!

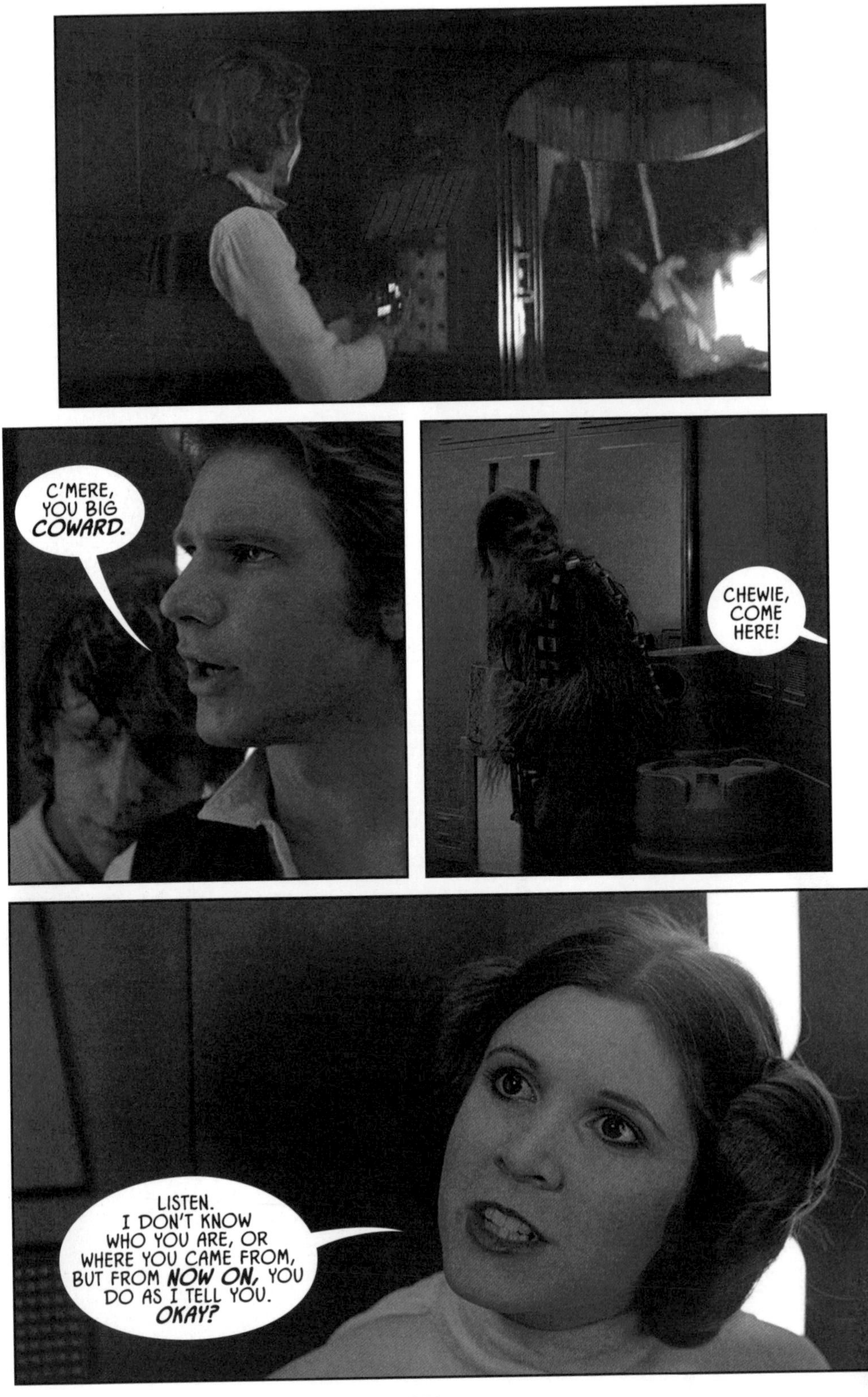
C'MERE, YOU BIG **COWARD.**
CHEWIE, COME HERE!
LISTEN. I DON'T KNOW WHO YOU ARE, OR WHERE YOU CAME FROM, BUT FROM **NOW ON,** YOU DO AS I TELL YOU. **OKAY?**

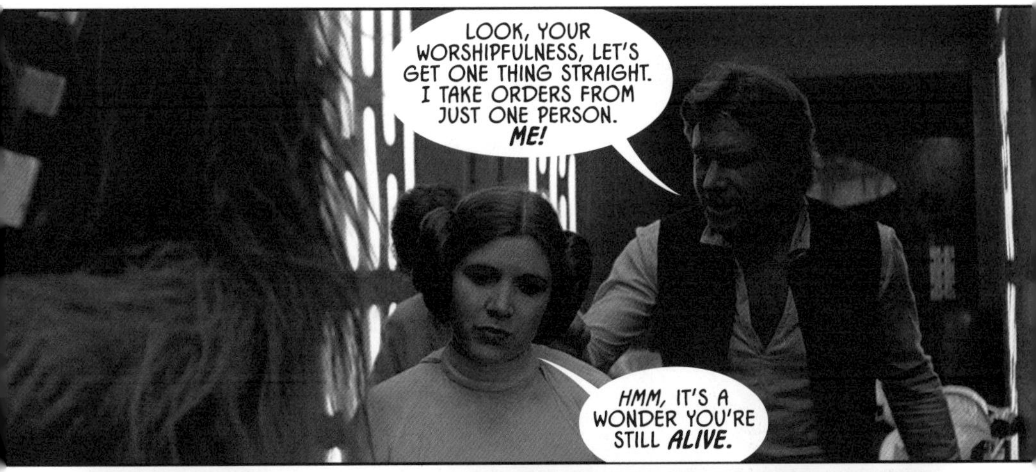
LOOK, YOUR WORSHIPFULNESS, LET'S GET ONE THING STRAIGHT. I TAKE ORDERS FROM JUST ONE PERSON. ***ME!***
HMM, IT'S A WONDER YOU'RE STILL ***ALIVE.***

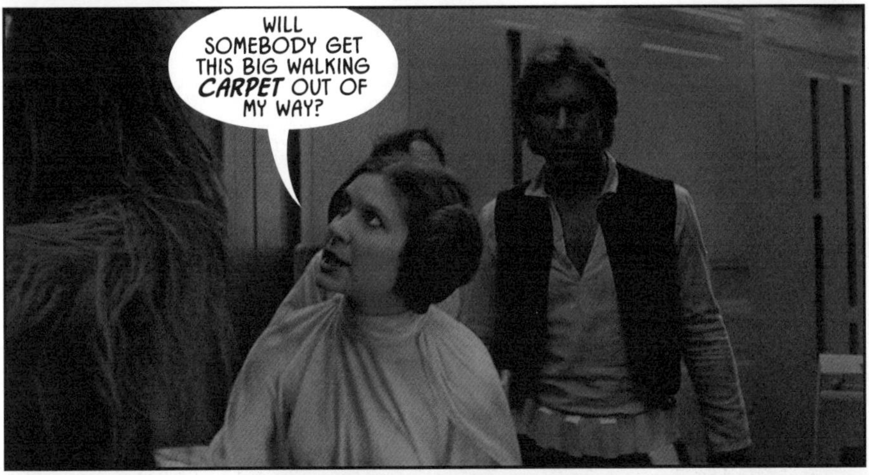
WILL SOMEBODY GET THIS BIG WALKING ***CARPET*** OUT OF MY WAY?

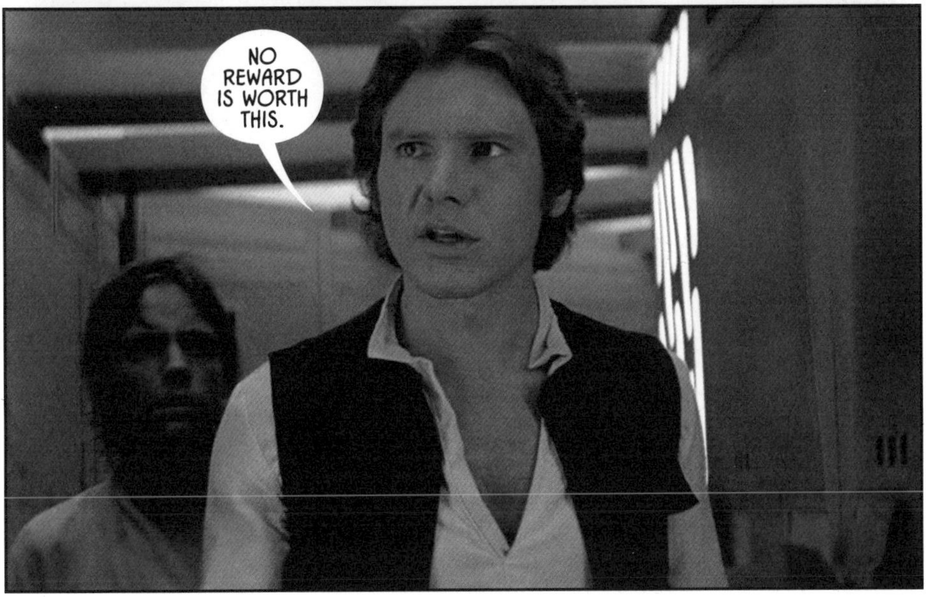
NO REWARD IS WORTH THIS.

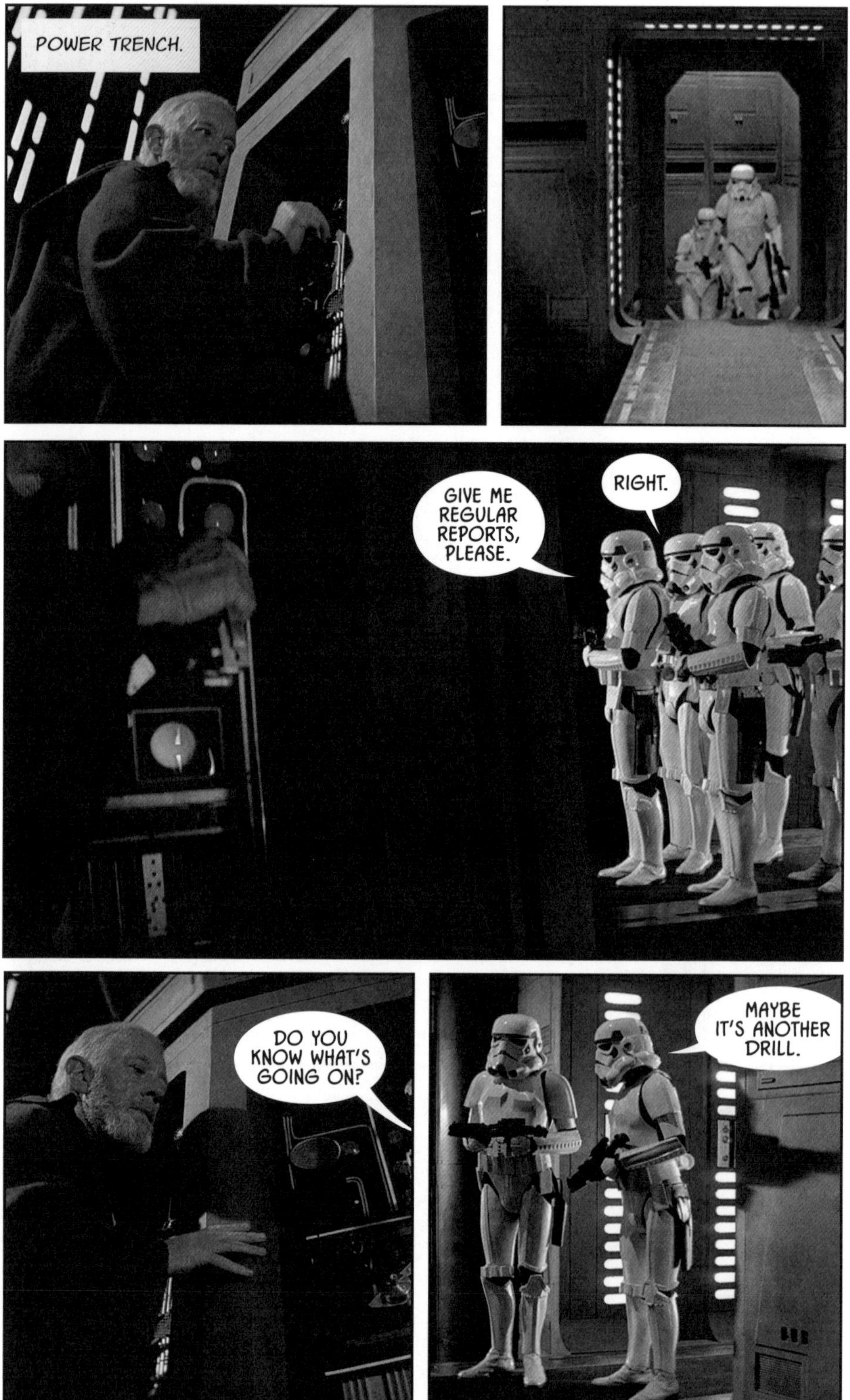
POWER TRENCH.
GIVE ME REGULAR REPORTS, PLEASE.
RIGHT.
DO YOU KNOW WHAT'S GOING ON?
MAYBE IT'S ANOTHER DRILL.

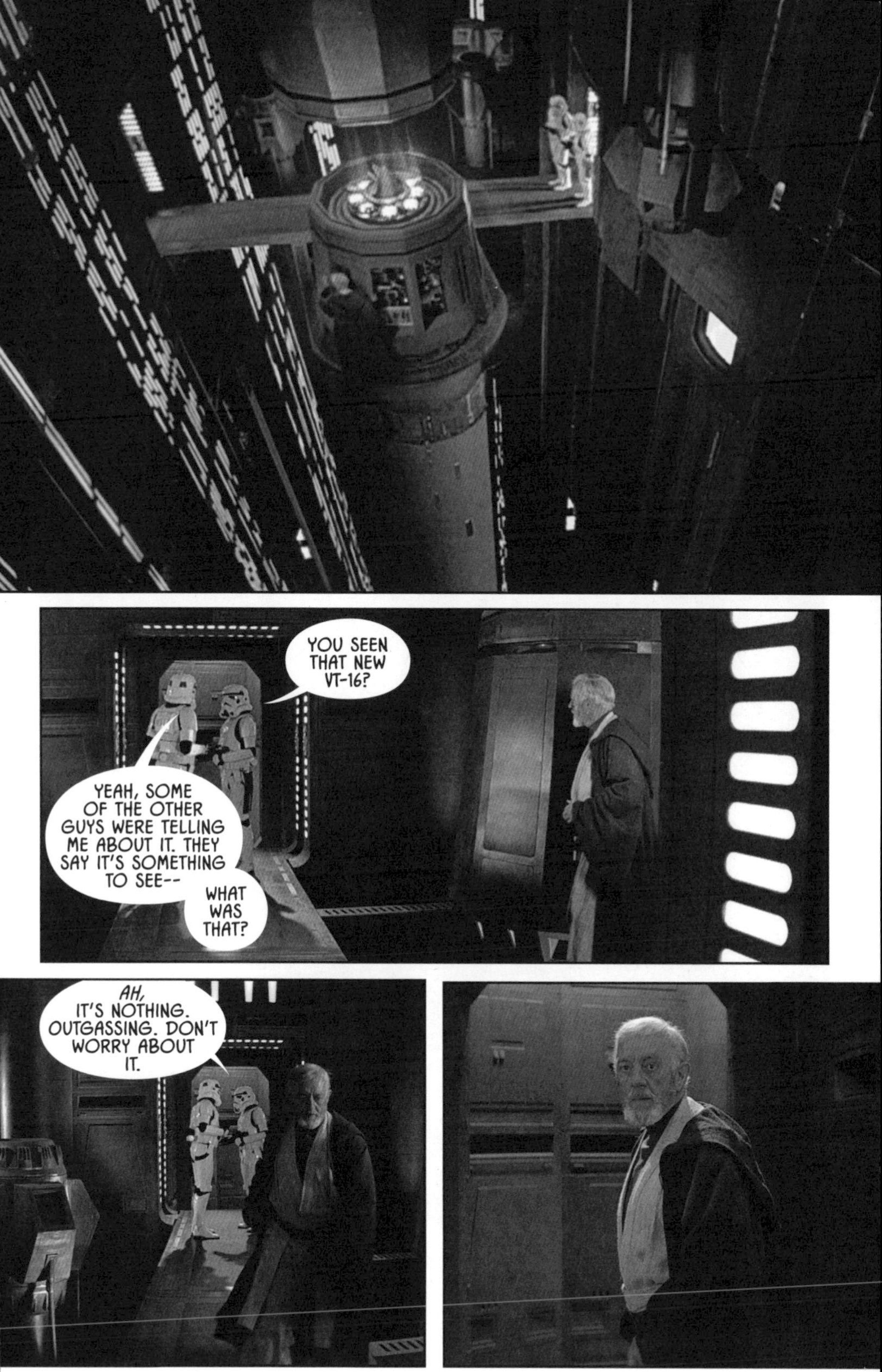
YOU SEEN THAT NEW VT-16?
YEAH, SOME OF THE OTHER GUYS WERE TELLING ME ABOUT IT. THEY SAY IT'S SOMETHING TO SEE--
WHAT WAS THAT?
AH, IT'S NOTHING. OUTGASSING. DON'T WORRY ABOUT IT.

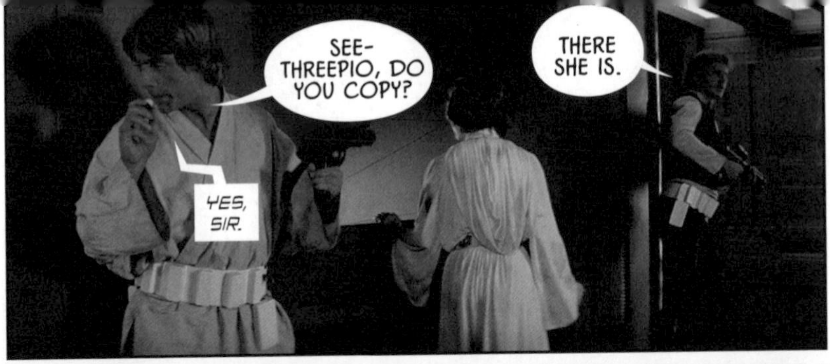
SEE-THREEPIO, DO YOU COPY?
YES, SIR.
THERE SHE IS.

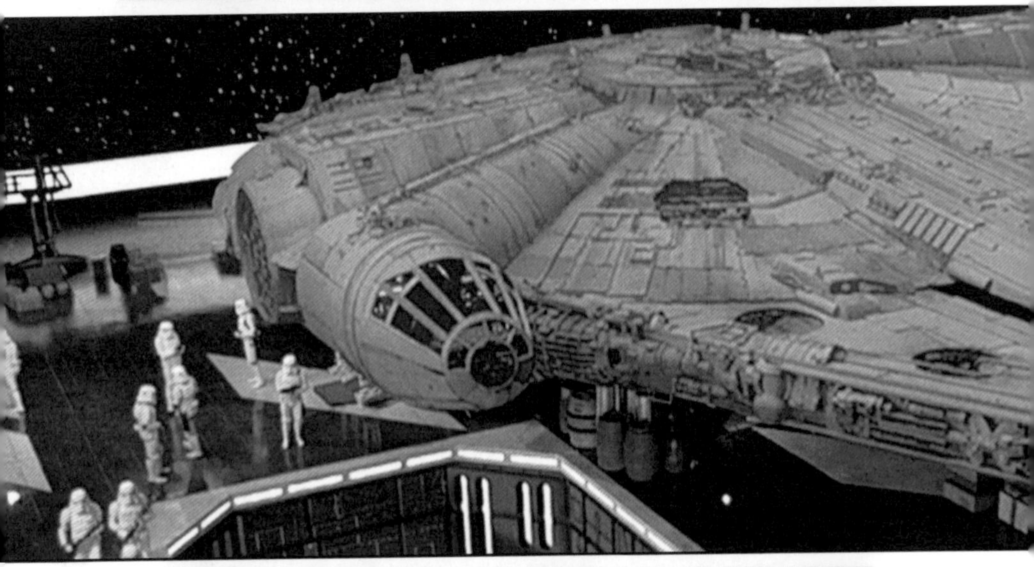

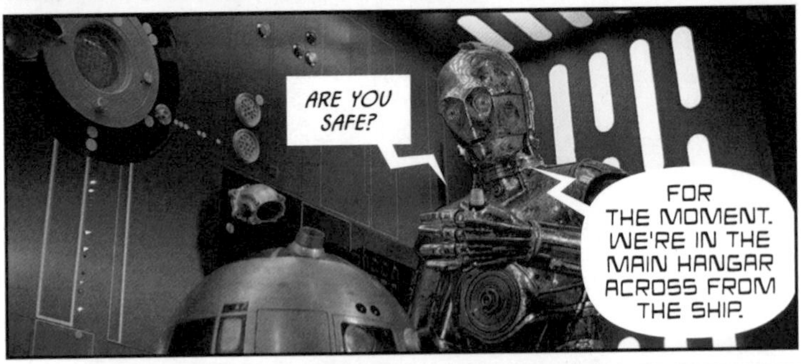
ARE YOU SAFE?
FOR THE MOMENT. WE'RE IN THE MAIN HANGAR ACROSS FROM THE SHIP.

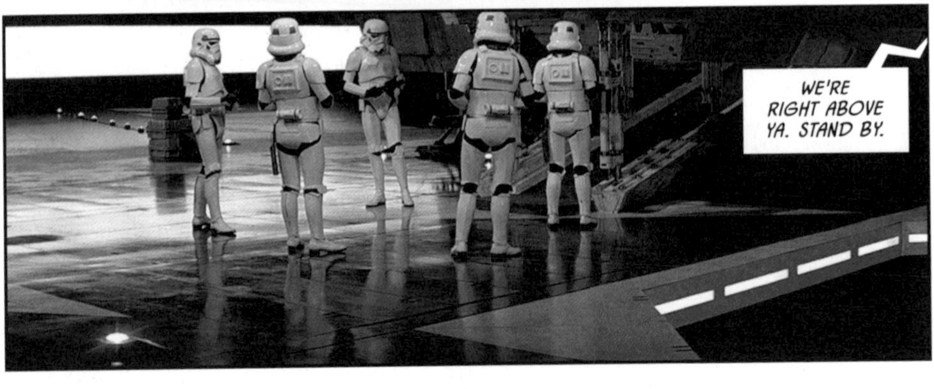
WE'RE RIGHT ABOVE YA. STAND BY.

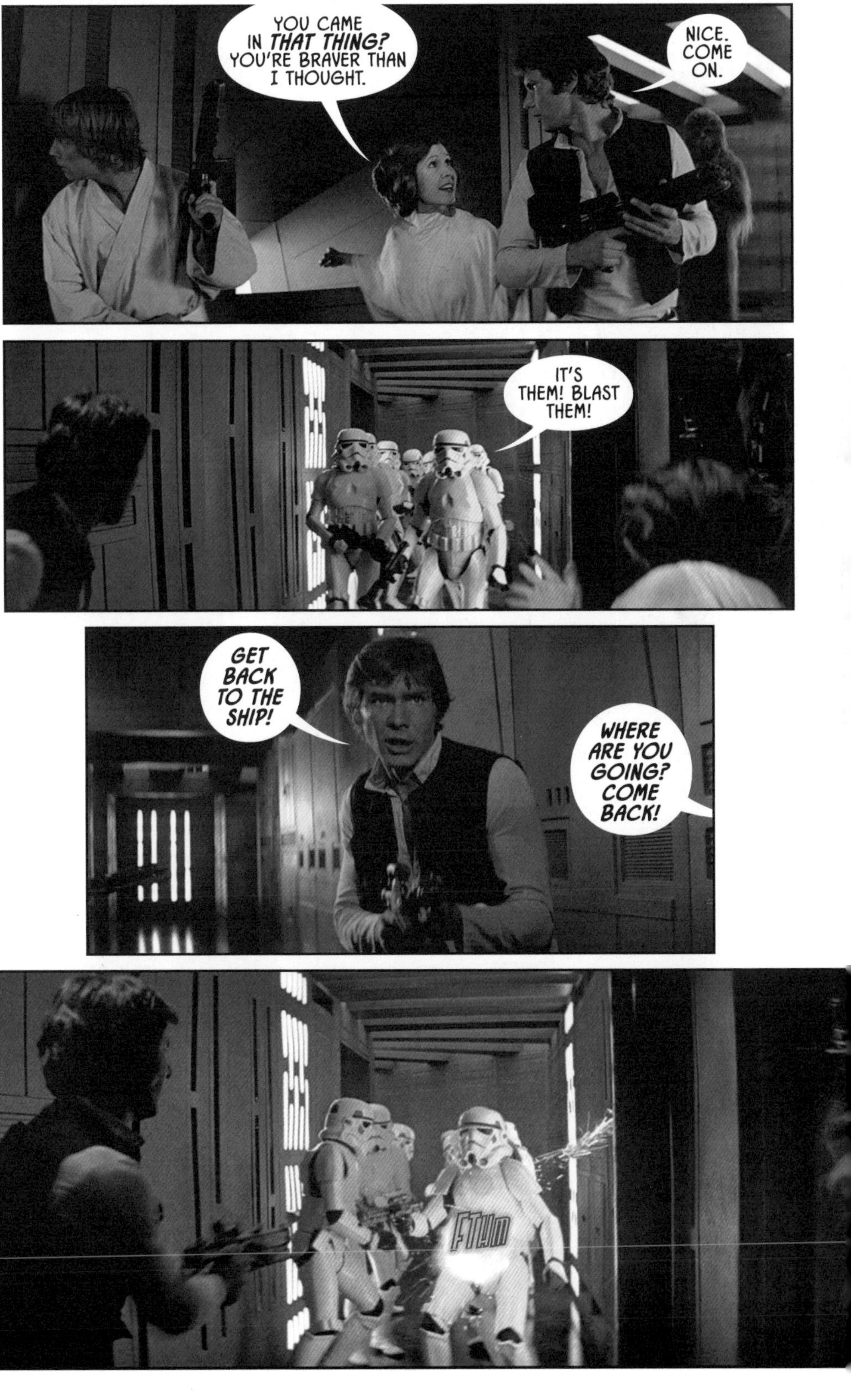
YOU CAME IN THAT THING? YOU'RE BRAVER THAN I THOUGHT.
NICE. COME ON.
IT'S THEM! BLAST THEM!
GET BACK TO THE SHIP!
WHERE ARE YOU GOING? COME BACK!
FTWM

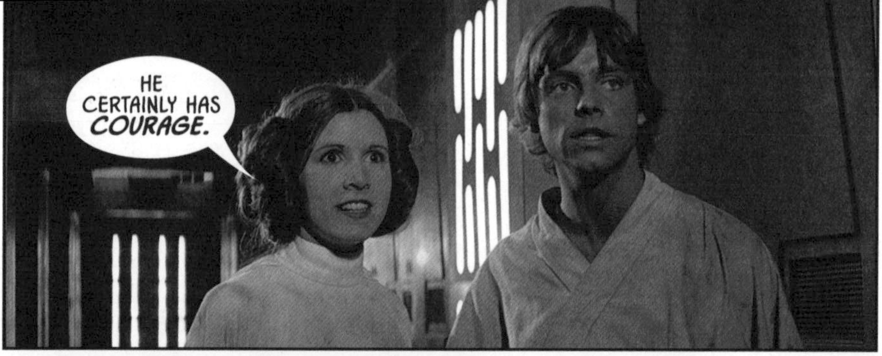
HE CERTAINLY HAS COURAGE.

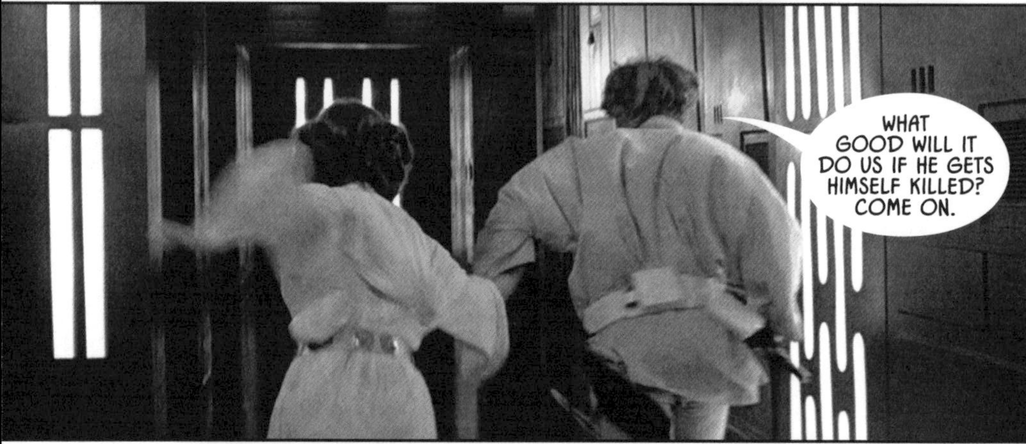
WHAT GOOD WILL IT DO US IF HE GETS HIMSELF KILLED? COME ON.

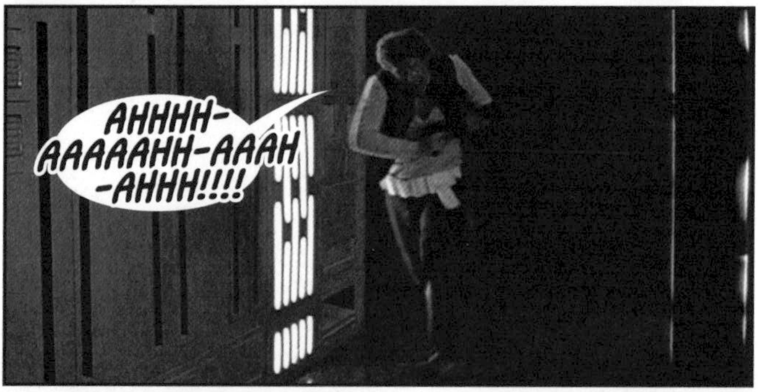
AHHHH-AAAAAHH-AAAH-AHHH!!!!

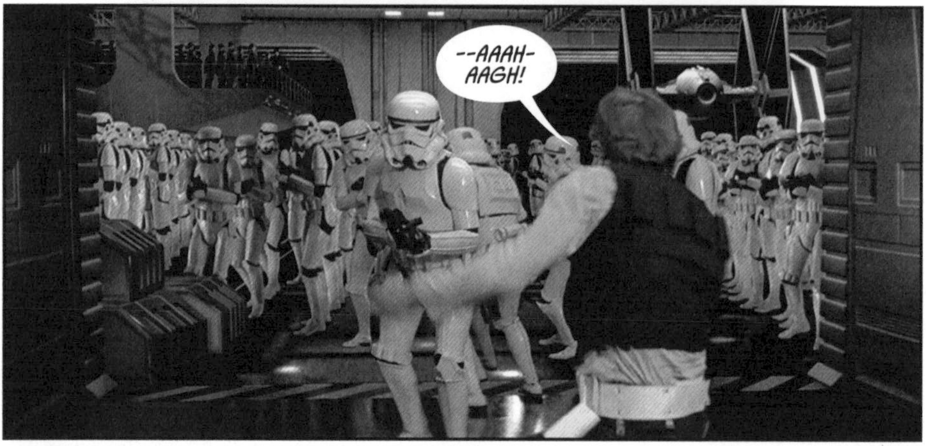
--AAAH-AAGH!

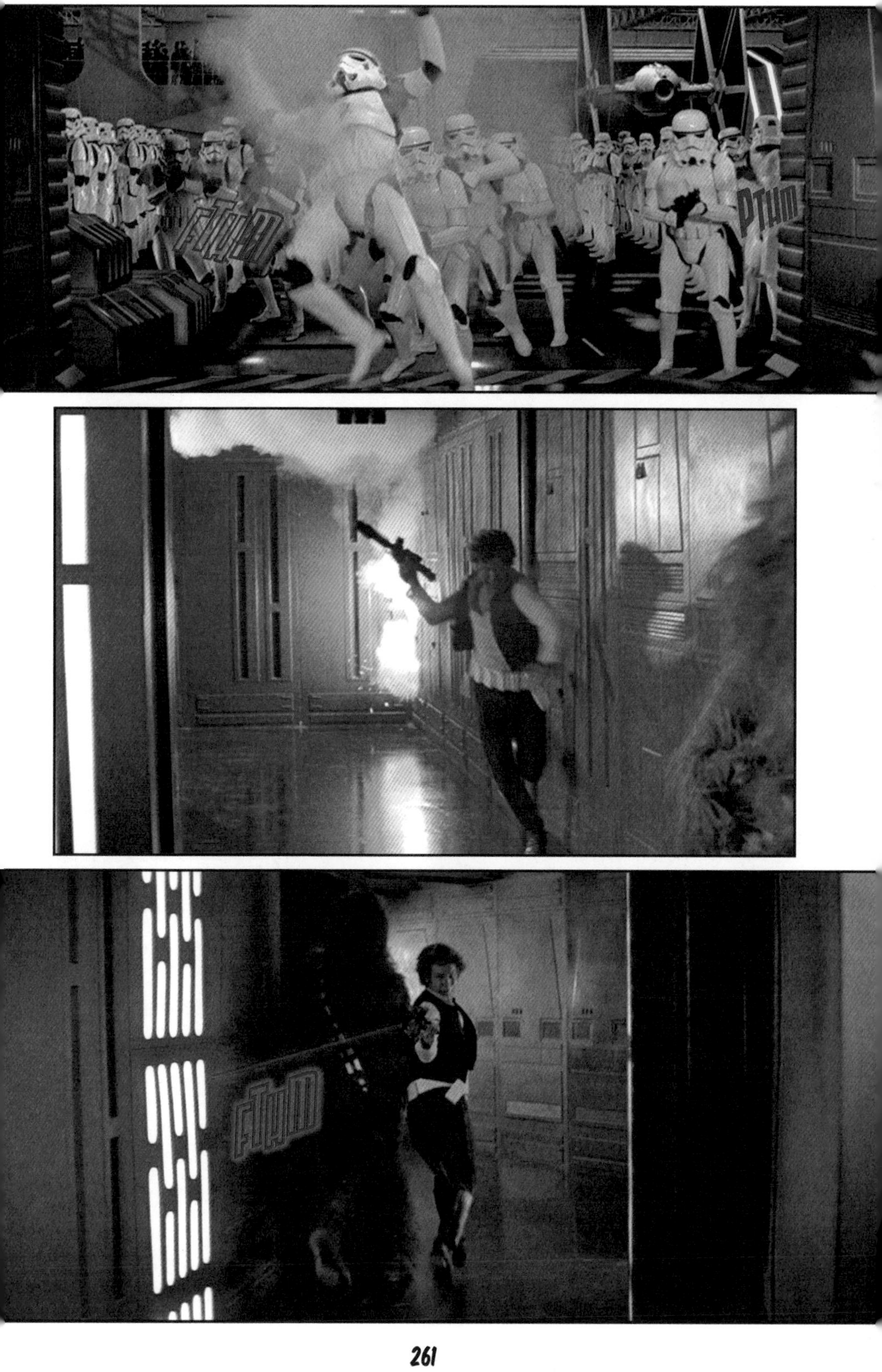
PTUM
PTUM

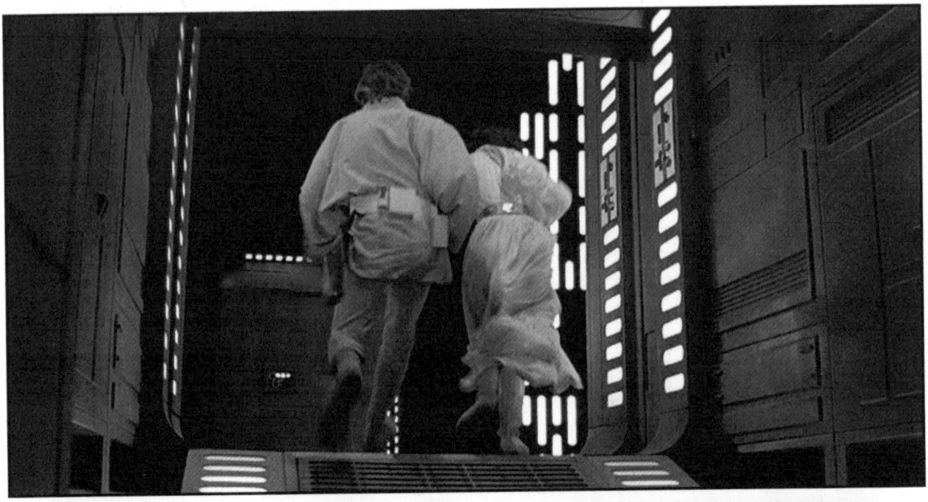

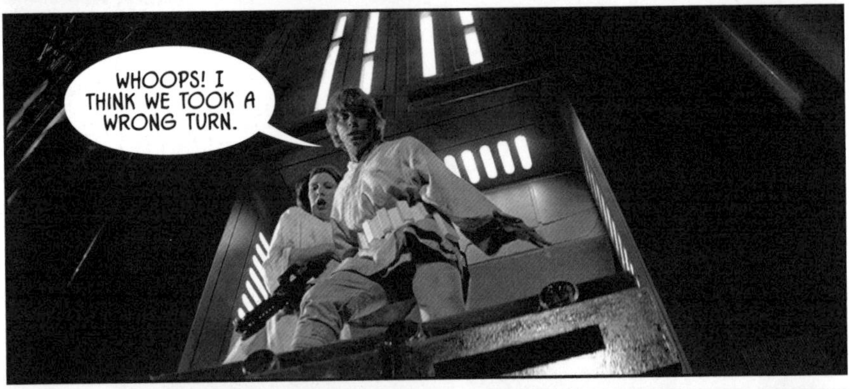
WHOOPS! I THINK WE TOOK A WRONG TURN.

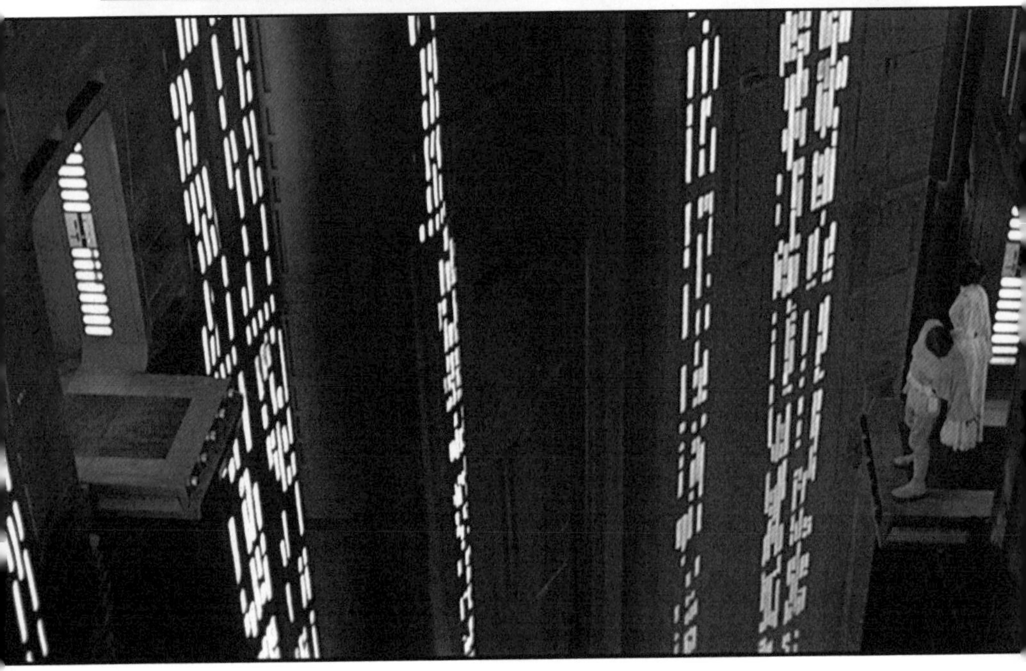

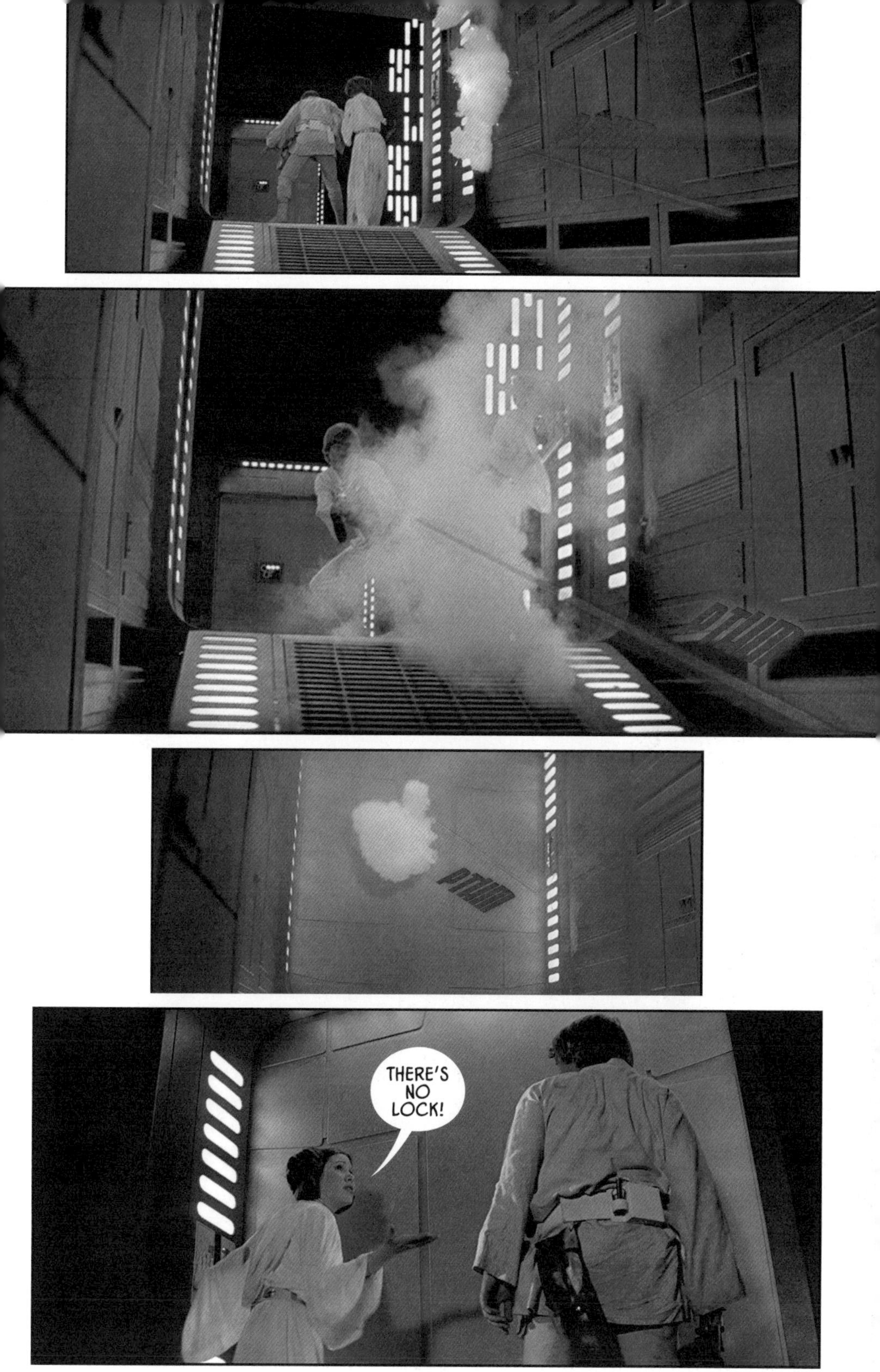
THERE'S NO LOCK!

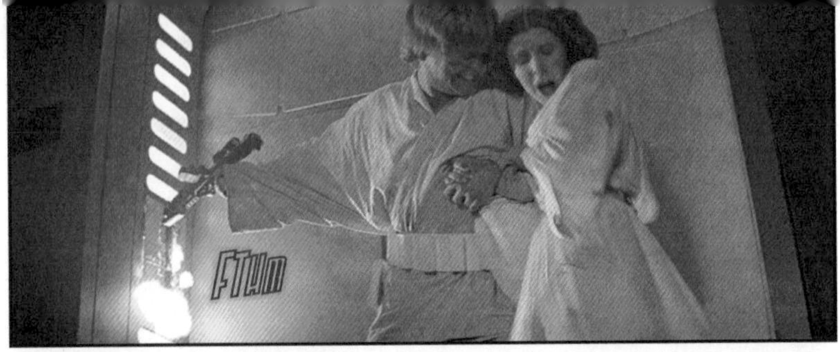

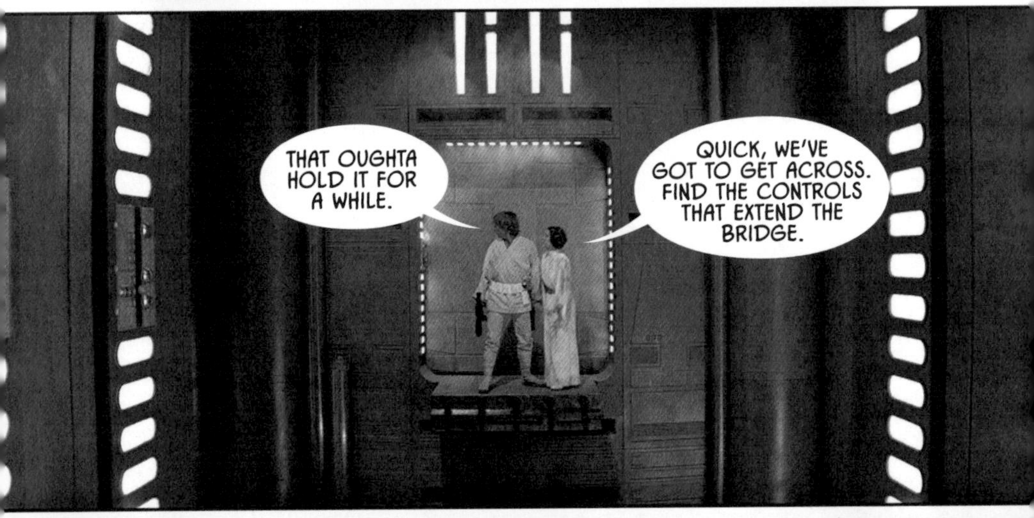

THAT OUGHTA HOLD IT FOR A WHILE.
QUICK, WE'VE GOT TO GET ACROSS. FIND THE CONTROLS THAT EXTEND THE BRIDGE.

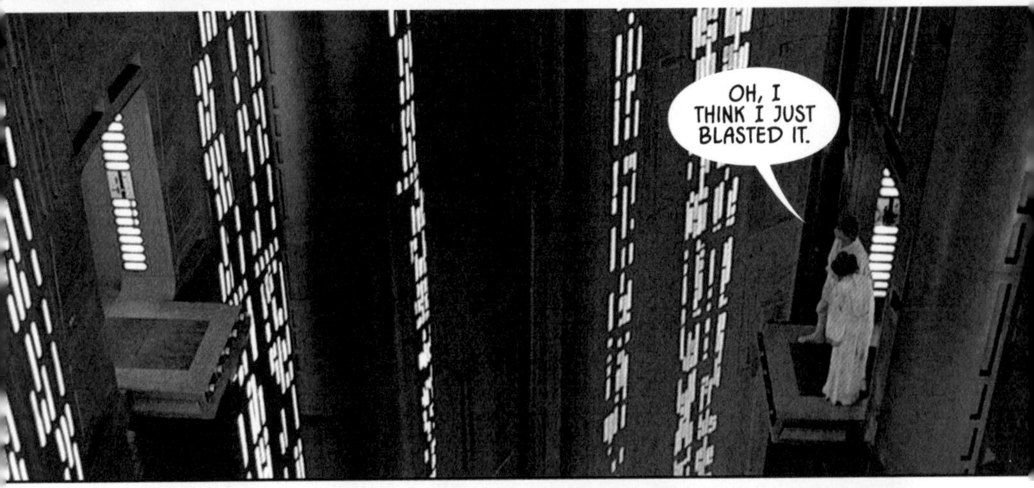

OH, I THINK I JUST BLASTED IT.

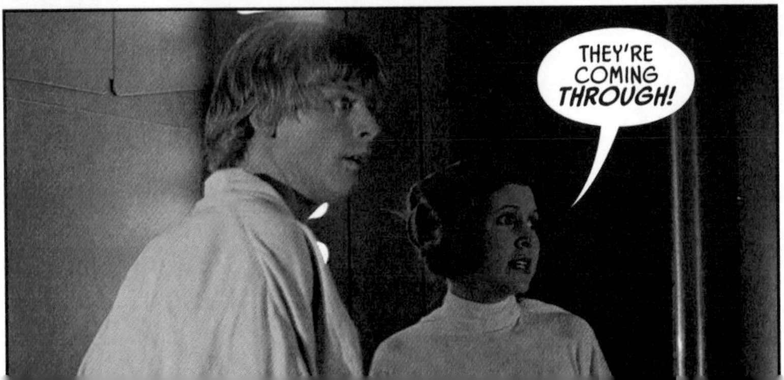

THEY'RE COMING *THROUGH!*

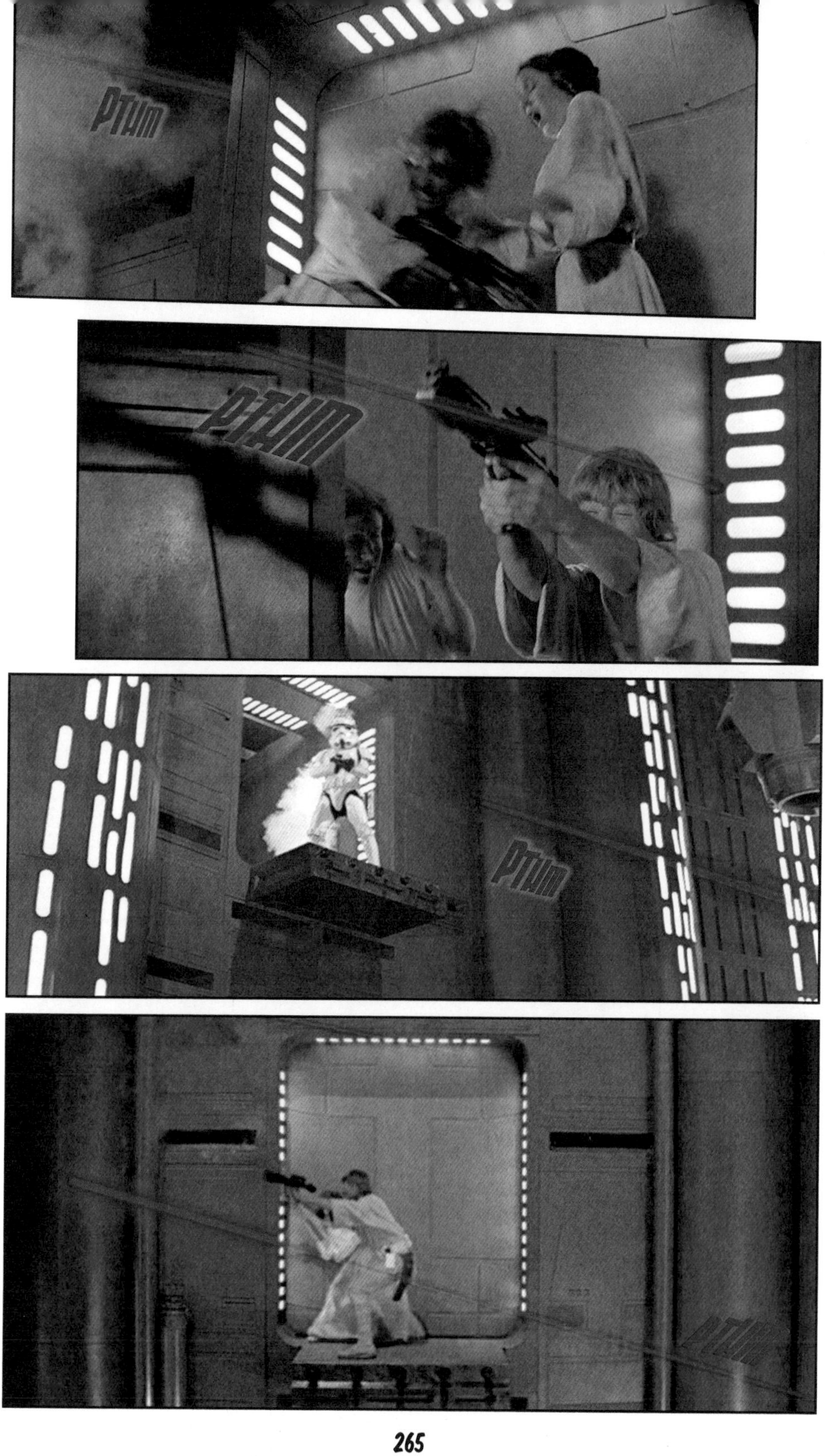

PTUM
PTUM
PTUM
PTUM

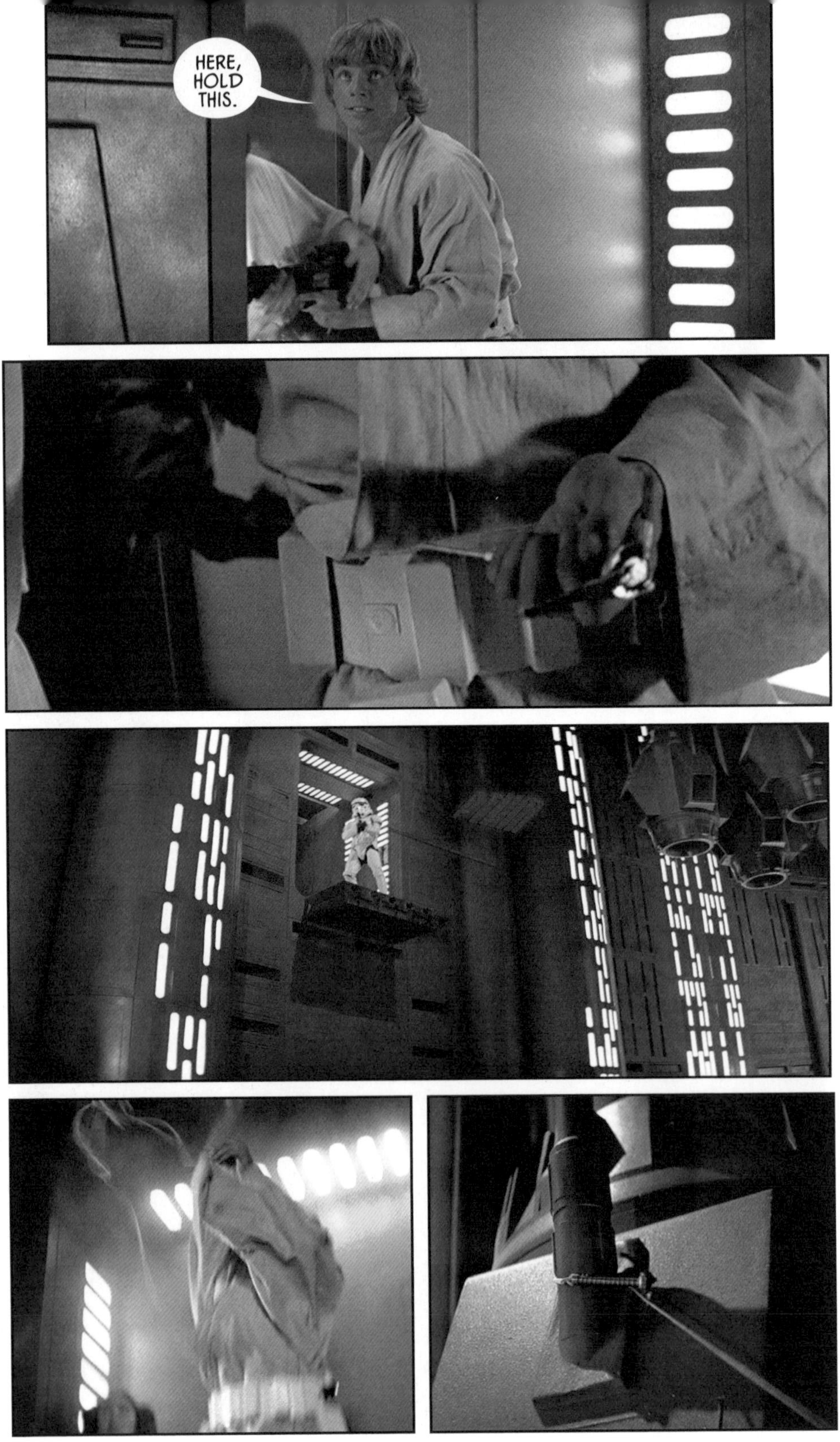
HERE, HOLD THIS.

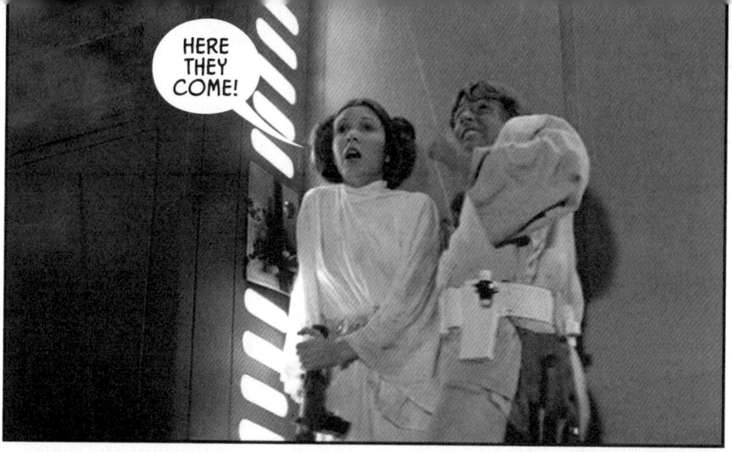
HERE THEY COME!

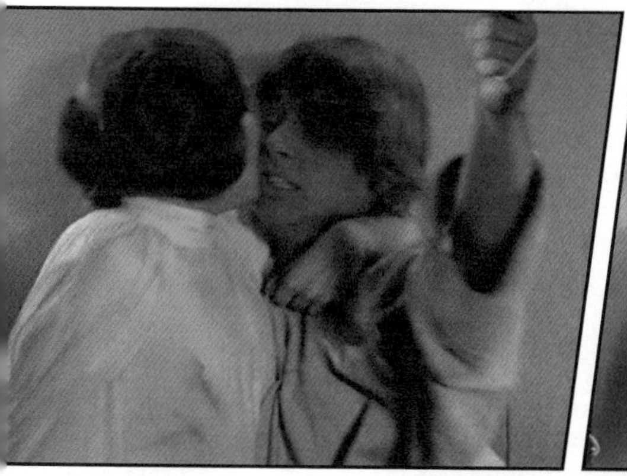

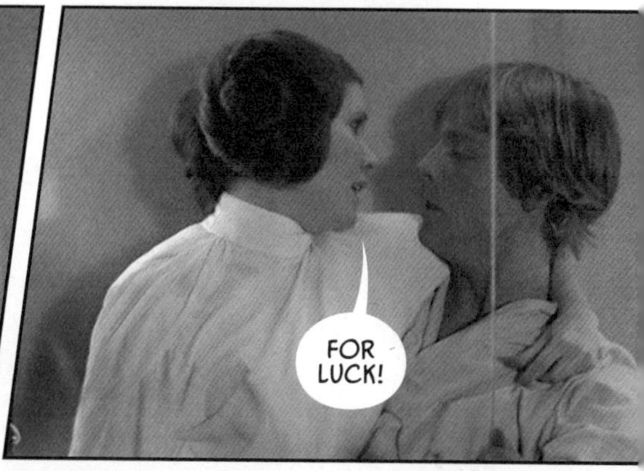
FOR LUCK!

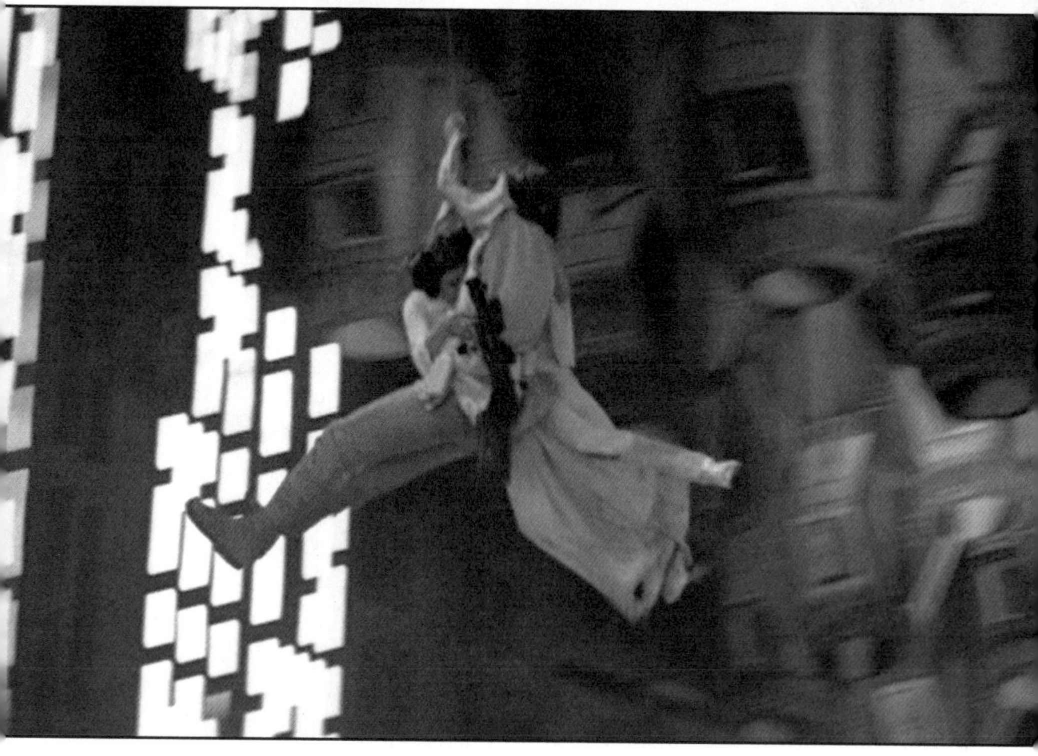

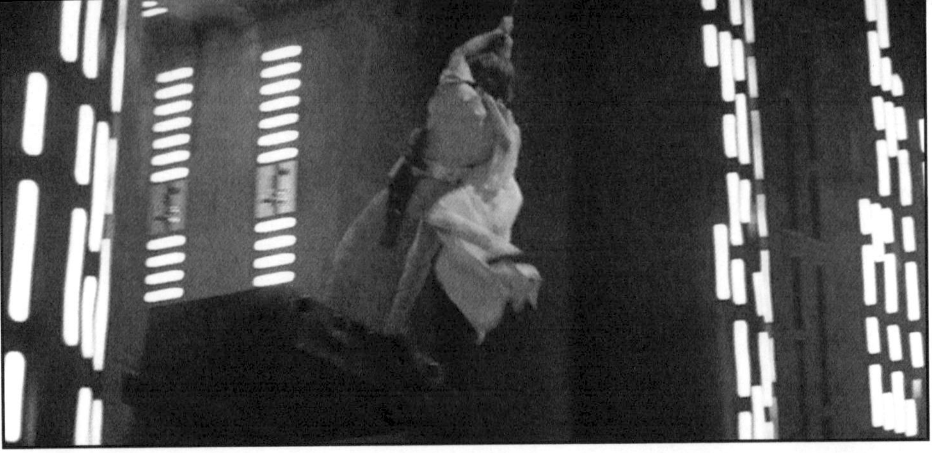

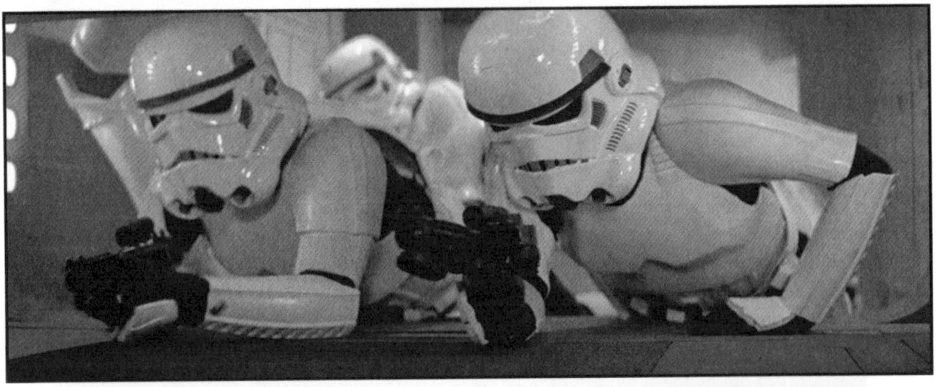

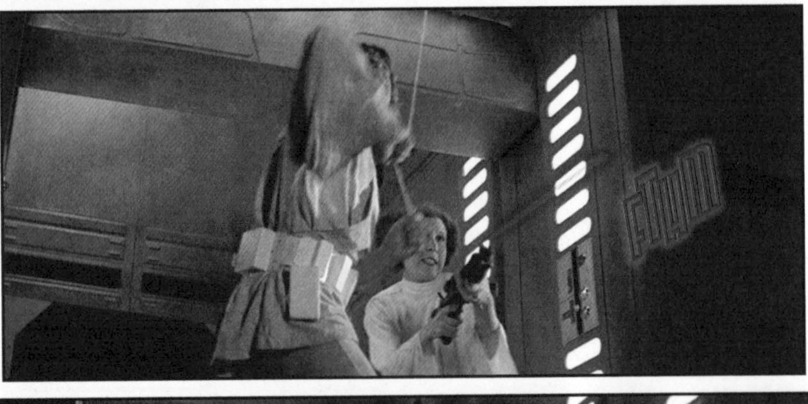

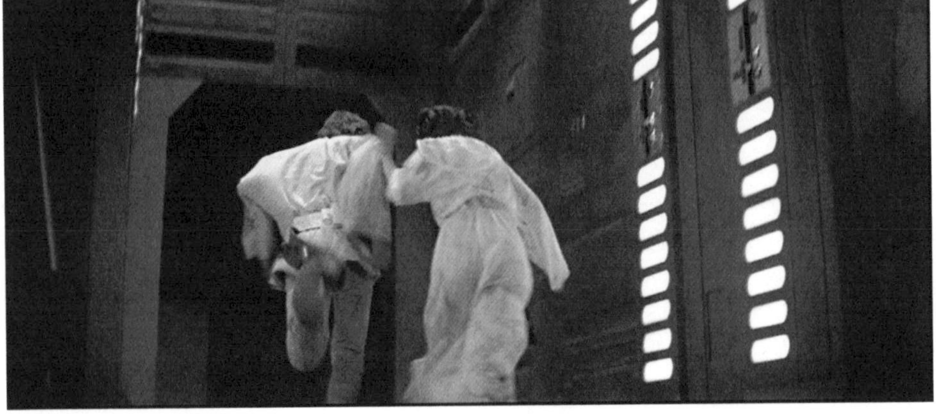

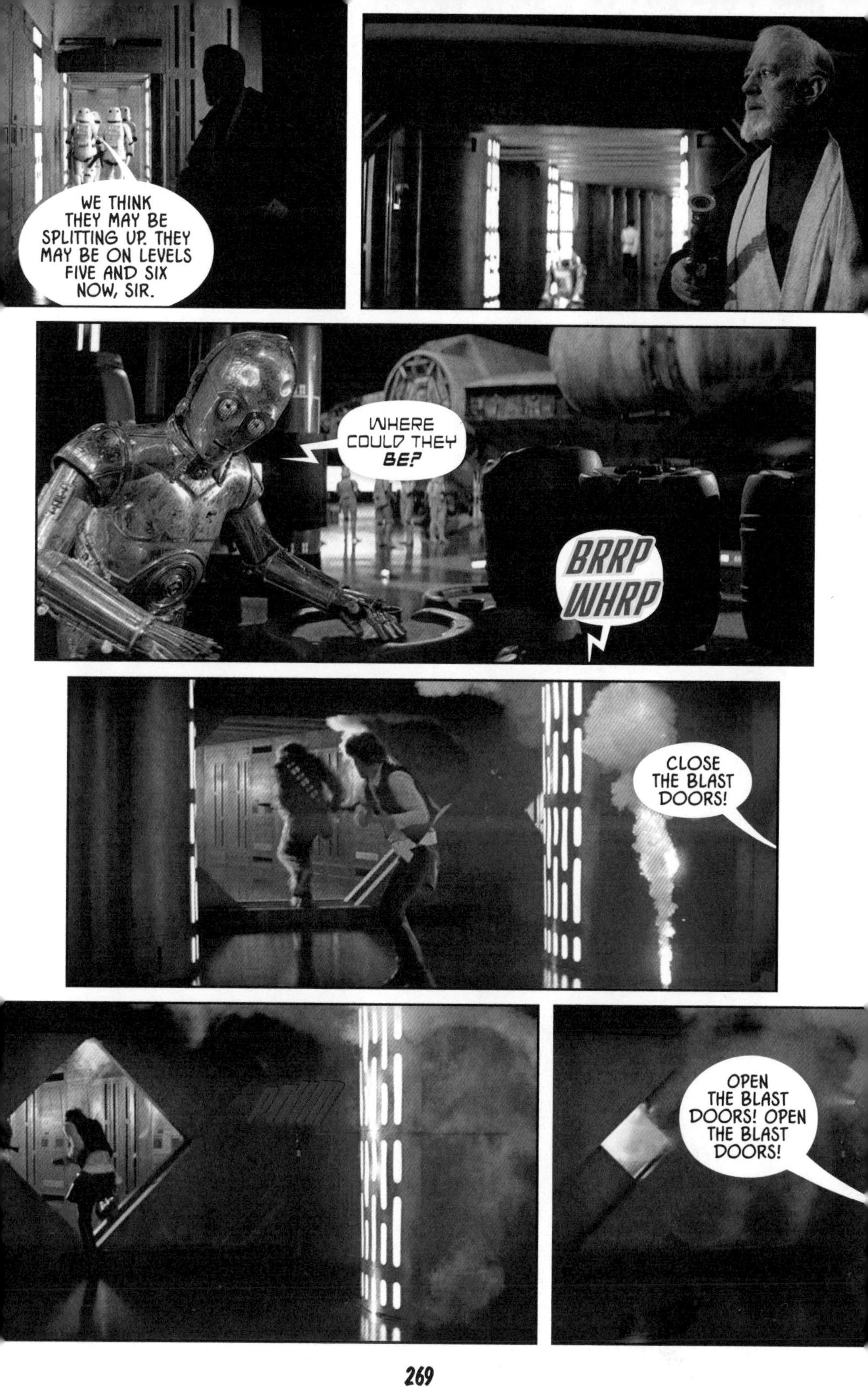
WE THINK THEY MAY BE SPLITTING UP. THEY MAY BE ON LEVELS FIVE AND SIX NOW, SIR.
WHERE COULD THEY BE?
BRRP WHRP
CLOSE THE BLAST DOORS!
OPEN THE BLAST DOORS! OPEN THE BLAST DOORS!

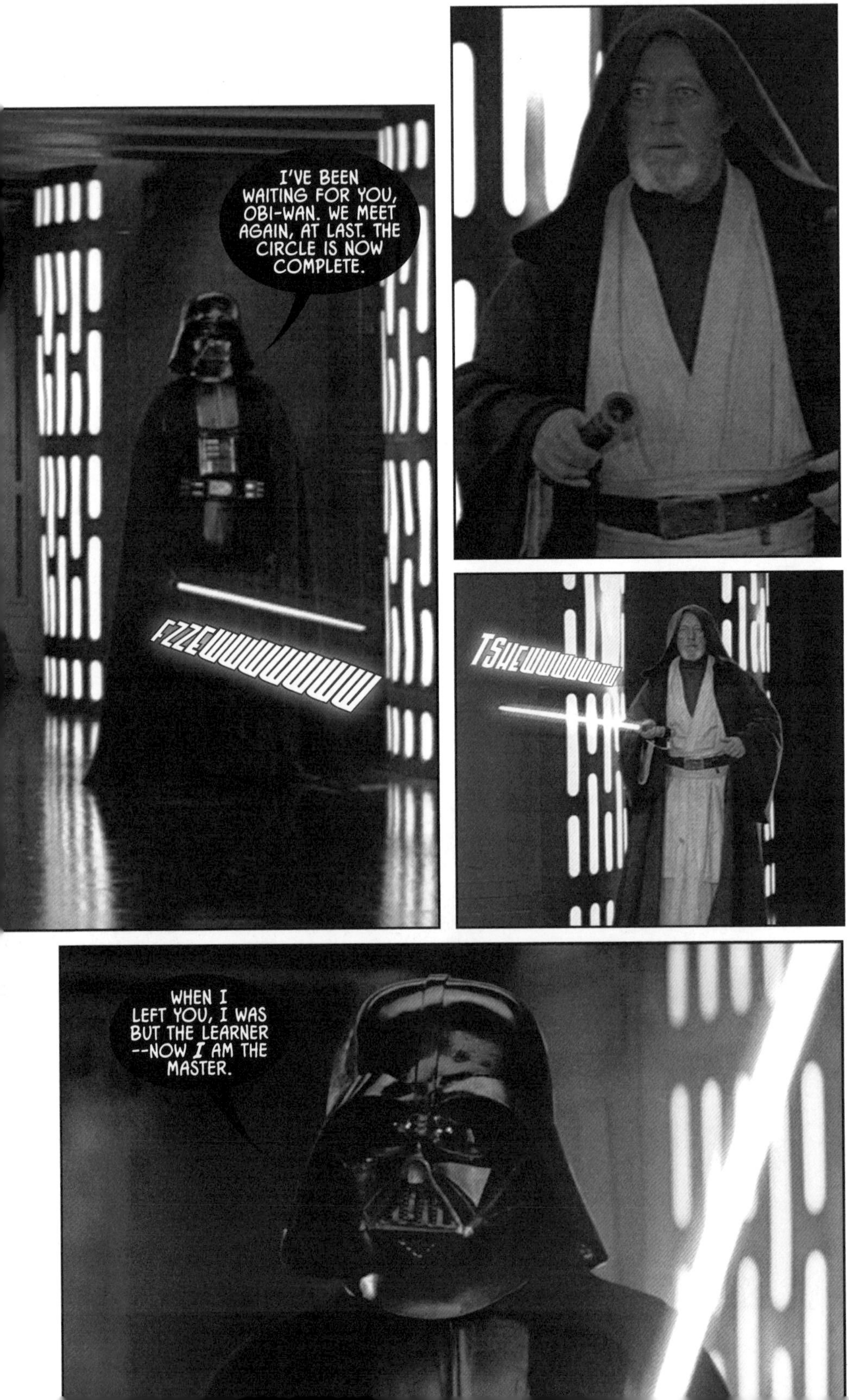
I'VE BEEN WAITING FOR YOU, OBI-WAN. WE MEET AGAIN, AT LAST. THE CIRCLE IS NOW COMPLETE.
FZZEWWWWWWWW
TSHEWWWWWWWW
WHEN I LEFT YOU, I WAS BUT THE LEARNER --NOW I AM THE MASTER.

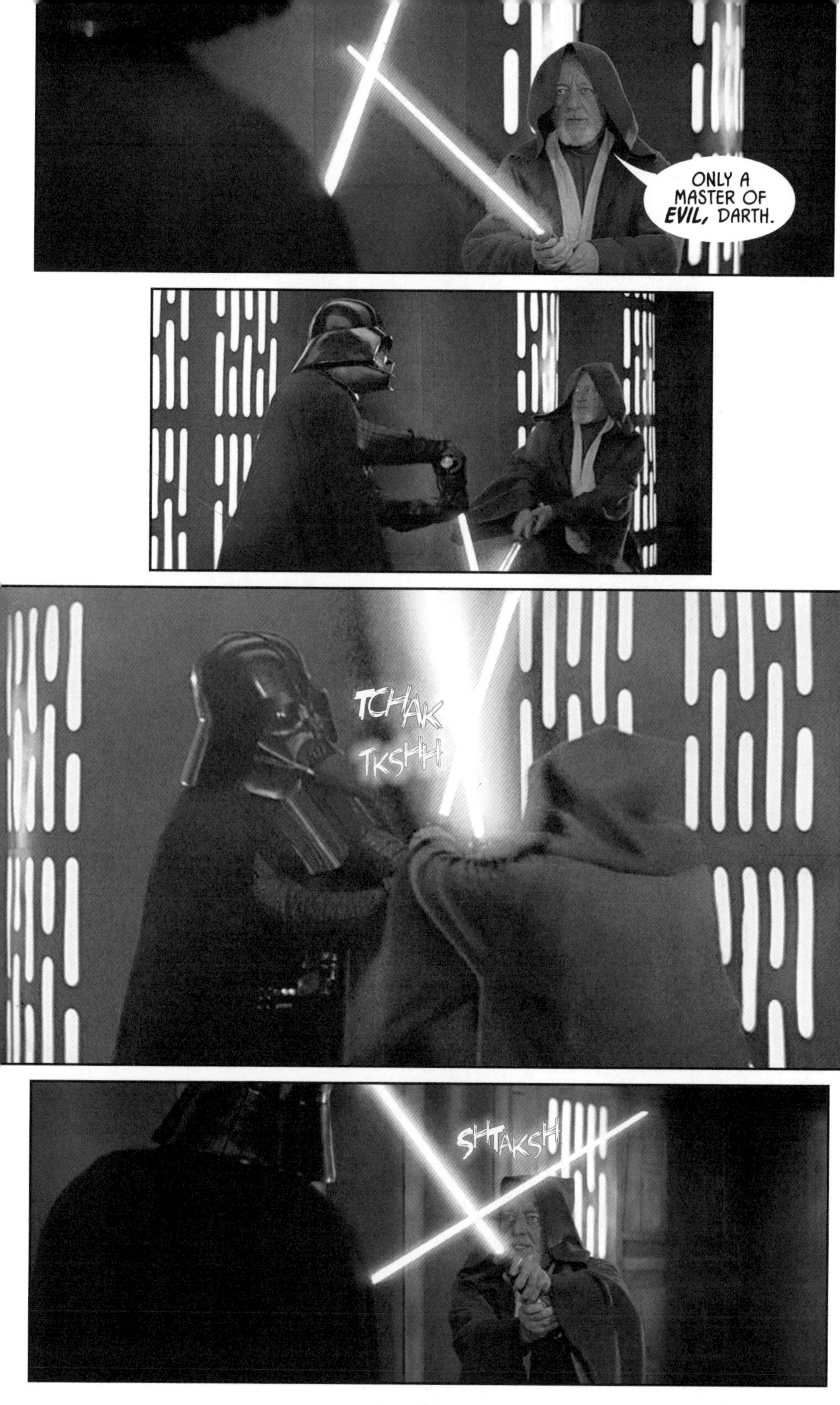
ONLY A MASTER OF EVIL, DARTH.
TCHAK
TKSHH
SHTAKSH

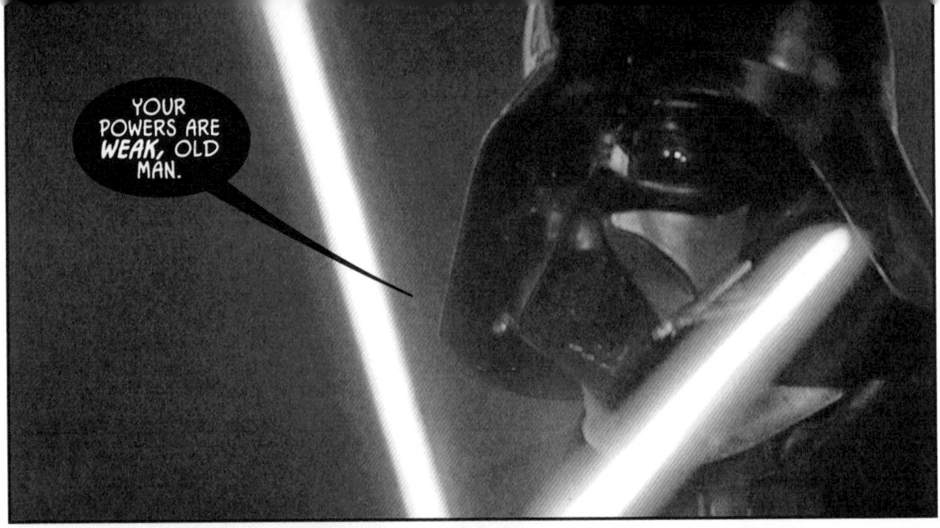
YOUR POWERS ARE WEAK, OLD MAN.

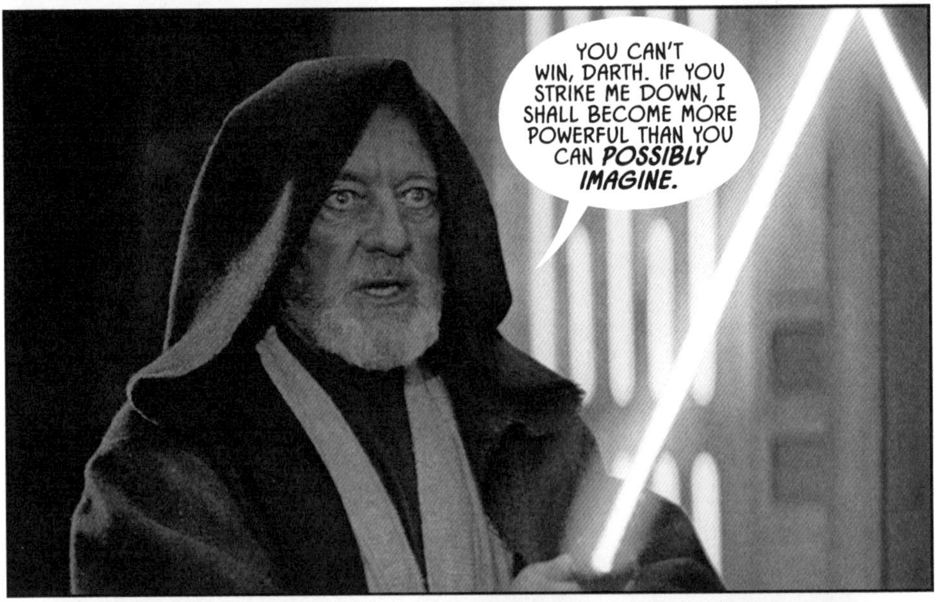
YOU CAN'T WIN, DARTH. IF YOU STRIKE ME DOWN, I SHALL BECOME MORE POWERFUL THAN YOU CAN POSSIBLY IMAGINE.

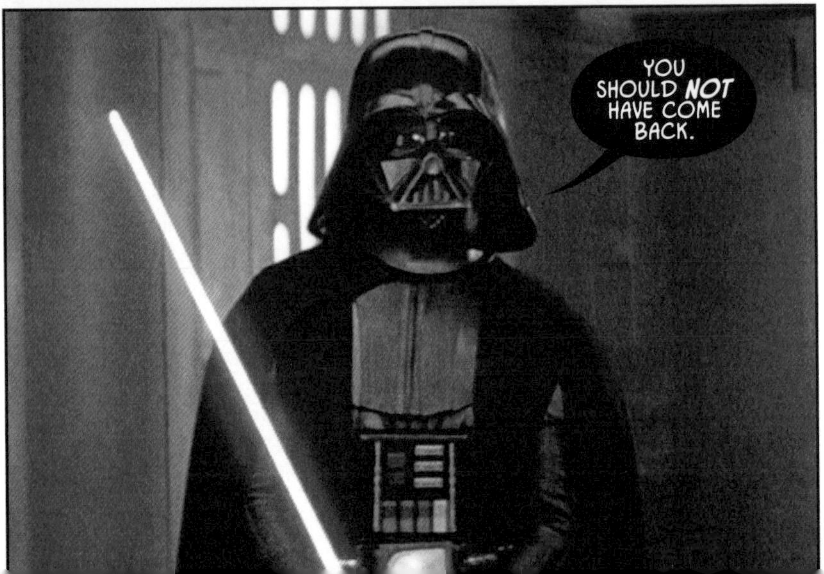
YOU SHOULD NOT HAVE COME BACK.

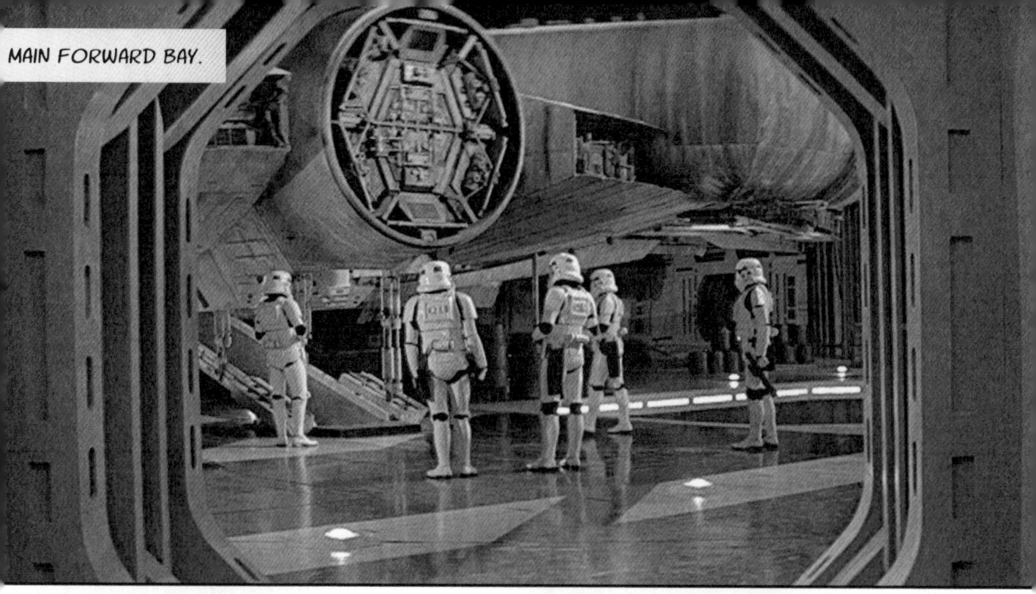
MAIN FORWARD BAY.

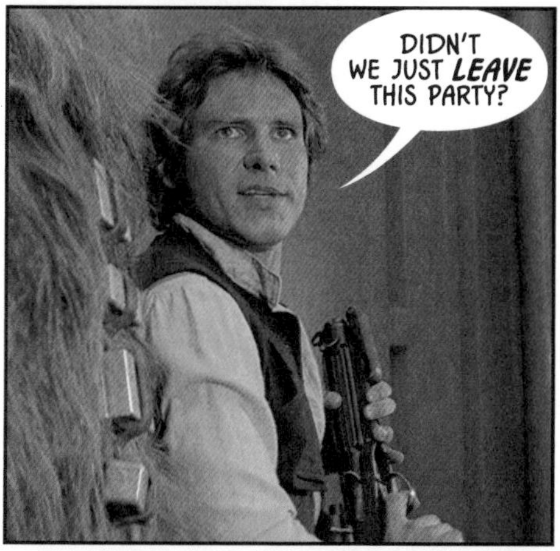
DIDN'T WE JUST *LEAVE* THIS PARTY?

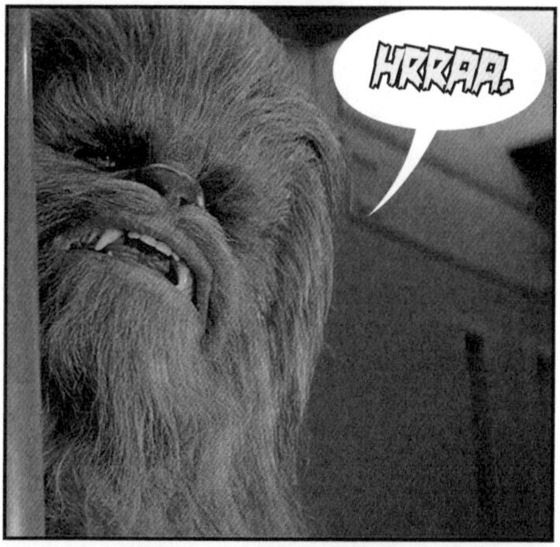
HRRAA.

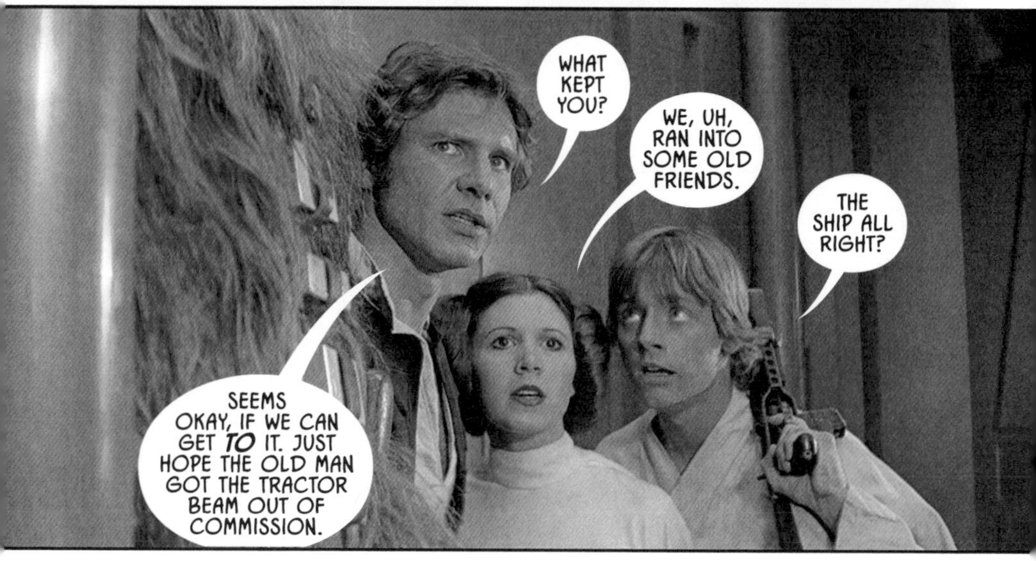
WHAT KEPT YOU?
WE, UH, RAN INTO SOME OLD FRIENDS.
THE SHIP ALL RIGHT?
SEEMS OKAY, IF WE CAN GET *TO* IT. JUST HOPE THE OLD MAN GOT THE TRACTOR BEAM OUT OF COMMISSION.

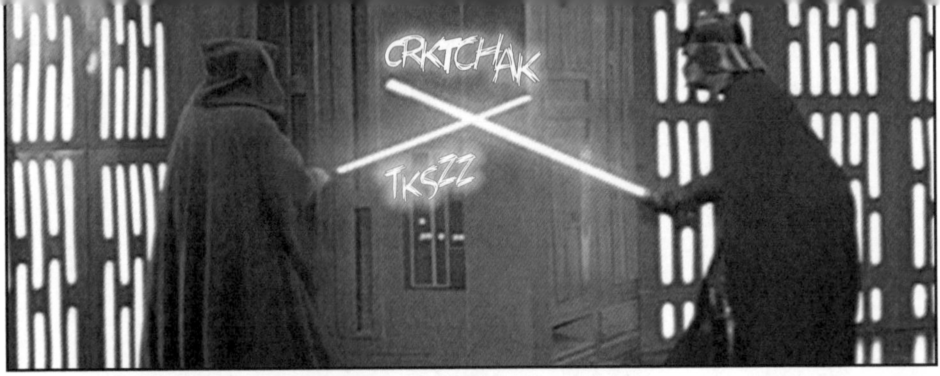
CRKTCHAK
TKSZZ

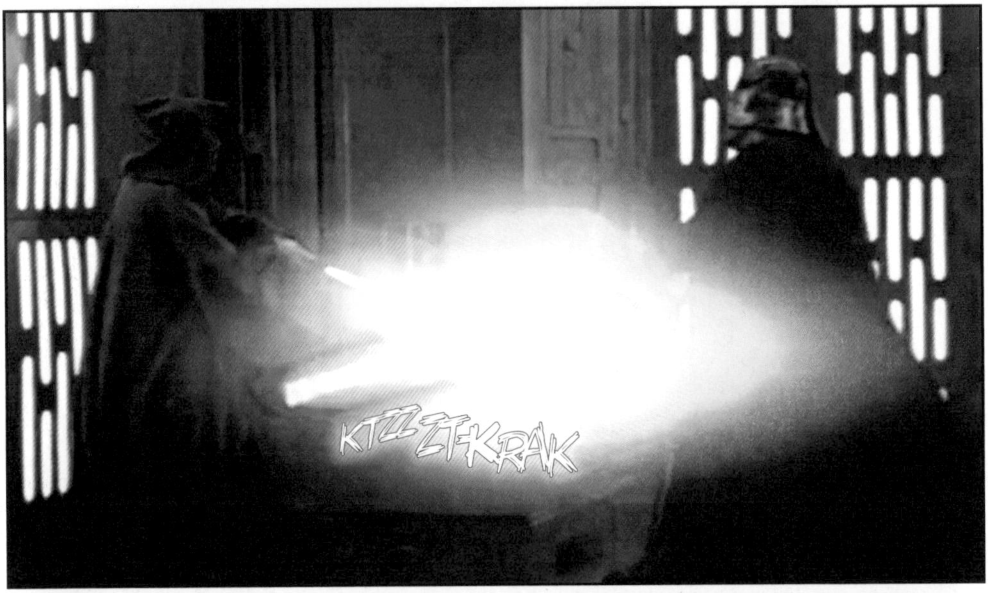
KTZZZT-KRAK

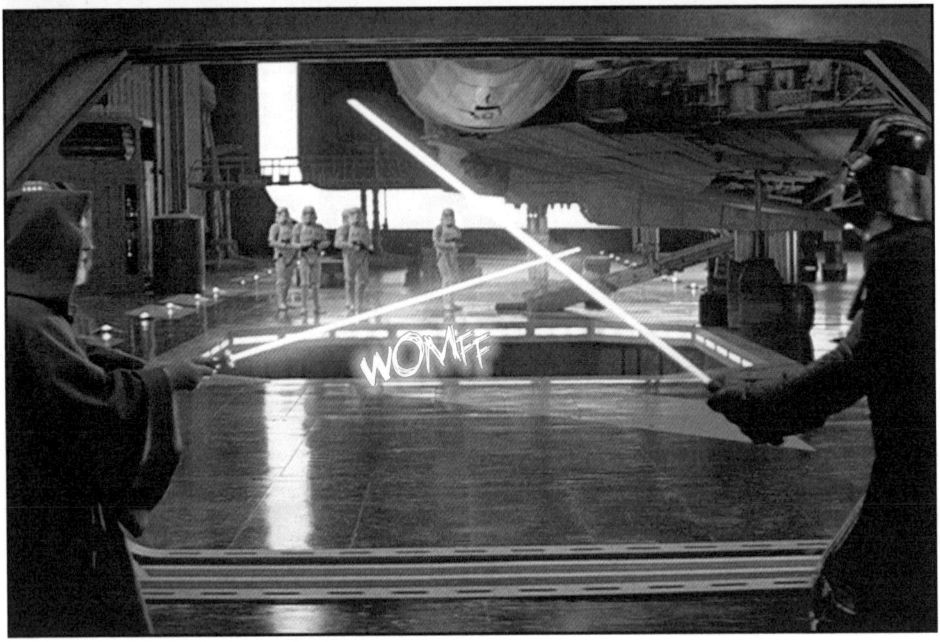
WOMFF

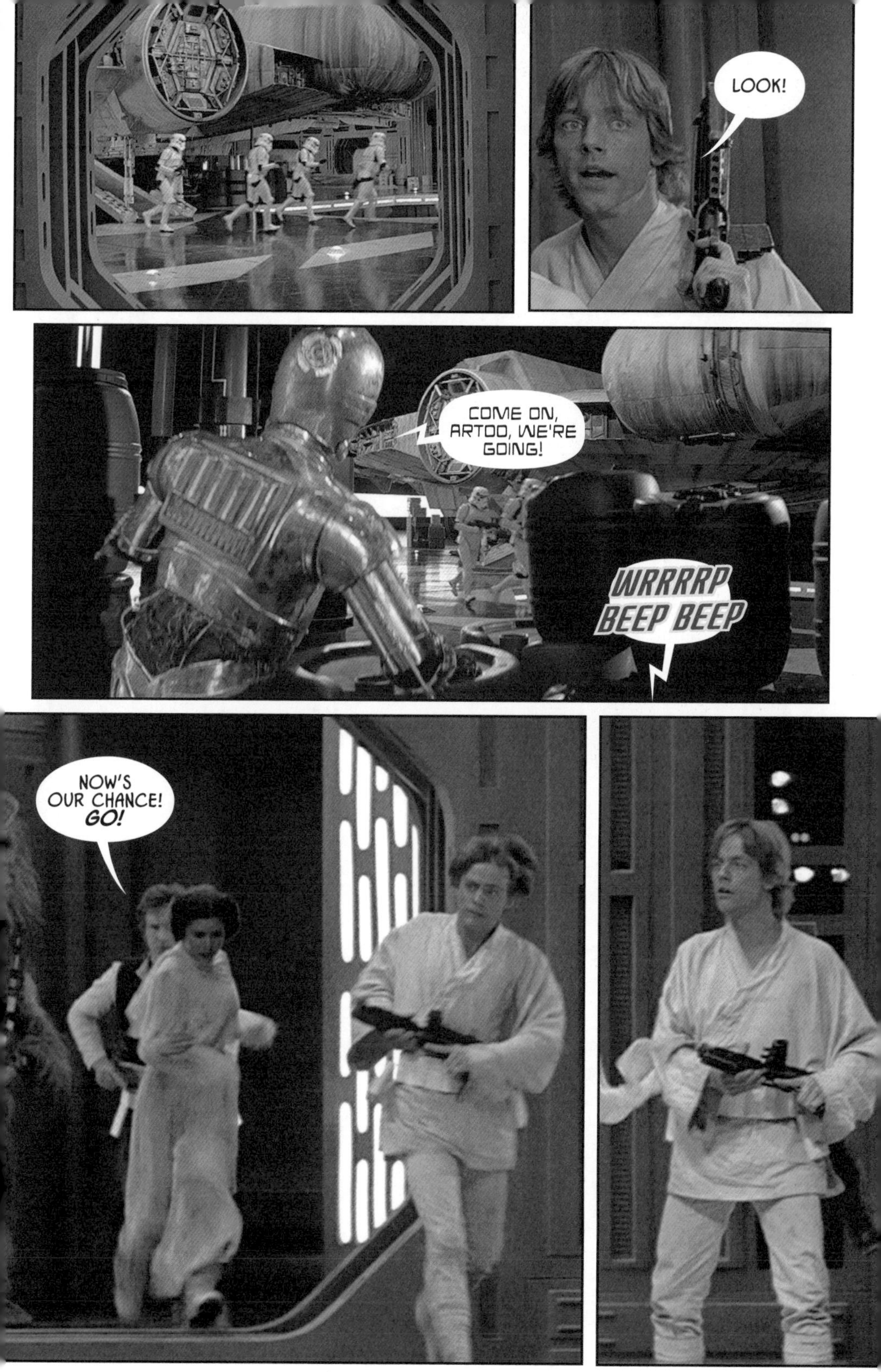
LOOK!
COME ON, ARTOO, WE'RE GOING!
WRRRRP BEEP BEEP
NOW'S OUR CHANCE! GO!

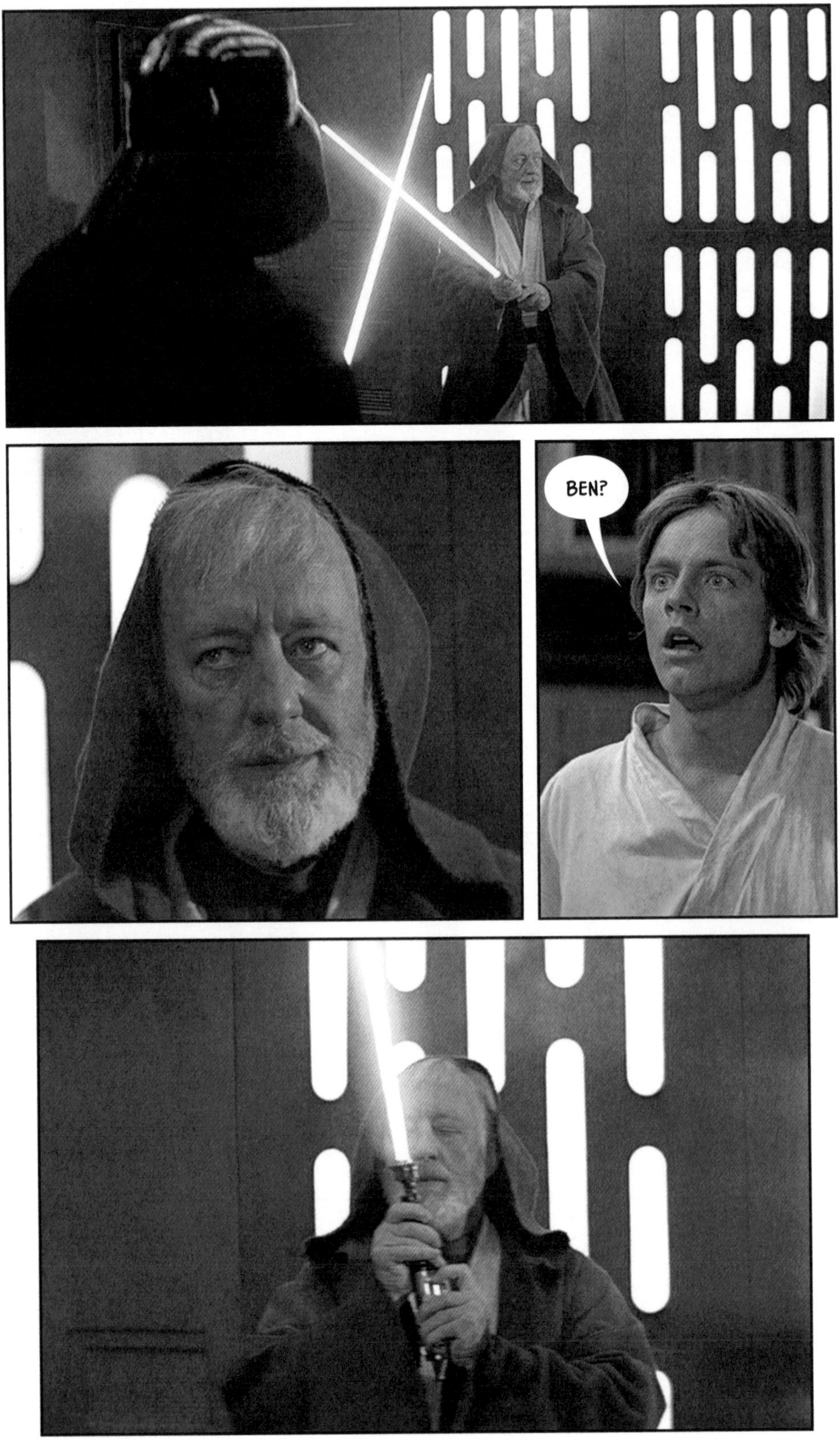
BEN?

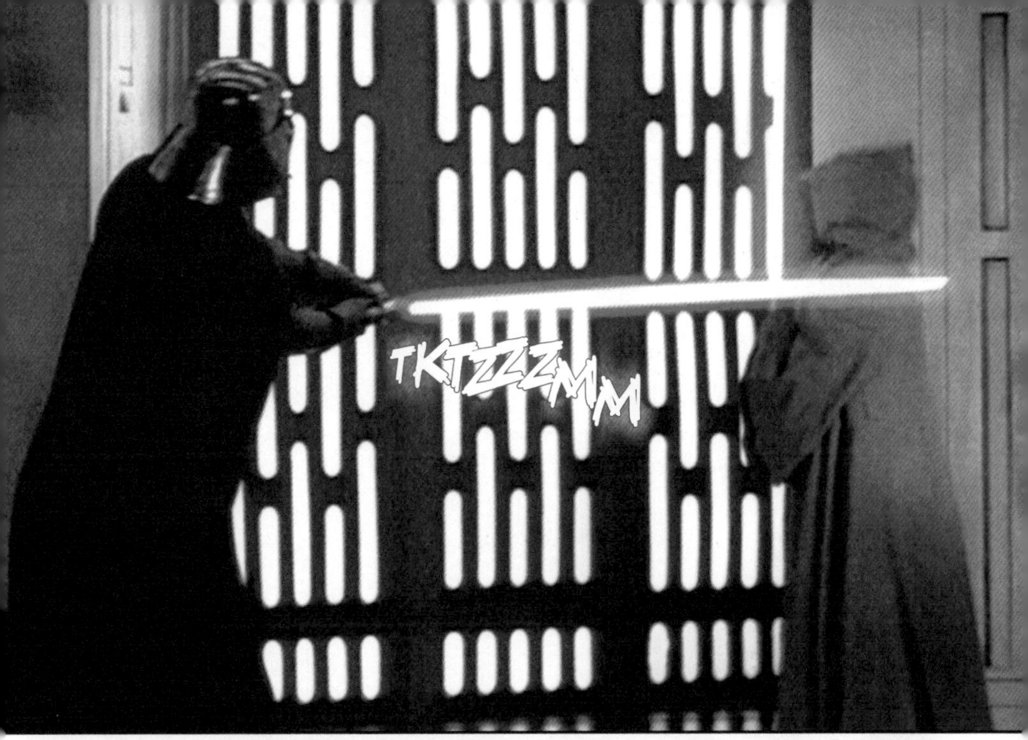
TKTZZZMM

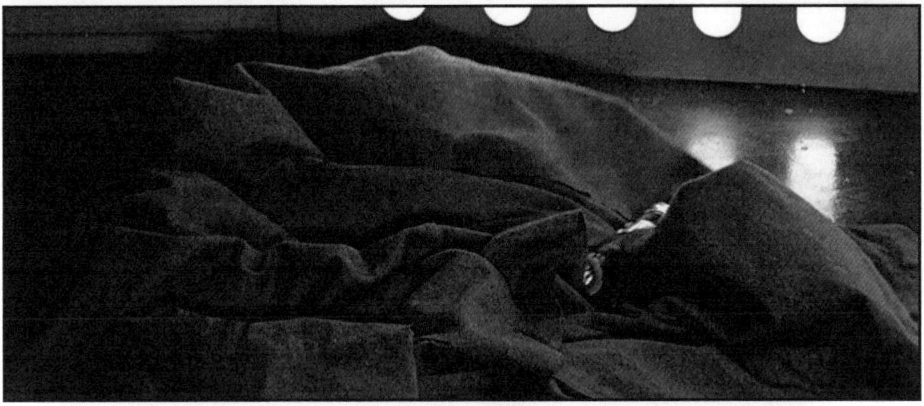

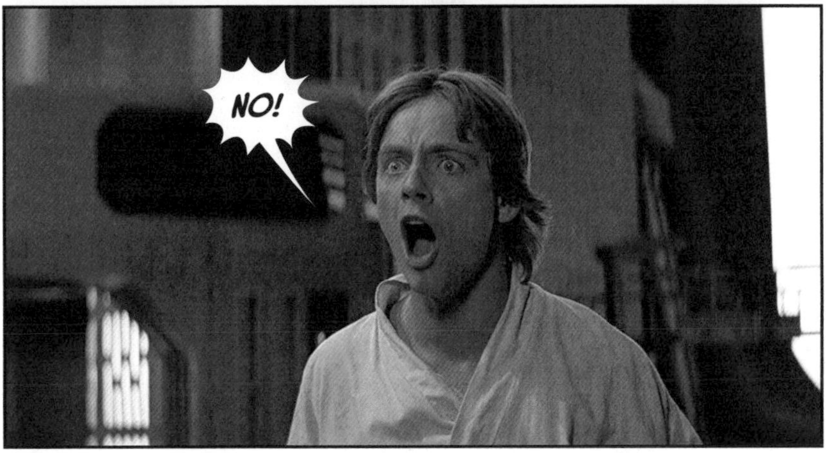
NO!

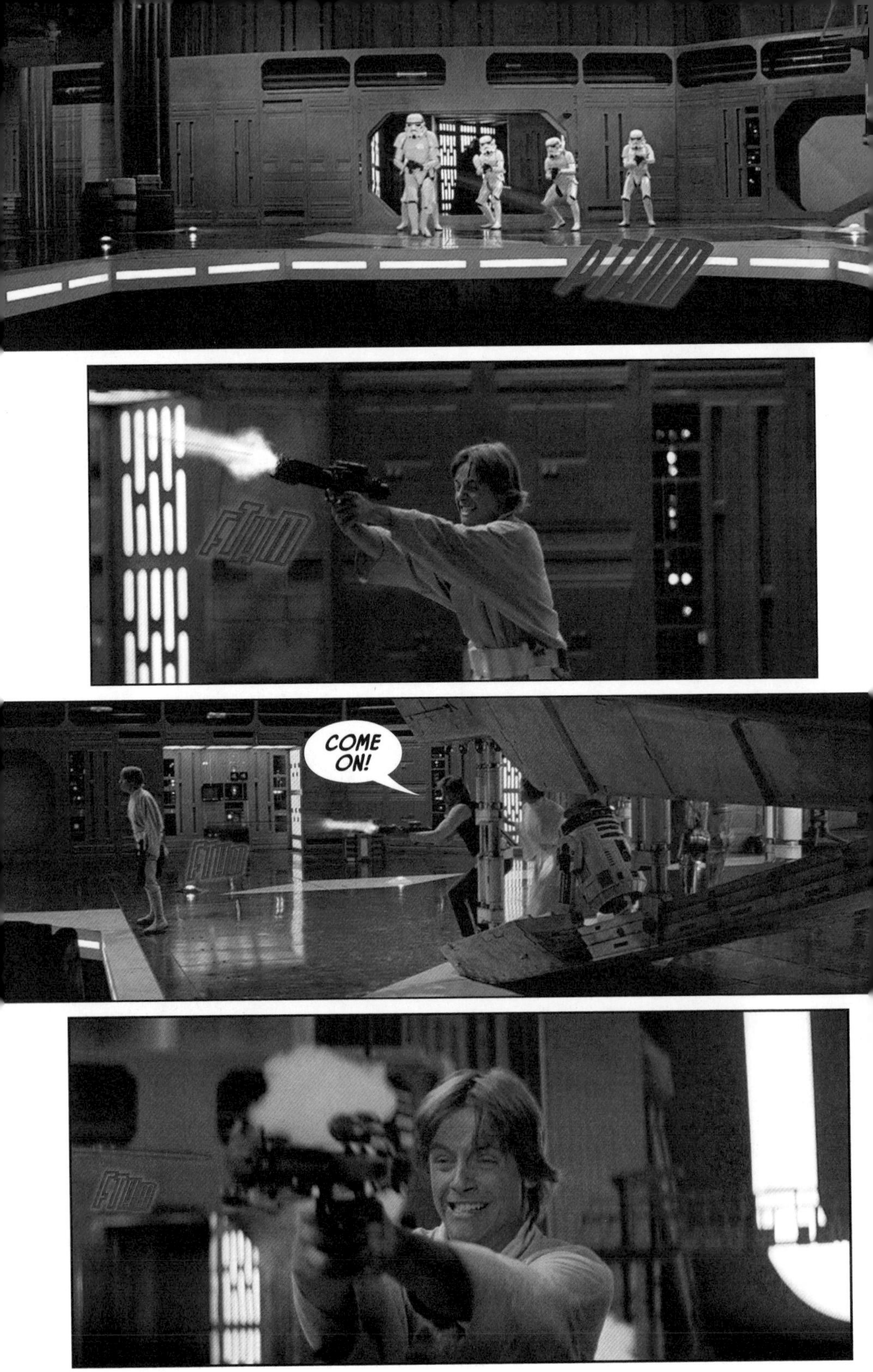
COME ON!

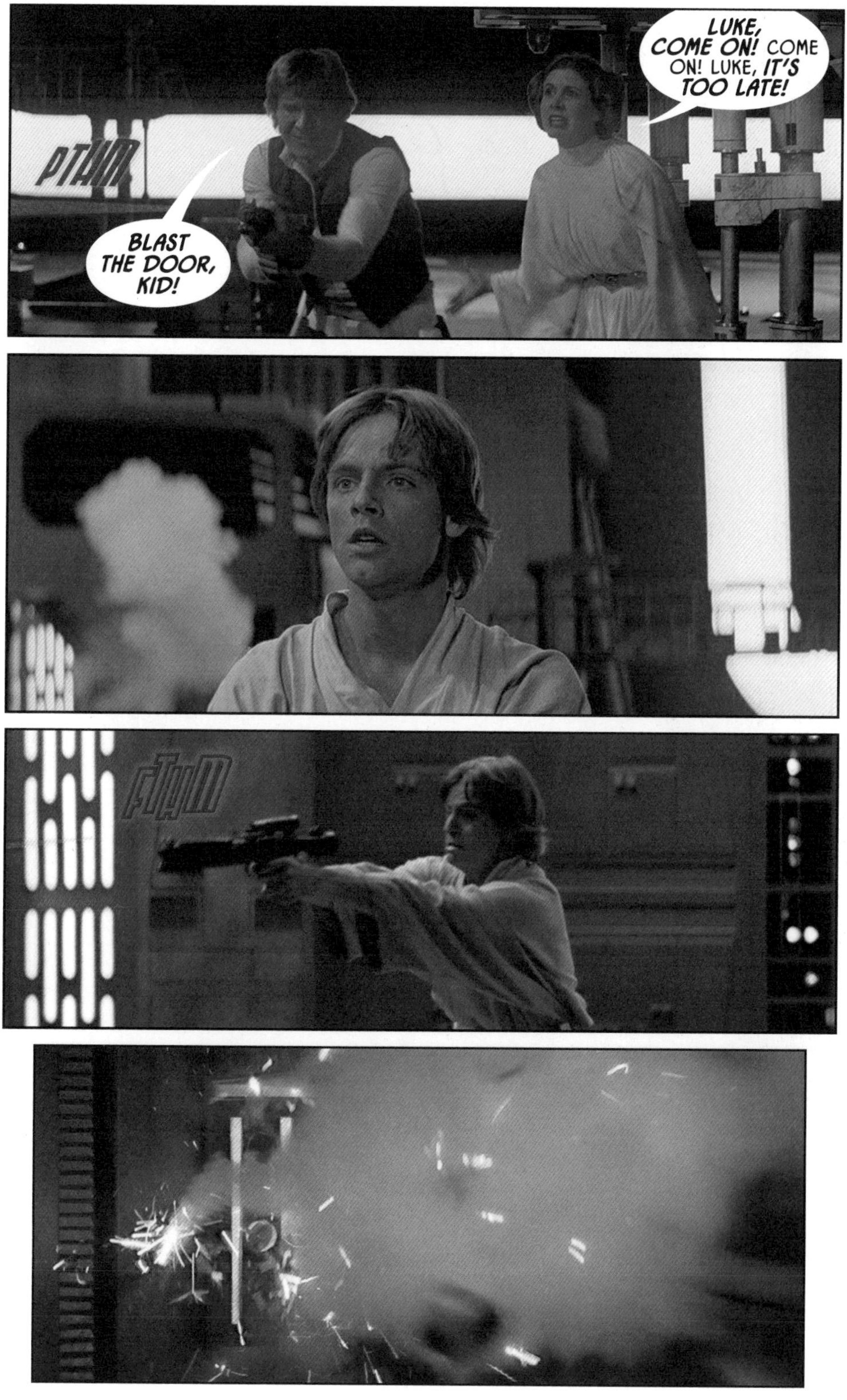
LUKE, COME ON! COME ON! LUKE, IT'S TOO LATE!
BLAST THE DOOR, KID!

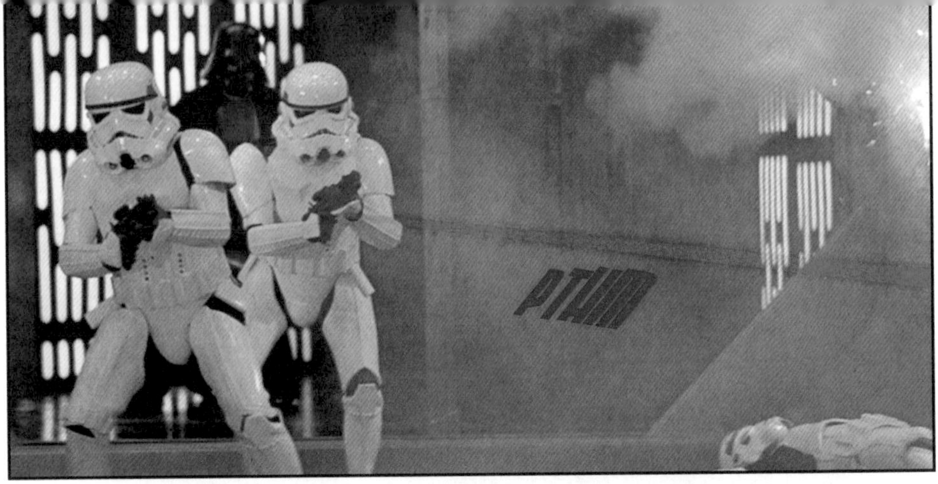

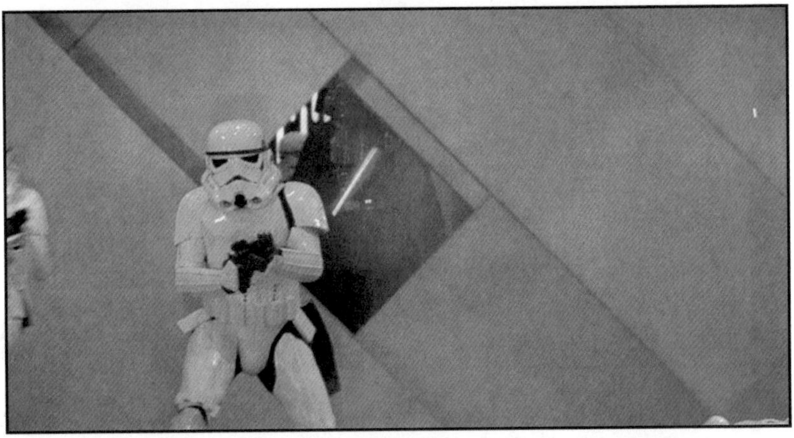

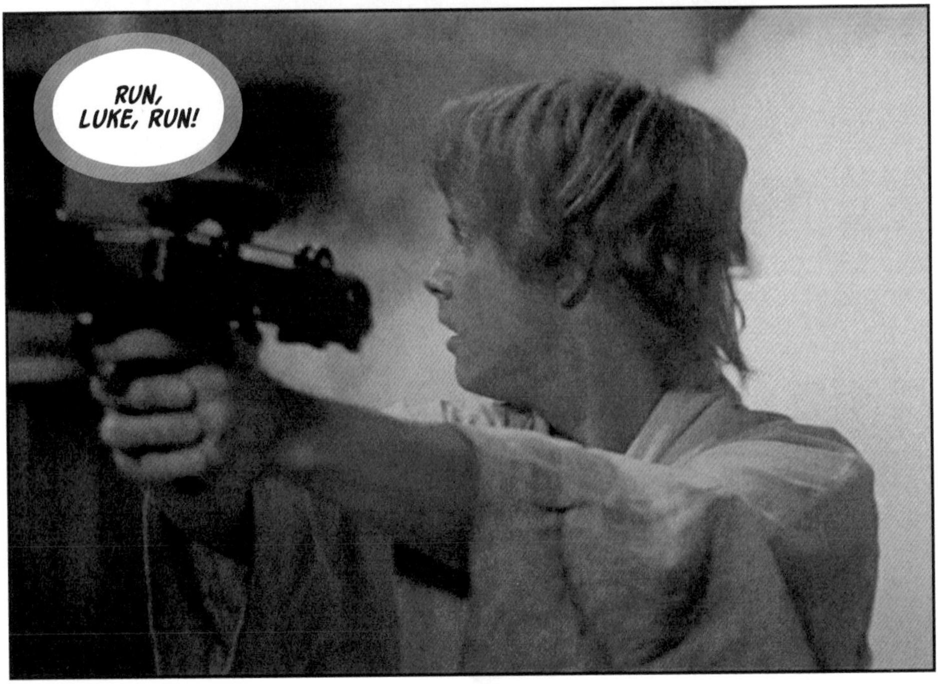
RUN, LUKE, RUN!

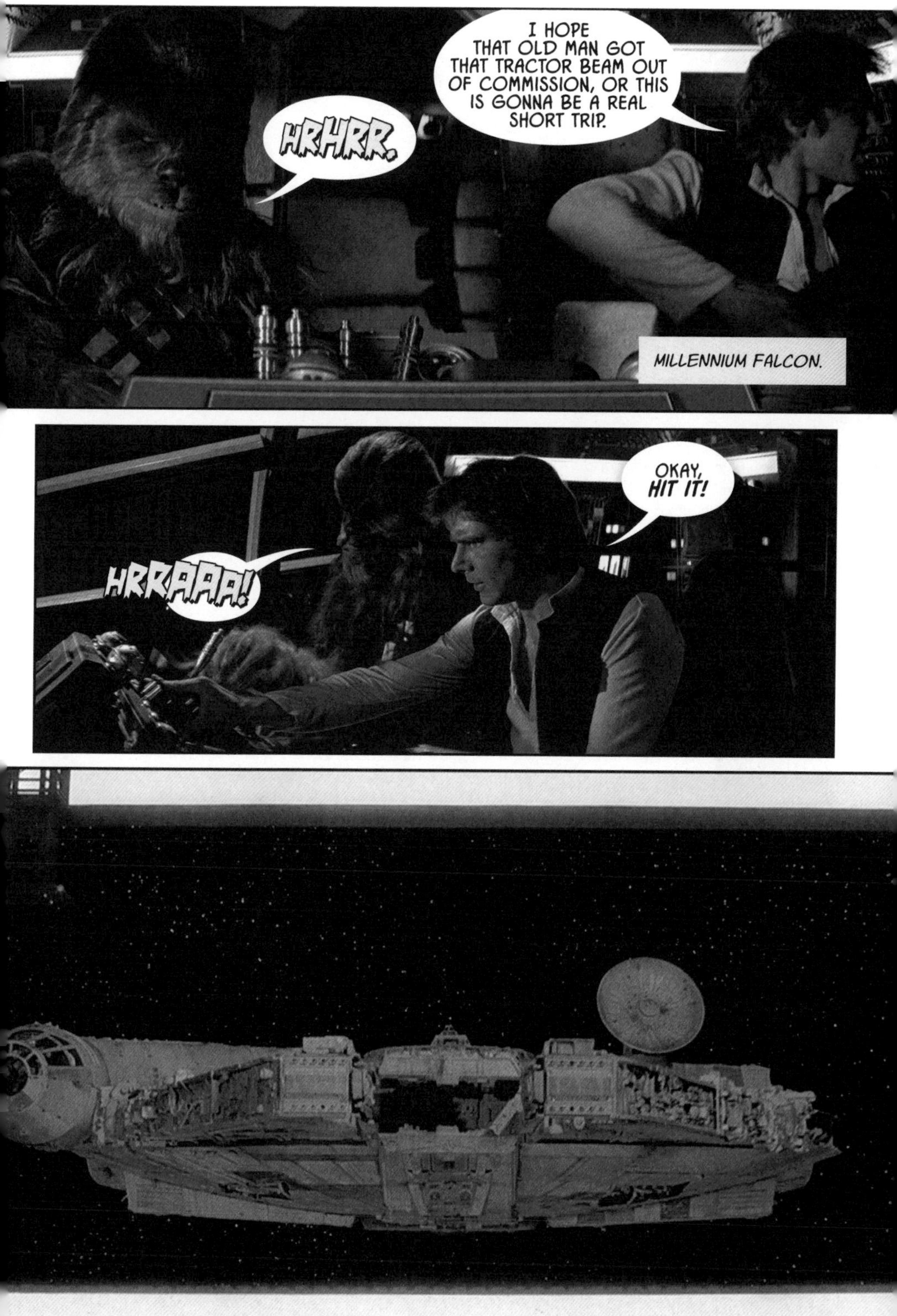
I HOPE THAT OLD MAN GOT THAT TRACTOR BEAM OUT OF COMMISSION, OR THIS IS GONNA BE A REAL SHORT TRIP.
HRHRR.
MILLENNIUM FALCON.
OKAY, HIT IT!
HRRAAA!

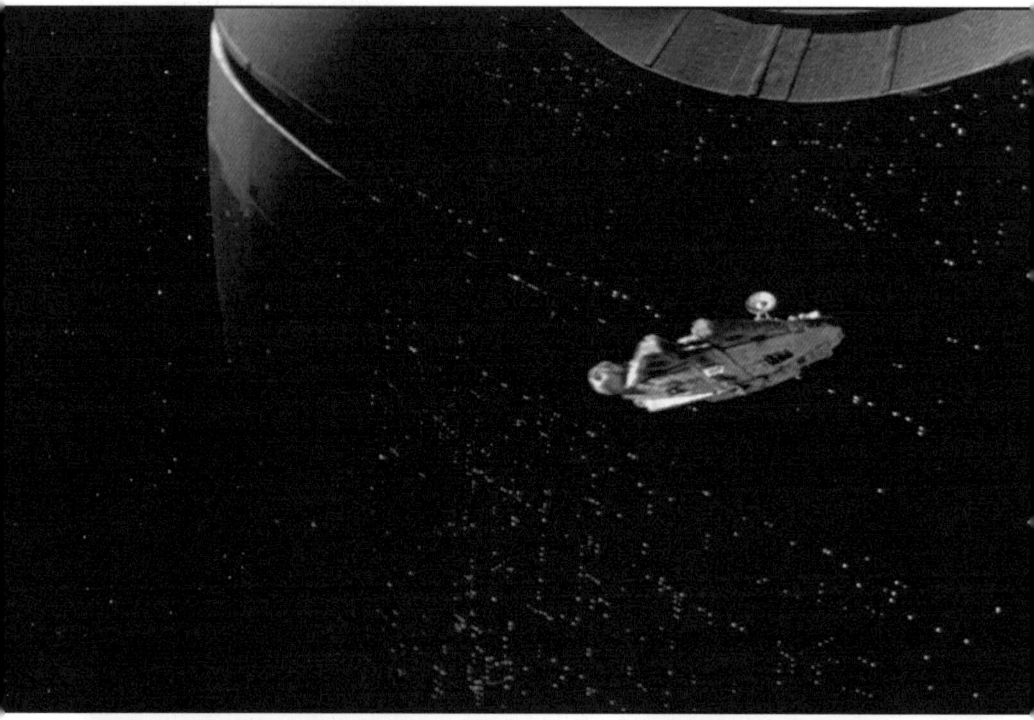

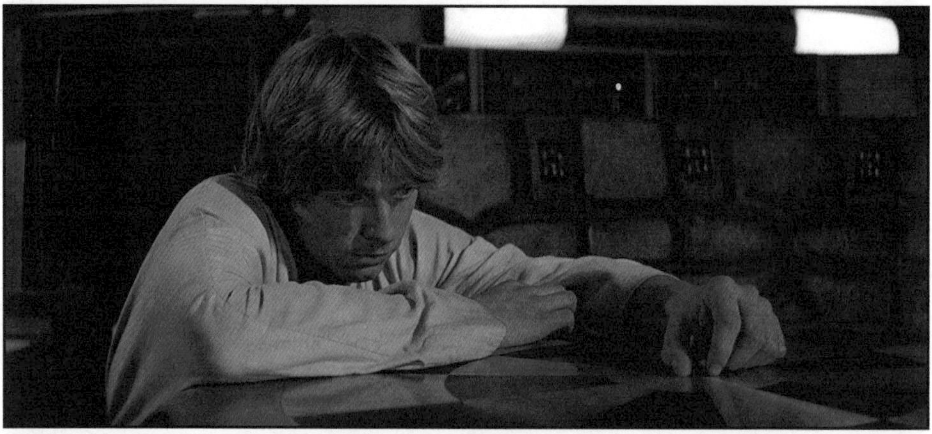

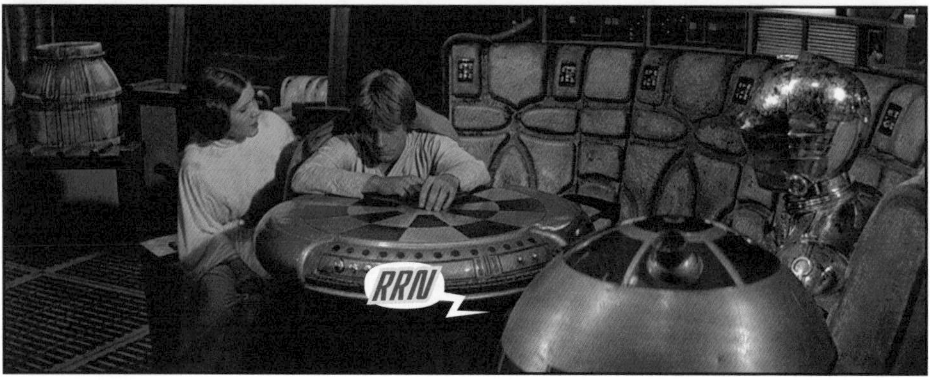
RRN

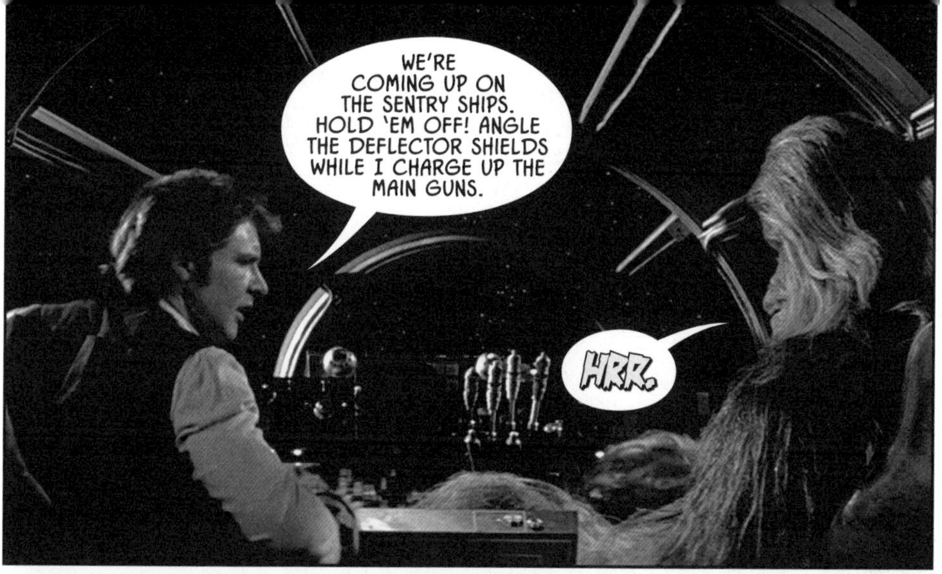
WE'RE COMING UP ON THE SENTRY SHIPS. HOLD 'EM OFF! ANGLE THE DEFLECTOR SHIELDS WHILE I CHARGE UP THE MAIN GUNS.
HRR.

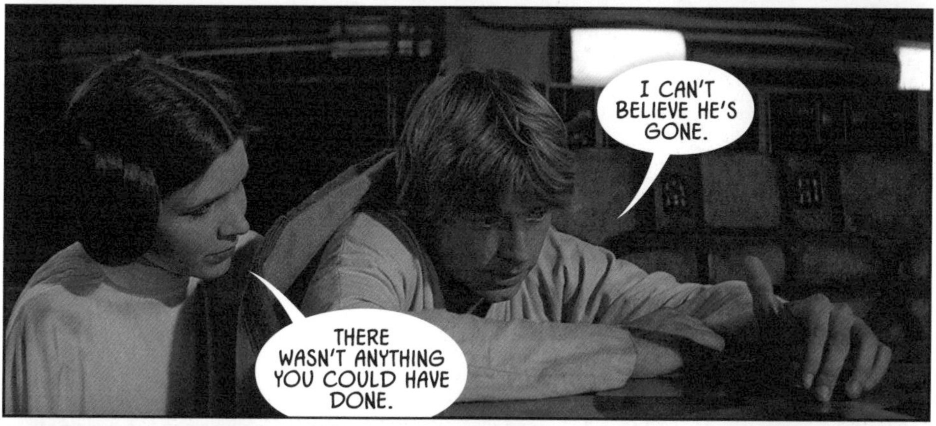
I CAN'T BELIEVE HE'S GONE.
THERE WASN'T ANYTHING YOU COULD HAVE DONE.

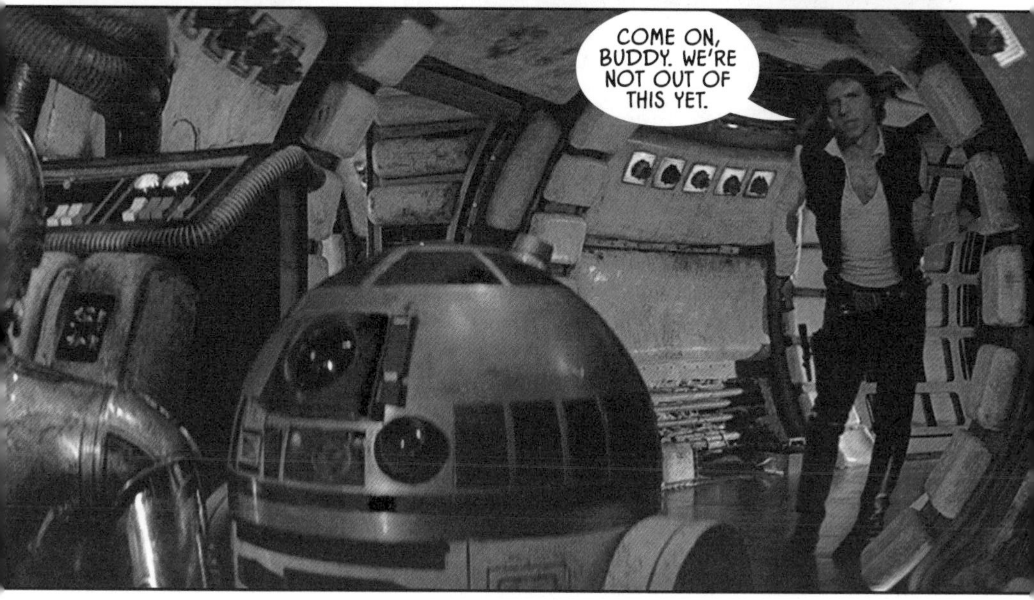
COME ON, BUDDY. WE'RE NOT OUT OF THIS YET.

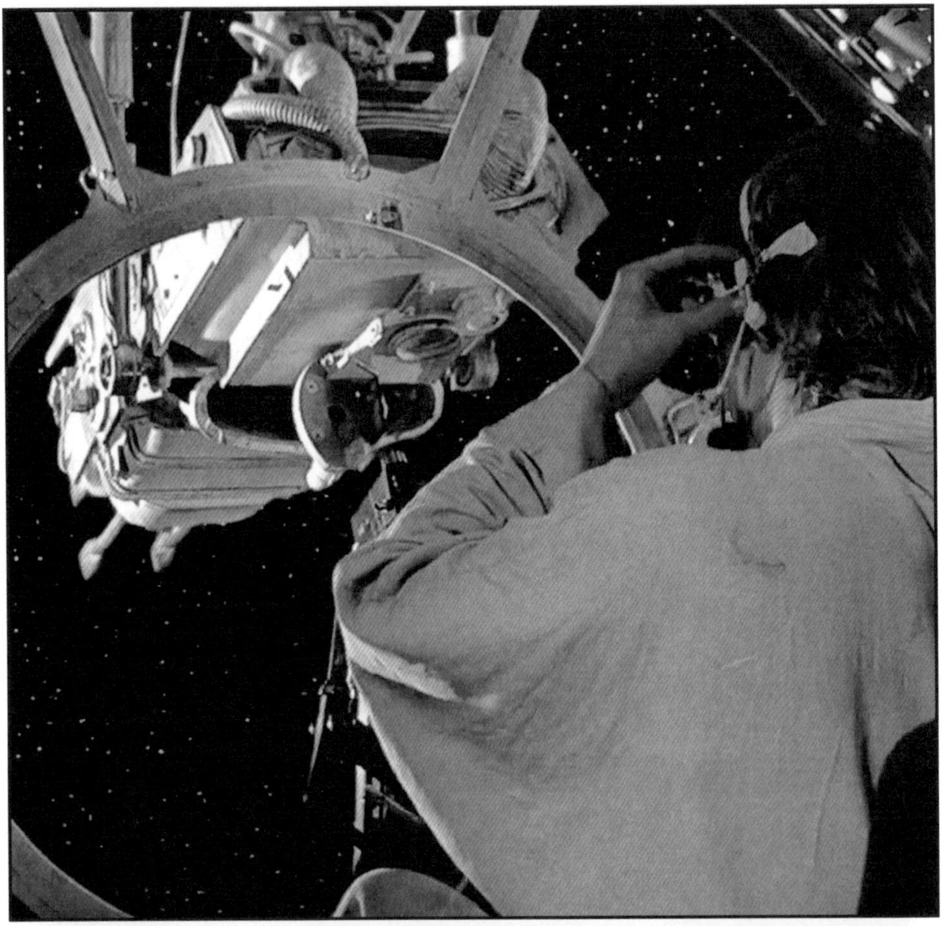

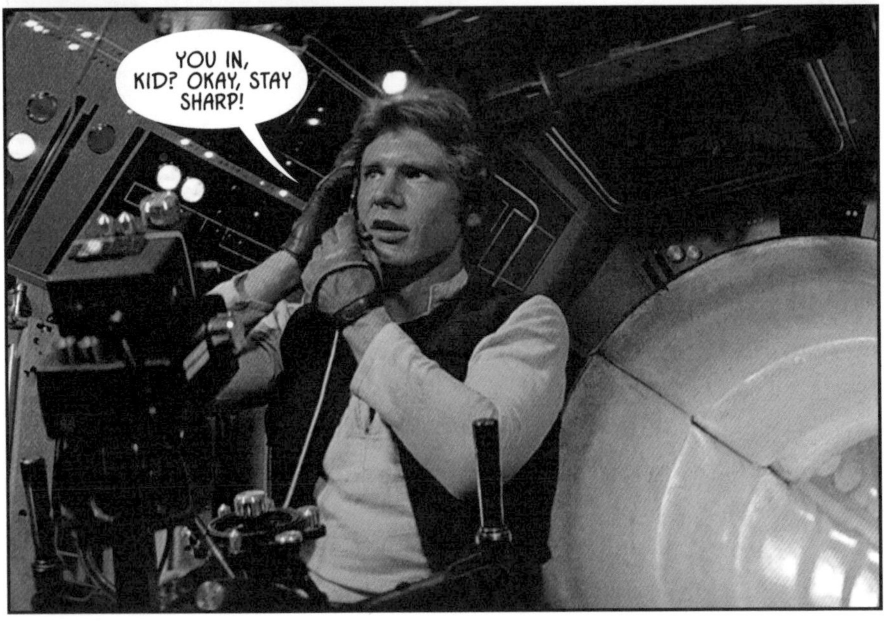
YOU IN, KID? OKAY, STAY SHARP!

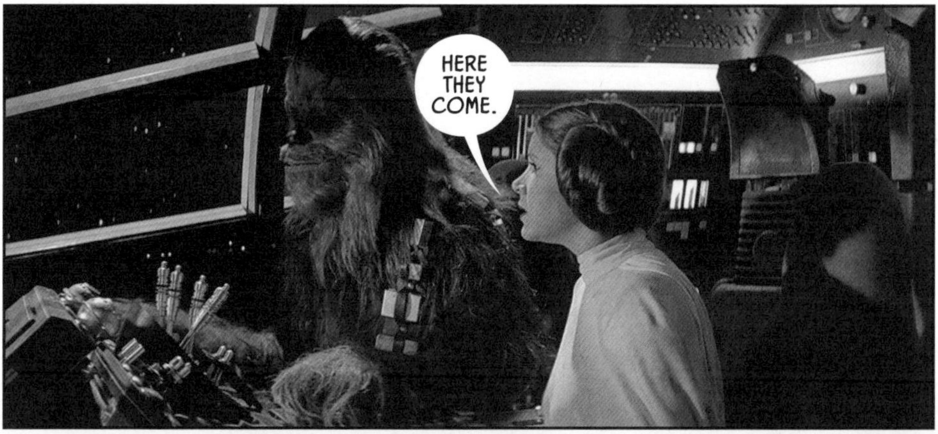
HERE THEY COME.

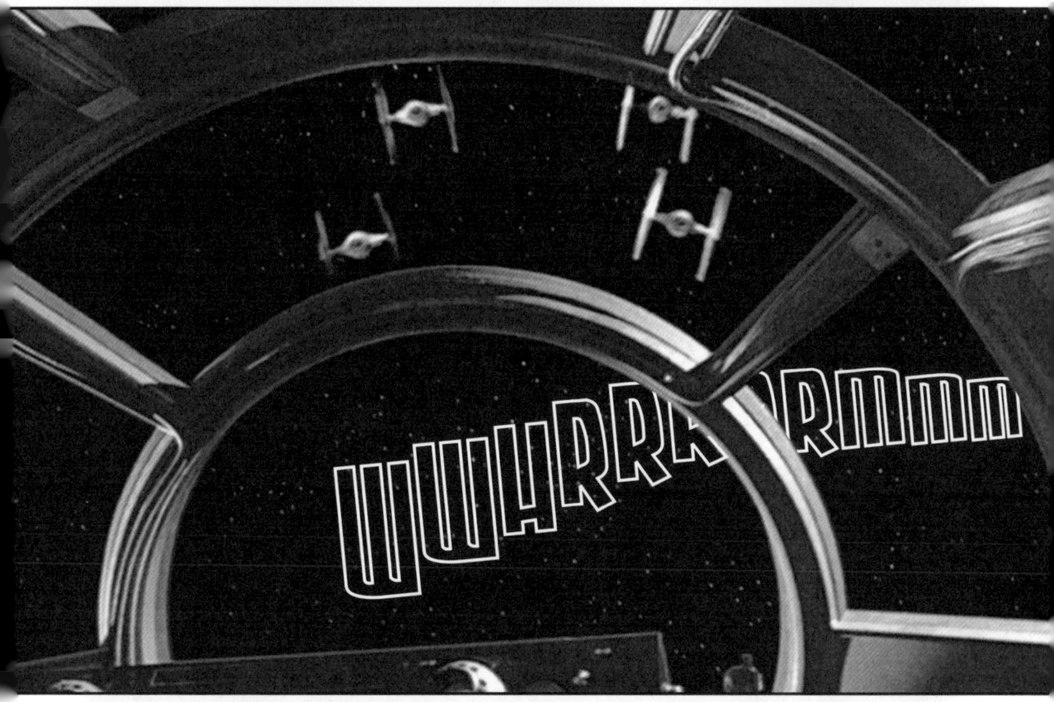
WWHRRRRMMM

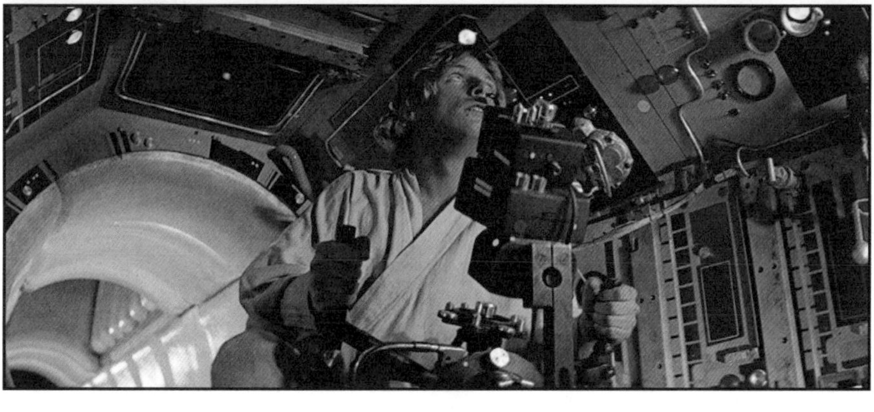

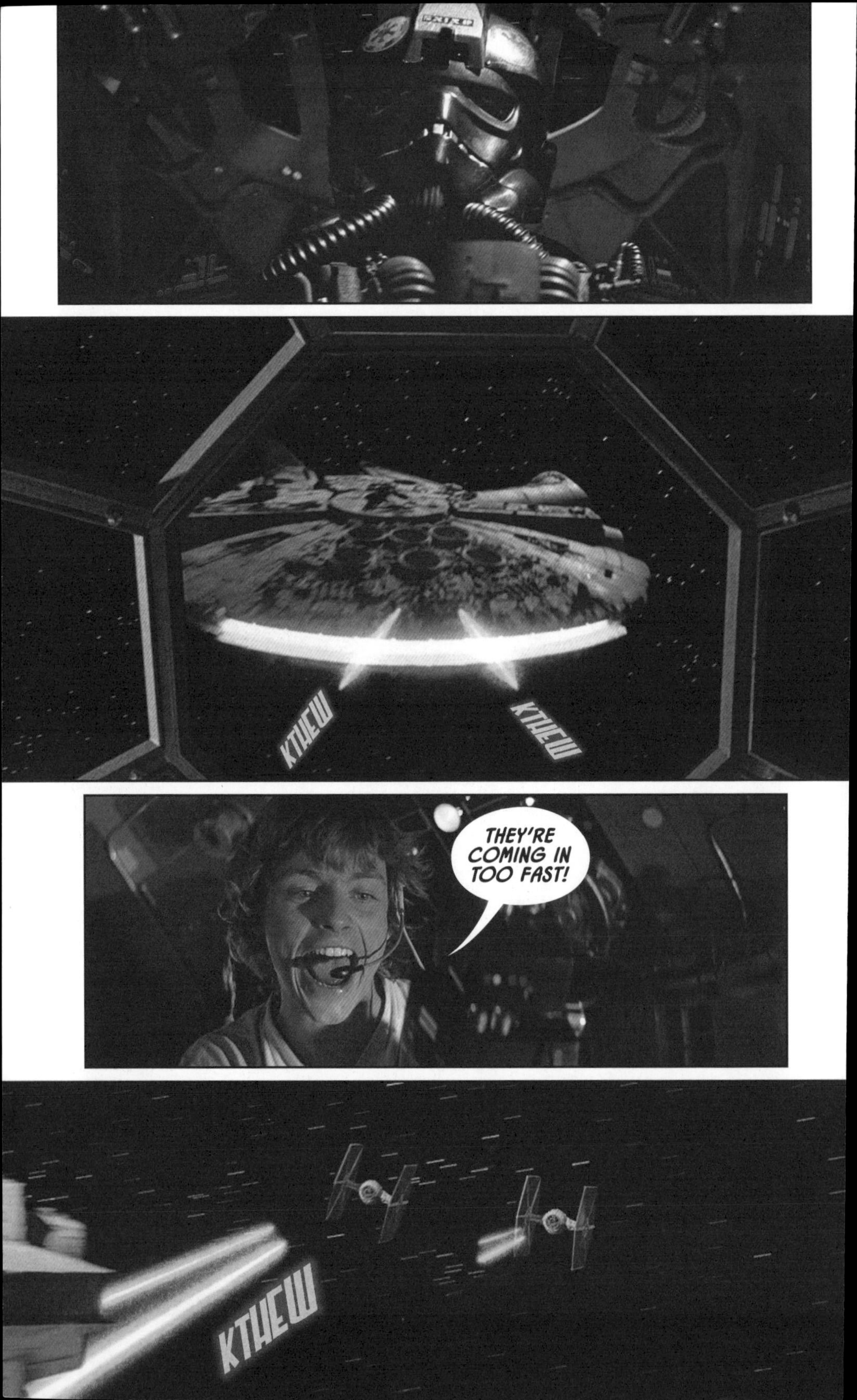
KTHEW
KTHEW
THEY'RE COMING IN TOO FAST!
KTHEW

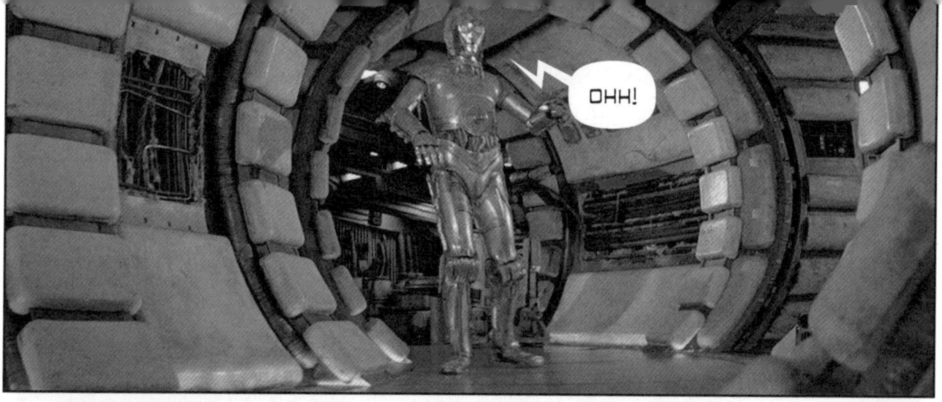
OHH!

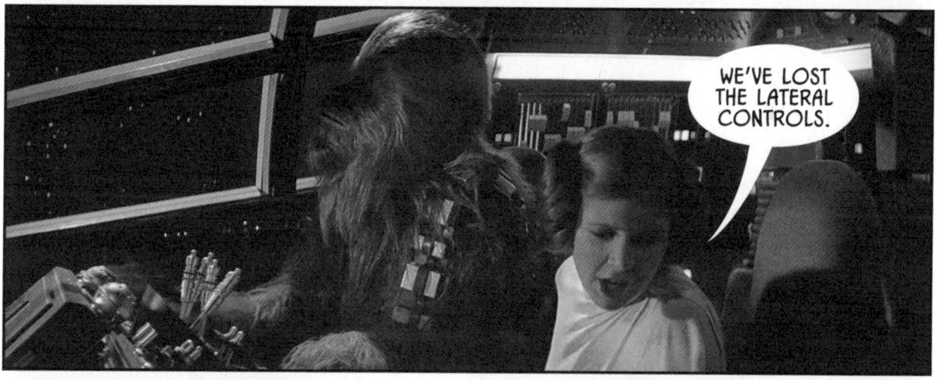
WE'VE LOST THE LATERAL CONTROLS.

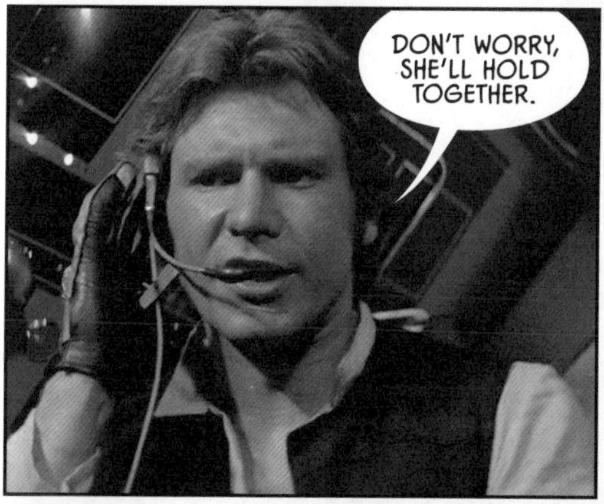
DON'T WORRY, SHE'LL HOLD TOGETHER.

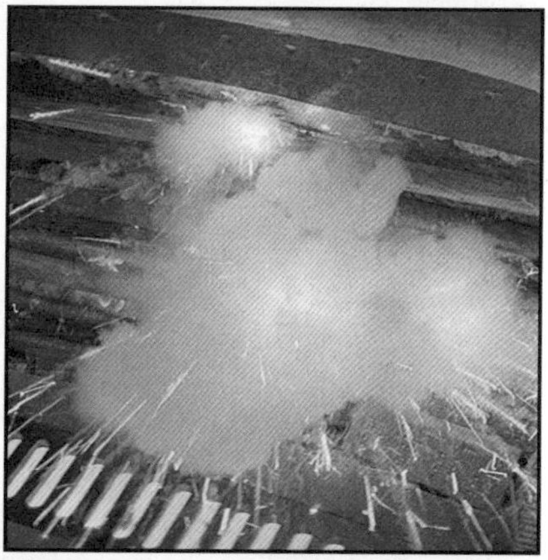

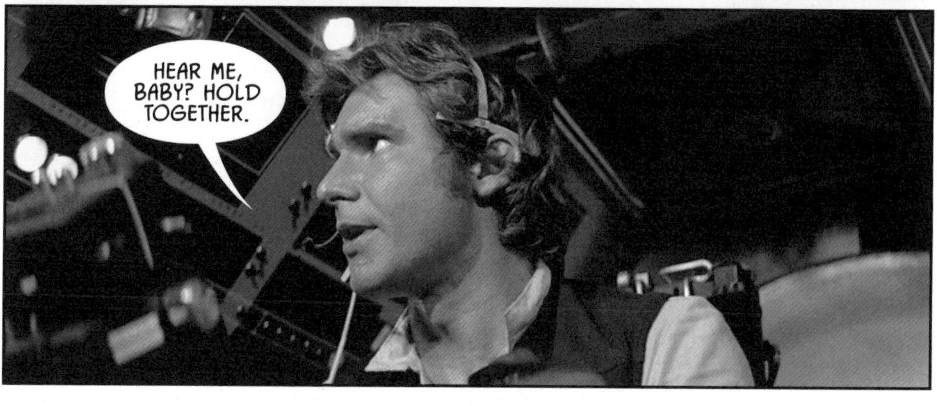
HEAR ME, BABY? HOLD TOGETHER.

KTHEW

THOOOM

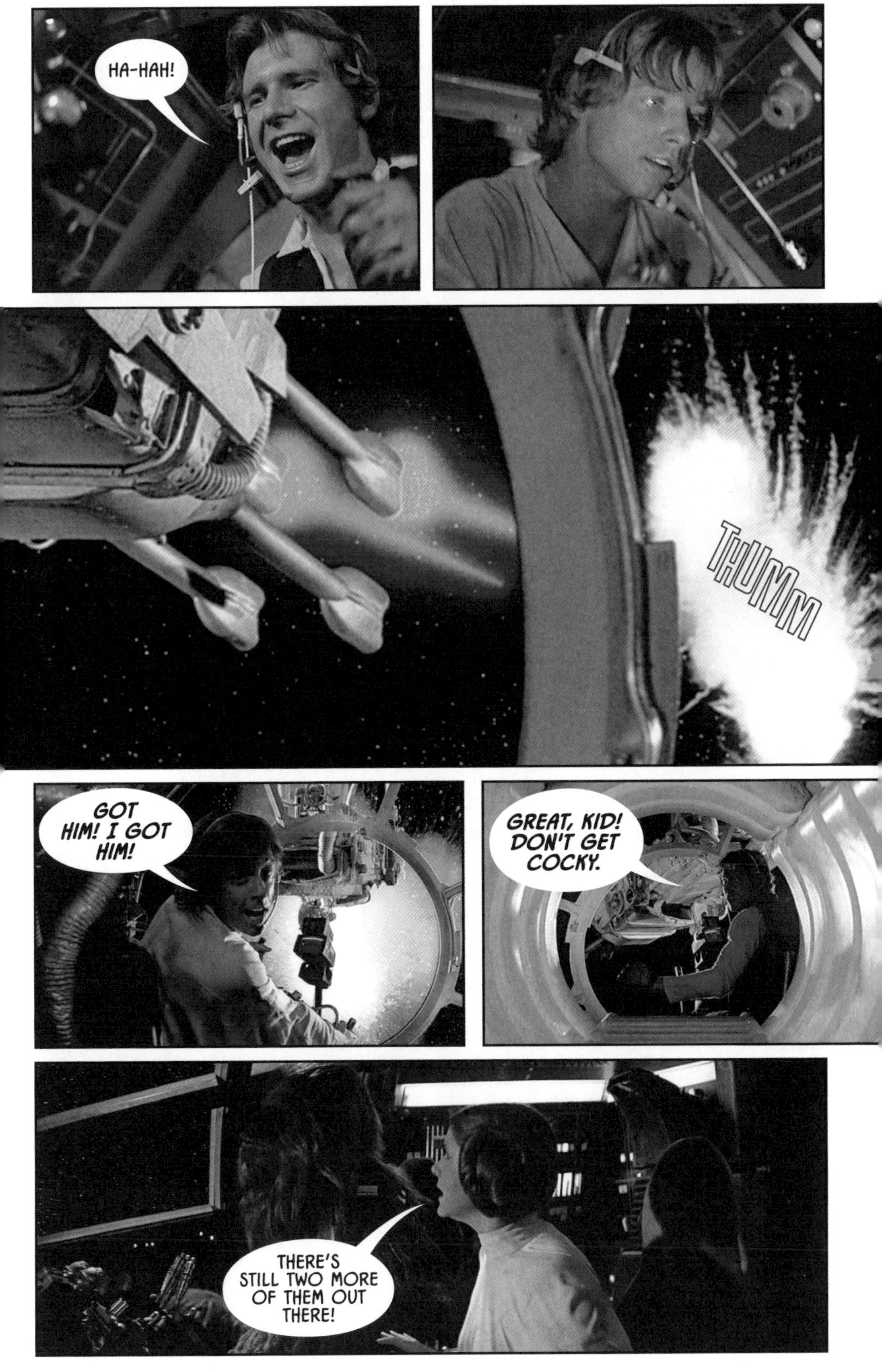
HA-HAH!
THUMM
GOT HIM! I GOT HIM!
GREAT, KID! DON'T GET COCKY.
THERE'S STILL TWO MORE OF THEM OUT THERE!

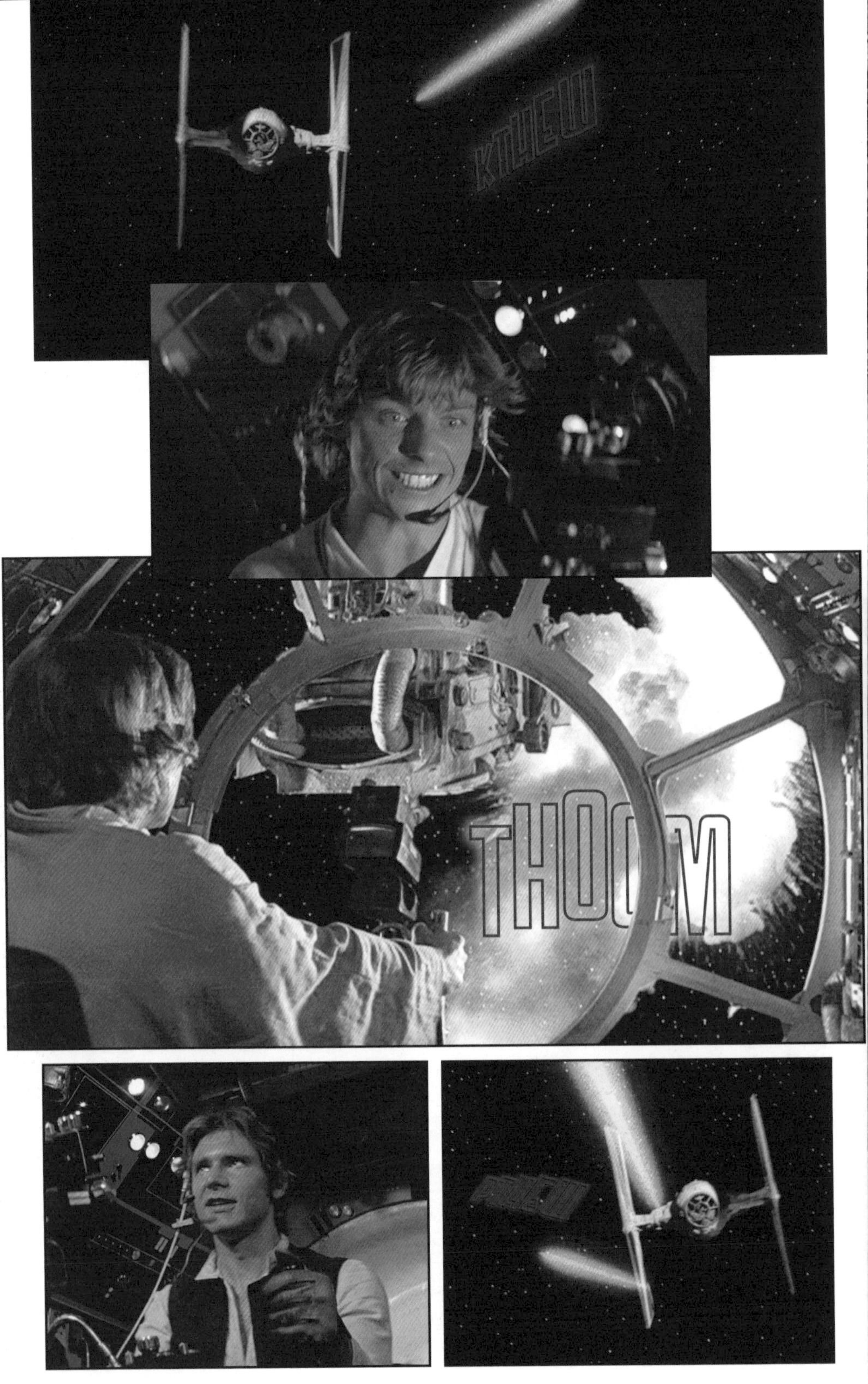
THOOM

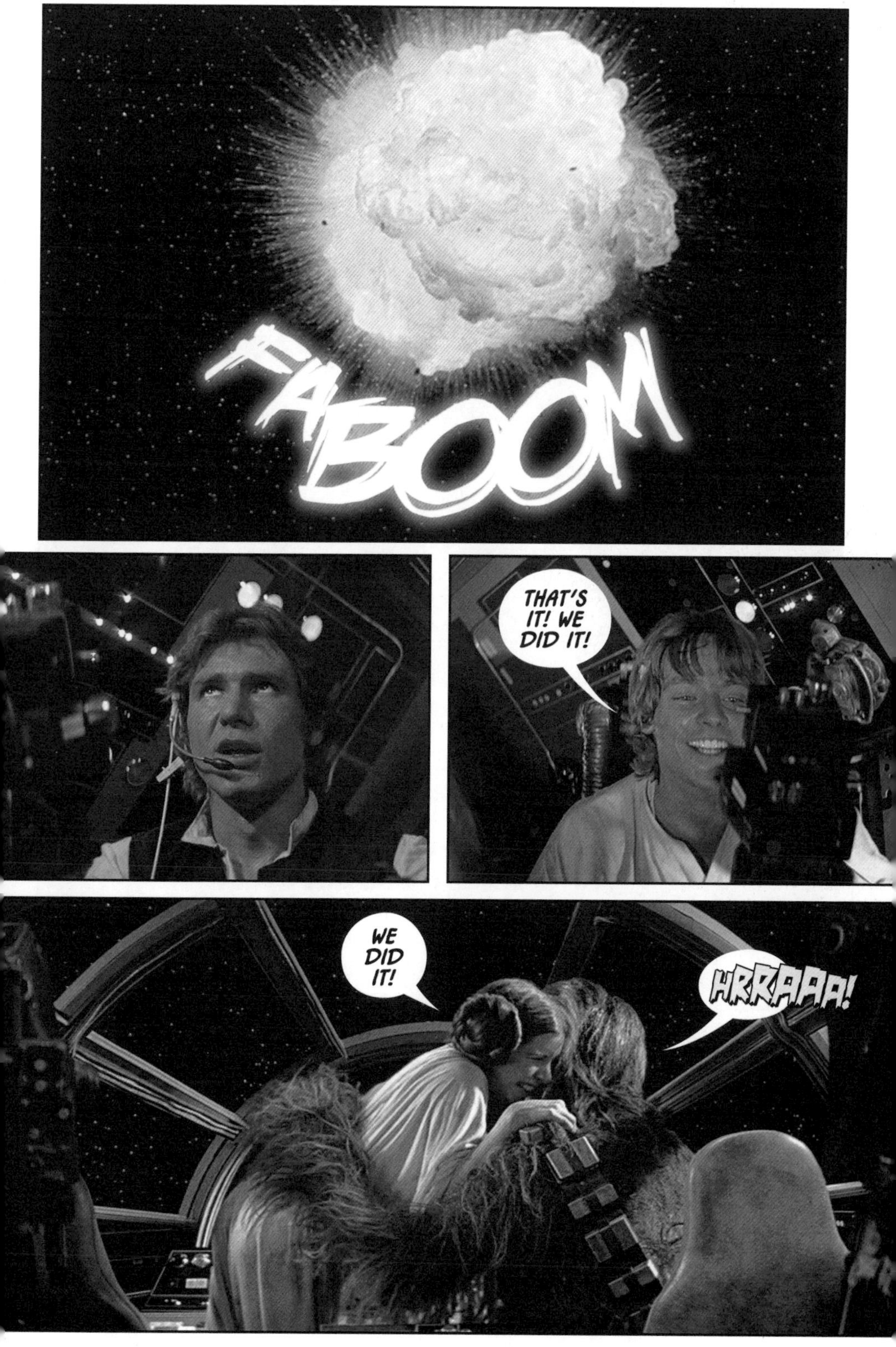
FA BOOM
THAT'S IT! WE DID IT!
WE DID IT!
HRRAAAA!

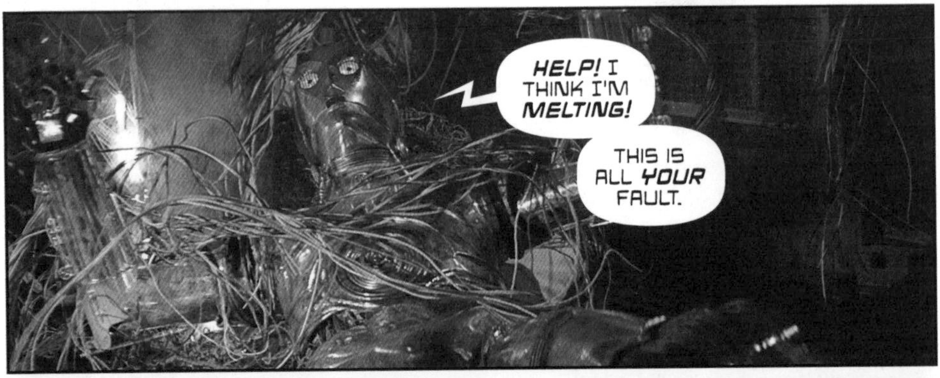
HELP! I THINK I'M MELTING!
THIS IS ALL YOUR FAULT.

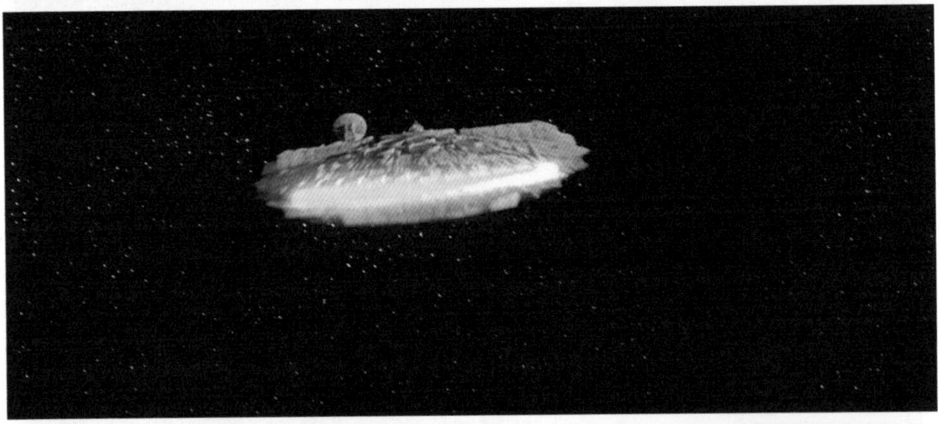

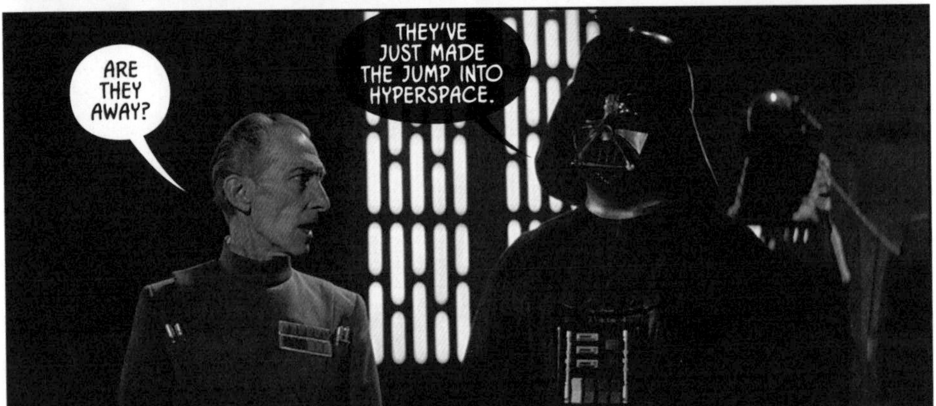
ARE THEY AWAY?
THEY'VE JUST MADE THE JUMP INTO HYPERSPACE.

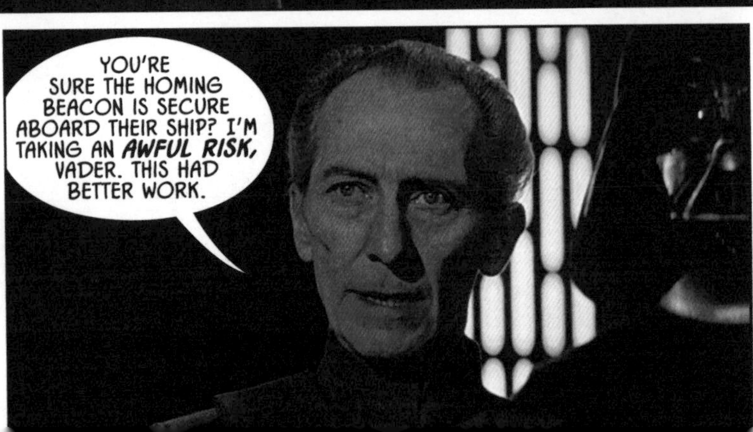
YOU'RE SURE THE HOMING BEACON IS SECURE ABOARD THEIR SHIP? I'M TAKING AN AWFUL RISK, VADER. THIS HAD BETTER WORK.

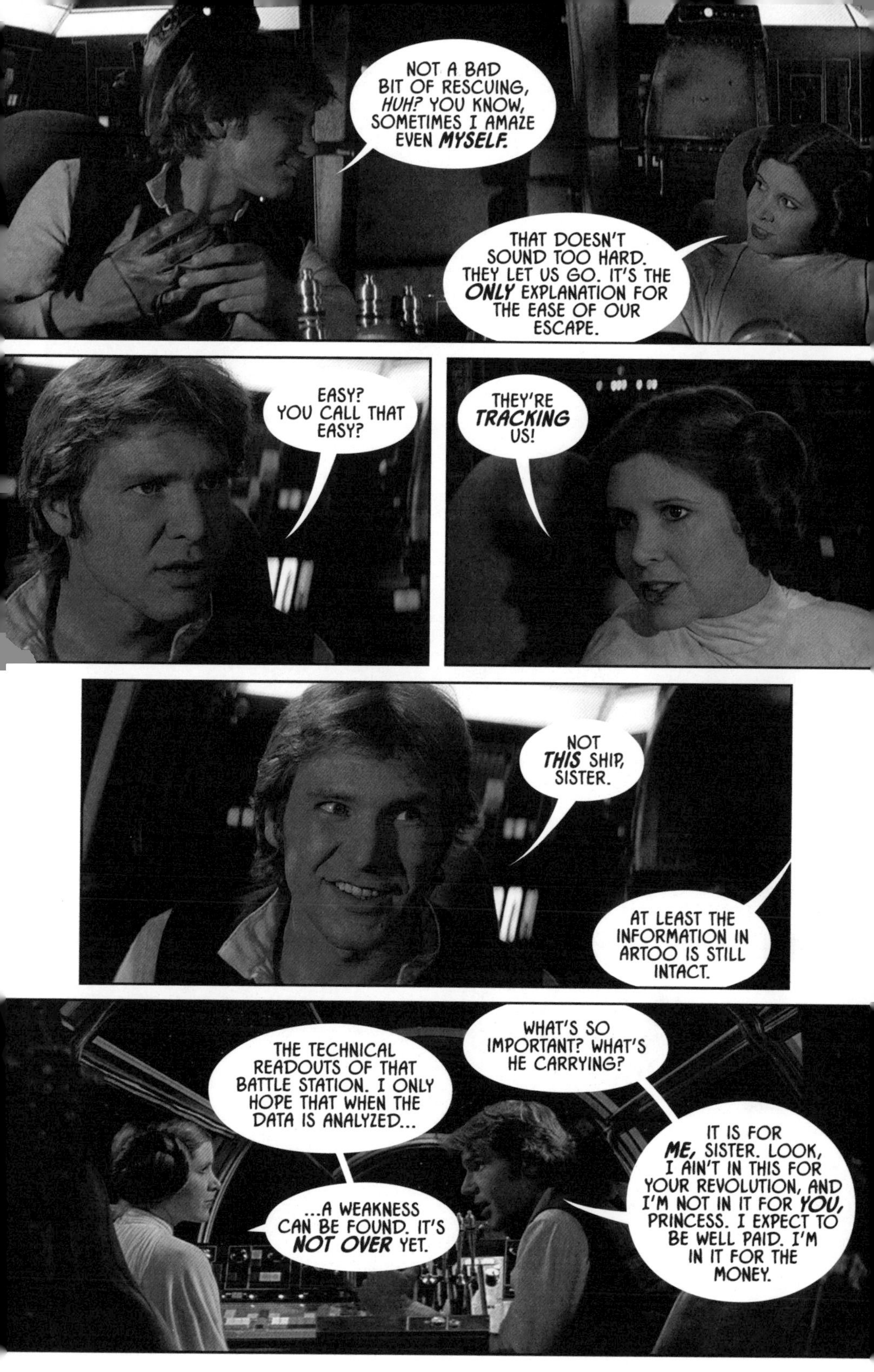
NOT A BAD BIT OF RESCUING, *HUH?* YOU KNOW, SOMETIMES I AMAZE EVEN ***MYSELF.***
THAT DOESN'T SOUND TOO HARD. THEY LET US GO. IT'S THE ***ONLY*** EXPLANATION FOR THE EASE OF OUR ESCAPE.
EASY? YOU CALL THAT EASY?
THEY'RE ***TRACKING*** US!
NOT ***THIS*** SHIP, SISTER.
AT LEAST THE INFORMATION IN ARTOO IS STILL INTACT.
WHAT'S SO IMPORTANT? WHAT'S HE CARRYING?
THE TECHNICAL READOUTS OF THAT BATTLE STATION. I ONLY HOPE THAT WHEN THE DATA IS ANALYZED...
...A WEAKNESS CAN BE FOUND. IT'S ***NOT OVER*** YET.
IT IS FOR ***ME,*** SISTER. LOOK, I AIN'T IN THIS FOR YOUR REVOLUTION, AND I'M NOT IN IT FOR ***YOU,*** PRINCESS. I EXPECT TO BE WELL PAID. I'M IN IT FOR THE MONEY.

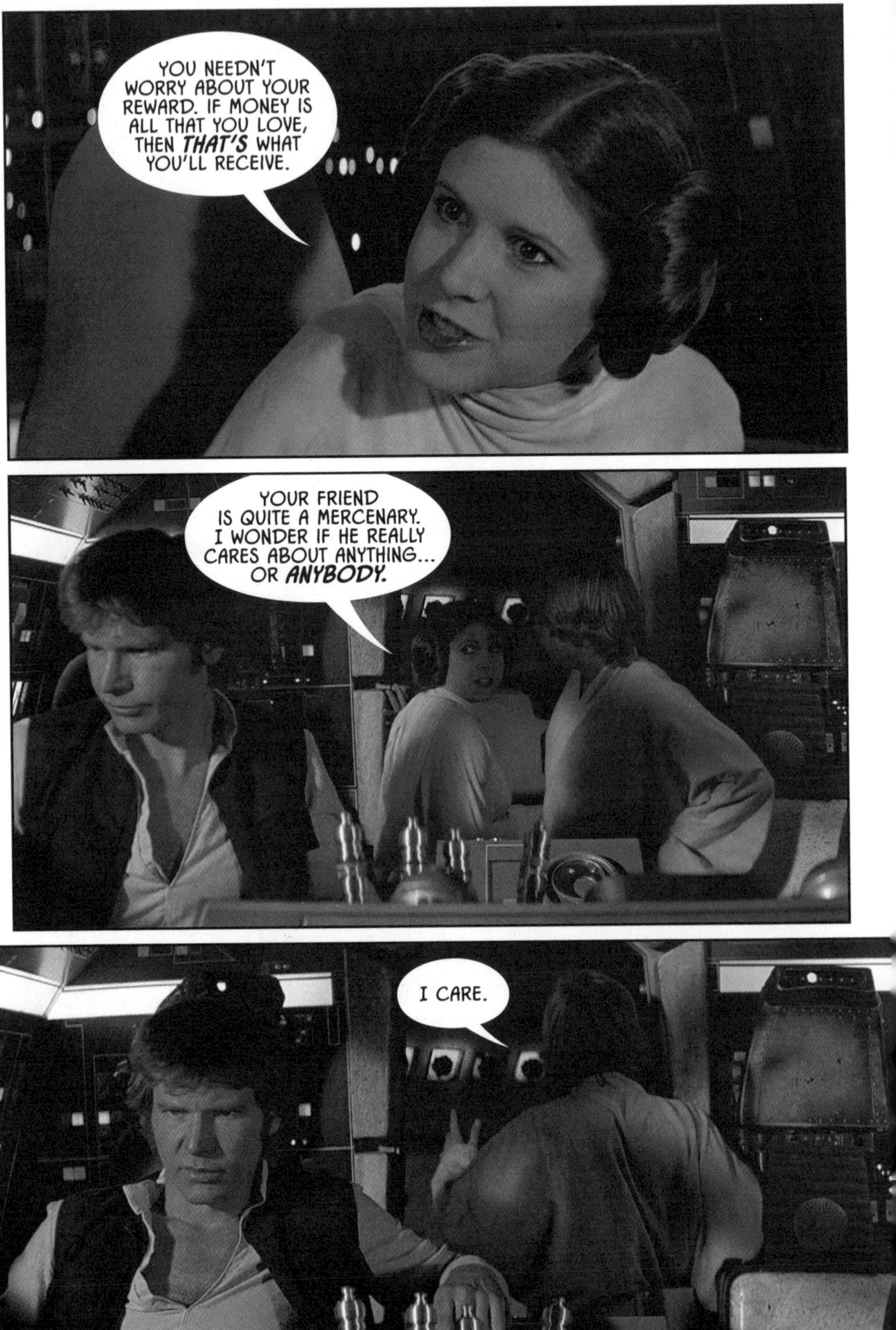
YOU NEEDN'T WORRY ABOUT YOUR REWARD. IF MONEY IS ALL THAT YOU LOVE, THEN ***THAT'S*** WHAT YOU'LL RECEIVE.
YOUR FRIEND IS QUITE A MERCENARY. I WONDER IF HE REALLY CARES ABOUT ANYTHING... OR ***ANYBODY.***
I CARE.

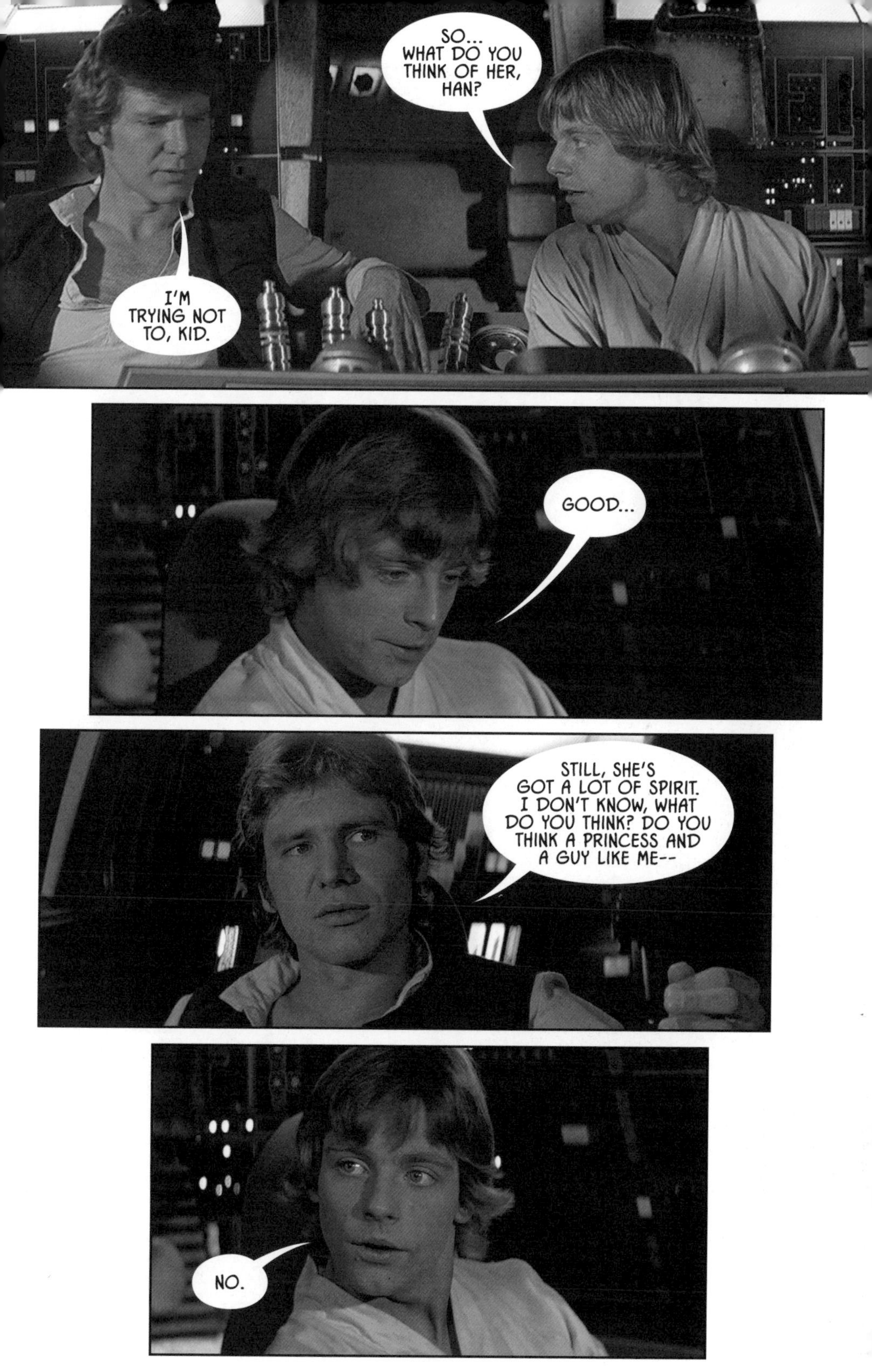
SO... WHAT DO YOU THINK OF HER, HAN?
I'M TRYING NOT TO, KID.
GOOD...
STILL, SHE'S GOT A LOT OF SPIRIT. I DON'T KNOW, WHAT DO YOU THINK? DO YOU THINK A PRINCESS AND A GUY LIKE ME--
NO.

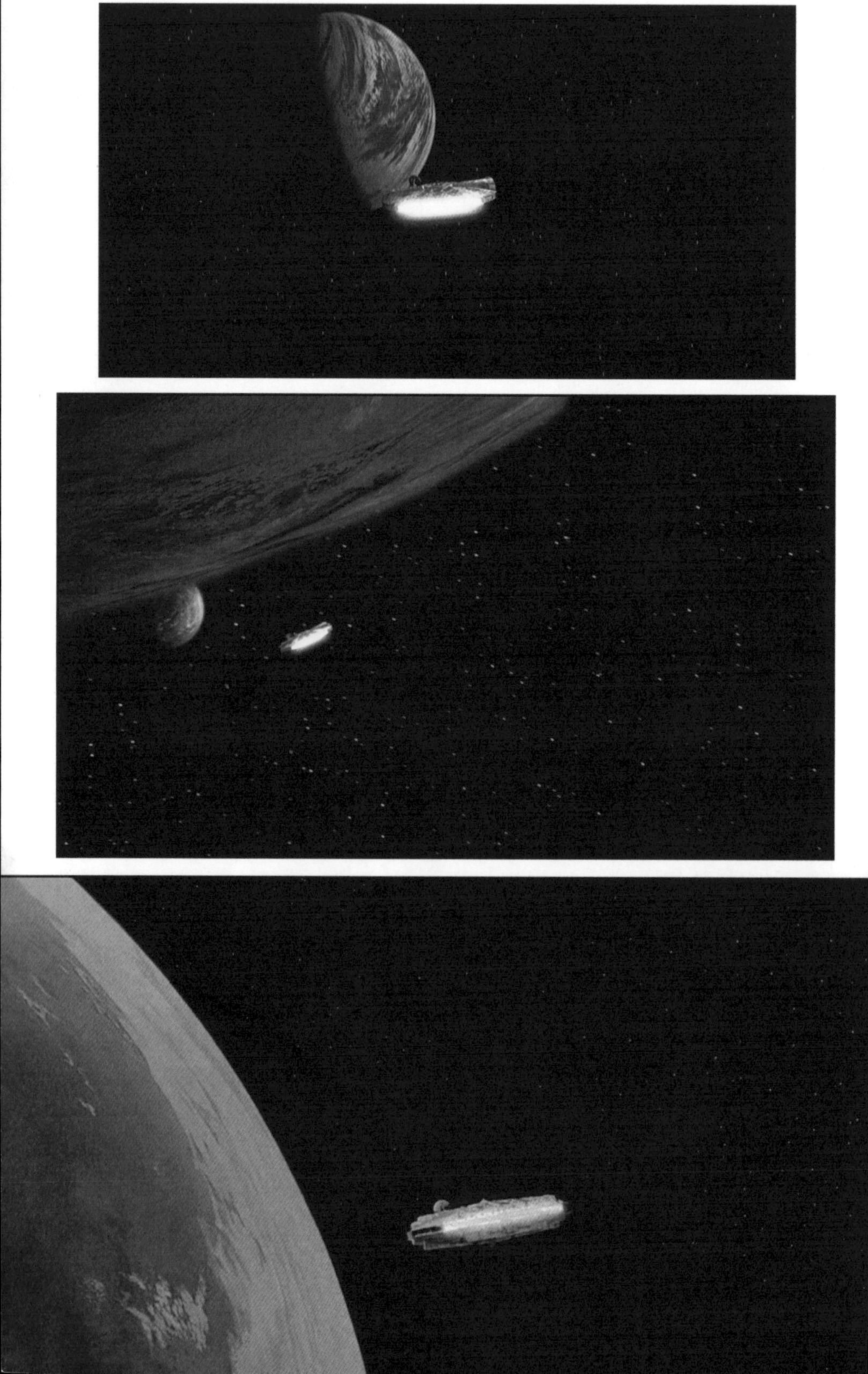

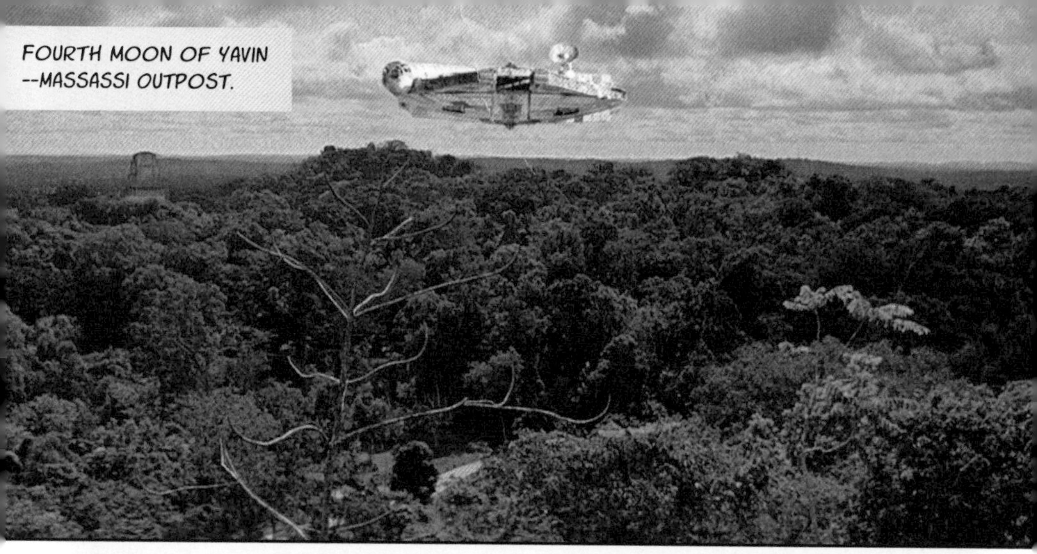
FOURTH MOON OF YAVIN
--MASSASSI OUTPOST.
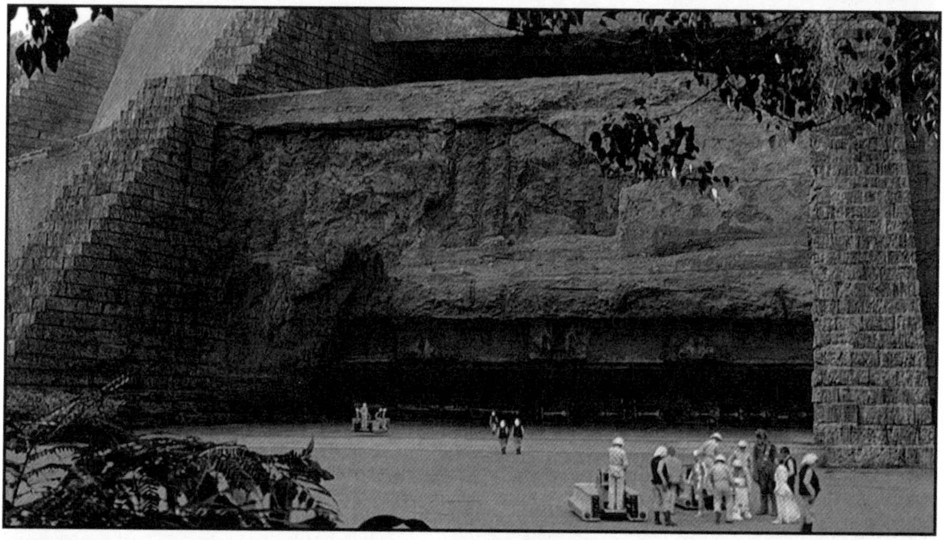
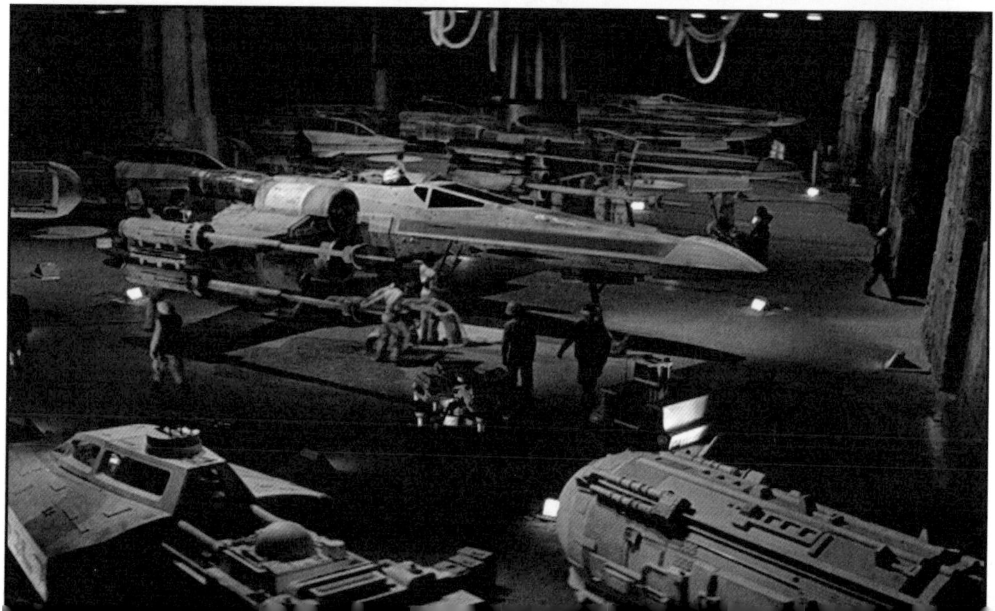

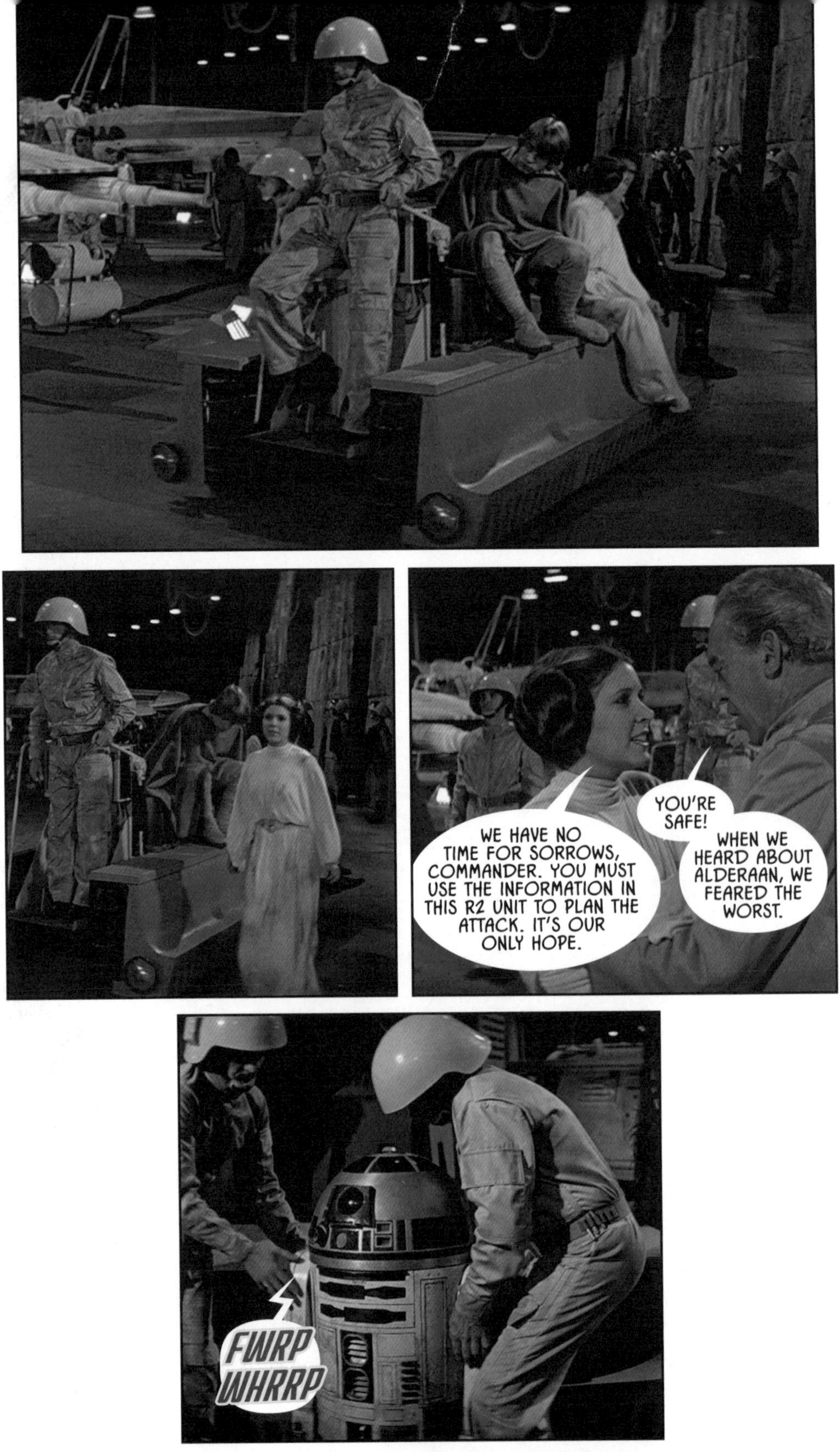
YOU'RE SAFE!
WHEN WE HEARD ABOUT ALDERAAN, WE FEARED THE WORST.
WE HAVE NO TIME FOR SORROWS, COMMANDER. YOU MUST USE THE INFORMATION IN THIS R2 UNIT TO PLAN THE ATTACK. IT'S OUR ONLY HOPE.
FWRP WHRRP

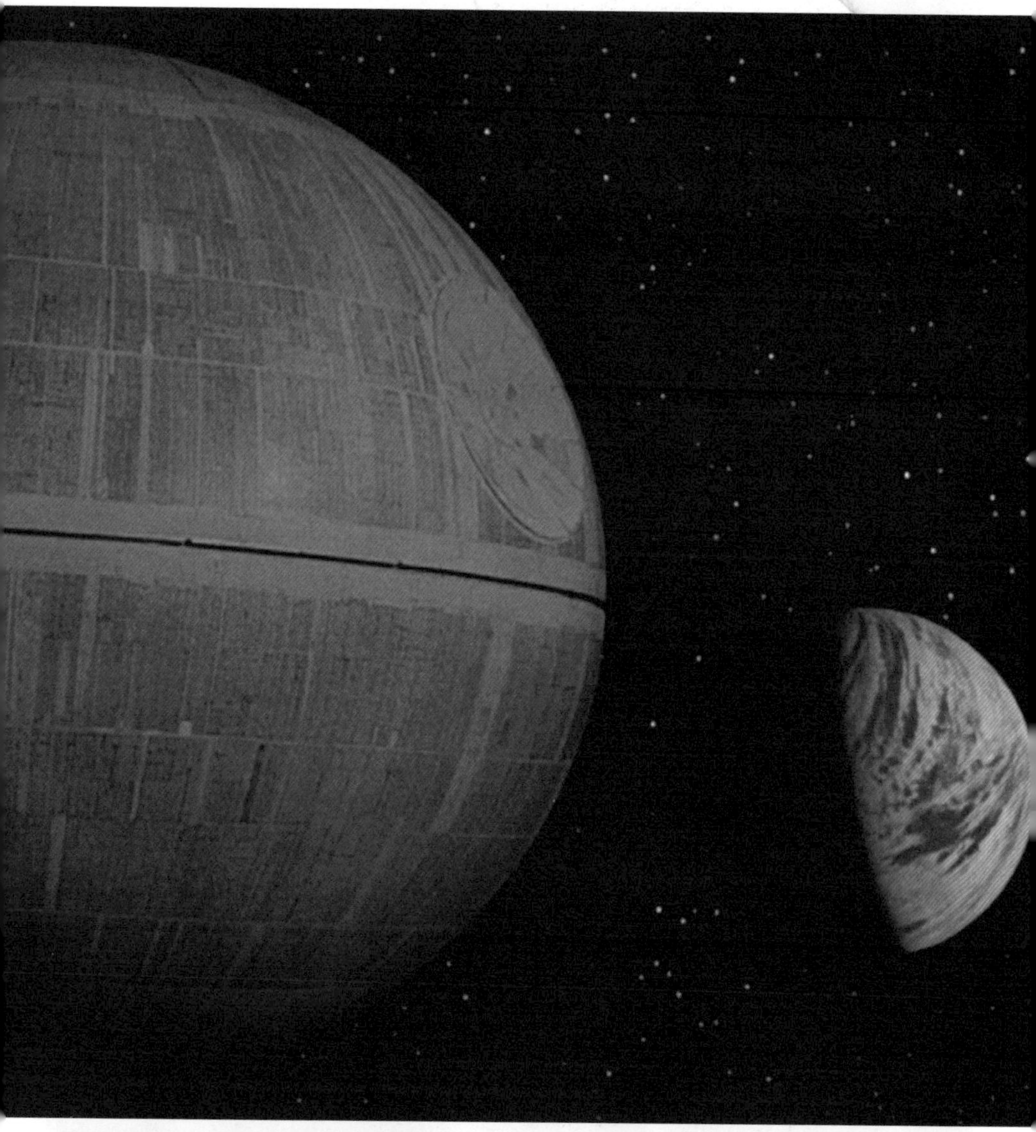

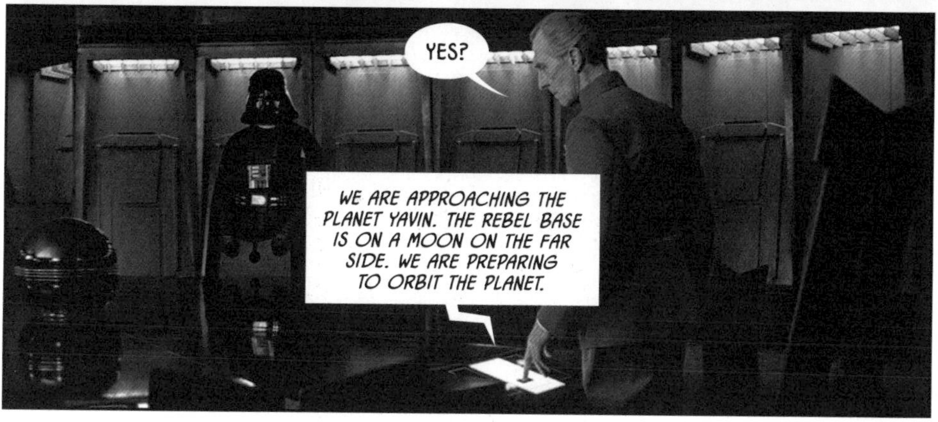

YES?
WE ARE APPROACHING THE PLANET YAVIN. THE REBEL BASE IS ON A MOON ON THE FAR SIDE. WE ARE PREPARING TO ORBIT THE PLANET.

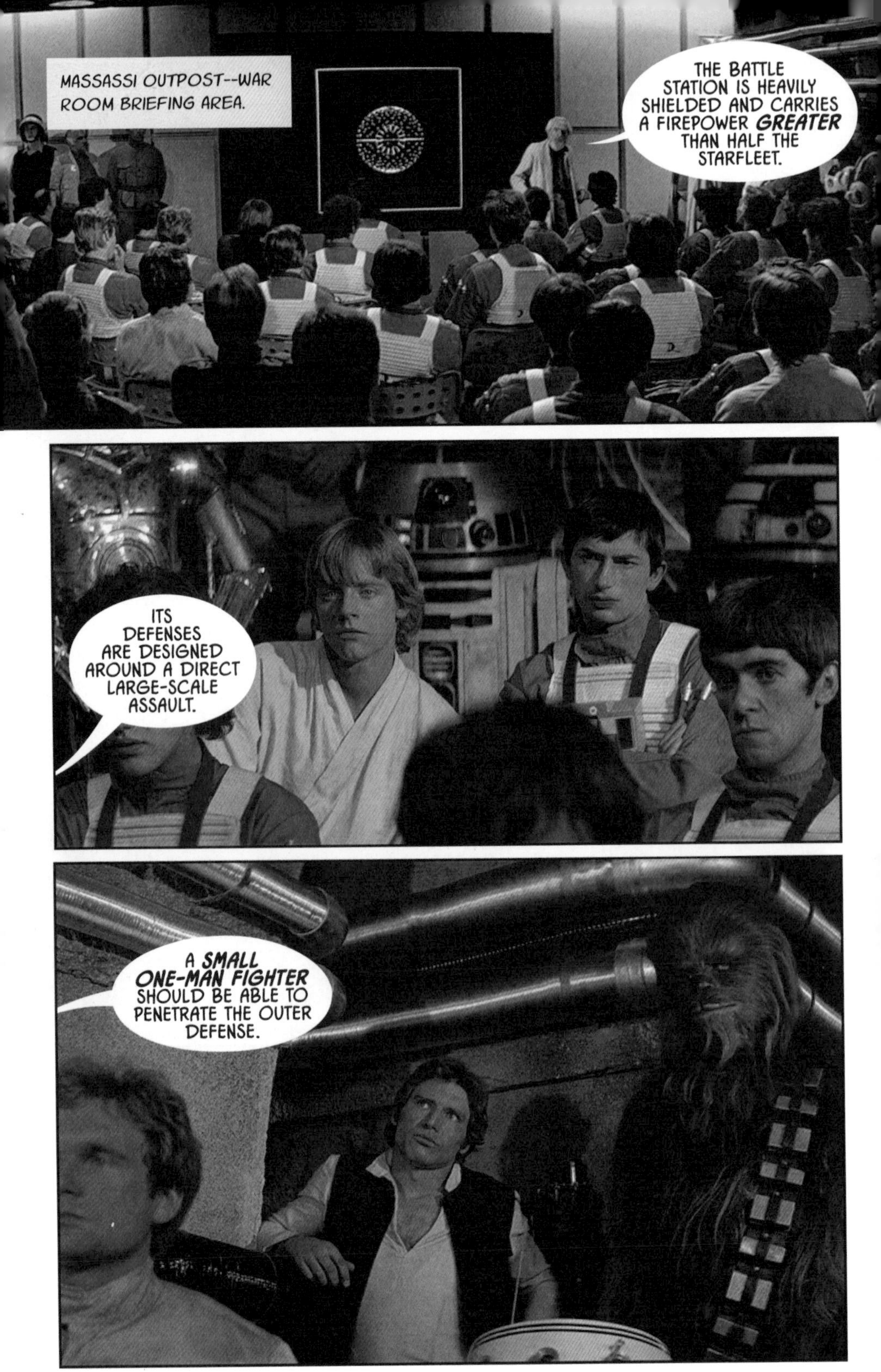
MASSASSI OUTPOST--WAR ROOM BRIEFING AREA.
THE BATTLE STATION IS HEAVILY SHIELDED AND CARRIES A FIREPOWER GREATER THAN HALF THE STARFLEET.
ITS DEFENSES ARE DESIGNED AROUND A DIRECT LARGE-SCALE ASSAULT.
A SMALL ONE-MAN FIGHTER SHOULD BE ABLE TO PENETRATE THE OUTER DEFENSE.

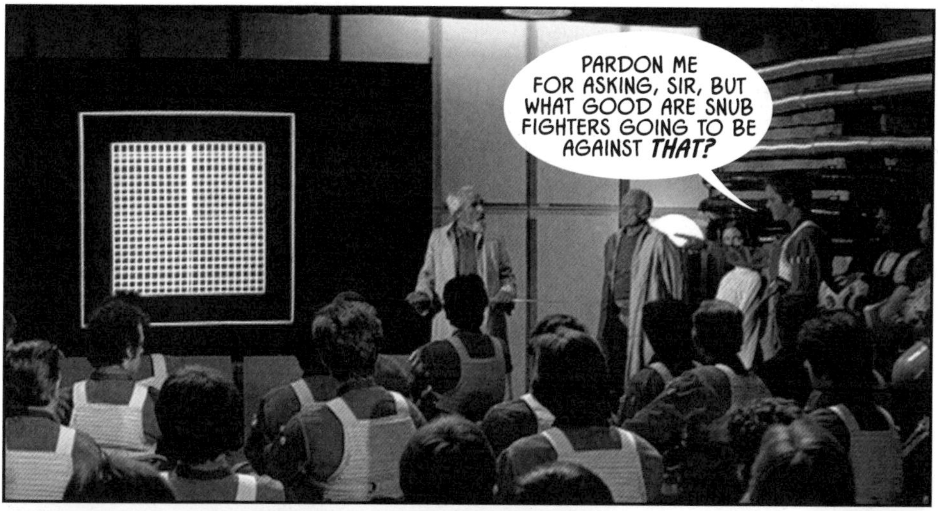
PARDON ME FOR ASKING, SIR, BUT WHAT GOOD ARE SNUB FIGHTERS GOING TO BE AGAINST *THAT?*

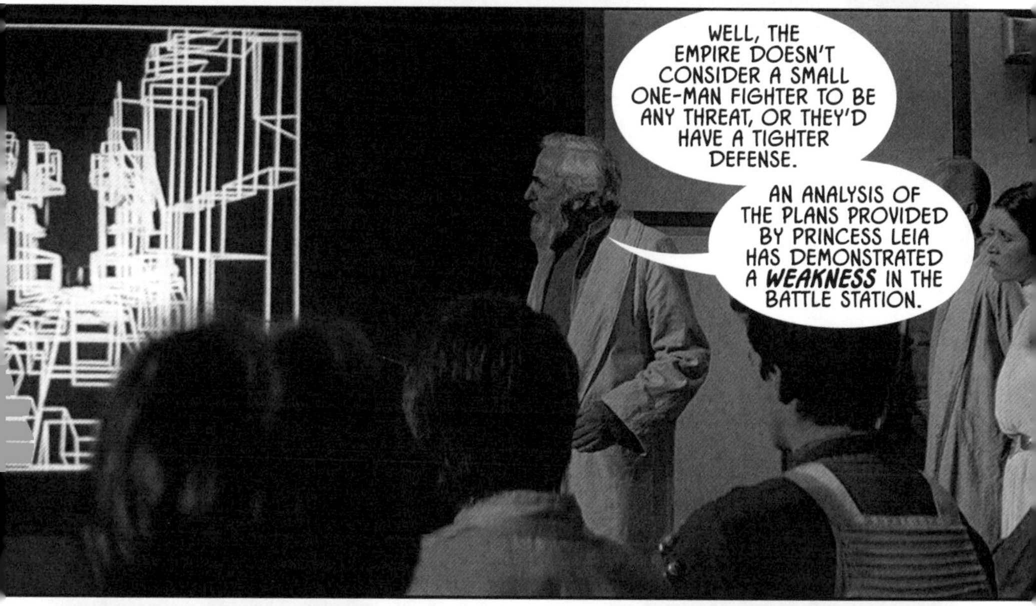
WELL, THE EMPIRE DOESN'T CONSIDER A SMALL ONE-MAN FIGHTER TO BE ANY THREAT, OR THEY'D HAVE A TIGHTER DEFENSE.
AN ANALYSIS OF THE PLANS PROVIDED BY PRINCESS LEIA HAS DEMONSTRATED A *WEAKNESS* IN THE BATTLE STATION.

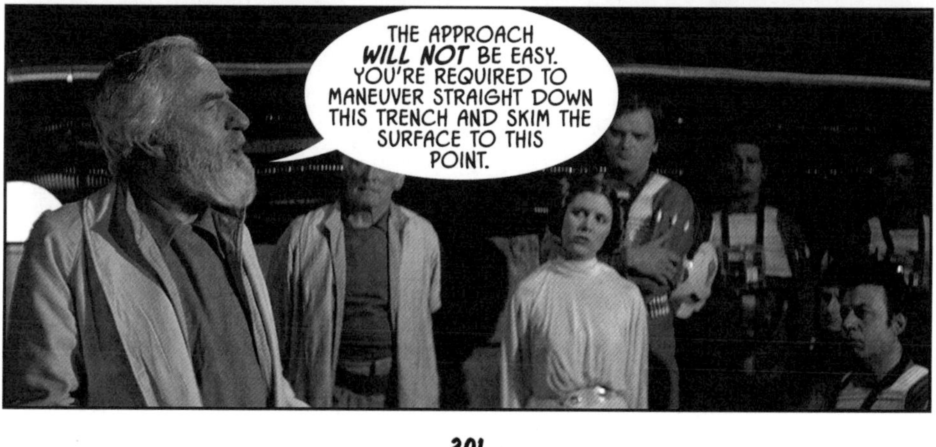
THE APPROACH *WILL NOT* BE EASY. YOU'RE REQUIRED TO MANEUVER STRAIGHT DOWN THIS TRENCH AND SKIM THE SURFACE TO THIS POINT.

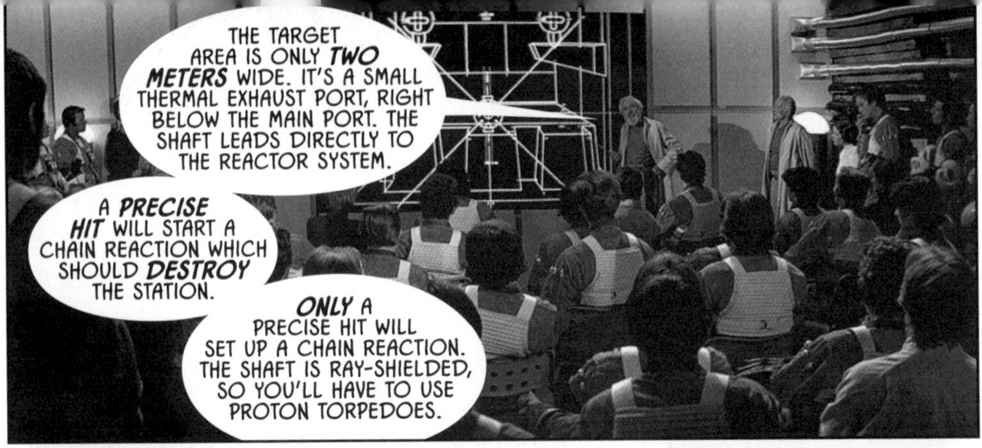
THE TARGET AREA IS ONLY TWO METERS WIDE. IT'S A SMALL THERMAL EXHAUST PORT, RIGHT BELOW THE MAIN PORT. THE SHAFT LEADS DIRECTLY TO THE REACTOR SYSTEM.
A PRECISE HIT WILL START A CHAIN REACTION WHICH SHOULD DESTROY THE STATION.
ONLY A PRECISE HIT WILL SET UP A CHAIN REACTION. THE SHAFT IS RAY-SHIELDED, SO YOU'LL HAVE TO USE PROTON TORPEDOES.

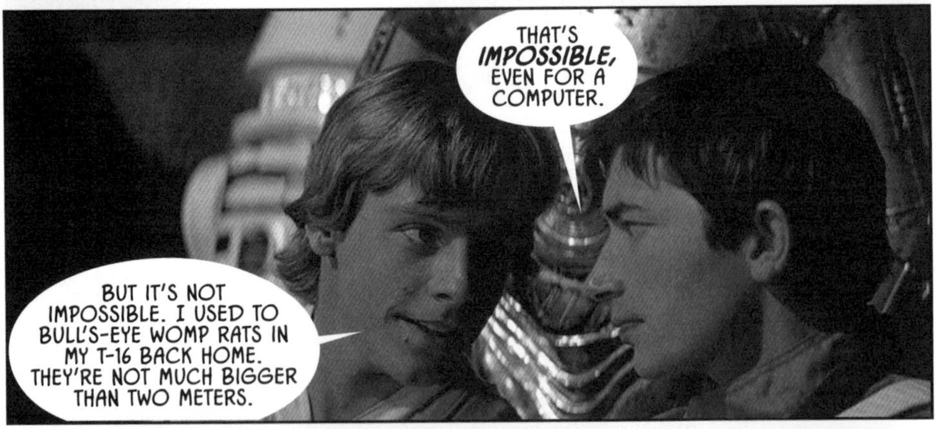
THAT'S IMPOSSIBLE, EVEN FOR A COMPUTER.
BUT IT'S NOT IMPOSSIBLE. I USED TO BULL'S-EYE WOMP RATS IN MY T-16 BACK HOME. THEY'RE NOT MUCH BIGGER THAN TWO METERS.

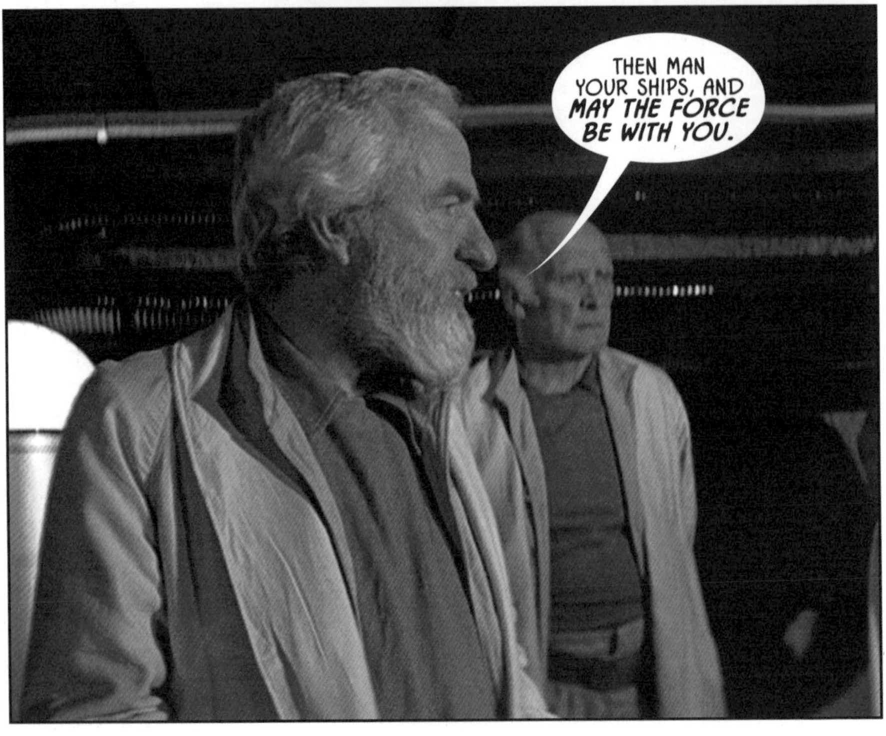
THEN MAN YOUR SHIPS, AND MAY THE FORCE BE WITH YOU.

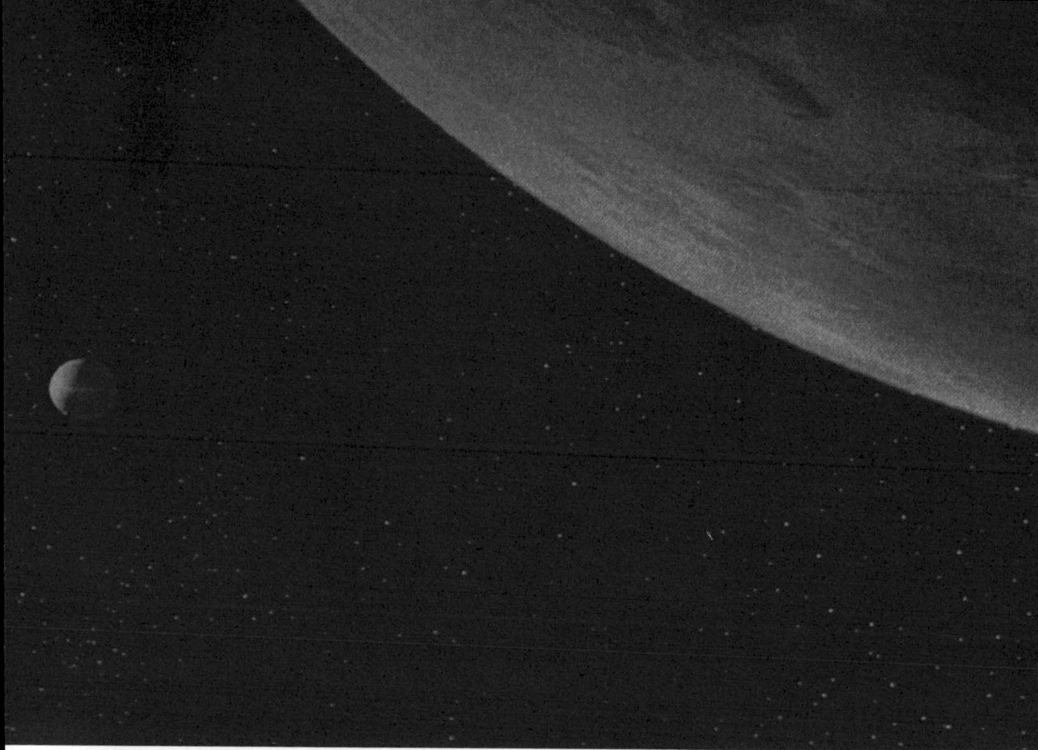

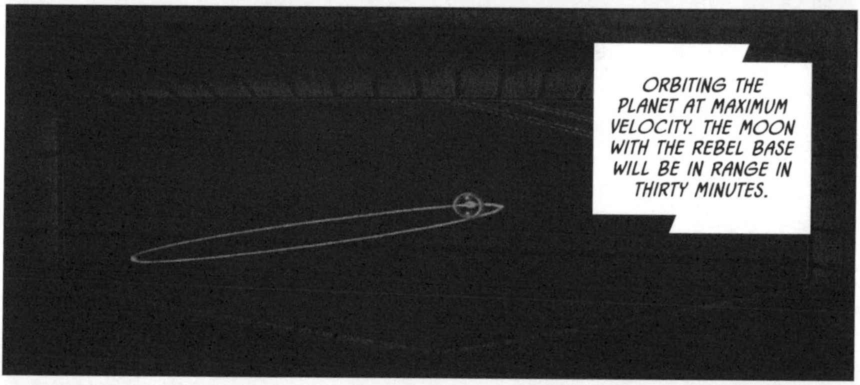
ORBITING THE PLANET AT MAXIMUM VELOCITY. THE MOON WITH THE REBEL BASE WILL BE IN RANGE IN THIRTY MINUTES.

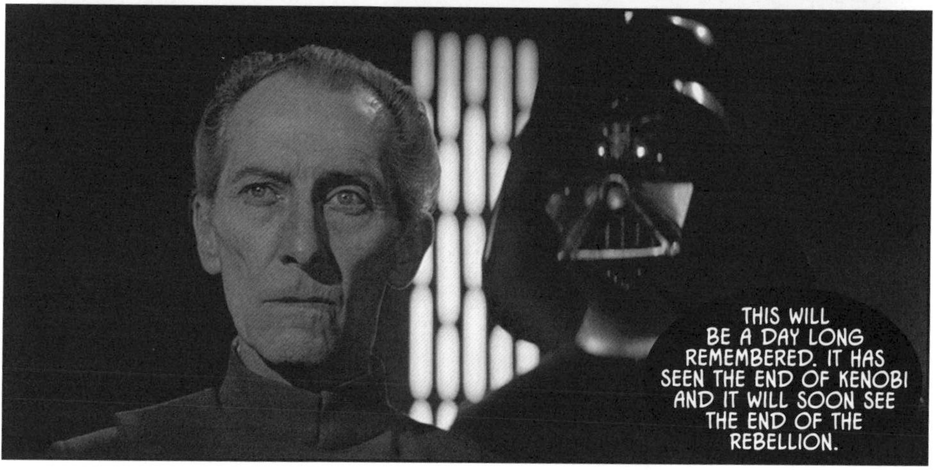
THIS WILL BE A DAY LONG REMEMBERED. IT HAS SEEN THE END OF KENOBI AND IT WILL SOON SEE THE END OF THE REBELLION.

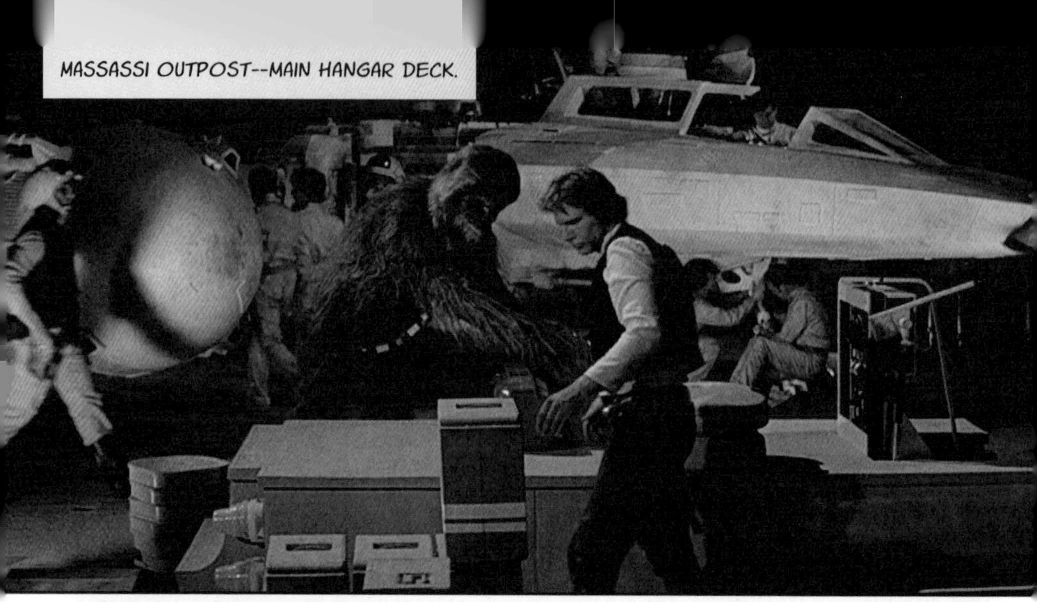
MASSASSI OUTPOST--MAIN HANGAR DECK.

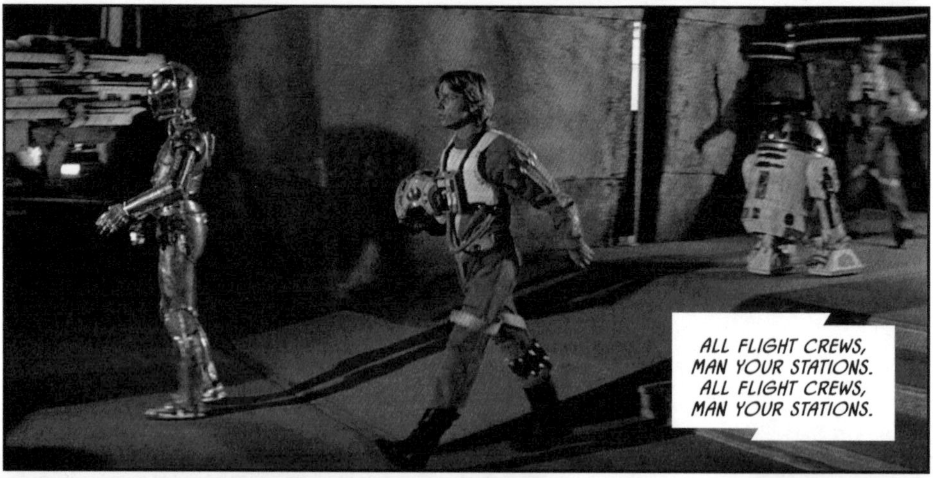
ALL FLIGHT CREWS, MAN YOUR STATIONS. ALL FLIGHT CREWS, MAN YOUR STATIONS.

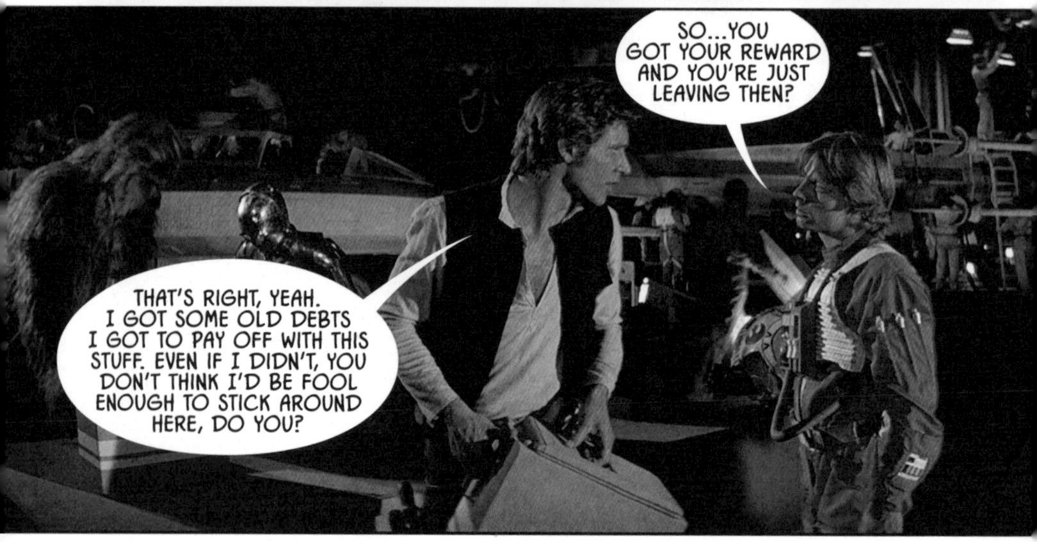
SO...YOU GOT YOUR REWARD AND YOU'RE JUST LEAVING THEN?
THAT'S RIGHT, YEAH. I GOT SOME OLD DEBTS I GOT TO PAY OFF WITH THIS STUFF. EVEN IF I DIDN'T, YOU DON'T THINK I'D BE FOOL ENOUGH TO STICK AROUND HERE, DO YOU?

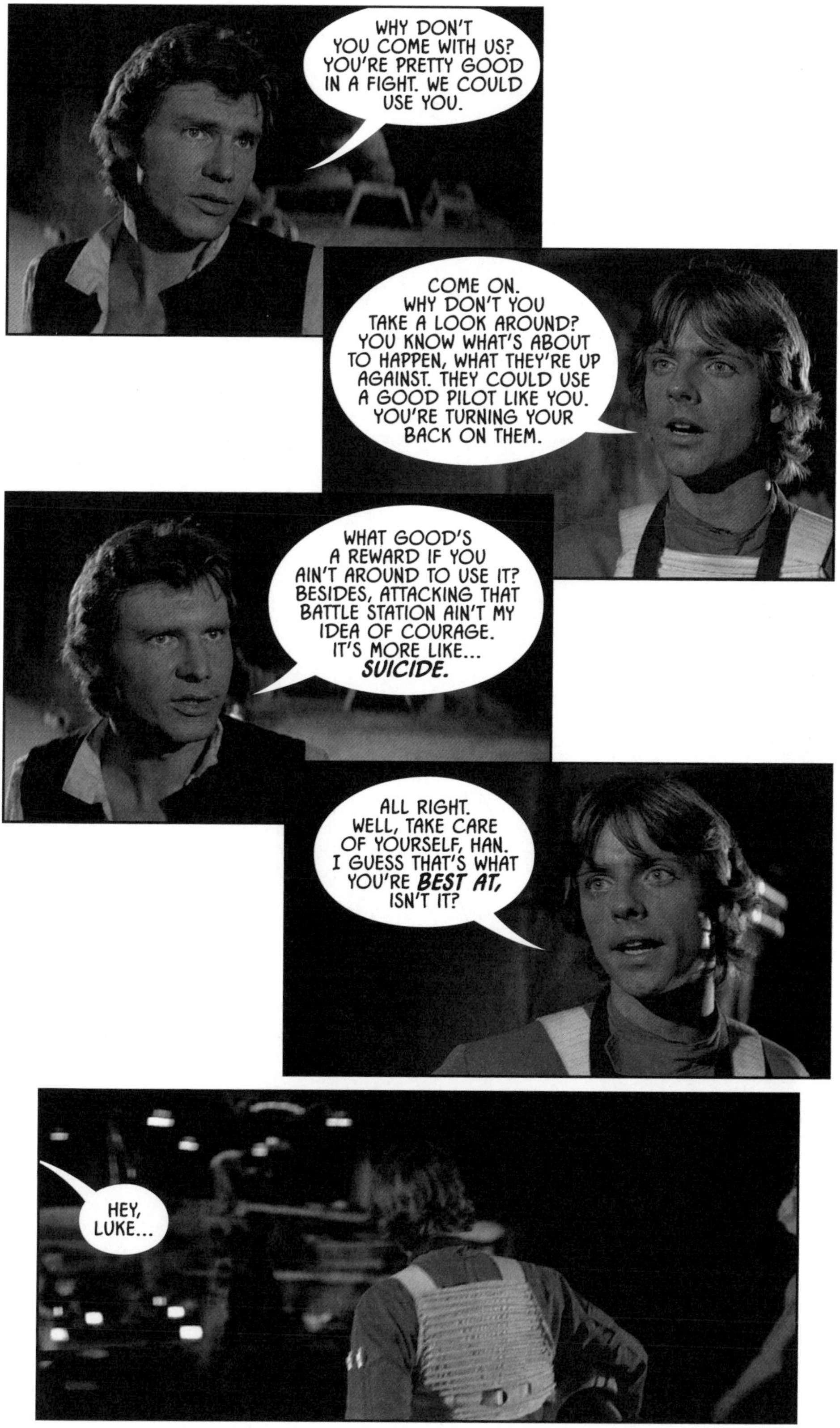
WHY DON'T YOU COME WITH US? YOU'RE PRETTY GOOD IN A FIGHT. WE COULD USE YOU.
COME ON. WHY DON'T YOU TAKE A LOOK AROUND? YOU KNOW WHAT'S ABOUT TO HAPPEN, WHAT THEY'RE UP AGAINST. THEY COULD USE A GOOD PILOT LIKE YOU. YOU'RE TURNING YOUR BACK ON THEM.
WHAT GOOD'S A REWARD IF YOU AIN'T AROUND TO USE IT? BESIDES, ATTACKING THAT BATTLE STATION AIN'T MY IDEA OF COURAGE. IT'S MORE LIKE... ***SUICIDE.***
ALL RIGHT. WELL, TAKE CARE OF YOURSELF, HAN. I GUESS THAT'S WHAT YOU'RE ***BEST AT,*** ISN'T IT?
HEY, LUKE...

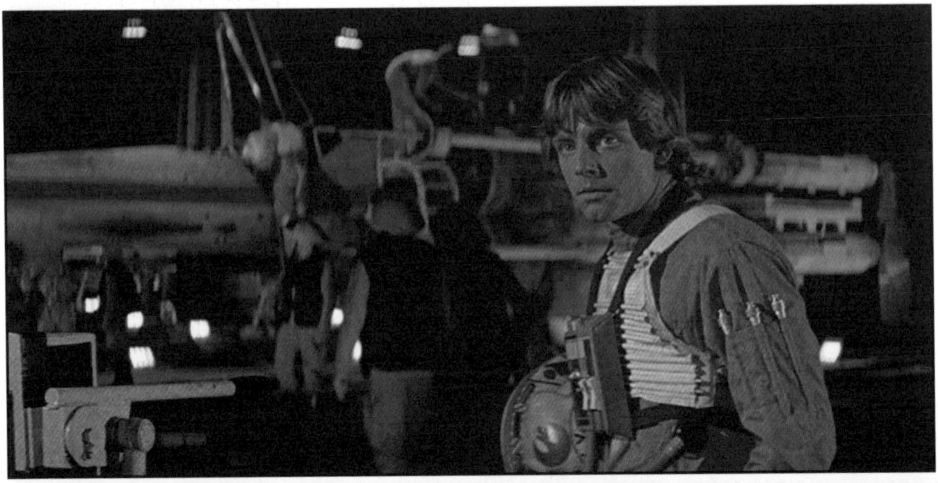

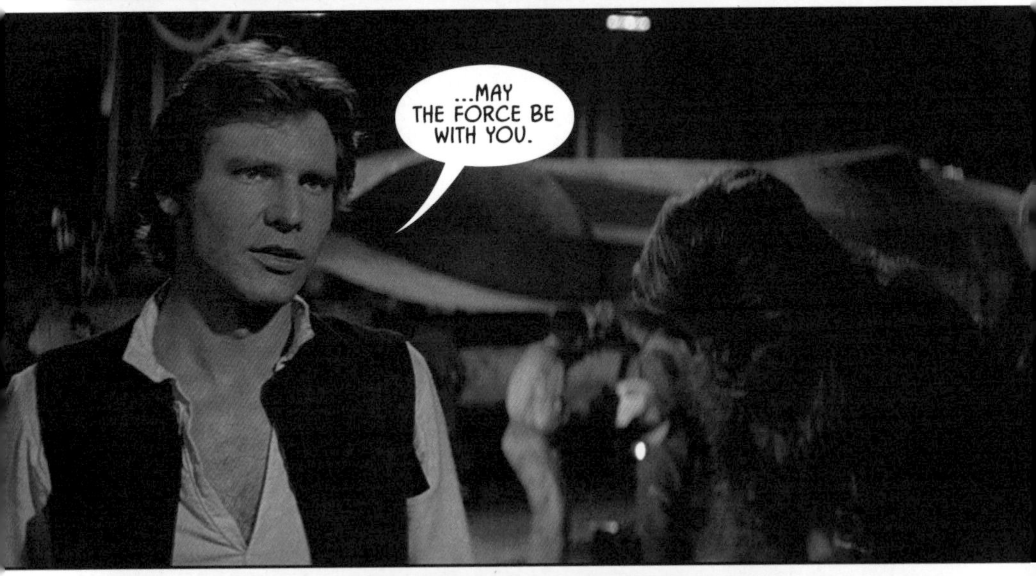
...MAY THE FORCE BE WITH YOU.

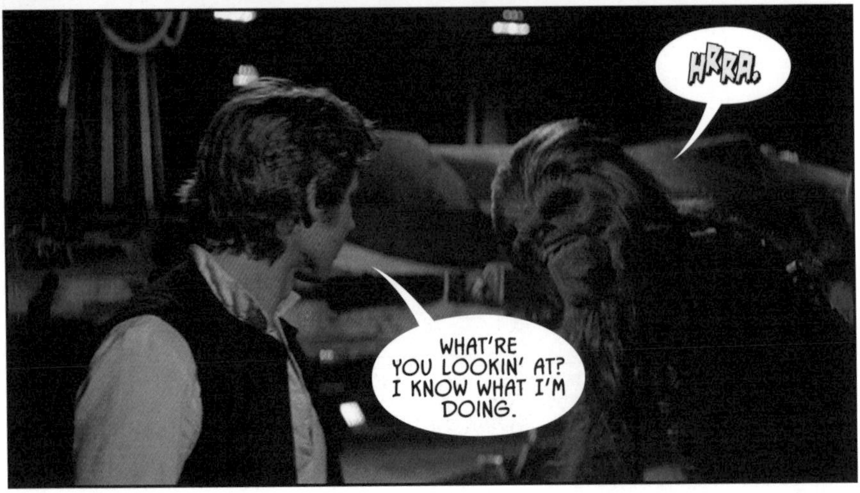
HRRA.
WHAT'RE YOU LOOKIN' AT? I KNOW WHAT I'M DOING.

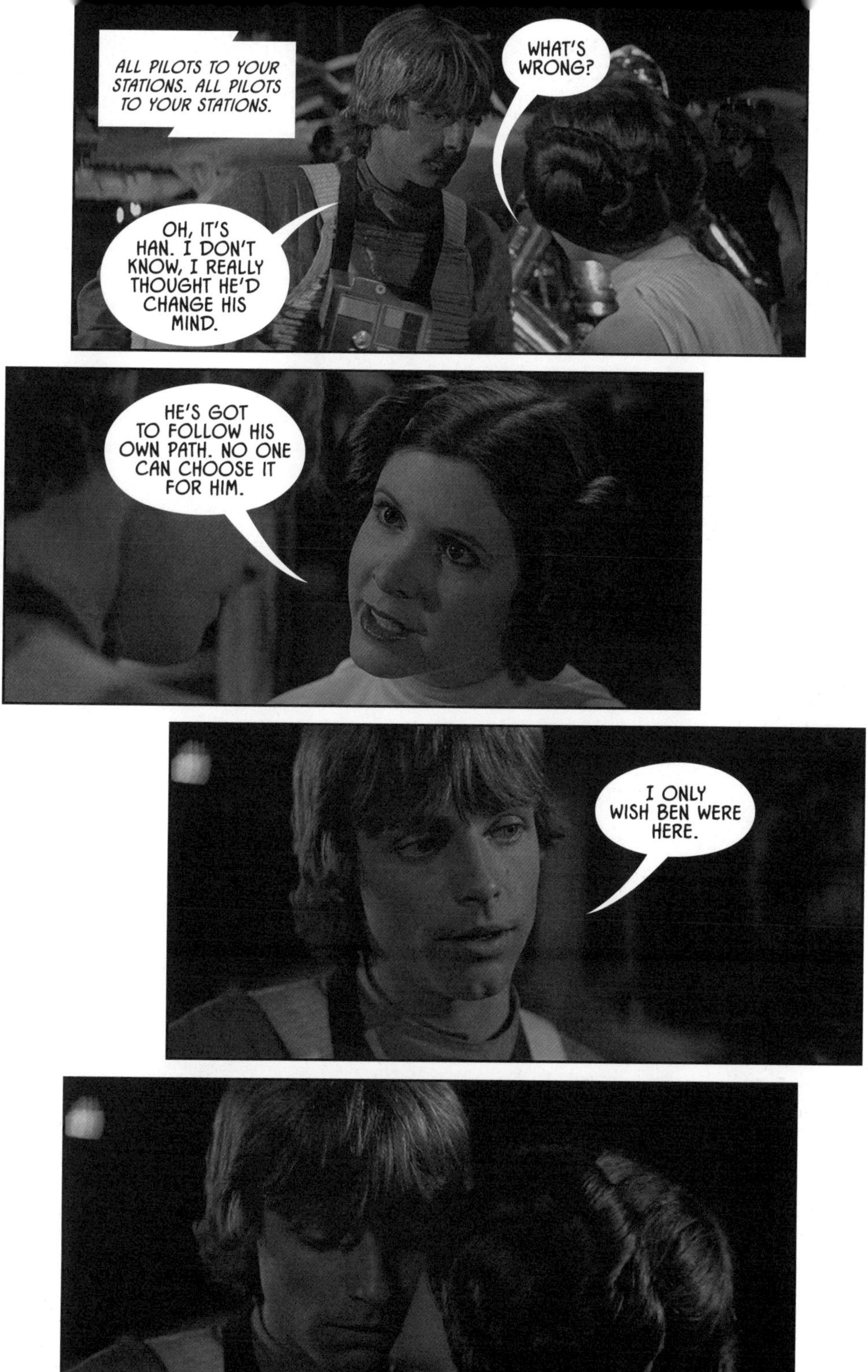
ALL PILOTS TO YOUR STATIONS. ALL PILOTS TO YOUR STATIONS.
WHAT'S WRONG?
OH, IT'S HAN. I DON'T KNOW, I REALLY THOUGHT HE'D CHANGE HIS MIND.
HE'S GOT TO FOLLOW HIS OWN PATH. NO ONE CAN CHOOSE IT FOR HIM.
I ONLY WISH BEN WERE HERE.

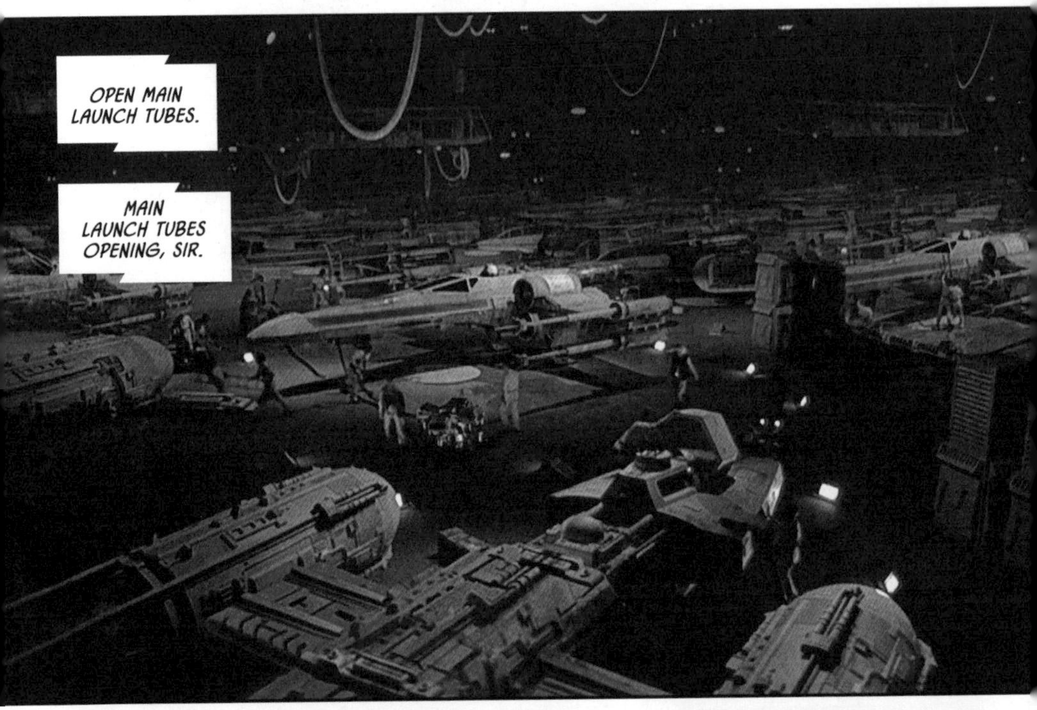
OPEN MAIN LAUNCH TUBES.
MAIN LAUNCH TUBES OPENING, SIR.

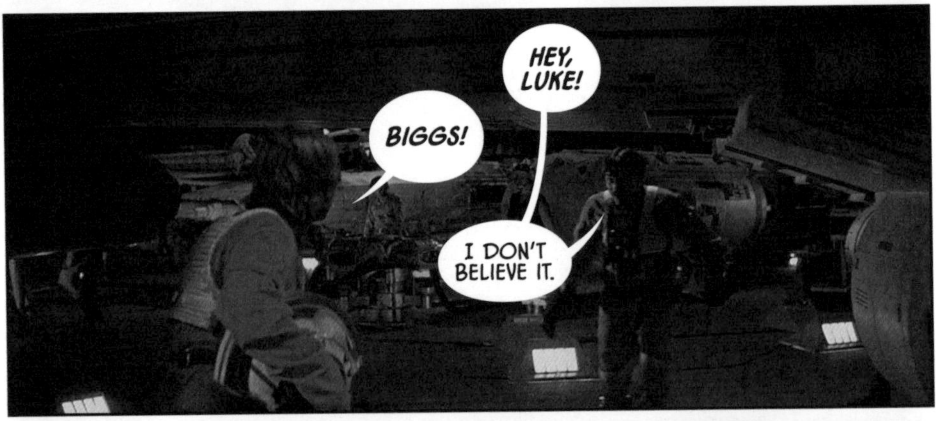
BIGGS!
HEY, LUKE!
I DON'T BELIEVE IT.

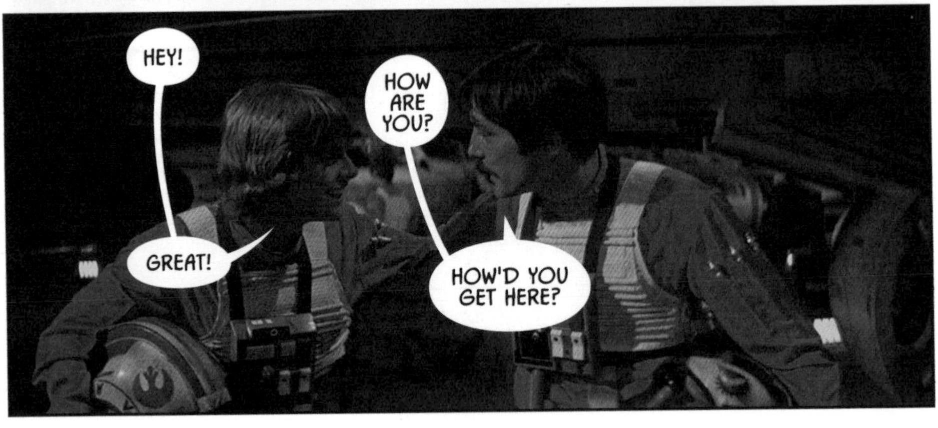
HEY!
HOW ARE YOU?
GREAT!
HOW'D YOU GET HERE?

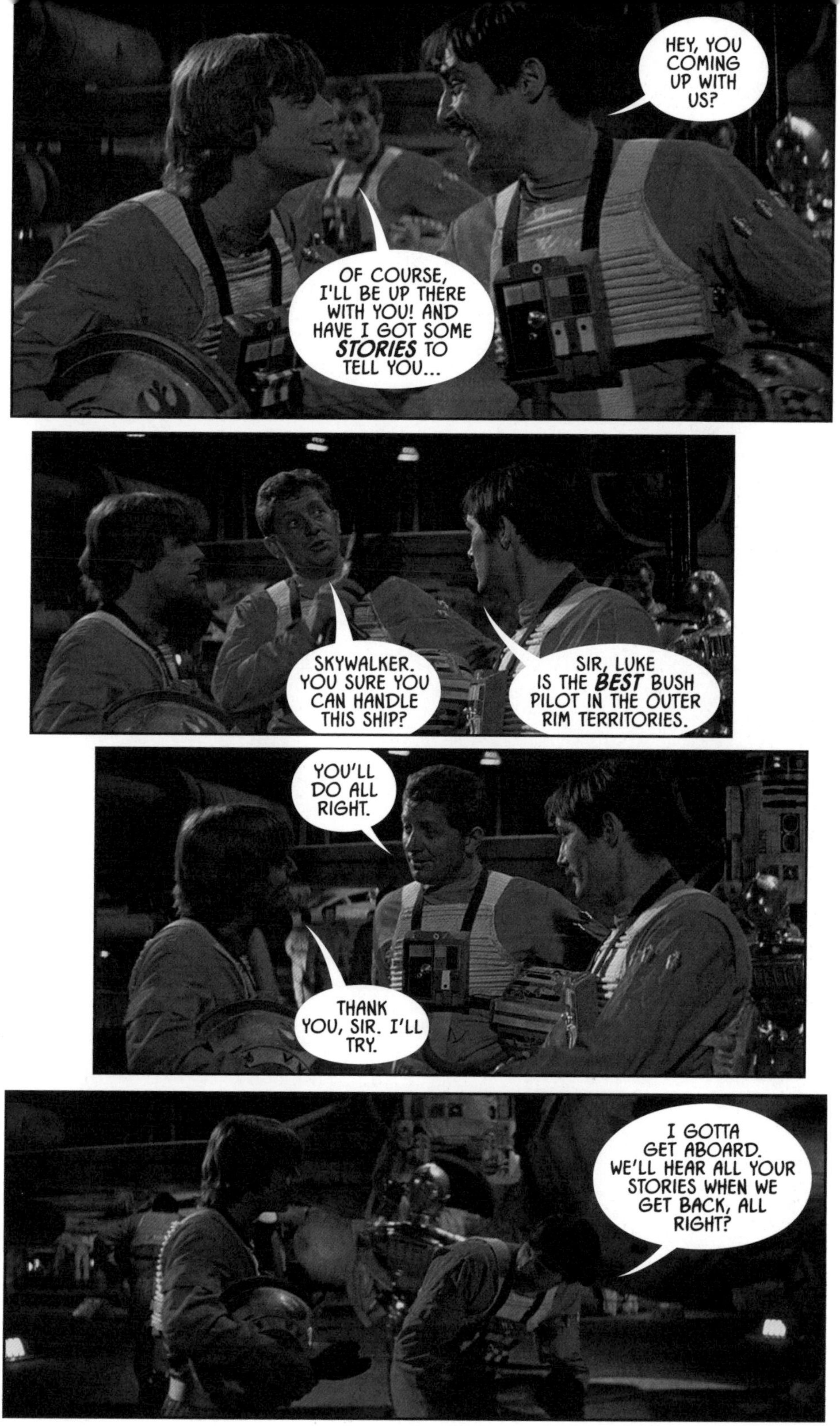
HEY, YOU COMING UP WITH US?
OF COURSE, I'LL BE UP THERE WITH YOU! AND HAVE I GOT SOME STORIES TO TELL YOU...
SKYWALKER. YOU SURE YOU CAN HANDLE THIS SHIP?
SIR, LUKE IS THE BEST BUSH PILOT IN THE OUTER RIM TERRITORIES.
YOU'LL DO ALL RIGHT.
THANK YOU, SIR. I'LL TRY.
I GOTTA GET ABOARD. WE'LL HEAR ALL YOUR STORIES WHEN WE GET BACK, ALL RIGHT?

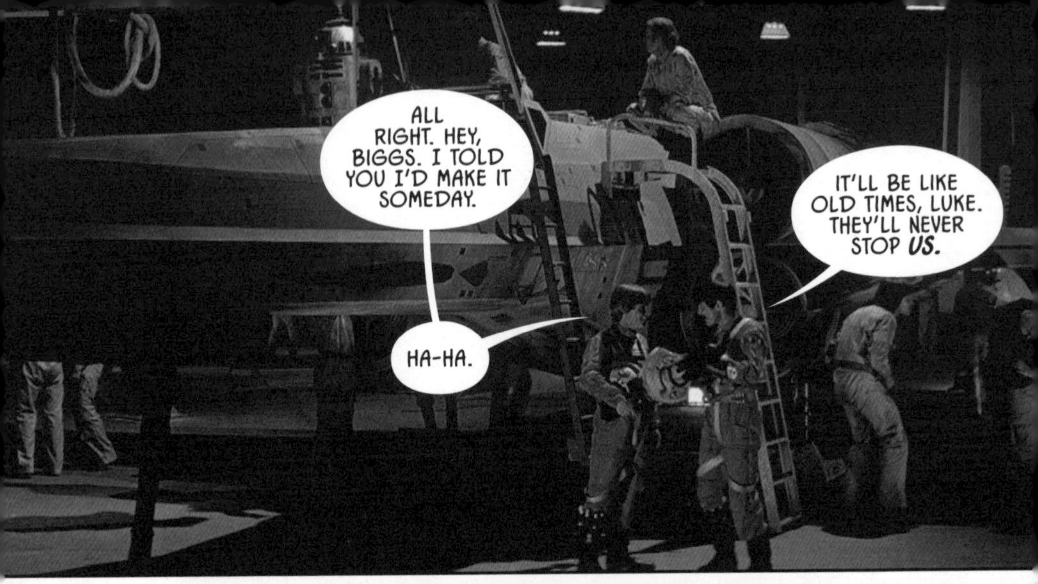
ALL RIGHT. HEY, BIGGS. I TOLD YOU I'D MAKE IT SOMEDAY.
HA-HA.
IT'LL BE LIKE OLD TIMES, LUKE. THEY'LL NEVER STOP *US.*

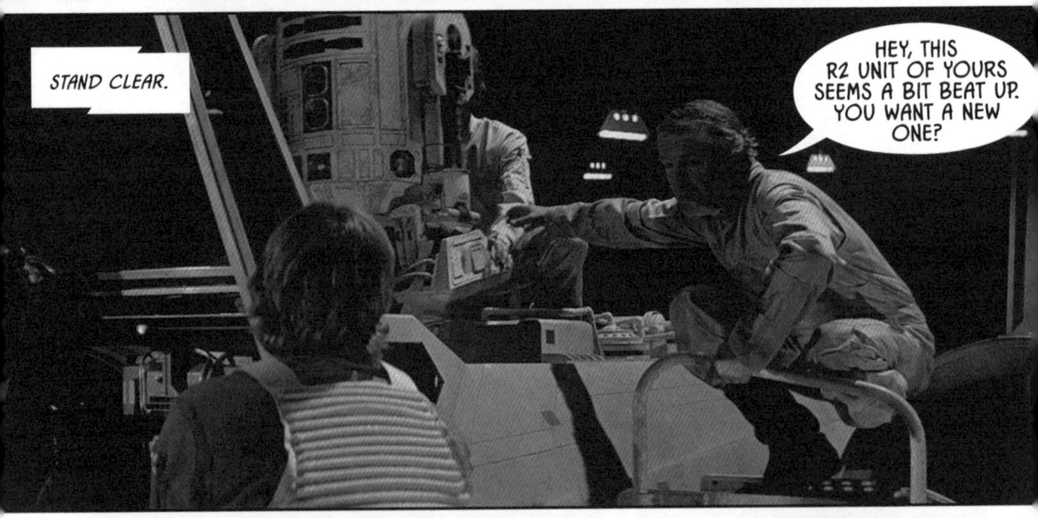
STAND CLEAR.
HEY, THIS R2 UNIT OF YOURS SEEMS A BIT BEAT UP. YOU WANT A NEW ONE?

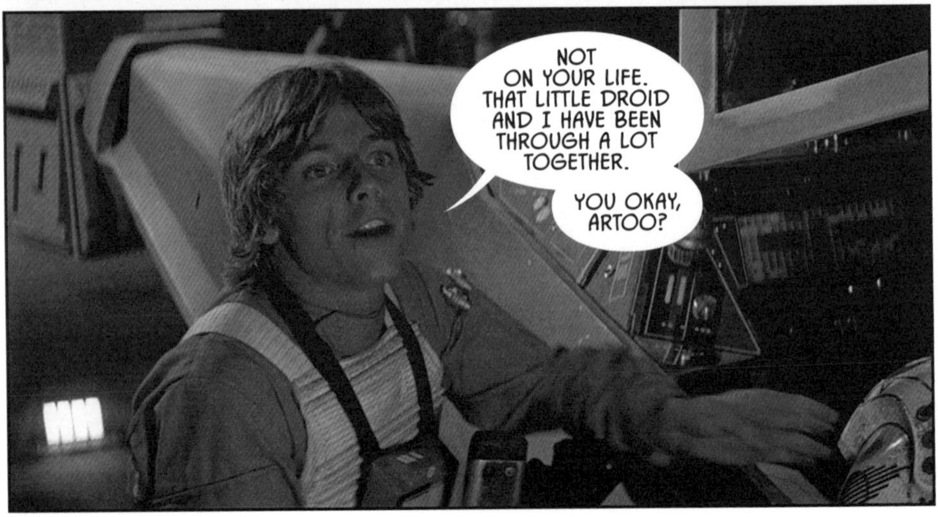
NOT ON YOUR LIFE. THAT LITTLE DROID AND I HAVE BEEN THROUGH A LOT TOGETHER.
YOU OKAY, ARTOO?

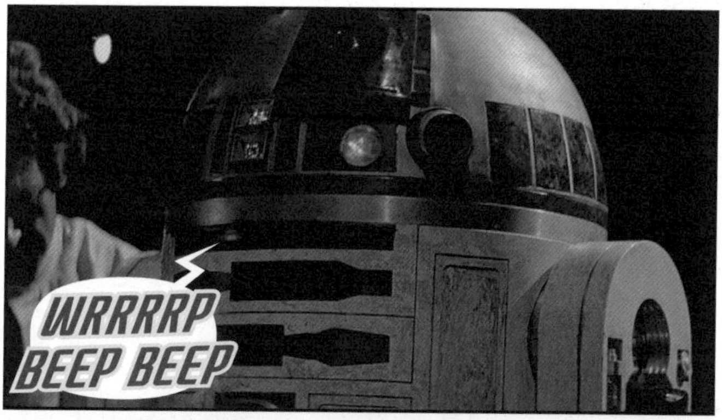
WRRRRP
BEEP BEEP

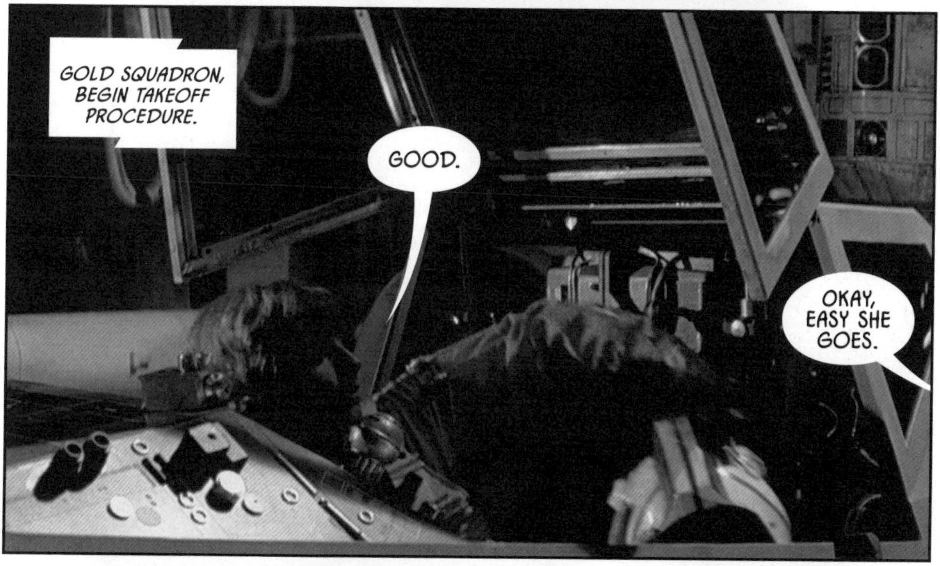
GOLD SQUADRON, BEGIN TAKEOFF PROCEDURE.
GOOD.
OKAY, EASY SHE GOES.

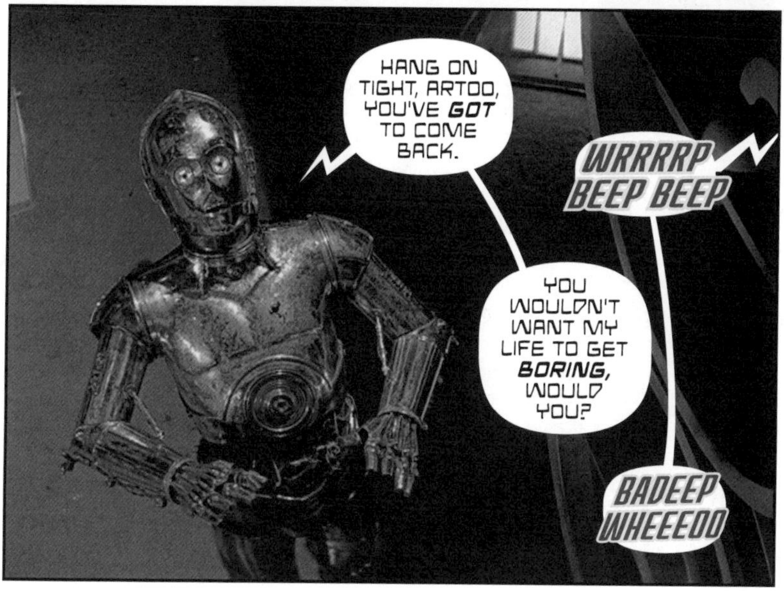
HANG ON TIGHT, ARTOO, YOU'VE GOT TO COME BACK.
WRRRRP BEEP BEEP
YOU WOULDN'T WANT MY LIFE TO GET BORING, WOULD YOU?
BADEEP WHEEEOO

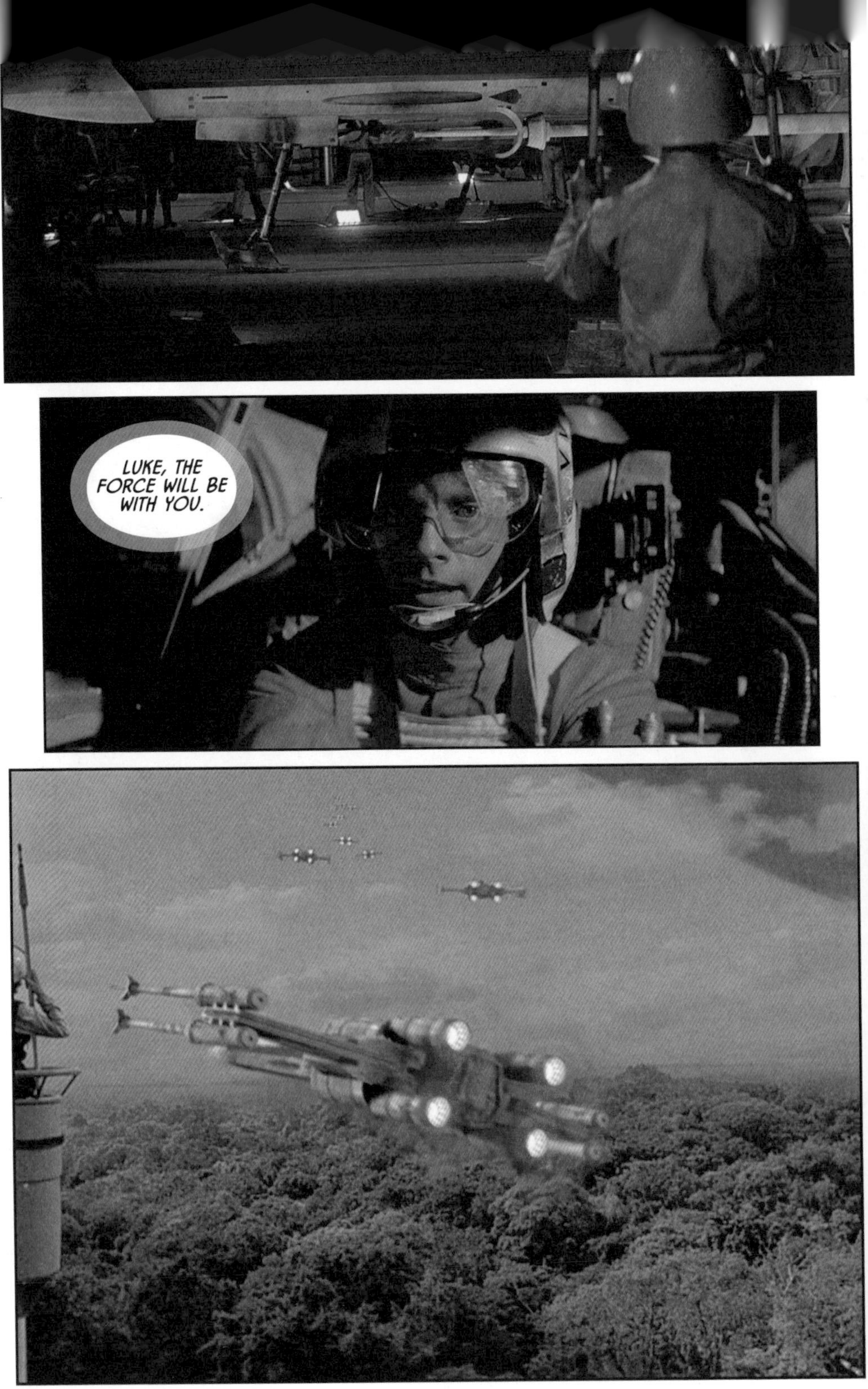
LUKE, THE FORCE WILL BE WITH YOU.

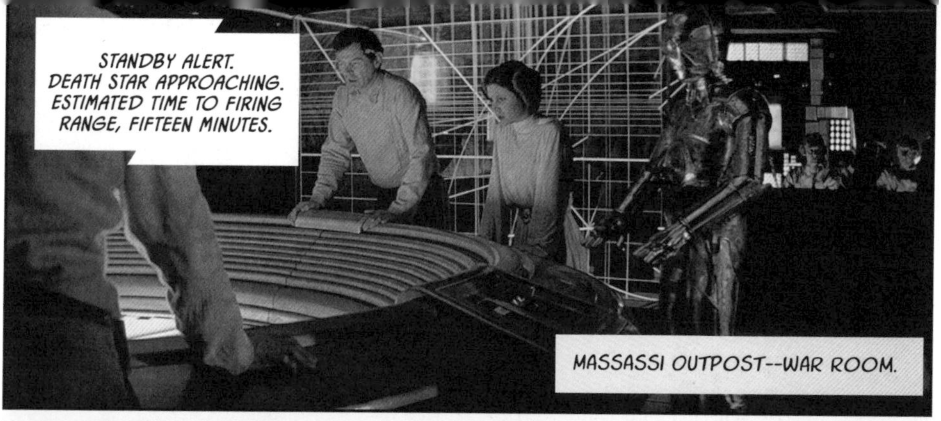
STANDBY ALERT. DEATH STAR APPROACHING. ESTIMATED TIME TO FIRING RANGE, FIFTEEN MINUTES.
MASSASSI OUTPOST--WAR ROOM.

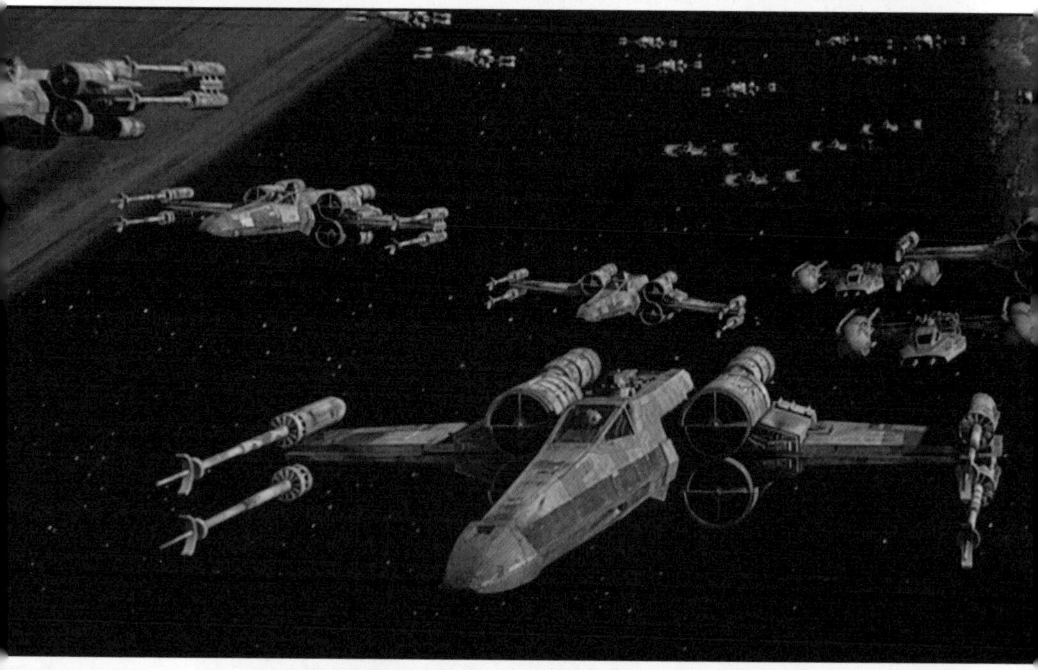

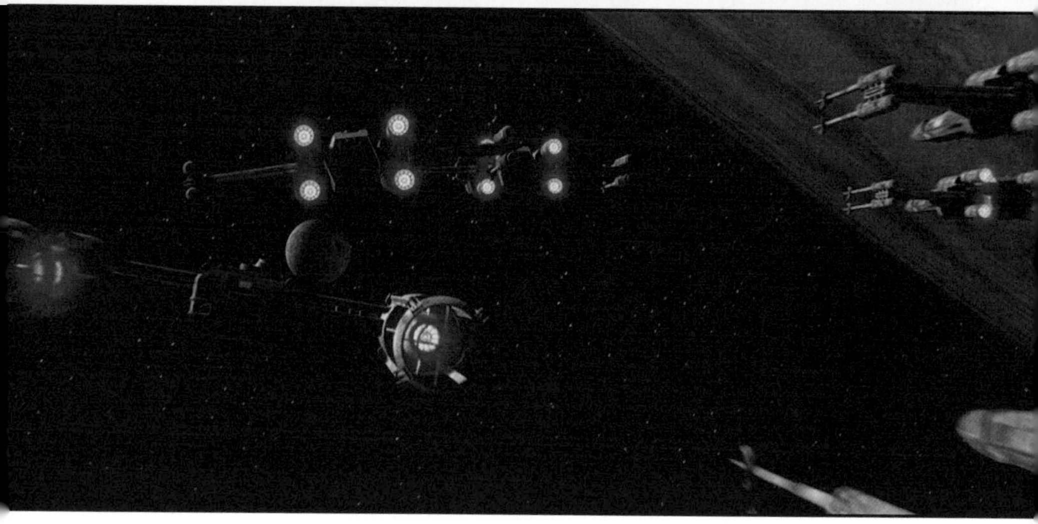

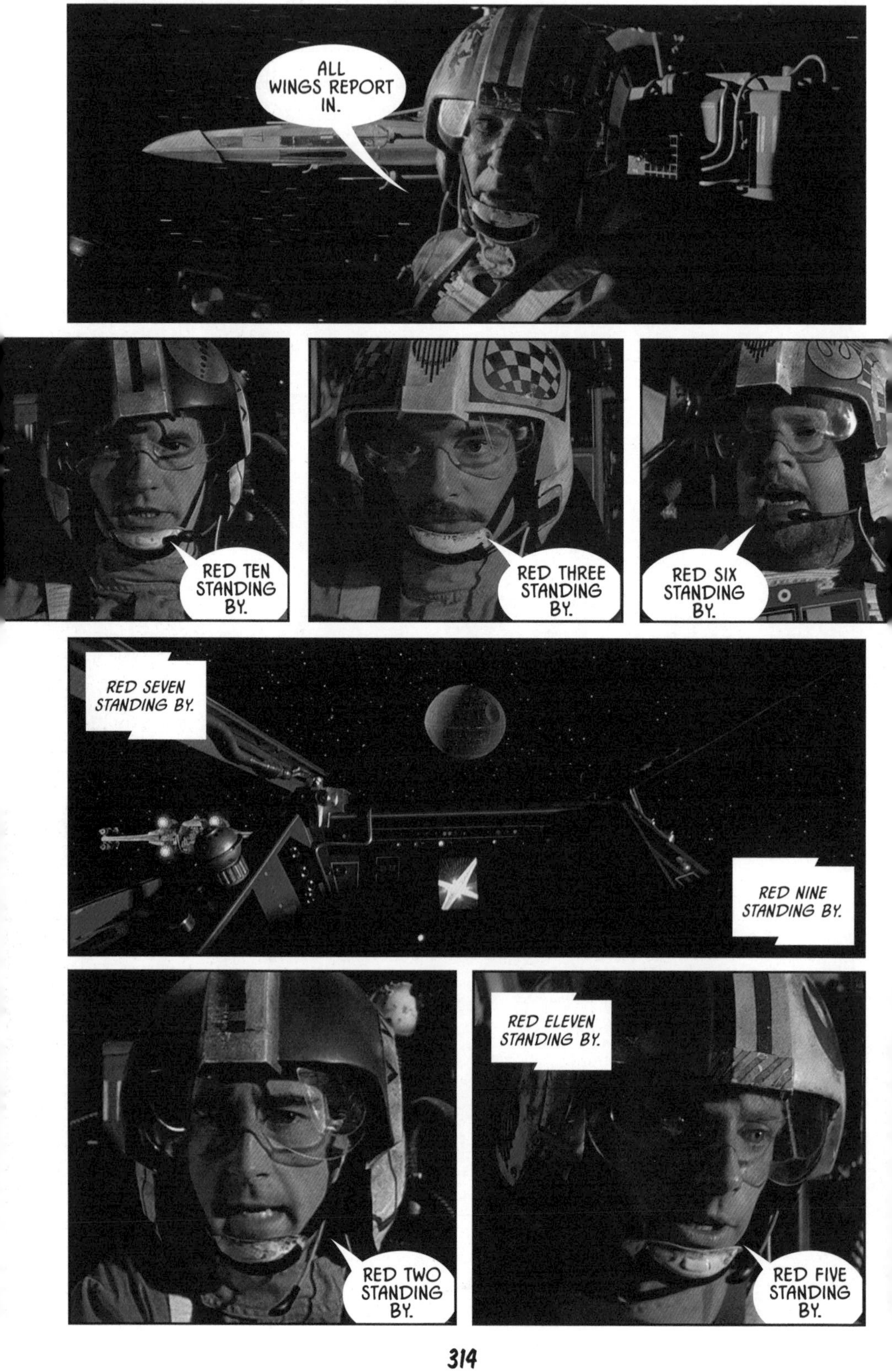
ALL WINGS REPORT IN.
RED TEN STANDING BY.
RED THREE STANDING BY.
RED SIX STANDING BY.
RED SEVEN STANDING BY.
RED NINE STANDING BY.
RED TWO STANDING BY.
RED ELEVEN STANDING BY.
RED FIVE STANDING BY.

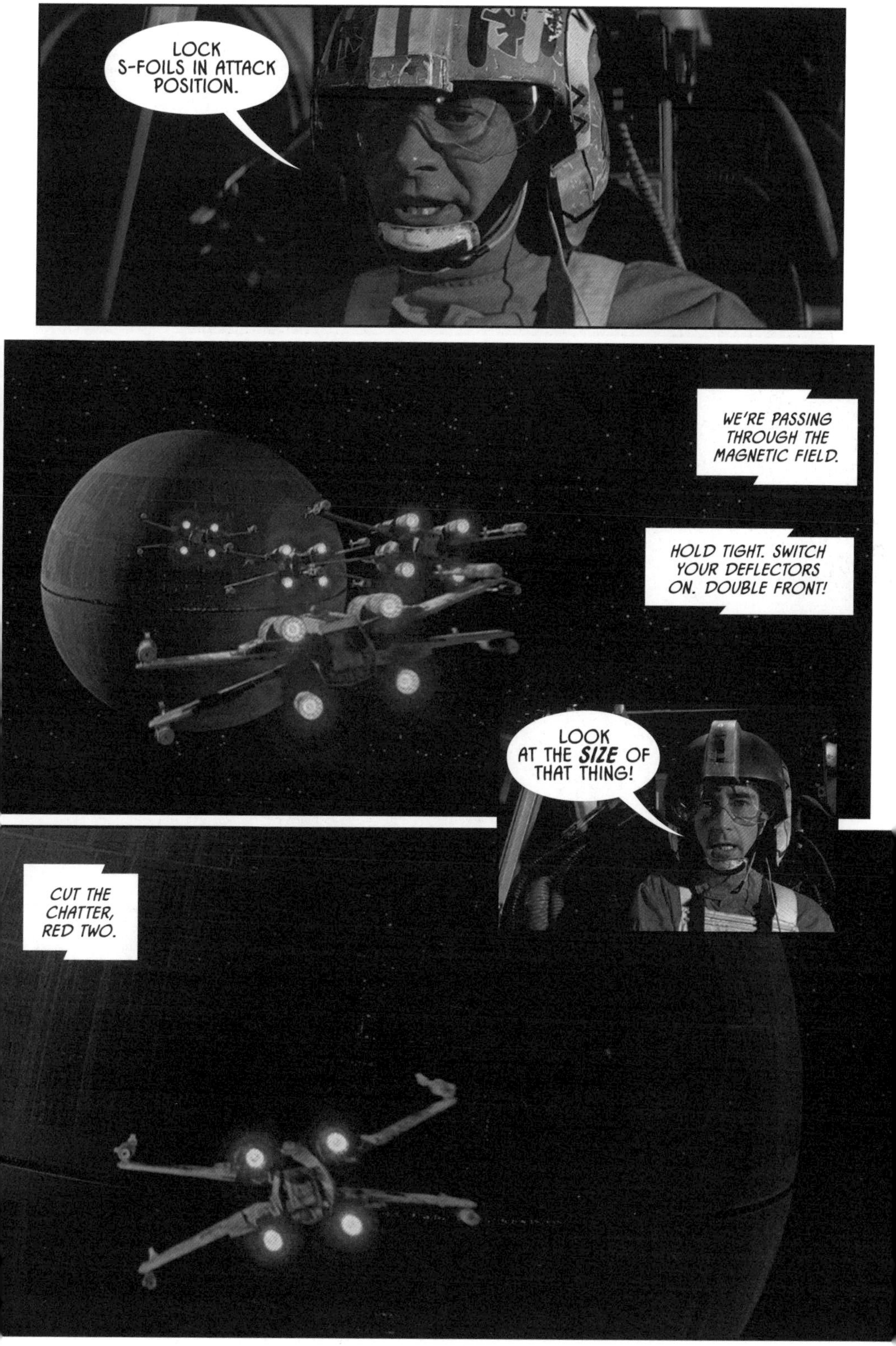
LOCK S-FOILS IN ATTACK POSITION.
WE'RE PASSING THROUGH THE MAGNETIC FIELD.
HOLD TIGHT. SWITCH YOUR DEFLECTORS ON. DOUBLE FRONT!
LOOK AT THE SIZE OF THAT THING!
CUT THE CHATTER, RED TWO.

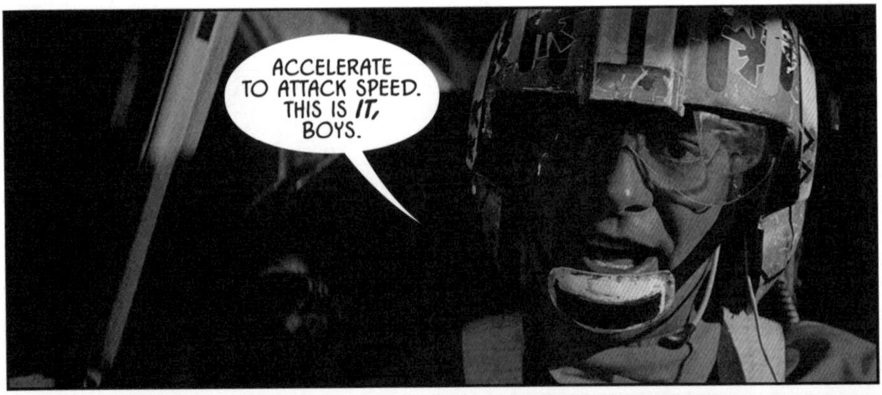
ACCELERATE TO ATTACK SPEED. THIS IS *IT,* BOYS.

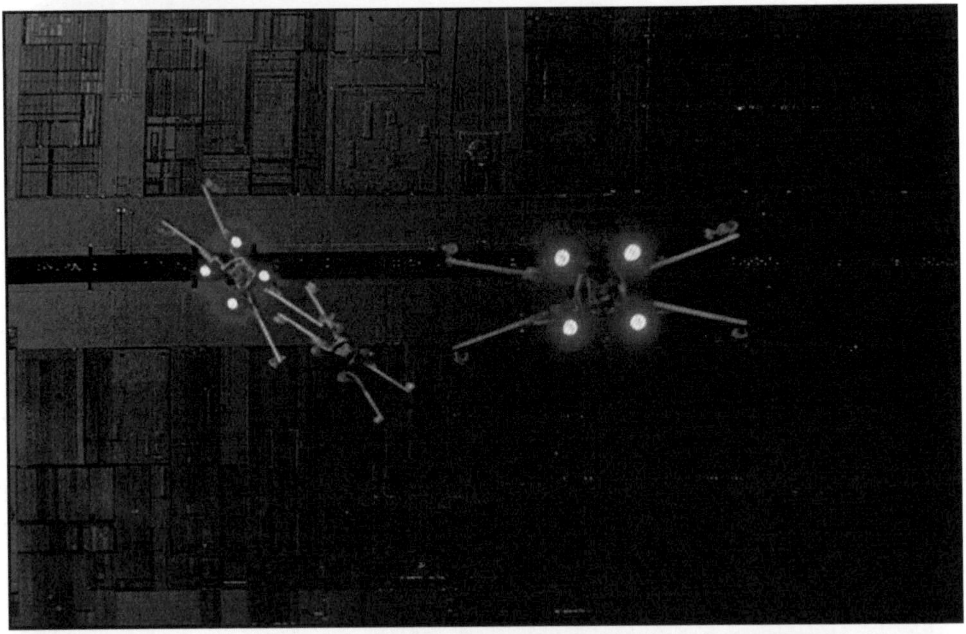

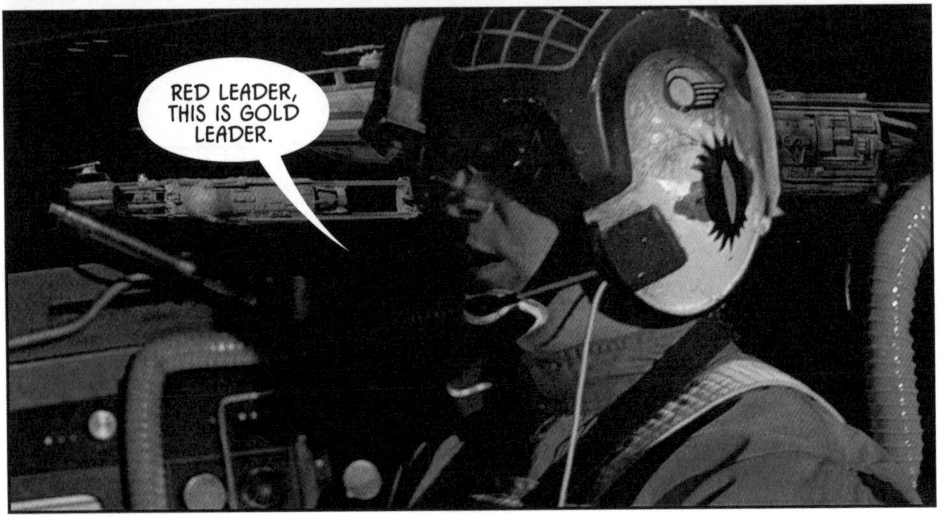
RED LEADER, THIS IS GOLD LEADER.

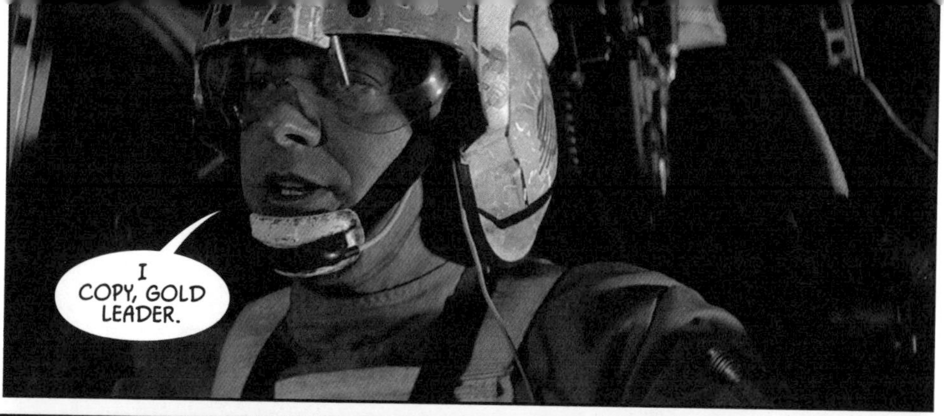
I COPY, GOLD LEADER.

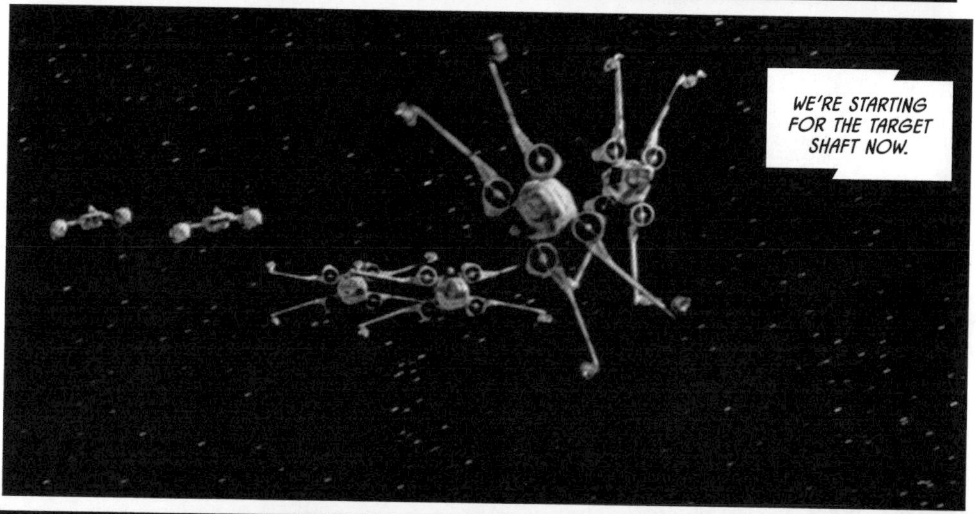
WE'RE STARTING FOR THE TARGET SHAFT NOW.

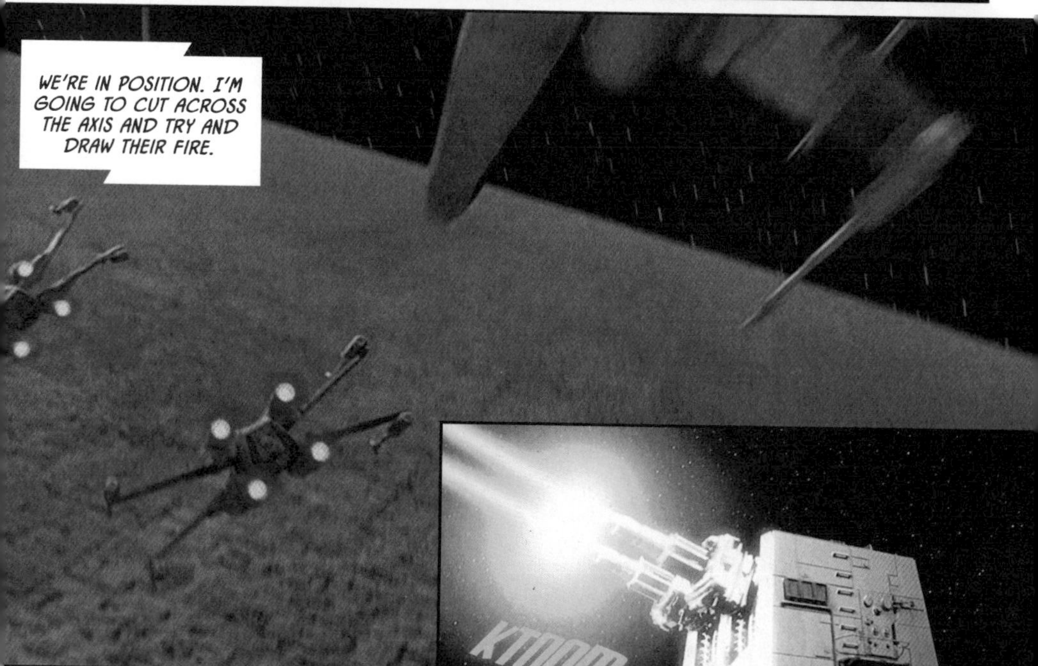
WE'RE IN POSITION. I'M GOING TO CUT ACROSS THE AXIS AND TRY AND DRAW THEIR FIRE.

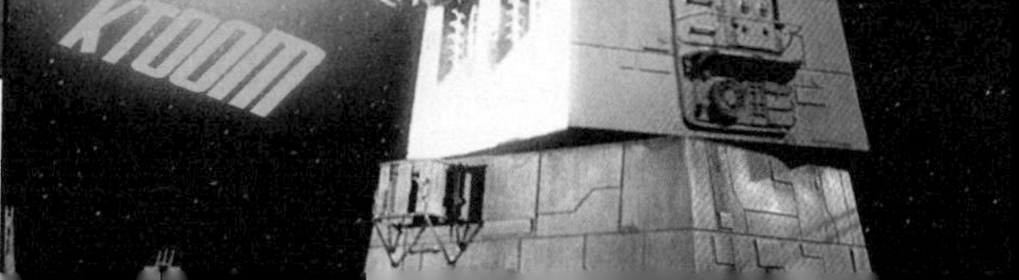
KTOOM

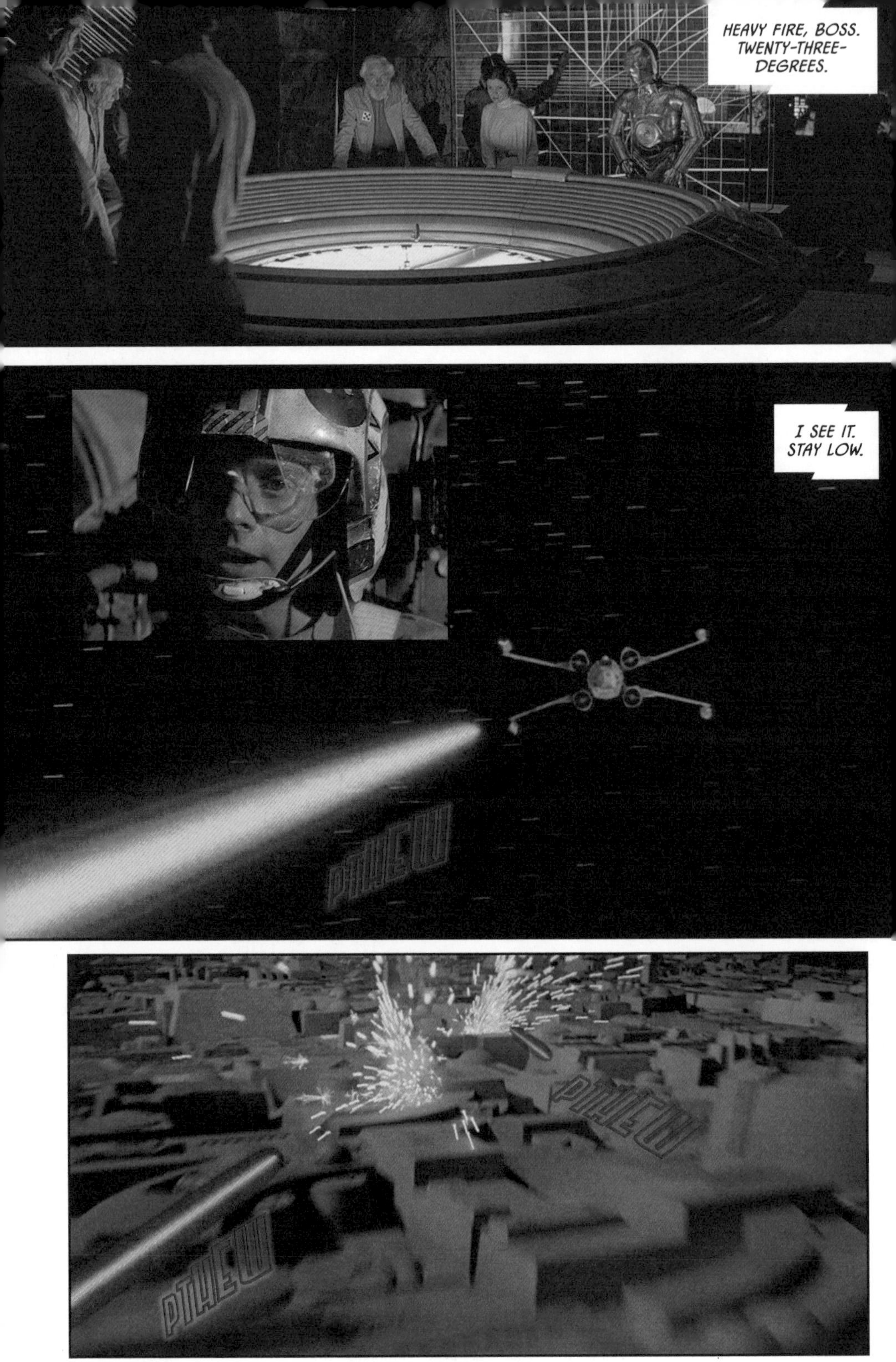
HEAVY FIRE, BOSS. TWENTY-THREE-DEGREES.
I SEE IT. STAY LOW.
PTHEW
PTHEW

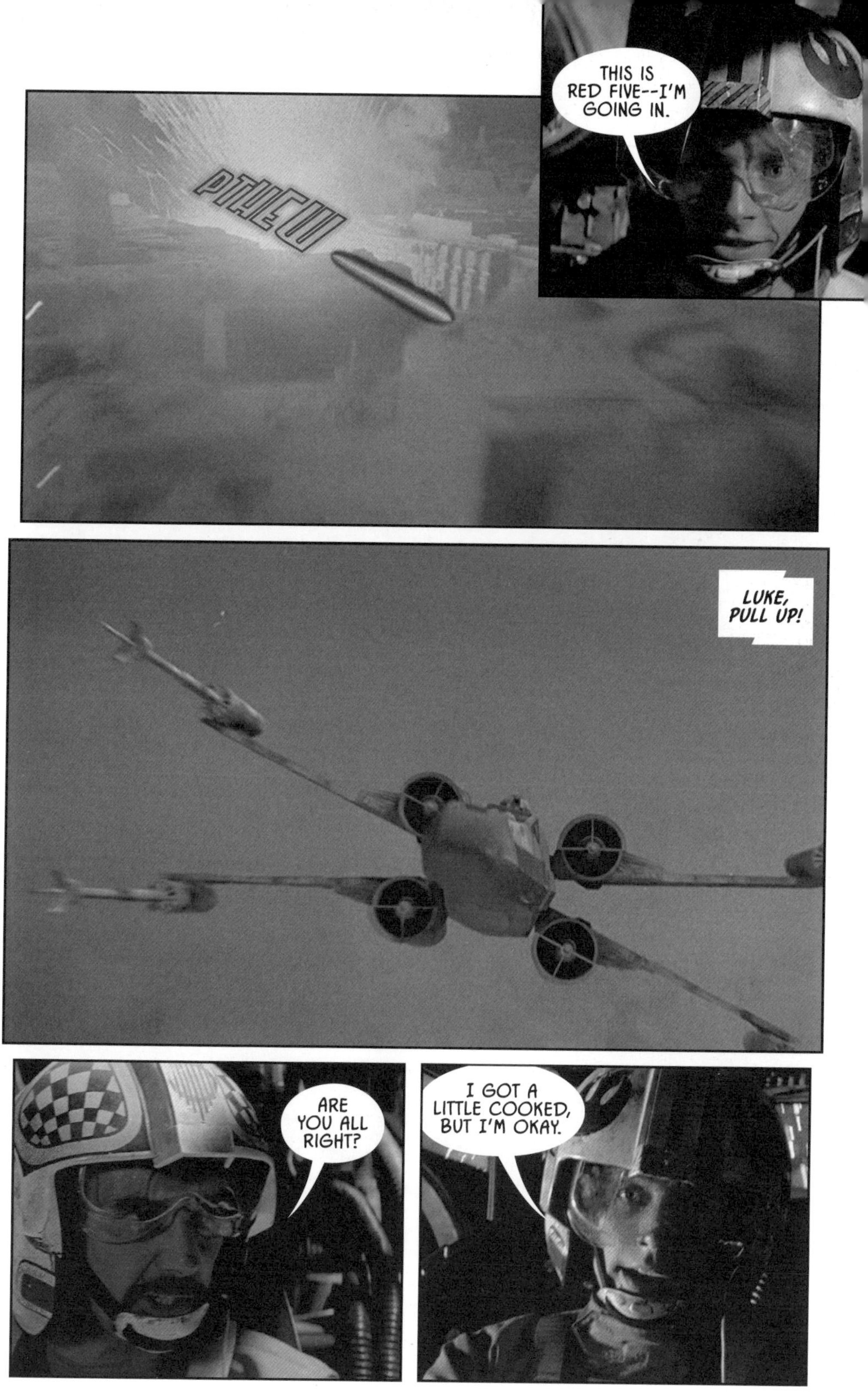
THIS IS RED FIVE--I'M GOING IN.
LUKE, PULL UP!
ARE YOU ALL RIGHT?
I GOT A LITTLE COOKED, BUT I'M OKAY.

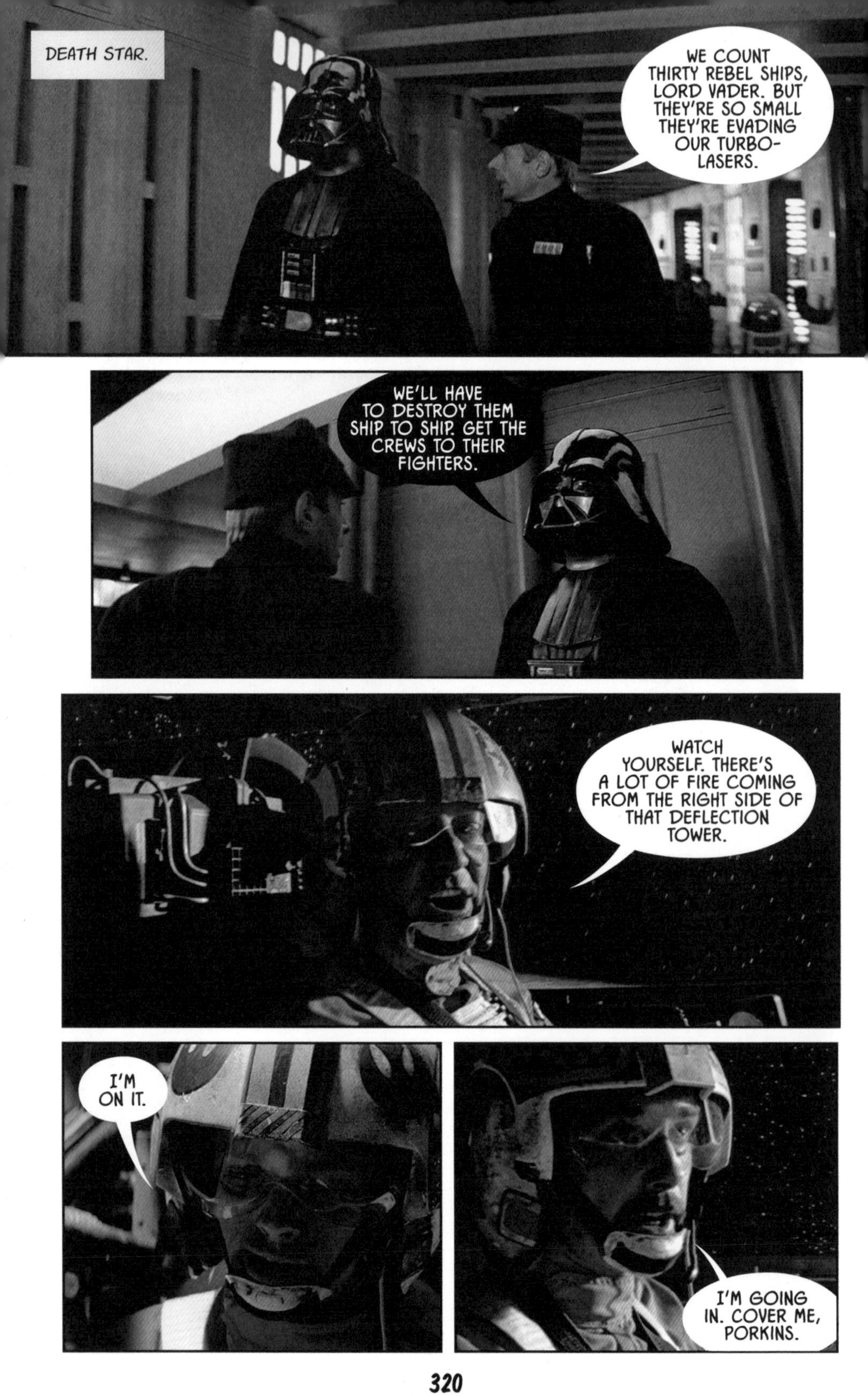
DEATH STAR.
WE COUNT THIRTY REBEL SHIPS, LORD VADER. BUT THEY'RE SO SMALL THEY'RE EVADING OUR TURBO-LASERS.
WE'LL HAVE TO DESTROY THEM SHIP TO SHIP. GET THE CREWS TO THEIR FIGHTERS.
WATCH YOURSELF. THERE'S A LOT OF FIRE COMING FROM THE RIGHT SIDE OF THAT DEFLECTION TOWER.
I'M ON IT.
I'M GOING IN. COVER ME, PORKINS.

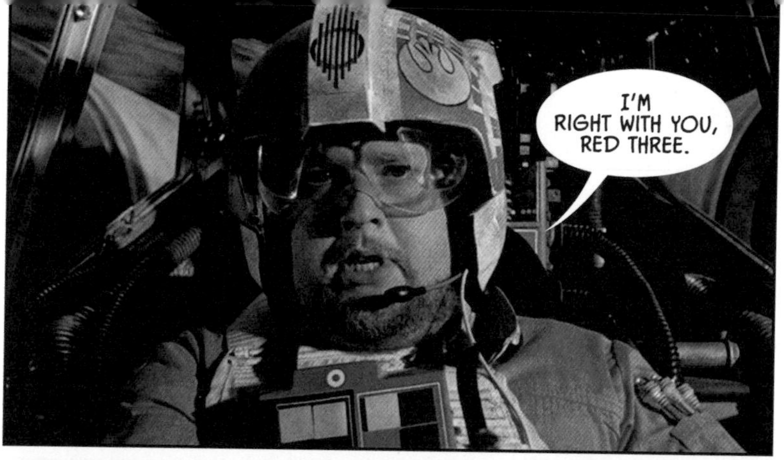
I'M RIGHT WITH YOU, RED THREE.

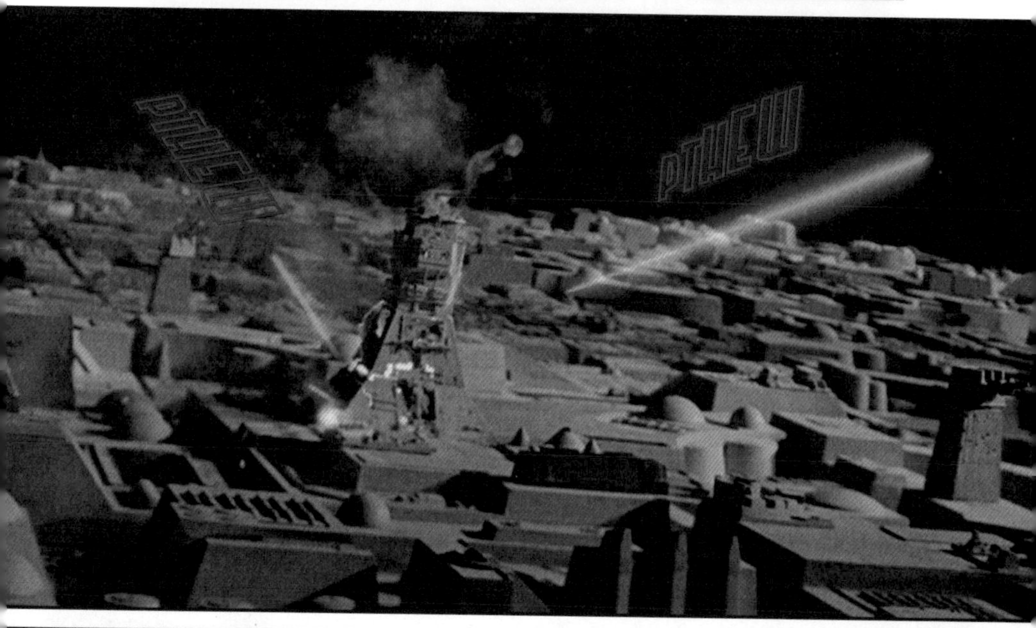
PTCHEW
PTCHEW

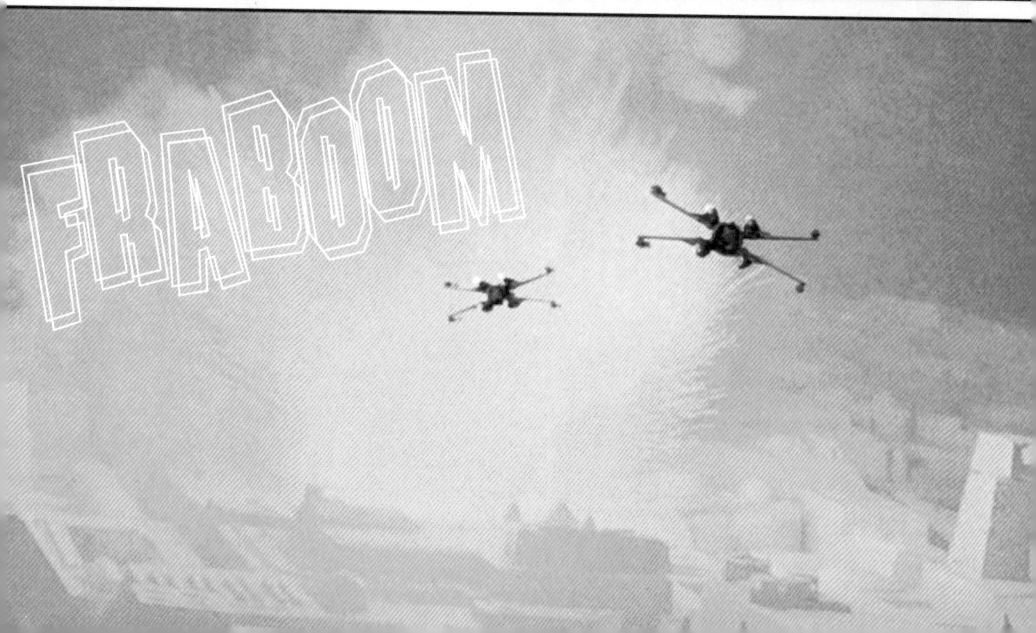
FRABOOM

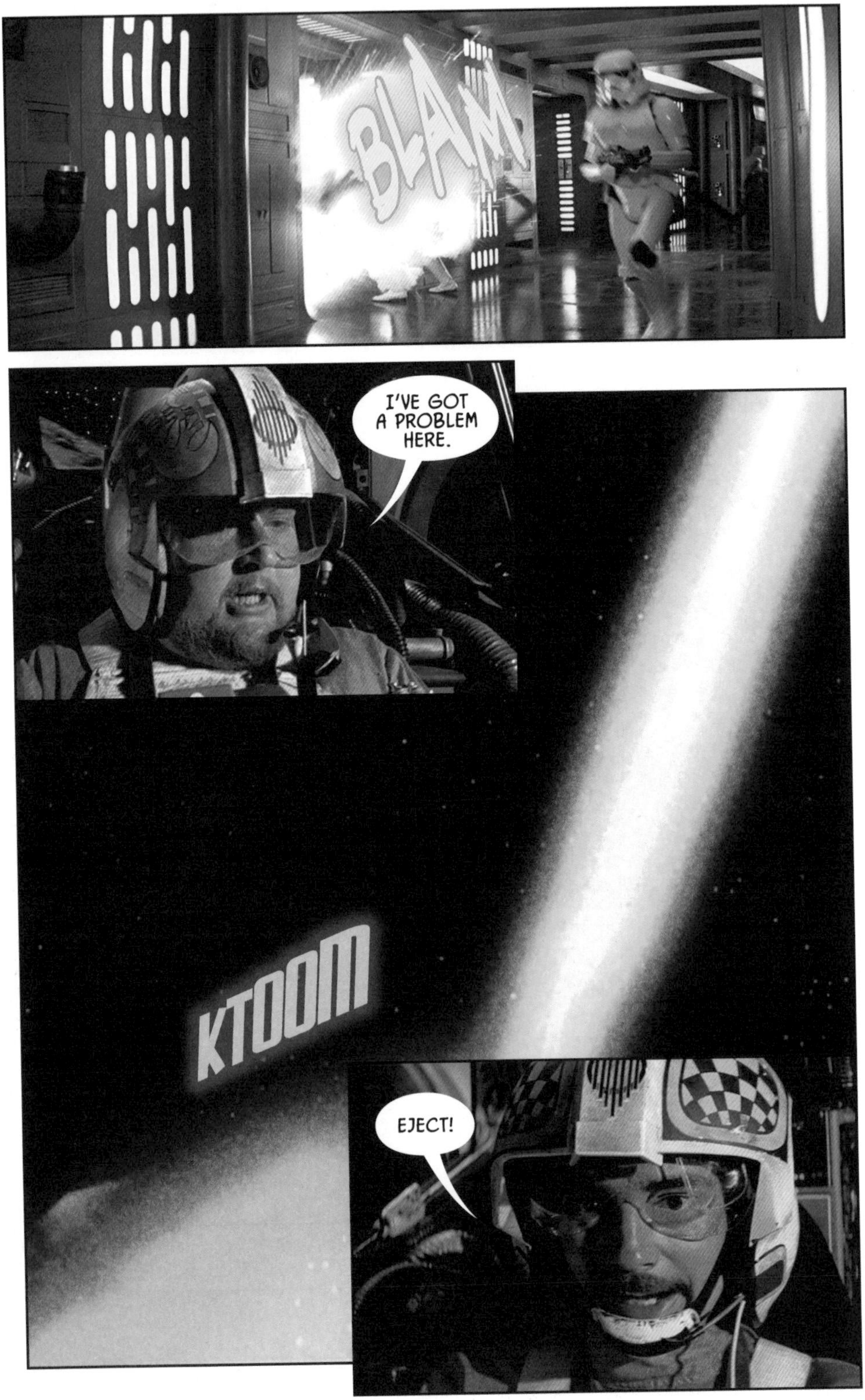
BLAM
I'VE GOT A PROBLEM HERE.
KTOOM
EJECT!

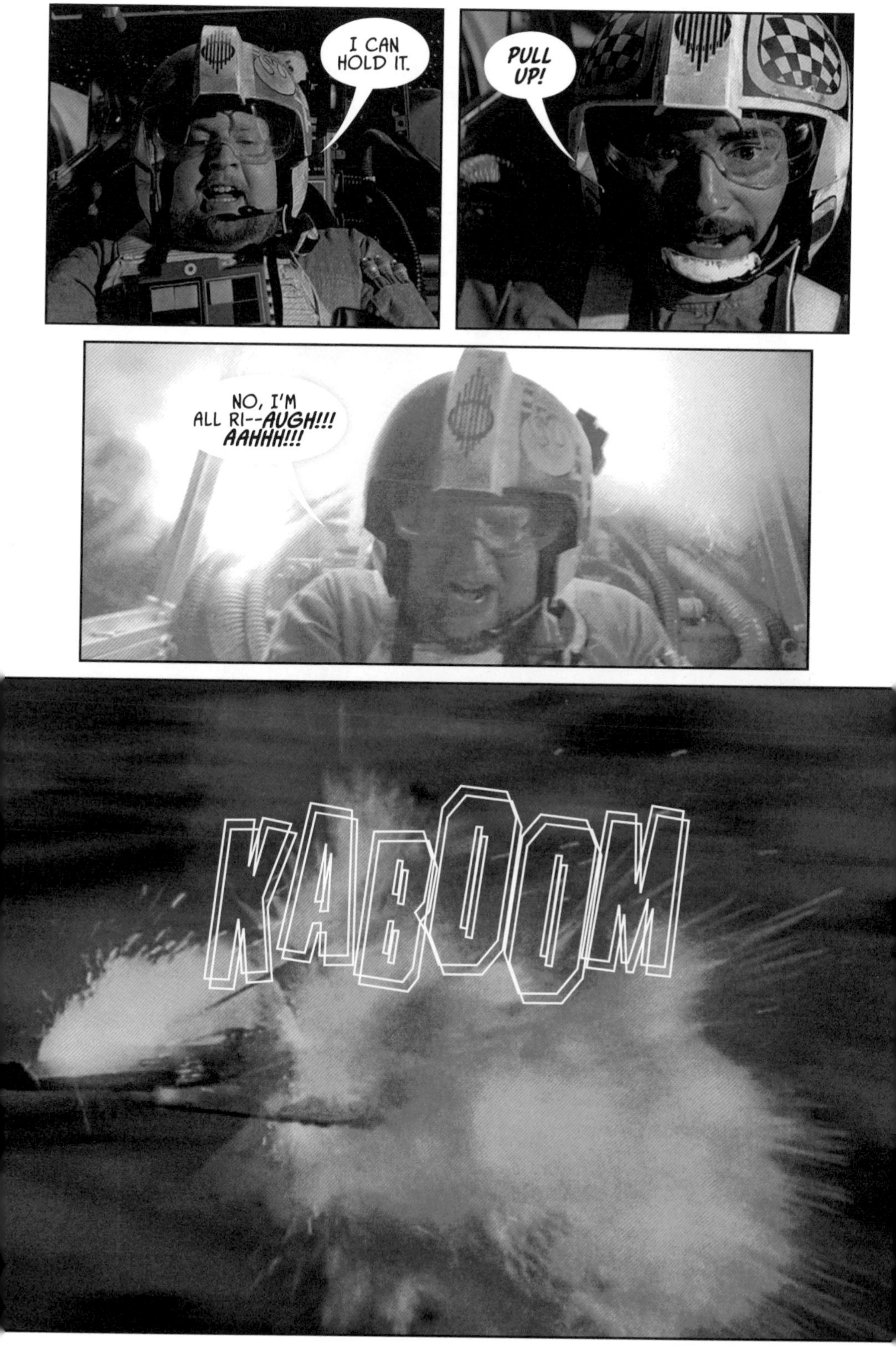
I CAN HOLD IT.
PULL UP!
NO, I'M ALL RI--AUGH!!! AAHHH!!!
KABOOM

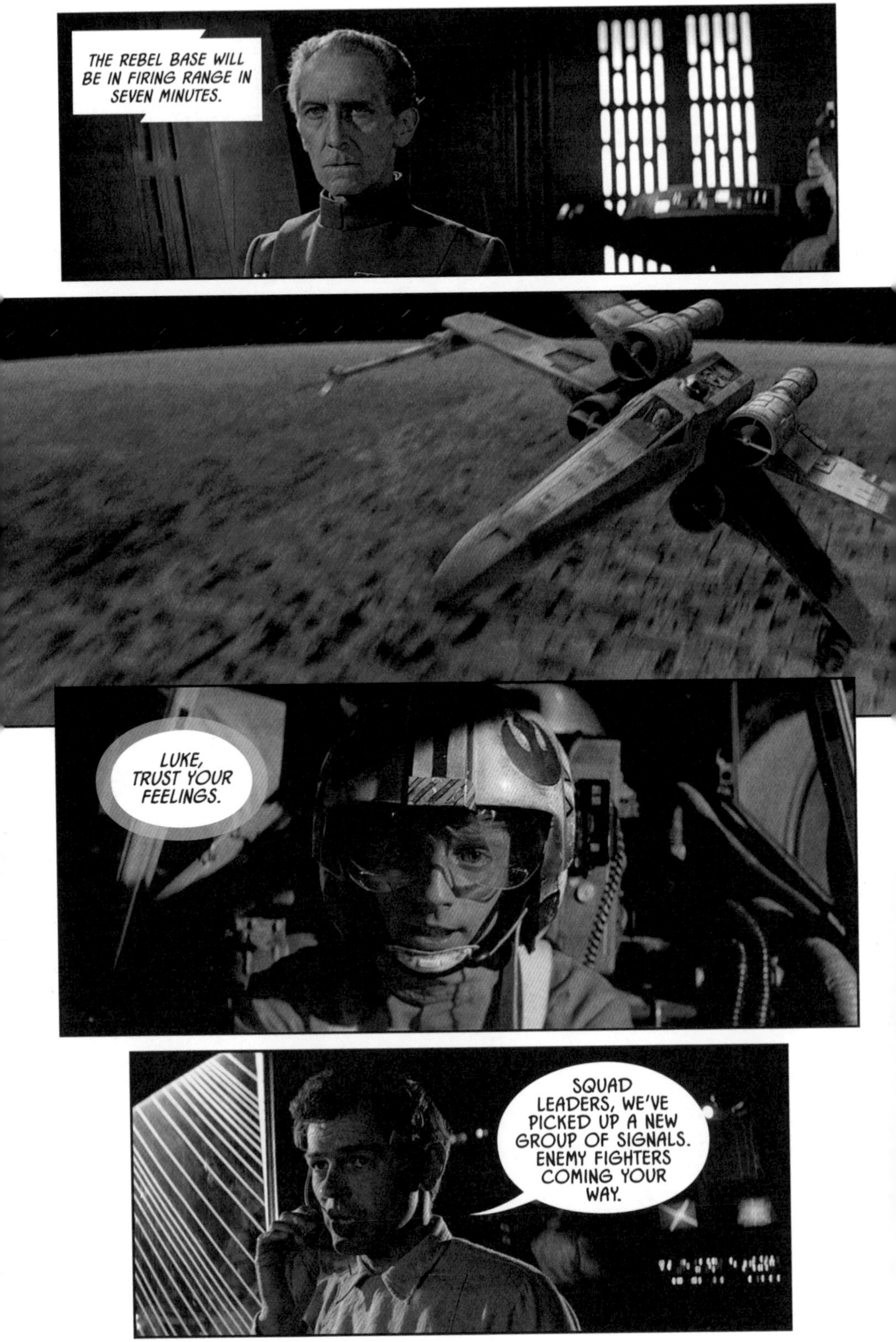
THE REBEL BASE WILL BE IN FIRING RANGE IN SEVEN MINUTES.
LUKE, TRUST YOUR FEELINGS.
SQUAD LEADERS, WE'VE PICKED UP A NEW GROUP OF SIGNALS. ENEMY FIGHTERS COMING YOUR WAY.

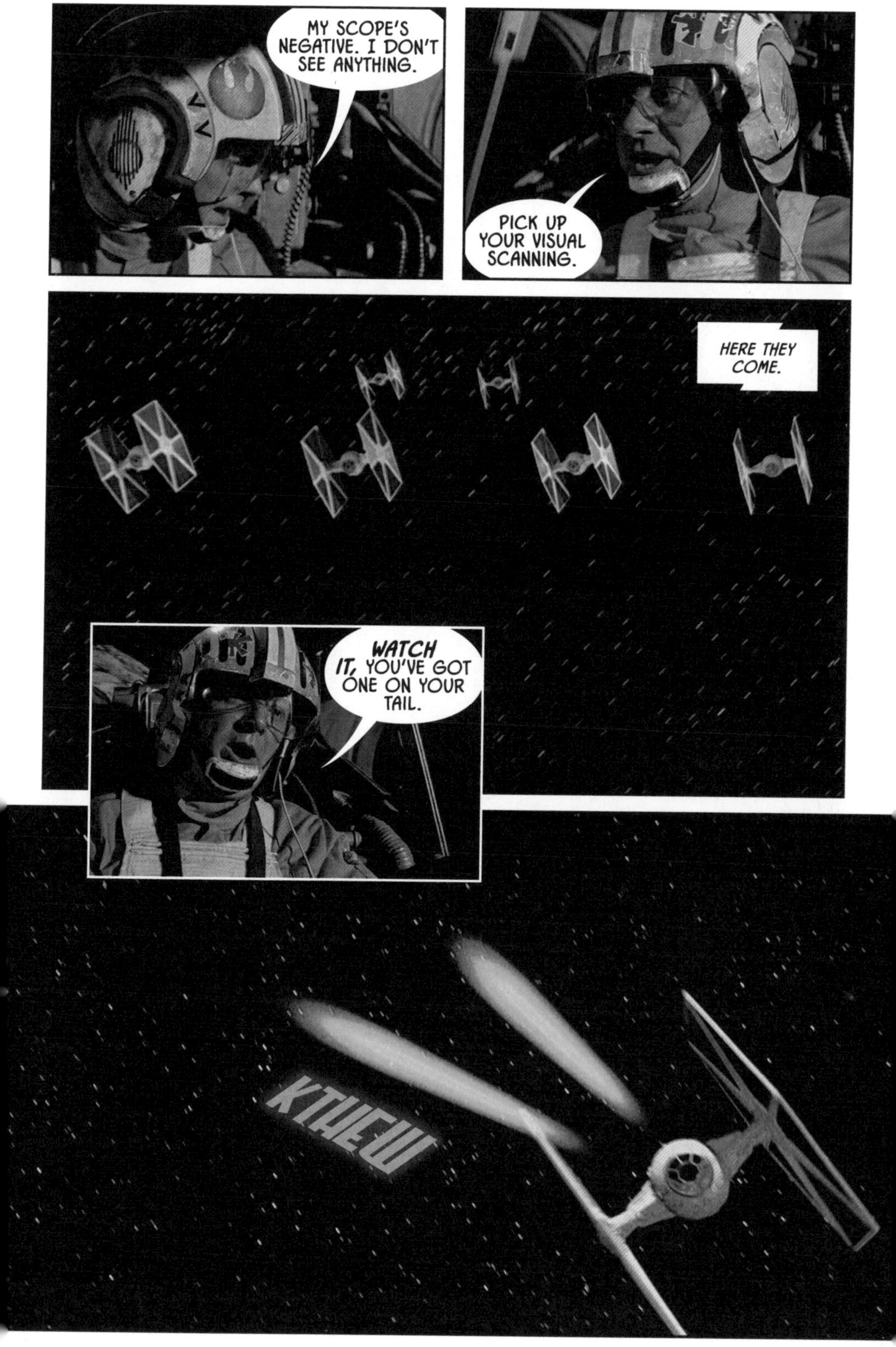
MY SCOPE'S NEGATIVE. I DON'T SEE ANYTHING.
PICK UP YOUR VISUAL SCANNING.
HERE THEY COME.
WATCH IT, YOU'VE GOT ONE ON YOUR TAIL.
KTHEW

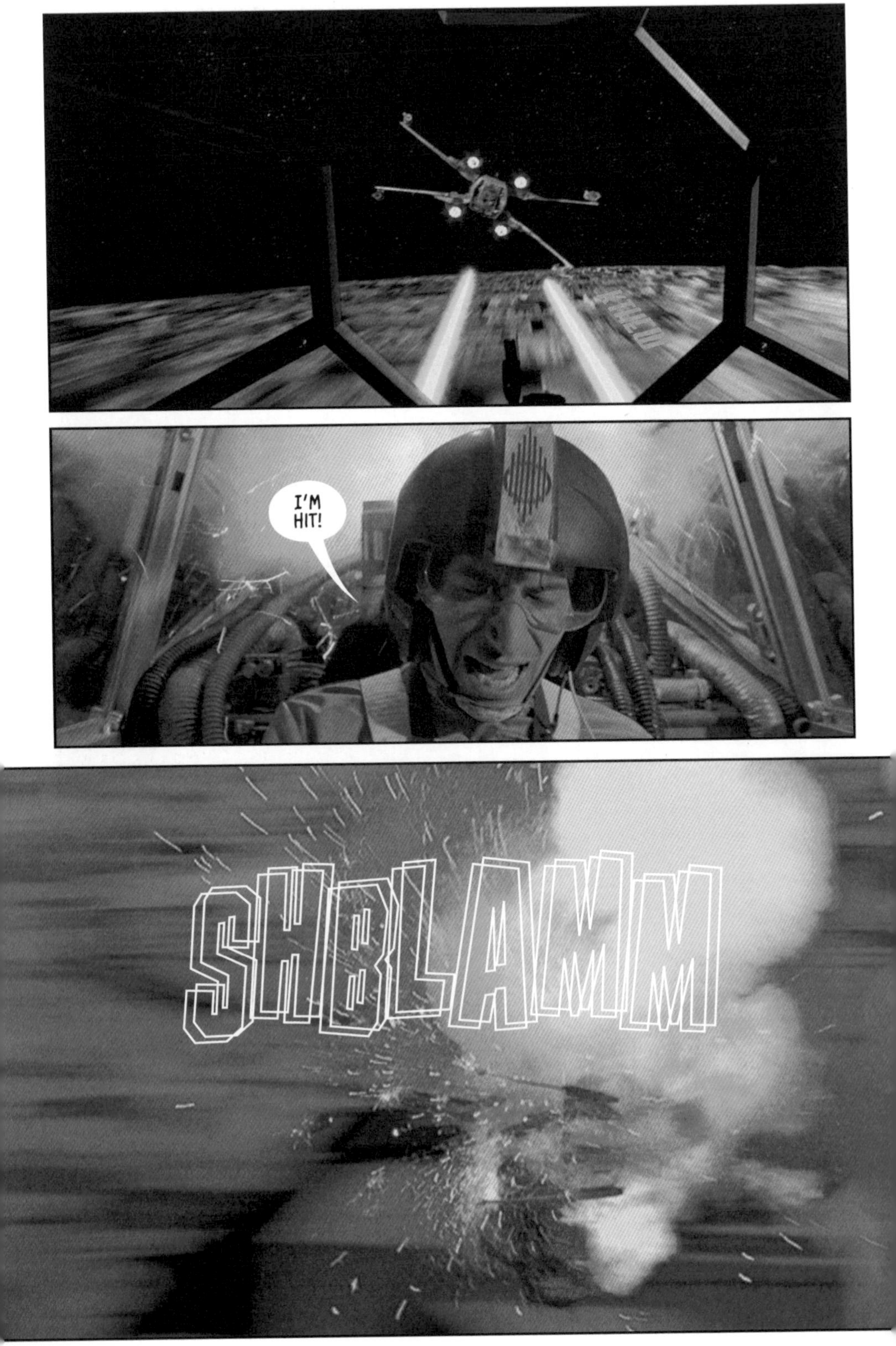
I'M HIT!
SHBLAMM

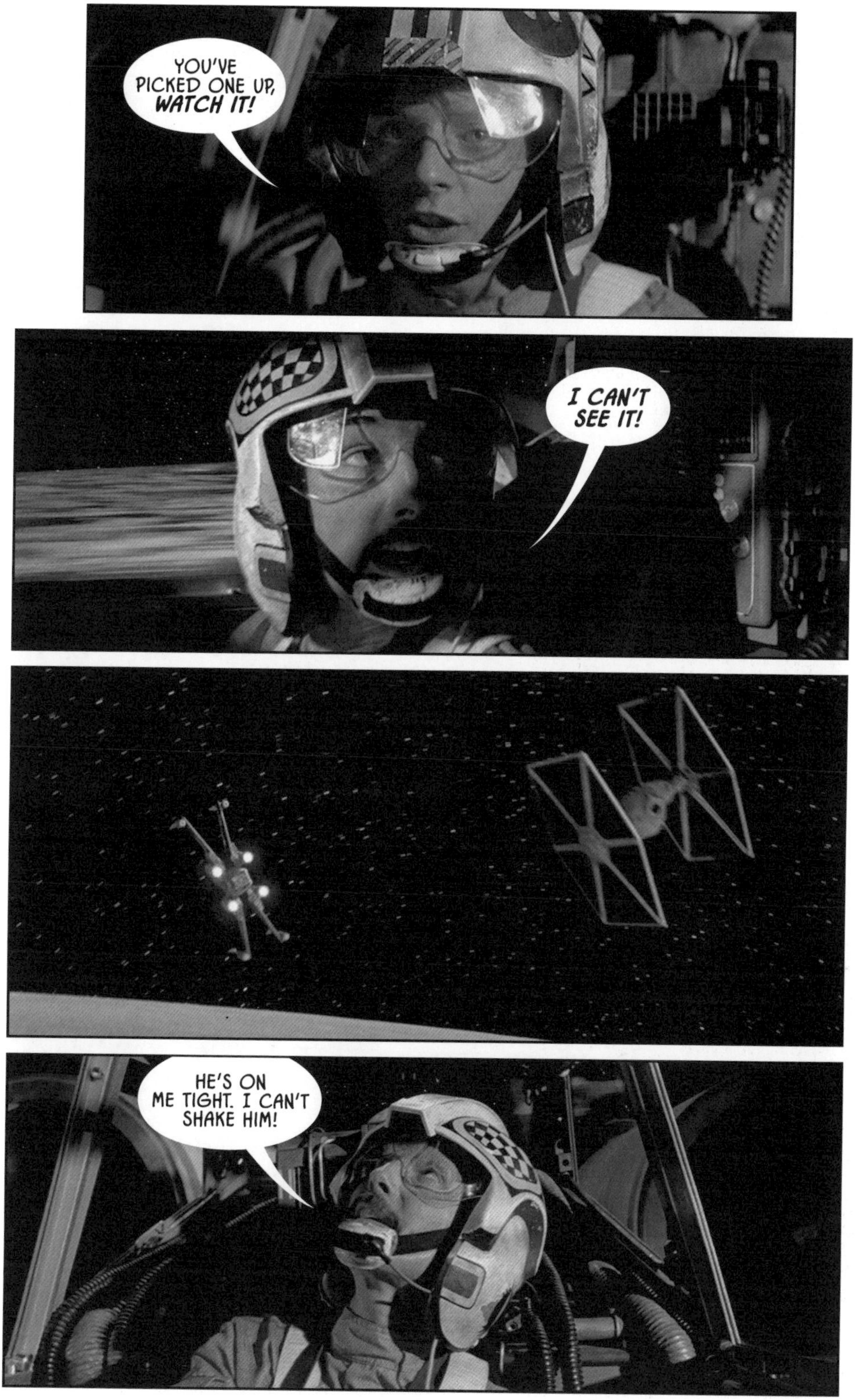
YOU'VE PICKED ONE UP, WATCH IT!
I CAN'T SEE IT!
HE'S ON ME TIGHT. I CAN'T SHAKE HIM!

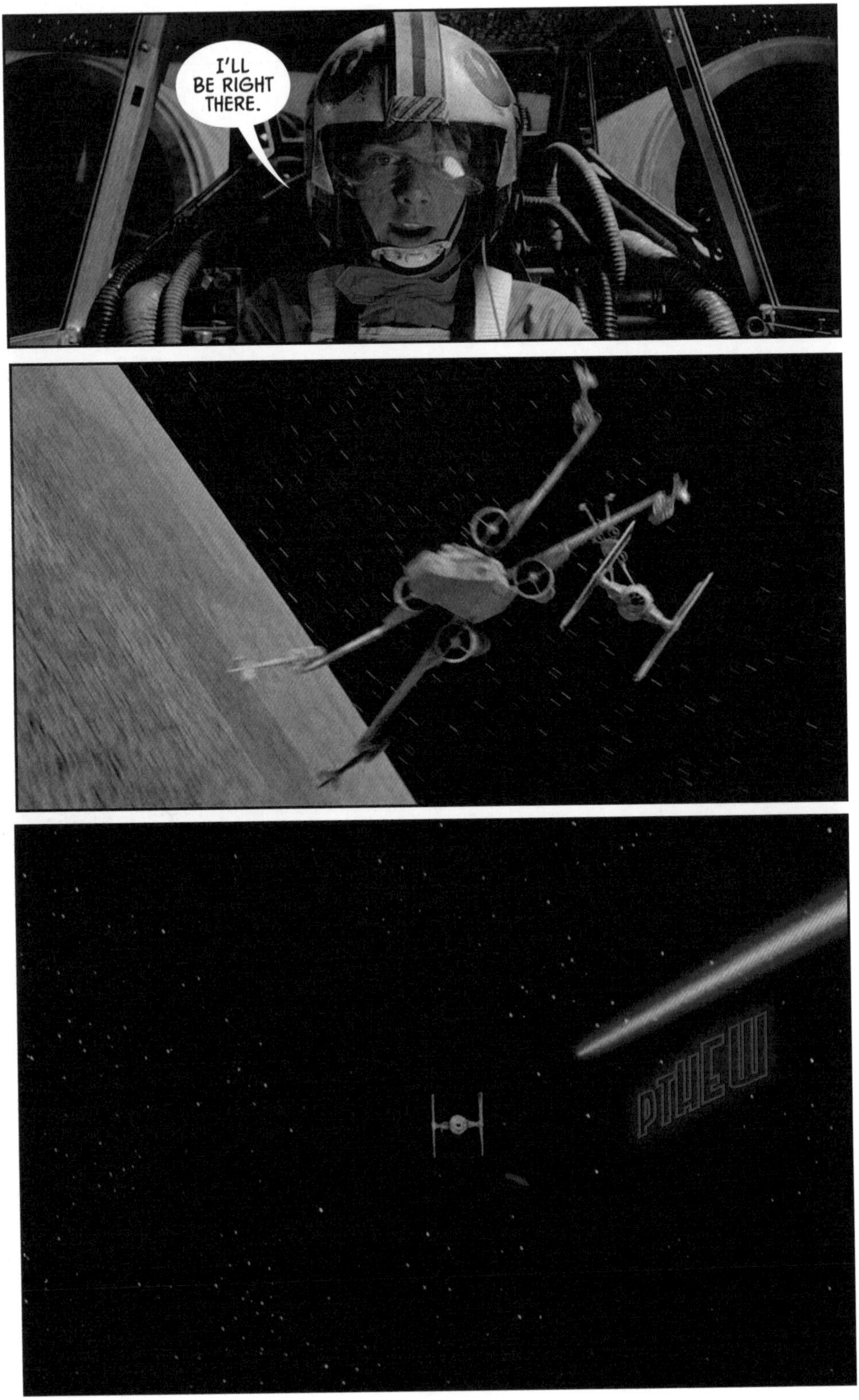
I'LL BE RIGHT THERE.
PTHEW

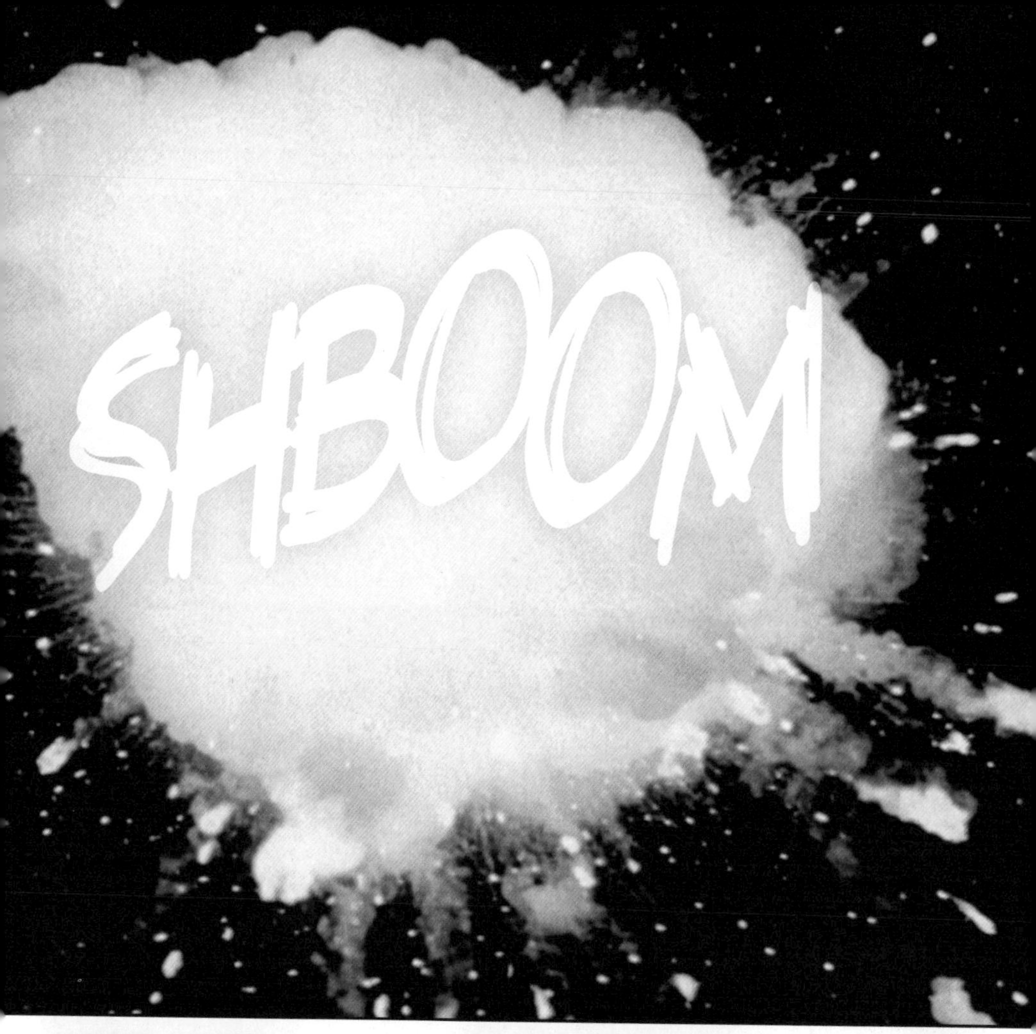
SHBOOM

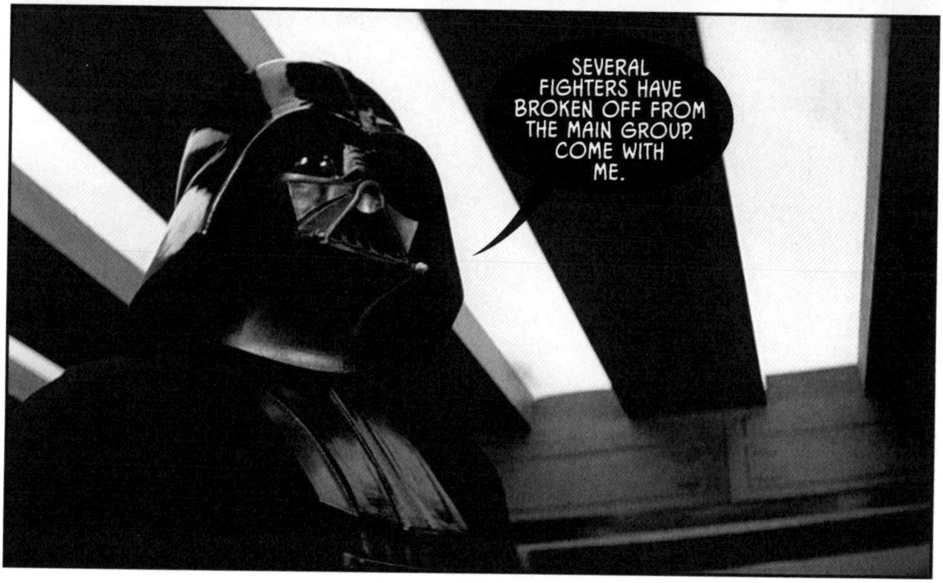
SEVERAL FIGHTERS HAVE BROKEN OFF FROM THE MAIN GROUP. COME WITH ME.

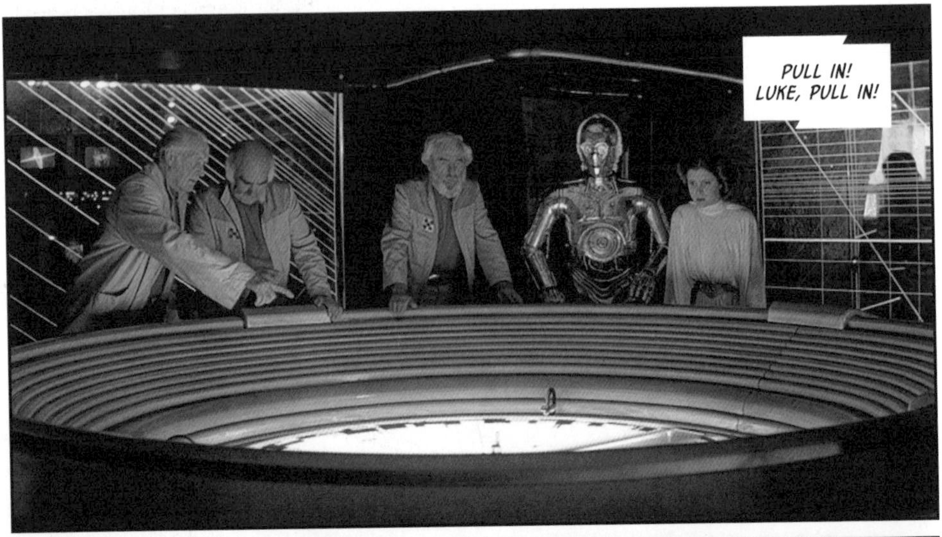
PULL IN!
LUKE, PULL IN!

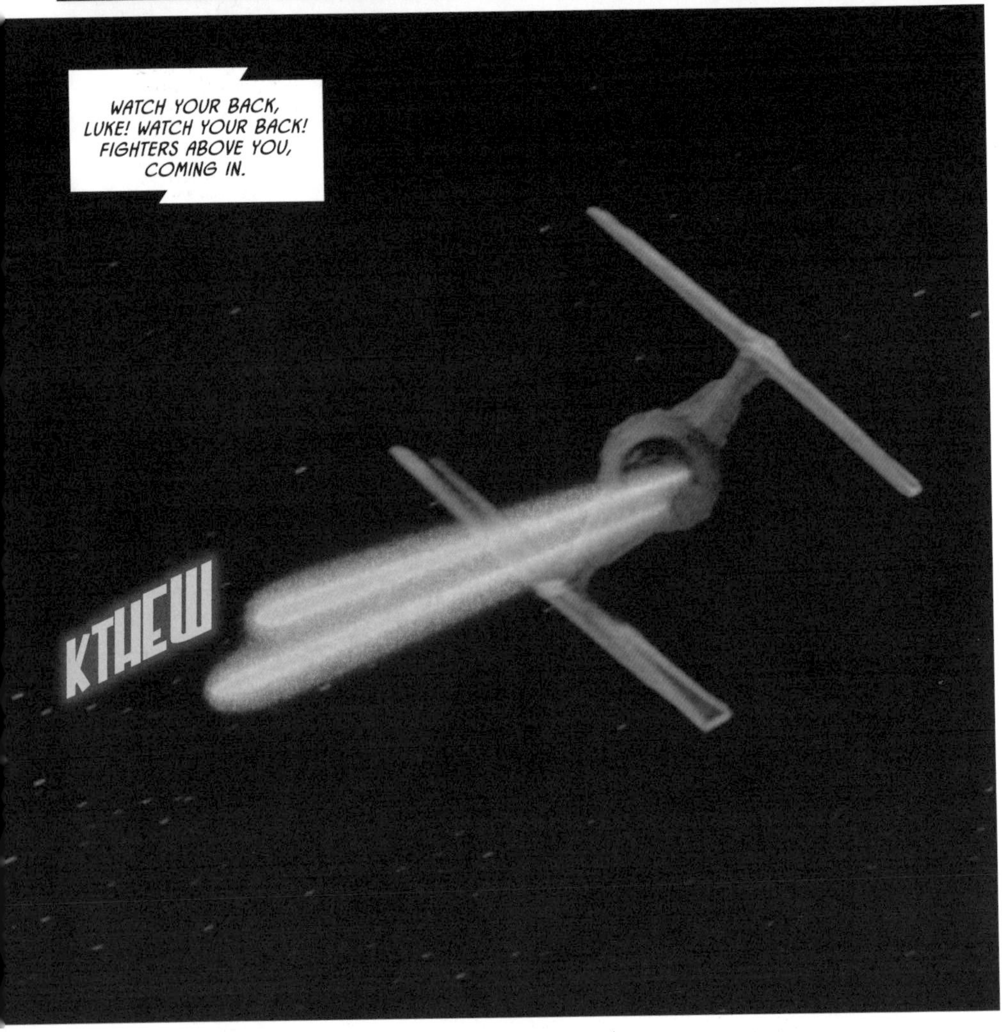
WATCH YOUR BACK,
LUKE! WATCH YOUR BACK!
FIGHTERS ABOVE YOU,
COMING IN.
KTHEW

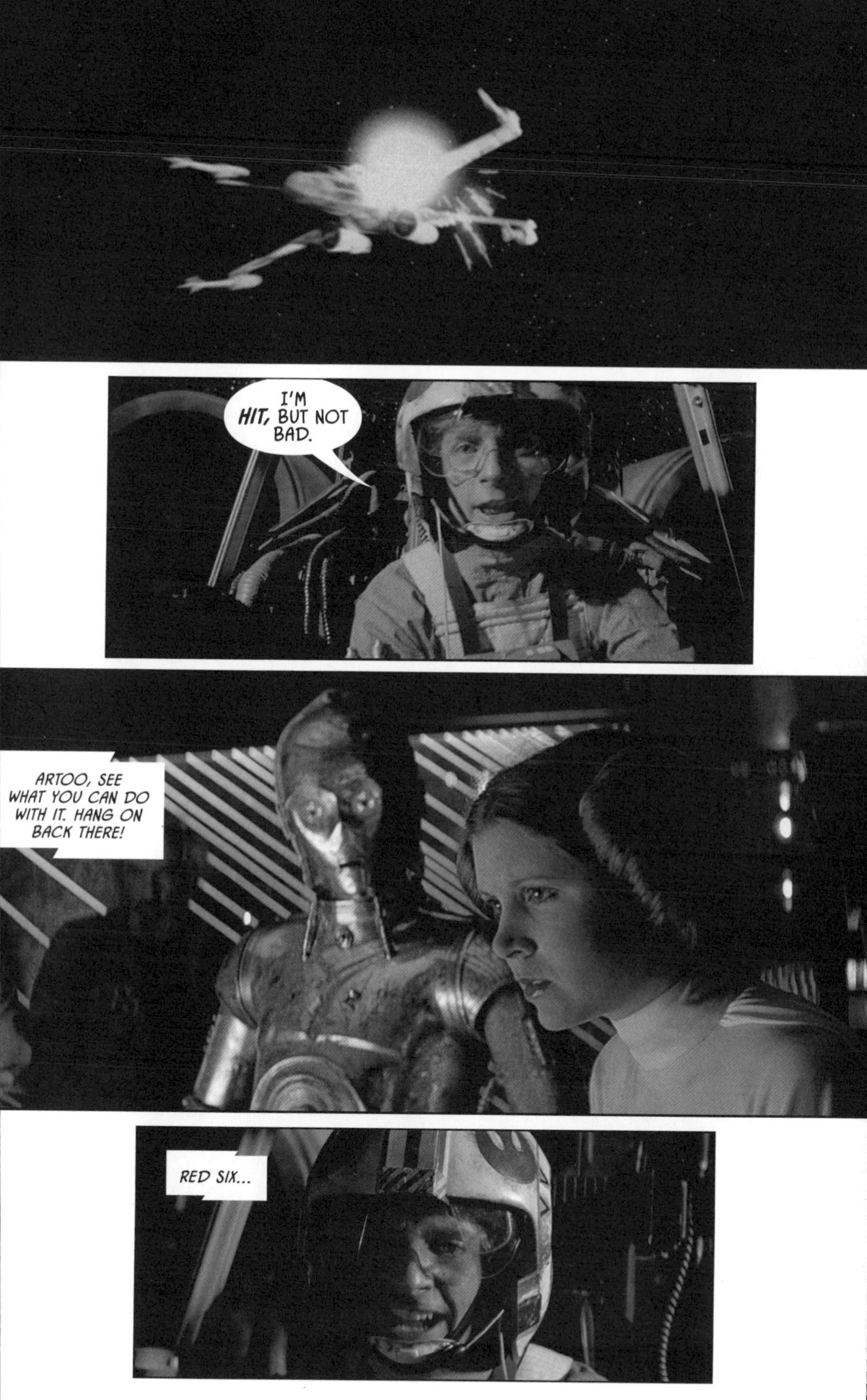
I'M HIT, BUT NOT BAD.
ARTOO, SEE WHAT YOU CAN DO WITH IT. HANG ON BACK THERE!
RED SIX...

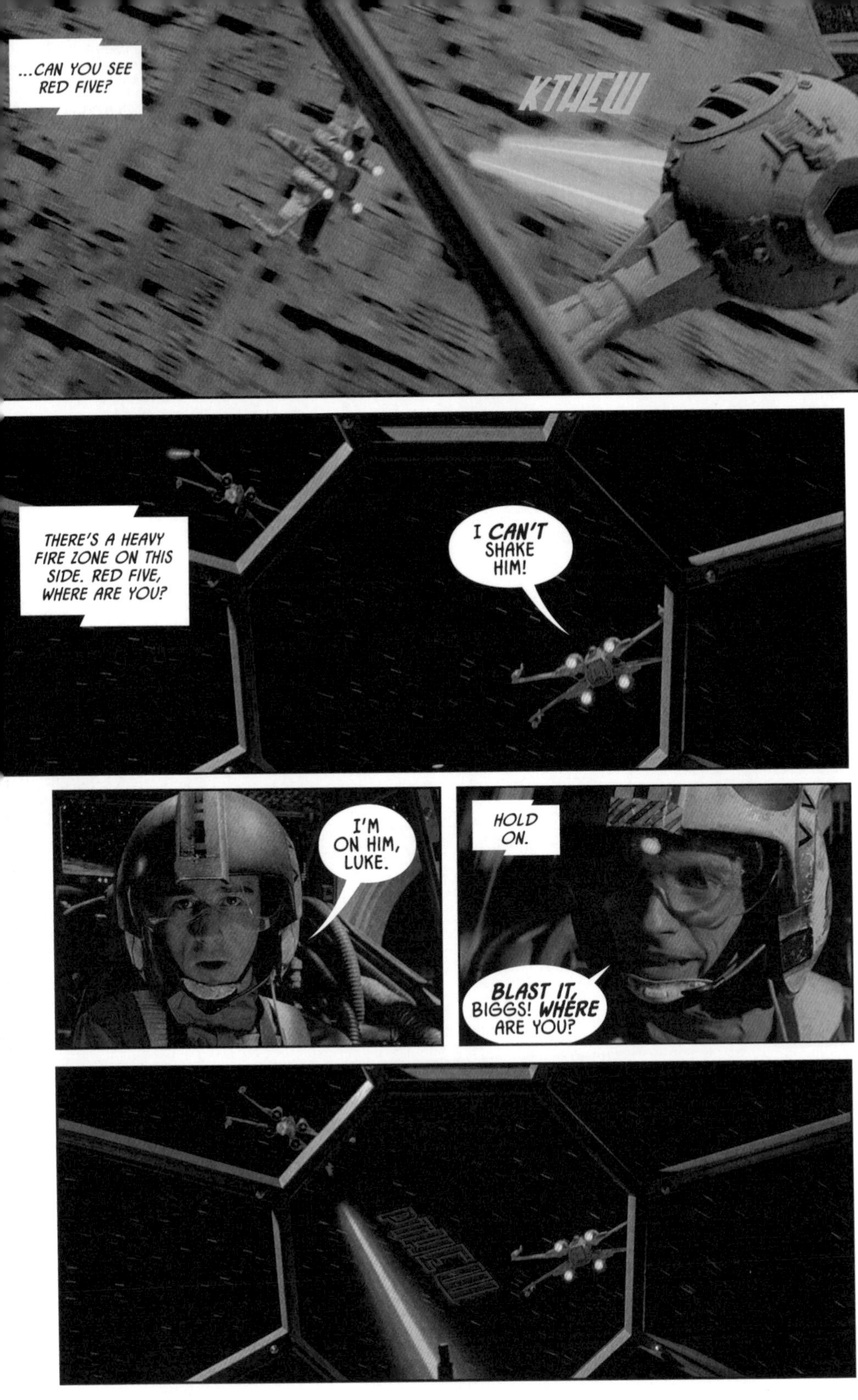
...CAN YOU SEE RED FIVE?
KTHEW
THERE'S A HEAVY FIRE ZONE ON THIS SIDE. RED FIVE, WHERE ARE YOU?
I CAN'T SHAKE HIM!
I'M ON HIM, LUKE.
HOLD ON.
BLAST IT, BIGGS! WHERE ARE YOU?

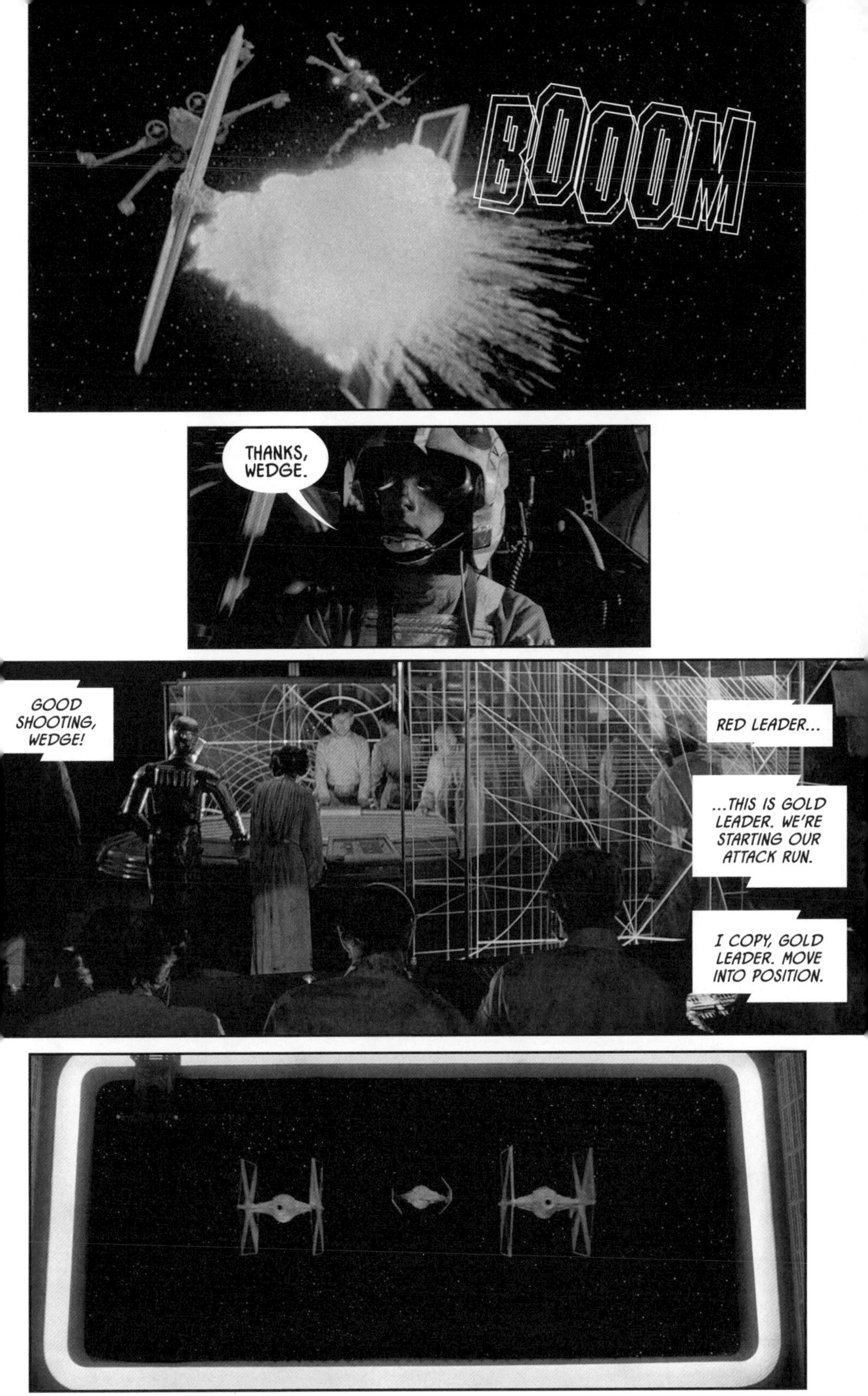
BOOOM
THANKS, WEDGE.
GOOD SHOOTING, WEDGE!
RED LEADER...
...THIS IS GOLD LEADER. WE'RE STARTING OUR ATTACK RUN.
I COPY, GOLD LEADER. MOVE INTO POSITION.

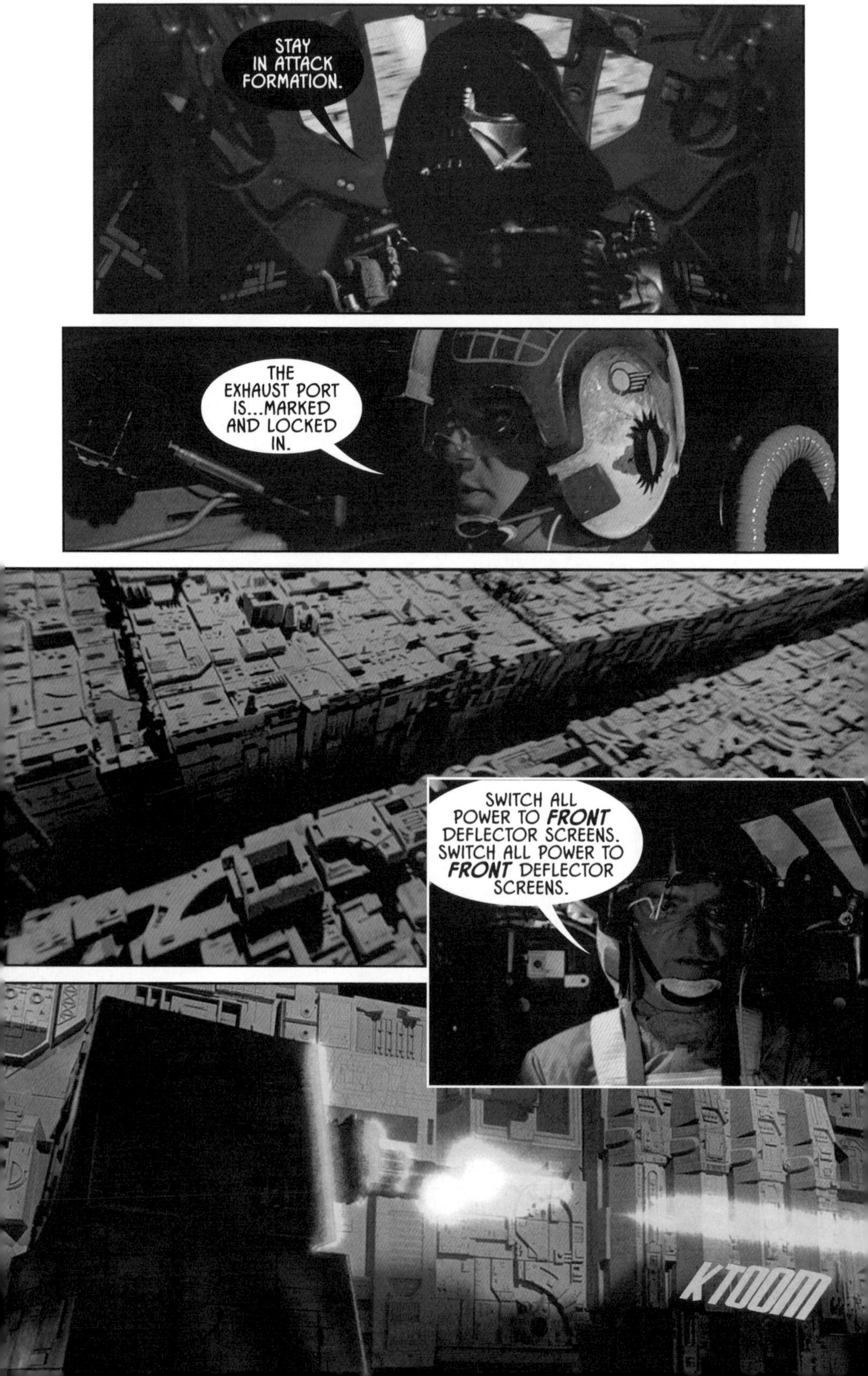
STAY IN ATTACK FORMATION.
THE EXHAUST PORT IS...MARKED AND LOCKED IN.
SWITCH ALL POWER TO *FRONT* DEFLECTOR SCREENS. SWITCH ALL POWER TO *FRONT* DEFLECTOR SCREENS.
KTOOM

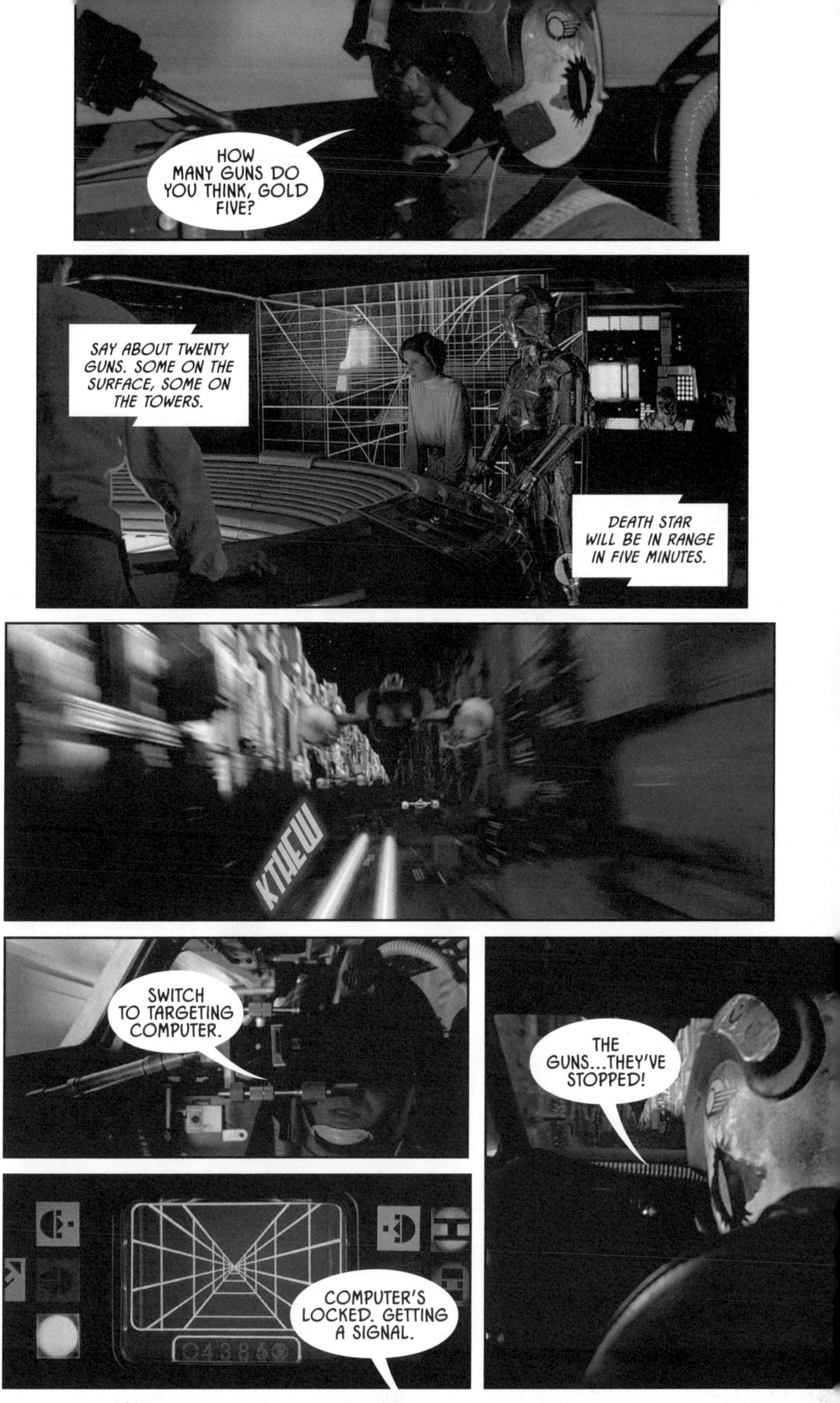
HOW MANY GUNS DO YOU THINK, GOLD FIVE?
SAY ABOUT TWENTY GUNS. SOME ON THE SURFACE, SOME ON THE TOWERS.
DEATH STAR WILL BE IN RANGE IN FIVE MINUTES.
KTHEW
SWITCH TO TARGETING COMPUTER.
THE GUNS...THEY'VE STOPPED!
COMPUTER'S LOCKED. GETTING A SIGNAL.

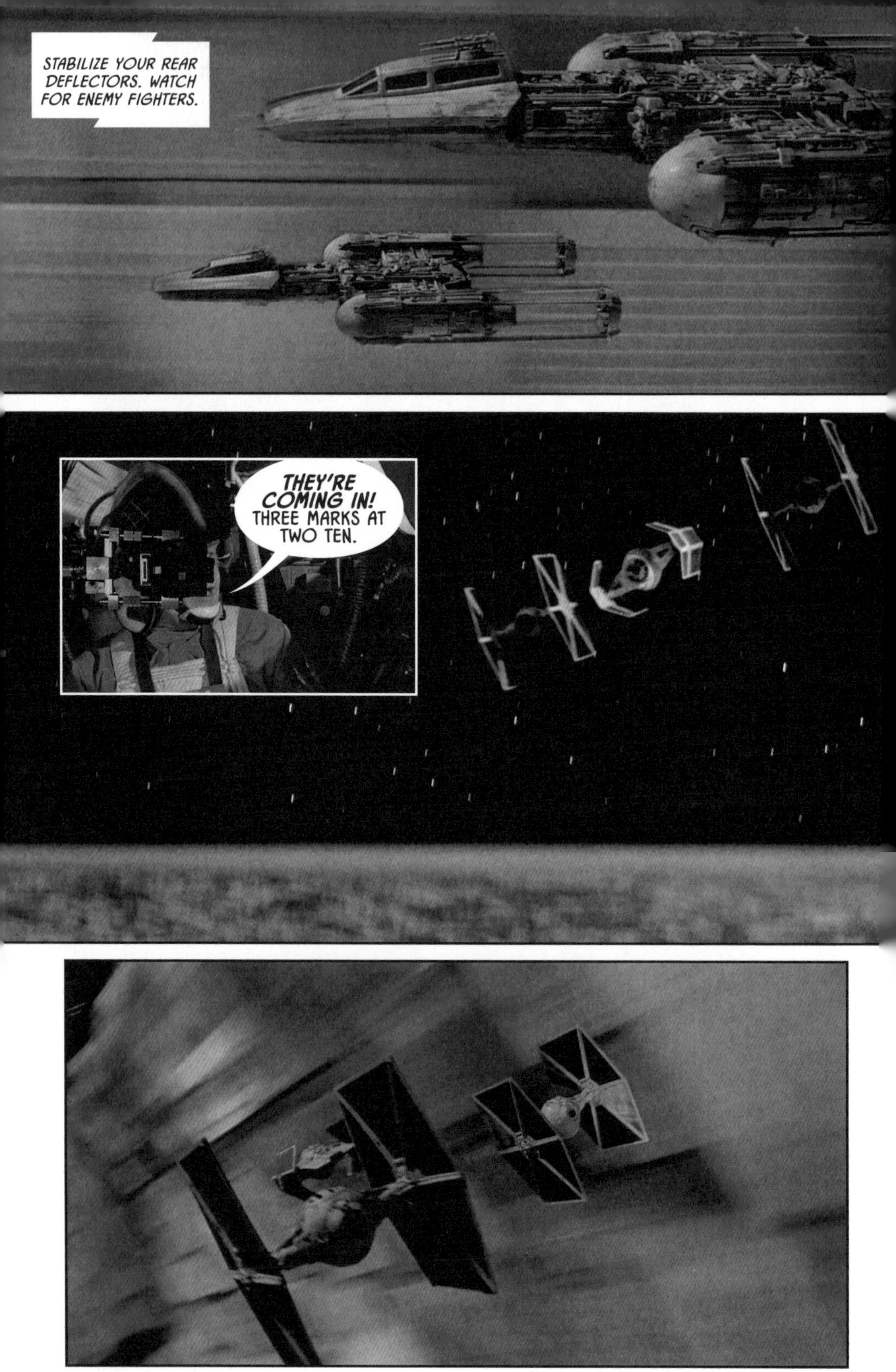
STABILIZE YOUR REAR DEFLECTORS. WATCH FOR ENEMY FIGHTERS.
THEY'RE COMING IN! THREE MARKS AT TWO TEN.

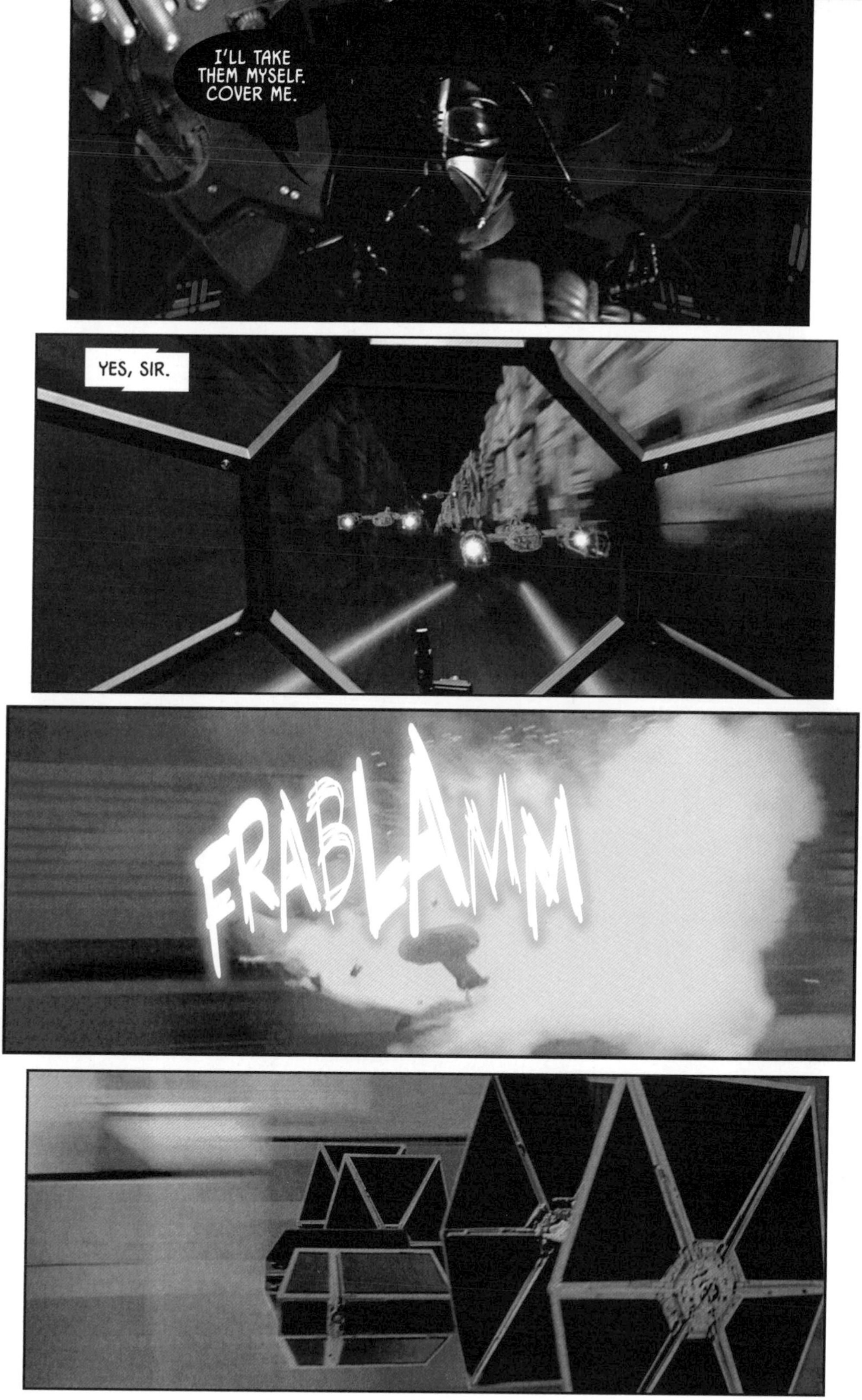
I'LL TAKE THEM MYSELF. COVER ME.
YES, SIR.
FRABLAMM

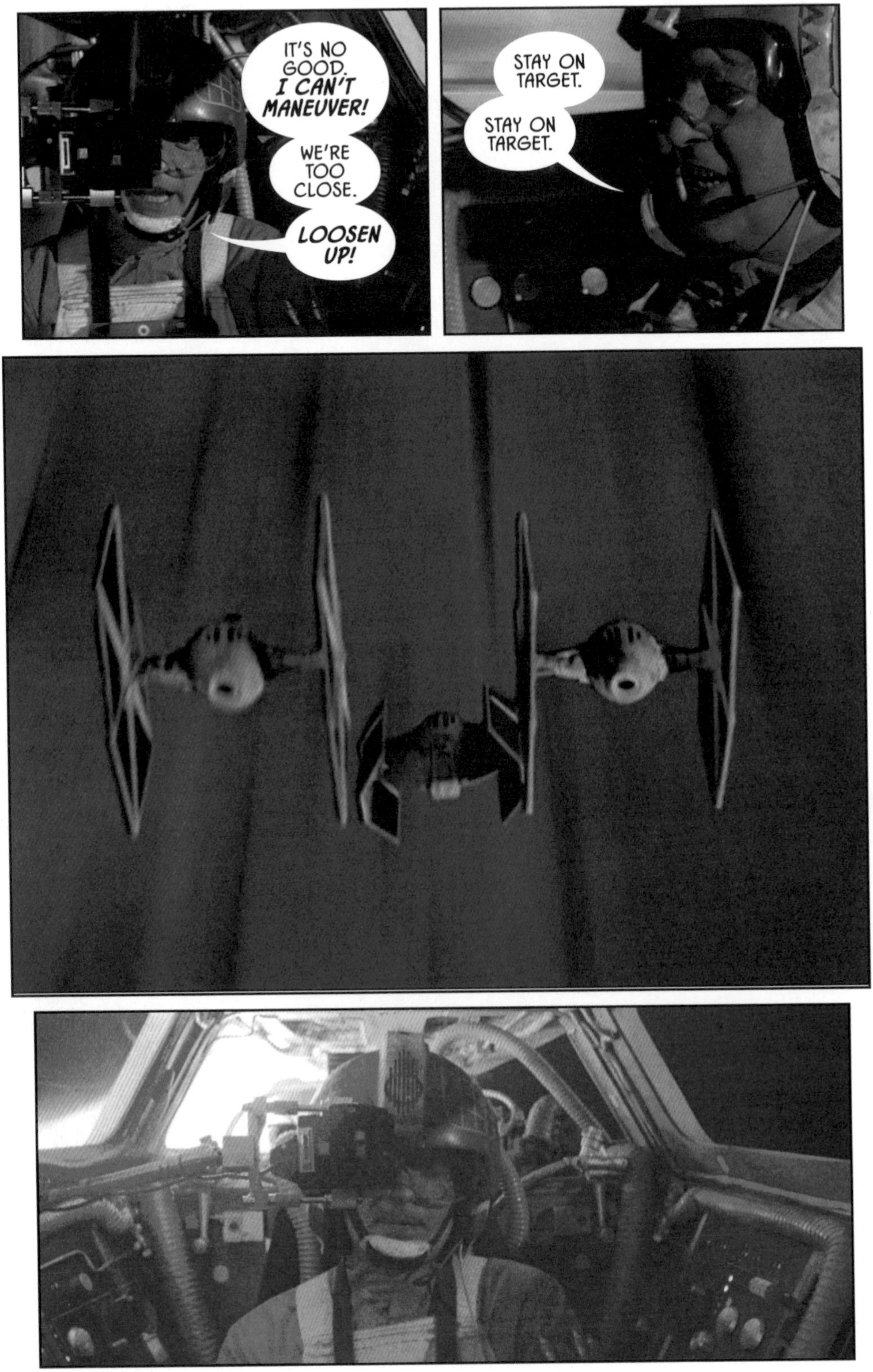
IT'S NO GOOD. I CAN'T MANEUVER!
WE'RE TOO CLOSE.
LOOSEN UP!
STAY ON TARGET.
STAY ON TARGET.

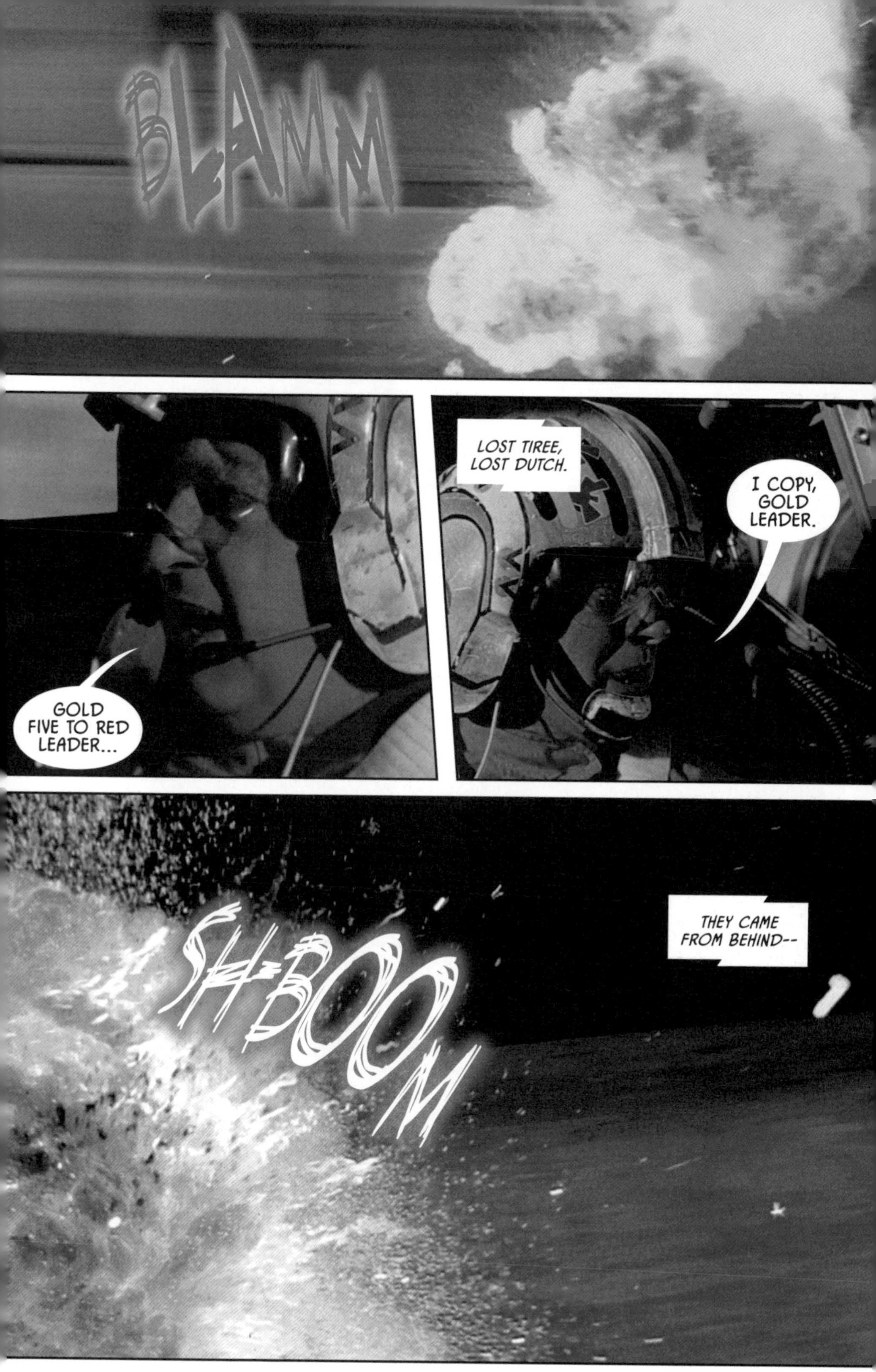
BLAMM
GOLD FIVE TO RED LEADER...
LOST TIREE, LOST DUTCH.
I COPY, GOLD LEADER.
SH-BOOM
THEY CAME FROM BEHIND--

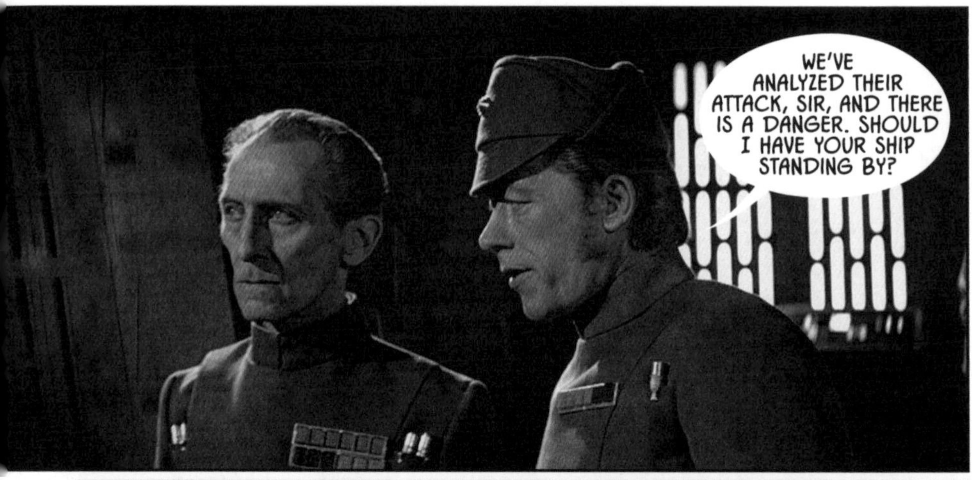
WE'VE ANALYZED THEIR ATTACK, SIR, AND THERE IS A DANGER. SHOULD I HAVE YOUR SHIP STANDING BY?

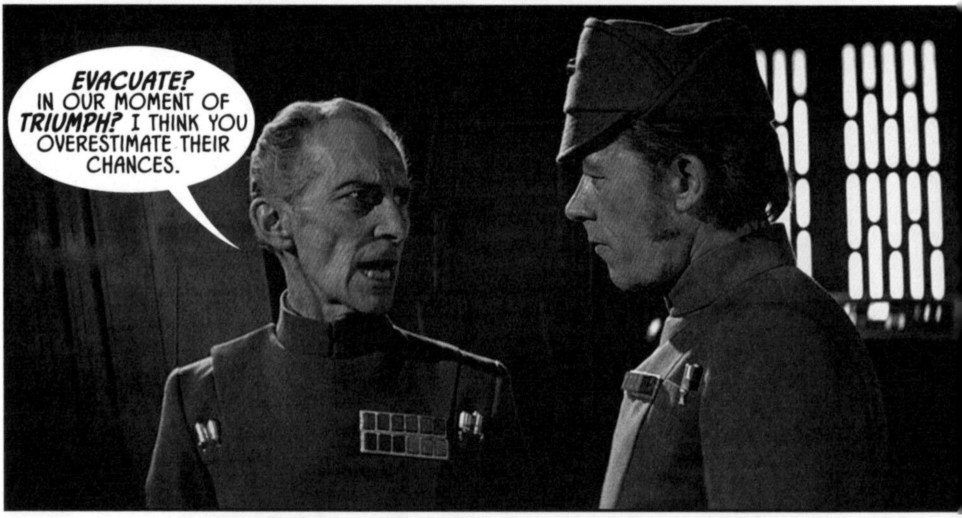
EVACUATE? IN OUR MOMENT OF TRIUMPH? I THINK YOU OVERESTIMATE THEIR CHANCES.

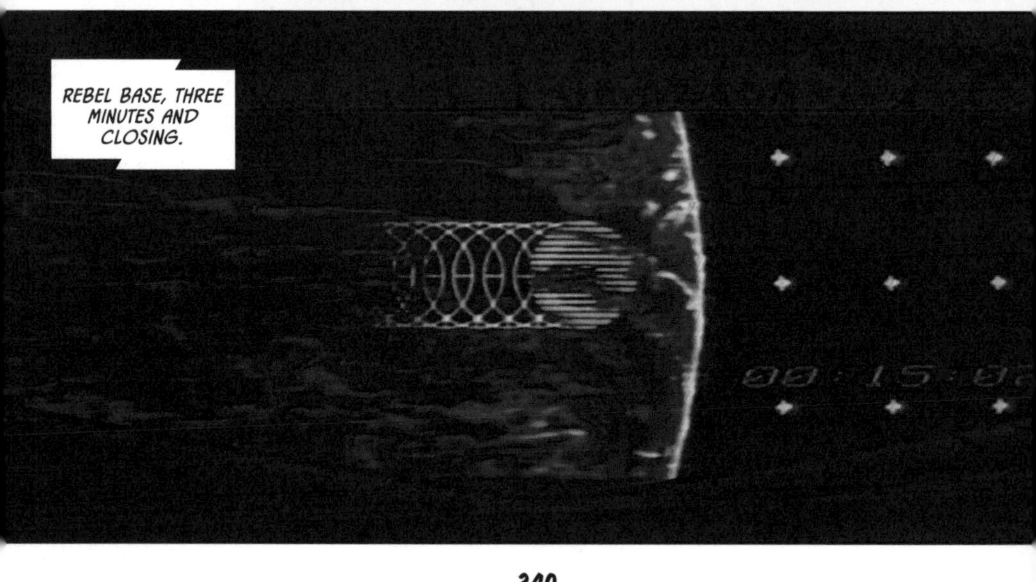
REBEL BASE, THREE MINUTES AND CLOSING.

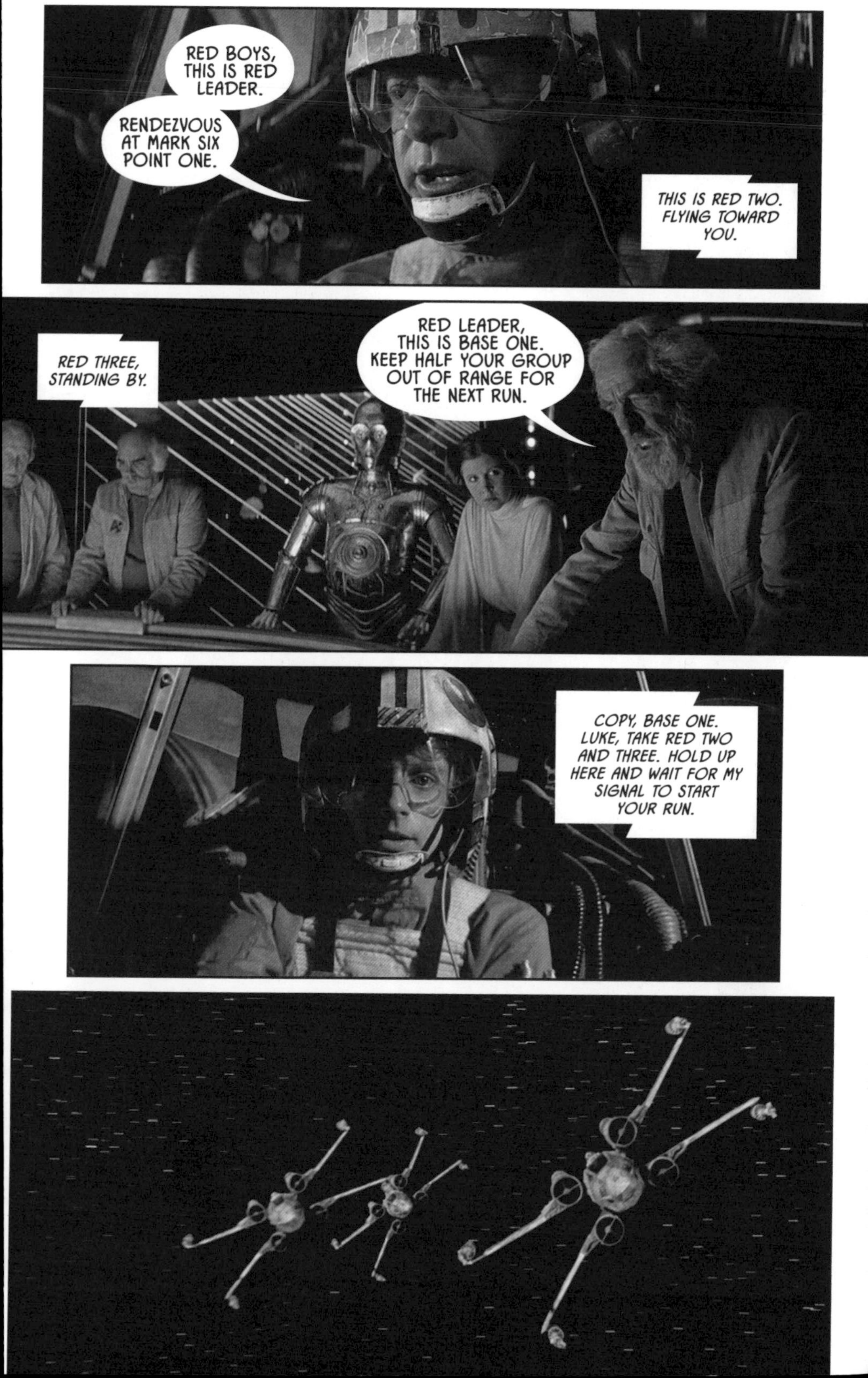
RED BOYS, THIS IS RED LEADER.
RENDEZVOUS AT MARK SIX POINT ONE.
THIS IS RED TWO. FLYING TOWARD YOU.
RED THREE, STANDING BY.
RED LEADER, THIS IS BASE ONE. KEEP HALF YOUR GROUP OUT OF RANGE FOR THE NEXT RUN.
COPY, BASE ONE. LUKE, TAKE RED TWO AND THREE. HOLD UP HERE AND WAIT FOR MY SIGNAL TO START YOUR RUN.

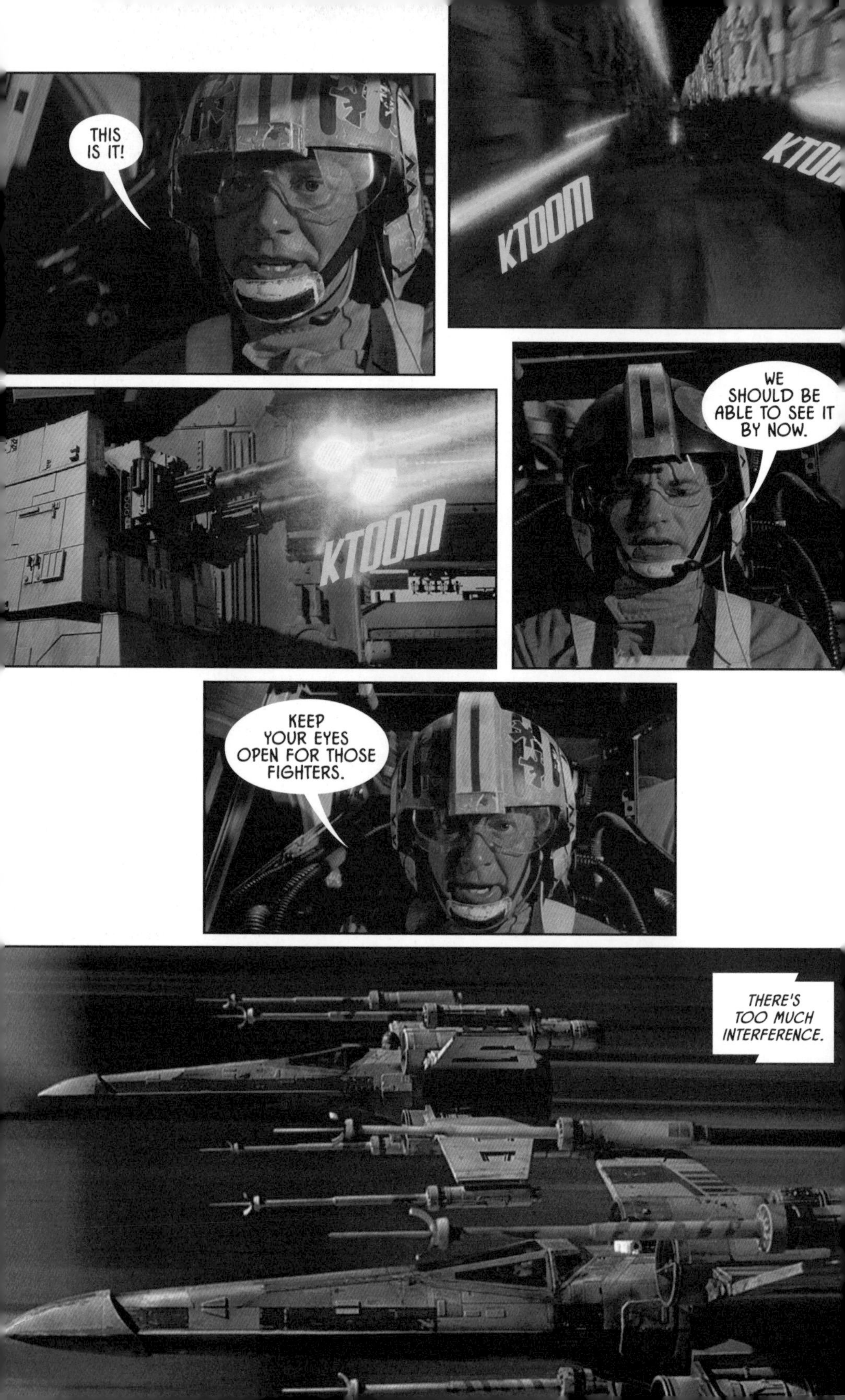
THIS IS IT!
KTOOM
KTOOM
KTOOM
WE SHOULD BE ABLE TO SEE IT BY NOW.
KEEP YOUR EYES OPEN FOR THOSE FIGHTERS.
THERE'S TOO MUCH INTERFERENCE.

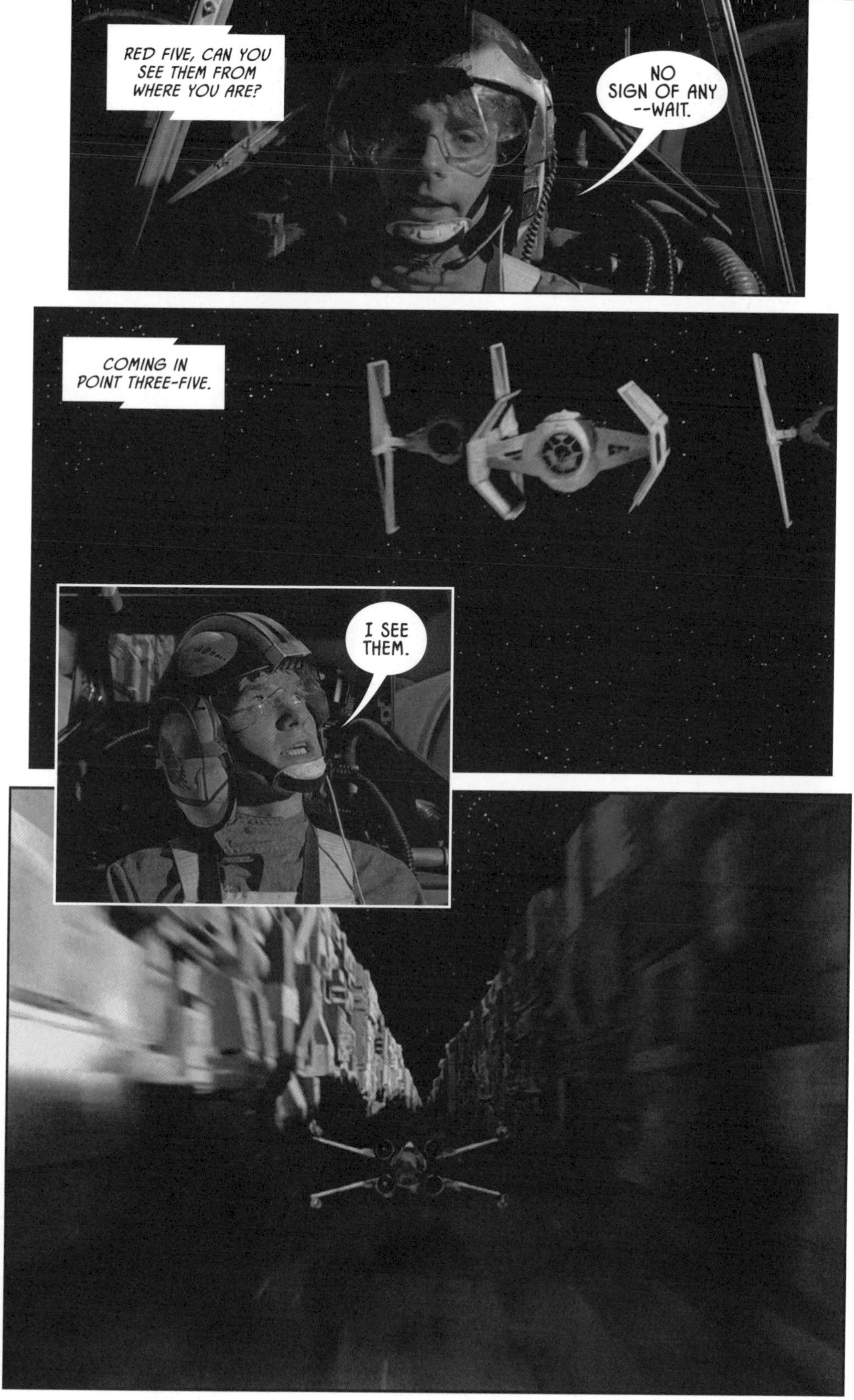
RED FIVE, CAN YOU SEE THEM FROM WHERE YOU ARE?
NO SIGN OF ANY --WAIT.
COMING IN POINT THREE-FIVE.
I SEE THEM.

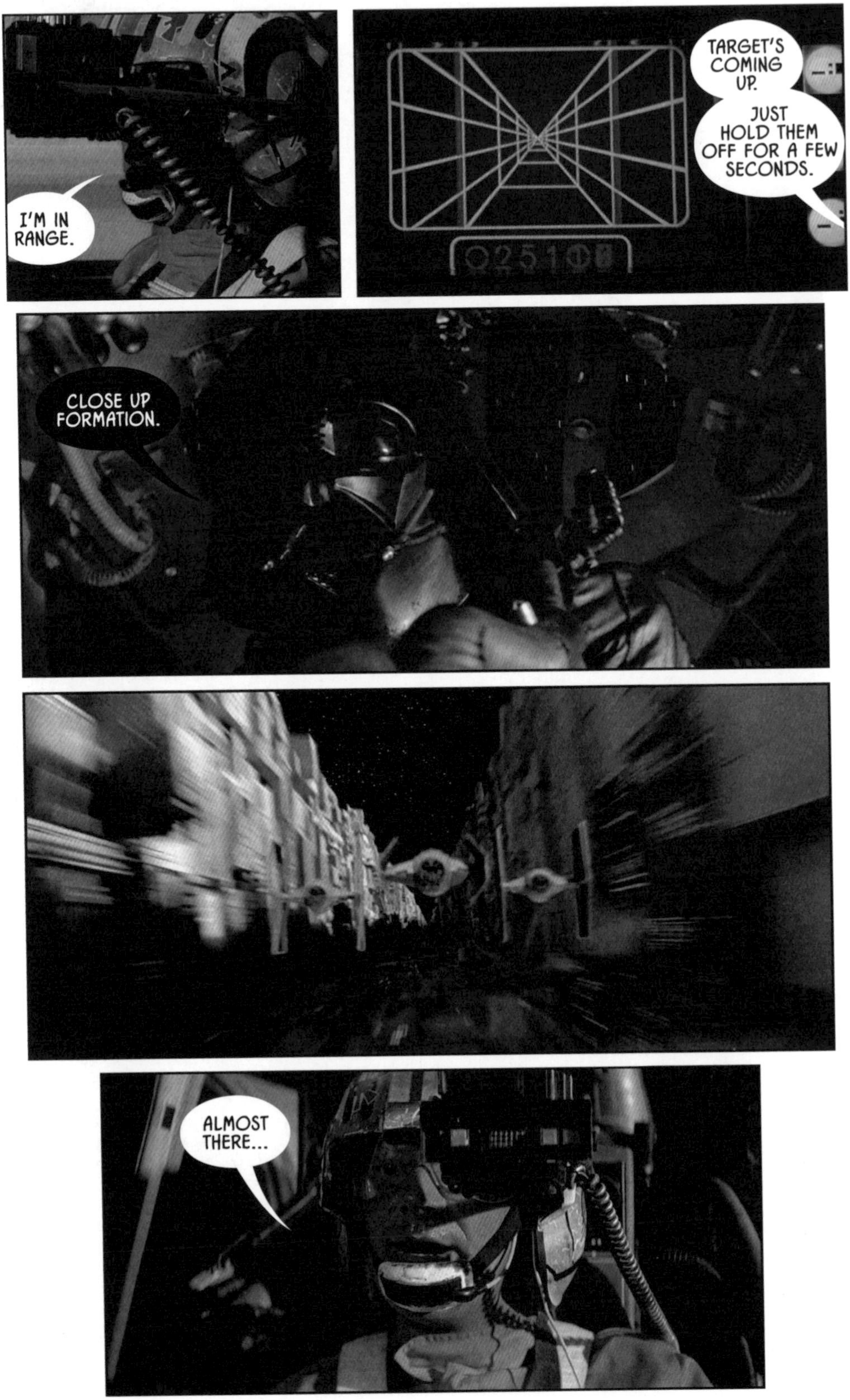
I'M IN RANGE.
TARGET'S COMING UP.
JUST HOLD THEM OFF FOR A FEW SECONDS.
CLOSE UP FORMATION.
ALMOST THERE...

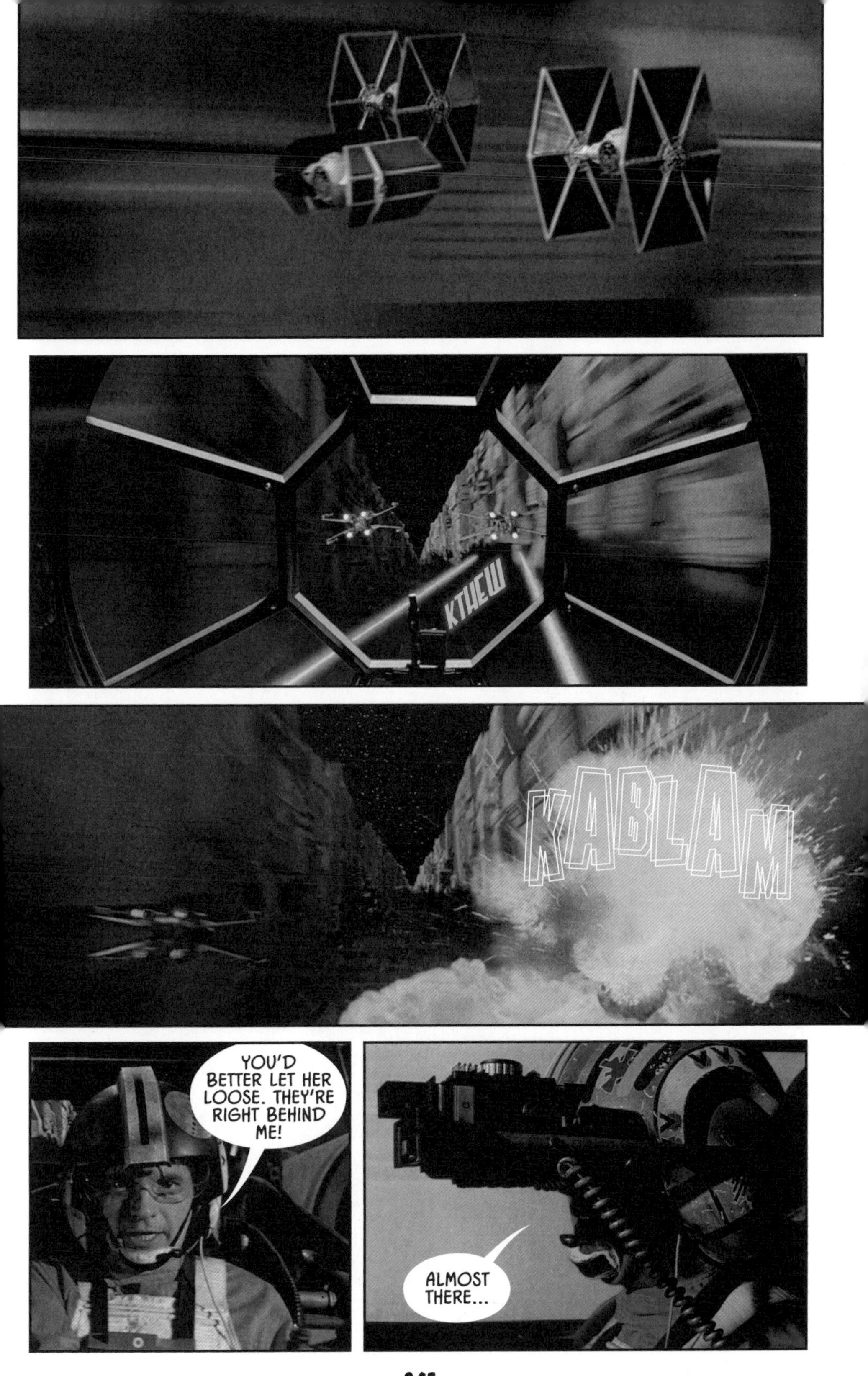
KTHEW
KABLAM
YOU'D BETTER LET HER LOOSE. THEY'RE RIGHT BEHIND ME!
ALMOST THERE...

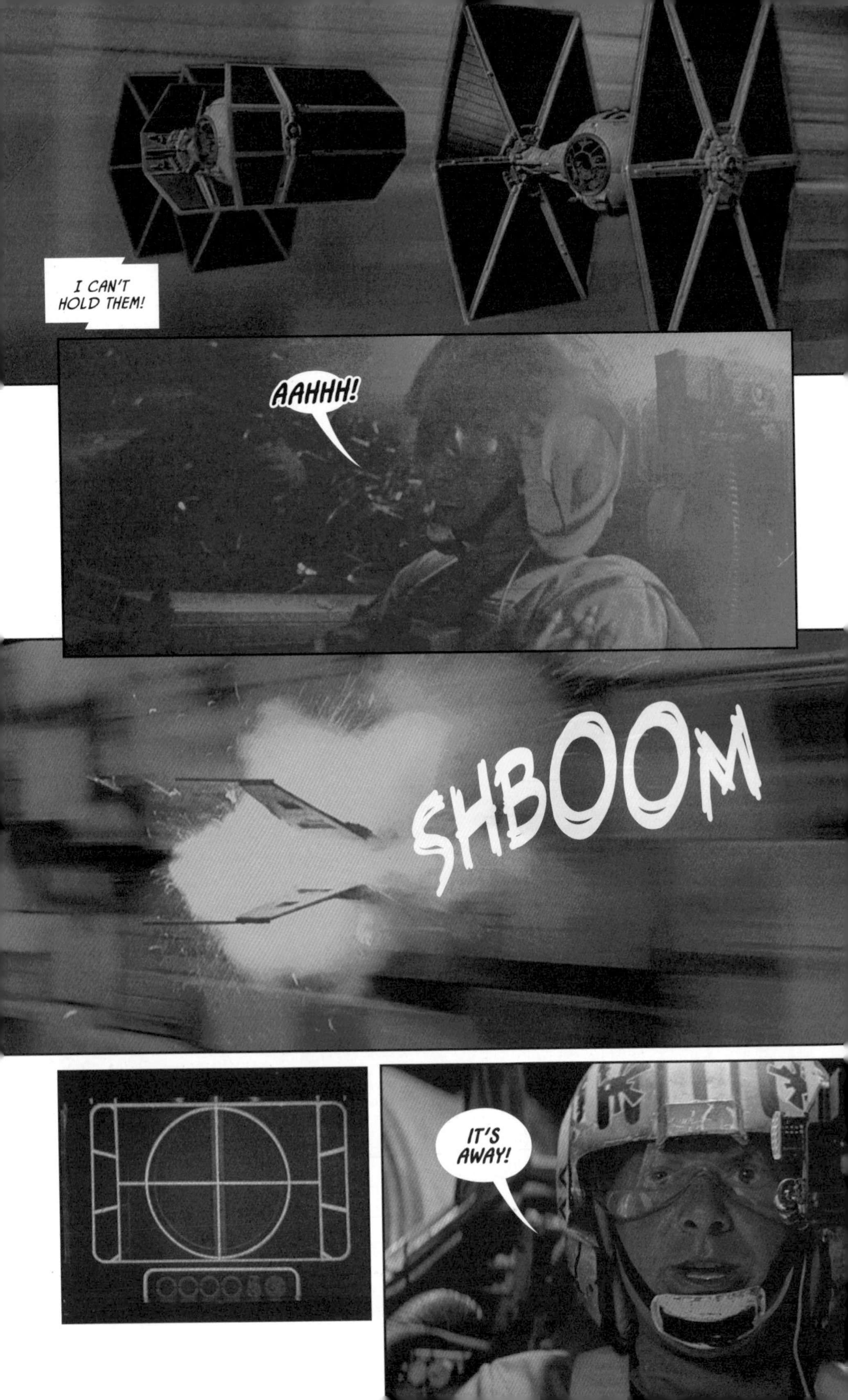
I CAN'T HOLD THEM!
AAHHH!
SHBOOM
IT'S AWAY!

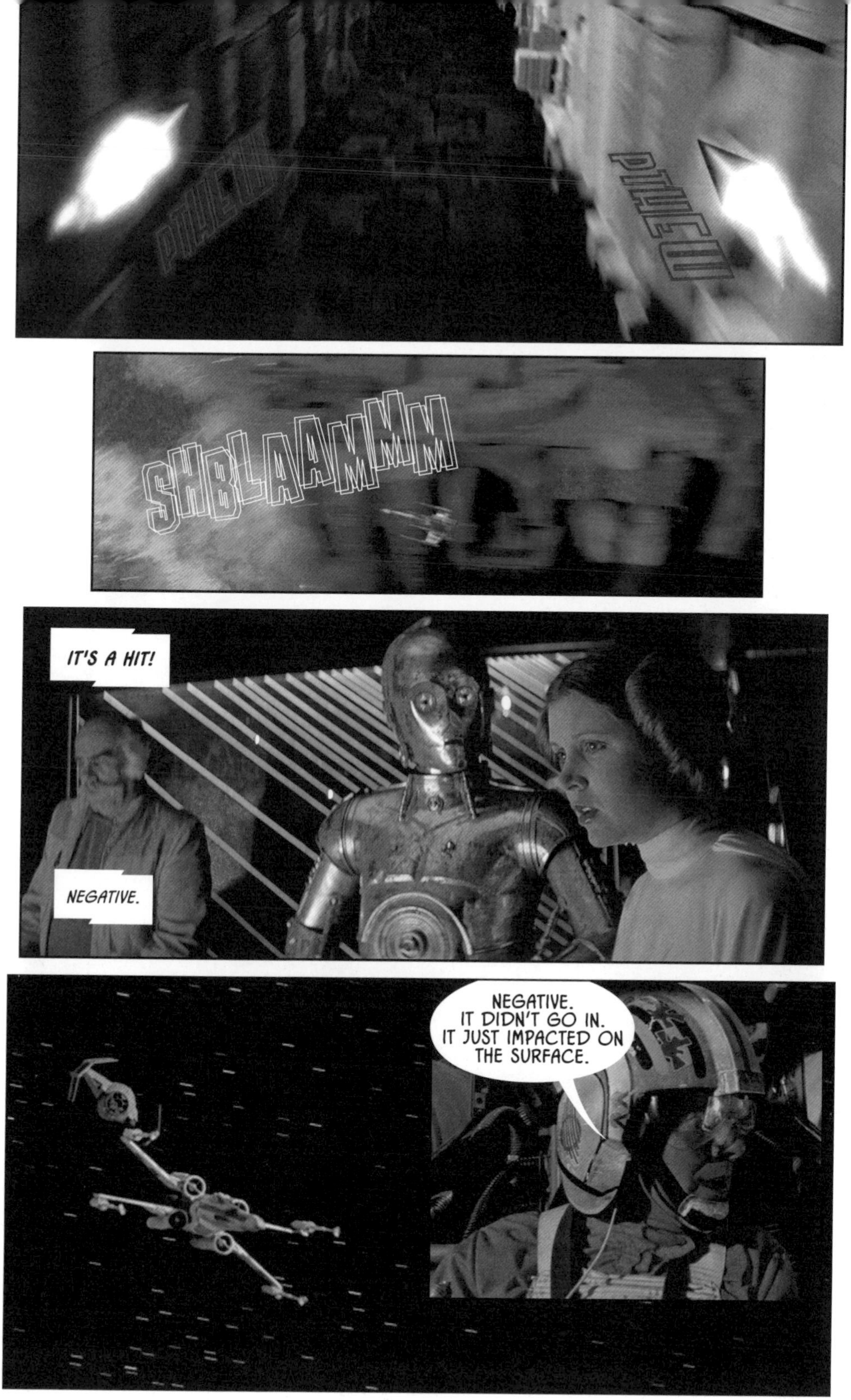
PTYEW
SHBLAAMMM
IT'S A HIT!
NEGATIVE.
NEGATIVE. IT DIDN'T GO IN. IT JUST IMPACTED ON THE SURFACE.

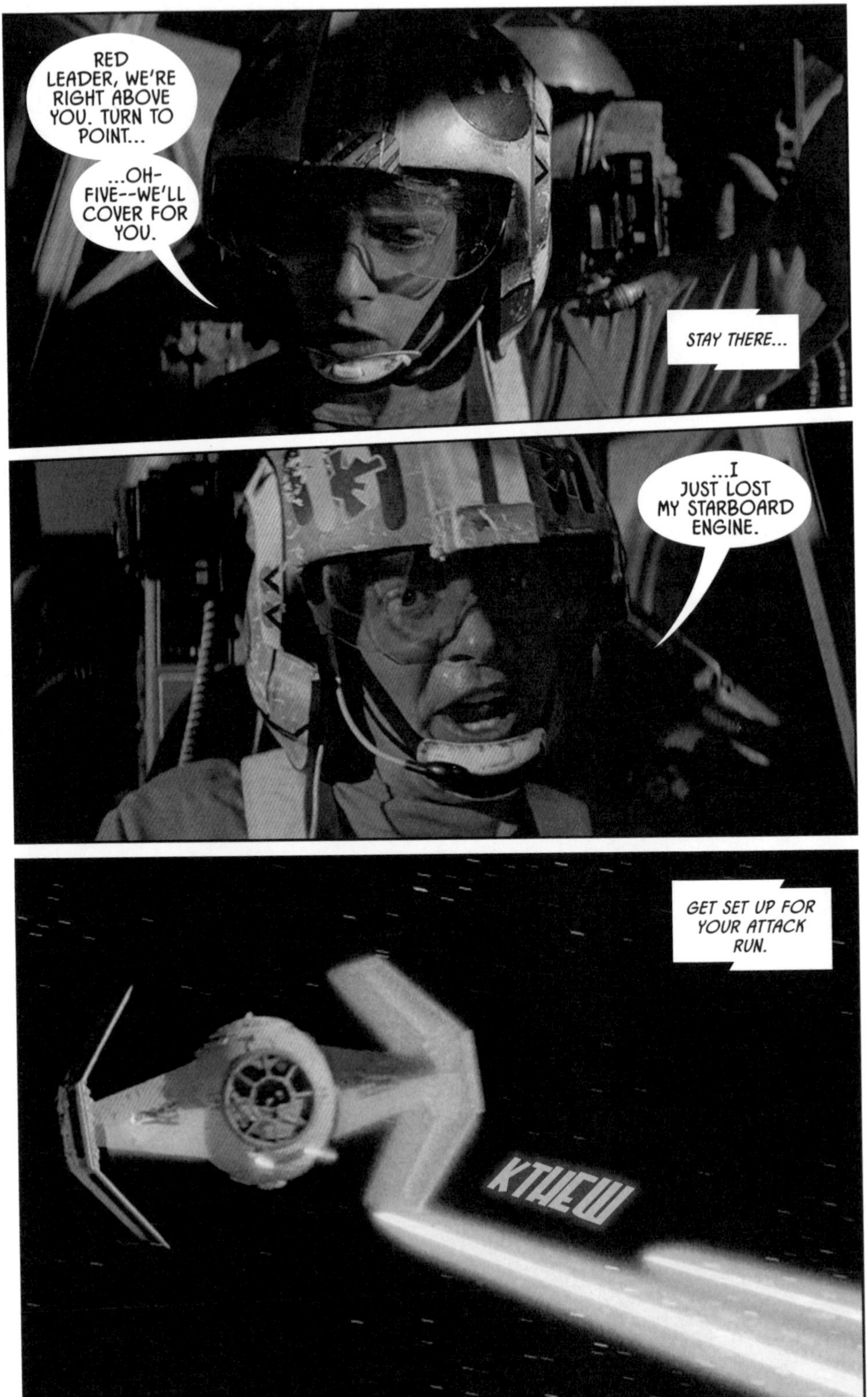
RED LEADER, WE'RE RIGHT ABOVE YOU. TURN TO POINT...
...OH-FIVE--WE'LL COVER FOR YOU.
STAY THERE...
...I JUST LOST MY STARBOARD ENGINE.
GET SET UP FOR YOUR ATTACK RUN.
KTHEW

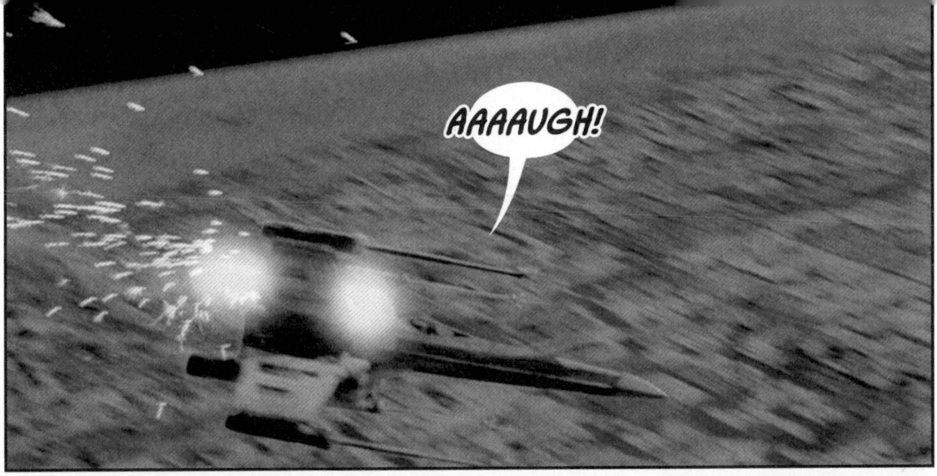
AAAAUGH!

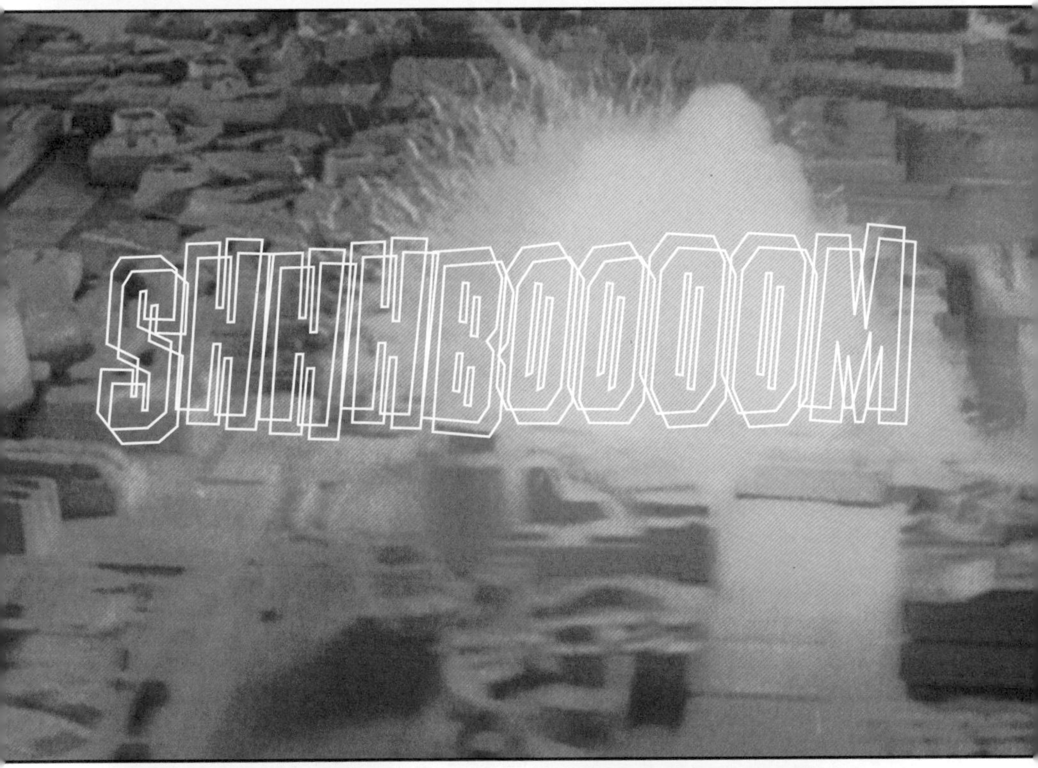
SHHHBOOOOOM

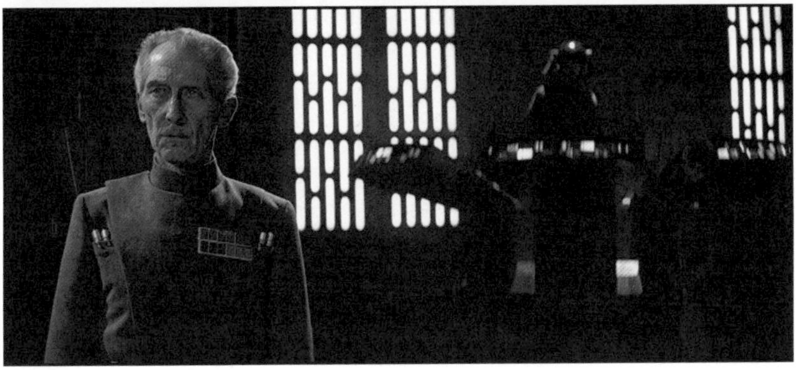

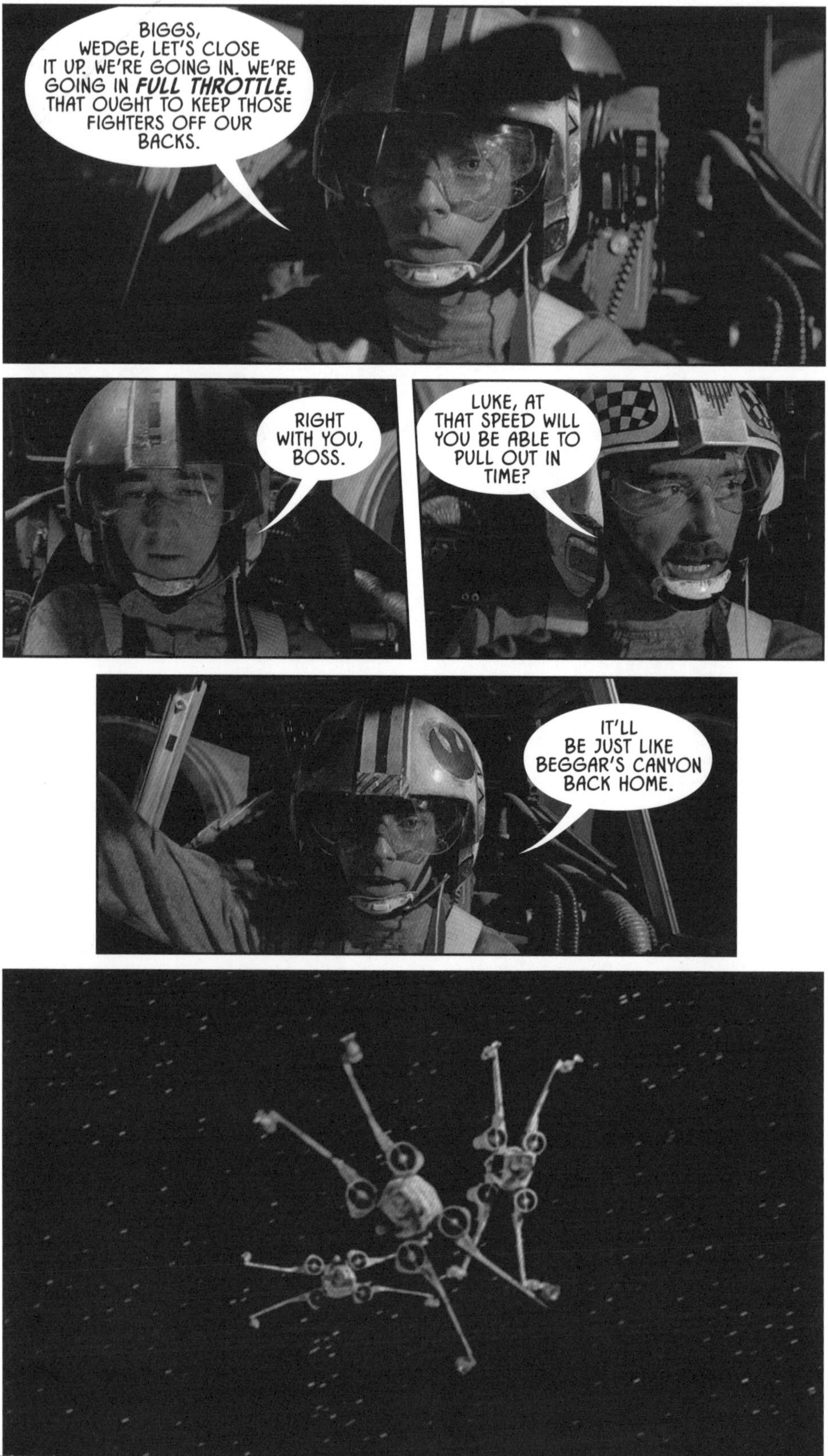
BIGGS, WEDGE, LET'S CLOSE IT UP. WE'RE GOING IN. WE'RE GOING IN **FULL THROTTLE.** THAT OUGHT TO KEEP THOSE FIGHTERS OFF OUR BACKS.
RIGHT WITH YOU, BOSS.
LUKE, AT THAT SPEED WILL YOU BE ABLE TO PULL OUT IN TIME?
IT'LL BE JUST LIKE BEGGAR'S CANYON BACK HOME.

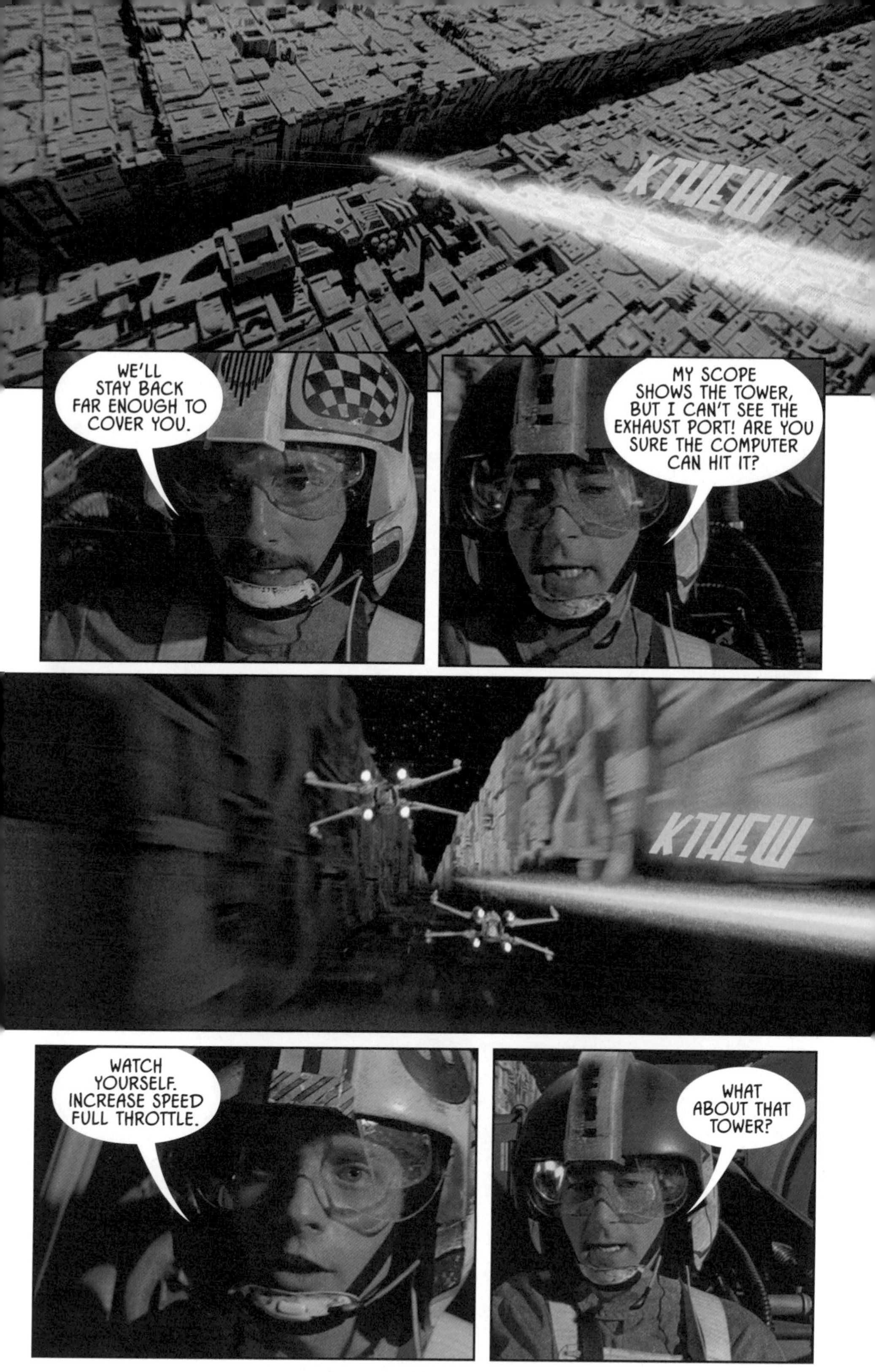
KTHEW
WE'LL STAY BACK FAR ENOUGH TO COVER YOU.
MY SCOPE SHOWS THE TOWER, BUT I CAN'T SEE THE EXHAUST PORT! ARE YOU SURE THE COMPUTER CAN HIT IT?
KTHEW
WATCH YOURSELF. INCREASE SPEED FULL THROTTLE.
WHAT ABOUT THAT TOWER?

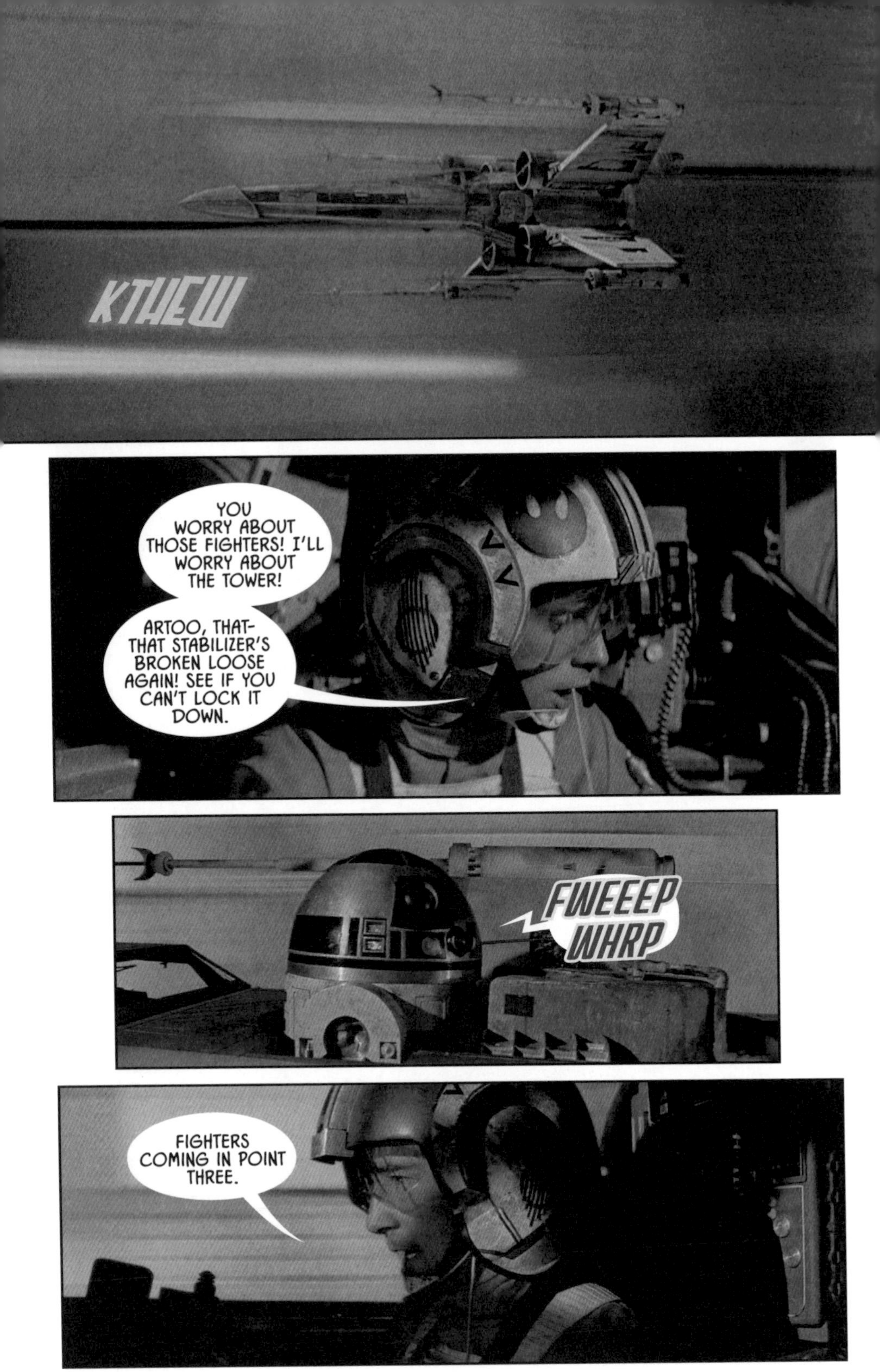
KTHEW
YOU WORRY ABOUT THOSE FIGHTERS! I'LL WORRY ABOUT THE TOWER!
ARTOO, THAT-THAT STABILIZER'S BROKEN LOOSE AGAIN! SEE IF YOU CAN'T LOCK IT DOWN.
FWEEEP WHRP
FIGHTERS COMING IN POINT THREE.

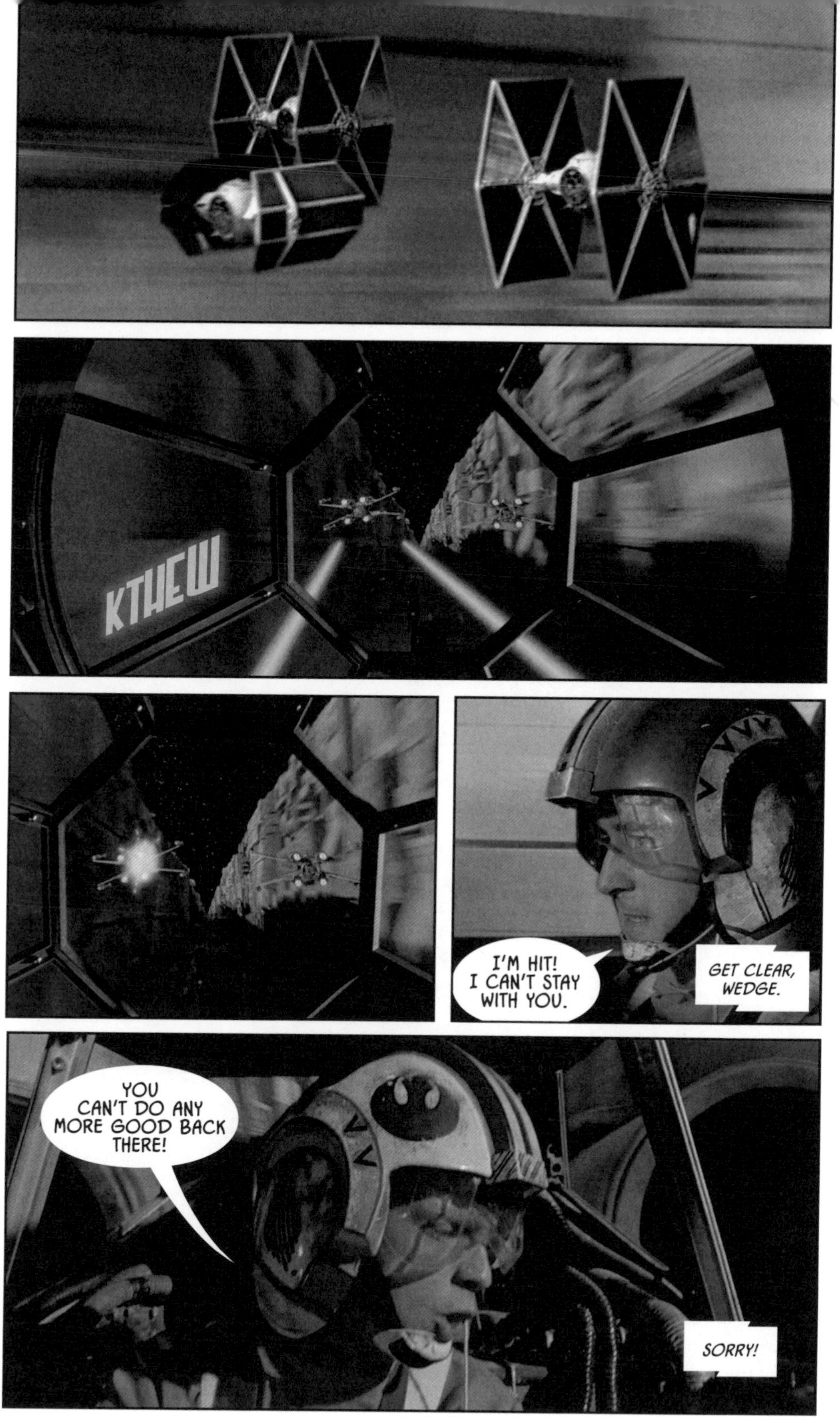
KTHEW
I'M HIT! I CAN'T STAY WITH YOU.
GET CLEAR, WEDGE.
YOU CAN'T DO ANY MORE GOOD BACK THERE!
SORRY!

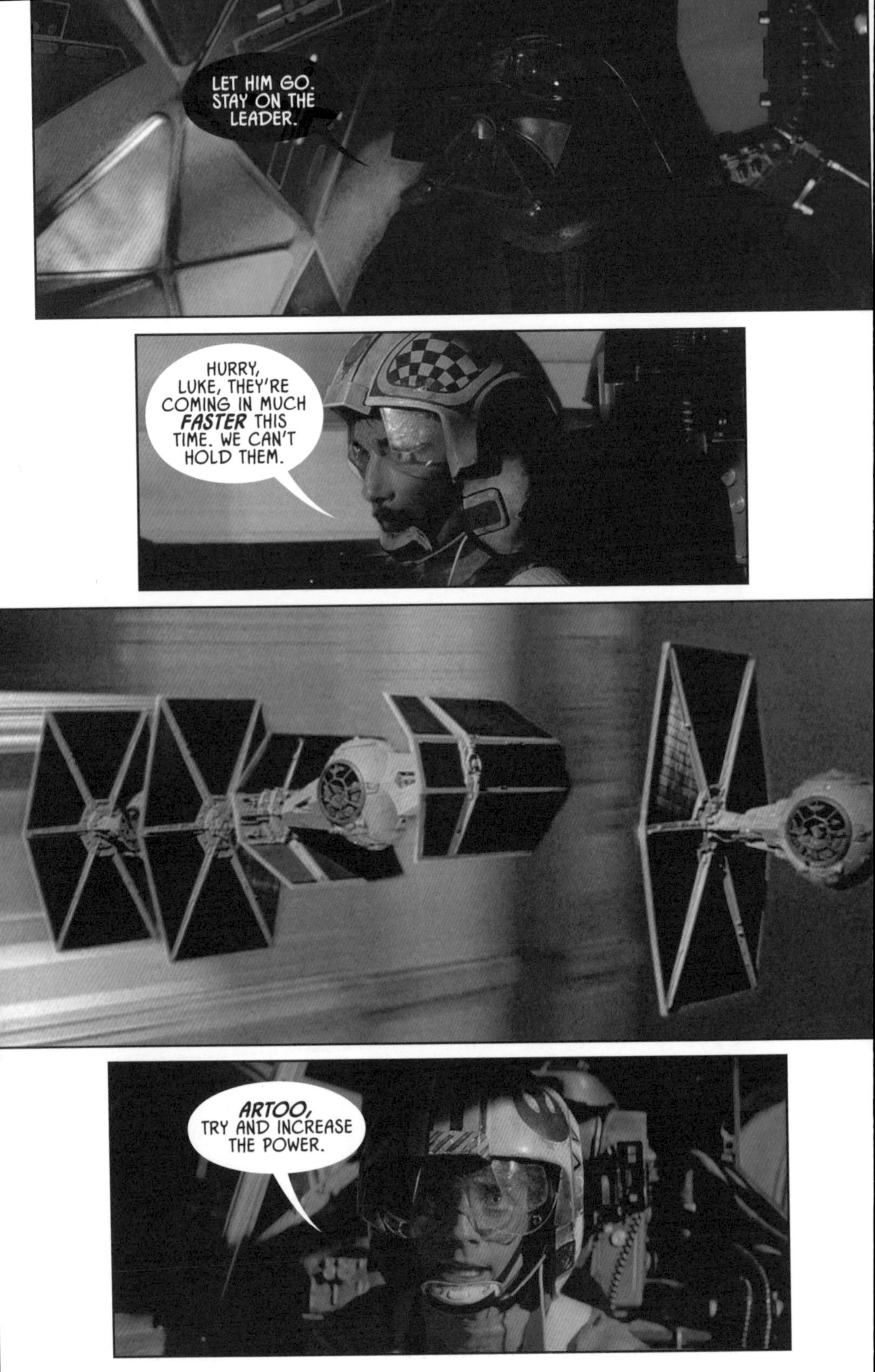
LET HIM GO. STAY ON THE LEADER.
HURRY, LUKE, THEY'RE COMING IN MUCH FASTER THIS TIME. WE CAN'T HOLD THEM.
ARTOO, TRY AND INCREASE THE POWER.

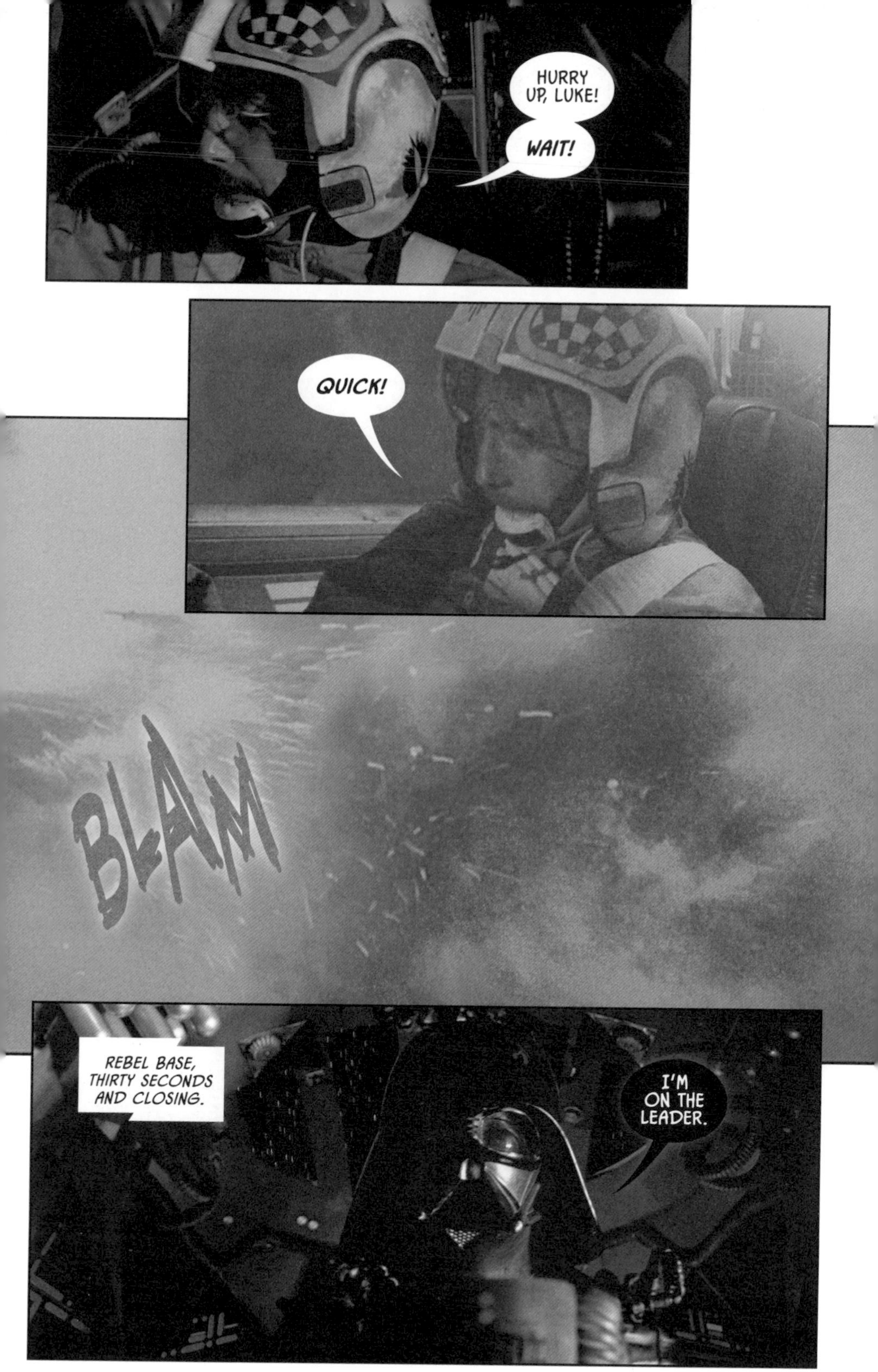
HURRY UP, LUKE!
WAIT!
QUICK!
BLAM
REBEL BASE, THIRTY SECONDS AND CLOSING.
I'M ON THE LEADER.

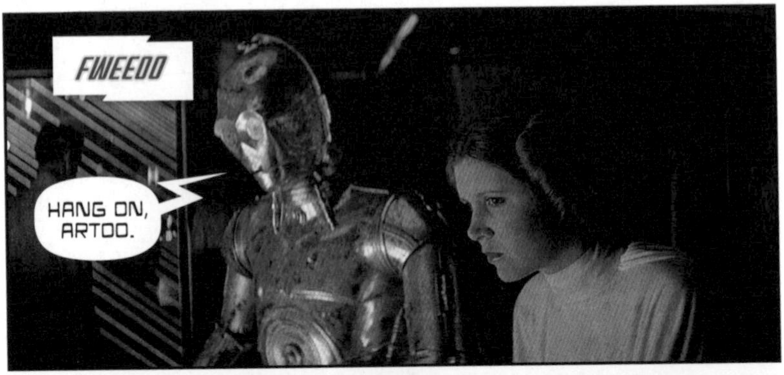
FWEEDO
HANG ON, ARTOO.

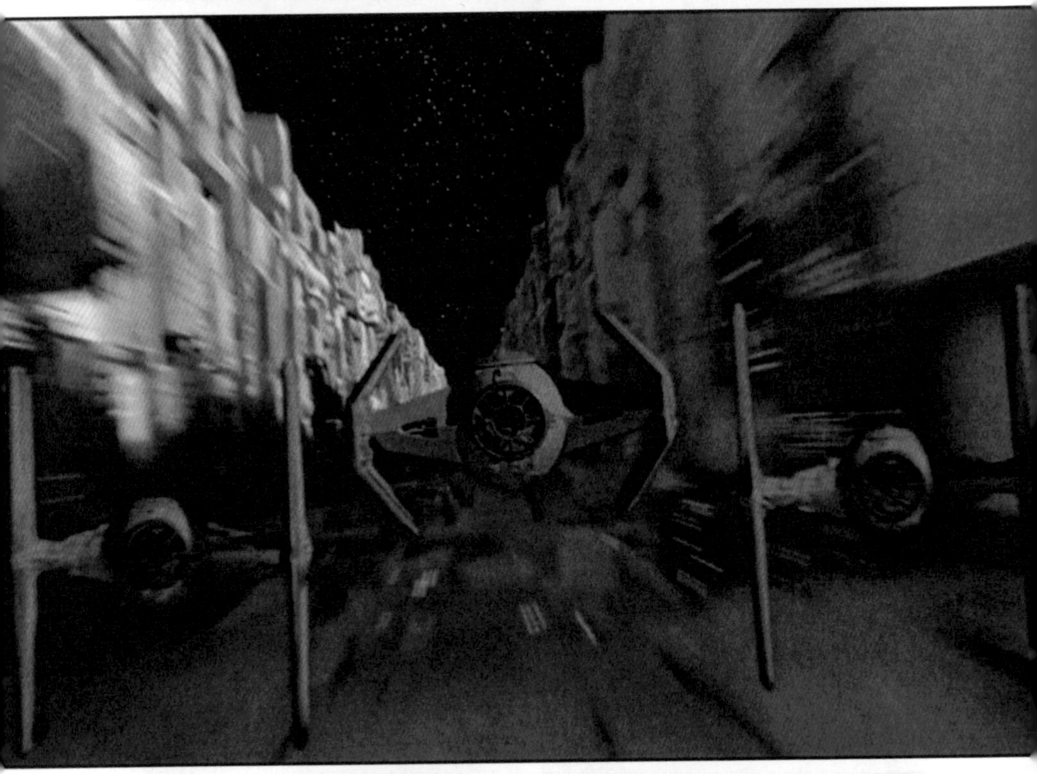

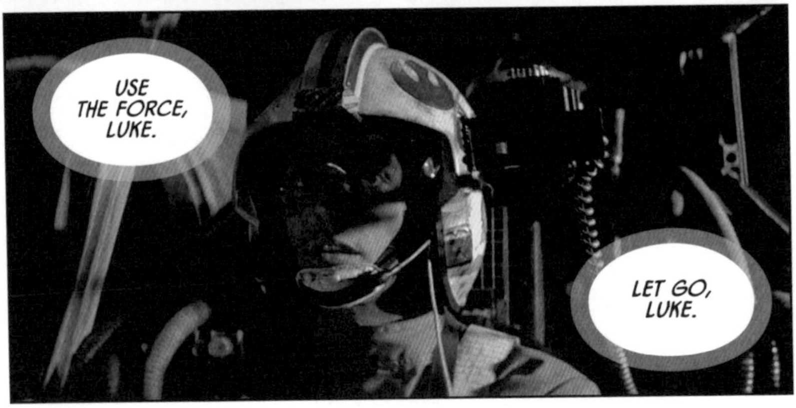
USE THE FORCE, LUKE.
LET GO, LUKE.

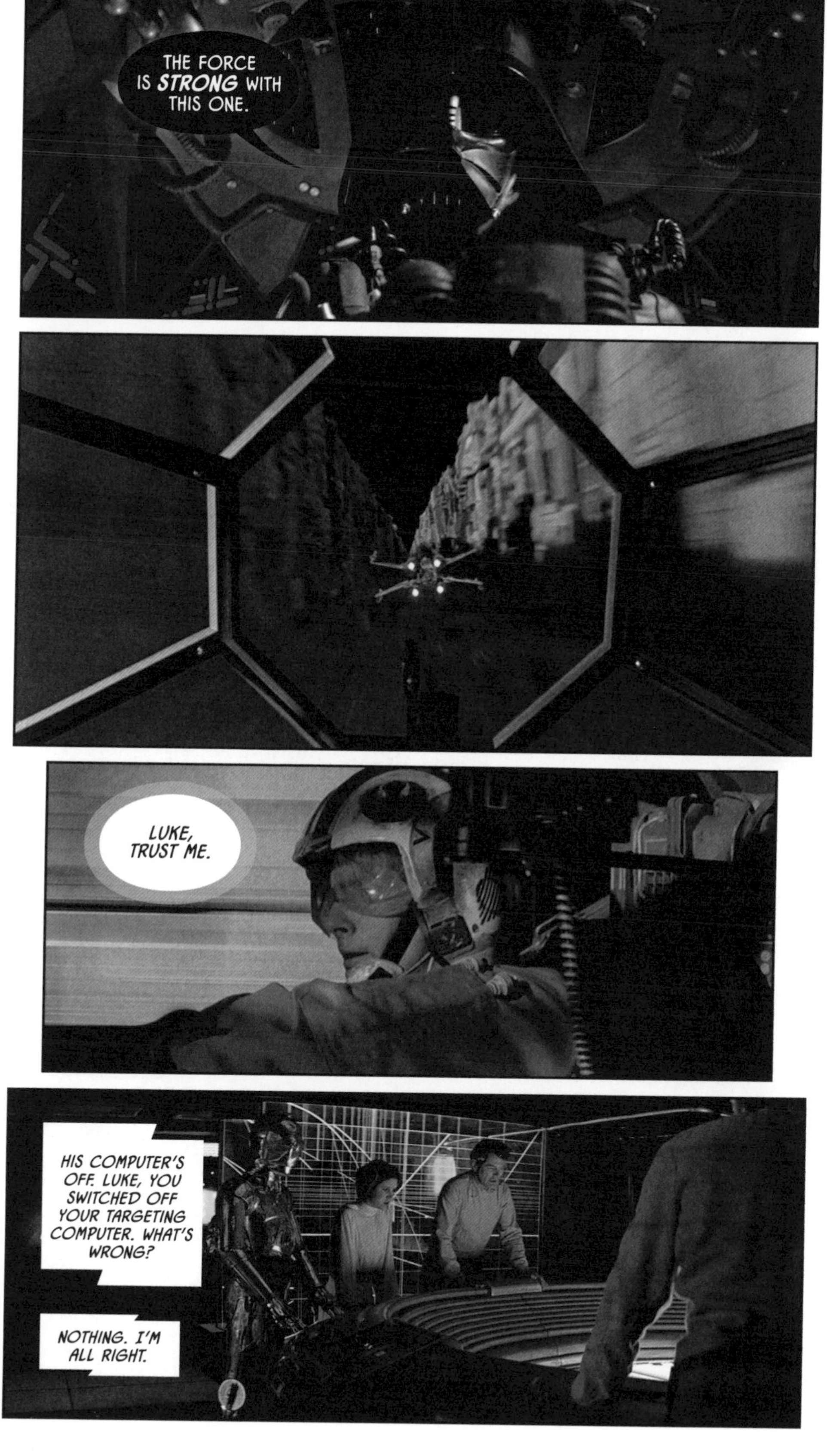
THE FORCE IS STRONG WITH THIS ONE.
LUKE, TRUST ME.
HIS COMPUTER'S OFF. LUKE, YOU SWITCHED OFF YOUR TARGETING COMPUTER. WHAT'S WRONG?
NOTHING. I'M ALL RIGHT.

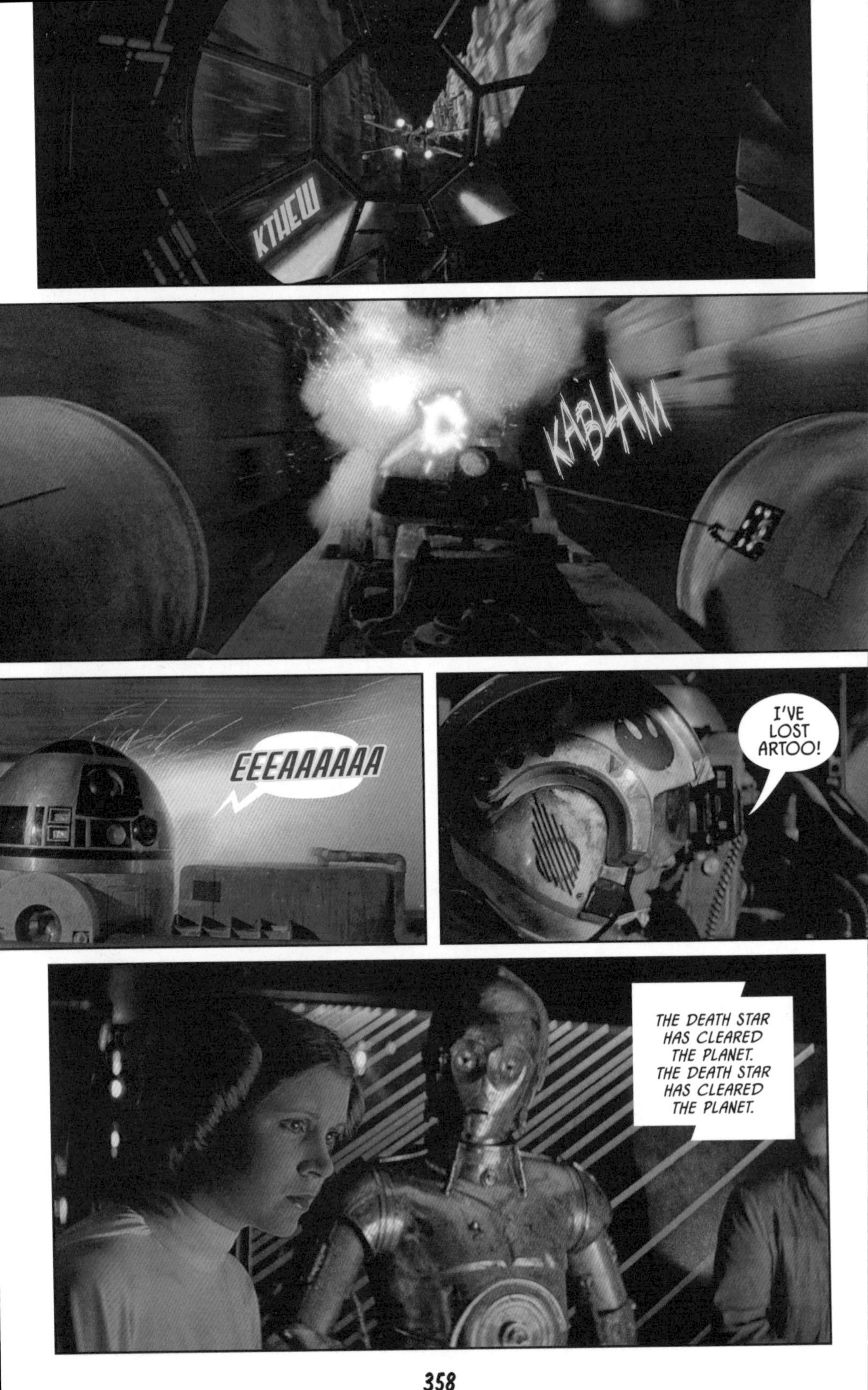
KTHEW
KABLAM
EEEAAAAAAA
I'VE LOST ARTOO!
THE DEATH STAR HAS CLEARED THE PLANET. THE DEATH STAR HAS CLEARED THE PLANET.

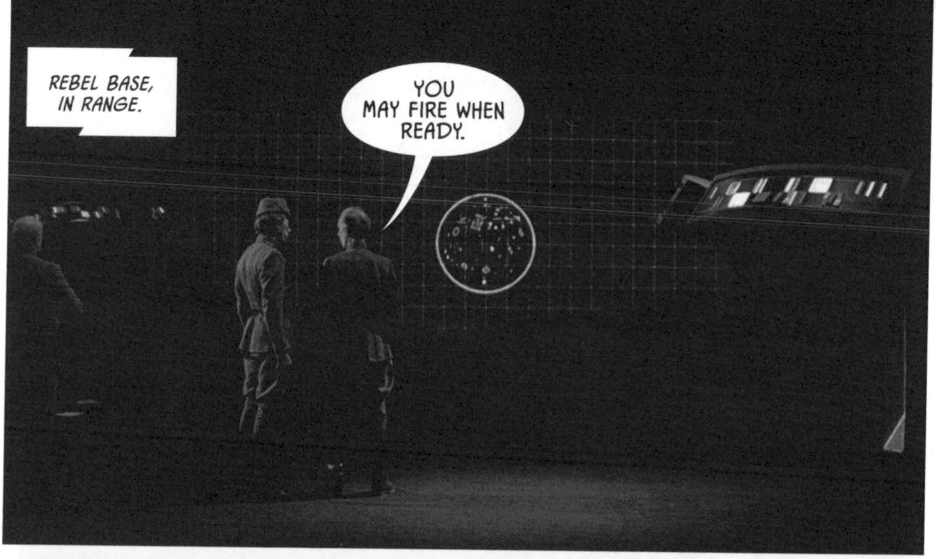
REBEL BASE, IN RANGE.
YOU MAY FIRE WHEN READY.

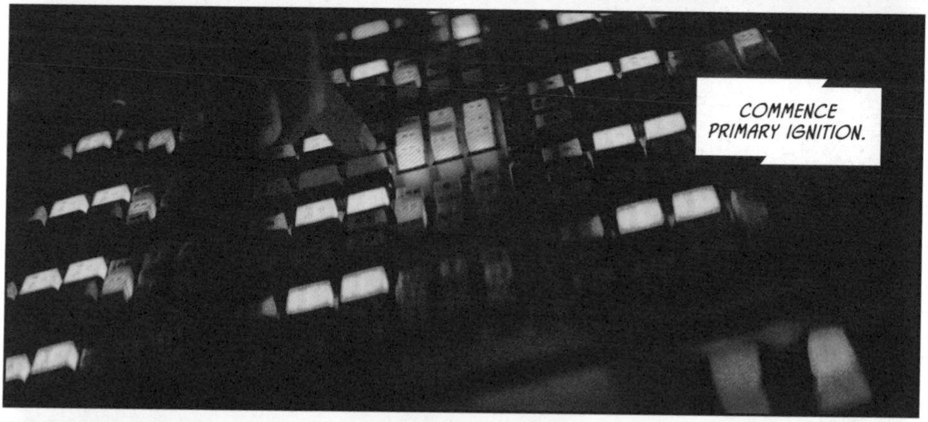
COMMENCE PRIMARY IGNITION.

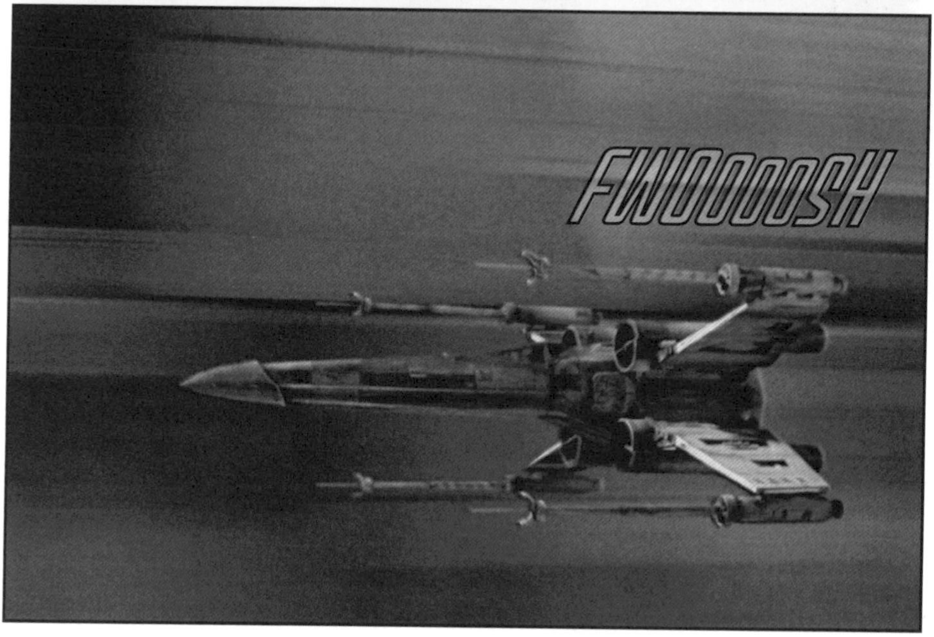
FWOOOOOSH

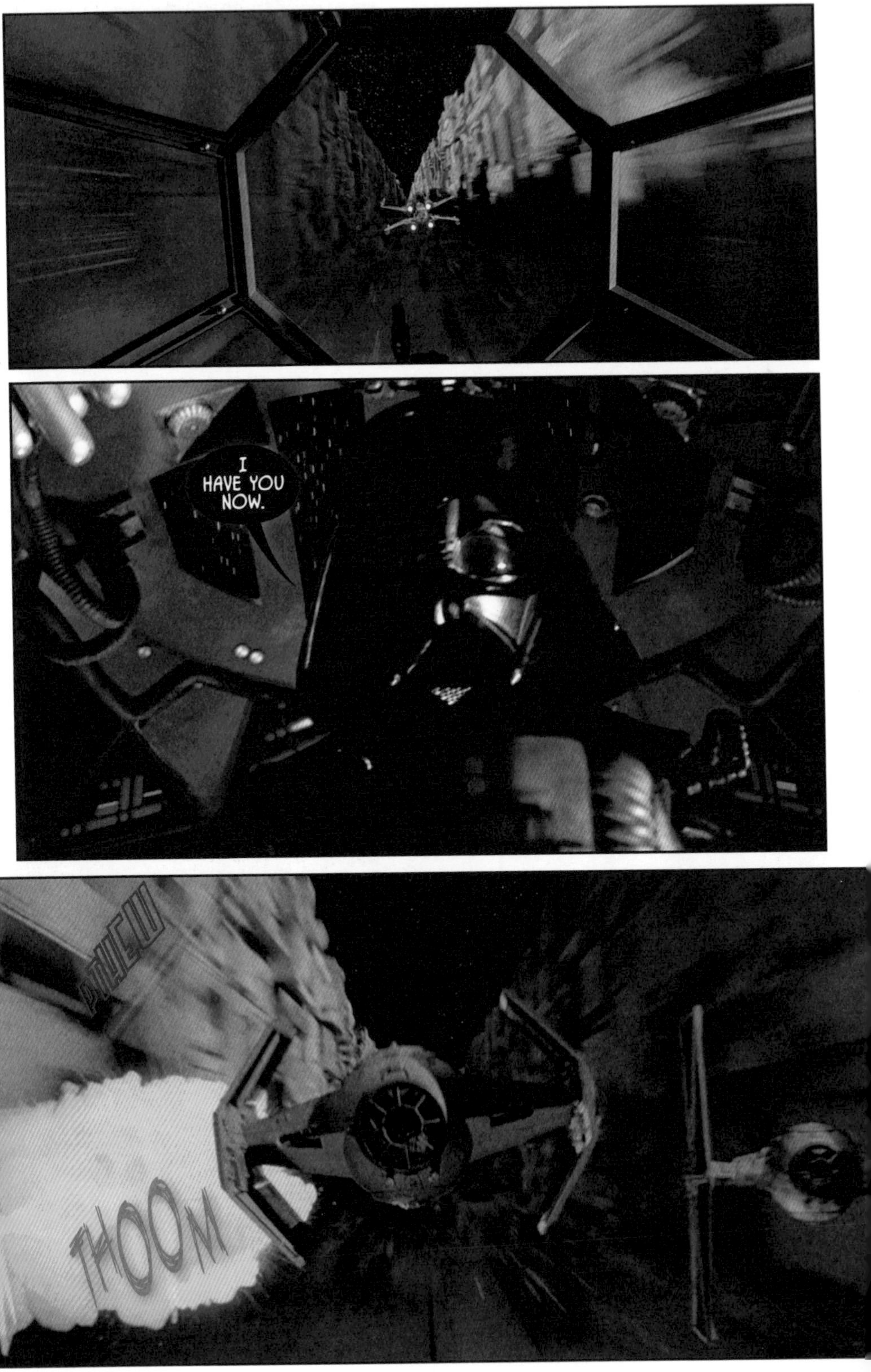
I HAVE YOU NOW.
THOOM

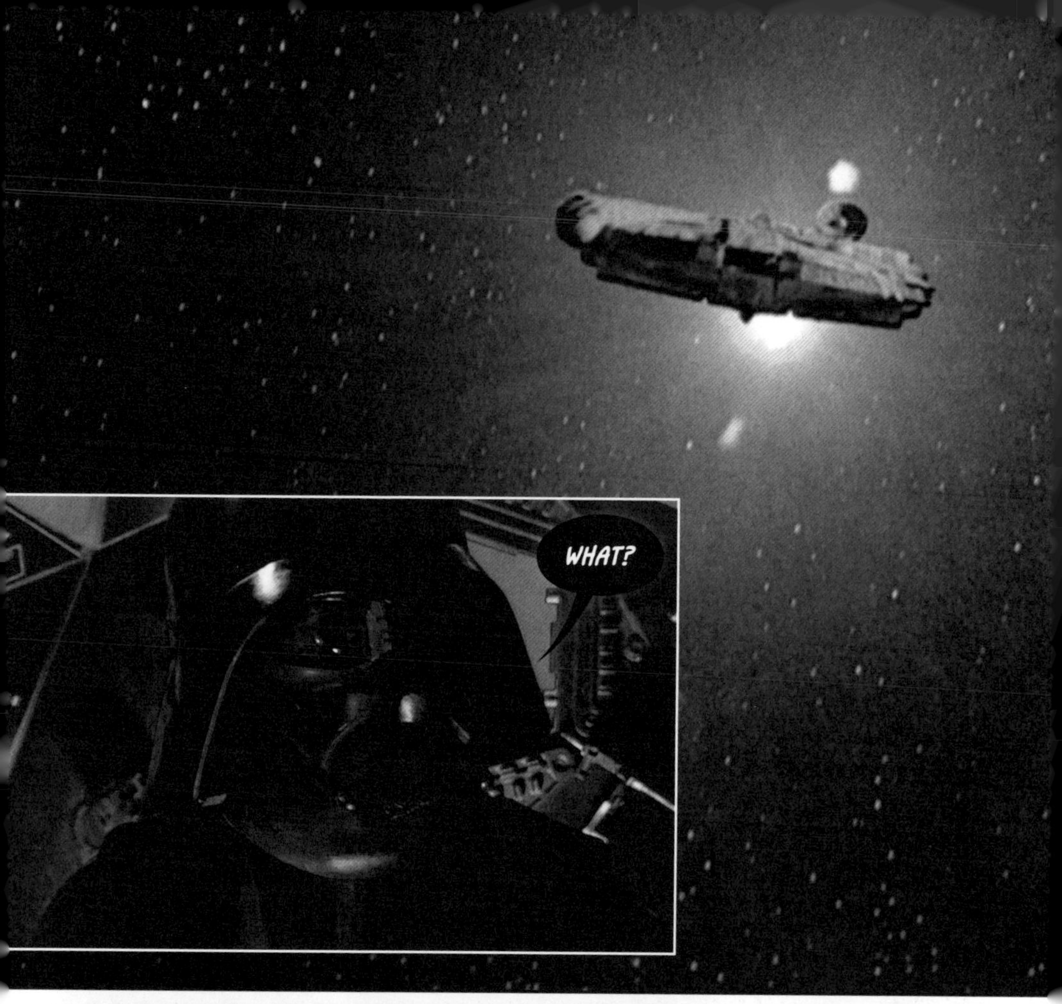
WHAT?

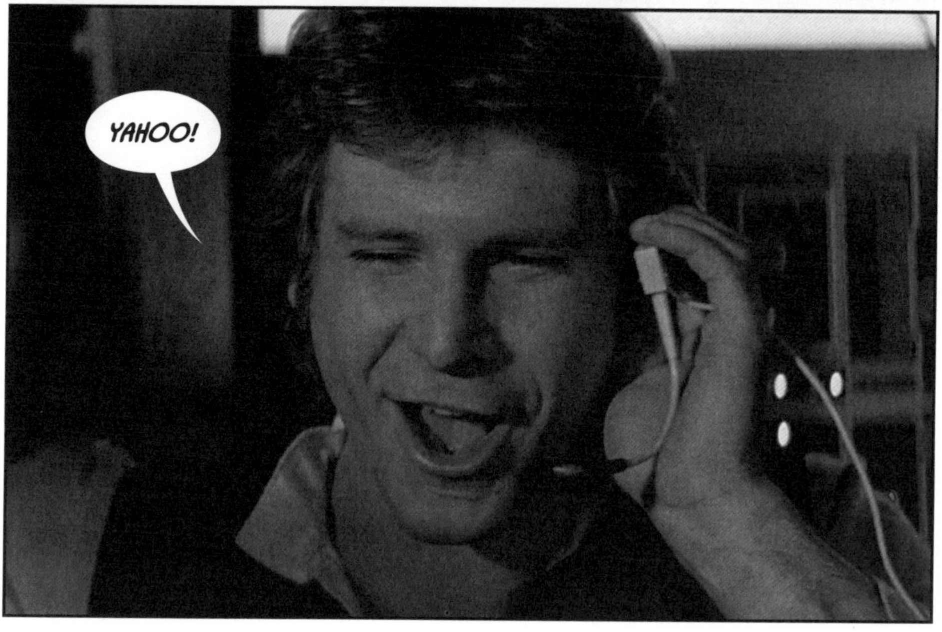
YAHOO!

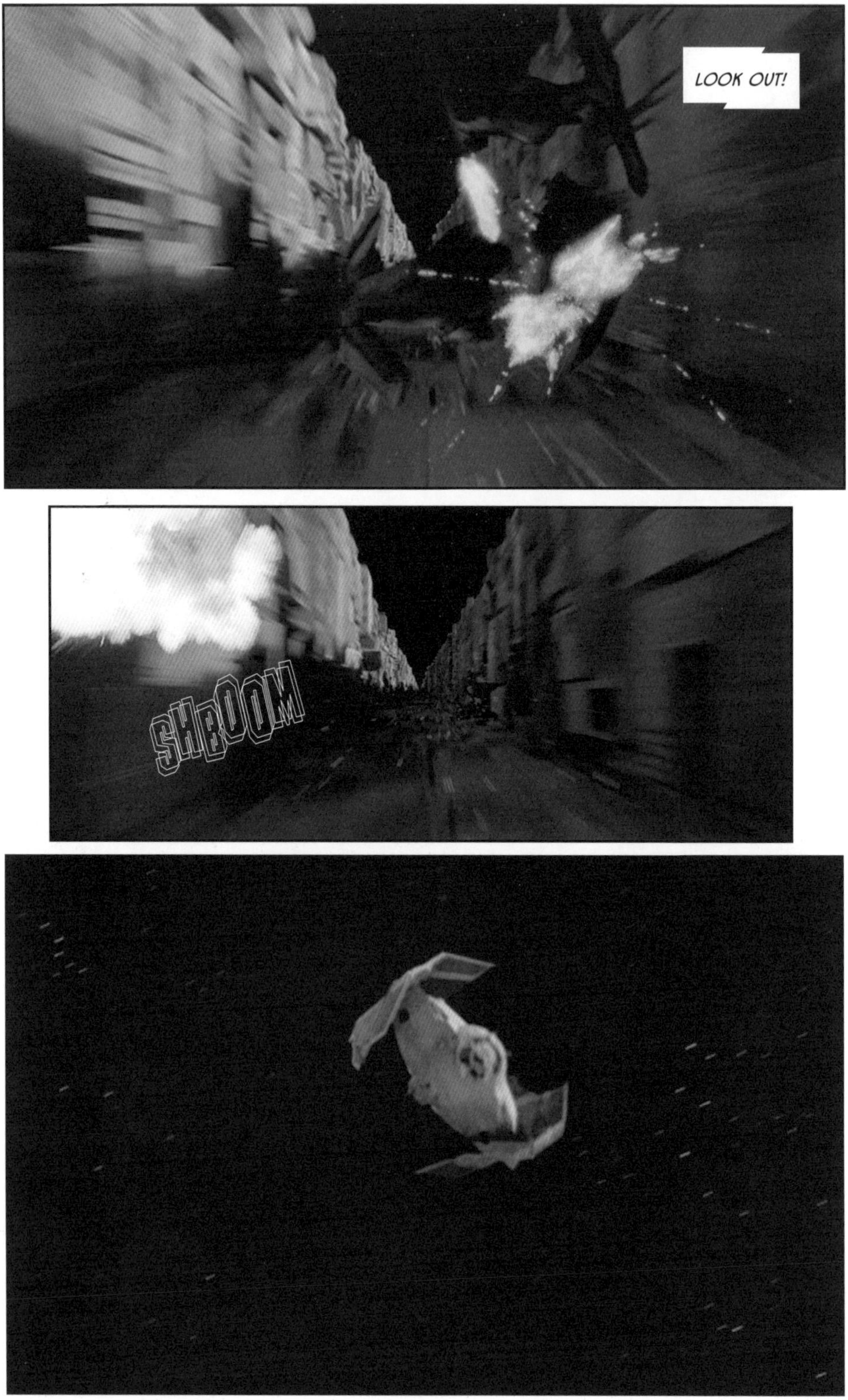
LOOK OUT!
SHBOOM

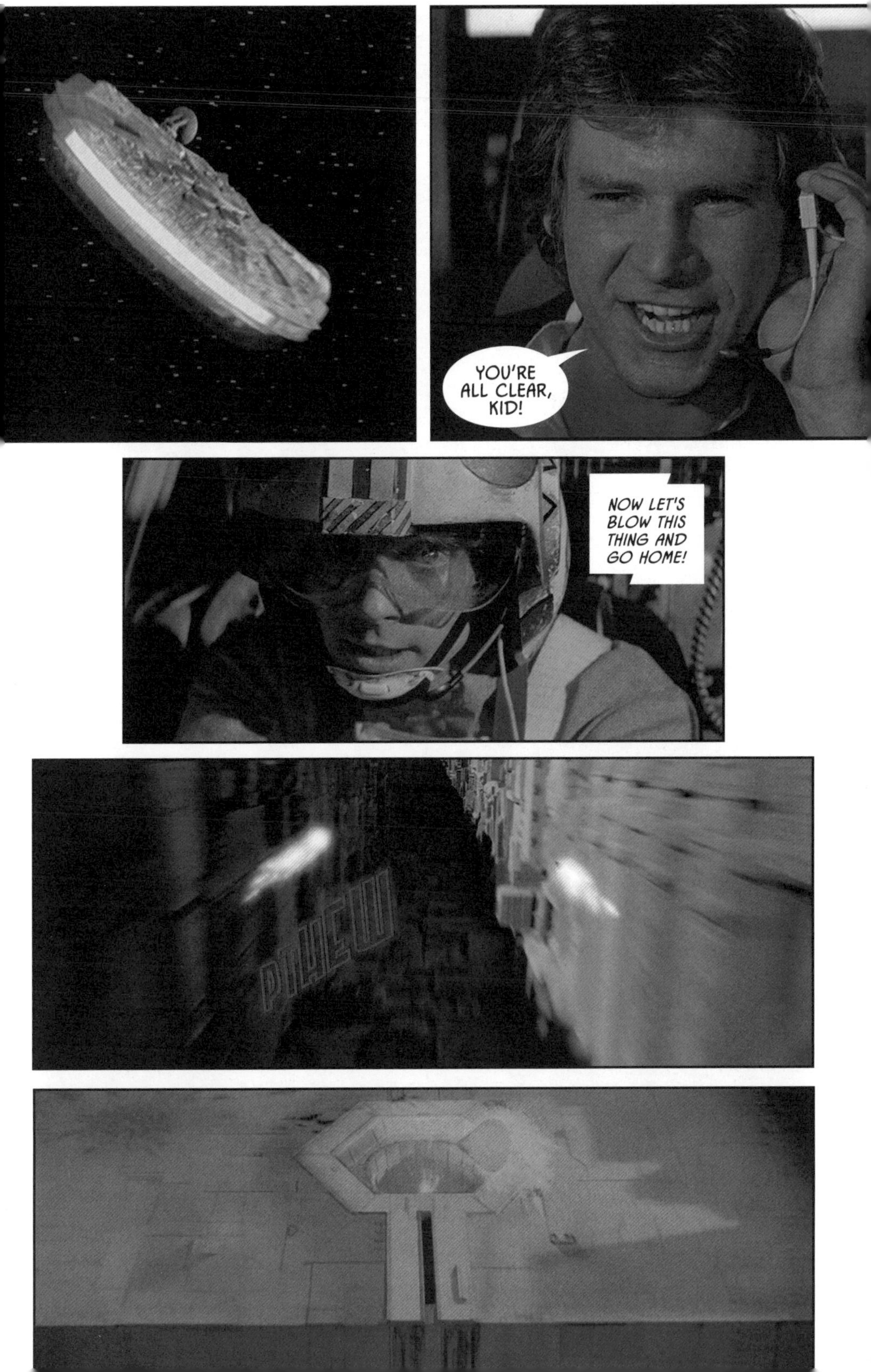
YOU'RE ALL CLEAR, KID!
NOW LET'S BLOW THIS THING AND GO HOME!
PTHEW

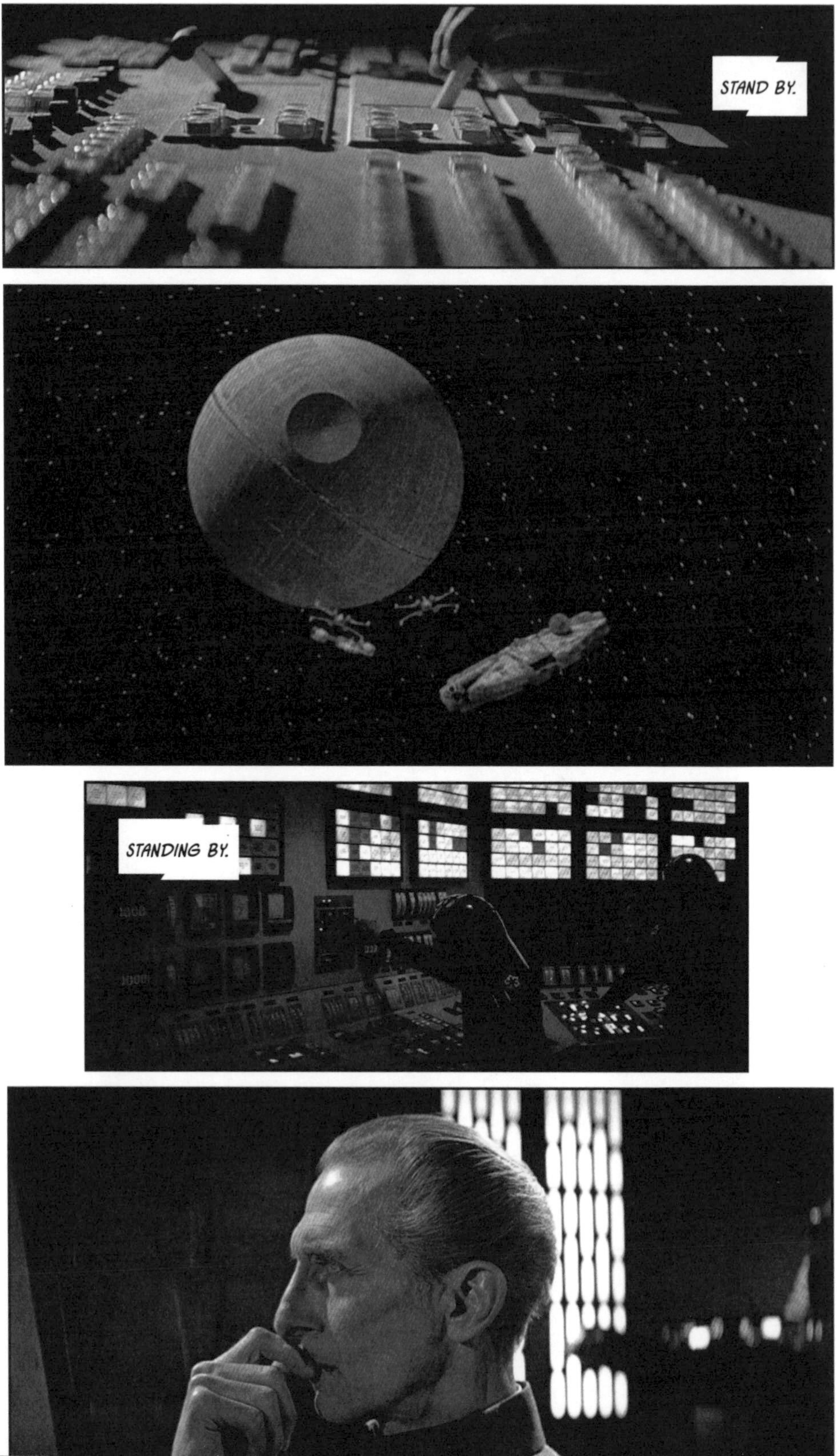
STAND BY.
STANDING BY.

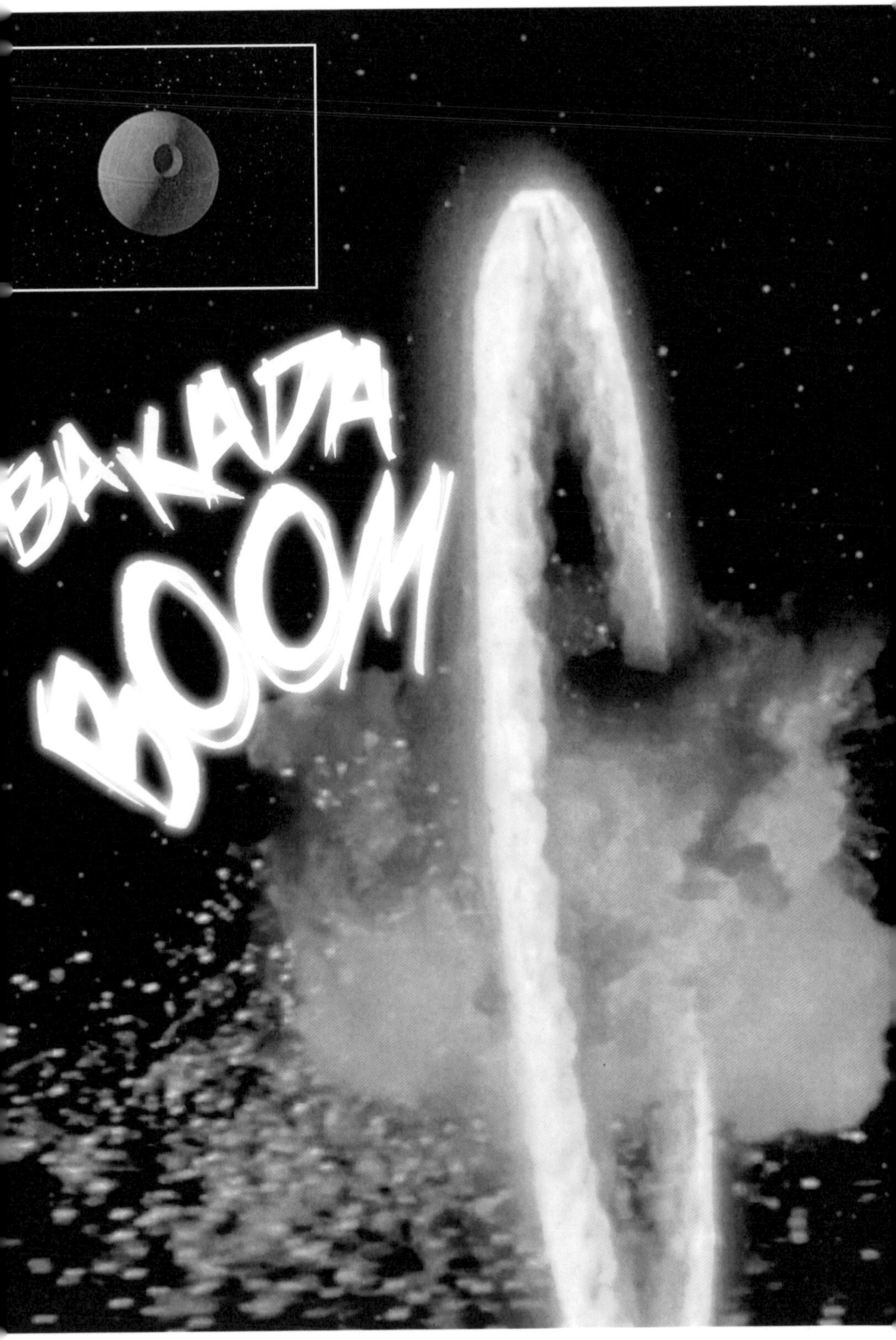
BAKADA
BOOM

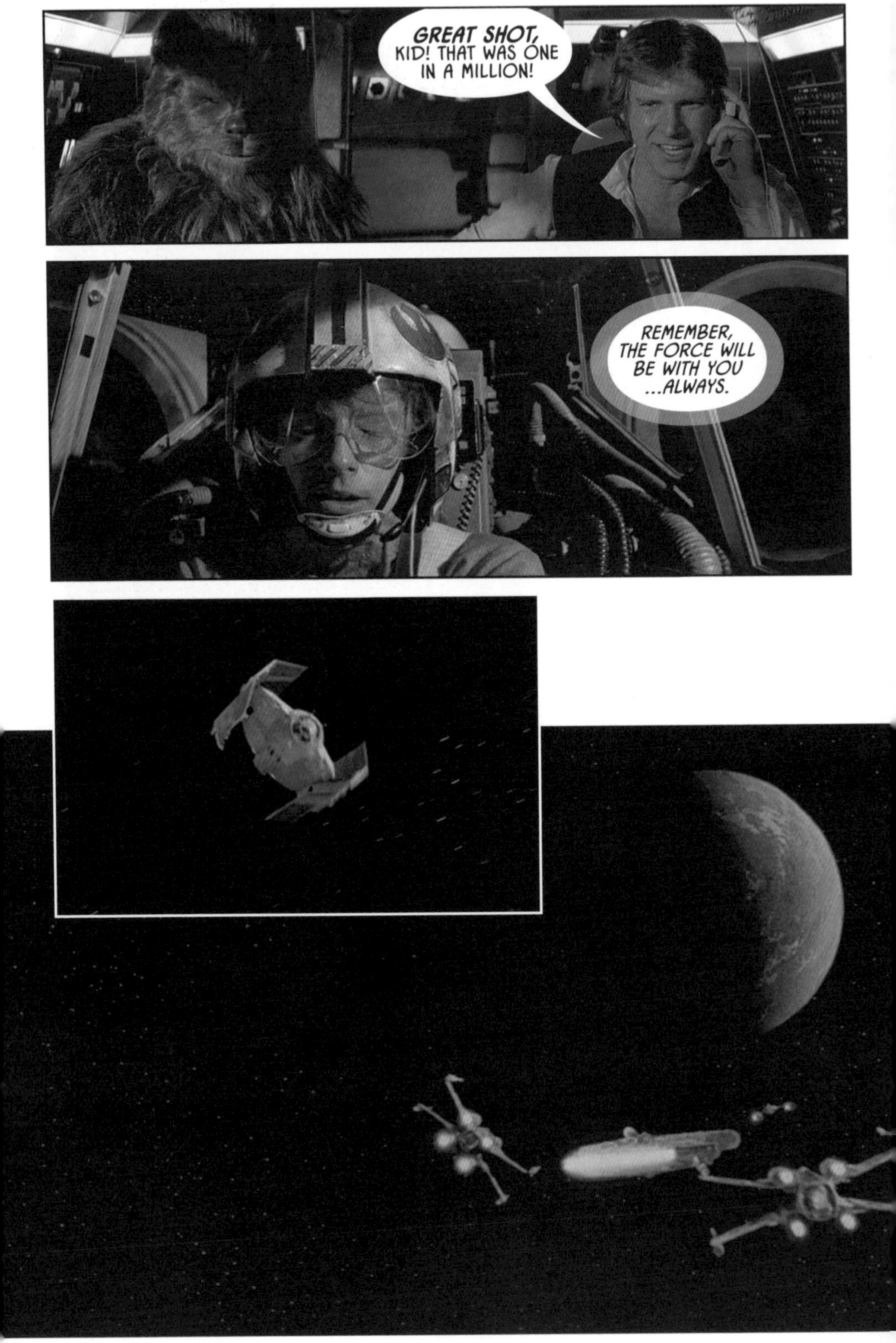
GREAT SHOT, KID! THAT WAS ONE IN A MILLION!
REMEMBER, THE FORCE WILL BE WITH YOU ...ALWAYS.

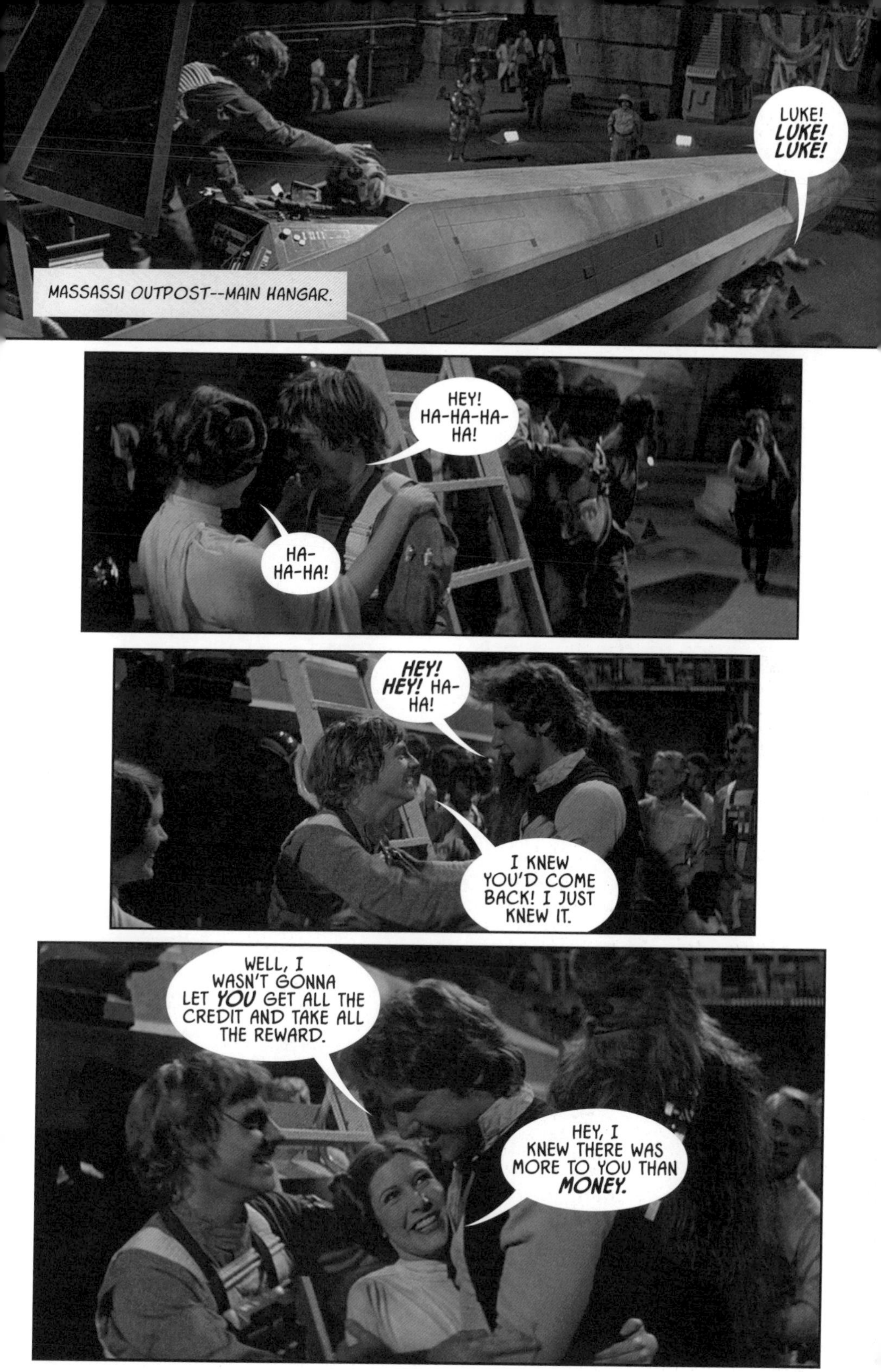
LUKE! LUKE! LUKE!
MASSASSI OUTPOST--MAIN HANGAR.
HEY! HA-HA-HA-HA!
HA-HA-HA!
HEY! HEY! HA-HA!
I KNEW YOU'D COME BACK! I JUST KNEW IT.
WELL, I WASN'T GONNA LET YOU GET ALL THE CREDIT AND TAKE ALL THE REWARD.
HEY, I KNEW THERE WAS MORE TO YOU THAN MONEY.

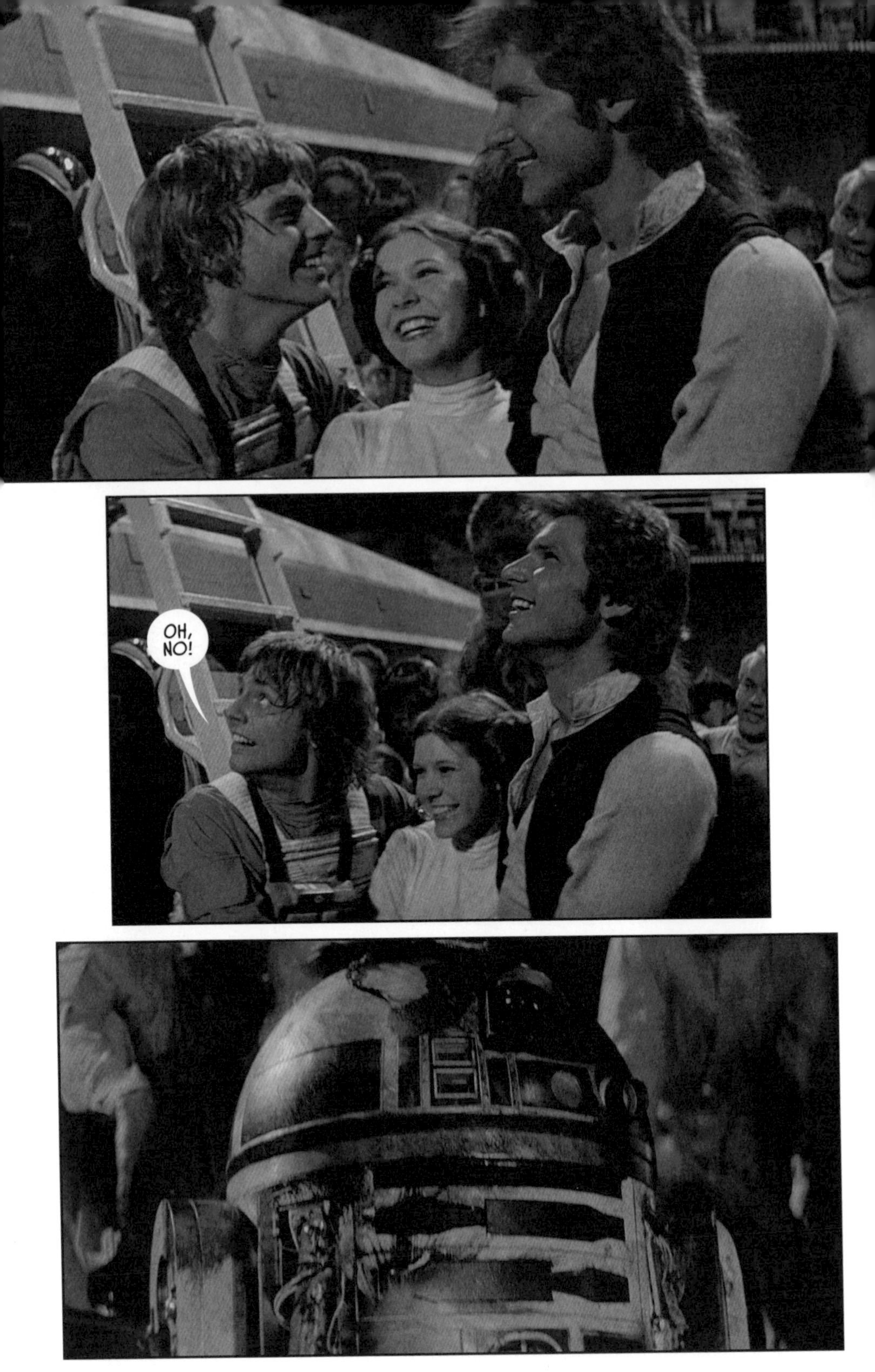
OH, NO!

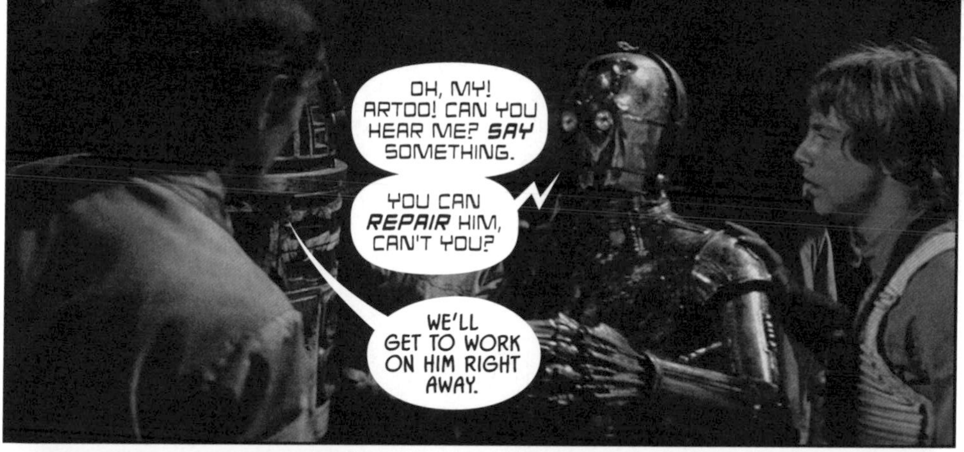
OH, MY! ARTOO! CAN YOU HEAR ME? SAY SOMETHING.
YOU CAN REPAIR HIM, CAN'T YOU?
WE'LL GET TO WORK ON HIM RIGHT AWAY.

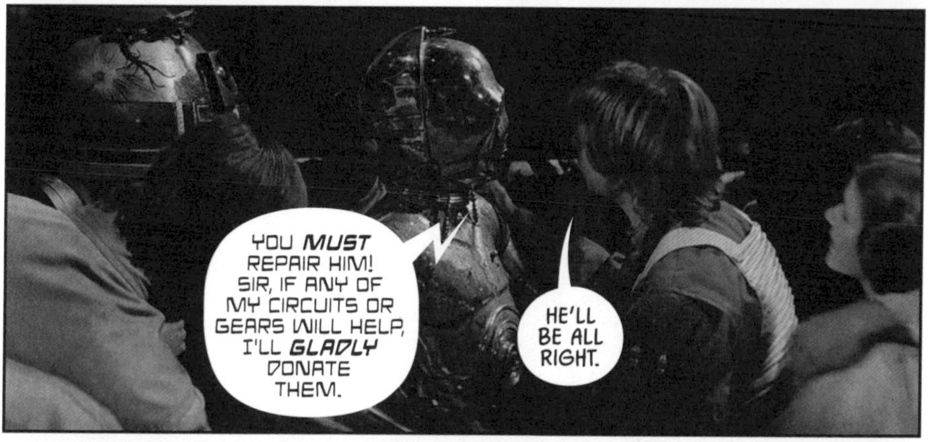
YOU MUST REPAIR HIM! SIR, IF ANY OF MY CIRCUITS OR GEARS WILL HELP, I'LL GLADLY DONATE THEM.
HE'LL BE ALL RIGHT.

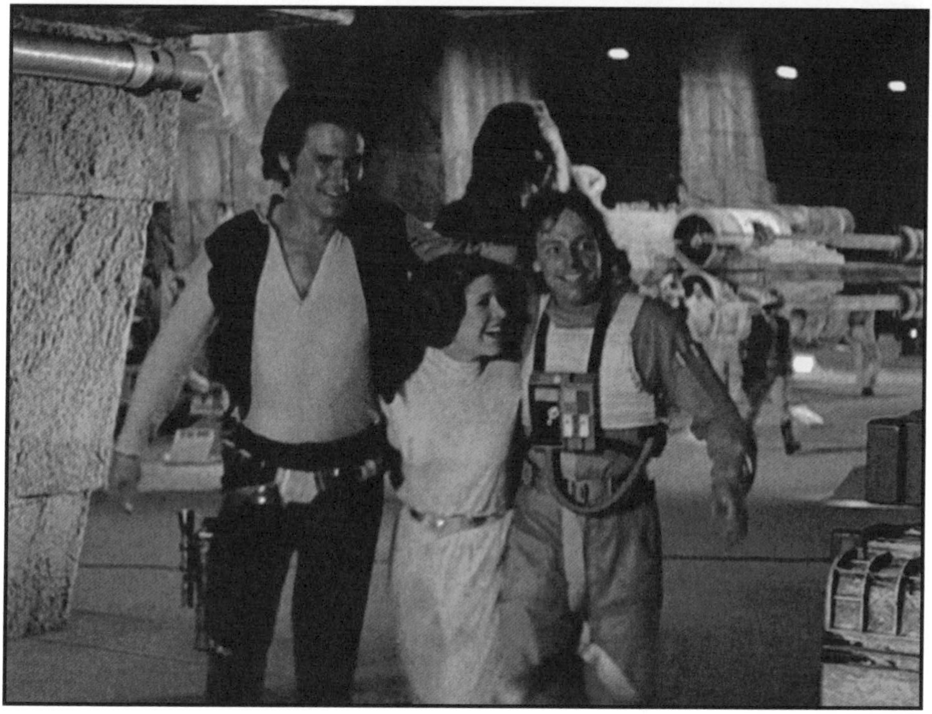

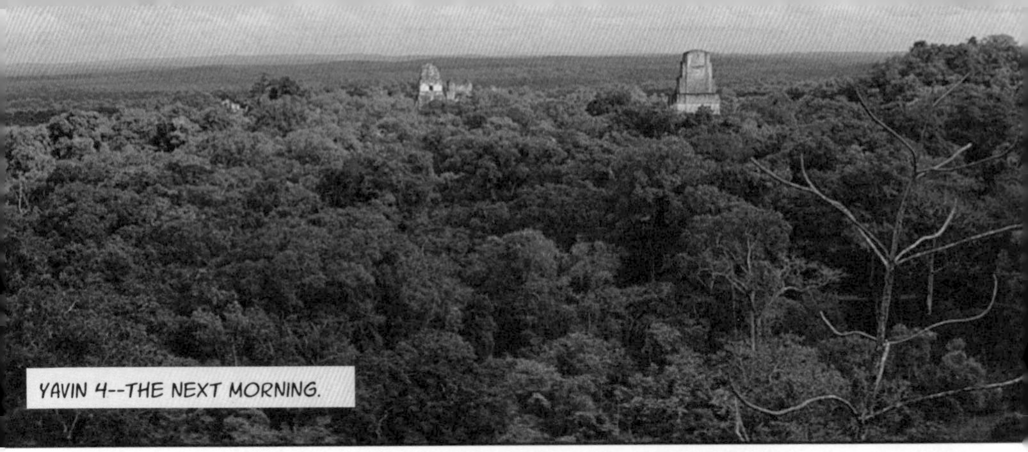
YAVIN 4--THE NEXT MORNING.

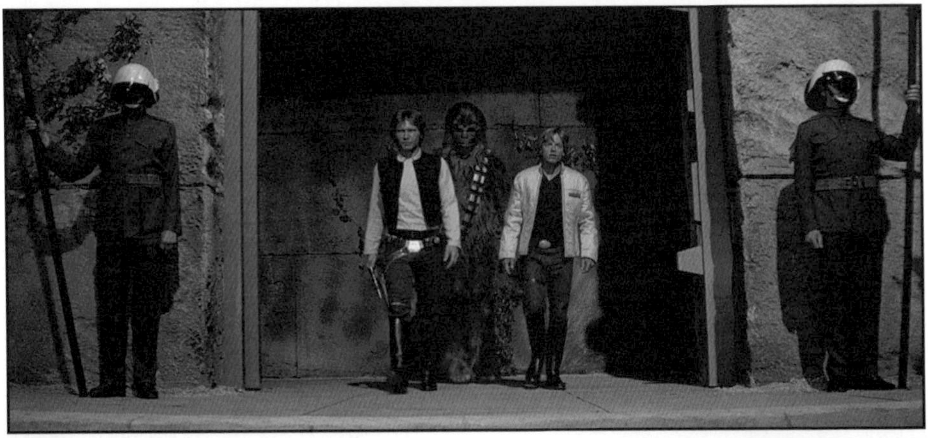

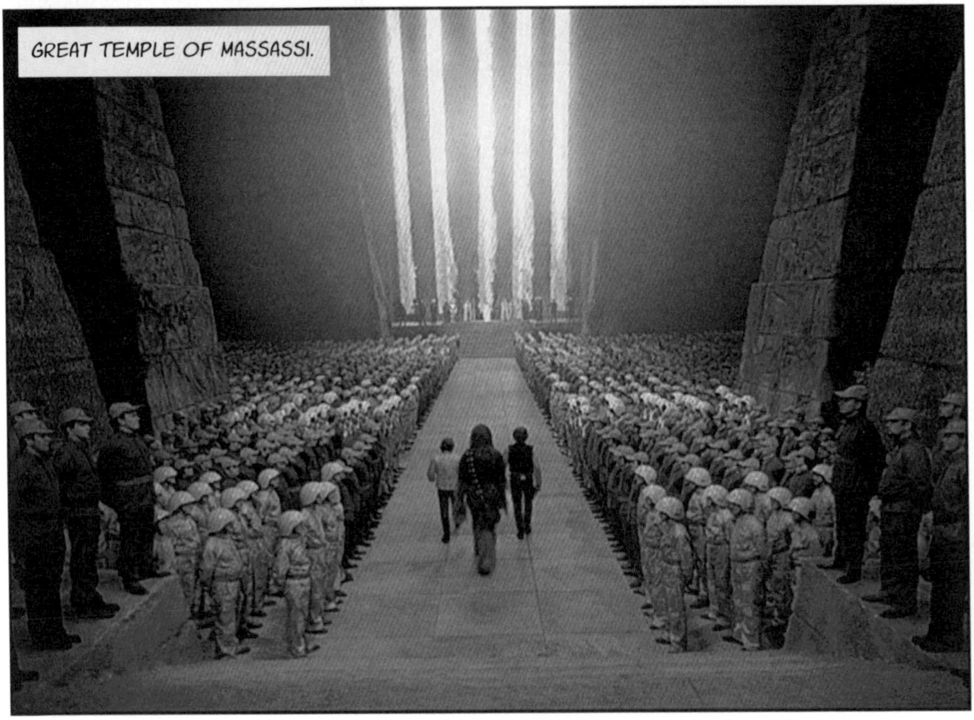
GREAT TEMPLE OF MASSASSI.

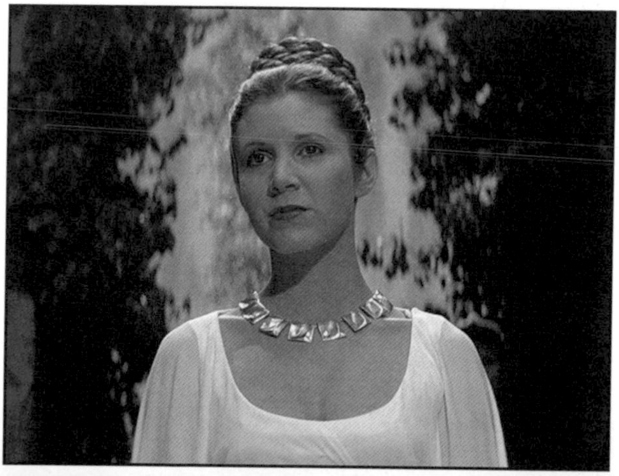

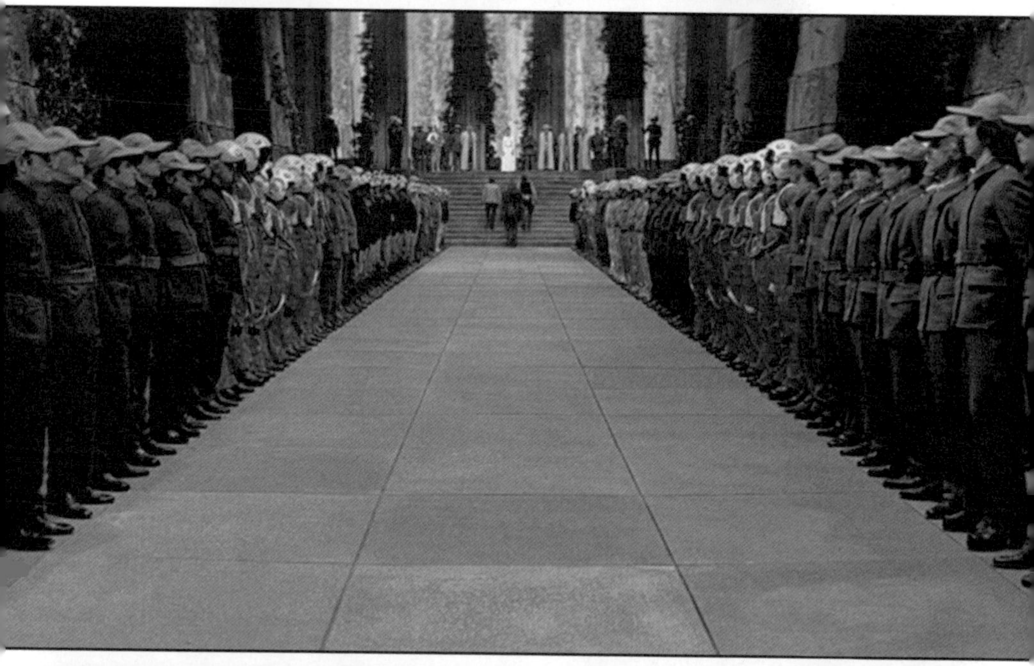

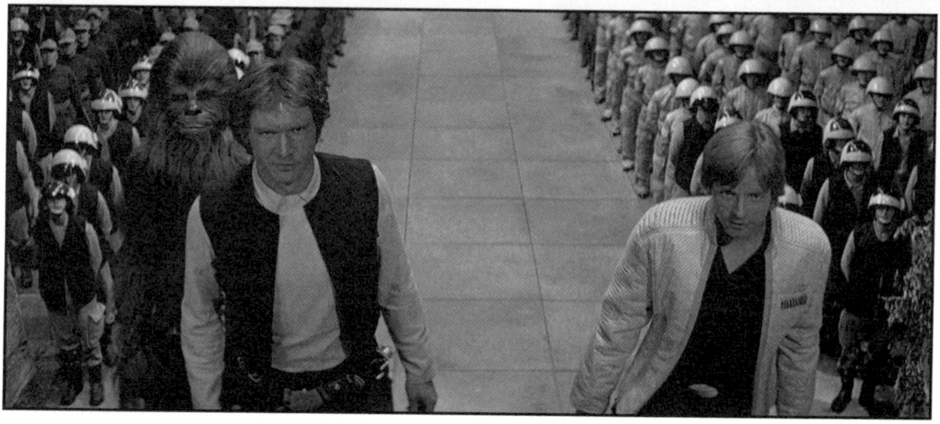

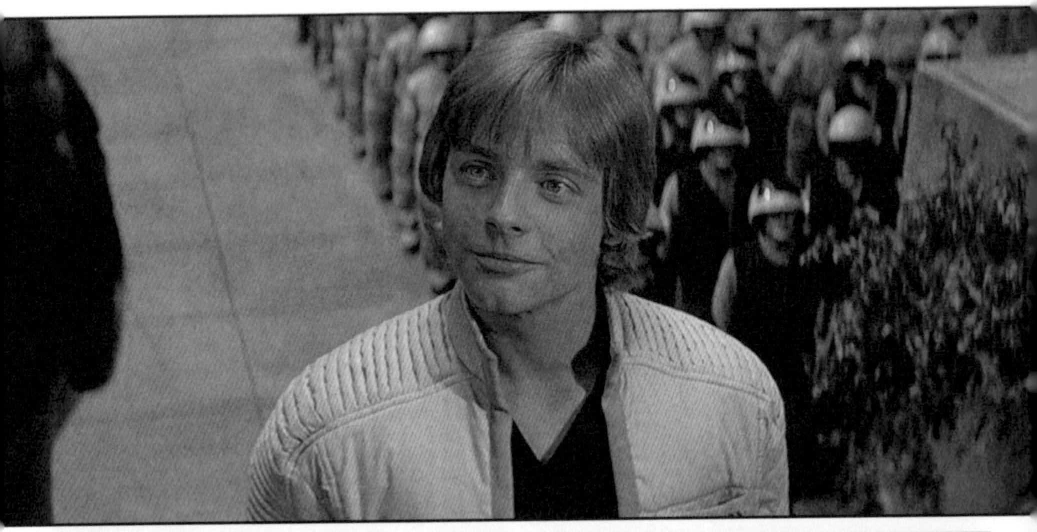

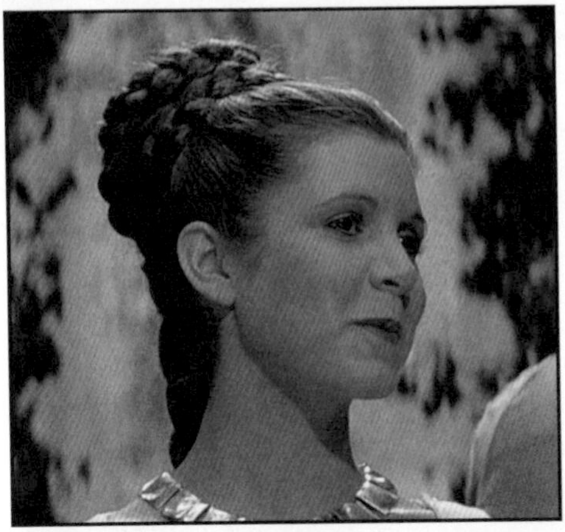

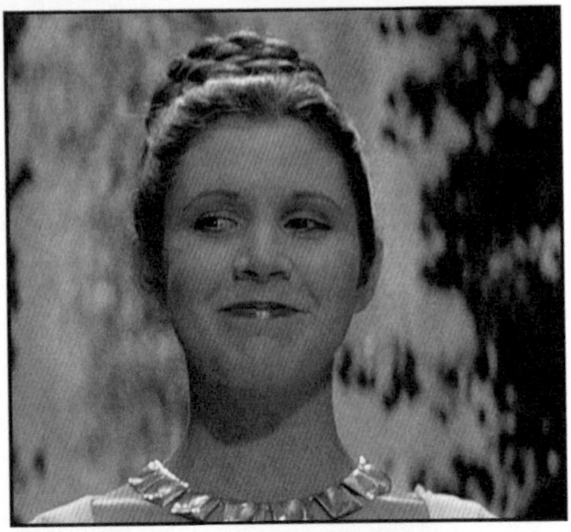

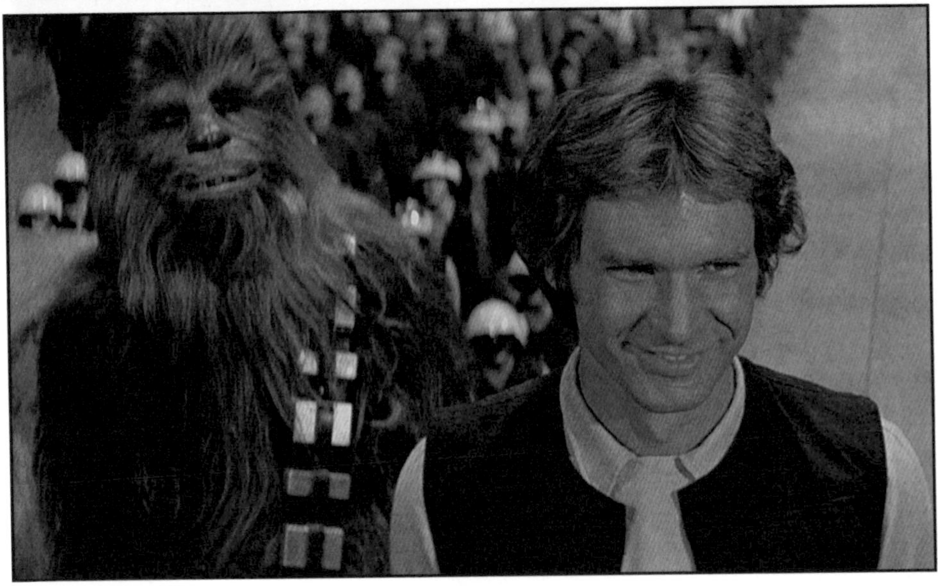

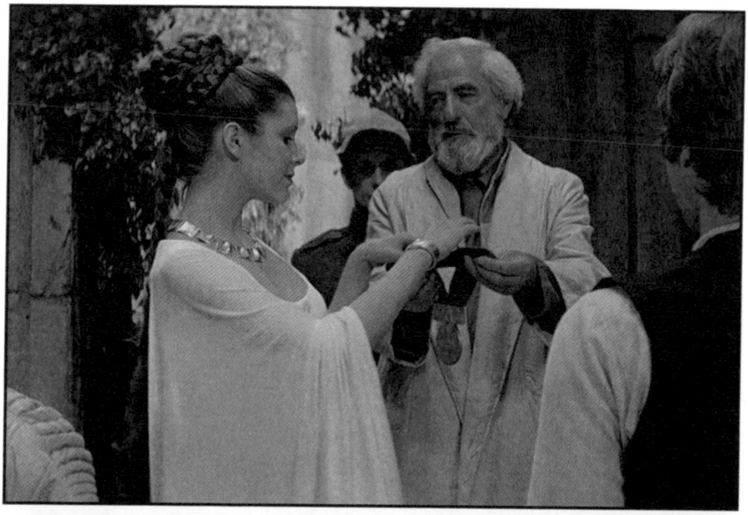

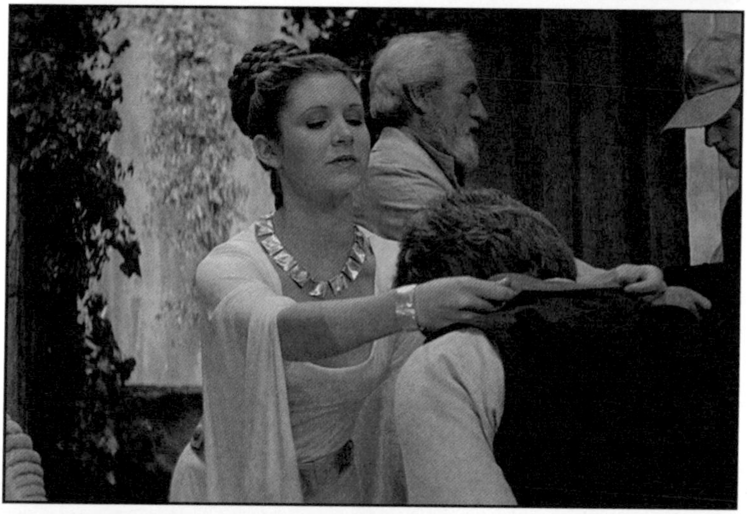

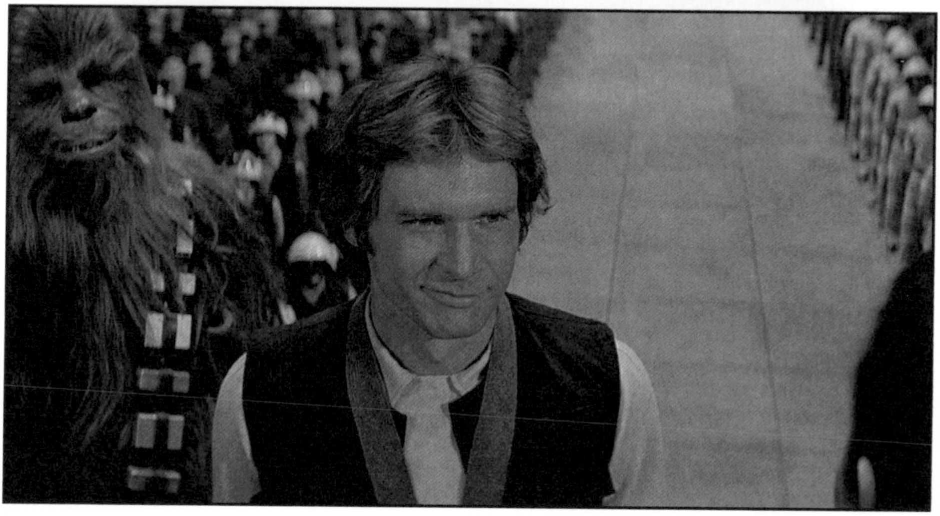

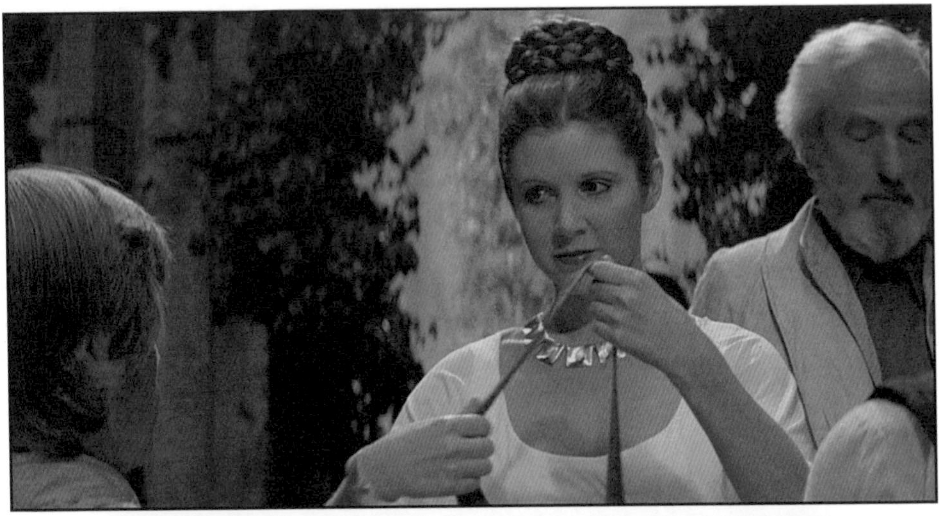

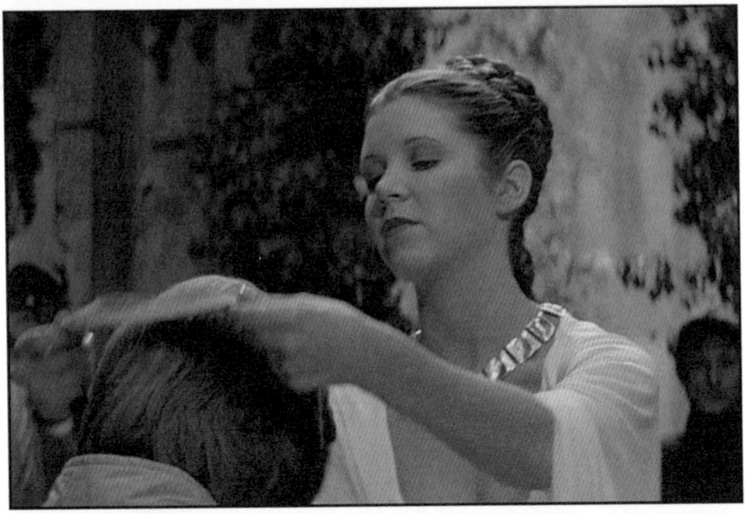

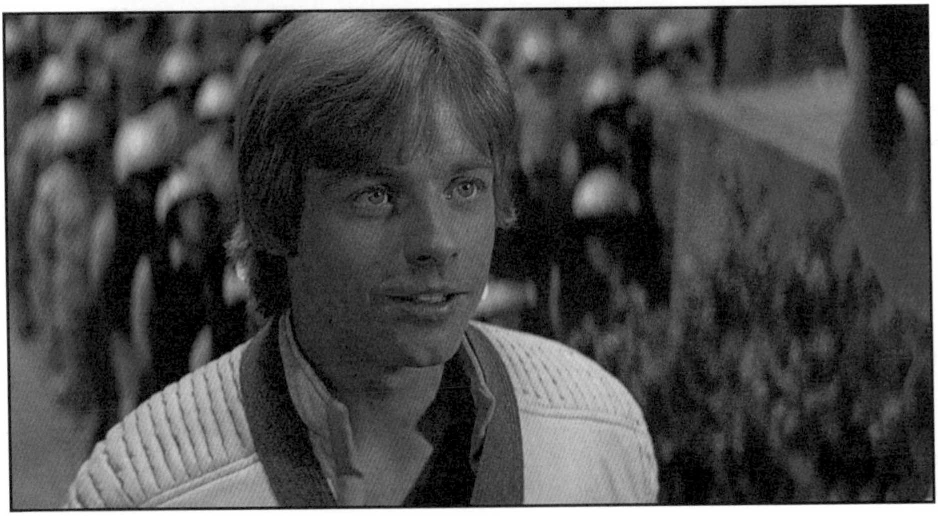

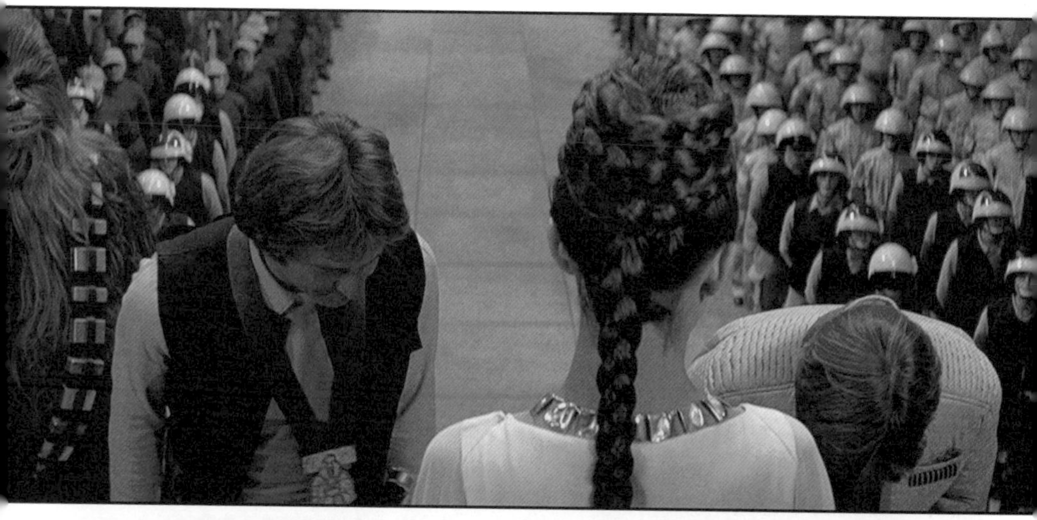

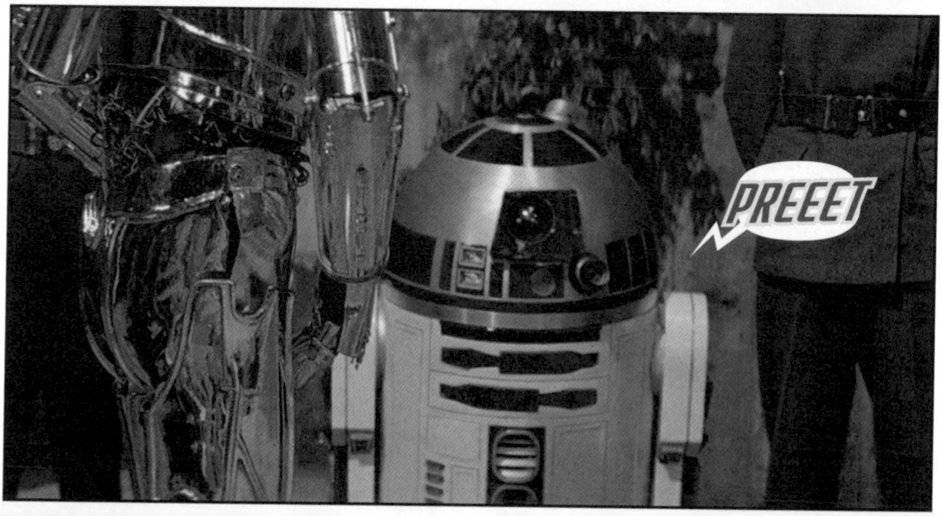
PREEET

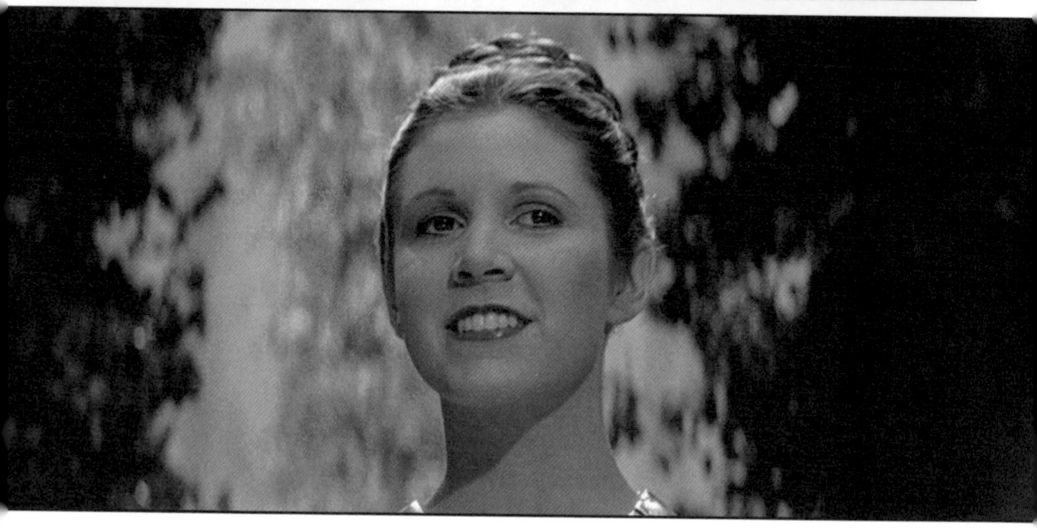

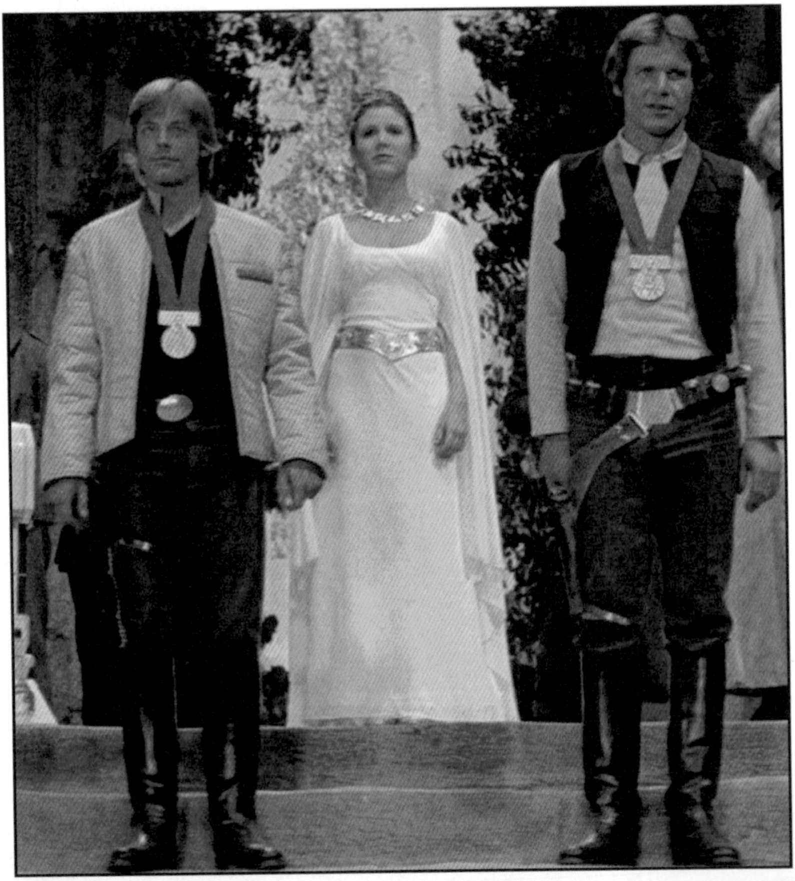

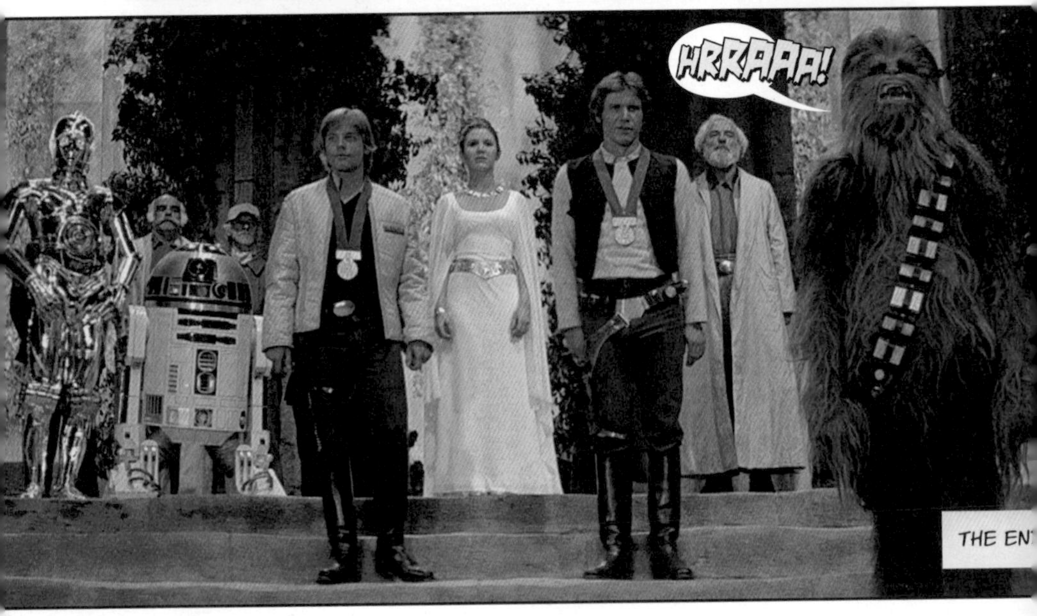
HRRAAA!
THE EN

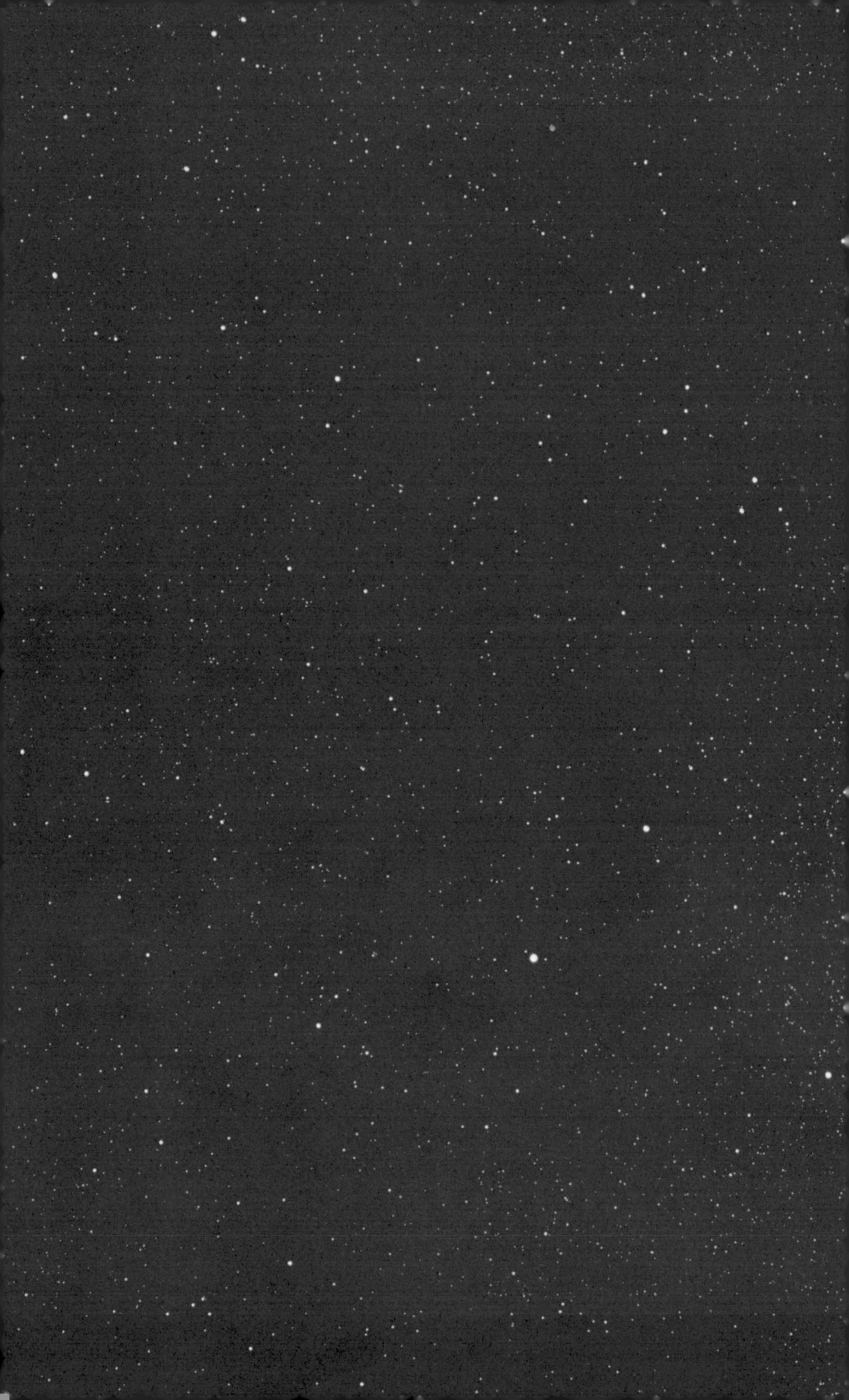